Penguin Books
Jeeves and Wooster

Pelham Grenville Wodehouse was born in 1881 in Guildford,
the son of a civil servant, and educated at Dulwich College. He
spent a brief period working for the Hong Kong and Shanghai
Bank before abandoning finance for writing, earning a living by
journalism and selling stories to magazines.

An enormously popular and prolific writer, he produced
about a hundred books. In Jeeves, the ever resourceful
'gentleman's personal gentleman', and the good-hearted young
blunderer Bertie Wooster, he created two of the best-known and
best-loved characters in twentieth-century literature. Their
exploits, first collected in *Carry on, Jeeves*, were chronicled in
fourteen books, and have been repeatedly adapted for television,
radio and the stage. Wodehouse also created many other comic
figures, notably Lord Emsworth, the Hon. Galahad
Threepwood, Psmith and the numerous members of the Drones
Club. He was part-author and writer of fifteen straight plays
and of 250 lyrics for some thirty musical comedies. *The Times*
hailed him as a 'comic genius recognized in his lifetime as a
classic and an old master of farce'.

P. G. Wodehouse said, 'I believe there are two ways of
writing novels. One is mine, making a sort of musical comedy
without music and ignoring real life altogether; the other is
going right deep down into life and not caring a damn.'

Wodehouse married in 1914 and took American citizenship
in 1955. He was created a Knight of the British Empire in the
1975 New Year's Honours List. In a BBC interview he said that
he had no ambitions left now that he had been knighted and
there was a waxwork of him in Madame Tussaud's. He died on
St Valentine's Day, 1975, at the age of ninety-three.

P. G. Wodehouse in Penguin

P. G. Wodehouse
Jeeves and Wooster: An Omnibus

P.G.Wodehouse

Jeeves and Wooster

Omnibus

An Omnibus volume containing
The Mating Season
The Code of the Woosters
Right Ho, Jeeves
with a Foreword by Hugh Laurie

PENGUIN BOOKS

PENGUIN BOOKS

Published by the Penguin Group
Penguin Books Ltd, 80 Strand, London WC2R 0RL, England
Penguin Putnam Inc., 375 Hudson Street, New York, New York 10014, USA
Penguin Books Australia Ltd, 250 Camberwell Road, Camberwell, Victoria 3124, Australia
Penguin Books Canada Ltd, 10 Alcorn Avenue, Toronto, Ontario, Canada M4V 3B2
Penguin Books India (P) Ltd, 11 Community Centre, Panchsheel Park, New Delhi – 110 017, India
Penguin Books (NZ) Ltd, Cnr Rosedale and Airborne Roads, Albany, Auckland, New Zealand
Penguin Books (South Africa) (Pty) Ltd, 24 Sturdee Avenue, Rosebank 2196, South Africa

Penguin Books Ltd, Registered Offices: 80 Strand, London WC2R 0RL, England

www.penguin.com

The Mating Season first published by Herbert Jenkins 1949
Copyright by the Trustees of the Wodehouse Estate

The Code of the Woosters first published by Herbert Jenkins 1937
Copyright by the Trustees of the Wodehouse Estate

Right Ho, Jeeves first published 1934
Published in Penguin Books 1953
Published in Penguin Books in the USA by arrangement with
Scott Meredith Literary Agency, Inc.
Copyright by the Trustees of the Wodehouse Estate

Foreword copyright © Hugh Laurie, 2001

This collection first published by Penguin Books 2001
5

Set in 9/11pt Monotype Trump
Typeset by Rowland Phototypesetting Ltd, Bury St Edmunds, Suffolk
Printed in England by Clays Ltd, St Ives plc

Contents

Foreword

This is the sort of honour that comes rarely in any man's life, let alone mine. This is rarity of a rare order. Halley's Comet seems like a blasted nuisance in comparison.

Let me put it this way. If you'd knocked on my head twenty years ago and told me that a time would come when I, Hugh Laurie – scraper-through of O levels, mover of lips (own) while reading, loafer, scrounger, pettifogger and general berk of this parish – would be asked to carve my initials in the broad bark of the Master's oak, I'm pretty certain that I would have said 'garn', or something like it.

So that you may have a chance of understanding how distant a prospect all this would have seemed to me back then, and therefore how remarkable its realization is to me now, I should probably tell you a little about my early life.

I was, in truth, a horrible child. Not much given to things of a bookery nature, I spent a large part of my youth smoking Number Six and cheating in French vocabulary tests. I wore platform boots with a brass skull-and-crossbones over the ankle, my hair was disgraceful and I somehow contrived to pull off the gruesome trick of being both fat and thin at the same time. If you had passed me in the street during those pimply years, I am confident that you would, at the very least, have quickened your pace. It's likely that the back of your neck would have started to feel hot and itchy, and the whole business might easily have started you in a habit of drinking spirits at lunchtime.

You think I exaggerate? I do not. Glancing over my

school reports from the year 1972, I observe that the words 'ghastly' and 'desperate' feature strongly, while 'no', 'not', 'never' and 'again' also crop up more often than one would expect in a random sample. My history teacher's report actually took the form of a postcard from Vancouver.

But this, you will be nauseated to learn, is a tale of redemption. Around my thirteenth year, it so happened that a copy of *Galahad at Blandings* by P. G Wodehouse entered my squalid universe, and things quickly began to change. From the very first sentence of my very first Wodehouse story, life appeared to grow somehow larger. There had always been height, depth, width and time, and in these prosaic dimensions I had hitherto snarled, and cursed, and not washed my hair. But now, suddenly, there was Wodehouse, and the discovery seemed to make me gentler every day. By the middle of the fifth chapter I was able to use a knife and fork, and I like to think that I have made some reasonable strides since.

I spent the following couple of years meandering happily back and forth through Blandings Castle and its environs – learning how often the trains ran, at what times the post was collected and delivered, how one could tell if the Empress was off-colour, why the Emsworth Arms was preferable to the Blue Boar – until the time came for me to roll up the map of adolescence and set forth into my first Jeeves novel. It was *The Code of the Woosters*, and things, as they used to say, would never be the same again.

Now, before I get to the main thrust of this essay, I must break off for a moment to deal with a question that's been worrying me. So far, I have been addressing you as a more or less homogeneous collection of bodies: a single mass, if you like, with a single face. I hope you won't be offended, but I have imagined you looking back at me with a wise, forgiving expression, your legs elegantly crossed, a glass of something at your elbow and a plate of something else at your other elbow. I've cast you as a better-than-average dancer (although, naturally, you don't go around the place boasting about it), and I fancy that, where it is safe to do so, you let other drivers in ahead of you. I have also assumed a shared liking for Keiller's Dundee Marmalade and a roughly mutual level of irritation at the use of graphics in television news reporting.

This picture, I now concede, is likely to be incomplete.

The truth is that you, as readers, are divided by many things. A Venn diagram of your assorted characteristics, attitudes, hobbies, beardedness, voting intentions, ability to do card tricks, etc. would be a complex, perhaps even a beautiful thing. Some of you will be old, some young; some short, some tall; some of you will be chaste and upstanding, while others may be reading this on a flight to Rio, with a suitcase full of drug money at your feet.

Whether or not you recognize yourself in any of the above, let me say that all, all are welcome. As your prefacer, there is only one distinction that concerns me, and that is – whether or not you have read a Jeeves story before.

A thing I never know, when I'm starting out to tell a story about a chap I've told a story about before, is how much explanation to bung in at the outset. It's a problem you've got to look at from every angle. I mean to say, in the present case, if I take it for granted that my public knows all about Gussie Fink-Nottle and just breeze ahead, those publicans who weren't hanging on my lips the first time are apt to be fogged. Whereas, if before kicking off I give about eight volumes of the man's life and history, other bimbos, who were so hanging, will stifle yawns and murmur 'Old stuff. Get on with it.'

The Code of the Woosters

Well, quite. My quandary precisely. How can one deal, simultaneously, with the knows and know-nots? If, for example, you should happen to style yourself a Wodehouse *aficionado* (and here I picture someone with a high forehead and more than one pair of moleskin trousers), then there is nothing I can say that will interest or surprise you in the slightest. In fact, if you have read this foreword at all, it will most probably have been in the grumpy expectation of coming across some heresy or other that will allow you to suck your teeth in a marked manner. I suspect that you will be, in these circumstances at least, unpleasable.

On the other hand, if this is your first Jeeves novel, then a lot of prattle from me about Sir Watkyn Bassett's fondness for silver knick-knacks isn't going to mean very much without some background material.

It's a tricky one.

The only way out that I can think of is to ask the old gang to let their attention wander for a bit – there are heaps of things they can be doing; washing the car, solving the crossword puzzle, taking the dog for a run – while I place the facts before the newcomers.

Much Obliged, Jeeves

The facts in this case, ladies and gentlemen, are simple. The first thing you should know, and probably the last too, is that P. G. Wodehouse is still the funniest writer ever to have put words on paper.

How can I be so sure? you may be wondering. Where do I get off, making assertions at that level of baldness? After all, do we not believe in eternal progress? Even if you grant that Wodehouse was funny *then*, what about now? Up against the modern titans, can he really cut the mustard?

I mean to say (this is still you wondering, by the way), we'd all give Fred Perry a cheer if he walked into the pub

– perhaps we'd even buy him a drink and ask for his autograph – but do any of us seriously believe that, even at his best, he could have taken a single game off Pete Sampras? Of course not. Tennis players are bigger, fitter, stronger, faster and, quite simply, *better* than they were fifty years ago. So why shouldn't the same be true of comic writers? (Last bit of wondering. Stick at it.) When all's said and done, isn't Wodehouse just a charming old buffer in long flannels, lolloping balls high over the net in flickery black and white?

Well, you can stop wondering now, because comic writing isn't tennis. It simply does not progress in the relentless athletic increments of an inch here, and a tenth of a second there. There are funny writers, and then there are no funny writers, and then there are funny writers again. They appear and disappear in cycles that it is not given to us to understand. All we need know is that, of the funny writers, Wodehouse was and is the funniest. He was a genius, the best ever, the number one seed. He could take them all, left-handed, then and now, and I ask that this be entered as fact number one.

Fact number two. With the Jeeves stories, Wodehouse created the best of the best. I speak as one whose first love was Blandings, and who later took immense pleasure from Psmith: but Jeeves is the jewel, and anyone who tries to tell you different can be shown the door, the mini-cab, the train station and Terminal 4 at Heathrow, with a clear conscience. The world of Jeeves is complete and integral; every bit as structured, layered, ordered, complex and self-contained as *King Lear*, and considerably funnier.

(Let me hasten to say that I do not mean to disparage Shakespeare with that last remark. That would be mad, and I don't believe that I am mad. But I do mean to champion Wodehouse against those who would call him light simply because he is funny. In the first place,

charging Wodehouse with 'lightness' is not so very far
away from accusing painters of relying heavily for the
achievement of their effects on paint. His lightness is, to
put it bluntly, the Whole Point.

And in the second place, in what sense do we actually
mean that Comedy is 'lighter' than Tragedy? Discuss.
And discuss it, if you would, with this question in mind:
when the final whistle is blown, and each one of us is
left to cower before the vast, immovable emptiness that
goes by the name of the Cosmos, what will our reaction
be? Or rather, what would we *want* it to be? Rage?
Despair? A recital of grievances and complaints? Hmm.
For some reason, they all seem fairly limp to me.
Petulant and egocentric. Light, even. The only reaction
that will *really* give us meaning, that will serve to
distinguish us from a lump of rock, or a standard lamp –
that will also, with a bit of luck, annoy the Vast
Immovable Cosmos beyond belief – is laughter.
Head-back, sinus-rupturing laughter. For this, in bulk
quantities, you come to P. G.Wodehouse.)

Now that the facts are before you, and you are
congratulating yourself on a wise purchase – or a wise
shoplift, if that happens to be your way of going about
things – I had better make it clear that I do not intend, in
the limited lifespan I have available, to tackle the
subject of *why* Wodehouse is funny. Discussions and
analyses of humour are almost always unsatisfactory,
and often leave one with a feeling similar to the one you
get when somebody takes a mallet to a crystal vase, then
holds up the pieces and tells you that, put together in a
vase-like shape, these bits could make quite a nice
crystal vase. Furthermore, I am convinced that a
foreword of the work in question is absolutely the worst
place to hold such a discussion: somewhat akin to
shouting out, 'Watch him, he's got something down the
back of his trousers', just as the conjurer takes the stage.
No, I will have none of it. The world needs a lot of

things just now – a renewable source of energy, more pens in banks – one could go on and on. What it most emphatically does *not* need is another attempt to 'explain' Wodehouse's funniness.

So let me confine myself, instead, to the business I know: namely, what it was like to portray Bertram W. Wooster in twenty-three hours of televised drama, opposite the internationally tall Stephen Fry in the role of Jeeves. Let the pages of the calendar tumble as autumn leaves, until ten years are understood to have passed.

A man came to us with a proposition.

'Fiddle,' one of us said. I forget which.

'Sticks,' said the other one. (See above.) 'Wodehouse on television? It's lunacy. A disaster in kit form. Get a grip, man.'

The man was a television producer called Brian Eastman, and he pressed home his argument with skill and determination.

'All right,' he said, getting up from the table and shrugging on his coat. 'I'll ask someone else.'

'Whoa, hold up,' said one of us, shooting a startled look at the other.

'Steady,' said the other, returning the s.l. with topspin.

There was a pause.

'You'll never get a cab in this weather,' we said, in unison.

And so it was that, a number of months later, I found myself slipping into a double-breasted suit in a Prince of Wales check, while my colleague made himself at home inside an enormous bowler hat, and the two of us embarked on our separate disciplines. Him for the noiseless opening of decanters, me for the twirling of the whangee.

As well as the practicalities of the thing – how to smoke plain cigarettes, how to drive a 1927 Aston Martin (throttle pedal in the middle and brake on the

right, which is a pretty entertaining set-up, let me tell
you), how to mix a martini with five parts water and one
part water, how to attach a pair of spats in less than a
day and a half, and so on – we also talked long and hard
about the sorts of things you'd expect actors to talk
about: the mood, the pace, the dynamics (whatever the
hell they are), the relationships between the characters;
all of which we dispatched within an hour or so. The
thing that really worried us, that had us stratching our
heads and saying 'crikey' for weeks on end, was this
business of the Words.

Let me give you an example. Bertie is leaving in a
huff:

'Tinkerty tonk,' I said, and I meant it to sting.

Now then, I ask you: how is one to do justice of even
the roughest sort to a line like that? How can any
human actor, with his clumsily attached ears, and his
irritating voice, and his completely misguided hair, hope
to deliver a line as pure as that? It can't be done. You
begin with a diamond on the page, and you end up with
a blob of Pritt, the Non-Sticky Sticky Stuff, on the
screen. Stands to reason. All we could do was belt the
stuff out with as much gusto as possible, shotgun-like,
and hope that, every so often, a pellet would penetrate
the constable's trousers. Some did, I think, but plenty
didn't.

The point is that Wodehouse on the page can be
taken in the reader's own time. When one fastens upon a
joyous sentence, as you are shortly to do, one can read it
once, twice, adjust an inflection and read it a third time,
imagine the expressions of the other characters in the
scene and have a fourth go, and so on. At each reading
the sentence becomes better, and funnier, and more
beautiful, until at least you become aware that other
people in the carriage are looking at you strangely, and

you're forced to convert the noise you've been making into a sort of cough.

On the screen, however, the experience is obviously different. The beautiful sentence often seems just to whip by, like an attractive member of the opposite sex glimpsed from the back of a cab, before being swallowed up in the crowd of jostling camera angles and jaunty music. You, as the viewer, try desperately to fix the image in your mind – but it's too late, because now you're into a commercial break and someone is chattering about o per cent finance on the Renault Laguna, and how your home may be at risk if you eat the wrong kind of breakfast cereal.

Naturally, one hopes there may be compensations in watching Wodehouse on the screen – pleasant scenery, amusing clothes, a particular actor's eyebrows – but, all in all, it can never replicate the experience of reading him. If I may go slightly culinary for a moment: a dish of *foie gras* nestling on a bed of truffles, with a side-order of lobster and caviar, may provide you with a wonderful sensation; but no matter how wonderful, you simply don't want to be spoon-fed the stuff by a perfect stranger. *You* need to hold the spoon, and decide yourself when to wolf and when to nibble.

That is your situation now, you lucky person. You have ordered the best of the best, in its best form. The spoon is in your hand, the dish is on its way and I, as your *maître d'hôtel*, am about to withdraw.

So what is there left to say? Nothing much, except to observe as I fold away my penknife and gaze up at the huge oak towering overhead, that this has been a real treat for me. The chance to write about Wodehouse, to think about him, to bathe in the novels, to hunt down a favourite passage, only to discover that the passages either side are just as good – all this has been a terrific pleasure, as well as an honour. If my history teacher could see me now . . .

But here it is, *enfin*. If you'll just allow me to top up your glass, whip off the cloche and spill a couple of sprouts in your lap, you can get stuck in.

Bon appetit.

HUGH LAURIE

The Mating Season

I

While I would not go so far, perhaps, as to describe the heart as actually leaden, I must confess that on the eve of starting to do my bit of time at Deverill Hall I was definitely short on chirpiness. I shrank from the prospect of being decanted into a household on chummy terms with a thug like my Aunt Agatha, weakened as I already was by having had her son Thomas, one of our most prominent fiends in human shape, on my hands for three days.

I mentioned this to Jeeves, and he agreed that the set-up could have been juicier.

'Still,' I said, taking a pop, as always, at trying to focus the silver lining, 'it's flattering, of course.'

'Sir?'

'Being the People's Choice, Jeeves. Having these birds going around chanting "We Want Wooster".'

'Ah, yes, sir. Precisely. Most gratifying.'

But half a jiffy. I'm forgetting that you haven't the foggiest what all this is about. It so often pans out that way when you begin a story. You whizz off the mark all pep and ginger, like a mettlesome charger going into its routine, and the next thing you know, the customers are up on their hind legs, yelling for footnotes.

Let me get into reverse and put you abreast.

My Aunt Agatha, the one who chews broken bottles and kills rats with her teeth, arriving suddenly in London from her rural lair with her son Thomas, had instructed me in her authoritative way to put the latter up in my flat for three days while he visited dentists and

3

Old Vics and things preparatory to leaving for his school at Bramley-on-Sea and, that done, to proceed to Deverill Hall, King's Deverill, Hants., the residence of some pals of hers, and lend my services to the village concert. Apparently they wanted to stiffen up the programme with a bit of metropolitan talent, and I had been recommended by the vicar's niece.

And that, of course, was that. It was no good telling her that I would prefer not to touch young Thos with a ten-foot pole and that I disliked taking on blind dates. When Aunt Agatha issues her orders, you fill them. But I was conscious, as I have indicated, of an uneasiness as to the shape of things to come, and it didn't make the outlook any brighter to know that Gussie Fink-Nottle would be among those present at Deverill Hall. When you get trapped in the den of the Secret Nine, you want something a lot better than Gussie to help you keep the upper lip stiff.

I mused a bit.

'I wish I had more data about these people, Jeeves,' I said. 'I like on these occasions to know what I'm up against. So far, all I've gathered is that I am to be the guest of a landed proprietor called Harris or Hacker or possibly Hassock.'

'Haddock, sir.'

'Haddock, eh?'

'Yes, sir. The gentleman who is to be your host is a Mr Esmond Haddock.'

'It's odd, but that name seems to strike a chord, as if I'd heard it before somewhere.'

'Mr Haddock is the son of the owner of a widely advertised patent remedy known as Haddock's Headache Hokies, sir. Possibly the specific is familiar to you.'

'Of course. I know it well. Not so sensationally good as those pick-me-ups of yours, but none the less a sound stand-by on the morning after. So he's one of those Haddocks, is he?'

'Yes, sir. Mr Esmond Haddock's late father married the late Miss Flora Deverill.'

'Before they were both late, of course?'

'The union was considered something of a *mésalliance* by the lady's sisters. The Deverills are a very old county family – like so many others in these days, impoverished.'

'I begin to get the scenario. Haddock, though not as posh as he might be on the father's side, foots the weekly bills?'

'Yes, sir.'

'Well, no doubt he can afford to. There's gold in them thar Hokies, Jeeves.'

'So I should be disposed to imagine, sir.'

A point struck me which often does strike me when chewing the fat with this honest fellow – viz. that he seemed to know a hell of a lot about it. I mentioned this, and he explained that it was one of those odd chances that had enabled him to get the inside story.

'My Uncle Charlie holds the post of butler at the Hall, sir. It is from him that I derive my information.'

'I didn't know you had an Uncle Charlie. Charlie Jeeves?'

'No, sir. Charlie Silversmith.'

I lit a rather pleased cigarette. Things were beginning to clarify.

'Well, this is a bit of a goose. You'll be able to give me all the salient facts, if salient is the word I want. What sort of a joint is this Deverill Hall? Nice place? Gravel soil? Spreading views?'

'Yes, sir.'

'Good catering?'

'Yes, sir.'

'And touching on the personnel. Would there be a Mrs Haddock?'

'No, sir. The young gentleman is unmarried. He resides at the Hall with his five aunts.'

'*Five?*'

'Yes, sir. The Misses Charlotte, Emmeline, Harriet and Myrtle Deverill and Dame Daphne Winkworth, relict of the late P. B. Winkworth, the historian. Dame Daphne's daughter, Miss Gertrude Winkworth, is, I understand, also in residence.'

On the cue 'five aunts' I had given at the knees a trifle, for the thought of being confronted with such a solid gaggle of aunts, even if those of another, was an unnerving one. Reminding myself that in this life it is not aunts that matter but the courage which one brings to them, I pulled myself together.

'I see,' I said. 'No stint of female society.'

'No, sir.'

'I may find Gussie's company a relief.'

'Very possibly, sir.'

'Such as it is.'

'Yes, sir.'

I wonder, by the way, if you recall this Augustus, on whose activities I have had occasion to touch once or twice before now? Throw the mind back. Goofy to the gills, face like a fish, horn-rimmed spectacles, drank orange juice, collected newts, engaged to England's premier pill, a girl called Madeline Bassett . . . Ah, you've got him? Fine.

'Tell me, Jeeves,' I said, 'how does Gussie come to be mixed up with these bacteria? Surely a bit of an inscrutable mystery that he, too, should be headed for Deverill Hall?'

'No, sir. It was Mr Fink-Nottle himself who informed me.'

'You've seen him, then?'

'Yes, sir. He called while you were out.'

'How did he seem?'

'Low-spirited, sir.'

'Like me, he shrinks from the prospect of visiting this ghastly shack?'

'Yes, sir. He had supposed that Miss Bassett would be accompanying him, but she has altered her arrangements at the last moment and gone to reside at The Larches, Wimbledon Common, with an old school friend who has recently suffered a disappointment in love. It was Miss Bassett's view that she needed cheering up.'

I was at a loss to comprehend how the society of Madeline Bassett could cheer anyone up, she being from topknot to shoe sole the woman whom God forgot, but I didn't say so. I merely threw out the opinion that this must have made Gussie froth a bit.

'Yes, sir. He expressed annoyance at the change of plan. Indeed, I gathered from his remarks, for he was kind enough to confide in me, that there has resulted a certain coolness between himself and Miss Bassett.'

'Gosh!' I said.

And I'll tell you why I goshed. If you remember Gussie Fink-Nottle, you will probably also remember the chain of circumstances which led up, if chains do lead up, to this frightful Bassett getting the impression firmly fixed in her woollen head that Bertram Wooster was pining away for love of her. I won't go into details now, but it was her conviction that if ever she felt like severing relations with Gussie, she had only to send out a hurry call for me and I would come racing round, all ready to buy the licence and start ordering the wedding cake.

So, knowing my view regarding this Bassett, M., you will readily understand why this stuff about coolnesses drew a startled 'Gosh!' from me. The thought of my peril had never left me, and I wasn't going to be really easy in my mind till these two were actually centre-aisling. Only when the clergyman had definitely pronounced sentence would Bertram start to breathe freely again.

'Ah, well,' I said, hoping for the best. 'Just a lovers' tiff, no doubt. Always happening, these lovers' tiffs.

7

Probably by this time a complete reconciliation has been effected and the laughing Love God is sweating away at the old stand once more with knobs on. Ha!' I proceeded as the front-door bell tootled, 'someone waits without. If it's young Thos, tell him that I shall expect him to be in readiness, all clean and rosy, at seven forty-five tonight to accompany me to the performance of *King Lear* at the Old Vic, and it's no good him trying to do a sneak. His mother said he had got to go to the Old Vic, and he's jolly well going.'

'I think it is more probable that it is Mr Pirbright, sir.'

'Old Catsmeat? What makes you think that?'

'He also called during your absence and indicated that he would return later. He was accompanied by his sister, Miss Pirbright.'

'Good Lord, really? Corky? I thought she was in Hollywood.'

'I understand that she has returned to England for a vacation, sir.'

'Did you give her tea?'

'Yes, sir. Master Thomas played host. Miss Pirbright took the young gentleman off subsequently to see a picture.'

'I wish I hadn't missed her. I haven't seen Corky for ages. Was she all right?'

'Yes, sir.'

'And Catsmeat? How was he?'

'Low-spirited, sir.'

'You're mixing him up with Gussie. It was Gussie, if you recall, who was low-spirited.'

'Mr Pirbright also.'

'There seems to be a lot of low-spiritedness kicking about these days.'

'We live in difficult times, sir.'

'True. Well, bung him in.'

He oozed out, and a few moments later oozed in again.

'Mr Pirbright,' he announced.

He had called his shots correctly. A glance at the young visitor was enough to tell me that he was low-spirited.

2

And mind you, it isn't often that you find the object under advisement in this condition. A singularly fizzy bird, as a rule. In fact, taking him by and large, I should say that of all the rollicking lads at the Drones Club, Claude Cattermole Pirbright is perhaps the most rollicking, both on the stage and off.

I say 'on the stage', for it is behind the footlights that he earns his weekly envelope. He comes of a prominent theatrical family. His father was the man who wrote the music of *The Blue Lady* and other substantial hits which I unfortunately missed owing to being in the cradle at the time. His mother was Elsie Cattermole, who was a star in New York for years. And his sister Corky has been wowing the customers with her oomph and *espièglerie*, if that's the word I want, since she was about sixteen.

It was almost inevitable, therefore, that, looking about him on coming down from Oxford for some walk in life which would ensure the three squares a day and give him time to play a bit of county cricket, he should have selected the sock and buskin. To-day he is the fellow managers pick first when they have a Society comedy to present and want someone for 'Freddie', the lighthearted friend of the hero, carrying the second love interest. If at such a show you see a willowy figure come bounding on with a tennis racket, shouting 'Hallo, girls' shortly after the kick-off, don't bother to look at the programme. That'll be Catsmeat.

On such occasions he starts off sprightly and continues sprightly till closing time, and it is the same

in private life. There, too, his sprightliness is a byword.
Pongo Twistleton and Barmy Phipps, who do each year
at the Drones smoker the knockabout Pat and Mike
cross-talk act of which he is the author and producer,
have told me that when rehearsing them in their lines
and business, he is more like Groucho Marx than
anything human.

Yet now, as I say, he was low-spirited. It stuck out a
mile. His brow was sicklied o'er with the pale cast of
thought and his air that of a man who, if he had said
'Hallo, girls', would have said it like someone in a
Russian drama announcing that Grandpapa had hanged
himself in the barn.

I greeted him cordially and said I was sorry I had been
out when he had come seeking an audience before,
especially as he had had Corky with him.

'I should have loved a chat with Corky,' I said. 'I had
no idea she was back in England. Now I'm afraid I've
missed her.'

'No, you haven't.'

'Yes, I have. I leave to-morrow for a place called
Deverill Hall in Hampshire to help at the village
concert. It seems that the vicar's niece insisted on
having me in the troupe, and what's puzzling me is how
this girl of God heard of me. One hadn't supposed one's
reputation was so far flung.'

'You silly ass, she's Corky.'

'Corky?'

I was stunned. There are few better eggs in existence
than Cora ('Corky') Pirbright, with whom I have been on
the matiest of terms since the days when in our
formative years we attended the same dancing class, but
nothing in her deportment had ever given me the idea
that she was related to the clergy.

'My Uncle Sidney is the vicar down there, and my
aunt's away at Bournemouth. In her absence, Corky is
keeping house for him.'

'My God! Poor old Sid! She tidies his study, no doubt?'

'Probably.'

'Straightens his tie?'

'I wouldn't be surprised.'

'And tells him he smokes too much, and every time he gets comfortably settled in an armchair boosts him out of it so that she can smooth the cushions. He must be feeling as if he were living in the book of Revelations. But doesn't she find a vicarage rather slow after Hollywood?'

'Not a bit. She loves it. Corky's different from me. I wouldn't be happy out of show business, but she was never really keen on it, though she's been such a success. I don't think she would have gone on the stage at all, if it hadn't been for Mother wanting her to so much. Her dream is to marry someone who lives in the country and spend the rest of her life knee-deep in cows and dogs and things. I suppose it's the old Farmer Giles strain in the Pirbrights coming out. My grandfather was a farmer. I can just remember him. Yards of whiskers, and always bellyaching about the weather. Messing about in the parish and getting up village concerts is her dish.'

'Any idea what she wants me to give the local yokels? Not the "Yeoman's Wedding Song", I trust?'

'No. You're billed to do the Pat part in that cross-talk act of mine.'

This came under the head of tidings of great joy. Too often at these binges the Brass Hats in charge tell you off to render the 'Yeoman's Wedding Song', which for some reason always arouses the worst passions of the tough eggs who stand behind the back row. But no rustic standees have ever been known not to eat a knockabout cross-talk act. There is something about the spectacle of Performer A sloshing Performer B over the head with an umbrella and Performer B prodding Performer A in the midriff with a similar blunt instrument that seems to

speak to their depths. Wearing a green beard and given
adequate assistance by my supporting cast, I could
confidently anticipate that I should have the clientele
rolling in the aisles.

'Right. Fine. Splendid. I can now face the future with
an uplifted heart. But if she wanted someone for Pat,
why didn't she get you? You being a seasoned
professional. Ah, I see what must have happened. She
offered you the role and you drew yourself up haughtily,
feeling that you were above this amateur stuff.'

Catsmeat shook the lemon sombrely.

'It wasn't that at all. Nothing would have pleased me
more than to have performed at the King's Deverill
concert, but the shot wasn't on the board. Those women
at the Hall hate my insides.'

'So you've met them? What are they like? A pretty
stiffish nymphery, I suspect.'

'No, I haven't met them. But I'm engaged to their
niece, Gertrude Winkworth, and the idea of her
marrying me gives them the pip. If I showed myself
within a mile of Deverill Hall, dogs would be set on me.
Talking of dogs, Corky bought one this morning at the
Battersea Home.'

'God bless her,' I said, speaking absently, for my
thoughts were concentrated on this romance of his and I
was trying to sort out his little ball of worsted from the
mob of aunts and what-have-you of whom Jeeves had
spoken. Then I got her placed. Gertrude, daughter of
Dame Daphne Winkworth, relict of the late P. B.
Winkworth, the historian.

'That's what I came to see you about.'

'Corky's dog?'

'No, this Gertrude business. I need your help. I'll tell
you the whole story.'

On Catsmeat's entry I had provided him with a
hospitable whisky and splash, and of this he had downed
up to this point perhaps a couple of sips and a gulp. He

now knocked back the residuum, and it seemed to touch the spot, for when it was down the hatch he spoke with animation and fluency.

'I should like to start by saying, Bertie, that since the first human crawled out of the primeval slime and life began on this planet nobody has ever loved anybody as I love Gertrude Winkworth. I mention this because I want you to realize that what you're sitting in on is not one of those light summer flirtations but the real West End stuff. I love her!'

'That's good. Where did you meet her?'

'At a house in Norfolk. They were doing some amateur theatricals and roped me in to produce. My God! Those twilight evenings in the old garden, with the birds singing sleepily in the shrubberies and the stars beginning to peep out in the – '

'Right ho. Carry on.'

'She's wonderful, Bertie. Why she loves me, I can't imagine.'

'But she does?'

'Oh yes, she does. We got engaged, and she returned to Deverill Hall to break the news to her mother. And when she did, what do you think happened?'

Well, of course, he had rather given away the punch of his story at the outset.

'The parent kicked?'

'She let out a yell you could have heard at Basingstoke.'

'Basingstoke being – '

'About twenty miles away as the crow flies.'

'I know Basingstoke. Bless my soul yes, know it well.'

'She – '

'I've stayed there as a boy. An old nurse of mine used to live at Basingstoke in a semi-detached villa called Balmoral. Her name was Hogg, oddly enough. Nurse Hogg. She suffered from hiccups.'

Catsmeat's manner became a bit tense. He looked

like a village standee hearing the 'Yeoman's Wedding Song'.

'Listen, Bertie,' he said, 'suppose we don't talk about Basingstoke or about your nurse either. To hell with Basingstoke and to hell with your ruddy nurse, too. Where was I?'

'We broke off at the point where Dame Daphne Winkworth was letting out a yell.'

'That's right. Her sisters, when informed that Gertrude was proposing to marry the brother of the Miss Pirbright down at the Vicarage and that this brother was an actor by profession, also let out yells.'

I toyed with the idea of asking if these, too, could have been heard at Basingstoke, but wiser counsels prevailed.

'They don't like Corky, and they don't like actors. In their young days, in the reign of Queen Elizabeth, actors were looked on as rogues and vagabonds, and they can't get it into their nuts that the modern actor is a substantial citizen who makes his sixty quid a week and salts most of it away in sound Government securities. Why, dash it, if I could think of some way of doing down the income-tax people, I should be a rich man. You don't know of a way of doing down the income-tax people do you, Bertie?'

'Sorry, no. I doubt if even Jeeves does. So you got the bird?'

'Yes. I had a sad letter from Gertrude saying no dice. You may ask why don't we elope?'

'I was just going to.'

'I couldn't swing it. She fears her mother's wrath.'

'A tough character, this mother?'

'Of the toughest. She used to be headmistress of a big girls' school. Gertrude was a member of the chain gang and has never got over it. No, elopements seem to be out. And here's the snag, Bertie. Corky has wangled a contract for me with her studio in Hollywood, and I may have to sail at any moment. It's a frightful situation.'

I was silent for a moment. I was trying to remember something I had read somewhere about something not quenching something, but I couldn't get at it. However, the general idea was that if a girl loves you and you are compelled to leave her in storage for a while, she will wait for you, so I put this point, and he said that was all very well but I didn't know all. The plot, he assured me, was about to thicken.

'We now come,' he said, 'to the hellhound Haddock. And this is where I want you to rally round, Bertie.'

I said I didn't get the gist, and he said of course I didn't get the damned gist, but couldn't I wait half a second, blast me, and give him a chance to explain, and I said Oh, rather, certainly.

'Haddock!' said Catsmeat, speaking between clenched teeth and exhibiting other signs of emotion. 'Haddock the Home Wrecker! Do you know anything about this Grade A louse, Bertie?'

'Only that his late father was the proprietor of those Headache Hokies.'

'And left him enough money to sink a ship. I'm not suggesting, of course, that Gertrude would marry him for his money. She would scorn such raw work. But in addition to having more cash than you could shake a stick at, he's a sort of Greek god in appearance and extremely magnetic. So Gertrude says. And, what is more, I gather from her letters that pressure is being brought to bear on her by the family. And you can imagine what the pressure of a mother and four aunts is like.'

I began to grasp the trend.

'You mean Haddock is trying to move in?'

'Gertrude writes that he is giving her the rush of a lifetime. And this will show you the sort of flitting and sipping butterfly the hound is. It's only a short while ago that he was giving Corky a similar rush. Ask her when you see her, but tactfully, because she's as sore as a gumboil about it. I tell you, the man is a public menace. He ought to be kept on a chain in the interests of pure womanhood. But we'll fix him, won't we?'

'Will we?'

'You bet we will. Here's what I want you to do. You'll agree that even a fellow like Esmond Haddock, who appears to be the nearest thing yet discovered to South American Joe, couldn't press his foul suit in front of you?'

'You mean he would need privacy?'

'Exactly. So the moment you are inside Deverill Hall, start busting up his sinister game. Be always at Gertrude's side. Stick to her like glue. See that he doesn't get her alone in the rose garden. If a visit to the rose garden is mooted, include yourself in. You follow me, Bertie?'

'I follow you, yes,' I said, a little dubiously. 'What you have in mind is something on the lines of Mary's lamb. I don't know if you happen to know the poem – I used to recite it as a child – but, broadly, the nub was that Mary had a little lamb with fleece as white as snow, and everywhere that Mary went the lamb was sure to go. You want me to model my technique on that of Mary's lamb?'

'That's it. Be on the alert every second, for the peril is frightful. Well, to give you some idea, his most recent suggestion is that Gertrude and he shall take sandwiches one of these mornings and ride out to a place about fifteen miles away, where there are cliffs and things. And do you know what he plans to do when they get there? Show her the Lovers' Leap.'

'Oh, yes?'

'Don't say "Oh, yes?" in that casual way. Think, man. Fifteen miles there, then the Lovers' Leap, then fifteen miles back. The imagination reels at the thought of what excesses a fellow like Esmond Haddock may

commit on a thirty-mile ride with a Lovers' Leap thrown
in half-way. I don't know what day the expedition is
planned for, but whenever it is, you must be with it
from start to finish. If possible riding between them.
And for God's sake don't take your eye off him for an
instant at the Lovers' Leap. That will be the danger spot.
If you notice the slightest disposition on his part, when
at the Lovers' Leap, to lean towards her and whisper in
her ear, break up the act like lightning. I'm relying on
you, Bertie. My life's happiness depends on you.'

Well, of course, if a man you've been at private
school, public school and Oxford with says he's relying
on you, you have no option but to let yourself be relied
on. To say that the assignment was one I liked would be
over-stating the facts, but I right-hoed, and he grasped
my hand and said that if there were more fellows like
me in it the world would be a better place – a view
which differed sharply from that of my Aunt Agatha,
and one which I had a hunch was going to differ sharply
from that of Esmond Haddock. There might be those at
Deverill Hall who would come to love Bertram, but my
bet was that E. Haddock's name would not be on the
roster.

'Well, you've certainly eased my mind,' said
Catsmeat, having released the hand and then re-grabbed
and re-squeezed it. 'Knowing that you are on the spot,
working like a beaver in my interests, will mean
everything. I have been off my feed for some little time
now, but I'm going to enjoy my dinner tonight. I only
wish there was something I could do for you in return.'

'There is,' I said.

A thought had struck me, prompted no doubt by his
mention of the word 'dinner'. Ever since Jeeves had told
me about the coolness which existed between Gussie
Fink-Nottle and Madeline Bassett I had been more than
a bit worried at the thought of Gussie dining by himself
that night.

I mean, you know how it is when you've had one of these lovers' tiffs and then go off to a solitary dinner. You start brooding over the girl with the soup and wonder if it wasn't a mug's game hitching up with her. With the fish this feeling deepens, and by the time you're through with the *poulet rôti au cresson* and are ordering the coffee you've probably come definitely to the conclusion that she's a rag and a bone and a hank of hair and that it would be madness to sign her on as a life partner.

What you need on these occasions is entertaining company, so that your dark thoughts may be diverted, and it seemed to me that here was the chance to provide Gussie with some.

'There is,' I said. 'You know Gussie Fink-Nottle? He's low-spirited, and there are reasons why I would prefer that he isn't alone tonight, brooding. Could you give him a spot of dinner?'

Catsmeat chewed his lip. I knew what was passing in his mind. He was thinking, as others have thought, that the first essential for an enjoyable dinner-party is for Gussie not to be at it.

'Give Gussie Fink-Nottle dinner?'

'That's right.'

'Why don't you?'

'My Aunt Agatha wants me to take her son Thomas to the Old Vic.'

'Give it a miss.'

'I can't. I should never hear the last of it.'

'Well, all right.'

'Heaven bless you, Catsmeat,' I said.

So Gussie was off my mind. It was with a light heart that I retired to rest that night. I little knew, as the expression is, what the morrow was to bring forth.

3

Though, as a matter of fact, in its early stages the morrow brought forth some pretty good stuff. As generally happens on these occasions when you are going to cop it in the quiet evenfall, the day started extremely well. Knowing that at 2.53 I was to shoot young Thos off to his seaside Borstal, I breakfasted with a song on my lips, and at lunch, I recall, I was in equally excellent fettle.

I took Thos to Victoria, bunged him into his train, slipped him a quid and stood waving a cousinly hand till he was out of sight. Then, after looking in at Queen's Club for a game or two of rackets, I went back to the flat, still chirpy.

Up till then everything had been fine. As I put hat on hat-peg and umbrella in umbrella-stand, I was thinking that if God wasn't in His heaven and all right with the world, these conditions prevailed as near as made no matter. Not the suspicion of an inkling, if you see what I mean, that round the corner lurked the bitter awakening, stuffed eelskin in hand, waiting to sock me on the occiput.

The first thing to which my attention was drawn on crossing the threshold was that there seemed to be a lot more noise going on than was suitable in a gentleman's home. Through the closed door of the sitting-room the ear detected the sound of a female voice raised in what appeared to be cries of encouragement and, mingled with this female voice, a loud barking, as of hounds on the trail. It was as though my boudoir had been selected by the management of the Quorn or the Pytchley as the site for their most recent meet, and my first instinct, as that of any householder would have been, was to look into this. Nobody can call Bertram Wooster a fussy man, but there are moments when he feels he has to take a firm stand.

I opened the door, accordingly, and was immediately knocked base over apex by some solid body with a tongue like an anteater's. This tongue it proceeded to pass enthusiastically over my upper slopes and, the mists clearing away, I perceived that what I was tangled up with was a shaggy dog of mixed parentage. And standing beside us, looking down like a mother watching the gambols of her first-born, was Catsmeat's sister Corky.

'Isn't he a lamb?' she said. 'Isn't he an absolute seraph?'

I was not able wholly to subscribe to this view. The animal appeared to have an agreeable disposition and to have taken an immediate fancy to me, but physically it was no beauty-prize winner. It looked like Boris Karloff made up for something.

Corky, on the other hand, as always, distinctly took the eye. Two years in Hollywood had left her even easier to look at than when last seen around these parts.

This young prune is one of those lissom girls of medium height, constructed on the lines of Gertrude Lawrence, and her map had always been worth more than a passing glance. In repose, it has a sort of meditative expression, as if she were a pure white soul thinking beautiful thoughts, and, when animated, so dashed animated that it boosts the morale just to look at her. Her eyes are a kind of browny-hazel and her hair rather along the same lines. The general effect is of an angel who eats lots of yeast. In fine, if you were called upon to pick something to be cast on a desert island with, Hedy Lamarr might be your first choice, but Corky

Pirbright would inevitably come high up in the list of Hon. Mentions.

'His name's Sam Goldwyn,' she proceeded, hauling the animal off the prostrate form. 'I bought him at the Battersea Home.'

I rose and dried the face.

'Yes, so Catsmeat told me.'

'Oh, you've seen Catsmeat? Good.'

At this point she seemed to become aware that we had skipped the customary pip-pippings, for she took time out to say how nice it was to see me again after all this time. I said how nice it was to see her again after all this time, and she asked me how I was, and I said I was fine. I asked her how she was, and she said she was fine. She enquired if I was still as big a chump as ever, and I satisfied her curiosity at this point.

'I looked in yesterday, hoping to see you,' she said, 'but you were out.'

'Yes, Jeeves told me.'

'A small boy with red hair entertained me. He said he was your cousin.'

'My Aunt Agatha's son and, oddly enough, the apple of her eye.'

'Why oddly enough?'

'He's the King of the Underworld. They call him The Shadow.'

'I liked him. I gave him fifty of my autographs. He's going to sell them to the boys at his school and expects to get sixpence apiece. He has long admired me on the screen, and we hit it off together like a couple of Yes-men. Catsmeat didn't seem to take to him so much.'

'He once put a drawing-pin on Catsmeat's chair.'

'Ah, that would account for the imperfect sympathy. Talking of Catsmeat, did he give you the Pat and Mike script?'

'Yes, I've got it. I was studying it in bed last night.'

22

'Good. It was sporting of you to rally round.'

I didn't tell her that my rallying round had been primarily due to *force majeure* on the part of an aunt who brooks, if that's the word, no back-chat. Instead, I asked who was to be my partner in the merry *mélange* of fun and topicality, sustaining the minor but exacting role of Mike, and she said an artiste of the name of Dobbs.

'Police Constable Dobbs, the local rozzer. And in this connection, Bertie, there is one thing I want to impress upon you with all the emphasis at my disposal. When socking Constable Dobbs with your umbrella at the points where the script calls for it, don't pull your punches. Let the blighter have it with every ounce of wrist and muscle. I want to see him come off that stage a mass of contusions.'

It seemed to me, for I am pretty quick, that she had it in for this Dobbs. I said so, and she concurred, a quick frown marring the alabaster purity of her brow.

'I have. I'm devoted to my poor old Uncle Sidney, and this uncouth bluebottle is a thorn in his flesh. He's the village atheist.'

'Oh, really? An atheist, is he? I never went in for that sort of thing much myself. In fact, at my private school I once won a prize for Scripture Knowledge.'

'He annoys Uncle Sidney by popping out at him from side streets and making offensive cracks about Jonah and the Whale. This cross-talk act has been sent from heaven. In ordinary life, I mean, you get so few opportunities of socking cops with umbrellas, and if ever a cop needed the treatment, it is Ernest Dobbs. When he isn't smirching Jonah and the Whale with his low sneers, he's asking Uncle Sidney where Cain got his wife. You can't say that sort of thing is pleasant for a sensitive vicar, so hew to the line, my poppet, and let the chips fall where they may.'

She had stirred the Wooster blood and aroused the

Wooster chivalry. I assured her that by the time they struck up 'God Save The King' in the old village hall Constable Dobbs would know he had been in a fight, and she thanked me prettily.

'I can see you're going to be good, Bertie. And I don't mind telling you your public is expecting big things. For days the whole village has been talking of nothing else but the coming visit of Bertram Wooster, the great London comic. You will be the high spot of the programme. And goodness knows it can do with a high spot or two.'

'Who are the performers?'

'Just the scourings of the neighbourhood . . . and Esmond Haddock. He's singing a song.'

The way she spoke that name, with a sort of frigid distaste as if it soiled her lips, told me that Catsmeat had not erred in saying that she was as sore as a gumboil about E. Haddock's in-and-out running. Remembering that he had warned me to approach the subject tactfully, I picked my words with care.

'Ah, yes. Esmond Haddock. Catsmeat was telling me about Esmond Haddock.'

'What did he tell you?'

'Oh, this and that.'

'Featuring me?'

'Yes, to a certain extent featuring you.'

'What did he say?'

'Well, he seemed to hint, unless I misunderstood him, that the above Haddock hadn't, as it were, done right by our Nell. According to Catsmeat, you and this modern Casanova were at one time holding hands, but after flitting and sipping for a while he cast you aside like a worn-out glove and attached himself to Gertrude Winkworth. Quite incorrect, probably. I expect he got the whole story muddled up.'

She came clean. I suppose a girl who has been going about for some weeks as sore as a gumboil, and with the

heart cracked in two places gets to feel that maidenly
pride is all very well but that what eases the soul is
confession. And, of course, making me her confidant
was not like spilling the inside stuff to a stranger. No
doubt the thought crossed her mind that we had
attended the same dancing class, and it may be that a
vision of the child Wooster in a Little Lord Fauntleroy
suit and pimples rose before her eyes.

'No, he didn't get the story muddled up. We were
holding hands. But Esmond didn't cast me aside like a
worn-out glove, I cast him aside like a worn-out glove. I
told him I wouldn't have any more to do with him
unless he asserted himself and stopped crawling to those
aunts of his.'

'He crawls to his aunts, does he?'

'Yes, the worm.'

I could not pass this. Better men than Esmond
Haddock have crawled to their aunts, and I said so, but
she didn't seem to be listening. Girls seldom do listen to
me, I've noticed. Her face was drawn and her eyes had a
misty look. The lips, I observed, were a-quiver.

'I oughtn't to call him a worm. It's not his fault,
really. They brought him up from the time he was six,
oppressing him daily, and it's difficult for him to cast off
the shackles, I suppose. I'm very sorry for him. But
there's a limit. When it came to being scared to tell
them we were engaged, I put my foot down. I said he'd
got to tell them, and he turned green and said Oh, he
couldn't, and I said All right, then, let's call the whole
thing off. And I haven't spoken to him since, except to
ask him to sing this song at the concert. And the
unfortunate part of it all is, Bertie, that I'm crazier about
him than ever. Just to think of him makes me want to
howl and chew the carpet.'

At this point she buried her face in Sam Goldwyn's
coat, ostensibly by way of showing a proprietress's
affection, but really, I could see, being shrewd, in order

to dry the starting tears. Personally, for the animal niffed to heaven, I would have preferred to use my cambric handkerchief, but girls will be girls.

'Oh, well,' she said, coming to the surface again.

It was a bit difficult to know how to carry on. A 'There, there, little woman' might have gone well, or it might not. After thinking it over for a moment, I too-badded.

'Oh, it's all right,' she said, stiffening the upper lip. 'Just one of those things. When do you go down to Deverill?'

'This evening.'

'How do you feel about it?'

'Not too good. A certain coolness in the feet. I'm never at my best in the society of aunts and, according to Jeeves, they assemble in gangs at Deverill Hall. There are five of them, he says.'

'That's right.'

'It's a lot.'

'Five too many. I don't think you'll like them, Bertie. One's deaf, one's dotty, and they're all bitches.'

'You use strong words, child.'

'Only because I can't think of any stronger. They're awful. They've lived all their lives at that mouldering old Hall, and they're like something out of a three-volume novel. They judge everybody by the county standard. If you aren't county, you don't exist. I believe they swooned for weeks when their sister married Esmond's father.'

'Yes, Jeeves rather suggested that in their opinion he soiled the escutcheon.'

'Nothing to the way I would have soiled it. Being in pix, I'm the scarlet woman.'

'I've often wondered about that scarlet woman. Was she scarlet all over, or was it just that her face was red? However, that is not germane to the issue. So that's how it is, is it?'

'That's how it is.'

I was rather glad that at this juncture the hound Sam Goldwyn made another of his sudden dives at my abdomen with the slogan 'Back to Bertram' on his lips, for it enabled me to bridge over an emotional moment. I was considerably concerned. What was to be done about it, I didn't know, but there was no gainsaying that when it came to making matrimonial plans, the Pirbrights were not a lucky family.

Corky seemed to be feeling this, too.

'It would happen, wouldn't it,' she said, 'that the only one of all the millions of men I've met that I've ever wanted to marry can't marry me because his aunts won't let him.'

'It's tough on you,' I agreed.

'And just as tough on poor old Catsmeat. You wouldn't think, just seeing him around, that Catsmeat was the sort of man to break his heart over a girl, but he is. He's full of hidden depths, if you really know him. Gertrude means simply everything to him. And I doubt if she will be able to hold out against a combination of Esmond and her mother and the aunts.'

'Yes, he told me pressure was being applied.'

'How did you think he seemed?'

'Low-spirited.'

'Yes, he's taking it hard,' said Corky.

Her face clouded. Catsmeat has always been her ewe lamb, if you understand what I mean by ewe lamb. It was plain that she mourned for him in spirit, and no doubt at this point we should have settled down to a long talk about his spot of bother, examining it from every angle and trying to decide what was to be done for the best, had not the door opened and he blown in in person.

'Hallo, Catsmeat,' I said.

'Hallo, Catsmeat, darling,' said Corky.

'Hallo,' said Catsmeat.

I looked at Corky. She looked at me. I rather think we pursed our lips and, speaking for myself, I know I raised my eyebrows. For the demeanour of this Pirbright was that of a man who has abandoned hope, and the voice in which he had said 'Hallo' had been to all intents and purposes a voice from the tomb. The whole set-up, in short, such as to occasion pity and terror in the bosoms of those who wished him well.

He sank into a chair and closed his eyes, and for some moments remained motionless. Then, as if a bomb had suddenly exploded inside the bean, he shot up with a stifled cry, clasping his temples, and I began to see daylight. His deportment, so plainly that of a man aware that only prompt action in the nick of time has prevented his head splitting in half, told me that we had been mistaken in supposing that this living corpse had got that way purely through disappointed love. I touched the bell, and Jeeves appeared.

'One of your special morning-afters, if you please, Jeeves.'

'Very good, sir.'

He shimmered out, and I subjected Catsmeat to a keen glance. I am told by those who know that there are six varieties of hangover – the Broken Compass, the Sewing Machine, the Comet, the Atomic, the Cement Mixer and the Gremlin Boogie, and his manner suggested that he had got them all.

'So you were lathered last night?' I said.

'I was perhaps a mite polluted,' he admitted.

'Jeeves has gone for one of his revivers.'

'Thank you, Bertie, thank you,' said Catsmeat in a low, soft voice, and closed his eyes again.

His intention obviously was to restore his tissues with a short nap, and personally I would have left him alone and let him go to it. But Corky was of sterner stuff. She took his head in both hands and shook it, causing him to shoot ceilingwards, this time with a cry so little stifled that it rang through the room like the death rattle of a hundred expiring hyenas. The natural consequence was that Sam Goldwyn began splitting the welkin, and with the view of taking him off the air I steered him to the door and bunged him out. I returned to find Corky ticking Catsmeat off in no uncertain manner.

'You promised me faithfully you wouldn't get pie-eyed, you poor fish,' she was saying with sisterly vehemence. 'What price the word of the Pirbrights?'

'That's all right "What price the word of the Pirbrights?"' retorted Catsmeat with some spirit. 'When I gave the word of the Pirbrights that I wouldn't get pie-eyed, I didn't know I should be dining with Gussie Fink-Nottle. Bertie will bear me out that it is not humanly possible to get through an evening alone with Gussie without large quantities of stimulants.'

I nodded.

'He's quite right,' I said. 'Even at the peak of his form Gussie isn't everybody's dream-comrade, and last night I should imagine he was low-spirited.'

'Very low-spirited,' said Catsmeat. 'In my early touring days I have sometimes arrived at Southport on a rainy Sunday morning. Gussie gave me that same sense of hopeless desolation. He sat there with his lower jaw drooping, goggling at me like a codfish –'

'Gussie,' I explained to Corky, 'has had a lovers' tiff with his betrothed.'

' – until after a bit I saw that there was only one thing to be done, if I was to survive the ordeal. I told the waiter to bring a magnum and leave it at my elbow. After that, things seemed to get better.'

'Gussie, of course, drank orange juice?'

'Throughout,' said Catsmeat with a slight shudder.

I could see that even though he had made this manly, straight-forward statement, Corky was still threatening to do the heavy sister and heap reproaches on a man who was in no condition to receive them, for even the best of women cannot refrain from saying their say the morning after, so I hastened to continue the conversation on a neutral note.

'Where did you dine?'

'At the Dorchester.'

'Go anywhere after dinner?'

'Oh, yes.'

'Where?'

'Oh, hither and thither. East Dulwich, Ponder's End, Limehouse –'

'Why Limehouse?'

'Well, I had always wanted to see it, and I may have had some idea of comparing its blues with mine. As to East Dulwich and Ponder's End, I am not sure. Perhaps I heard someone recommend them, or possibly I just felt that the thing to do was to get about and see fresh faces. I had chartered a taxi for the evening and we roamed around, taking in the sights. Eventually we fetched up in Trafalgar Square.'

'What time was this?'

'About five in the morning. Have you ever been in Trafalgar Square at five in the morning? Very picturesque, that fountain in the first early light of the dawn. It was as we stood on its brink with the sun just beginning to gild the house-tops that I got an idea which I can now see, though it seemed a good one at the time, was a mistake.'

'What was that?'

'It struck me as a possibility that there might be newts in the fountain, and knowing how keen Gussie is on newts I advised him to wade in and hunt around.'

'With all his clothes on?'

'Yes, he had his clothes on. I remember noticing.'

'But you can't go wading in the Trafalgar Square fountain with all your clothes on.'

'Yes, you can. Gussie did. My recollection of the thing

is a trifle blurred, but I seem to recall that he took a bit of persuading. Yes, I've got it now,' said Catsmeat, brightening. 'I told him to wade, and he wouldn't wade, and I said if he didn't wade I would bean him with my magnum. So he waded.'

'You still had the magnum?'

'This was another one, which we had picked up in Limehouse.'

'And Gussie waded?'

'Yes, Gussie waded.'

'I wonder he wasn't pinched.'

'He was,' said Catsmeat. 'A cop came along and gaffed him, and this morning he was given fourteen days without the option at Bosher Street police court.'

The door opened. Sam Goldwyn came bounding in and flung himself on my chest as if we had been a couple of lovers meeting at journey's end.

He was followed by Jeeves, bearing a salver with a glass on it containing one of his dynamite specials.

4

When I was a piefaced lad of some twelve summers,
doing my stretch at Malvern House, Bramley-on-Sea, the
private school conducted by the Rev. Aubrey Upjohn, I
remember hearing the Rev. Aubrey give the late Sir
Philip Sidney a big build-up because, when wounded at
the battle of somewhere and offered a quick one by a
companion in arms, he told the chap who was setting
them up to leave him out of that round and slip his spot
to a nearby stretcher-case, whose need was greater than
his. This spirit of selfless sacrifice, said the Rev. Aubrey,
was what he would like to see in you boys – particularly
you, Wooster, and how many times have I told you not
to gape at me in that half-witted way? Close your
mouth, boy, and sit up.

Well, if he had been one of our little circle, he would
have seen it now. My primary impulse was to charge
across and grab that glass from that salver and lower it at
a gulp, for if ever I needed a bracer, it was then. But I
stayed my hand. Even in that dreadful moment I was
able to tell myself that Catsmeat's need was greater than
mine. I stood back, shimmying in every limb, and he got
the juice and drained it, and after going through the
motions of a man struck by lightning, always the
immediate reaction to these pick-me-ups of Jeeves's,
said 'Ha!' and looked a lot better.

I passed a fevered hand across the brow.

'Jeeves!'

'Sir?'

'Do you know what?'

'No, sir.'

'Gussie Fink-Nottle is in stir.'

'Indeed, sir?'

I passed another hand across the brow, and the blood pressure rose several notches. I ought, I suppose, to have got it into my nut by this time that no news item, however front page, is going to make Jeeves roll his eyes and leap about, but that 'Indeed, sir?' stuff of his never fails to get the Wooster goat.

'Don't say "Indeed, sir?" I repeat. Wading in the Trafalgar Square fountain at five ack emma this morning, Augustus Fink-Nottle was apprehended by the police and is in the coop for fourteen days. And he's due at Deverill Hall this evening.'

Catsmeat, who had closed his eyes, opened them for a moment.

'Shall I tell you something?' he said. 'He won't be there.'

He reclosed the eyes, and I passed a third hand across the brow.

'You see the ghastly position, Jeeves? What is Miss Bassett going to say? What will her attitude be when she learns the facts? She opens to-morrow's paper. She sees that loved name in headlines in the police court section . . .'

'No, she doesn't,' said Catsmeat. 'Because Gussie, showing unexpected intelligence, gave his name as Alfred Duff Cooper.'

'Well, what's going to happen when he doesn't turn up at the Hall?'

'Yes, there's that,' said Catsmeat, and fell into a refreshing sleep.

'I'll tell you what Miss Bassett is going to say. She is going to say . . . Jeeves!'

'Sir?'

'You are letting your attention wander.'

'I beg your pardon, sir. I was observing the dog. If you notice, sir, he has commenced to eat the sofa cushion.'

'Never mind about the dog.'

'I think it would be advisable to remove the little fellow to the kitchen, sir,' he said with respectful firmness. Jeeves is a great stickler for having things just right. 'I will return as soon as he is safely immured.'

He withdrew, complete with dog, and Corky caught the speaker's eye. For some moments she had been hovering on the outskirts with the air of one not completely abreast of the continuity.

'But, Bertie,' she said, 'why all the excitement and agony? I could understand this Mr Fink-Nottle being a little upset, but why are you skipping like the high hills?'

I was glad that Jeeves had temporarily absented himself from the conference-table, as it would have been impossible for me to unbosom myself freely about Madeline Bassett in his presence. Naturally he knows all the circumstances *in re* the Bassett, and I know he knows them, but we do not discuss her. To do so would be bandying a woman's name. The Woosters do not bandy a woman's name. Nor, for the matter of that, do the Jeeveses.

'Hasn't Catsmeat told you about me and Madeline Bassett?'

'Not a word.'

'Well, I'll tell you why I'm skipping like the high hills,' I said, and proceeded to do so.

The Bassett-Wooster imbroglio or mix-up will, of course, be old stuff to those of my public who were hanging on my lips when I told of it before, but there are always new members coming along, and for the benefit of these new members I will give a brief what's-it-called of the facts.

The thing started at Brinkley Court, my Aunt Dahlia's place in Worcestershire, when Gussie and I and this blighted Bassett were putting in a spell there during

the previous summer. It was one of those cases you so
often read about where Bloke A loves a girl but fears to
speak and a friend of his, Bloke B, out of the kindness of
his heart, offers to pave the way for him with a few
well-chosen words – completely overlooking, poor
fathead, the fact that by doing so he will be sticking his
neck out and simply asking for it. What I'm driving at is
that Gussie, though very much under the influence,
could not bring himself to start the necessary
pourparlers, and like an ass I told him to leave this to
me.

And so, steering the girl out into the twilight one
evening, I pulled some most injudicious stuff about
there being hearts at Brinkley Court that ached for love
of her. And the first thing I knew, she was saying that of
course she had guessed how I felt, for a girl always
knows, doesn't she, but she was so, so sorry it could not
be, for she was sold on Gussie. But, she went on, and it
was this that had made peril lurk ever since, if there
should come a time when she found that Gussie was not
the rare, stainless soul she thought him, she would hand
him his hat and make me happy.

And, as I have related elsewhere, there had been
moments when it had been touch and go, notably on the
occasion when Gussie got lit up like a candelabra and in
that condition presented the prizes to the young scholars
of Market Snodsbury Grammar School. She had
scratched his nomination then, though subsequently
relenting, and it could not but be that she would scratch
it again, should she discover that the man on whom she
looked as a purer, loftier spirit than other men had
received an exemplary sentence for wading in the
Trafalgar Square fountain. Nothing puts an idealistic girl
off a fellow more than the news that he is doing fourteen
days in the jug.

All this I explained to Corky, and she said Yes, she
saw what I meant.

'I should think you do see what I mean. I shan't have a hope. Let Madeline Bassett become hep to what has occurred, and there can be but one result. Gussie will get the bum's rush, and the bowed figure you will see shambling down the aisle at her side, while the customers reach for their hats and the organ plays "The Voice That Breathed O'er Eden", will be that of Bertram Wilberforce Wooster.'

'I didn't know your name was Wilberforce.'

I explained that except in moments of great emotion one hushed it up.

'But Bertie, I can't understand why you don't want to shamble down aisles at her side. I've seen a photograph of her at the Hall, and she's a pippin.'

This is a very common error into which people fall who have never met Madeline Bassett but have only seen her photograph. As far as the outer crust is concerned, there is little, I fully realize, to cavil at in this pre-eminent bit of bad news. The eyes are large and lustrous, the features delicately moulded, the hair, nose, teeth and ears well up to, if not above, the average standard. Judge her by the photograph alone, and you have something that would be widely accepted as a pin-up girl.

But there is a catch, and a very serious catch.

'You ask me why I do not wish to shamble down aisles at her side,' I said. 'I will tell you. It is because, though externally, as you say, a pippin, she is the sloppiest, mushiest, sentimentalest young Gawd-help-us who ever thought the stars were God's daisy chain and that every time a fairy hiccoughs a wee baby is born. She is squashy and soupy. Her favourite reading is Christopher Robin and Winnie the Pooh. I can perhaps best sum it up by saying that she is the ideal mate for Gussie Fink-Nottle.'

'I've never met Mr Fink-Nottle.'

'Well, ask the man who has.'

She stood pondering. It was plain that she appreciated the gravity of the situation.

'Then you think that, if she finds out, you will be in for it?'

'Definitely and indubitably. I shall have no option but to take the rap. If a girl thinks you love her, and comes and says she is returning her betrothed to store and is now prepared to sign up with you, what can you do except marry her? One must be civil.'

'Yes, I see. Difficult. But how are you going to keep her from finding out? When she hears that Mr Fink-Nottle hasn't arrived at the Hall, she's bound to make inquiries.'

'And those inquiries, once made, must infallibly lead her to the awful truth? Exactly. But there is always Jeeves.'

'You think he will be able to fix things?'

'He never fails. He wears a number fourteen hat, eats tons of fish, and moves in a mysterious way his wonders to perform. See, here he comes, looking as intelligent as dammit. Well, Jeeves? Have you speared a solution?'

'Yes, sir. But –'

'You see,' I said to Corky. I paused, knitting the brow a bit. 'Did I hear you use the word "but", Jeeves? Why "but"?'

'It is merely that I entertained a certain misgiving as to whether the solution which I am about to put forward would meet with your approval, sir.'

'If it's a solution, that's all I want.'

'Well, sir, to obviate the inquiries which would inevitably be set on foot, should Mr Fink-Nottle not present himself at Deverill Hall this evening, it would appear to be essential that a substitute, purporting to be Mr Fink-Nottle, should take his place.'

I reeled.

'You aren't suggesting that I should check in at this leper colony as Gussie?'

'Unless you can persuade one of your friends to do so, sir.'

I laughed. One of those hollow, mirthless ones.

'You can't go about London asking people to pretend to be Gussie Fink-Nottle. At least, you can, I suppose, but what a hell of a life. Besides, there isn't time to . . .' I paused. 'Catsmeat!' I cried.

Catsmeat opened his eyes.

'Hallo, there,' he said, seeming much refreshed. 'How's it coming?'

'It's come. Jeeves has found the way.'

'I thought he would. What does he suggest?'

'He thinks . . . What was it, Jeeves?'

'To obviate the inquiries which would inevitably be set on foot should Mr Fink-Nottle not present himself at Deverill Hall this evening –'

'Follow this closely, Catsmeat.'

' – it would appear to be essential that a substitute, purporting to be Mr Fink-Nottle, should take his place.'

Catsmeat nodded, and said he considered that very sound.

'You mean Bertie, of course?'

I massaged his coat sleeve tenderly.

'We thought of you,' I said.

'Me?'

'Yes.'

'You want me to say I'm Gussie Fink-Nottle?'

'That's right.'

'No,' said Catsmeat. 'A thousand times no. What a revolting idea!'

The shuddering horror with which he spoke made me realize how deeply his experiences of the previous night must have affected him. And, mind you, I could understand his attitude. Gussie is a fellow you can take or leave alone, and anyone having him as a constant companion from eight at night till five on the following

morning might well become a bit allergic to him. I began
to see that a good deal of silver-tongued eloquence
would be needed in order to obtain service and
co-operation from C. C. Pirbright.

'It would enable you to be beneath the same roof as
Gertrude Winkworth,' I urged.

'Yes,' said Corky, 'you would be at your Gertrude's
side.'

'Even to be at my Gertrude's side,' said Catsmeat
firmly, 'I won't have people going about thinking I'm
Gussie Fink-Nottle. Besides, I couldn't get away with it.
I shouldn't be even adequate in the role. I'm much too
obviously a man of intelligence and brains and gifts and
all that sort of thing, and Gussie must have been widely
publicized as the fat-headedest ass in creation. After five
minutes' conversation with me the old folks would
penetrate the deception like a dose of salts. No, what
you want if you are putting on an understudy for Gussie
Fink-Nottle is someone *like* Gussie Fink-Nottle, so that
the eye is deceived. You get the part, Bertie.'

A cry escaped me.

'You don't think I'm like Gussie?'

'You might be twins.'

'I still think you're a chump, Catsmeat,' said Corky.
'If you were at Deverill Hall you could protect Gertrude
from Esmond Haddock's advances.'

'Bertie's attending to that. I agree that I would much
enjoy a brief visit to Deverill Hall, and if only there were
some other way . . . But I won't say I'm Gussie
Fink-Nottle.'

I bowed to the inev.

'Right ho,' I said, with one of those sighs. 'In all
human affairs there has got to be a goat or Patsy doing
the dirty work, and in the present crisis I see it has got
to be me. It generally happens that way. Whenever there
is a job to be taken on of a kind calculated to make
Humanity shudder, the cry goes up "Let Wooster do it".

I'm not complaining, I'm just mentioning it. Very well.
No need to argue. I'll be Gussie.'

'Smiling, the boy fell dead. That's the way I like to
hear you talk,' said Catsmeat. 'On the way down be
thinking out your business.'

'What do you mean – my business?'

'Well, for instance, would it or would it not be a good
move to kiss Gussie's girl's godmother when you meet?
Those are the little points you will have to give thought
to. And now, Bertie, if you don't mind, I'll be pushing
along to your bedroom and taking a short nap. Too many
interruptions in here, and sleep is what I must have, if I
am to face the world again. What was it I heard you call
sleep the other day, Jeeves?'

'Tired Nature's sweet restorer, sir.'

'That was it. And you said a mouthful.'

He crawled off, and Corky said she would have to be
going too. A hundred things to attend to.

'Well, it all looks pretty smooth now, thanks to
your quick thinking, Jeeves,' she said. 'The only
nuisance is that there will be disappointment in the
village when they hear they're going to get a Road
Company Number Four Fink-Nottle as Pat, and not the
celebrated Bertram Wooster. I rather played you up,
Bertie, in the advance billing and publicity. Still, it can't
be helped. Good-bye. We shall meet at Philippi.
Good-bye, Jeeves.'

'Good-bye, miss.'

'Here, half a second,' I said. 'You're forgetting your
dog.'

She paused at the door.

'Oh, I had been meaning to tell you about that, Bertie.
I want you to take him to the Hall with you for a day or
two, so as to give me time to prepare Uncle Sidney's
mind. He's not too keen on dogs, and Sam will have to
be broken to him gently.'

I put in an instant *nolle prosequi*.

'I'm not going to appear at the Hall with a dog like that. It would ruin my prestige.'

'Mr Fink-Nottle's prestige, you mean. And I don't suppose he has any. As Catsmeat said, they have been told all about him, and will probably be relieved that you aren't rolling in with half a dozen bowls of newts. Well, good-bye again.'

'Hey!' I yipped, but she had gone.

I turned to Jeeves.

'So, Jeeves!'

'Yes, sir.'

'What do you mean, "Yes, sir"?'

'I was endeavouring to convey my appreciation of the fact that your position *is* in many respects somewhat difficult, sir. But I wonder if I might call your attention to an observation of the Emperor Marcus Aurelius. He said: "Does aught befall you? It is good. It is part of the destiny of the Universe ordained for you from the beginning. All that befalls you is part of the great web."'

I breathed a bit stertorously.

'He said that, did he?'

'Yes, sir.'

'Well, you can tell him from me he's an ass. Are my things packed?'

'Yes, sir.'

'The two-seater is at the door?'

'Yes, sir.'

'Then lead me to it, Jeeves. If I'm to get to this lazar-house before midnight, I'd better be starting.'

5

Well, I did get there before midnight, of course, but I was
dashed late, all the same. As might have been expected
on a day like this, the two-seater, usually as reliable as
an Arab steed, developed some sort of pox or sickness
half-way through the journey, with the result that the
time schedule was shot to pieces and it was getting on
for eight when I turned in at the main gates. A quick
burst up the drive enabled me to punch the front-door
bell at about twenty to.   I remember once when he and
I arrived at a country house where the going threatened
to be sticky, Jeeves, as we alighted, murmured in my ear
the words 'Childe Roland to the Dark Tower came, sir',
and at the time I could make nothing of the crack.
Subsequent inquiry, however, revealed that this Roland
was one of those knights of the Middle Ages who spent
their time wandering to and fro, and that on fetching up
one evening at a dump known as the Dark Tower he had
scratched the chin a bit dubiously, not liking the look of
things.

It was the same with me now. I admired Deverill
Hall, I could appreciate that it was a fine old pile, with
battlements and all the fixings, and if the Deverill who
built it had been with me at the moment, I would have
slapped him on the back and said 'Nice work, Deverill'.
But I quailed at the thought of what lay within. Behind
that massive front door lurked five aunts of early
Victorian vintage and an Esmond Haddock who, when
he got on to the fact that I was proposing to pull a
Mary's lamb on him, was quite likely to forget the
obligations of a host and break my neck. Considerations

like these prevent one feasting the eye on Tudor architecture with genuine enjoyment and take from fifty to sixty per cent off the entertainment value of spreading lawns and gay flower-beds.

The door opened, revealing some sixteen stone of butler.

'Good evening, sir,' said this substantial specimen. 'Mr Wooster?'

'Fink-Nottle,' I said hastily, to correct this impression.

As a matter of fact, it was all I could do to speak at all, for the sudden impact of Charlie Silversmith had removed the breath almost totally. He took me right back to the days when I was starting out as a *flâneur* and man about town and used to tremble beneath butlers' eyes and generally feel very young and bulbous.

Older now and tougher, I am able to take most of these fauna in my stride. When they open front doors to me, I shoot my cuffs nonchalantly. 'Aha, there, butler,' I say. 'How's tricks?' But Jeeves's Uncle Charlie was something special. He looked like one of those steel engravings of nineteenth-century statesmen. He had a large, bald head and pale, protruding gooseberry eyes, and those eyes, resting on mine, heightened the Dark Tower feeling considerably. The thought crossed my mind that if something like this had popped out at Childe Roland, he would have clapped spurs to his charger and been off like a jack-rabbit.

Sam Goldwyn, attached by a stout cord to the windscreen, seemed to be thinking along much the same lines, for, after one startled glance at Uncle Charlie, he had thrown his head back and was now uttering a series of agitated howls. I sympathized with his distress. A South London dog belonging to the lower middle classes or, rather, definitely of the people, I don't suppose he had ever seen a butler before, and it was a dashed shame that he should have drawn something like Uncle Charlie first crack out of the box. With an apologetic jerk of the thumb I directed the latter's attention to him.

'A dog,' I said, this seeming about as good a way as any other of effecting the introductions, and Uncle Charlie gave him an austere look, as if he had found him using a fish fork for the entrée.

'I will have the animal removed to the stables, sir,' he said coldly, and I said Oh, thanks, that would be fine.

'And now,' I said, 'I'd better be nipping along and dressing, what? I don't want to be late for dinner.'

'Dinner has already commenced, sir. We dine at seven-thirty punctually. If you would care to wash your hands, sir,' he said, and indicated a door to the left.

In the circles in which I move it is pretty generally recognized that I am a resilient sort of bimbo, and in circumstances where others might crack beneath the strain, may frequently be seen rising on stepping-stones of my dead self to higher things. Look in at the Drones and ask the first fellow you meet 'Can the fine spirit of the Woosters be crushed?' and he will offer you attractive odds against such a contingency. However tough the going, he will say, and however numerous what are called the slings and arrows of outrageous fortune, you will still find Bertram in there swinging.

But I had never before been thrust into the position of having to say I was Gussie Fink-Nottle and slap on top of that of having to dine in a strange house without dressing, and I don't mind admitting that for an instant everything went black. It was a limp and tottering Bertram Wooster who soaped, rinsed and dried the outlying portions and followed Uncle Charlie to the dining-room. And what with the agony of feeling like a tramp cyclist and the embarrassment of having to bolt my rations with everybody, or so it seemed to my inflamed imag., clicking their tongues and drumming on the table and saying to one another in undertones what a hell of a nuisance this hold-up was, because they wanted the next course to appear so that they could start digging in and getting theirs, it was not for some time that I was sufficiently restored to be able to glance around the board and take a dekko at the personnel. There had been introductions of a sort, of course – I seemed to recall Uncle Charlie saying 'Mr Fink-Nottle' in a reserved sort of voice, as if wishing to make it clear that it was no good blaming *him* – but they hadn't really registered.

As far as the eye could reach, I found myself gazing on a surging sea of aunts. There were tall aunts, short aunts, stout aunts, thin aunts, and an aunt who was carrying on a conversation in a low voice to which nobody seemed to be paying the slightest attention. I was to learn later that this was Miss Emmeline Deverill's habitual practice, she being the aunt of whom Corky had spoken as the dotty one. From start to finish of every meal she soliloquized. Shakespeare would have liked her.

At the top of the table was a youngish bloke in a well-cut dinner jacket which made me more than ever conscious of the travel-stained upholstery in which I had been forced to appear. E. Haddock, presumably. He was sitting next to a girl in white, so obviously the junior member of the bunch that I deduced that here we had Catsmeat's Gertrude.

Drinking her in, I could see how Catsmeat had got that way. The daughter of Dame Daphne, relict of the late P. B. Winkworth, was slim and blonde and fragile, in sharp contradistinction to her mother, whom I had now identified as the one on my left, a rugged light-heavyweight with a touch of Wallace Beery in her make-up. Her eyes were blue, her teeth pearly, and in other respects she had what it takes. I was quite able to follow Catsmeat's thought processes. According to his own statement, he had walked with this girl in an old garden on twilight evenings, with the birds singing sleepily in the shrubberies and the stars beginning to peep out, and no man of spirit could do that with a girl like this without going under the ether.

I was musing on these two young hearts in springtime and speculating with a not unmanly touch of sentiment on their chances of spearing the happy ending, when the subject of the concert came up.

The conversation at the table up to this point had been pretty technical stuff, not easy for the stranger within the gates to get a toe-hold on. You know the sort of thing I mean. One aunt saying that she had had a letter from Emily by the afternoon post, and another aunt saying Had she said anything about Fred and Alice, and the first aunt saying Yes, everything was all right about Fred and Alice, because Agnes had now told Edith what Jane had said to Eleanor. All rather mystic.

But now an aunt in spectacles said she had met the vicar that evening and the poor old gook was spitting blood because his niece, Miss Pirbright, insisted on introducing into the programme of the concert what she described as a knockabout cross-talk act by Police Constable Dobbs and Agatha Worplesdon's nephew, Mr Wooster. What a knockabout cross-talk act was, she had no idea. Perhaps you can tell us, Augustus?

I was only too glad to have the opportunity of saying a few words, for, except for a sort of simpering giggle at the outset, I hadn't uttered since joining the party, and I felt it was about time, for Gussie's sake, that I came out of the silence. Carry along on these lines much longer, and the whole gang would be at their desks writing letters to the Bassett entreating her to think twice before entrusting her happiness to a dumb brick who would probably dish the success of the honeymoon by dashing off in the middle of it to become a Trappist monk.

'Oh, rather,' I said. 'It's one of those Pat and Mike things. Two birds come on in green beards, armed with umbrellas, and one bird says to the other bird "Who was that lady I saw you coming down the street with?" and the second bird says to the first bird "Faith and begob, that was no lady, that was my wife." And then the second bird busts the first bird over the bean with his umbrella, and the first bird, not to be behindhand, busts the second bird over the head with *his* umbrella. And so the long day wears on.'

It didn't go well. There was a sharp intake of breath from one and all.

'Very vulgar!' said one aunt.

'Terribly vulgar!' said another.

'Disgustingly vulgar,' said Dame Daphne Winkworth. 'But how typical of Miss Pirbright to suggest such a performance at a village concert.'

The rest of the aunts didn't say 'You betcher' or 'You've got something there, Daph', but their manner suggested these words. Lips were pursed and noses looked down. I began to get on to what Catsmeat had meant when he had said that these females did not approve of Corky. Her stock was plainly down in the cellar and the market sluggish.

'Well, I am glad,' said the aunt in spectacles, 'that it is this Mr Wooster and not you, Augustus, who is disgracing himself by taking part in this degrading horseplay. Imagine how Madeline would feel!'

'Madeline would never get over it,' said a thin aunt.

'Dear Madeline is so spiritual,' said Dame Daphne Winkworth.

A cold hand seemed to clutch at my heart. I felt like a Gadarene swine that has come within a toucher of doing a nose-dive over the precipice. You'll scarcely believe it, but it had never so much as crossed my mind that Madeline Bassett, on learning that her lover had been going about in a green beard socking policemen with umbrellas, would be revolted to the depths of her soul. Why, dash it, the engagement wouldn't go on functioning for a minute after the news had reached her. You can't be too careful how you stir up these romantic girls with high ideals. A Gussie in a green beard would be almost worse than a Gussie in the cooler.

It gave me a pang to hand in my portfolio, for I had been looking forward to a sensational triumph, but I know when I'm licked. I resolved that bright and early tomorrow morning word must be sent to Corky that Bertram was out and that she would have to enlist the services of another artist for the role of Pat.

'From all I have heard of Mr Wooster,' said an aunt with a beaky nose, continuing the theme, 'this kind of vulgar foolery will be quite congenial to him. By the way, where *is* Mr Wooster?'

'Yes,' chimed in the aunt with spectacles. 'He was to have arrived this afternoon, and he has not even sent a telegram.'

'He must be a most erratic young man,' said a third aunt, who would have been the better for a good facial.

Dame Daphne took command of the conversation like a headmistress at a conference of her subordinates.

'"Erratic",' she said, 'is a kindly term. He appears to be completely irresponsible. Agatha tells me that sometimes she despairs of him. She says she often wonders if the best thing would not be to put him in a home of some kind.'

You may picture the emotions of Bertram on learning that his flesh and blood was in the habit of roasting the pants off him in this manner. One doesn't demand much in the way of gratitude, of course, but when you have gone to the expense and inconvenience of taking an aunt's son to the Old Vic, you are justified, I think, in expecting her to behave like an aunt who has had her son taken to the Old Vic – in expecting her, in other words, to exhibit a little decent feeling and a modicum of the live-and-let-live spirit. How sharper than a serpent's tooth, I remember Jeeves saying once, it is to have a thankless child, and it isn't a dashed sight better having a thankless aunt.

I flushed darkly, and would have drained my glass if it had contained anything restorative. But it didn't. Champagne of a sound vintage was flowing like water elsewhere, Uncle Charlie getting a stiff wrist pouring the stuff, but I, in deference to Gussie's known tastes, had been served with that obscene beverage which is produced by putting half an orange on a squeezer and pushing.

'There seems,' proceeded Dame Daphne in the cold and disapproving voice which in the old days she would have employed when rebuking Maud or Beatrice for smoking gaspers in the shrubbery, 'to be no end to his escapades. It is not so long ago that he was arrested and fined for stealing a policeman's helmet in Piccadilly.'

I could put her straight there, and did so.

'That,' I explained, 'was due to an unfortunate oversight. In pinching a policeman's helmet, as of course I don't need to tell you, it is essential before lifting to give a forward shove in order to detach the strap from the officer's chin. This Wooster omitted to do, with the results you have described. But I think you ought to take into consideration the fact that the incident occurred pretty late on Boat Race night, when the best of men are not quite themselves. Still, be that as it may,' I said, quickly sensing that I had not got the sympathy of the audience and adroitly changing the subject, 'I wonder if you know the one about the strip-tease dancer and the performing flea. Or, rather, no, not that one,' I said, remembering that it was a *conte* scarcely designed for the gentler sex and the tots. 'The one about the two men in the train. It's old, of course, so stop me if you've heard it before.'

'Pray go on, Augustus.'

'It's about these two deaf men in the train.'

'My sister Charlotte has the misfortune to be deaf. It is a great affliction.'

49

The thin aunt bent forward.

'What is he saying?'

'Augustus is telling us a story, Charlotte. Please go on, Augustus.'

Well, of course, this had damped the fire a bit, for the last thing one desires is to be supposed to be giving a maiden lady the horse's laugh on account of her physical infirmities, but it was too late now to take a bow and get off, so I had a go at it.

'Well, there were these two deaf chaps in the train, don't you know, and it stopped at Wembley, and one of them looked out of the window and said "This is Wembley", and the other said "I thought it was Thursday", and the first chap said "Yes, so am I".'

I hadn't had much hope. Right from the start something had seemed to whisper in my ear that I was about to lay an egg. I laughed heartily to myself, but I was the only one. At the point where the aunts should have rolled out of their seats like one aunt there occurred merely a rather ghastly silence as of mourners at a death-bed, which was broken by Aunt Charlotte asking what I had said.

I would have been just as pleased to let the whole thing drop, but the stout aunt spoke into her ear, spacing her syllables carefully.

'Augustus was telling us a story about two men in a train. One of them said "To-day is Wednesday", and the other said "I thought it was Thursday", and the first man said "Yes, so did I".'

'Oh?' said Aunt Charlotte, and I suppose that about summed it up.

Shortly after this, the browsing and sluicing being concluded, the females rose and filed from the room. Dame Daphne told Esmond Haddock not to be too long over his port, and popped off. Uncle Charlie brought the decanter, and also popped off. And Esmond Haddock and

I were alone together, self wondering how chances were for getting a couple of glassfuls.

I moved up to his end of the table, licking the lips.

6

Esmond Haddock, seen close to, fully bore out Catsmeat's description of him as a Greek god, and I could well understand the concern of a young lover who saw his girl in danger of being steered into rose gardens by such a one. He was a fine, upstanding – sitting at the moment, of course, but you know what I mean – broad-shouldered bozo of about thirty, with one of those faces which I believe, though I should have to check up with Jeeves, are known as Byronic. He looked like a combination of a poet and an all-in wrestler.

It would not have surprised you to learn that Esmond Haddock was the author of sonnet sequences of a fruity and emotional nature which had made him the toast of Bloomsbury, for his air was that of a man who could rhyme 'love' and 'dove' as well as the next chap. Nor would you have been astonished if informed that he had recently felled an ox with a single blow. You would simply have felt what an ass the ox must have been to get into an argument with a fellow with a chest like that.

No, what was extraordinary was that this superman was in the habit, as testified to by the witness Corky, of crawling to his aunts. But for Corky's evidence I would have said, looking at him, that there sat a nephew capable of facing the toughest aunt and making her say Uncle. Not that you can ever tell, of course, by the outward appearance. Many a fellow who looks like the dominant male and has himself photographed smoking a pipe curls up like carbon paper when confronted with one of these relatives.

He helped himself to port, and there was a momentary silence, as so often occurs when two strong men who have not been formally introduced sit face to face. He worked painstakingly through his snootful, while I continued to fix my bulging eyes on the decanter. It was one of those outsize decanters, full to the brim.

He swigged away for some little while before opening the conversation. His manner was absent, and I got the impression that he was thinking deeply. Presently he spoke.

'I say,' he said, in an odd, puzzled voice. 'That story of yours.'

'Oh, yes?'

'About the fellows in the train.'

'Quite.'

'I was a bit *distrait* when you were telling it, and I think I may possibly have missed the point. As I got it, there were two men in a train, and it stopped at a station.'

'That's right.'

'And one of them said "This is Woking", and the other chap said "I'm thirsty". Was that how it went?'

'Not quite. It was Wembley the train stopped at, and the fellow said he thought it was Thursday.'

'Was it Thursday?'

'No, no, these chaps were deaf, you see. So when the first chap said "This is Woking", the other chap, thinking he had said "Wednesday", said "So am I". I mean –'

'I see. Yes, most amusing,' said Esmond Haddock.

He refilled his glass, and I think that as he did so he must have noticed the tense, set expression on my face, rather like that of a starving wolf giving a Russian peasant the once-over, for he started, as if realizing that he had been remiss.

'I say, I suppose it's no good offering you any of this?'

I felt the table-talk could not have taken a more satisfactory turn.

'Well, do you know,' I said, 'I wouldn't mind trying it. It would be an experience. It's whisky, or claret or something, isn't it?'

'Port. You may not like it.'

'Oh, I think I shall.'

And a moment later I was in a position to state that I did. It was a very fine old port, full of buck and body, and though my better self told me that it should be sipped, I lowered a beakerful at a gulp.

'It's good,' I said.

'It's supposed to be rather special. More?'

'Thanks.'

'I'll have another myself,' he said. 'One needs a lot of bracing up these days, I find. Do you know the expression "These are the times that try men's souls"?'

'New to me. Your own?'

'No, I heard it somewhere.'

'It's very neat.'

'It is, rather. Another?'

'Thanks.'

'I'll join you. Shall I tell you something?'

'Do.'

I inclined the ear invitingly. Three goblets of the right stuff had left me with a very warm affection for this man. I couldn't remember when I had liked a fellow more at a first meeting, and if he wanted to tell me his troubles, I was prepared to listen as attentively as any barman to an old and valued customer.

'The reason I mentioned the times that try men's souls is that I am right up against those identical times at this very moment. My soul is on the rack. More port?'

'Thanks. I find this stuff rather grows on you. Why is your soul on the rack, Esmond? You don't mind me calling you Esmond?'

'I prefer it. I'll call you Gussie.'

This, of course, came as rather an unpleasant shock, Gussie being to my mind about the ultimate low in names. But I quickly saw that in the role I had undertaken I must be prepared to accept the rough with the smooth. We drained our glasses, and Esmond Haddock refilled them. A princely host, he struck me as.

'Esmond,' I said, 'you strike me as a princely host.'

'Thank you, Gussie,' he replied. 'And you're a princely guest. But you were asking me why my soul was on the rack. I will tell you, Gussie. I must begin by saying that I like your face.'

I said I liked his.

'It is an honest face.'

I said his was, too.

'A glance at it tells me that you are trustworthy. By that I mean that I can trust you.'

'Quite.'

'If I couldn't, I wouldn't, if you follow what I mean. Because what I am about to tell you must go no further, Gussie.'

'Not an inch, Esmond.'

'Well, then, the reason my soul is on the rack is that I love a girl with every fibre of my being, and she has given me the brush-off. Enough to put anyone's soul on the rack, what?'

'I should say so.'

'Her name . . . But naturally I can't mention names.'

'Of course not.'

'Not cricket.'

'Not at all.'

'So I will merely say that her name is Cora Pirbright. Corky to her pals. You don't know her, of course. I remember when I told her you were coming here she said she had heard from mutual friends that you were a freak of the first water and practically dotty, but she had never met you. But she is probably familiar to you on

the screen. The name she goes by professionally is Cora
Starr. You've seen her?'

'Oh, rather.'

'An angel in human shape, didn't you think?'

'Definitely.'

'That was my view, too, Gussie. I was in love with her
long before I met her. I had frequently seen her pictures
in Basingstoke. And when old Pirbright, the vicar here,
mentioned that his niece was coming to keep house for
him and that she was just back from Hollywood and I
said "Oh really? Who is she?" and he said "Cora Starr",
you could have knocked me down with a feather,
Gussie.'

'I bet I could, Esmond. Proceed. You are interesting
me strangely.'

'Well, she arrived. Old Pirbright introduced us. Our
eyes met.'

'They would, of course.'

'And it wasn't more than about two days after that
that we talked it over and agreed that we were twin
souls.'

'And then she gave you the brusheroo?'

'And then she gave me the brusheroo. But mark this,
Gussie. Even though she has given me the brusheroo,
she is still the lodestar of my life. My aunts . . . More
port?'

'Thanks.'

'My aunts, Gussie, will try to kid you that I love my
cousin Gertrude. Don't believe a word of it. I'll tell you
how that mistake arose. Shortly after Corky handed
me my papers, I went to the pictures in Basingstoke,
and in the thing they were showing there was a
fellow who had been turned down by a girl, and in
order to make her think a bit and change her mind
he started surging around another girl.'

'To make her jealous?'

'Exactly. I thought it a clever idea.'

'Very clever.'

'And it occurred to me that if I started surging round Gertrude, it might make Corky change her mind. So I surged.'

'I see. A bit risky, wasn't it?'

'Risky?'

'Suppose you overdid it and got too fascinating. Broke her heart, I mean.'

'Corky's heart?'

'No, your cousin Gertrude's heart.'

'Oh, that's all right. She's in love with Corky's brother. No chance of breaking Gertrude's heart. We might drink to the success of my scheme, don't you think, Gussie?'

'An excellent idea, Esmond.'

I was, as you may imagine, profoundly bucked. What this meant was that the dark menace of Esmond Haddock had passed from Catsmeat's life. No more need for him to worry about that rose garden. You could unleash Esmond Haddock in the rose gardens with Gertrude Winkworth by the hour, and no business would result. I raised my glass and emptied it to Catsmeat's happiness. Whether or not a tear stole into my eye, I couldn't say, but I should think it very probable.

It was a pity, of course, that, being supposed never to have met Corky, I couldn't electrify Esmond Haddock and bring the sunshine breezing back into his life by telling him what she had told me – viz. that she loved him still. All I could do was to urge him not to lose hope, and he said he hadn't lost hope, not by a jugful.

'And I'll tell you why I haven't lost hope, Gussie. The other day a very significant thing happened. She came to me and asked me to sing a song at this ghastly concert she's getting up. Well, of course, it wasn't a thing I would have gone out of my way to do, had the circumstances been different. I've never sung at a village concert. Have you?'

'Oh, rather. Often.'

'A terrible ordeal, was it not?'

'Oh, no. I enjoyed it. I don't say it was all jam for the audience, but a good time was had by me. You feel nervous at the prospect, do you, Esmond?'

'There are moments, Gussie, when the thought of what is before me makes me break into a cold perspiration. But then I say to myself that I'm the young Squire and pretty popular around these parts, so I'll probably get by all right.'

'That's the attitude.'

'But you're wondering why I said it was significant that she should have come to me and asked me to sing a song at this foul concert. I'll tell you. I take it as definite evidence that the old affection still lingers. Well, I mean, if it didn't would she come asking me to sing at concerts? I am banking everything on that song, Gussie. Corky is an emotional girl, and when she hears that audience cheering me to the echo, it will do something to her. She will melt. She will relent. I wouldn't be surprised if she didn't say "Oh, Esmond!" and fling herself into my arms. Always provided, of course, that I don't get the bird.'

'You won't get the bird.'

'You think not?'

'Not a chance. You'll go like a breeze.'

'You're a great comfort, Gussie.'

'I try to be, Esmond. What are you going to sing? The "Yeoman's Wedding Song"?'

'No, it's a thing written by my Aunt Charlotte, with music by my Aunt Myrtle.'

I pursed the lips. This didn't sound too good. Nothing that I had seen of Aunt Charlotte had led me to suppose that the divine fire lurked within her. One didn't want to condemn her unheard, of course, but I was prepared to

bet that anything proceeding from her pen would be well
on the lousy side.

'I say,' said Esmond Haddock, struck by an idea,
'would you mind if I just ran through it for you now?'

'Nothing I'd like better.'

'Except perhaps another spot of port?'

'Except that, perhaps. Thanks.'

Esmond Haddock drained his glass.

'I won't sing the verse. It's just a lot of guff about the
sun is high up in the sky and the morn is bright and fair,
and so forth.'

'Quite.'

'The chorus is what brings home the bacon. It goes
like this.'

He assumed the grave, intent expression of a stuffed
frog, and let it rip.

' "Hallo, hallo, hallo, hallo . . ." '

I raised a hand.

'Just a second. What are you supposed to be doing?
Telephoning?'

'No, it's a hunting song.'

'Oh, a hunting song? I see. I thought it might be one of
those "I'm going to telephone ma baby" things. Right
ho.'

He resumed.

' "Hallo, hallo, hallo, hallo!
A-hunting we will go, pom pom,
A-hunting we will go, Gussie." '

I raised the hand again.

'I don't like that.'

'What?'

'That "pom pom".'

'Oh, that's just in the accompaniment.'

'And I don't like that "Gussie". It lets the side down.'

'Did I say "Gussie"?'

'Yes. You said "A-hunting we will go, pom pom,
a-hunting we will go, Gussie".'

59

'Just a slip of the tongue.'

'It isn't in the script?'

'No, it isn't in the script.'

'I'd leave it out on the night.'

'I will. Shall I continue?'

'Do.'

'Where was I?'

'Better start again at the beginning.'

'Right. Another drop of port?'

'Just a trickle, perhaps.'

'Well, then, starting again at the beginning and omitting, as before, all the-sun-is-high-up-in-the-sky stuff, "Hallo, hallo, hallo, hallo! A-hunting we will go, pom pom, a-hunting we will go. To-day's the day, so come what may, a-hunting we will go".'

I began to see that I had been right about Charlotte. This wouldn't do at all. Young Squire or no young Squire, a songster singing this sort of thing at a village concert was merely asking for the raspberry.

'All wrong,' I said.

'All wrong?'

'Well, think it out for yourself. You start off "A-hunting we will go, a-hunting we will go", and then, just as the audience is all keyed up for a punch line, you repeat that a-hunting we will go. There will be a sense of disappointment.'

'You think so, Gussie?'

'I'm sure of it, Esmond.'

'Then what would you advise?'

I pondered a moment.

'Try this,' I said. ' "Hallo, hallo, hallo, hallo! A-hunting we will go, my lads, a-hunting we will go, pull up our socks and chase the fox and lay the blighter low." '

'I say, that's good!'

'Stronger, I think?'

'Much stronger.'

'How do you go on from there?'

He switched on the stuffed-frog expression once more:

' "Oh, hearken to the merry horn!
Over brake and over thorn
Upon this jolly hunting morn
A-hunting we will go." '

I weighed this.

'I pass the first two lines,' I said. ' "Merry horn." "Brake and thorn." Not bad at all. At-a-girl, Charlotte, we always knew you had it in you! But not the finish.'

'You don't like it?'

'Weak. Very weak. I don't know what sort of standees you get at King's Deverill, but if they're like the unshaven thugs behind the back row at every village concert I've ever known, you're simply inviting them to chi-yike and make a noise like tearing calico. No, we must do better than that. Born . . . corn . . . pawn . . . torn . . . Ha!' I said, reaching out for the decanter, 'I think I have it. "Oh, hearken to the merry horn! Over brake and over thorn we'll ride although our bags get torn! What ho! What ho! What ho!" '

I had more or less expected it to knock him cold and it did.

For an instant he was speechless with admiration, then he said it lifted the whole thing and he couldn't thank me enough.

'It's terrific!'

'I was hoping you would like it.'

'How do you think of these things?'

'Oh, they just come to one.'

'We might run through the authorized version, old man, shall we?'

'No time like the present, dear old chap.'

It's curious how, looking back, you can nearly always spot where you went wrong in any binge or enterprise. Take this little slab of community singing of ours, for instance. In order to give the thing zip, I stood on my chair and waved the decanter like a baton, and this, I see now, was a mistake. It helped the composition enormously, but it tended to create a false impression in the mind of the observer, conjuring up a picture of drunken revels.

And if you are going to say that on the present occasion there was no observer, I quietly reply that you are wrong. We had just worked through the 'brake and thorn' and were going all out for the rousing finish, when a voice spoke behind us.

It said:

'Well!'

There are, of course, many ways of saying 'Well!' The speaker who had the floor at the moment – Dame Daphne Winkworth – said it rather in the manner of the prudish Queen of a monarch of Babylon who has happened to wander into the banqueting hall just as the Babylonian orgy is beginning to go nicely.

'*Well*!' she said.

Of course, what Corky had told me about Esmond Haddock's aunt-fixation ought to have prepared me for it, but I must say I was shocked at his deportment at this juncture. It was the deportment of a craven and a worm. Possibly stimulated by my getting on a chair, he had climbed onto the table and was using a banana as a hunting-crop, and he now came down like an apologetic sack of coals, his whole demeanour so crushed and cringing that I could hardly bear to look at him.

'It's all right, Aunt Daphne!'

'All right!'

'We were rehearsing. For the concert, you know. With the concert so near, one doesn't want to lose a minute.'

'Oh? Well, we are expecting you in the drawing-room.'

'Yes, Aunt Daphne.'

'Gertrude is waiting to play backgammon with you.'

'Yes, Aunt Daphne.'

'If you feel capable of playing backgammon.'

'Oh, yes, Aunt Daphne.'

He slunk from the room with bowed head, and I was about to follow, when the old geezer checked me with an imperious gesture. One noted a marked increase in the resemblance to Wallace Beery, and the thought crossed my mind that life for the unfortunate moppets who had drawn this Winkworth as a headmistress must have been like Six Weeks on Sunny Devil's Island. Previous to making her acquaintance, I had always supposed the Rev. Aubrey Upjohn to be the nearest thing to the late Captain Bligh of the *Bounty* which the scholastic world had provided to date, but I could see now that compared with old Battling Daphne he was a mere prelim boy.

'Augustus, did you bring a great, rough dog with you this evening?' she demanded.

It shows how the rush and swirl of events at Deverill Hall had affected me when I say that for an instant nothing stirred.

'Dog?'

'Silversmith says it belongs to you.'

'Oh, ah,' I said, memory returning to its throne. 'Yes, yes, yes, of course. Yes, to be sure. You mean Sam Goldwyn. But he's not mine. He belongs to Corky.'

'To *whom*?'

'Corky Pirbright. She asked me to put him up for a day or two.'

The mention of Corky's name, as had happened at the dinner-table, caused her to draw in her breath and do a quick-take-um. There was no getting away from the fact that the girl's popularity at Deverill Hall was but slight.

'Is Miss Pirbright a great friend of yours?'

'Oh, rather,' I said, remembering too late that this scarcely squared with what Corky had told Esmond Haddock. I was glad that he was no longer with us. 'She

was a trifle dubious about springing the animal on her
uncle without a certain amount of preliminary spadework, he being apparently not very dog-minded, so she
turned it over to me. It's in the stables.'

'It is not in the stables.'

'Then Silversmith was pulling my leg. He said he
would have it taken there!'

'He did have it taken there, but it broke loose and
came rushing into the drawing-room just now like a
mad thing.'

I saw that here was where the soothing word was
required.

'Sam Goldwyn isn't dotty,' I assured her. 'I wouldn't
say he was one of our great minds, but he's perfectly
compos. In *re* his rushing into the drawing-room, that
was because he thought I was there. He has conceived a
burning passion for me and counts every minute lost
when he is not in my society. No doubt his first act on
being tied up in the stables was to start gnawing through
the rope in order to be free to come and look for me.
Rather touching.'

Her manner suggested that she did not think it in the
least touching. Her eye was alight with anti-Sam
sentiment.

'Well, it was most unpleasant. We had left the french
windows open, as the night was so warm, and suddenly
this disgusting brute came galloping in. My sister
Charlotte received a nervous shock from which it will
take her a long time to recover. The animal leaped upon
her back and chased her all over the room.'

I did not give the thought utterance, for if there is one
thing the Woosters are, it is tactful, but it did occur to
me that this had come more or less as a judgement on
Charlotte for writing all that Hallo-hallo-hallo-hallo,
a-hunting-we-will-go stuff and would be a lesson to her
next time she took pen in hand. She was now in a
position to see the thing from the fox's point of view.

'And when we rang for Silversmith, the creature bit him.'

I must confess to feeling a thrill of admiration as I heard these words. 'You're a better man than I am, Gunga Din', I came within a toucher of saying. I wouldn't have bitten Silversmith myself to please a dying grandmother.

'I'm frightfully sorry,' I said. 'Is there anything I can do?'

'No, thank you.'

'I have considerable influence with this hound. I might be able to induce him to call it a day and go back to the stables and get his eight hours.'

'It will not be necessary. Silversmith succeeded in overpowering the animal and locking it in a cupboard. Now that you tell me its home is at the Vicarage, I will send it there at once.'

'I'll take him, shall I?'

'Pray do not trouble. I think it would be better if you were to go straight to bed.'

This seemed to me the most admirable suggestion. From the moment when the females had legged it from the dinner-table, I had been musing somewhat apprehensively on the quiet home evening which would set in as soon as Esmond and I were through with the port. You know what these quiet home evenings are like at country houses where the personnel of the ensemble is mainly feminine. You get backed into corners and shown photograph albums. Folk songs are sung at you. You find the head drooping like a lily on its stem and have to keep jerking it back into position one with an effort that taxes the frail strength to the utmost. Far, far better to retire to my sleeping quarters now, especially as I was most anxious to get in touch with Jeeves, who long 'ere this must have arrived by train with the heavy luggage.

I am not saying that this woman's words, with their

65

underlying suggestion that I was fried to the tonsils, had not wounded me. It was all too plainly her opinion that, if let loose in drawing-rooms, I would immediately proceed to create an atmosphere reminiscent of a waterfront saloon when the Fleet is in. But the Woosters are essentially fair-minded, and I did not blame her for holding these views. I could quite see that when you come into a dining-room and find a guest leaping about on a chair with a decanter in his hand, singing Hallo, hallo, hallo, hallo, a-hunting we will go, my lads, a-hunting we will go, you are pretty well bound to fall into a certain train of thought.

'I do feel a little fatigued after my journey,' I said.

'Silversmith will show you to your room,' she replied, and I perceived that Uncle Charlie was in our midst. I had not seen or heard him arrive. Like Jeeves, he had manifested himself silently out of the void. No doubt these things run in families.

'Silversmith.'

'Madam?'

'Show Mr Fink-Nottle to his room,' said Dame Daphne, though I could see that she was feeling that 'help' would have been more the *mot juste*.

'Very good, madam.'

I noticed that the man was limping slightly, seeming to suggest that Sam Goldwyn had connected with his calf, but I forbore to probe and question, realizing that the subject, like the calf, might be a sore one. I followed him up the stairs to a well-appointed chamber and wished him a cheery good night.

'Oh, Silversmith,' I said.

'Sir?'

'Has my man arrived?'

'Yes, sir.'

'You might send him along.'

'Very good, sir.'

He withdrew, and a few minutes later there entered a familiar form.

But it wasn't the familiar form of Jeeves. It was the familiar form of Claude Cattermole Pirbright.

7

Well, I suppose if I had been a Seigneur of the Middle Ages – somebody like Childe Roland, for instance – in the days when you couldn't throw a brick without beaning a magician or a wizard or a sorcerer and people were always getting changed into something else, I wouldn't have given the thing a second thought. I would just have said 'Ah, so Jeeves has had a spell cast on him and been turned into Catsmeat, has he? Too bad. Still, that's life', and carried on regardless, calling for my pipe and my bowl and my fiddlers three.

But nowadays you tend to lose this easy outlook, and it would be wilfully deceiving my public to say that I did not take it big. I stared at the man, my eyes coming out of the parent sockets like a snail's and waving about on their stems.

'Catsmeat!' I yipped.

He waggled his head frowningly, like a conspirator when a fellow-conspirator has said the wrong thing.

'Meadowes,' he corrected.

'What do you mean, Meadowes?'

'That is my name while I remain in your employment. I'm your man.'

A solution occurred to me. I have already mentioned that the port which I had swigged perhaps a little too freely in Esmond Haddock's society was of a fine old vintage and full of body. It now struck me that it must have had even more authority than I had supposed and that Dame Daphne Winkworth had been perfectly correct in assuming that I was scrooched. And I was about to turn my face to the wall and try to sleep it off, when he proceeded.

'Your valet. Your attendant. Your gentleman's personal gentleman. It's quite simple. Jeeves couldn't come.'

'What!'

'No.'

'You mean Jeeves isn't going to be at my side?'

'That's right. So I am taking his place. What are you doing?'

'Turning my face to the wall.'

'Why?'

'Well, wouldn't you turn your face to the wall if you were trapped in a place like this with everybody thinking you were Gussie Fink-Nottle and without Jeeves to comfort and advise? Oh, hell! Oh, blast! Oh, damn! Why couldn't Jeeves come? Is he ill?'

'I don't think so. I speak only as a layman, of course, not as a medical man, but the last I saw of him he seemed pretty full of vitamins. Sparkling eyes. Rosy cheeks. No, Jeeves isn't ill. What stopped him coming was the fact that his Uncle Charlie is the butler here.'

'Why the devil should that stop him?'

'My good Bertie, use your intelligence, if any. Uncle Charlie knows that Jeeves is your keeper. No doubt Jeeves writes him weekly letters, saying how happy he is with you and how nothing would ever induce him to switch elsewhere. Well, what would happen if he suddenly showed up in attendance on Gussie Fink-Nottle? I'll tell you what would happen. Uncle Charlie's suspicions would be aroused. "Something fishy here," he would say to himself. And before you knew where you were he would be tearing off your whiskers and denouncing you. Obviously Jeeves couldn't come.'

I was forced to admit that there was something in this. But I still chafed.

'Why didn't he tell me?'

'It only occurred to him after you had left.'

'And why couldn't he have squared Silversmith?'

'That point came up when we were discussing the thing, and Jeeves said his Uncle Charlie was one of those fellows who can't be squared. A man of very rigid principles.'

'Every man has his price.'

'Not Jeeves's Uncle Charlie. My gosh, Bertie, what a lad! He received me when I arrived, and my bones turned to water. Do you remember the effect King Solomon had on the Queen of Sheba at their first meeting? My reactions were somewhat similar. "The half was not told unto me," I said to myself. If it hadn't been for Queenie leading me from the presence and buoying me up with a quick cooking sherry, I might have swooned in my tracks.'

'Who's Queenie?'

'Haven't you met her? The parlourmaid. Delightful girl. Engaged to the village policeman, a fellow named Dobbs. Have you ever tasted cooking sherry, Bertie? Odd stuff.'

I felt that we were wandering from the nub. This was no time for desultory chit-chat about cooking sherry.

'But, look here, dash it, I can understand Jeeves's reasons for backing out, but I can't see why you had to come.'

He raised a couple of eyebrows.

'You can't see why I had to come? Didn't you yourself say with your own lips, when we were discussing the idea of me understudying Gussie, that this was the one place where I ought to be? It's vital that I should be on the spot, seeing Gertrude constantly, pleading with her, reasoning with her, trying to break down her sales resistance.' He paused, and gave me a penetrating look. 'You've nothing against my being here, have you?'

'Well . . .'

'So!' he said, and his voice was cold and hard, like a

picnic egg. 'You have some far-fetched objection to the scheme, have you? You don't want me to win the girl I love?'

'Of course I want you to win the bally girl you love.'

'Well, I can't do it by mail.'

'But I don't see why you've got to be at the Hall. Why couldn't you have stayed at the Vicarage?'

'You couldn't expect Uncle Sidney to have Corky *and* me on the premises. The mixture would be too rich.'

'At the inn, then.'

'There isn't an inn. Only what they call beer-houses.'

'You could have got a bed at a cottage.'

'And shared it with the cottager? No, thanks. How many beds do you think these birds have?'

I relapsed into a baffled silence. But it is never any good repining on these occasions. When I next spoke, I doubt if Catsmeat spotted the suspicion of a tremor in the voice. We Woosters are like that. In moments of mental anguish we resemble those Red Indians who, while getting cooked to a crisp at the stake, never failed to be the life and soul of the party.

'Have you seen her?' I asked.

'Gertrude? Yes, just before I came up here. I was in the hall, and she suddenly appeared from the drawing-room.'

'I suppose she was surprised.'

'Surprised is right. She swayed and tottered. Queenie said "Oh, miss, are you ill?" and rushed off to get sal volatile.'

'Oh, Queenie was there?'

'Yes, Queenie was there with her hair in a braid. She had just been telling me how worried she was about her betrothed's spiritual outlook. He's an atheist.'

'So Corky told me.'

'And every time she tries to make him see the light, he just twirls his moustache and talks Ingersoll at her. This upsets the poor girl.'

'She's very pretty.'

'Extraordinarily pretty. I don't remember ever having seen a prettier parlourmaid.'

'Gertrude. Not Queenie.'

'Oh, Gertrude. Well, dash it, you don't need to tell me that. She's the top. She begins where Helen of Troy left off.'

'Did you get a chance to talk to her?'

'Unfortunately no. A couple of aunts came out of the drawing-room, and I had to leg it. That's the trouble about being a valet. You can't mix. By the way, Bertie, I've found out something of the utmost importance. That Lovers' Leap binge is fixed for next Thursday. Queenie told me. She's cutting the sandwiches. I hope you haven't weakened? You are still in your splendid, resolute frame of mind of yesterday? I can rely on you to foil and battle that foul blot, Esmond Haddock?'

'I like Esmond Haddock.'

'Then you ought to be ashamed of yourself.'

I smiled an indulgent smile.

'It's all right, Catsmeat. You can simmer down. Gertrude Winkworth means nothing to Esmond Haddock. He's not really pursuing her with his addresses.'

'Don't be an ass. How about the Lovers' Leap? What price the sandwiches?'

'All that stuff is just to make Corky jealous.'

'What!'

'He thinks it will bring her round. You see, he didn't give Corky the brush-off. You had your facts twisted. She gave him the brush-off, because they had differed on a point of policy, and she is still the lodestar of his life. I had this from his own lips. We got matey over the port. So you can cease to regard him as a menace.'

He gaped at me. You could see hope beginning to dawn.

'Is this official?'

'Absolutely.'

'You say Corky is the lodestar of his life?'

'That's what he told me.'

'And all this rushing Gertrude is just a ruse?'

'That's right.'

Catsmeat expelled a deep breath. It sounded like the final effort of a Dying Rooster.

'My gosh, you've taken a weight off my mind.'

'I thought you'd be pleased.'

'You bet I'm pleased. Well, good night.'

'You're off?'

'Yes, I shall leave you now, Bertie, much as I enjoy your society, because I have man's work to do elsewhere. When I was chatting with Queenie, she happened to mention that she knows where Uncle Charlie keeps the key of the cellar. So long. I shall hope to see more of you later.'

'Just a second. Will you be seeing Corky shortly?'

'First thing to-morrow morning. I must let her know I'm here and put her in touch with the general situation, so that she will be warned against making any floaters. Why?'

'Tell her from me that she has got to find somebody else for Pat.'

'You're walking out on the act?'

'Yes, I am,' I said, and put him abreast.

He listened intelligently, and said he quite understood.

'I see. Yes, I think you're right. I'll tell her.'

He withdrew, walking on the tips of his toes and conveying in his manner the suggestion that if he had had a hat and that hat had contained roses, he would have started strewing them from it, and for a while the thought that I had been instrumental in re-sunshining a pal's life bucked me up no little.

But it takes more than that to buck a fellow up permanently who is serving an indeterminate sentence

in a place like Deverill Hall, and it was not long before I
was in sombre mood again, trying to find the bluebird
but missing it by a wide margin.

I have generally found on these occasions when the
heart is heavy that the best thing to do is to curl up with
a good goose-flesher and try to forget, and fortunately I
had packed among my effects one called *Murder At
Greystone Grange*. I started to turn its pages now, and
found that I couldn't have made a sounder move. It was
one of those works in which Baronets are constantly
being discovered dead in libraries and the heroine can't
turn in for a night without a Thing popping through a
panel in the wall of her bedroom and starting to chuck
its weight about, and it was not long before I was so
soothed that I was able to switch off the light and fall
into a refreshing sleep, which lasted, as my refreshing
sleeps always do, till the coming of the morning cup of
tea.

My last thought, just before the tired eyelids closed,
was that I had had an idea that I had heard the front-door
bell ring and a murmur of distant voices, seeming to
indicate the blowing-in of another guest.

It was Silversmith who brought me my tea ration,
and though his manner, on the chilly side, suggested
that the overnight activities of Sam Goldwyn still
rankled, I had a dash at setting the conversational ball
rolling. I always like, if I can, to establish matey
relations between tea bringer and tea recipient.

'Oh, good morning, Silversmith, good morning,' I said.
'What sort of a day is it, Silversmith? Fine?'

'Yes, sir.'

'The lark on the wing and the snail on the thorn and
all that?'

'Yes, sir.'

'Splendid. Oh, Silversmith,' I said, 'I don't know if it
was but a dream, but latish last night I fancied I heard
the front-door bell doing its stuff and a good lot of

off-stage talking going on. Was I right? Did someone arrive after closing time?'

'Yes, sir. Mr Wooster.'

He gave me a cold look, as if to remind me that he would prefer not to be drawn into conversation with the man responsible for introducing Sam Goldwyn into his life, and vanished, leaving not a wrack behind.

And it was, as you may well imagine, a pensive Bertram with a puzzled frown on his face who propped himself against the pillows and sipped from the teacup. I could make nothing of this.

'Mr Wooster', the man had said, and only two explanations seemed to offer themselves – (a) that, like the fellows in the train at Wembley, I had not heard correctly and (b) that I had recently been in the presence of a butler who had been having a couple.

Neither theory satisfied me. From boyhood up my hearing has always been of the keenest, and as for the possibility of Silversmith having had one over the eight, I dismissed that instanter. It is a very frivolous butler who gets a load before nine in the morning, and I have gone sadly astray in my delineation of character if I have given my public the impression that Jeeves's Uncle Charlie was frivolous. You could imagine Little Lord Fauntleroy getting a skinful, but not Silversmith.

And yet he had unquestionably said 'Mr Wooster'.

I was still pondering like billy-o and nowhere near spiking a plausible solution of the mystery, when the door opened and the ghost of Jeeves entered, carrying a breakfast tray.

8

I say 'the ghost of Jeeves' because in that first awful
moment that was what I had the apparition docketed as.
The words 'What ho! A spectre!' trembled on my lips,
and I reacted rather like the heroine of *Murder At
Greystone Grange* on discovering that the Thing had
come to doss in her room. I don't know if you have ever
seen a ghost, but the general effect is to give you quite a
start.

Then the scent of bacon floated to the nostrils, and
feeling that it was improbable that a wraith would be
horsing about the place with dishes of eggs and b., I
calmed down a bit. That is to say, I stopped upsetting
the tea and was able to stutter. It is true that all I
said was 'Jeeves!' but that wasn't such bad going for
one whose tongue had so recently been tangled up
with the uvula, besides cleaving to the roof of the
mouth.

He dumped the tray on my lap.

'Good morning, sir,' he said. 'I fancied that you would
possibly wish to enjoy your breakfast in the privacy of
your apartment, rather than make one of the party in the
dining-room.'

Cognizant as I was of the fact that in that
dining-room there would be five aunts, one of them deaf,
one of them dotty, one of them Dame Daphne
Winkworth, and all of them totally unfit for human
consumption on an empty stomach, I applauded the
kindly gesture; all the more heartily because it had
just occurred to me that in a house like this, where
things were sure to be run on old-fashioned lines

rather than in a manner of keeping with the trend of modern thought, the butler probably waited at the breakfast-table.

'Does he?' I asked. 'Does Silversmith minister to the revellers at the morning meal?'

'Yes, sir.'

'My God!' I said, paling beneath the tan. 'What a man, Jeeves!'

'Sir?'

'Your Uncle Charlie.'

'Ah, yes, sir. A forceful personality.'

'Forceful is correct. What's that thing of Shakespeare's about someone having an eye like Mother's?'

'An eye like Mars, to threaten and command, is possibly the quotation for which you are groping, sir.'

'That's right. Uncle Charlie has an eye like that. You really call him Uncle Charlie?'

'Yes, sir.'

'Amazing. To me, to think of him as Uncle Charlie is like thinking of him as Jimmy or Reggie, or, for the matter of that, Bertie. Used he in your younger days to dandle you on his knee?'

'Quite frequently, sir.'

'And you didn't quail? You must have been a child of blood and iron.' I addressed myself to the platter once more. 'Extraordinarily good bacon, this, Jeeves.'

'Home cured, I understand, sir.'

'And made, no doubt, from contented pigs. Kippers, too, not to mention toast, marmalade and, unless my senses deceive me, an apple. Say what you will of Deverill Hall, its hospitality is lavish. I don't know if you have ever noticed it, Jeeves, but a good, spirited kipper first thing in the morning seems to put heart into you.'

'Very true, sir, though I myself am more partial to a slice of ham.'

For some moments we discussed the relative merits

of ham and kippers as buckers-up of the morale, there
being much, of course, to be said on both sides, and then
I touched on something which I had been meaning to
touch on earlier. I can't think how it came to slip my
mind.

'Oh, Jeeves,' I said, 'I knew there was something I
wanted to ask you. What in the name of everything
bloodsome are you doing here?'

'I fancied that you might possibly be curious on that
point, sir, and I was about to volunteer an explanation. I
have come here in attendance on Mr Fink-Nottle.
Permit me, sir.'

He retrieved the slab of kipper which a quick jerk of
the wrist had caused me to send flying from the fork,
and replaced it on the dish. I stared at him wide-eyed as
the expression is.

'Mr Fink-Nottle?'

'Yes, sir.'

'But Gussie's not here?'

'Yes, sir. We arrived at a somewhat late hour last
night.'

A sudden blinding light flashed upon me.

'You mean it was Gussie to whom Uncle Charlie was
referring when he said that Mr Wooster had punched the
time-clock? I'm here saying I'm Gussie, and now Gussie
has blown in, saying he's me?'

'Precisely, sir. It is a curious and perhaps somewhat
complex situation that has been precipitated –'

'You're telling me, Jeeves!'

Only the fact that by doing so I should have upset the
tray prevented me turning my face to the wall. When
Esmond Haddock in our exchanges over the port had
spoken of the times that try men's souls, he hadn't had a
notion of what the times that try men's souls can really
be, if they spit on their hands and get right down to it. I
levered up a forkful of kipper and passed it absently over
the larynx, endeavouring to adjust the faculties to a

set-up which even the most intrepid would have had to admit was a honey.

'But how did Gussie get out of stir?'

'The magistrate decided on second thoughts to substitute a fine for the prison sentence, sir.'

'What made him do that?'

'Possibly the reflection that the quality of mercy is not strained, sir.'

'You mean it droppeth as the gentle rain from heaven?'

'Precisely, sir. Upon the place beneath. His Worship would no doubt have taken into consideration the fact that it blesseth him that gives and him that takes and becomes the throned monarch better than his crown.'

I mused. Yes, there was something in that.

'What did he soak him? Five quid?'

'Yes, sir.'

'And Gussie brassed up and was free?'

'Yes, sir.'

I put my finger on the nub.

'Why?' I said.

I thought I had him there, but I hadn't. Where a lesser man would have shuffled his feet and twiddled his fingers and mumbled 'Yes, I see what you mean, that is the problem, is it not?' he had his explanation all ready to serve and dished it up without batting an eyelid.

'It was the only course to pursue, sir. On the one hand, her ladyship, your aunt, was most emphatic in her desire that you should visit the Hall, and on the other Miss Bassett was equally insistent on Mr Fink-Nottle doing so. In the event of either of you failing to arrive, inquiries would have been instituted, with disastrous results. To take but one aspect of the matter, Miss Bassett is expecting to receive daily letters from Mr Fink-Nottle, giving her all the gossip of the Hall and

79

describing in detail his life there. These will, of course, have to be written on the Hall notepaper and postmarked "King's Deverill".'

'True. You speak sooth, Jeeves. I never thought of that.'

I swallowed a sombre chunk of toast and marmalade. I was thinking how easily all this complex stuff could have been avoided, if only the beak had had the sense to fine Gussie in the first place, instead of as an afterthought. I have said it before, and I will say it again, all magistrates are asses. Show me a magistrate and I will show you a fathead.

I started on the apple.

'So here we are.'

'Yes, sir.'

'I'm Gussie and Gussie's me.'

'Yes, sir.'

'And ceaseless vigilance will be required if we are not to gum the game. We shall be walking on eggshells.'

'A very trenchant figure, sir.'

I finished the apple, and lit a thoughtful cigarette.

'Well, I suppose it had to be,' I said. 'But lay off the Marcus Aurelius stuff, because I don't think I could stand it if you talk about it all being part of the great web. How's Gussie taking the thing?'

'Not blithely, sir. I should describe him as disgruntled. I learn from Mr Pirbright –'

'Oh, you've seen Catsmeat?'

'Yes, sir, in the servants' hall. He was helping Queenie, the parlourmaid, with her crossword puzzle. He informed me that he had contrived to obtain an interview with Miss Pirbright and had apprised her of your reluctance to play the part of Pat in the Hibernian entertainment at the concert, and that Miss Pirbright fully appreciated your position and said that now that Mr Fink-Nottle had arrived he would, of course, sustain the role. Mr Pirbright has seen Mr Fink-Nottle and informed him of the arrangement, and it is this that has caused Mr Fink-Nottle to become disgruntled.'

'He shrinks from the task?'

'Yes, sir. He is also somewhat exercised in his mind by what he has heard the ladies of the Hall saying with regard to – '

'My doings?'

'Yes, sir.'

'The dog?'

'Yes, sir.'

'The port?'

'Yes, sir.'

'And the hallo, hallo, a-hunting we will go?'

'Yes, sir.'

I whooshed out a remorseful puff of smoke.

'Yes,' I said, 'I'm afraid I haven't given Gussie a very good send-off. Quite inadvertently I fear that I have established him in the eyes of mine hostesses as one of those whited sepulchres which try to kid the public that they drink nothing but orange juice and the moment that public's back is turned, start doing the *Lost Week-End* stuff with the port. Of course, I could put up a pretty good case for myself. Esmond Haddock thrust the decanter on me, and I was dying of thirst. You wouldn't blame a snowbound traveller in the Alps for accepting a drop of brandy at the hands of a St Bernard dog. Still, one hopes that they will keep it under their hats and not pass it along to Miss Bassett. One doesn't want spanners bunged into Gussie's romance.'

We were silent for a moment, musing on what the harvest would be, were anything to cause Madeline Bassett to become de-Gussied. Then I changed a distasteful subject.

'Talking of romances, I suppose Catsmeat confided in you about his?'

'Yes, sir.'

'I thought he would. Amazing, the way all these

81

birds come to you and sob out their troubles on your chest.'

'I find it most gratifying, sir, and am always eager to lend such assistance as may lie within my power. One desires to give satisfaction. Shortly after your departure yesterday, Mr Pirbright devoted some little time to an exposition of the problems confronting him. It was after learning the facts that I ventured to suggest that he should take my place here as your attendant.'

'I wish one of you had thought to tip me off with a telegram. I should have been spared a nasty shock. The last thing one wants on top of what might be termed a drinking bout is to have a changeling ring himself in on you without warning. You'd look pretty silly yourself if you came into my room one morning with the cup of tea after a thick night and found Ernie Bevin or someone propped up in the bed. When you saw Catsmeat just now, did he tell you the Stop Press news?'

'Sir?'

'About Esmond Haddock and Corky.'

'Ah, yes, sir. He informed me of what you had said to him with reference to Mr Haddock's unswerving devotion to Miss Pirbright. He appeared greatly relieved. He feels that the principal obstacle to his happiness has now been removed.'

'Yes, Catsmeat's sitting pretty. One wishes one could say the same of poor old Esmond.'

'You think that Miss Pirbright does not reciprocate Mr Haddock's sentiments, sir?'

'Oh, she reciprocates them, all right. She freely admits that he is the lodestar of her life, and you're probably saying to yourself that in these circs everything should be hunkadory. I mean, if she's the lodestar of his life and he's the lodestar of hers, the thing ought to be in the bag. But you're wrong, and so is Esmond Haddock. His view, poor deluded clam, is that he will make such a whale of a hit with this song he's singing at the concert that when she hears the audience cheering him to the echo she will say "Oh, Esmond!" and fling herself into his arms. Not a hope.'

'No, sir?'

'Not a hope, Jeeves. There's a snag. The trouble is that she refuses to consider the idea of hitching up with him unless he defies his aunts, and he very naturally gets the vapours at the mere idea. It is what I have sometimes heard described as an impasse.'

'Why does the young lady wish Mr Haddock to defy his aunts, sir?'

'She says he has allowed them to oppress him from childhood, and it's time he threw off the yoke. She wants him to show her that he is a man of intrepid courage. It's the old dragon gag. In the days when knights were bold, as you probably know, girls used to hound fellows into going out and fighting dragons. I expect your old pal Childe Roland had it happen to him a dozen times. But dragons are one thing, and aunts are another. I have no doubt that Esmond Haddock would spring to the task of taking on a fire-breathing dragon, but there isn't the remotest chance of him ever standing up to Dame Daphne Winkworth, and the Misses Charlotte, Emmeline, Harriet and Myrtle Deverill and making them play ball.'

'I wonder, sir?'

'What do you mean, you wonder, Jeeves?'

'It crossed my mind as a possibility, sir, that were Mr Haddock's performance at the concert to be the success he anticipates, his attitude might become more resolute. I have not myself had the opportunity of studying the young gentleman's psychology, but from what my Uncle Charlie tells me I am convinced that he is one of those gentlemen on whom popular acclamation might have sensational effects. Mr Haddock's has been, as you say, a repressed life, and he has, no doubt, a very marked inferiority complex. The cheers of the multitude

frequently act like a powerful drug upon young
gentlemen with inferiority complexes.'

I began to grasp the gist.

'You mean that if he makes a hit he will get it up his
nose to such an extent that he will be able to look his
aunts in the eye and make them wilt?'

'Precisely, sir. You will recall the case of Mr Little.'

'Golly, yes, that's right. Bingo became a changed man,
didn't he? Jeeves, I believe you've got something.'

'At least the theory which I have advanced is a tenable
one, sir.'

'It's more than tenable. It's a pip. Then what we've got
to do is to strain every nerve to see that he makes a hit.
What are those things people have?'

'Sir?'

'Opera singers and people like that.'

'You mean a claque, sir?'

'That's right. The word was on the tip of my tongue.
He must be provided with a claque. It will be your task,
Jeeves, to move about the village, dropping a word here,
standing a beer there, till the whole community is
impressed with the necessity of cheering Esmond
Haddock's song till their eyes bubble. I can leave this to
you?'

'Certainly, sir. I will attend to the matter.'

'Fine. And now I suppose I ought to be getting up and
seeing Gussie. There are probably one or two points he
will want to discuss. Is there a ruined mill around here?'

'Not to my knowledge, sir.'

'Well, any landmark where you could tell him to meet
me? I don't want to roam the house and grounds,
looking for him. My aim is rather to sneak down the
back stairs and skirt around the garden via the
shrubberies. You follow me, Jeeves?'

'Perfectly, sir. I would suggest that I arrange with Mr
Fink-Nottle to meet you in, say, an hour's time outside
the local post office.'

'Right,' I said. 'Outside the post office in an hour or sixty minutes. And now, Jeeves, if you will be so good as to turn it on, the refreshing bath.'

9

What with one thing and another, singing a bit too much in the bath and so on, I was about five minutes behind scheduled time in reaching the post office, and when I got there I found Gussie already at the tryst.

Jeeves, in speaking of this Fink-Nottle, had, if you remember, described him as disgruntled, and it was plain at a glance that the passage of time had done nothing to gruntle him. The eyes behind their horn-rimmed spectacles were burning with fury and resentment and all that sort of thing. He looked like a peevish halibut. In moments of emotion Gussie's resemblance to some marine monster always becomes accentuated.

'Well,' he said, starting in without so much as a What-ho. 'This is a pretty state of things!'

It seemed to me that a cheery, pep-giving word would be in order. I proceeded, accordingly, to shoot it across. Assenting to his opinion that the state of things was pretty, I urged him to keep the tail up, pointing out that though the storm clouds might lower, he was better off at Deverill Hall than he would have been in a dark dungeon with dripping walls and a platoon of resident rats, if that's where they put fellows who have been given fourteen days without the option at Bosher Street police court.

He replied curtly that he entirely disagreed with me.

'I would greatly have preferred prison,' he said. 'When you're in prison, you don't have people calling you Mr Wooster. How do you suppose I feel, knowing that everybody thinks I'm you?'

This startled me, I confess. Of all the things I had to worry about, the one that was gashing me like a knife most was the thought that the populace, beholding Gussie, were under the impression that there stood Bertram Wooster. When I reflected that the little world of King's Deverill would go to its grave believing that Bertram Wooster was an undersized gargoyle who looked like Lester de Pester in that comic strip in one of the New York papers, the iron entered my soul. It was a bit of a jar to learn that Gussie was suffering the same spiritual agonies.

'I don't know if you are aware,' he proceeded, 'what your reputation is in these parts? In case you are under any illusions, let me inform you that your name is mud. Those women at breakfast were drawing their skirts away as I passed. They shivered when I spoke to them. From time to time I would catch them looking at me in a way that would have wounded a smash-and-grab man. And, as if that wasn't bad enough, you seem in a single evening to have made my name mud, too. What's all this I hear about you getting tight last night and singing hunting songs?'

'I didn't get tight, Gussie. Just pleasantly mellowed, as you might say. And I sang hunting songs because my host seemed to wish it. One has to humour one's host. So they mentioned that, did they?'

'They mentioned it, all right. It was the chief topic of conversation at the breakfast-table. And what's going to happen if they mention it to Madeline?'

'I advise stout denial.'

'It wouldn't work.'

'It might,' I said, for I had been giving a good deal of thought to the matter and was feeling more optimistic than I had been. 'After all, what can they prove?'

'Madeline's godmother said she came into the dining-room and found you on a chair, waving a decanter and singing A-hunting we will go.'

'True. We concede that. But who is to say that that decanter was not emptied exclusively by Esmond Haddock, who, you must remember, was on the table, also singing A-hunting we will go and urging his horse on with a banana? I feel convinced that, should the affair come to Madeline's ears, you can get away with it with stout denial.'

He pondered.

'Perhaps you're right. But all the same I wish you'd be more careful. The whole thing has been most annoying and upsetting.'

'Still,' I said, feeling that it was worth trying, 'it's part of the great web, what?'

'Great web?'

'One of Marcus Aurelius's cracks. He said: "Does aught befall you? It is good. It is part of the destiny of the Universe ordained for you from the beginning. All that befalls you is part of the great web." '

From the brusque manner in which he damned and blasted Marcus Aurelius, I gathered that, just as had happened when Jeeves sprang it on me, the gag had failed to bring balm. I hadn't had much hope that it would. I doubt, as a matter of fact, if Marcus Aurelius's material is ever the stuff to give the troops at a moment when they have just stubbed their toe on the brick of Fate. You want to wait till the agony has abated.

To ease the strain, I changed the subject, asking him if he had been surprised to find Catsmeat in residence at the Hall, and immediately became aware that I had but poured kerosene on the flames. Heated though his observations on Marcus Aurelius had been, they were mildness itself compared with what he had to say about Catsmeat.

It was understandable, of course. If a fellow has forced you against your better judgement to go wading in the Trafalgar Square fountain at five in the morning, ruining your trousers and causing you to be pinched and jugged and generally put through it by the machinery of the Law, no doubt you do find yourself coming round to the view that what he needs is disembowelling with a blunt bread-knife. This, among other things, was what Gussie hoped some day to be able to do to Catsmeat, if all went well, and, as I say, one could follow the train of thought.

Presently, having said all he could think of on the topic of Catsmeat, he turned, as I had rather been expecting he would, to that of the cross-talk act of which the other was the originator and producer.

'What's all this Pirbright was saying about something he called a cross-talk act?' he asked, and I saw that we had reached a point in the exchanges where suavity and the honeyed word would be needed.

'Ah, yes, he mentioned that to you, did he not? It's an item on the programme of the concert which his sister is impresarioing at the village hall shortly. I was to have played Pat in it, but owing to the changed circumstances you will now sustain the role.'

'Will I! We'll see about that. What the devil is the damned thing?'

'Haven't you seen it? Pongo Twistleton and Barmy Phipps do it every year at the Drones smoker.'

'I never go to the Drones smoker.'

'Oh? Well, it's a . . . How shall I put it? . . . It's what is known as a cross-talk act. The principals are a couple of Irishmen named Pat and Mike, and they come on and . . . But I have the script here,' I said, producing it. 'If you glance through it, you'll get the idea.'

He took the script and studied it with a sullen frown. Watching him, I realized what a ghastly job it must be writing plays. I mean, having to hand over your little effort to a hardfaced manager and stand shuffling your feet while he glares at it as if it hurt him in a tender spot, preparatory to pushing it back at you with a curt 'It stinks'.

'Who wrote this?' asked Gussie, as he turned the final

89

page, and when I told him that Catsmeat was the author
he said he might have guessed it. Throughout his
perusal, he had been snorting at intervals, and he snorted
again, a good bit louder, as if he were amalgamating
about six snorts into one snort.

'The thing is absolute drivel. It has no dramatic
coherence. It lacks motivation and significant form.
Who are these two men supposed to be?'

'I told you. A couple of Irishmen named Pat and
Mike.'

'Well, perhaps you can explain what their social
position is, for it is frankly beyond me. Pat, for instance,
appears to move in the very highest circles, for he
describes himself as dining at Buckingham Palace, and
yet his wife takes in lodgers.'

'I see what you mean. Odd.'

'Inexplicable. Is it credible that a man of his class
would be invited to dinner at Buckingham Palace,
especially as he is apparently completely without social
savoir-faire? At this dinner-party to which he alludes he
relates how the Queen asked him if he would like some
mulligatawny and he, thinking that there was nothing
else coming, had six helpings, with the result that, to
quote his words, he spent the rest of the evening sitting
in a corner full of soup. And in describing the incident
he prefaces his remarks at several points with the
expressions "Begorrah" and "faith and begob". Irishmen
don't talk like that. Have you ever read Synge's *Riders to
the Sea*? Well, get hold of it and study it, and if you can
show me a single character in it who says "Faith and
begob", I'll give you a shilling. Irishmen are poets. They
talk about their souls and mist and so on. They say
things like "An evening like this, it makes me wish I
was back in County Clare, watchin' the cows in the tall
grass".'

He turned the pages frowningly, his nose wrinkled as
if it had detected some unpleasant smell. It brought back

to me the old days at Malvern House, Bramley-on-Sea, when I used to take my English essay to be blue-pencilled by the Rev. Aubrey Upjohn.

'Here's another bit of incoherent raving. "My sister's in the ballet." "You say your sister's in the ballet?" "Yes, begorrah, my sister's in the ballet." "What does your sister do in the ballet?" "She comes rushing in, and then she goes rushing out." "What does she have to rush like that for?" "Faith and begob, because it's a Rushin' ballet." It simply doesn't make sense. And now we come to something else that is quite beyond me, the word "*bus*". After the line "Because it's a Rushin' ballet" and in other places throughout the script the word "*bus*" in brackets occurs. It conveys nothing to me. Can you explain it?'

'It's short for "*business*". That's where you hit Mike with your umbrella. To show the audience that there has been a joke.'

Gussie started.

'Are these things jokes?'

'Yes.'

'I see. I *see*. Well, of course, that throws a different light on . . .' He paused, and eyed me narrowly. 'Did you say that I am supposed to strike my colleague with an umbrella?'

'That's right.'

'And if I understood Pirbright correctly, the other performer in this extraordinary production is the local policeman?'

'That's right.'

'The whole thing is impossible and utterly out of the question,' said Gussie vehemently. 'Have you any idea what happens when you hit a policeman with an umbrella? I did so on emerging from the fountain in Trafalgar Square, and I certainly do not intend to do it again.' A sort of grey horror came into his face, as if he had been taking a quick look into a past which he had hoped to forget. 'Well, let me put you quite straight, Wooster, as to what my stand is in this matter. I shall not say "Begorrah". I shall not say "Faith and begob". I shall not assault policemen with an umbrella. In short, I absolutely and positively refuse to have the slightest association with this degraded buffoonery. Wait till I meet Miss Pirbright. I'll tell her a thing or two. I'll show her she can't play fast and loose with human dignity like this.'

He was about to speak further, but at this point his voice died away in a sort of gurgle and I saw his eyes bulge. Glancing around, I perceived Corky approaching. She was accompanied by Sam Goldwyn and was looking, as is her wont, like a million dollars, gowned in some clinging material which accentuated rather than hid her graceful outlines, if you know what I mean.

I was delighted to see her. With Gussie in this non-cooperative mood, digging his feet in and refusing to play ball, like Balaam's ass, it seemed to me that precisely what was needed was the woman's touch. To decide to introduce them and leave her to take on the job of melting his iron front was with me the work of a moment.

I had high hopes that she would be able to swing the deal. Though differing from my Aunt Agatha in almost every possible respect, Corky has this in common with that outstanding scourge: she is authoritative. When she wants you to do a thing, you find yourself doing it. This has been so from her earliest years. I remember her on one occasion at our mutual dancing class handing me an antique orange, a blue and yellow mass of pips and mildew, and bidding me bung it at our instructress, who had incurred her displeasure for some reason which has escaped my recollection. And I did it without a murmur, though knowing full well how bitter the reckoning would be.

'Hoy!' I said, eluding the cheesehound's attempts to

place his front paws on my shoulders and strop his tongue on my face. I jerked a thumb. 'Gussie,' I said.

Corky's face lit up in a tickled-to-death manner. She proceeded immediately to turn on the charm.

'Oh, is *this* Mr Fink-Nottle? How do you do, Mr Fink-Nottle? I *am* so glad to see you, Mr Fink-Nottle. How lucky meeting you. I wanted to talk to you about the act.'

'We've just been having a word or two on that subject,' I said, 'and Gussie's kicking a bit at playing Pat.'

'Oh, *no*?'

'I thought you might like to reason with him. I'll leave you to it,' I said and biffed off. Looking around as I turned the corner, I saw that she had attached herself with one slim hand to the lapel of Gussie's coat and with the other was making wide, appealing gestures, indicating to the most vapid and irreflective observer that she was giving him Treatment A.

Well pleased, I made my way back to the Hall, keeping an eye skinned for prowling aunts, and won through without disaster to my room. I was enjoying a thoughtful smoke there about half an hour later when Gussie came in, and I could see right away that this was not the morose, sullen Fink-Nottle who had so uncompromisingly panned the daylights out of Pat and Mike in the course of our recent get-together. His bearing was buoyant. His face glowed. He was wearing in his buttonhole a flower which had not been there before.

'Hallo, there, Bertie,' he said. 'I say, Bertie, why didn't you tell me that Miss Pirbright was Cora Starr, the film actress? I have long been one of her warmest admirers. What a delightful girl she is, is she not, and how unlike her brother, whom I consider and always shall consider England's leading louse. She has made me see this cross-talk act in an entirely new light.'

'I thought she might.'

'It's extraordinary that a girl as pretty as that should also have a razor-keen intelligence and that amazing way of putting her arguments with a crystal clarity which convinces you in an instant that she is right in every respect.'

'Yes, Corky's a persuasive young gumboil.'

'I would prefer that you did not speak of her as a gumboil. Corky, eh? That's what you call her, is it? A charming name.'

'What was the outcome of your conference? Are you going to do the act?'

'Oh, yes, it's all settled. She overcame my objections entirely. We ran through the script after you had left us, and she quite brought me round to her view that there is nothing in the least degrading in this simple, wholesome form of humour. Hokum, yes, but, as she pointed out good theatre. She is convinced that I shall go over big.'

'You'll knock 'em cold. I'm sorry I can't play Pat myself –'

'A good thing, probably. I doubt if you are the type.'

'Of course I'm the type,' I retorted hotly. 'I should have given a sensational performance.'

'Corky thinks not. She was telling me how thankful she was that you had stepped out and I had taken over. She said the part wants broad, robust treatment and you would have played it too far down. It's a part that calls for personality and the most precise timing, and she said that the moment she saw me she felt that here was the ideal Pat. Girls with her experience can tell in a second.'

I gave it up. You can't reason with hams, and twenty minutes of Corky's society seemed to have turned Augustus Fink-Nottle from a blameless newt-fancier into as pronounced a ham as ever drank small ports in Bodegas and called people 'laddie'. In another half jiffy, I felt, he would be addressing me as 'laddie'.

'Well, it's no use talking about it,' I said, 'because I

could never have taken the thing on. Madeline wouldn't have approved of her affianced appearing in public in a green beard.'

'No, she's an odd girl.'

It seemed to me that I might wipe that silly smile off his face by reminding him of something he appeared to have forgotten.

'And how about Dobbs?'

'Eh?'

'When last heard from, you were a bit agitated at the prospect of having to slosh Police Constable Dobbs with your umbrella.'

'Oh, Dobbs? He's out. He's been given his notice. He came along when we were rehearsing and started to read Mike's lines, but he was hopeless. No technique. No personality. And he wouldn't take direction. Kept arguing every point with the management, until finally Corky got heated and began raising her voice, and he got heated and began raising his voice, and the upshot was that that dog of hers, excited no doubt by the uproar, bit him in the leg.'

'Good Lord!'

'Yes, it created an unpleasant atmosphere. Corky put the animal's case extremely well, pointing out that it had probably been pushed around by policemen since it was a slip of a puppy and so was merely fulfilling a legitimate aspiration if it took an occasional nip at one, but Dobbs refused to accept her view that the offence was one calling for a mere reprimand. He took the creature into custody and is keeping it at the police station until he has been able to ascertain whether this was its first bite. Apparently a dog that has had only one bite is in a strong position legally.'

'Sam Goldwyn bit Silversmith last night.'

'Did he? Well, if that comes out, I'm afraid counsel for the prosecution will have a talking-point. But, to go on with my story, Corky, incensed, and quite rightly, by

Dobbs's intransigent attitude, threw him out of the act and is getting her brother to play the part. There is the risk, of course, that the vicar will recognize him, which would lead to an unfortunate situation, but she thinks the green beard will form a sufficient disguise. I am looking forward to having Pirbright as a partner. I can think of few men whom it would give me more genuine pleasure to hit with an umbrella,' said Gussie broodingly, adding that the first time his weapon connected with Catsmeat's head, the latter would think he had been struck by a thunderbolt. It was plain that Time, the great healer, would have to put in a lot of solid work before he forgot and forgave.

'But I can't stay here talking,' he went on. 'Corky has asked me to lunch at the Vicarage, and I must be getting along. I just looked in to give you those poems.'

'Those what?'

'Those Christopher Robin poems. Here they are.'

He handed me a slim volume of verse, and I gave it the perplexed eye.

'What's this for?'

'You recite them at the concert. The ones marked with a cross. I was to have recited them, Madeline making a great point of it – you know how fond she is of the Christopher Robin poems – but now, of course, we have switched acts. And I don't mind telling you that I feel extremely relieved. There's one about the little blighter going hoppity-hoppity-hop which . . . Well, as I say, I feel extremely relieved.'

The slim volume fell from my nerveless fingers, and I goggled at him.

'But, dash it!'

'It's no good saying "But, dash it!" Do you think I didn't say "But, dash it!" when she forced these nauseous productions on me? You've got to do them. She insists. The first thing she will want to know is how they went.'

'But the tough eggs at the back of the row will rush the stage and lynch me.'

'I shouldn't wonder. Still, you've got one consolation.'

'What's that?'

'The thought that all that befalls you is part of the great web, ha, ha, ha,' said Gussie, and exited smiling.

And so the first day of my sojourn at Deverill Hall wore to a close, full to the brim of V-shaped depressions and unsettled outlooks.

10

And as the days went by, these unsettled outlooks became more unsettled, those V-shaped depressions even V-er. It was on a Friday that I had clocked in at Deverill Hall. By the morning of Tuesday I could no longer conceal it from myself that I was losing the old pep and that, unless the clouds changed their act and started dishing out at an early date a considerably more substantial slab of silver lining than they were coming across with at the moment, I should soon be definitely down among the wines and spirits.

It is bad to be trapped in a den of slavering aunts, lashing their tails and glaring at you out of their red eyes. It is unnerving to know that in a couple of days you will be up on a platform in a village hall telling an audience, probably well provided with vegetables, that Christopher Robin goes hoppity-hoppity-hop. It degrades the spirit to have to answer to the name of Augustus, and there are juicier experiences than being in a position where you are constantly asking yourself if an Aunt Agatha or a Madeline Bassett won't suddenly arrive and subject you to shame and exposure. No argument about that. We can take that, I think, as read.

But it was not these chunks of the great web that were removing the stiffening from the Wooster upper lip. No, the root of the trouble, the thing that was giving me dizzy spells and night sweats and making me look like the poor bit of human wreckage in the 'before taking' pictures in the advertisements of Haddocks' Headache Hokies, was the sinister behaviour of Gussie

Fink-Nottle. Contemplating Gussie, I found my soul
darkened by a nameless fear.

I don't know if you have ever had your soul darkened
by a nameless fear. It's a most unpleasant feeling. I used
to get it when I was one of the resident toads beneath
the harrow at Malvern House, Bramley-on-Sea, on
hearing the Rev. Aubrey Upjohn conclude a series of
announcements with the curt crack that he would like
to see Wooster in his study after evening prayers. On the
present occasion I had felt it coming on during the
conversation with Gussie which I have just related, and
in the days that followed it had grown and grown until
now I found myself what is known as a prey to the
liveliest apprehension.

I wonder if you spotted anything in the conversation
to which I refer? Did it, I mean, strike you as significant
and start you saying 'What ho!' to yourself? It didn't?
Then you missed the gist.

The first day I had had merely a vague suspicion. The
second day this suspicion deepened. By nightfall on the
third day suspicion had become a certainty. The
evidence was all in, and there was no getting round it.
Reckless of the fact that there existed at The Larches,
Wimbledon Common, a girl to whom he had plighted
his troth and who would be madder than a bull-pup
entangled in a fly-paper were she to discover that he was
moving in on another, Augustus Fink-Nottle had fallen
for Corky Pirbright like a ton of bricks.

You may say 'Come, come, Bertram, you are
imagining things' or 'Tush, Wooster, this is but an idle
fancy', but let me tell you that I wasn't the only one
who had noticed it. Five solid aunts had noticed it.

'Well, really,' Dame Daphne Winkworth had observed
bitterly just before lunch, when Silversmith had blown
in with the news that Gussie had once again telephoned
to say he would be taking pot-luck at the Vicarage. 'Mr
Wooster seems to live in Miss Pirbright's pocket. He

appears to regard Deverill Hall as a hotel which he can drop into or stay away from as he feels inclined.'

And Aunt Charlotte, when the facts had been relayed to her through her ear-trumpet, for she was wired for sound, had said with a short, quick sniff that she supposed they ought to consider themselves highly honoured that the piefaced young bastard condescended to sleep in the bally place, or words to that effect.

Nor could one fairly blame them for blinding and stiffing. Nothing sticks the gaff into your chatelaine more than a guest being constantly AWOL, and it was only on the rarest occasions nowadays that Gussie saw fit to put on the nosebag at Deverill Hall. He lunched, tea-ed and dined with Corky. Since that first meeting outside the post office he had seldom left her side. The human poultice, nothing less.

You can readily understand, then, why there were dark circles beneath my eyes and why I had almost permanently now a fluttering sensation at the pit of the stomach, as if I had recently swallowed far more mice than I could have wished. It only needed a word from Dame Daphne Winkworth to Aunt Agatha to the effect that her nephew Bertram had fallen into the toils of a most undesirable girl – a Hollywood film actress, my dear – I could see her writing it as clearly as if I had been peeping over her shoulder – to bring the old relative racing down to Deverill Hall with her foot in her hand. And then what? Ruin, desolation and despair.

The obvious procedure, of course, when the morale is being given the sleeve across the windpipe like this, is to get in touch with Jeeves and see what he has to suggest. So, encountering the parlourmaid, Queenie, in the passage outside my room after lunch, I enquired as to his whereabouts.

'I say,' I said, 'I wonder if you happen to know where Jeeves is? Wooster's man, you know.'

She stood staring at me goofily. Her eyes, normally

like twin stars, were dull and a bit reddish about the
edges, and I should have described her face as drawn.
The whole set-up, in short, seeming to indicate that here
one had a parlourmaid who had either gone off her onion
or was wrestling with a secret sorrow.

'Sir?' she said, in a tortured sort of voice.

I repeated my remarks, and this time they penetrated.

'Mr Jeeves isn't here, sir. Mr Wooster let him go to
London. There was a lecture he wanted to be at.'

'Oh thanks,' I said, speaking dully, for this was a
blow. 'You don't know when he'll be back?'

'No, sir.'

'I see. Thanks.'

I went on into my room and took a good, square look
at the situation.

If you ask any of the nibs who move in diplomatic
circles and are accustomed to handling tricky affairs of
state, he will tell you that when matters have reached a
deadlock, it is not a bit of good just sitting on the seat of
the pants and rolling the eyes up to heaven – you have
got to turn stones and explore avenues and take prompt
steps through the proper channels. Only thus can you
hope to find a formula. And it seemed to me, musing
tensely, that in the present crisis something
constructive might be accomplished by rounding up
Corky and giving her a straight-from-the-shoulder talk,
pointing out the frightful jeopardy in which she was
placing an old friend and dancing-class buddy by
allowing Gussie to spend his time frisking and bleating
round her.

I left the room, accordingly, and a few minutes later
might have been observed stealing through the sunlit
grounds en route for the village. In fact, I was observed,
and by Dame Daphne Winkworth. I was nearing the
bottom of the drive and in another moment should have
won through to safety, when somebody called my name
– or, rather, Gussie's name – and I saw the formidable

old egg standing in the rose garden. From the fact that
she had a syringe in her hand I deduced that she was in
the process of doing the local green-fly a bit of no good.

'Come here, Augustus,' she said.

It was the last thing I would have done, if given the
choice, for even at the best of times this dangerous
specimen put the wind up me pretty vertically, and she
was now looking about ten degrees more forbidding than
usual. Her voice was cold and her eye was cold, and I
didn't like the way she was toying with that syringe. It
was plain that for some reason I had fallen in her
estimation to approximately the level of a green-fly, and
her air was that of a woman who for two pins would
press the trigger and let me have a fluid ounce of
whatever the hell-brew was squarely in the mazzard.

'Oh, hallo,' I said, trying to be *debonair* but missing
by a mile. 'Squirting the rose trees?'

'Don't talk to me about rose trees!'

'Oh, no, rather not,' I said. Well, I hadn't wanted to
particularly. Just filling in with *ad lib* stuff.

'Augustus, what is this I hear?'

'I beg your pardon?'

'You would do better to beg Madeline's.'

Mystic stuff. I didn't get it. The impression I received
was of a Dame of the British Empire talking through the
back of her neck.

'When I was in the house just now,' she proceeded, 'a
telegram arrived for you from Madeline. It was
telephoned from the post office. Sometimes they
telephone, and sometimes they deliver personally.'

'I see. According to the whim of the moment.'

'Please do not interrupt. This time it happened that
the message was telephoned, and as I was passing
through the hall when the bell rang, I took it down.'

'Frightfully white of you,' I said, feeling that I couldn't
go wrong in giving her the old oil.

I had gone wrong, however. She didn't like it. She

frowned, raised the syringe, then, as if remembering in time that she was a Deverill, lowered it again.

'I have already asked you not to interrupt. I took down the message, as I say, and I have it here. No,' she said, having searched through her costume, 'I must have left it on the hall table. But I can tell you its contents. Madeline says she has not received a single letter from you since you arrived at the Hall, and she wishes to know why. She is greatly distressed at your abominable neglect, and I am not surprised. You know how sensitive she is. You ought to have been writing to her every day. I have no words to express what I think of your heartless behaviour. That is all, Augustus,' she said, and dismissed me with a gesture of loathing, as if I had been a green-fly that had fallen short of even the very moderate level of decency of the average run-of-the-mill green-fly. And I tottered off and groped my way to a rustic bench and sank onto it.

The information which she had sprung on me had, I need scarcely say, affected me like the impact behind the ear of a stocking full of wet sand. Only once in my career had I experienced an emotion equally intense, on the occasion when Freddie Widgeon at the Drones, having possessed himself of a motor horn, stole up behind me as I crossed Dover Street in what is known as a reverie and suddenly tooted the apparatus in my immediate ear.

It had never so much as occurred to me to suppose that Gussie was not writing daily letters to the Bassett. It was what he had come to this Edgar Allan Poe residence to do, and I had taken it for granted that he was doing it. I didn't need a diagram to show me what the run of events would be, if he persisted in this policy of ca'canny. A spot more silence on his part, and along would come La Bassett in person to investigate, and the thought of what would happen then froze the blood and made the toes curl.

I suppose it may have been for a matter of about ten
minutes that I sat there inert, the jaw drooping, the eyes
staring sightlessly at the surrounding scenery. Then I
pulled myself together and resumed my journey. It has
been well said of Bertram Wooster that though he may
sink onto rustic benches and for a while give the
impression of being licked to a custard, the old spirit
will always come surging back sooner or later.

As I walked, I was thinking hard and bitter thoughts
of Corky, the *fons et origo*, if you know what I mean by
fons et origo, of all the trouble. It was she who, by
shamelessly flirting with him, by persistently giving
him the flashing smile and the quick sidelong look out
of the corner of the eye, had taken Gussie's mind off his
job and slowed him up as our correspondent on the spot.
Oh, Woman, Woman, I said to myself, not for the first
time, feeling that the sooner the sex was suppressed, the
better it would be for all of us.

At the age of eight, in the old dancing-class days,
incensed by some incisive remarks on her part about my
pimples, of which I had a notable collection at that time,
I once forgot myself to the extent of socking Corky
Pirbright on the top-knot with a wooden dumb-bell, and
until this moment I had always regretted the unpleasant
affair, considering my action a blot on an otherwise
stainless record and, no matter what the provocation,
scarcely the behaviour of a *preux chevalier*. But now, as I
brooded on the Delilah stuff she was pulling, I found
myself wishing I could do it again.

I strode on, rehearsing in my mind some opening
sentence to be employed when we should meet, and not
far from the Vicarage came upon her seated at the wheel
of her car by the side of the road.

But when I confronted her and said I wanted a word
with her, she regretted that it couldn't be managed at
the moment. It was, she explained, her busy afternoon.
In pursuance of her policy of being the Little Mother to

her uncle, the sainted Sidney, she was about to take a bowl of strengthening soup to one of his needy parishioners.

'A Mrs Clara Wellbeloved, if you want to keep the record straight,' she proceeded. 'She lives in one of those picturesque cottages off the High Street. And it's no good you waiting, because after delivering the bouillon I sit and talk to her about Hollywood. She's a great fan, and it takes hours. Some other time, my lamb.'

'Listen, Corky –'

'You are probably saying to yourself "Where's the soup?" I unfortunately forgot to bring it along, and Gussie has trotted back for it. What a delightful man he is, Bertie. So kind. So helpful. Always on hand to run errands, when required, and with a fund of good stories about newts. I've given him my autograph. Speaking of autographs, I heard from your cousin Thomas this morning.'

'Never mind about young Thos. What I want –'

She broke into speech again, as girls always do. I have had a good deal of experience of this tendency on the part of the female sex to refrain from listening when you talk to them, and it has always made me sympathize with those fellows who tried to charm the deaf adder and had it react like a Wednesday matinée audience.

'You remember I gave him fifty of my autographs, and he expected to sell them to his playmates at sixpence apiece? Well, he tells me that he got a bob, not sixpence, which will give you a rough idea of how I stand with the boys at Bramley-on-Sea. He says a genuine Ida Lupino only fetches ninepence.'

'Listen, Corky –'

'He wants to come and spend his midterm holiday at the Vicarage, and, of course, I've written to say that I shall be delighted. I don't think Uncle Sidney is too happy at the prospect, but it's good for a clergyman to have these trials. Makes him more spiritual, and consequently hotter at his job.'

'Listen, Corky. What I want to talk to you about –'

'Ah, here's Gussie,' she said, once more doing the deaf adder.

Gussie came bounding up with a look of reverent adoration on his face and a steaming can in his hands. Corky gave him a dazzling smile which seemed to go through him like a red-hot bullet through a pat of butter, and stowed the can away in the rumble seat.

'Thank you, Gussie darling,' she said. 'Well, good-bye all. I must rush.'

She drove off, Gussie standing gaping after her transfixed, like a goldfish staring at an ant's egg. He did not, however, remain transfixed long, because I got him between the third and fourth ribs with a forceful finger, causing him to come to life with a sharp 'Ouch!'

'Gussie,' I said, getting down to brass tacks and beating about no bushes. 'What's all this about you not writing to Madeline?'

'Madeline?'

'Madeline.'

'Oh, Madeline?'

'Yes, Madeline. You ought to have been writing to her every day.'

This seemed to annoy him.

'How on earth could I write to her every day? What chance do I get to write letters when my time is all taken up with memorizing my lines in this cross-talk act and thinking up effective business? I haven't a moment.'

'Well, you'll jolly well have to find a moment. Do you realize she's started sending telegrams about it? You must write to-day without fail.'

'What, to Madeline?'

'Yes, blast you, to Madeline.'

I was surprised to see that he was glowering sullenly through his windshields.

'I'll be blowed if I write to Madeline,' he said, and would have looked like a mule if he had not looked so like a fish. 'I'm teaching her a lesson.'

'You're what?'

'Teaching her a lesson. I'm not at all pleased with Madeline. She wanted me to come to this ghastly house, and I consented on the understanding that she would come, too, and give me moral support. It was a clear-cut gentlemen's agreement. And at the last moment she coolly backed out on the flimsy plea that some school friend of hers at Wimbledon needed her. I was extremely annoyed, and I let her see it. She must be made to realize that she can't do that sort of thing. So I'm not writing to her. It's a sort of system.'

I clutched at the brow. The mice in my interior had now got up an informal dance and were buck-and-winging all over the place like a bunch of Nijinskys.

'Gussie,' I said, 'once and for all, will you or will you not go back to the house and compose an eight-page letter breathing love in every syllable?'

'No, I won't,' he said and left me flat.

Baffled and despondent, I returned to the Hall. And the first person I saw there was Catsmeat. He was in my room, lying on the bed with one of my cigarettes in his mouth.

There was a sort of dreamy look on his dial, as if he were thinking of Gertrude Winkworth.

11

Observing me, he switched off the dreamy look.

'Oh, hallo, Bertie,' he said. 'I wanted to see you.'

'Oh, yes?' I riposted, quick as a flash, and I meant it to sting, for I was feeling a bit fed up with Catsmeat.

I mean of his own free will he had taken on the job of valeting me, and in his capacity of my gentleman's personal gentleman should have been in and out all the time, brushing here a coat, pressing there a trouser and generally making himself useful, and I hadn't set eyes on him since the night we had arrived. One frowns on this absenteeism.

'I wanted to tell you the good news.'

I laughed hollowly.

'Good news? Is there such a thing?'

'You bet there's such a thing. Things are looking up. The sun is smiling through. I believe I'm going to swing this Gertrude deal. Owing to the footling social conventions which prevent visiting valets hobnobbing with the daughter of the house, I haven't seen her, of course, to speak to, but I've been sending her notes by Jeeves and she has been sending me notes by Jeeves, and in her latest she shows distinct signs of yielding to my prayers. I think about two more communications, if carefully worded, should do the trick. Don't actually buy the fish-slice yet, but be prepared.'

My pique vanished. As I have said before, the Woosters are fairminded. I knew what a dickens of a sweat these love letters are, a whole-time job calling for incessant concentration. If Catsmeat had been tied up with a lot of correspondence of this type, he wouldn't have had much time for attending to my wardrobe, of course. You can't press your suit and another fellow's trousers simultaneously.

'Well, that's fine,' I said, pleased to learn that, though the general outlook was so scaly, someone was getting a break. 'I shall watch your future progress with considerable interest. But pigeon-holing your love life for the moment, Catsmeat, a most frightful thing has happened, and I should be glad if you could come across with anything in the aid-and-comfort line. That criminal lunatic Gussie – '

'What's he been doing?'

'It's what he's not been doing that's the trouble. You could have flattened me with a toothpick just now when I found out that he hasn't written a single line to Madeline Bassett since he got here. And, what's more, he says he isn't going to write to her. He says he's teaching her a lesson,' I said, and in a few brief words placed the facts before him.

He looked properly concerned. Catsmeat's is a kindly and feeling heart, readily moved by the spectacle of an old friend splashing about in the gumbo, and he knows how I stand with regard to Madeline Bassett, because she told him the whole story one day when they met at a bazaar and the subject of me happened to come up.

'This is rather serious,' he said.

'You bet it's serious. I'm shaking like a leaf.'

'Girls of the Madeline Bassett type attach such importance to the daily letter.'

'Exactly. And if it fails to arrive, they come and make inquiries on the spot.'

'And you say Gussie was not to be moved?'

'Not an inch. I pleaded with him, I may say passionately, but he put his ears back and refused to co-operate.'

Catsmeat pondered.

'I think I know what's behind all this. The trouble is

that Gussie at the moment is slightly off his rocker.'

'What do you mean, at the moment? And why slightly?'

'He's infatuated with Corky. Sorry to use such long words. I mean he's got a crush on her.'

'I know he has. So does everybody else for miles around. His crush is the favourite topic of conversation when aunt meets aunt.'

'There has been comment in the servants' hall, too.'

'I'm not surprised. I'll bet they're discussing the thing in Basingstoke.'

'You can't blame him, of course.'

'Yes, I can.'

'I mean, it isn't his fault, really. This is springtime, Bertie, the mating season, when, as you probably know, a livelier iris gleams upon the burnished dove and a young man's fancy lightly turns to thoughts of love. The sudden impact plumb spang in the middle of spring, of a girl like Corky on a fathead like Gussie, weakened by constantly swilling orange juice, must have been terrific. Corky, when she's going nicely, bowls over the strongest. No one knows that better than you. You were making a colossal ass of yourself over her at one time.'

'No need to rake up the dead past.'

'I only raked it up to drive home my point, which is that he is more to be pitied than censured.'

'She's the one that wants censuring. Why does she encourage him?'

'I don't think she encourages him. He just adheres.'

'She does encourage him. I've seen her doing it. She deliberately turns on the charm and gives him the old personality. Don't tell me that a girl like Corky, accustomed to giving Hollywood glamour men the brusheroo, couldn't put Gussie on ice, if she wanted to.'

'But she doesn't.'

'That's what I'm beefing about.'

'And I'll tell you why she doesn't. I haven't actually asked her, but I'm pretty sure she's working this Gussie continuity with the idea of sticking the harpoon into Esmond Haddock. To show him that if he doesn't want her, there are others who do.'

'But he does want her.'

'She doesn't know that. Unless you've told her.'

'I haven't.'

'Why not?'

'I wasn't sure if it would be the correct procedure. You see, he dished out all that stuff about his inner feelings under the seal of the confessional, as you might say, and he said he didn't want it to go any further. "This must go no further," he said. On the other hand, a word in season might quite easily reunite a couple of sundered hearts. The whole thing is extraordinarily moot.'

'I'd go ahead and tell her. Bung in the word in season. I'm all for reuniting sundered hearts.'

'Me, too. But I think we've left it too late. Already the Bassett is burning up the wires with telegrams asking what it's all about. A hot one just arrived. I found it on the hall table when I came in. It was the telegram of a girl on the verge of becoming fed to the eye teeth. I tell you, Catsmeat, I see no ray of light. I'm sunk.'

'No, you're not.'

'I am. When I told Gussie about this telegram, urging upon him that now was the time for all good men to come to the aid of the party, he merely as I say, stuck his ears back and said he was teaching the girl a lesson and not a smell of a letter should she get from him till that lesson had been learned. The man's *non compos*, and I repeat that I see no ray of light.'

'It seems to me it's all quite simple.'

'You mean you have something to suggest?'

'Of course I've something to suggest. I always have something to suggest. The thing's obvious. If Gussie won't write to this girl, you must write to her yourself.'

'But she doesn't want to hear from me. She wants to hear from Gussie.'

'And so she will, bless her heart. Gussie has sprained his wrist, so had to dictate the letter to you.'

'Gussie hasn't sprained his wrist.'

'Pardon me. He gave it a nasty wrench while stopping a runaway horse and at great personal risk saving a little child from a hideous death. A golden-haired child, if you will allow yourself to be guided by me, with blue eyes, pink cheeks and a lisp. I think a lisp is good box-office?'

I gasped. I had got his drift.

'Catsmeat, this is terrific! You'll write the thing?'

'Of course. It'll be pie. I've been writing Gertrude that sort of letter since I was so high.'

He seated himself at the table, took pen and paper and immediately became immersed in composition, as the expression is. I could see that it had been no idle boast on his part that the thing would be pie. He didn't even seem to have to stop and think. In almost no time he was handing me the finished script and bidding me get a jerk on and copy it out.

'It ought to go off at once, every moment being vital. Trot down to the post office with it yourself. Then she'll get it first thing in the morning. And now, Bertie, I must leave you. I promised to play gin rummy with Queenie, and I am already late. She wants cheering up, poor child. You've heard about her tragedy? The severing of her engagement to the flatty Dobbs?'

'No, really? Is her engagement off? Then that's why she was looking like that, I suppose. I ran into her after lunch,' I explained, 'and I got the impression that the heart was heavy. What went wrong?'

'She didn't like him being an atheist, and he wouldn't stop being an atheist, and finally he said something about Jonah and the Whale which it was impossible for her to overlook. This morning, she returned the ring, his letters and a china ornament with "A Present From

Blackpool" on it, which he bought her last summer
while visiting relatives in the north. It's hit her pretty
hard, I'm afraid. She's passing through the furnace. She
loves him madly and yearns to be his, but she can't take
that stuff about Jonah and the Whale. One can only hope
that gin rummy will do something to ease the pain.
Right ho, Bertie, get on with that letter. It's not actually
one of my best, perhaps, because I was working against
time and couldn't prune and polish, but I think you'll
like it.'

He was correct. I studied the communication
carefully, and was enchanted with its virtuosity. If it
wasn't one of his best, his best must have been pretty
good, and I was not surprised that upon receipt of a
series Gertrude Winkworth was weakening. There are
letters which sow doubts as to whether this bit here
couldn't have been rather more neatly phrased and that
bit there gingered up a trifle, and other letters of which
you say to yourself 'This is the goods. Don't alter a
word'. This was one of the latter letters. He had got just
the right modest touch into the passage about the
runaway horse, and the lisping child was terrific. She
stuck out like a sore thumb and hogged the show. As for
the warmer portions about missing Madeline every
minute and wishing she were here so that he could fold
her in his arms and what not, they simply couldn't have
been improved upon.

I copied the thing out, stuffed it in an envelope and
took it down to the post office. And scarcely had it
plopped into the box, when I was hailed from behind by
a musical soprano and, turning, saw Corky heaving
alongside.

I felt profoundly bucked. The very girl I wanted to see. I grabbed her by the arm, so that she couldn't do another of her sudden sneaks.

'Corky,' I said, 'I want a long, heart to heart talk with you.'

'Not about Hollywood?'

'No, not about Hollywood.'

'Thank God. I don't think I could have stood any more Hollywood chatter this afternoon. I wouldn't have believed,' she said, proceeding, as always, to collar the conversation, 'that anybody except Louella Parsons and Hedda Hopper could be such an authority on the film world as is Mrs Clara Wellbeloved. She knows much more about it than I do, and I'll have been moving in celluloid circles two years come Lammas Eve. She knows exactly how many times everybody's been divorced and why, how much every picture for the last twenty years has grossed, and how many Warner brothers there are. She even knows how many times Artie Shaw has been married, which I'll bet he couldn't tell you himself. She asked if I had ever married Artie Shaw, and when I said No, seemed to think I was pulling her leg or must have done it without noticing. I tried to explain that when a girl goes to Hollywood she doesn't *have* to marry Artie Shaw, it's optional, but I don't think I convinced her. A very remarkable old lady, but a bit exhausting after the first hour or two. Did you say you wanted to speak to me about something.'

'Yes, I did.'

'Well, why don't you?'

'Because you won't let me get a word in edgeways.'

'Oh, have I been talking? I'm sorry. What's on your mind, my king?'

'Gussie.'

'Fink-Nottle?'

'Fink-Nottle is correct.'

'The whitest man I know.'

'The fatheadest man you know. Listen, Corky, I've just been talking to Catsmeat –'

'Did he tell you that he expects shortly to persuade Gertrude Winkworth to elope with him?'

'Yes.'

She smiled in a steely sort of way, like one of those women in the Old Testament who used to go about driving spikes into people's heads.

'I'm just waiting for that to happen,' she said, 'so that I can get a good laugh out of seeing Esmond's face when he finds out that his Gertrude has gone off with another. Most amusing it will be. Ha, ha,' she added.

That 'Ha, ha', so like the expiring quack of a duck dying of a broken heart, told me all I wanted to know. I saw that Catsmeat had not erred in his diagnosis of this young shrimp's motives in giving Gussie the old treatment, and I had no option but to slip her the lowdown without further delay. I tapped her on the shoulder, and bunged in the word in season.

'Corky,' I said, 'you're a chump. You've got a completely wrong angle on this Haddock. So far from being enamoured of Gertrude Winkworth, I don't suppose he would care, except in a distant, cousinly way, if she choked on a fish-bone. You are the lodestar of his life.'

'What!'

'I had it from his own lips. He was a bit pickled at the time, which makes it all the more impressive, because *in vino* what's-the-word.'

Her eyes had lighted up. She gave a quick gulp.

'He said I was the lodestar of his life?'

'With a "still" in front of the "lodestar". "Mark this," he said, helping himself to port, of which he was already nearly full. "Though she has given me the brusheroo, she is still the lodestar of my life."'

'Bertie, if you're kidding –'

'Of course I'm not.'

'I hope you're not, because if you are I shall put the curse of the Pirbrights on you, and it's not at all the sort of curse you will enjoy. Tell me more.'

I told her more. In fact I told her all. When I had finished, she laughed like a hyena and also, for girls never make sense, let fall a pearly tear or two.

'Isn't that just the sort of thing he would think up, bless him!' she said, alluding to the hot idea Esmond Haddock had brought back with him from the Basingstoke cinema. 'What a woolly lambkin that man is!'

I was not sure if 'woolly lambkin' was quite the phrase I would have used myself to describe Esmond Haddock, but I let it go, it being no affair of mine. If she elected to regard a fellow with a forty-six-inch chest and muscles like writhing snakes as a woolly lambkin, that was up to her. My task, having started a good thing, was to push it along.

'In these circs,' I said, 'you will probably be glad of a word of advice from a knowledgeable man of the world. Catsmeat appears to have obtained excellent results on the Gertrude front from pouring out his soul in the form of notes, and if you take my tip, you will do the same. Drop Esmond Haddock a civil line telling him you are aching for his presence, and he will lower the world's record racing round to the Vicarage to fold you in his arms. He's only waiting for the green light.'

She shook her head.

'No,' she said.

'Why no?'

'We should simply be where we were before.'

I saw what she was driving at, of course.

'I know what's in your mind,' I said. 'You are alluding to his civil disobedience *in re* defying his aunts. Well, let me assure you that that little difficulty will very shortly yield to treatment. Listen. Esmond Haddock is singing a hunting song at the concert, words by his Aunt Charlotte, music by his Aunt Myrtle. You don't dispute that.'

'All correct so far.'

'Well, suppose that hunting song is a smackerino.'

And in a few well-chosen words I informed her of Jeeves's tenable theory.

'You get the idea?' I concluded. 'The cheers of the multitude frequently act like a powerful drug on these birds with inferiority complexes. Rouse such birds, as, for instance, by whistling through your fingers and yelling "*Bis! Bis!*" when they sing hunting songs, and they become changed men. Their morale stiffens. Their tails shoot up like rockets. They find themselves regarding the tough eggs before whom they have always been accustomed to crawl as less than the dust beneath their chariot wheels. If Esmond Haddock goes with the bang I anticipate, it won't be long before those aunts of his will be climbing trees and pulling them up after them whenever he looks squiggle-eyed at them.'

My eloquence had not been wasted. She started considerably, and said something about 'Out of the mouths of babes and sucklings', going on to explain that the gag was not her own but one of her Uncle Sidney's. And in return I told her that the tenable theory I had been outlining was not mine, but Jeeves's. Each giving credit where credit was due.

'I believe he's right, Bertie.'

'Of course he's right. Jeeves is always right. It's happened before. Do you know Bingo Little?'

'Just to say Hallo to. He married some sort of female novelist, didn't he?'

'Rosie M. Banks, author of *Mervyn Keene, Clubman*, and *Only A Factory Girl*. And their union was blessed. In due season a bouncing baby was added to the strength. Keep your eye on that baby, for the plot centres round it. Well, since you last saw Bingo, Mrs Bingo, by using her substantial pull, secured for him the post of editor of *Wee Tots*, a journal for the nursery and the home, a very good job in most respects but with this flaw, that the salary attached to it was not all it might have been. His proprietor, P. P. Purkiss, being one of those parsimonious birds in whose pocket-books moths nest and raise large families. It was Bingo's constant endeavour, accordingly, to try to stick old Gaspard the Miser for a raise. All clear so far?'

'I've got it.'

'Week after week he would creep into P. P. Purkiss's presence and falter out apologetic sentences beginning "Oh, Mr Purkiss, I wonder if . . ." and "Oh, Mr Purkiss, do you think you could possibly . . ." only to have the blighter gaze at him with fishy eyes and talk about the tightness of money and the growing cost of pulp paper. And Bingo would say "Oh, quite, Mr Purkiss," and "I see, Mr Purkiss, yes I see," and creep out again. That's Act One.'

'But mark the sequel?'

'You're right, mark the sequel. Came a day when Bingo's bouncing baby, entered in a baby contest against some of the warmest competition in South Kensington, scooped in the first prize, a handsome all-day sucker, getting kissed in the process by the wife of a Cabinet Minister and generally fawned upon by all and sundry. And next morning Bingo, with a strange light on his face, strode into P. P. Purkiss's private office without knocking, banged the desk with his fist and said he wished to see an additional ten fish in his pay envelope from now on, and to suit everybody's convenience the new arrangement would come into effect on the following Saturday. And when P. P. Purkiss started to go into his act, he banged the desk again and said he hadn't come there to argue. "Yes or no, Purkiss!" he said, and P. P. Purkiss, sagging like a wet sock, said "Why, yes, yes, of course, most certainly, Mr Little", adding that he had been on the point of suggesting some such idea himself. Well, I mean, that shows you.'

It impressed her. No mistaking that. She uttered a meditative 'Golly!' and stood on one leg, looking like 'The Soul's Awakening'.

'And so,' I proceeded, 'we are going to strain every nerve to see that Esmond Haddock's hunting song is the high-spot of the evening. Jeeves is to go about the village, scattering beers, so as to assemble what is known as a claque and ensure the thunderous applause. You will be able to help in that direction, too.'

'Of course I will. My standing in the village is terrific. I have the place in my pocket. I must get after this right away. I can't wait. You don't mind me leaving you?'

'Not at all, not at all, or, rather, yes, I jolly well do. Before you go, we've got to get this Gussie thing straight.'

'What Gussie thing?'

I clicked my tongue.

'You know perfectly well what Gussie thing. For reasons into which we need not go, you have recently been making Augustus Fink-Nottle the plaything of an idle hour, and it has got to stop. I don't have to tell you again what will happen if you continue carrying on as of even date. In our conference at the flat I made the facts clear to the meanest intelligence. You are fully aware that should the evil spread, should sand be shoved into the gears of the Fink-Nottle-Bassett romance to such an extent that it ceases to tick over, Bertram Wooster will be faced with the fate that is worse than death – viz. marriage. I feel sure that, now that you have been reminded of the hideous peril that looms, your good heart will not allow you to go on encouraging the above Fink-Nottle as, according to the evidence of five aunts, you are doing now. Appalled by the thought of poor old Wooster pressing the wedding trousers and packing the trunks for a honeymoon with that ghastly Bassett, you will obey the dictates of your better self and cool him off.'

She saw my point.

'You want me to restore Gussie to circulation?'

'Exactly.'

'Switch off the fascination? Release him from my clutches?'

'That's right.'

'Why, of course. I'll attend to it immediately.'

And on these very satisfactory terms we parted. A great weight had been lifted from my mind.

Well, I don't know what your experience has been, but mine is that there is very little percentage in having a weight lifted off your mind, because the first thing you know another, probably a dashed sight heavier, is immediately shoved on. It would appear to be a game you can't beat.

I had scarcely got back to my room, all soothed and relaxed, when in blew Catsmeat, and there was that in his mere appearance that chilled my merry mood like a slap in the eye with a wet towel. His face was grave, and his deportment not at all the sprightly deportment of a man who has recently been playing gin rummy with parlourmaids.

'Bertie,' he said, 'hold on tight to something. A very serious situation has arisen.'

The floor seemed to heave beneath me like a stage sea. The mice, which since that latter sequence and the subsequent chat with Corky had been taking a breather, sprang into renewed activity, as if starting training for some athletic sports.

'Oh, my sainted aunt!' I moaned, and Catsmeat said I might well say 'My sainted aunt', because she was the spearhead of the trouble.

'Here comes the bruise,' he said. 'When I was in the servants' hall a moment ago, Silversmith rolled in. And do you know what he had just been told by the girls higher up? He had been told that your Aunt Agatha is coming here. I don't know when, but in the next day or so. Dame Daphne Winkworth had a letter from her by the afternoon post, and in it she announced her intention of shortly being a pleasant visitor at this ruddy hencoop. So now what?'

13

It was a Bertram Wooster with a pale, careworn face and a marked disposition to start at sudden noises who sat in his bedroom on the following afternoon, rising occasionally to pace the floor. Few, seeing him, would have recognized in this limp and shivering chunk of human flotsam the suave, dapper *boulevardier* of happier years. I was waiting for Catsmeat to return from the metropolis and make his report.

Threshing the thing out on the previous evening, we had not taken long in reaching the conclusion that it would be madness to attempt to cope with this major crisis ourselves, and that the whole conduct of the affair must at the earliest moment be handed over to Jeeves. And as Jeeves was in London and it might have looked odd for me to dash away from the Big House for the night, Catsmeat had gone up to confer with him. He had tooled off secretly in my two-seater, expecting to be back around lunch-time.

But lunch had come and gone, the duck and green peas turning to ashes in my mouth, and still no sign of him. It was past three when he finally showed up.

At the sight of him, my heart, throwing off its burden of care, did a quick soft-shoe dance. No fellow, I reasoned, unless he was bringing good news, could look so like the United States Marines. When last seen, driving off on his mission, his air had been sober and downcast, as if he feared that even Jeeves would have to confess himself snookered by this one. He was now gay, bobbish and boomps-a-daisy.

'Sorry I'm late,' he said. 'I had to wait for Jeeves's

brain to gather momentum. He was a little slower off
the mark than usual.'

I clutched his arm.

'Did he click?' I cried, quivering in every limb.

'Oh, yes, he clicked. Jeeves always clicks. But this
time only after brooding for what seemed an eternity. I
found him in the kitchen at your flat, sipping a cup of
tea and reading Spinoza, and put our problem before
him, bidding him set the little grey cells in operation
without delay and think of some way of preventing your
blasted aunt from fulfilling her evil purpose of coming to
infest Deverill Hall. He said he would, and I went back
to the sitting-room, where I took a seat, put my feet on
the mantelpiece and thought of Gertrude. From time to
time I would rise and look in at the kitchen and ask him
how it was coming, but he motioned me away with a
silent wave of the hand and let the brain out another
notch. Finally he emerged and announced that he had
got it. He had been musing, as always, on the psychology
of the individual.'

'What individual? My Aunt Agatha?'

'Naturally, your Aunt Agatha. What other individual's
psychology would you have expected him to muse on?
Sir Stafford Cripps's? He then proceeded to outline a
scheme which I think you will agree was a ball of fire.
Tell me, Bertie, have you ever stolen a cub from a
tigress?'

I said no, for one reason and another I never had, and
he asked me what, if I ever did, I supposed the reactions
of the tigress would be, always assuming that she was a
good wife and mother. And I said that, while I didn't set
myself up as an authority on tigresses, I imagined that
she would be as sick as mud.

'Exactly. And you would expect the animal, the loss of
its child having been drawn to its attention, to drop
everything and start looking for it, would you not? It
would completely revise its social plans, don't you

think? If, for instance, it had arranged to visit other tigresses in a nearby cave, it would cancel the date and begin hunting around for clues. You agree?'

I said Yes, I thought this probable.

'Well, that is what Jeeves feels will happen in the case of your Aunt Agatha when she learns that her son Thomas has vanished from his school at Bramley-on-Sea.'

I can't tell you offhand what I had been expecting, but it certainly wasn't this. Having recovered sufficient breath to enable me to put the question, I asked what it was that he had said, and he repeated his words at dictation speed, and I said, 'But dash it!' and he said 'Well?'

'You aren't telling me that Jeeves is going to kidnap young Thos?'

He t'chk-t'chked impatiently.

'You don't have to kidnap dyed-in-the-wool fans like your cousin Thomas, if you inform them that their favourite film star is hoping that they will be able to get away and come and spend a few days at the Vicarage where she is staying. That is the message which Jeeves has gone to Bramley-on-Sea to deliver, and I confidently expect it to work like a charm.'

'You mean he'll run away from school?'

'Of course he'll run away from school. Like lightning. However, to clinch the thing, I empowered Jeeves in your name to offer a fee of five quid in the event of any hesitation. I gather from Jeeves, in whom he confided, that young Thomas is more than ordinarily out for the stuff just now. He's saving up to buy a camera.'

I applauded the shrewd thought, but I didn't think that this introduction of the sordid note would really be necessary. Thos is a boy of volcanic passions, the sort of boy who, if he had but threepence in the world, would spend it on a stamp, writing to Dorothy Lamour for her autograph, and the message which Catsmeat had outlined would, I felt, be in itself amply sufficient to get him on the move.

'Yes,' Catsmeat agreed, 'I think we should shortly have the young fellow with us. But not your Aunt Agatha, who will be occupied elsewhere. It's a pity she has to be temporarily deprived of her cub, of course, and one sympathizes with a mother's anxiety. It would have been nice if the thing could have been arranged some other way, but that's how it goes. One has simply got to say to oneself that into each life some rain must fall.'

My own view was that Aunt Agatha wouldn't be anxious so much as hopping mad.

'Thos,' I said, 'makes rather a speciality of running away from school. He's done it twice before this, once to attend a cup final and once to go hunting for buried treasure in the Caribbees, and I don't remember Aunt Agatha on either occasion as the stricken mother. Thos was the one who got stricken. Six of the best on the old spot, he tells me. This, I should imagine, will probably occur again, and I think that even if he takes the assignment on for love alone, I will slip him that fiver as added money.'

'It would be a graceful act.'

'After all, what's money? You can't take it with you.'

'The right spirit.'

'But isn't Corky going to be a bit at a loss when he suddenly shows up?'

'That's all fixed. I met her in the village and told her.'

'And she approved?'

'Wholeheartedly. Corky always approves of anything that seems likely to tend to start something.'

'She's a wonderful girl.'

'A very admirable character. By the way, she tells me you put in that word in season.'

'Yes. I thought she seemed braced.'

'That's how she struck me, too. Odd that she should be so crazy about Esmond Haddock. I've only seen him

from a distance, of course, but I should have imagined he
would have been a bit on the stiff side for Corky.'

'He's not really stiff. You should see him relaxing over
the port.'

'Perhaps you're right. And, anyway, love's a thing you
can't argue about. I suppose it would perplex thousands
that Gertrude, bless her, loves me. Yet she does. And
look at poor little Queenie. Heartbroken over the loss of
a rozzer I wouldn't be seen in a ditch with. And talking
of Queenie, I was thinking of taking her to the pictures
in Basingstoke this afternoon, if you'll lend me your car.'

'Of course. You feel it would cheer her up?'

'It might. And I should like to slap balm on that
wounded spirit, if it can be managed. It's curious how,
when you're in love, you yearn to go about doing acts of
kindness to everybody. I am bursting with a sort of
yeasty benevolence these days, like one of those chaps in
Dickens. I very nearly bought you a tie in London. Gosh!
Who's that?'

Someone had knocked on the door.

'Come in,' I said, and Catsmeat dashed at the
wardrobe and dashed out festooned in trousers and
things. Striking the professional note.

Silversmith came navigating over the threshold. This
majestic man always had in his deportment a suggestion
of the ambassador about to deliver important State
papers to a reigning monarch, and now the resemblance
was heightened by the fact that in front of his ample
stomach he was bearing a salver with a couple of
telegrams on it. I gathered them in, and he went
navigating out again.

Catsmeat replaced the trousers. He was quivering a
little.

'What effect does that bloke have on you, Bertie?' he
asked in a hushed voice, as if he were speaking in a
cathedral. 'He paralyses me. I don't know if you are

familiar with the works of Joseph Conrad, but there's a chap in his *Lord Jim* of whom he says "Had you been the Emperor of the East and West, you could not have ignored your inferiority in his presence". That's Silversmith. He fills me with an awful humility. He shrivels my immortal soul to the size of a parched pea. He's the living image of some of those old time pros who used to give me such a hell of a time when I first went on the stage. Well, go on. Open them.'

'You mean these telegrams?'

'What did you think I meant?'

'They're addressed to Gussie.'

'Of course they're addressed to Gussie. But they're for you.'

'We don't know that.'

'They must be. One's probably from Jeeves, telling you that the balloon has gone up.'

'But the other? It may be a tender bob's-worth from Madeline.'

'Ah, go on.'

I was firm.

'No, Catsmeat. The code of the Woosters restrains me. The code of the Woosters is more rigid than the code of the Catsmeats. A Wooster cannot open a telegram addressed to another, even if for the moment he is that other, if you see what I mean. I'll have to submit them to Gussie.'

'All right, if you see it that way. I'll be off, then, to try to bring a little sunshine into Queenie's life.'

He legged it, and I took a seat and went on being firm. The hour was then three-forty-five.

I continued firm till about five minutes to four.

The catch about the code of the Woosters is that if you start examining it with a couple of telegrams staring you in the face, one of them almost certainly containing news of vital import, you find yourself after a while

beginning to wonder if it's really so hot, after all. I mean
to say, the thought creeps in that maybe, if one did but
know, the Woosters are priceless asses to let themselves
be ruled by a code like that. By four o'clock I wasn't
quite so firm as I had been. By ten past my fingers were
definitely twitching.

It was at four-fifteen sharp that I opened the first
telegram. As Catsmeat had predicted, it was a cautiously
worded communication from Jeeves, handed in at
Bramley-on-Sea and signed Bodger's Stores, guardedly
intimating that everything had gone according to plan.
The goods, it said, were in transit and would be
delivered in a plain van in the course of the evening.
Highly satisfactory.

I put a match to it and reduced it to ashes, for you
can't be too careful, and having done so was concerned
to find, as I looked at the other envelope, that my fingers
were still twitching. I took the thing and twiddled it
thoughtfully.

I can guess what you're going to say. You're going to
say that, having perused the first one and mastered its
contents, there was no need whatever for me to open the
other, and you are perfectly right. But you know how it
is. Ask the first lion cub you meet, and it will tell you
that, once you've tasted blood, there is no pulling up,
and it's the same with opening telegrams. Conscience
whispered that this one, addressed to Gussie and
intended for Gussie, was for Gussie's eyes alone, and I
agreed absolutely. But I could no more stop myself
opening it than you can stop yourself eating another
salted almond.

I ripped the envelope, and the quick blush of shame
mantled the cheek as my eye caught the signature
'Madeline'.

Then my eye caught the rest of the bally thing.

It read as follows:

Fink-Nottle
Deverill Hall
King's Deverill
Hants.

Letter received. Cannot understand why not had reassuring telegram. Sure you concealing accident terribly serious. Fever anxiety. Fear worst. Arriving Deverill Hall to-morrow afternoon. Love. Kisses. Madeline.

14

Yes, that was the torpedo that exploded under my bows,
and I had the feeling you get sometimes that some
practical joker has suddenly removed all the bones from
your legs, substituting for them an unsatisfactory jelly. I
reread the thing, to make sure I had seen what I thought
I had seen, and, finding I had, buried the face in the
hands.

It was the being without advisers that made the
situation so bleak. On these occasions when Fate,
having biffed you in the eye, proceeds to kick you in the
pants, you want to gather the boys about you and thresh
things out, and there weren't any boys to gather. Jeeves
was in London, Catsmeat in Basingstoke. It made me
feel like a Prime Minister who starts to call an
important Cabinet meeting and finds that the Home
Secretary and the Lord President of the Council have
nipped over to Paris and the Minister of Agriculture
and Fisheries and the rest of the gang are at the dog
races.

There seemed to be nothing to do but wait till
Catsmeat, having sat through the news and the main
feature and the two-reel Silly Symphony, wended
homeward. And though Reason told me that he couldn't
get back for another two hours or more and that even
when he did get back it was about a hundred to eight
against him having any constructive policy to put
forward, I went down to the main gate and paced up and
down, scanning the horizon like Sister what-was-her-
name in that story one used to read.

The evening was well advanced, and the local birds

had long since called it a day, when I spotted the two-seater coming down the road. I flagged it, and Catsmeat applied the brakes.

'Oh, hallo, Bertie,' he said in a subdued sort of voice, and when he had alighted and I had drawn him apart he explained the reason for his sober deportment.

'Most unfortunate,' he said, throwing a commiserating glance at the occupant of the other seat, who was staring before her with anguished eyes and from time to time taking a dab at them with her handkerchief. 'With these tough films so popular, I suppose I might have foreseen that something like this would happen. The picture was full of cops, scores of cops racing to and fro saying "Oh, so you won't talk?" and it was too much for poor little Queenie. Just twisted the knife in the wound, as you might say. She's better now, though still sniffing.'

I suppose if you went through the W1 postal district of London with a fine-tooth comb and a brace of bloodhounds, you wouldn't find more than about three men readier than Bertram Wooster to sympathize with a woman's distress, and in ordinary circumstances I would unquestionably have given a low, pitying whistle and said 'Too bad, too bad.' But I hadn't time now to mourn over stricken parlourmaids. All the mourning at my disposal was earmarked for Wooster, B.

'Read this,' I said.

He cocked an eye at me.

'Hallo!' he said, in what is known as a sardonic manner. 'So the code of the Woosters sprang a leak? I had an idea it would.'

I think he was about to develop the theme and be pretty dashed humorous at my expense, but at this moment he started to scan the document and the gist hit him in the eyeball.

'H'm!' he said. 'This will want a little management.'

'Yes,' I concurred.

'It calls for sophisticated handling. We shall have to think this over.'

'I've been thinking it over for hours.'

'Yes, but you've got one of those cheap substitute brains which are never any good. It will be different when a man like me starts giving it the cream of his intellect.'

'If only Jeeves were here!'

'Yes, we could use Jeeves. It's a pity he is not with us.'

'And it's a pity,' I couldn't help pointing out, though the man of sensibility dislikes rubbing these things in, 'that you started the whole trouble by making Gussie wade in the Trafalgar Square fountain.'

'True. One regrets that. Yet at the time it seemed so right, so inevitable. There he was, I mean, and there was the fountain. I felt very strongly that here was an opportunity which might not occur again. And while I would be the last to deny that the aftermath hasn't been too good, it was certainly value for money. A man who has seen Gussie Fink-Nottle chasing newts in the Trafalgar Square fountain in correct evening costume at five o'clock in the morning is a man who has lived. He has got something he can tell his grandchildren. But if we are apportioning the blame, we can go further back than that. Where the trouble started was when you insisted on me giving him dinner. Madness. You might have known something would crack.'

'Well, it's no good talking about it.'

'No. Action is what we want. Sharp, decisive action as dished out by Napoleon. I suppose you will shortly be going in and dressing for dinner?'

'I suppose so.'

'How soon after dinner will you be in your room?'

'As soon as I can jolly well manage it.'

'Expect me there, then, probably with a whole plan of campaign cut and dried. And now I really must be getting back to Queenie. She will be on duty before long and will want to powder her nose and remove the tear stains. Poor little soul! If you knew how my heart bleeds for that girl, Bertie, you would shudder.'

And, of course, it being so vital that we should get together with the minimum of delay, that night turned out to be the one night when it was impossible to take an early powder. Instead of the ordinary dinner, a regular binge had been arranged, with guests from all over the countryside. No fewer than ten of Hampshire's more prominent stiffs had been summoned to the trough, and they stuck on like limpets long after any competent chucker-out would have bounced them. No doubt, if you have gone to the sweat of driving twenty miles to a house to dine, you don't feel like just snatching a chop and dashing off. You hang on for the musical evening and the drinks at ten-thirty.

Be that as it may, it wasn't till close on midnight that the final car rolled away. And when I bounded to my room, off duty at last, there was no sign of Catsmeat.

There was, however, a note from him lying on the pillow, and I tore it open with a feverish flick of the finger.

It was dated eleven p.m., and its tone was reproachful. He rebuked me for what he described as sitting gorging and swilling with my fine friends when I ought to have been at the conference table doing a bit of honest work. He asked me if I thought he was going to remain seated on his fanny in my damned room all night, and hoped that I would have a hangover next day, as well as indigestion from too much rich food. He couldn't wait any longer, he said, it being his intention to take my car and drive to London so as to be at Wimbledon Common bright and early to-morrow morning for an interview with Madeline Bassett. And at that interview, he went on, concluding on a cheerier note, he would fix everything up just the same as Mother makes it, for he had got the idea of a lifetime, an idea so superb that I could set my mind, if I called it a mind, completely at rest. He doubted, he said, whether Jeeves himself, even if full to the brim of fish, could have dug up a better *modus operandi*.

Well, this was comforting, of course, always provided that one could accept the theory that he was as good as he thought he was. You never know with Catsmeat. In one of his school reports, which I happened to see while prowling about the Rev. Aubrey Upjohn's study one night in search of biscuits, the Rev. Aubrey had described him as 'brilliant but unsound', and if ever a headmaster with a face like a cassowary rang the bell and entitled himself to receive a cigar or a coco-nut, this headmaster was that headmaster.

However, I will own that his communication distinctly eased the spirit. It is a pretty well established fact that the heart bowed down with weight of woe to weakest hope will cling, and that's what mine did. It was in quite an uplifted frame of mind that I shed the soup and fish and climbed into the slumberwear. I rather think, though I wouldn't swear to it, that I sang a bar or two of a recent song hit.

I had just donned the dressing-gown and was preparing for a final cigarette, when the door opened and Gussie came in.

Gussie was in peevish mood. He hadn't liked the stiffs, and he complained with a good deal of bitterness at having had to waste in their society an evening which might have been spent *chez* Corky.

'You couldn't oil out of a big dinner-party,' I urged.

'No, that's what Corky said. She said it wouldn't do. *Noblesse oblige* was one of the expressions she used. Amazing what high principles she has. You don't often find a girl as pretty as that with such high principles. And how pretty she is, isn't she, Bertie? Or, rather, when I say pretty, I mean angelically lovely.'

I agreed that Corky's face wouldn't stop a clock, and

he retorted warmly what did I mean it wouldn't stop a clock.

'She's divine. She's the most beautiful girl I've ever seen. It seems so extraordinary that she should be Pirbright's sister. You would think any sister of Pirbright's would be as repulsive as he is.'

'I'd call Catsmeat rather good-looking.'

'I disagree with you. He's a hellhound, and it comes out in his appearance. "There are newts in that fountain, Gussie," he said to me. "Get after them without a second's delay." And wouldn't take No for an answer. Urged me on with sharp hunting cries. "Yoicks!" he said, and "Tallyho!" But what I came about, Bertie,' said Gussie, breaking off abruptly as if this dip into the past pained him, 'was to ask if you could lend me that tie of yours with the pink lozenges on the dove-grey background. I shall be dropping in at the Vicarage to-morrow morning, and I want to look my best.'

Apart from the fleeting thought that he was a bit of an optimist if he expected a tie with pink lozenges on a dove-grey background to undo Nature's handiwork to the extent of making him look anything but a fish-faced gargoyle, my reaction to these words was a feeling of profound relief that I had had that talk with Corky and obtained her promise that she would lose no time in choking Gussie off and putting him on the ice.

For it was plain that there was no time to be lost. Every word this super-heated newt-fancier uttered showed more clearly the extent to which he had got it up his nose. Chatting with Augustus Fink-Nottle about Corky was like getting the inside from Mark Antony on the topic of Cleopatra, and every second he spent out of the Frigidaire was fraught with peril. It was only too plain that The Larches, Wimbledon Common, had ceased to mean a thing in his life and instead of being a holy shrine housing the girl of his dreams, had become just an address in the suburban telephone book.

I gave him the tie, and he thanked me and started out.

'Oh, by the way,' he said, pausing at the door, 'you remember pestering me to write to Madeline. Well, I've done it. I wrote to her this afternoon. Why are you looking like a dying duck?'

I was looking like a dying duck because I had, of course, instantly spotted the snag. What, I was asking myself, was Madeline Bassett going to think when on top of the letter about the sprained wrist she got one in Gussie's handwriting with no reference in it whatever to runaway horses and completely silent on the theme of golden-haired children with lisps?

I revealed to Gussie the recent activities of the Catsmeat-Wooster duo, and he frowned disapprovingly. Most officious, he said, writing people's love letters for them, and not in the best of taste.

'However,' he proceeded, 'it doesn't really matter, because what I said in my letter was that everything was off.'

I tottered and would have fallen, had I not clutched at a passing chest of drawers.

'*Off?*'

'I've broken the engagement. I've been feeling for some days now that Madeline, though a nice girl, won't do. My heart belongs to Corky. Good night again, Bertie. Thanks for the tie.'

He withdrew, humming a sentimental ballad.

15

The Larches, Wimbledon Common, was one of those
eligible residences standing in commodious grounds
with Company's own water both h. and c. and the usual
domestic offices and all that sort of thing, which you
pass on the left as you drive out of London by way of
Putney Hill. I don't know who own these joints, though
obviously citizens who have got the stuff in sackfuls,
and I didn't know who owned The Larches. All I knew
was that Gussie's letter to Madeline Bassett would be
arriving at that address by the first postal delivery, and it
was my intention, should the feat prove to be within the
scope of human power, to intercept and destroy it.

In tampering with His Majesty's mails in this
manner, I had an idea that I was rendering myself liable
to about forty years in the coop, but the risk seemed to
me well worth taking. After all, forty years soon pass,
and only by preventing that letter reaching its
destination could I secure the bit of breathing space so
urgently needed in order to enable me to turn round and
think things over.

That was why on the following morning the
commodious grounds of The Larches, in addition to a
lawn, a summer-house, a pond, flower-beds, bushes and
an assortment of trees, contained also one Wooster,
noticeably cold about the feet and inclined to rise from
twelve to eighteen inches skywards every time an early
bird gave a sudden *cheep* over its worm. This Wooster to
whom I allude was crouching in the interior of a bush
not far from the french windows of what, unless the
architect had got the place all cockeyed, was the

dining-room. He had run up from King's Deverill on the 2.54 milk train.

I say 'run', but perhaps 'sauntered' would be more the *mot juste*. When milk moves from spot to spot, it takes its time, and it was not until very near zero hour that I had sneaked in through the gates and got into position one. By the time I had wedged myself into my bush, the sun was high up in the sky, as Esmond Haddock's Aunt Charlotte would have said, and I found myself musing, as I have so often had occasion to do, on the callous way in which Nature refuses to chip in and do its bit when the human heart is in the soup.

Though howling hurricanes and driving rainstorms would have been a more suitable accompaniment to the run of the action, the morning – or morn, if you prefer to string along with Aunt Charlotte – was bright and fair. My nervous system was seriously disordered, and one of God's less likeable creatures with about a hundred and fourteen legs had crawled down the back of my neck and was doing its daily dozen on the sensitive skin, but did Nature care? Not a hoot. The sky continued blue, and the fatheaded sun which I have mentioned shone smilingly throughout.

Beetles on the spine are admittedly bad, calling for all that a man has of fortitude and endurance, but when embarking on an enterprise which involved parking the carcass in bushes one more or less budgets for beetles. What was afflicting me much more than the activities of the undersigned was the reflection that I didn't know what was going to happen when the postman arrived. It might quite well be, I felt, that everybody at The Larches fed in bed of a morning, in which event a maid would take Gussie's bit of trinitrotoluol up to Madeline's room on a tray, thus rendering my schemes null and void.

It was just as this morale-lowering thought came into my mind that something suddenly bumped against my leg, causing the top of my head to part from its moorings. My initial impression that I had been set upon by a powerful group of enemies lasted, though it seemed a year, for perhaps two seconds. Then, the spots clearing from before my eyes and the world ceasing to do the adagio dance into which it had broken, I was able to perceive that all that had come into my life was a medium-sized ginger cat. Breathing anew, as the expression is, I bent down and tickled it behind the ear, such being my invariable policy when closeted with cats, and was still tickling when there was a bang and a rattle and somebody threw back the windows of the dining-room.

Shortly afterwards, the front door opened and a housemaid came out onto the steps and started shaking a mat in a languid sort of way.

Able now to see into the dining-room and observing that the table was laid for the morning meal, I found my thoughts taking a more optimistic turn. Madeline Bassett, I told myself, was not the girl to remain sluggishly in bed while others rose. If the gang took their chow downstairs she would be with them. One of those plates now under my inspection, therefore, was her plate, and beside it the fateful letter would soon be deposited. A swift dash, and I should be able to get my hooks on it before she came down. I limbered up the muscles, so as to be ready for instant action, and was on my toes and all set to go, when there was a whistle to the south-west and a voice said 'Oo-oo!' and I saw that the postman had arrived. He was standing at the foot of the steps, giving the housemaid the eye.

'Hallo, beautiful!' he said.

I didn't like it. My heart sank. Now that I could see this postman steadily and see him whole, he stood out without disguise as a jaunty young postman, lissom of limb and a mass of sex-appeal, the sort of postman who, when off duty, is a devil of a fellow at the local hops and,

when engaged on his professional rounds, considers the
day wasted that doesn't start with about ten minutes
intensive flirtation with the nearest domestic handy. I
had been hoping for something many years older and
much less the Society playboy. With a fellow like this at
the helm, the delivery of the first post was going to take
time. And every moment that passed made more
probable the arrival on the scene of Madeline Bassett
and others.

My fears were well founded. The minutes went by
and still this gay young postman stood rooted to the
spot, dishing out the brilliant badinage as if he were
some carefree gentleman of leisure who was just passing
by in the course of an early morning stroll. It seemed to
me monstrous that a public servant, whose salary I
helped to pay, should be wasting the Government's time
in this frivolous manner, and it wouldn't have taken
much to make me write a strong letter to *The Times*
about it.

Eventually, awakening to a sense of his obligations,
he handed over a wad of correspondence and with a final
sally went on his way, and the housemaid disappeared,
to manifest herself a few moments later in the
dining-room. There, having read a couple of postcards in
rather a bored way, as if she found little in them to grip
and interest, she did what she ought to have done at
least a quarter of an hour earlier – viz. placed them and
the letters beside the various plates.

I perked up. Things, I felt, were moving. What would
happen now, I assumed, was that she would pop off and
go about her domestic duties, leaving the terrain
unencumbered, and it was with something of the
emotions of the war-horse that sayeth 'Ha!' among the
trumpets that I once more braced the muscles. Ignoring
the cat, which was weaving in and out between my legs
with a camaraderie in its manner that suggested that it
had now got me definitely taped as God's gift to the

animal kingdom of Wimbledon, I made ready for the leap.

Picture, then, my chagrin and agony of spirit when, instead of hoofing it out of the door, this undisciplined housemaid came through the window, and having produced a gasper stood leaning against the wall, puffing luxuriously and gazing dreamily at the sky, as if thinking of postmen.

I don't know anything more sickening than being baffled by an unforeseen stymie at the eleventh hour, and it would not be overstating it to say that I writhed with impotent fury. As a rule, my relations with housemaids are cordial and sympathetic. If I meet a housemaid, I beam at her and say 'Good morning', and she beams at me and says 'Good morning', and all is joy and peace. But this one I would gladly have socked on the napper with a brick.

I stood there cursing. She stood there smoking. How long I cursed and she smoked I couldn't say, but I was just wondering if this degrading exhibition was going on for ever when she suddenly leaped, looked hastily over her shoulder and, hurling the gasper from her, legged it round the side of the house. The whole thing rather reminiscent of a nymph surprised while bathing.

And it wasn't long before I was able to spot what had caused her concern. I had thought for a moment that the voice of conscience must have whispered in her ear, but this was not so. Somebody was coming out of the front door, and my heart did a quick double somersault as I saw that it was Madeline Bassett.

And I was just saying 'This is the end', for it seemed inevitable that in another two ticks she would be inside the dining-room absorbing the latest news from Deverill Hall, when my *joie de vivre*, which had hit a new low, was restored by the sight of her turning to the left instead of to the right, and I perceived, what had failed

to register in that first awful moment, that she was
carrying a basket and gardening scissors. One sprang to
the conclusion that she was off for a bit of pre-breakfast
nosegay gathering, and one was right. She disappeared,
and I was alone once more with the cat.

There is, as Jeeves rather neatly put it once, a tide in
the affairs of men which, taken at the flood, leads on to
fortune, and I could see clearly enough that this was it.
What is known as the crucial moment had
unquestionably arrived, and any knowledgeable adviser,
had such a one been present, would have urged me to
make it snappy and get moving while the going was
good.

But recent events had left me weak. The spectacle of
Madeline Bassett so close to me that I could have tossed
a pebble into her mouth – not that I would, of course –
had had the effect of numbing the sinews. I was for the
nonce a spent force, incapable even of kicking the cat,
which, possibly under the impression that this rigid
Bertram was a tree, had now started to sharpen its claws
on my leg.

And it was lucky I was – a spent force, I mean, not a
tree – for at the very moment when, had I had the
horse-power, I would have been sailing through the
dining-room window, a girl came out of it carrying a
white, woolly dog. And a nice ass I should have looked if
I had taken at the flood the tide which leads on to
fortune, because it wouldn't have led on to fortune or
anything like it. It would have resulted in a nasty
collision on the threshold.

She was a solid, hefty girl, of the type which plays
five sets of tennis without turning a hair, and from the
fact that her face was sombre and her movements on the
listless side, I deduced that this must be Madeline
Bassett's school friend, the one whose sex life had
recently stubbed its toe. Too bad, of course, and one was
sorry that she and the dream man hadn't been able to

make a go of it, but at the moment I wasn't thinking very much about her troubles, my attention being riveted on the disturbing fact that I was dished. Thanks to the delay caused by the dilatory methods of that sprightly young postman, my plan of campaign was a total loss. I couldn't possibly start to function, with solid girls cluttering up the fairway.

There was but one hope. Her demeanour was that of a girl about to take the dog for a run, and it might be that she and friend would wander far enough afield to enable me to bring the thing off. I was just speculating on the odds for and against this, when she put the dog on the ground and with indescribable emotion I saw that it was heading straight for my bush and in another moment would be noting contents and barking its head off. For no dog, white or not white, woolly or not woolly, accepts with a mere raised eyebrow the presence of strangers in bushes. The thing, I felt, might quite possibly culminate not only in exposure, disgrace and shame, but in a quick nip on the ankle.

It was the cat who eased a tense situation. Possibly because it had not yet breakfasted and wished to do so, or it may be because the charm of Bertram Wooster's society had at last begun to pall, it selected this moment to leave me. It turned on its heel and emerged from the bush with its tail in the air, and the white, woolly dog, sighting it, broke into a canine version of Aunt Charlotte's a-hunting-we-will-go song and with a brief 'Hallo, hallo, hallo, hallo' went a-hunting. The pursuit rolled away over brake and over thorn, with Madeline Bassett's school friend bringing up the rear.

Position at the turn:

1. Cat
2. Dog
3. Madeline Basset's school friend.

The leaders were well up in a bunch. Several lengths separated 2 and 3.

I did not linger and dally. All a passer-by, had there been a passer-by, would have seen, was a sort of blur. Ten seconds later, I was standing beside the breakfast-table, panting slightly, with Gussie's letter in my hand.

To trouser it was with me the work of an instant; to reach the window with a view to the quick getaway that of an instant more. And I was on the point of passing through in the same old bustling way, when I suddenly perceived the solid girl returning with the white, woolly dog in her arms, and I saw what must have happened. These white, woolly dogs lack staying power. All right for the quick sprint, but hopeless across country. This one must have lost the hallo-hallo spirit in the first fifty yards or so and, pausing for breath, allowed itself to be gathered in.

In moments of peril, the Woosters act swiftly. One way out being barred to me, I decided in a flash to take the other. I nipped through the door, nipped across the hall and, still nipping, reached the temporary safety of the room on the other side of it.

16

The room in which I found myself was bright and cheerful, in which respect it differed substantially from Bertram Wooster. It had the appearance of being the den or snuggery of some female interested in sports and pastimes and was, I assumed, the headquarters of Madeline Bassett's solid school friend. There was an oar over the mantelpiece, a squash racket over the book-shelf, and on the walls a large number of photographs which even at a cursory glance I was able to identify as tennis and hockey groups.

A cursory glance was all I was at leisure to bestow upon them at the moment, for the first thing to which my eye had been attracted on my entry was a serviceable french window, and I made for it like a man on a walking tour diving into a village pub two minutes before closing time. It opened on a sunken garden at the side of the house, and offered an admirable avenue of escape to one whose chief object in life was to detach himself from this stately home of Wimbledon and never set eyes on the bally place again.

When I say that it offered an admirable avenue of escape, it would be more correct to put it that it would have done, had there not been standing immediately outside it, leaning languidly on a spade, a short, stout gardener in corduroy trousers and a red and yellow cap which suggested – erroneously, I imagine – that he was a member of the Marylebone Cricket Club. His shirt was brown, his boots black, his face cerise and his whiskers grey.

I am able to supply this detailed record of the colour

scheme because for some considerable time I stood submitting this son of toil to a close inspection. And the closer I inspected him, the less I found myself liking the fellow. Just as I had felt my spirit out of tune with the gasper-smoking housemaid of The Larches, so did I now look askance at the establishment's gardener, feeling very strongly that what he needed was a pound and a half of dynamite exploded under his fat trouser seat.

Presently, unable to stand the sight of him any longer, I turned away and began to pace the room like some caged creature of the wild, the only difference being that whereas a caged creature of the wild would not have bumped into and come within a toucher of upsetting a small table with a silver cup, a golf ball in a glass case and a large framed photograph on it, I did. It was only by an outstanding feat of legerdemain that I succeeded in catching the photograph as it fell, thereby averting a crash which would have brought every inmate of the house racing to the spot. And having caught it, I saw that it was a speaking likeness of Madeline Bassett.

It was one of those full-face speaking likenesses. She was staring straight out of the picture with large, sad, saucerlike eyes, and the lips seemed to quiver with a strange, reproachful appeal. And as I gazed at those sad eyes and took a square look at those quivery lips, something went off inside my bean like a spring. I had had an inspiration.

Events were to prove that my idea, like about ninety-four per cent of Catsmeat's, was just one of those that seem good at the time, but at the moment I was convinced that if I were to snitch this studio portrait and confront Gussie with it, bidding him drink it in and let conscience be his guide, all would be well. Remorse would creep in, his better self would get it up the nose, and all the old love and affection would come surging back. I believe this sort of thing frequently happens. Burglars, catching sight of photographs of their mothers, instantly turn in their tools and resolve to lead a new life, and the same is probably true of footpads, con men and fellows who have not paid their dog licence. I saw no reason to suppose that Gussie would be slower off the mark.

It was at this moment that I heard the sound of a Hoover being wheeled along the hall, and realized that the housemaid was on her way to do the room.

If there is anything that makes you feel more like a stag at bay than being in a room where you oughtn't to be and hearing housemaids coming to do it, I don't know what is. If you described Bertram Wooster at this juncture as all of a doodah, you would not be going far astray. I sprang to the window. The gardener was still there. I sprang back, and nearly knocked the table over again. Finally, thinking quick, I sprang sideways. My eye had been caught by a substantial sofa in the corner of the room, and I could have wished no more admirable cover. I was behind it with perhaps two seconds to spare.

To say that I now breathed freely again would be putting it perhaps too strongly. I was still far from being at my ease. But I did feel that in this little nook of mine I ought to be reasonably secure. One of the things you learn, when you have knocked about the world a bit, is that housemaids don't sweep behind sofas. Having run the Hoover over the exposed portions of the carpet, they consider the day well spent and go off and have a cup of tea and a slice of bread and jam.

On the present occasion even the exposed portions of the carpet did not get their doing, for scarcely had the girl begun to ply the apparatus when she was called off the job by orders from up top.

''Morning, Jane,' said a voice, which from the fact that it was accompanied by a shrill bark such as could have proceeded only from a white, woolly dog I took to be that of the solid school friend. 'Never mind about doing the room now.'

'No, miss,' said the housemaid, seeming well pleased with the idea, and pushed off, no doubt to have another gasper in the scullery. There followed a rustling of paper as the solid girl, seating herself on the sofa, skimmed through the morning journal. Then I heard her say 'Oh, hallo, Madeline', and was aware that the Bassett was with us.

'Good morning, Hilda,' said the Bassett in that soupy, treacly voice which had got her so disliked by all right-thinking men. 'What a lovely, lovely morning.'

The solid girl said she didn't see what was so particularly hot about it, adding that personally she found all mornings foul. She spoke morosely, and I could see that her disappointment in love had soured her, poor soul. I mourned for her distress, and had the circumstances been different, might have reached up and patted her on the head.

'I have been gathering flowers,' proceeded the Bassett. 'Beautiful smiling flowers, all wet with the morning dew. How *happy* flowers seem, Hilda.'

The solid girl said why shouldn't they, what had they got to beef about, and there was a pause. The solid girl said something about the prospects of the Surrey Cricket Club, but received no reply, and a moment later it was evident that Madeline Bassett's thoughts had been elsewhere.

'I have just been in the dining-room,' she said, and one spotted the tremor in the voice. 'There was no letter from Gussie. I'm so worried, Hilda. I think I shall go down to Deverill by an earlier train.'

'Suit yourself.'

'I can't help having an awful feeling that he is seriously injured. He said he had only sprained his wrist, but has he? That is what I ask myself. Suppose the horse knocked him down and trampled on him?'

'He'd have mentioned it.'

'But he wouldn't. That's what I mean. Gussie is so

unselfish and considerate. His first thought would be to spare me anxiety. Oh, Hilda, do you think his spine is fractured?'

'What rot! Spine fractured, my foot. If there isn't a letter, all it means is that this other fellow – what's his name – Wooster – has kicked at acting as an amanuensis. I don't blame him. He's dippy about you, isn't he?'

'He loves me very, very dearly. It's a tragedy. I can't describe to you, Hilda, the pathos of that look of dumb suffering in his eyes when we meet.'

'Well, then, the thing's obvious. If you're dippy about a girl, and another fellow has grabbed her, it can't be pleasant to sit at a writing-table, probably with a rotten pen, sweating away while the other fellow dictates "My own comma precious darling period I worship you comma I adore you period How I wish comma my dearest comma that I could press you to my bosom and cover your lovely face with burning kisses exclamation mark". I don't wonder Wooster kicked.'

'You're very heartless, Hilda.'

'I've had enough to make me heartless. I've sometimes thought of ending it all. I've got a gun in that drawer there.'

'Hilda!'

'Oh, I don't suppose I shall. Lot of fuss and trouble. Have you seen the paper this morning? It says there's some talk of altering the leg-before-wicket rule again. Odd how your outlook changes when your heart's broken. I can remember a time when I'd have been all excited if they altered the leg-before-wicket rule. Now I don't give a damn. Let 'em alter it, and I hope they have a fine day for it. What sort of a fellow is this Wooster?'

'Oh, a dear.'

'He must be, if he writes Gussie's love letters for him. Either that or a perfect sap. If I were in your place, I'd give Gussie the air and sign up with him. Being a man, I presume he's a louse, like all other men, but he's rich, and money's the only thing that matters.'

From the way Madeline said, 'Oh, Hilda, *darling*!' – the wealth of reproach in the voice, I mean, and all that sort of thing – I could tell that these cynical words had got in amongst her, shocking her and wounding her finer feelings, and I found myself in complete accord with her attitude. I thoroughly disapproved of this girl and her whole outlook, and wished she wouldn't say things like that. The position of affairs was black enough already, without having old school friends egging Madeline Bassett on to give Gussie the air and sign up with me.

I think that Madeline would have gone on to chide and rebuke, but at this point, instead of speaking, she suddenly uttered a squeal or wordless exclamation, and the solid girl said 'Now what?'

'My photograph!'

'What about it?'

'Where is it?'

'On the table.'

'But it's not. It's gone.'

'Then I suppose Jane has smashed it. She always does smash everything that isn't made of sheet-iron, and I see no reason why she should have made an exception in favour of your photograph. You'd better go and ask her.'

'I will,' said Madeline, and I heard her hurrying out.

A few moments passed, self inhaling fluff and the solid girl presumably scanning her paper for further facts about the leg-before-wicket rule, and then I heard her say 'Sit still', no doubt addressing the white, woolly dog, for shortly afterwards she said 'Oh, all right, blast you, buzz off if you want to', and there was a thud; not a dull, sickening thud but the sort of thud a white, woolly dog makes when landing on a carpet from a sofa of medium height. And it was almost immediately after this that there came a sound of sniffing in my vicinity, and with a considerable lowering of the already low morale I realized that the animal must have picked up the characteristic Wooster smell and was now in the process of tracking it to its source.

And so it proved. Glancing round, I suddenly found its face about six inches from mine, its demeanour that of a dog that can hardly believe its eyes. Backing away with a startled 'Ooops!' it retreated to the centre of the room and began barking.

'What's the matter, you silly ass?' said the solid girl, and then there was a silence. On her part, that is. The white, woolly dog continued to strain its vocal cords.

Madeline Bassett re-entered.

'Jane says –' she began, then broke off with a piercing scream. '*Hilda*! Oh, Hilda, *what* are you doing with that pistol?'

The solid girl calmed her fears, though leaving mine in *status quo*.

'Don't get excited. I'm not going to shoot myself. Though it would be a pretty good idea, at that. There's a man behind the sofa.'

'Hilda!'

'I've been wondering for some time where that curious, breathing sound was coming from. Percy spotted him. At-a-boy, Percy, nice work. Come on out of it, you.'

Rightly concluding that she meant me, I emerged, and Madeline uttered another of her piercing screams.

'A dressy criminal, though shopsoiled,' said the solid girl, scrutinizing me over the young cannon which she was levelling at my waistcoat. 'One of those Mayfair men you read about, I suppose. Hallo, I see he's got that photograph you were looking for. And probably half a dozen other things as well. I think the first move is to make him turn out his pockets.'

The thought that in one of those pockets lay Gussie's letter caused me to reel and utter a strangled cry, and the solid girl said if I was going to have a fit, that was all right with her, but she would be obliged if I would step through the window and have it outside.

It was at this point that Madeline Bassett most fortunately found speech. During the preceding exchanges, if you can call it exchanges when one person has taken the floor and is doing all the talking, she had been leaning against the wall with a hand to her heart, giving an impersonation, and not at all a bad one either, of a cat with a herring-bone in its throat. She now made her first contribution to the dialogue.

'Bertie!' she cried.

The solid girl seemed puzzled.

'Bertie?'

'This is Bertie Wooster.'

'The complete letter-writer? Well, what's he doing here? And why has he swiped your photograph?'

Madeline's voice sank to a tremulous whisper.

'I think I know.'

'Then you're smarter than I am. Goofy, the whole proceeding strikes me as.'

'Will you leave us, Hilda? I want to speak to Bertie . . . alone.'

'Right ho. I'll be shifting along to the dining-room. I don't suppose, feeling the way I do, there's a dog's chance of my being able to swallow a mouthful, but I can be counting the spoons.'

The solid girl pushed off, accompanied by the white, woolly dog, leaving us all set for a *tête-à-tête* which I for one would willingly have avoided. In fact, though it would, of course, have been a near thing with not much in it either way, I think I would have preferred a *tête-à-tête* with Dame Daphne Winkworth.

17

The proceedings opened with one of those long, sticky
silences which give you the same unpleasant feeling you
get when you let them rope you in to play 'Bulstrode, a
butler' in amateur theatricals and you go on and find you
have forgotten your opening lines. She was standing
gazing at me as if I had been a photographer about to
squeeze the bulb and take a studio portrait in sepia and
silver-grey wash, and after a while it seemed to me that
it was about time one of us said something. The great
thing on these occasions is to get the conversation going.

'Nice day,' I said. 'I thought I'd look in.'

She enlarged the eyes a bit, but did not utter, so I
proceeded.

'It occurred to me that you might be glad to have the
latest bulletin about Gussie, so I popped up on the milk
train. Gussie, I am glad to say, is getting along fine. The
wrist is still stiff, but the swelling is subsiding and there
is no pain. He sends his best.'

She remained *sotto voce* and the silent tomb, and I
carried on. I thought a word or two touching upon my
recent activities might now be in order. I mean, you
can't just come bounding up from behind the furniture
and let it go at that. You have to explain and clarify your
motives. Girls like to know these things.

'You are probably asking yourself,' I said, 'what I was
doing behind that sofa. I parked myself there on a
sudden whim. You know how one gets these sudden
whims. And you may be thinking it a bit odd that I
should be going around with this studio portrait in my
possession. Well, I'll tell you. I happened to see it on the

table there, and I took it to give to Gussie. I thought he
would like to have it, to buck him up in your absence.
He misses you sorely, of course, and it occurred to me
that it would be nice for him to shove it on the
dressing-table and study it from time to time. No doubt
he already has several of these speaking likenesses, but a
fellow can always do with one more.'

Not too bad, it seemed to me, considering that the
material had had to be thrown together rather against
time, and I was hoping for the bright smile and the
cordial 'Why, yes, to be sure, a capital idea'. Instead of
which, she waggled her head in a slow, mournful sort of
way, and a teardrop stood in her eye.

'Oh, Bertie!' she said.

I have always found it difficult to think of just the
right comeback when people say 'Oh, Bertie!' to me. My
Aunt Agatha is always doing it, and she has me stymied
every time. I found myself stymied now. It is true that
this 'Oh, Bertie!' of the Bassett's differed in many
respects from Aunt Agatha's 'Oh, Bertie!' its tone being
one of soupiness rather than asperity, but the effect was
the same. I stood there at a loss.

'Oh, Bertie!' she said again. 'Do you read Rosie M.
Banks's novels?' she asked.

I was a bit surprised at her changing the subject like
this, but equally relieved. A talk about current
literature, I felt, might ease the strain. These booksy
chats often do.

'Not very frequently,' I said. 'They sell like hot cakes,
Bingo tells me.'

'You have not read *Mervyn Keene, Clubman*?'

'No, I missed that. Good stuff?'

'It is very, very beautiful.'

'I must put it on my library list.'

'You are sure you have not read it?'

'Oh, quite. As a matter of fact, I've always steered
rather clear of Mrs Bingo's stuff. Why?'

'It seemed such an extraordinary coincidence . . . Shall I tell you the story of Mervyn Keene?'

'Do.'

She took time out to gulp a bit. Then she carried on in a low voice with a goodish amount of throb to it.

'He was young and rich and handsome, an officer in the Coldstream Guards and the idol of all who knew him. Everybody envied him.'

'I don't wonder, the lucky stiff.'

'But he was not really to be envied. There was a tragedy in his life. He loved Cynthia Grey, the most beautiful girl in London, but just as he was about to speak his love, he found that she was engaged to Sir Hector Mauleverer, the explorer.'

'Dangerous devils, these explorers. You want to watch them like hawks. In these circs, of course, he would have refrained from speaking his love? Kept it under his hat, I suppose, what?'

'Yes, he spoke no word of love. But he went on worshipping her, outwardly gay and cheerful, inwardly gnawed by a ceaseless pain. And then one night her brother Lionel, a wild young man who had unfortunately got into bad company, came to his rooms and told him that he had committed a very serious crime and was going to be arrested, and he asked Mervyn to save him by taking the blame himself. And, of course, Mervyn said he would.'

'The silly ass! Why?'

'For Cynthia's sake. To save her brother from imprisonment and shame.'

'But it meant going to chokey himself. I suppose he overlooked that?'

'No. Mervyn fully realized what must happen. But he confessed to the crime and went to prison. When he came out, grey and broken, he found that Cynthia had married Sir Hector and he went out to the South Sea Islands and became a beachcomber. And time passed.

And then one day Cynthia and her husband arrived at the island on their travels and stayed at Government House, and Mervyn saw her drive by, and she was just as beautiful as ever, and their eyes met, but she didn't recognize him, because of course he had a beard and his face was changed because he had been living the pace that kills, trying to forget.'

I remembered a good one I had read somewhere about the pace that kills nowadays being the slow, casual walk across a busy street, but I felt that this was not the moment to spring it.

'He found out that she was leaving next morning, and he had nothing to remember her by, so he broke into Government House in the night and took from her dressing-table the rose she had been wearing in her hair. And Cynthia found him taking it, and, of course, she was very upset when she recognized him.'

'Oh, she recognized him this time? He'd shaved, had he?'

'No, he still wore his beard, but she knew him when he spoke her name, and there was a very powerful scene in which he told her how he had always loved her and had come to steal her rose, and she told him that her brother had died and confessed on his death-bed that it was he who had been guilty of the crime for which Mervyn had gone to prison. And then Sir Hector came in.'

'Good situation. Strong.'

'And, of course, he thought Mervyn was a burglar, and he shot him, and Mervyn died with the rose in his hand. And, of course, the sound of the shot roused the house, and the Governor came running in and said: "Is anything missing?" And Cynthia in a low, almost inaudible voice said: "Only a rose." That is the story of Mervyn Keene, Clubman.'

Well, it was difficult, of course, to know quite what comment to make. I said 'Oh, ah!' but I felt at the time

that it could have been improved on. The fact is, I was
feeling a bit stunned. I had always known in a sort of
vague, general way that Mrs Bingo wrote the world's
worst tripe – Bingo generally changes the subject
nervously if anyone mentions the little woman's output
– but I had never supposed her capable of bilge like this.

But the Bassett speedily took my mind off literary
criticism. She had resumed her saucerlike stare, and
the teardrop in the eye was now more noticeable than
ever.

'Oh, Bertie,' she said, and her voice, like Cynthia's,
was low and almost inaudible, 'I ought to have given you
my photograph long ago. I blame myself. But I thought it
would be too painful for you, too sad a reminder of all
that you had lost. I see now that I was wrong. You found
the strain too great to bear. At all costs you had to have
it. So you stole into the house, like Mervyn Keene, and
took it.'

'What!'

'Yes, Bertie. There need be no pretences between you
and me. And don't think I am angry. I am touched, more
deeply touched than I can say, and oh, so, so sorry. How
sad life is!'

I was with her there.

'You betcher,' I said.

'You saw my friend Hilda Gudgeon. There is another
tragedy. Her whole happiness has been ruined by a
wretched quarrel with the man she loves, a man called
Harold Anstruther. They were playing in the Mixed
Doubles in a tennis tournament not long ago and –
according to her – I don't understand tennis very well –
he insisted on hogging the game, as she calls it. I think
she means that when the ball came near her and she was
going to strike it, he rushed across and struck it himself,
and this annoyed her very much. She complained to
him, and he was very rude and said she was a rabbit and
had better leave everything to him, and she broke off the

engagement directly the game was finished. And now she is broken-hearted.'

I must say she didn't sound very broken-hearted. Just as the Bassett said these words, there came from without the uproar of someone singing, and I identified the voice as that of the solid school friend. She was rendering that old number 'Give yourself a pat on the back', and the general effect was of an exhilarated foghorn. The next moment, she came leaping into the room, and I have never seen anything more radiant. If she hadn't had the white, woolly dog in her arms, I wouldn't have recognized the sombre female of so short a while ago.

'Hi, Madeline,' she cried. 'What do you think I found on the breakfast-table? A grovelling letter from the boy friend, no less. He's surrendered unconditionally. He says he must have been mad to call me a rabbit. He says he can never forgive himself, but can I forgive him. Well, I can answer that one. I'm going to forgive him the day after tomorrow. Not earlier, because we must have discipline.'

'Oh, Hilda! How glad I am!'

'I'm pretty pleased about it myself. Good old Harold! A king among men, but, of course, needs keeping in his place from time to time and has to be taught what's what. But I mustn't run on about Harold. What I came to tell you was that there's a fellow outside in a car who says he wants to see you.'

'To see me?'

'So he says. Name of Pirbright.'

Madeline turned to me.

'Why, it must be your friend Claude Pirbright, Bertie. I wonder what he wants. I'd better go and see.' She threw a quick glance at the solid girl, and seeing that she had stepped through the french window, no doubt to give the gardener the devil about something, came to me and pressed my hand. 'You must be brave, Bertie,' she said in a low, roopy voice. 'Some day another girl will come into your life and you will be happy. When we are both old and grey, we shall laugh together over all this . . . laugh, but I think with a tear behind the smile.'

She popped off, leaving me feeling sick. The solid girl, whom I had dimly heard telling the gardener he needn't be afraid of breaking that spade by leaning on it, came back and immediately proceeded, in which I considered an offensively familiar manner, to give me a hearty slap on the back.

'Well, Wooster, old bloke,' she said.

'Well, Gudgeon, old bird,' I replied courteously.

'Do you know, Wooster, I keep feeling there's something familiar about your name? I must have heard Harold mention it. Do you know Harold Anstruther?'

I had recognized the name directly I heard Madeline Bassett utter it. Beefy Anstruther had been my partner at Rackets my last year at Oxford, when I had represented the establishment at that sport. I revealed this to the solid girl, and she slapped my back again.

'I thought I wasn't wrong. Harold speaks very highly of you, Wooster, old-timer, and I'll tell you something. I have a lot of influence with Madeline, and I'll exert it on your behalf. I'll talk to her like a mother. Dash it all, we can't have her marrying a pill like Gussie Fink-Nottle, when there's a Rackets Blue on her waiting list. Courage, Wooster, old cock. Courage and patience. Come and have a bit of breakfast.'

'Thanks awfully, no,' I said, though I needed it sorely. 'I must be getting along.'

'Well, if you won't, you won't. But I will. I'm going to have the breakfast of a lifetime. I haven't felt so roaring fit since I won the tennis singles at Roedean.'

I had braced myself for another slap on the back, but with a swift change of policy she prodded me in the ribs, depriving me of what little breath her frightful words had left inside me. At the thought of what might result from a girl of her dominating personality talking to

Madeline Bassett like a mother, I had wilted where I stood. It was with what are called leaden steps that I passed through the french window and made my way to the road. I was anxious to intercept Catsmeat when he drove out, so that I might learn from him the result of his interview.

And, of course, when he did drive out, he was hareing along at such a pace that it was impossible to draw myself to his attention. He vanished over the skyline as if he had been competing in some event at Brooklands, leaving me standing.

In sombre mood, bowed down with dark forebodings, I went off to get a bit of breakfast and catch a train back to King's Deverill.

18

The blokes who run the railway don't make it easy for
you to get from Wimbledon to King's Deverill, feeling no
doubt – and I suppose it's a kindly thought – that that
abode of thugs and ghouls is a place you're better away
from. You change twice before you get to Basingstoke
and then change again and take the branch line. And
once you're on the branch line, it's quicker to walk.

The first person I saw when I finally tottered out at
journey's end, feeling as if I had been glued to the
cushioned seat since early boyhood and a bit surprised
that I hadn't put out tendrils like a Virginia creeper, was
my cousin Thomas. He was buying motion-picture
magazines at the bookstall.

'Oh, hallo,' I said. 'So you got here all right?'

He eyed me coldly and said 'Crumbs!' a word of
which he is far too fond. This Thos is one of those
tough, hardboiled striplings, a sort of juvenile James
Cagney with a touch of Edward G. Robinson. He has
carroty hair and a cynical expression, and his manner is
supercilious. You would think that anyone conscious of
having a mother like my Aunt Agatha and knowing it
could be proved against him, would be crushed and
apologetic, but this is not the case. He swanks about the
place as if he'd bought it, and in conversation with a
cousin lacks tact and is apt to verge on the personal.

He became personal now, on the subject of my
appearance, which I must confess was not spruce. Night
travel in milk trains always tends to remove the gloss,
and you can't hobnob with beetles in bushes and remain
dapper.

'Crumbs!' he said. 'You look like something the cat brought in.'

You see what I mean? The wrong note. In no frame of mind to bandy words, I clouted the child moodily on the head and passed on. And as I emerged into the station yard, somebody yoo-hooed and I saw Corky sitting in her car.

'Hallo, Bertie,' she said. 'Where did you spring from, moon of my delight?' She looked about her in a wary and conspiratorial manner, as if she had been registering snakiness in a spy film. 'Did you see what was in the station?' she asked, lowering the voice.

'I did.'

'Jeeves delivered him as per memo last night. Uncle Sidney looked a little taken aback for a moment, and seemed as if he were on the point of saying some of the things he gave up saying when he took Orders, but everything has turned out for the best. He loves his game of chess, and it seems that Thomas is the undisputed champion of his school, brimming over with gambits and openings and things, so they get along fine. And I love him. What a sympathetic, sweet-natured boy he is, Bertie.'

I blinked.

'You are speaking of my cousin Thomas?'

'He's so *loyal*. When I told him about the heel Dobbs arresting Sam Goldwyn, he simply boiled with generous indignation. He says he's going to cosh him.'

'To what him?'

'It's something people do to people in detective stories. You use a small but serviceable rubber bludgeon.'

'He hasn't got a small but serviceable rubber bludgeon.'

'Yes, he has. He bought it in Seven Dials when he was staying at your flat. His original idea was to employ it on a boy called Stinker at Bramley-on-Sea, but it is now earmarked for Dobbs.'

'Oh, my God!'

'It will do Dobbs all the good in the world to be coshed. It may prove a turning-point in his life. I have a feeling that things are breaking just right these days and that very shortly an era of universal happiness will set in. Look at Catsmeat, if you want Exhibit A. Have you seen him?'

'Not to speak to,' I said, speaking in a *distrait* manner, for my mind was still occupied with Thos and his plans. The last thing you want, when the nervous system is in a state of hash, are your first cousins socking policemen with rubber bludgeons. 'What about Catsmeat?'

'I met him just now, and he was singing like a linnet all over the place. He had a note from Gertrude last night, and she says that, if and when she can elude her mother's eye, she will elope with him. His cup of joy is full.'

'I'm glad someone's is.'

The sombreness of my tone caused her to look sharply at me, and her eyes widened as she saw the disorder of my outer crust.

'Bertie! My lamb!' she cried, visibly moved. 'What have you been doing to yourself? You look like –'

'Something the cat brought in?'

'I was going to say something excavated from Tutankhamen's tomb, but your guess is as good as mine. What's been happening?'

I passed a weary hand over the brow.

'Corky,' I said, 'I've been through hell.'

'About the only place I thought you didn't have to go through to get to King's Deverill. And how were they all?'

'I have a frightful story to relate.'

'Did somebody cosh you?'

'I've just come from Wimbledon.'

'From Wimbledon? But Catsmeat was attending to the Wimbledon end. He told me all about it.'

'He didn't tell you all about it, because all about it is precisely what he doesn't know. If you've only heard Catsmeat's reminiscences, you simply aren't within a million miles of being in possession of the facts. He barely scratched the surface of Wimbledon, whereas I . . . Would you care to have the ghastly details?'

She said she would love to, and I slipped them to her, and for once she listened attentively from start to finish, an agreeable deviation from her customary deaf-adder tactics. I found her a good audience. She was properly impressed when I spoke of Gussie's letter, nor did she omit to draw the breath in sharply as I touched on the Gudgeon and the sinister affair of the studio portrait. The facts in connection with the white, woolly dog also went over big.

'Golly!' she said, as I wore to a close. 'You do live, don't you, Bertie?'

I agreed that I lived, but expressed a doubt as to whether, the circumstances being what they were it was worthwhile continuing to do so. One was rather inclined, I said, to murmur 'Death, where is thy sting?' and turn the toes up.

'The best one can say,' I concluded, 'is that one has obtained a brief respite, if respite is the word. And that only if Catsmeat was successful in dissuading the Bassett from her awful purpose. For all I know, she may be coming on the next train.'

'No, she's not. He headed her off.'

'You had that straight from the horse's mouth?'

'Direct from his personal lips.'

I drew a deep breath. This certainly put a brighter aspect on the cloud wreck. In fact, it seemed to me that 'Hallelujah!' about summed it up, and I mentioned this.

I was concerned to note that she appeared a bit dubious.

'Yes, I suppose "Hallelujah!" sums it up . . . to a

certain extent. I mean you can make your mind easy
about her coming here. She isn't coming. But in the light
of what you tell me about Mervyn Keene, Clubman, and
the studio portrait, it's a pity Catsmeat didn't hit on
some other method of heading her off. I do feel that.'

My heart stood still. I clutched at the windscreen for
support, and what-whatted.

'The great thing to remember, the thing to bear in
mind and keep the attention fixed on, is that he meant
well.'

My heart stood stiller. In your walks about London
you will sometimes see bent, haggard figures that look
as if they had recently been caught in some powerful
machinery. They are those of fellows who got mixed up
with Catsmeat when he was meaning well.

'What he told Miss Bassett was this. He said that on
hearing that she was coming to the Hall you betrayed
agitation and concern, and finally he got it out of you
what the trouble was. Loving her hopelessly as you do,
you shrank from the agony of having to see her day after
day in Gussie's society.'

My heart, ceasing to stand still, gave a leap and tried
to get out through my front teeth.

'He told Madeline Bassett that?' I quavered, shaking
on my stem.

'Yes, and implored her to stay away and not subject
you to this anguish. He says he was terrific and wished
one or two managers had been there to catch his work,
and I think he must have been pretty good, because Miss
Bassett cried buckets and said she quite understood and,
of course, would cancel her visit, adding something in a
low voice about the desire of the moth for the star and
how sad life was. What did you say?'

I explained that I had not spoken, merely uttered one
of those hollow groans, and she agreed that in the circs
hollow groans were perhaps in order.

'But, of course, it wasn't easy for the poor angel to

think of a good way of stopping her coming,' she argued.
'And the great thing was to stop her somehow.'

'True.'

'So, if I were you, I would try to look on the bright
side. Count your blessings one by one, if you know what
I mean.'

This is an appeal which, when addressed to Bertram
Wooster, rarely falls on deaf ears. The stunned sensation
which her words had induced did not actually leave me,
but it diminished somewhat in intensity. I saw her
point.

'There is much in what you say,' I agreed, rising on
stepping-stones of my dead self to higher things, as I
have mentioned is my custom. 'The great thing, as you
justly remark, was to stop the Bassett blowing in, and, if
that has been accomplished, one does wrong to be fussy
about the actual mechanism. And, after all, she was
already firmly convinced of my unswerving devotion, so
Catsmeat hasn't really plunged me so very much deeper
in the broth than I was before.'

'That's my brave little man. That's the way to
talk.'

'We now have a respite, and all depends on how
quickly you can put Gussie on ice. The moment that is
done, the whole situation will clarify. Released from
your fatal spell, he will automatically return to the old
love, feeling that the cagey thing is to go where he is
appreciated. When do you expect to cool him off?'

'Very soon.'

'Why not instanter?'

'Well, I'll tell you, Bertie. There's a little job I want
him to do for me first.'

'What job?'

'Ah, here's Thomas at last. He seems to have bought
every fan magazine in existence. To read at the concert,
if he's sensible. You haven't forgotten the concert is this
evening? Well, mind you don't. And when you see

Jeeves, ask him how that claque of Esmond's has come out. Hop in, Thomas.'

Thos hopped in, giving me another of his supercilious looks, and when in, leaned across and slipped a penny into my hand, saying 'Here, my poor man' and urging me not to spend it on drink. At any other moment this coarse ribaldry would have woken the fiend that sleeps in Bertram Wooster and led to the young pot of poison receiving another clout on the head, but I had no time now for attending to Thoses. I fixed Corky with a burning eye.

'What job?' I repeated.

'Oh, it wouldn't interest you,' she said. 'Just a trivial little job about the place.'

And she drove off, leaving me a prey to a nameless fear.

I was hoofing along the road that led to the Hall, speculating dully as to what precisely she had meant by the expression 'trivial little job', when, as I rounded a corner, something large and Norfolk-coated hove in sight, and I identified it as Esmond Haddock.

19

Owing to the fact that on the instructions of Dame Daphne ('Safety First') Winkworth port was no longer served after dinner and the male and female members of the gang now left the table in a body at the conclusion of the evening repast, I had not enjoyed a *tête-à-tête* with Esmond Haddock since the night of my arrival. I had seen him around the place, of course, but always in the company of a brace of assorted aunts or that of his cousin Gertrude, in each case looking Byronic. (Checking up with Jeeves, I find that that is the word all right. Apparently it means looking like the late Lord Byron, who was a gloomy sort of bird, taking things the hard way.)

We came together, he approaching from the nor'-nor'-east and self approaching from the sou'-sou'-west, and he greeted me with a moody twitch of the cheek muscles, as if he had thought of smiling and then thought again and said 'Oh, to hell with it'.

'Hallo,' he said.

'Hallo,' I said.

'Nice day,' he said.

'Yes,' I said. 'Out for a walk?'

'Yes,' he said. 'You out for a walk?'

Prudence compelled me to descend to subterfuge.

'Yes,' I said. 'I'm out for a walk. I just ran into Miss Pirbright.'

At the mention of that name, he winced as if troubled by an old wound.

'Oh?' he said. 'Miss Pirbright, eh?'

He swallowed a couple of times. I could see a

question trembling on his lips, but it was plainly one
that nauseated him, for after uttering the word 'Was' he
kept right along swallowing. I was just about to touch on
the situation in the Balkans in order to keep the
conversation going, when he got it out.

'Was Wooster with her?'

'No, she was alone.'

'You're sure?'

'Certain.'

'He may have been lurking in the background. Behind
a tree or something.'

'The meeting occurred in the station yard.'

'He wasn't skulking in a doorway?'

'Oh, no.'

'Strange. You don't often see her without Wooster
these days,' he said, and ground his teeth a trifle.

I had a shot at trying to mitigate his anguish, which I
could see was considerable. He, too, had obviously noted
Gussie's spotty work, and it was plain that what is
technically known as the green-eyed monster had been
slipping it across him properly.

'They're old friends, of course,' I said.

'Are they?'

'Oh, rather. We – I should say they – have known each
other since childhood. They went to the same dancing
class.'

The moment I had mentioned that, I was wishing I
hadn't, for it seemed to affect him as though some
hidden hand had given him the hotfoot. You couldn't
say his brow darkened because it had been dark to start
with, but he writhed visibly. Like Lord Byron reading a
review of his last slim volume of verse and finding it a
stinker. I wasn't surprised. A man in love and viewing
with concern the competition of a rival does not like to
think of the adored object and that rival pirouetting about
together at dancing classes and probably splitting a
sociable milk and biscuit in the eleven o'clock interval.

'Oh?' he said, and gave a sort of whistling sigh like the last whoosh of a dying soda-water syphon. 'The same dancing class? The same dancing class, eh?'

He brooded a while. When he spoke again, his voice was hoarse and rumbling.

'Tell me about this fellow Wooster, Gussie. He is a friend of yours?'

'Oh, yes.'

'Known him long?'

'We were at school together.'

'I suppose he was a pretty loathsome boy? The pariah of the establishment?'

'Oh, no.'

'Changed after he grew up, eh? Well, he certainly made up leeway all right, because of all the slinking snakes it has ever been my misfortune to encounter, he is the slimiest.'

'Would you call him a slinking snake?'

'I did call him a slinking snake, and I'll do it again as often as you wish. The fishfaced trailing arbutus!'

'He's not a bad chap.'

'That may be your opinion. It is not mine, nor, I should imagine, that of most decent-minded people. Hell is full of men like Wooster. What the devil does she see in him?'

'I don't know.'

'Nor anyone else. I've studied the fellow carefully and without bias, and he seems to me entirely lacking in charm. Have you ever turned over a flat stone?'

'From time to time.'

'And what came crawling out? A lot of obscene creatures that might have been his brothers. I tell you, Gussie, if you were to put a bit of gorgonzola cheese on the slide of a microscope and tell me to take a look, the first thing I'd say on getting it focused would be: "Why, hallo, Wooster!"'

He brooded Byronically for a moment.

'I know the specious argument you are going to put forward, Gussie,' he proceeded. 'You are going to say that it is not Wooster's fault that he looks like a slightly enlarged cheesemite. Very true. One strives to be fair. But it is not only the man's revolting appearance that distresses the better element. He is a menace to the community.'

'Oh, come.'

'What do you mean, "Oh, come"? You heard what my Aunt Daphne was telling us at dinner the night you arrived. About this ghastly Wooster perpetually stealing policemen's helmets.'

'Not perpetually. Just as a treat on Boat Race night.'

He frowned.

'I don't like the way you stick up for the fellow, Gussie. You probably consider that you are being broadminded, but you want to be careful how you let that so-called broadmindedness grow on you. It is apt to become mere moral myopia. The facts are well documented. Whenever Wooster has a spare moment, he goes about London persecuting unfortunate policemen, assaulting them, hampering them in their duties, making their lives a hell on earth. That's the kind of man Wooster is.'

He paused, and became for a moment lost in thought. Then there flitted across his map another of those quick twitches which he seemed to be using nowadays, on the just-as-good principle, as a substitute for smiles.

'Well, I'll tell you one thing, Gussie. I only hope he intends to start something on those lines here, because we're ready for him.'

'Eh?'

'Ready and waiting. You know Dobbs?'

'The flatty?'

'Our village constable, yes. A splendid fellow, tireless in the performance of his duties.'

'I've not met him. I hear his engagement is broken off.'

'So much the better, for it will remove the last trace of pity and weakness from his heart. I have told Dobbs all about Wooster and warned him to be on the alert. And he is on the alert. He is straining at the leash. Let Wooster so much as lift a finger in the direction of Dobbs's helmet, and he's for it. You might not think so at a casual glance, Gussie, but I'm a Justice of the Peace. I sit on the Bench at our local Sessions and put it across the criminal classes when they start getting above themselves. It is my earnest hope that the criminal streak in Wooster will come to the surface and cause him to break out, because in that event Dobbs will be on him like a leopard and he will come up before me and I shall give him thirty days without the option, regardless of his age or sex.'

I didn't like the sound of this.

'You wouldn't do that, Esmond?'

'I would. I'm looking forward to it. Let Wooster stray one inch from the straight and narrow path – just one inch – and you can kiss him good-bye for thirty days. Well, I'll be moving along, Gussie. I find it helps a little to keep walking.'

He disappeared over the horizon at five m.p.h., and I stood there aghast. The sense of impending peril was stronger on the wing than ever. 'Oh, that Jeeves were here!' I said to myself.

I found he was. For some little time past I had been conscious of some substance in the offing that was saying 'Good morning, sir', and, turning to see where the noise was coming from, I beheld him at my side, looking bronzed and fit, as if his visit to Bramley-on-Sea had done him good.

20

'Good morning, sir,' he said. 'May I make a remark?'

'Certainly, Jeeves. Carry on. Make several.'

'It is with reference to your appearance, sir. If I might take the liberty of suggesting –'

'Go on. Say it. I look like something the cat found in Tutankhamen's tomb, do I not?'

'I would not go so far as that, sir, but I have unquestionably seen you more *soigné*.'

It crossed my mind for an instant that with a little thought one might throw together something rather clever about 'Way down upon the *soigné* river', but I was too listless to follow it up.

'If you will allow me, sir, I will take the suit which you are wearing and give it my attention.'

'Thank you, Jeeves.'

'I will sponge and press it.'

'Thank you, Jeeves.'

'Very good, sir. A beautiful morning, is it not, sir?'

'Thank you, Jeeves.'

He raised an eyebrow.

'You appear *distrait*, sir.'

'I am *distrait*, Jeeves. About as *distrait* as I can stick. And there's enough to make me *distrait*.'

'But surely, sir, matters are proceeding most satisfactorily. I delivered Master Thomas at the Vicarage. And I learn from my Uncle Charlie that her ladyship, your aunt, has postponed her visit to the Hall.'

'Quite. But these things are mere side issues. I don't say they aren't silver linings in their limited way, but take a look at the clouds that lower elsewhere. First and foremost, that man is in again.'

'Sir?'

I pulled myself together with a strong effort, for I saw that I was being obscure.

'Sorry to speak in riddles, Jeeves,' I said. 'What I meant was that Gussie had once more become a menace of the first water.'

'Indeed, sir? In what way?'

'I will tell you. What started all this rannygazoo?'

'The circumstances of Mr Fink-Nottle being sent to prison, sir.'

'Exactly. Well, it's an odds on bet that he's going to be sent to prison again.'

'Indeed, sir?'

'I wish you wouldn't say "Indeed, sir?" Yes, the shadow of the Pen is once more closing in on Augustus Fink-Nottle. The Law is flexing its muscles and waiting to pounce. One false step – and he's bound to make at least a dozen in the first minute – and into the coop he goes for thirty days. And we know what'll happen then, don't we?'

'We do indeed, sir.'

'I don't mind you saying "Indeed, sir" if you tack it on to something else like that. Yes, we know what will happen, and the flesh creeps, what?'

'Distinctly, sir.'

I forced myself to a sort of calm. Only a frozen calm, but frozen calms are better than nothing.

'Of course, it may be, Jeeves, that I am mistaken in supposing that this old lag is about to resume his life of crime, but I don't think so. Here are the facts. Just now I encountered Miss Pirbright in the station yard. We naturally fell into conversation, and after a while the subject of Gussie came up. And we had been speaking of him for some moments when she let fall an observation that filled me with a nameless fear. She said there was a little job she was getting him to do for her. And when I said "What job?" she replied "Oh, just a trivial little job about the place". And her manner was evasive. Or shall I say furtive?'

'Whichever you prefer, sir.'

'It was the manner of a girl guiltily conscious of being in the process of starting something. "What ho!" I said to myself. "Hallo, hallo, hallo, hallo!"'

'If I might interrupt for a moment, sir, I am happy to inform you that my efforts to secure a claque for Mr Esmond Haddock at the concert have been crowned with gratifying success. The back of the hall will be thronged with his supporters and well-wishers.'

I frowned.

'This is excellent news, Jeeves, but I'm dashed if I can see what it's got to do with the *res* under discussion.'

'No, sir. I am sorry. It was your observing "Hallo, hallo, hallo, hallo", that put the matter into my mind. Pardon me, sir. You were saying – '

'Well, what *was* I saying? I've forgotten.'

'You were commenting on Miss Pirbright's furtive and evasive manner, sir.'

'Ah, yes. It suggested that she was in the process of starting something. And the thought that smote me like a blow was this. If Corky is starting something, it's a hundred to eight it's something in the nature of reprisals against Constable Dobbs. Am I right or wrong, Jeeves?'

'The probability certainly lies in that direction, sir.'

'I know Corky. Her psychology is an open book to me. Even in the distant days when she wore rompers and had a tooth missing in front, hers was always a fiery and impulsive nature, quick to resent anything in the shape of oompus-boompus. And it is inevitably as oompus-boompus that she will have classed the zealous officer's recent arrest of her dog. And if she had it in for him merely on account of their theological differences, how much more will she have it in for him now. The unfortunate hound is languishing in a dungeon with gyves upon his wrists, and a girl of her spirit is not likely to accept such a state of things supinely.'

'No, sir.'

'You're right, No, sir. The facts are hideous, but we must face them. Corky is planning direct action against Constable Dobbs, taking we cannot say what form, and it seems only too sickeningly certain that Gussie, whom it is so imperative to keep from getting embroiled again with the Force, is going to lend himself as an instrument to her sinister designs. And here's something that'll make you say "Indeed, sir?" I've just been talking to Esmond Haddock, and he turns out to be a J.P. He has the powers of the High, the Middle and the Low Justice in King's Deverill, and is consequently in a position to give anyone thirty days without the option as soon as look at them. And what's more, he has taken a violent dislike to Gussie and told me in so many words that it is his dearest wish to see the darbies clapped on him. Try that one on your pianola, Jeeves.'

He seemed about to speak, but I raised a restraining hand.

'I know what you're going to say, and I quite agree. Left to himself, with Conscience as his guide, Gussie is the last person likely to commit a tort or malfeasance and start J.P.s ladling out exemplary sentences. Quite true. From boyhood up, his whole policy, instilled into him, no doubt, at his mother's knee, has been to give the primrose path a solid miss and sedulously avoid those rash acts which put wilder spirits in line for thirty days in the jug. But one knows that he is easily swayed. Catsmeat, for instance, swayed him in Trafalgar Square by threatening to bean him with a bottle. I shall be vastly surprised if Corky doesn't sway him, too. And I know from personal experience,' I said, thinking of that orange at the dancing school, 'that when Corky sways people, the sky is the limit.'

'You think that Mr Fink-Nottle will lend a willing ear
to the young lady's suggestions?'

'Her word is law to him. He will be wax in her hands.
I tell you, Jeeves, the spirits are low. I don't know if you
have ever been tied hand and foot to a chair in front of a
barrel of gunpowder with an inch of lighted candle on
top of it?'

'No, sir, I have not had that experience.'

'Well, that's how I am feeling. I'm just clenching the
teeth and waiting for the bang.'

'Would you wish me to speak a word to Mr
Fink-Nottle, sir, warning him of the inadvisability of
doing anything rash?'

'There's nothing I'd like better. He might listen to
you.'

'I will make a point of doing so at the earliest
opportunity, sir.'

'Thank you, Jeeves. It's a black business, isn't it?'

'Extremely, sir.'

'I don't know when I've come across a blacker. Very,
very murky everything is.'

'With perhaps the exception of the affairs of Mr
Pirbright, sir?'

'Ah, yes, Catsmeat. I was informed of his lucky strike.
His hat is on the side of his head, they tell me.'

'It was distinctly in that position when I last saw him,
sir.'

'Well, that's something. Yes, that cheers the heart a
bit,' I said, for even when preoccupied with the
stickiness of their own concerns, the Woosters can
always take time out to rejoice over a buddy's bliss. 'One
may certainly chalk up Catsmeat's happy ending as a ray
of light. And you say that the village toughs are going to
rally round Mr Haddock this evening?'

'In impressive numbers, sir.'

'Well, dash it, that's two rays of light. And if you can
talk Gussie out of making an ass of himself, that'll be

three. We're getting on. All right, Jeeves, push off and
see what you can do with him. I should imagine you will
find him at the Vicarage.'

'Very good, sir.'

'Oh, and, Jeeves, most important. When at the
Vicarage, get in touch with young Thos and remove
from his possession a blunt instrument known as a cosh,
which he has managed to acquire. It's a species of rubber
bludgeon, and you know as well as I do how reluctantly
one would trust him with such a thing. You could go
through the telephone book from A to Z without hitting
on the name of anyone one wouldn't prefer to see with
his hooks on a rubber bludgeon. You will get an idea of
what I mean when I tell you that he speaks freely of
beaning Constable Dobbs with the weapon. So choke it
out of him without fail. I shan't be easy in my mind till I
know you've got it.'

'Very good, sir. I will give the matter my attention,' he
said and we parted with mutual civilities, he to do his
day's good deed at the Vicarage, I to resume my hoofing
in the opposite direction.

And I had hoofed perhaps a matter of two hundred
yards, when I was jerked out of the reverie into which I
had fallen by a sight which froze the blood and caused
the two eyes, like stars, to start from their spheres. I had
seen Gussie coming out of a gate of a picturesque
cottage standing back from the road behind a neat
garden.

King's Deverill was one of those villages where
picturesque cottages breed like rabbits, but what
distinguished this picturesque cottage from the others
was that over its door were the Royal Arms and the words

POLICE STATION

And evidence that the above legend was not just a gag
was supplied by the fact that accompanying Gussie, not
actually with a hand on his collar and another gripping

the seat of his trousers but so nearly so that the casual observer might have been excused for supposing that this was a pinch, was a stalwart figure in a blue uniform and a helmet, who could be no other than Constable Ernest Dobbs.

21

It was the first time I had been privileged to see this celebrated rozzer, of whom I had heard so much, and I think that even had the circumstances been less tense I would have paused to get an eyeful, for his, like Silversmith's, was a forceful personality, arresting the attention and causing the passer-by to draw the breath in quite a bit.

The sleepless guardian of the peace of King's Deverill was one of those chunky, nobbly officers. It was as though Nature, setting out to assemble him, had said to herself 'I will not skimp'. Nor had she done so, except possibly in the matter of height. I believe that in order to become a member of the Force you have to stand five feet nine inches in your socks, and Ernest Dobbs can only just have got his nose under the wire. But this slight perpendicular shortage had the effect of rendering his bulk all the more impressive. He was plainly a man who, had he felt disposed, could have understudied the village blacksmith and no questions asked, for it could be seen at a glance that the muscles of his brawny arms were strong as iron bands.

To increase the similarity, his brow at the moment was wet with honest sweat. He had the look of a man who has recently passed through some testing emotional experience. His eyes were aglow, his moustache a-bristle and his nose a-wiggle.

'Grrh!' he said and spat. Only that and nothing more. A man of few words, apparently, but a good spitter.

Gussie, having reached the great open spaces, smiled weakly. He, too, appeared to be in the grip of some strong emotion. And as I was, also, that made three of us.

'Well, good day, officer,' he said.

'Good day, sir,' said the constable shortly.

He went back into the cottage and banged the door, and I sprang at Gussie like a jumping bean.

'What's all this?' I quavered.

The door of the cottage opened, and Constable Dobbs reappeared. He had a shovel in his hand, and in this shovel one noted what seemed to be frogs. Yes, on a closer inspection, definitely frogs. He gave the shovel a jerk, shooting the dumb chums through the air as if he had been scattering confetti. They landed on the grass and went about their business. The officer paused, directed a hard look at Gussie, spat once more with all the old force and precision and withdrew, and Gussie, removing his hat, wiped his forehead.

'Let's get out of this,' he urged, and it was not until we were some quarter of a mile distant that he regained a certain measure of calm. He removed his glasses, polished them, replaced them on his nose and seemed the better for it. His breathing became more regular.

'That was Constable Dobbs,' he said.

'So I deduced.'

'From the uniform, no doubt?'

'That and the helmet.'

'Quite,' said Gussie. 'I see. Quite. I see. Quite. I see.'

It seemed possible that he would go rambling on like this for a goodish while, but after saying 'Quite' about another six times and 'I see' about another seven he snapped out of it.

'Bertie,' he said, 'you have frequently been in the hands of the police, haven't you?'

'Not frequently. Once.'

'It is a ghastly experience, is it not? Your whole life seems to rise before you. By Jove, I could do with a drink of orange juice!'

I paused for a moment, to allow a dizzy feeling to pass.

'What was happening?' I asked, when I felt stronger.

'Eh?'

'What had you been doing?'

'Who, me?'

'Yes, you.'

'Oh,' said Gussie in an offhand way, as if it were only what might have been expected of an English gentleman, 'I had been strewing frogs.'

I goggled.

'Doing *what*?'

'Strewing frogs. In Constable Dobbs's boudoir. The Vicar suggested it.'

'The Vicar?'

'I mean it was he who gave Corky the idea. She had been brooding a lot, poor girl, on Dobbs's high-handed behaviour in connection with her dog, and last night the Vicar happened to speak of Pharaoh and all those Plagues he got when he wouldn't let the Children of Israel go. You probably recall the incident? His words started a train of thought. It occurred to Corky that if Dobbs were visited by a Plague of Frogs, it might quite possibly change his heart and make him let Sam Goldwyn go. So she asked me to look in at his cottage and attend to the matter. She said it would please her and be good for Dobbs and would only take a few minutes of my time. She felt that the Plague of Lice might be even more effective, but she is a practical, clear-thinking girl and realized that lice are hard to come by, whereas you can find frogs in any hedgerow.'

Every mouse in my interior sprang into renewed life. With a strong effort I managed to refrain from howling like a lost soul. It seemed incredible to me that this super-goof should have gone through life all this while without fetching up in some loony bin. You would have thought that some such establishment as Colney Hatch, with its talent scouts out all over the place, would have snapped him up years ago.

'Tell me exactly what happened. He caught you?'

'Fortunately, no. He came in about half a minute too late. I had bided my time, and having ascertained that the cottage was empty I went in and distributed my frogs.'

'And he was somewhere round the corner?'

'Exactly. In a sort of shed place by the back door, where I think he must have been potting geraniums or something, for his hands were all covered with mould. I suppose he had come in to wash them. It was a most embarrassing moment. One didn't quite know how to begin the conversation. Eventually I said "Oh, hallo, there you are!" and he stared at the frogs for some time, and then he said, "What's all this?" They were hopping about a bit. You know how frogs hop.'

'Hither and thither, you mean?'

'That's right. Hither and thither. Well, I kept my presence of mind. I said "What's all what, officer?" And he said "All these frogs". And I said "Ah, yes, there do seem to be quite a few frogs in here. You are fond of them?" He then asked if these frogs were my doing. And I said "In what sense do you use the word 'doing', officer?" and he said "Did you bring these frogs in here?" Well, then, I'm afraid, I wilfully misled him, for I said No. It went against the grain to tell a deliberate falsehood, of course, but I do think there are times when one is justified in –'

'Get on!'

'You bustle me so, Bertie. Where was I? Ah, yes. I said No, I couldn't account for their presence in any way. I said it was just one of those things we should never be able to understand. Probably, I said, we were not meant to understand. And, of course, he could prove nothing. I mean, anyone could wander innocently into a room where there happened to be some frogs hopping about –

the Archbishop of Canterbury or anyone. I think he
must have appreciated this, for all he did was mutter
something about it being a very serious offence to bring
frogs into a police station and I said I supposed it was
and what a pity one could never hope to catch the fellow
who had done it. And then he asked me what I was
doing there, and I said I had come to ask him to release
Sam Goldwyn, and he said he wouldn't because he had
now established that the bite Sam had given him was his
second bite and that the animal was in a very serious
position. So I said "Oh, well, then, I think I'll be going",
and I went. He came with me, as you saw, growling
under his breath. I can't say I liked the man. His manner
is bad. Brusque. Abrupt. Not at all the sort of chap likely
to win friends and influence people. Well, I suppose I
had better be getting along and reporting to Corky.
That stuff about the second bite will worry her, I'm
afraid.'

Repeating his remark about being in the vein for a
drink of orange juice, he set a course for the Vicarage and
pushed off, and I resumed my progress to the
Deverilleries, speculating dully as to what would be the
next horror to come into my life. It only needed a
meeting with Dame Daphne Winkworth, I felt sombrely,
to put the tin hat on this dark day.

My aim was to sneak in unobserved, and it seemed at
first as though luck were with me. From time to time, as
I slunk through the grounds, keeping in the shelter of
the bushes and trying not to let a twig snap beneath my
feet, I could hear the distant baying of aunts, but I
wasn't spotted. With something approaching a 'Tra-la'
on my lips I passed through the front door into the hall,
and – *bing* – right in the middle of the fairway, arranging
flowers at a table, Dame Daphne Winkworth.

Well, I suppose Napoleon or Attila the Hun or one of
those fellows would just have waved a hand and said
'Aha, there!' and hurried on, but the feat was beyond me.

Her eye, swivelling round, stopped me like a bullet. The Wedding Guest, if you remember, had the same trouble with the Ancient Mariner.

'Ah, there you are, Augustus.'

It was fruitless to deny it. I stood on one leg and dashed a bead of persp from the brow.

'I had no time to ask you last night. Have you written to Madeline?'

'Oh, yes, rather.'

'I hope you were properly apologetic.'

'Oh, rather, yes.'

'And why are you looking as if you had slept in your clothes?' she asked, giving the upholstery a look of distaste.

The thing about the Woosters is that they know when to speak out and when not to speak out. Something told me that here was where manly frankness might pay dividends.

'Well, as a matter of fact,' I said, 'I did. I ran up to Wimbledon last night on the milk train. To see Madeline, don't you know. You know how it is. You can't say all you want to in letters, and I thought . . . well, the personal touch, if you see what I mean.'

It couldn't have gone better. I have never actually seen a shepherd welcoming a strayed lamb back into the fold, but I should imagine that his manner on such an occasion would closely parallel that of this female twenty-minute egg as she heard my words. The eyes softened. The face split in a pleased smile. That wrinkling of the nose which had been so noticeable a moment before, as if I had been an escape of gas or a not-quite-up-to-sample egg, disappeared totally. It would not be putting it too strongly to say that she beamed.

'Augustus!'

'I think it was a good move.'

'It was, indeed. It is just the sort of thing that would

appeal to Madeline's romantic nature. Why, you are
quite a Romeo, Augustus. In the *milk* train? You must
have been travelling all night.'

'Pretty well.'

'You poor boy! I can see you're worn out. I will ring
for Silversmith to bring you some orange juice.'

She pressed the bell. There was a stage wait. She
pressed it again, and there was another stage wait. She
was on the point of giving it a third prod, when the hour
produced the man. Uncle Charlie entered left, and I was
amazed to see that there was an indulgent smile on his
face. It is true that he switched it off immediately and
resumed his customary aspect of a respectful chunk of
dough, but the facial contortion had unquestionably
been there.

'I must apologize for my delay in answering the bell,
m'lady,' he said. 'When your ladyship rang, I was in the
act of making a speech, and it was not until some
moments had elapsed that I became aware of the
summons.'

Dame Daphne blinked. Me, too.

'Making a speech?'

'In honour of the happy event, m'lady. My daughter
Queenie has become affianced, m'lady.'

Dame Daphne oh-really-ed, and I very nearly said
'Indeed, sir?' for the information had come as a complete
surprise. For one thing I hadn't suspected for an instant
that ties of blood linked this bulging butler and that
lissom parlourmaid, and for another, it seemed to me
that she had got over her spot of Dobbs trouble pretty
snappily. So this is what Woman's constancy amounts
to, is it, I remember saying to myself, and I'm not at all
sure I didn't add the word 'Faugh!'

'And who is the happy man, Silversmith?'

'A nice steady young fellow, m'lady. A young fellow
called Meadowes.'

I had a feeling I had heard the name before somewhere, but I couldn't place it. Meadowes? Meadowes? No, it eluded me.

'Indeed? From the village?'

'No, m'lady. Meadowes is Mr Fink-Nottle's personal attendant,' said Silversmith, now definitely unshipping a smile and directing it at me. He seemed to be trying to indicate that after this he looked on me as one of the boys and practically a relation by marriage and that, on his side at least, no more would be said of my weakness for singing hunting songs over the port and introducing into country houses dogs that bit like serpents.

I suppose the gasp that had escaped my lips sounded to Dame Daphne like the gurgle of a man dying of thirst, for she instantly put in her order for orange juice.

'Silversmith had better take it to your room. You will be wanting to change your clothes.'

'He might tell Meadowes to bring it,' I said faintly.

'Why, of course. You will want to wish him happiness.'

'That's right,' I said.

It was not immediately that Catsmeat presented himself. No doubt if you have made all your plans for marrying the daughter of the house and then suddenly find yourself engaged to the parlourmaid you need a little time to adjust the faculties. When he finally did appear, it seemed to me from his dazed expression that he had still a longish way to go in that direction. His air was that of a man who has recently been coshed by a small but serviceable rubber bludgeon.

'Bertie,' he said, 'a rather unfortunate thing has happened.'

'I know.'

'Oh, you know, do you? Then what do you advise?'

There could be but one answer to this.

'You'd better place the whole matter before Jeeves.'

'I will. That great brain may find a formula. I'll lay the facts before Jeeves and bid him brood on them.'

'But what are the facts? How did it happen?'

'I'll tell you. Do you want this orange juice?'

'No.'

'Then I'll have it. It may help a little.'

He drank deeply, and mopped the forehead.

'It all comes of letting that Dickens spirit creep over you, Bertie. The advice I give to every young man starting life is Never get Dickensy. You remember I told you that for some days I have been bursting with a sort of yeasty benevolence? This morning it came to a head. I had had Gertrude's note saying that she would elope with me, and I was just a solid chunk of sweetness and light. In ecstasies myself, I wanted to see happiness all around me. I loved my species and yearned to do it a bit of good. And with these sentiments fizzing about inside me, with the milk of human kindness sloshing up against my back teeth, I wandered into the servants' hall and found Queenie there in tears.'

'Your heart bled?'

'Profusely. I said "There, there". I took her hand and patted it. And then, as I didn't seem to be making any headway, almost unconsciously I drew her on to my knee and put my arm around her waist and started kissing her. Like a brother.'

'H'm.'

'Don't say "H'm", Bertie. It was only what Sir Galahad or someone like that would have done in my place. Dash it, there's nothing wrong, is there, in acting like a sympathetic elder brother when a girl is in distress? Pretty square behaviour, I should have thought. But don't run away with the idea that I don't wish I hadn't yielded to the kindly impulse. I regret it sincerely, because at that moment Silversmith came in. And what do you think? He's her father.'

'I know.'

'You seem to know everything.'

'I do.'

'Well, there's one thing you don't know, and that is that he was accompanied by Gertrude.'

'Gosh!'

'Yes. Her manner on beholding me was a bit reserved. Silversmith's, on the other hand, wasn't. He looked like a minor prophet without a beard suddenly confronted with the sins of the people, and started in immediately to thunder denunciations. There are fathers who know how to set about an erring daughter, and fathers who do not. Silversmith is one of the former. And then, in a sort of dream, I heard Queenie telling him that we were engaged. She has since informed me that it seemed to her the only way out. It did, of course, momentarily ease the strain.'

'How did Gertrude appear to take it?'

'Not very blithely. I've just had a brief note from her, cancelling our arrangements.'

He groaned the sort of hollow groan I had been groaning so much of late.

'You see before you, Bertie, a spent egg, a man in whom hope is dead. You don't happen to have any cyanide on you?' He groaned another hollow one. 'And on top of all this,' he said, 'I've got to put on a green beard and play Mike in a knockabout cross-talk act!'

I was sorry for the unhappy young blister, of course, but it piqued me somewhat that he seemed to consider that he was the only one who had any troubles.

'Well, I've got to recite Christopher Robin poems.'

'Pah!' he said. 'It might have been Winnie the Pooh.'

Well, there was that, of course.

22

The village hall stood in the middle of the High Street, just abaft the duck-pond. Erected in the year 1881 by Sir Quintin Deverill, Bart, a man who didn't know much about architecture but knew what he liked, it was one of those mid-Victorian jobs in glazed red brick which always seem to bob up in these olde-worlde hamlets and do so much to encourage the drift to the towns. Its interior, like those of all the joints of its kind I've ever come across, was dingy and fuggy and smelled in about equal proportions of apples, chalk, damp plaster, Boy Scouts and the sturdy English peasantry.

The concert was slated to begin at eight-fifteen, and a few minutes before the kick-off, my own little effort not being billed till after the intermission, I wandered in and took my place among the standees at the back, noting dully that I should be playing to absolute capacity. The populace had rolled up in droves, though I could have warned them that they were asking for it. I had seen the programme, and I knew the worst.

The moment I scanned the bill of fare, I was able to understand why Corky, that afternoon at my flat, had spoken so disgruntledly of the talent at her disposal, like a girl who has been thwarted and frustrated and kept from fulfilling herself and what not. I knew what had happened. Starting out to arrange this binge with high hopes and burning ideals and all that sort of thing, poor child, she had stubbed her toe on the fatal snag which always lurks in the path of the impresario of this type of entertainment. I allude to the fact that at every village concert there are certain powerful vested interests which have to be considered. There are, that is to say, divers local nibs who, having always done their bit, are going to be pretty cold and sniffy if not invited to do it again this time. What Corky had come up against was the Kegley-Bassington clan.

To a man of my wide experience, such items as 'Solo: Miss Muriel Kegley-Bassington' and 'Duologue (A Pair of Lunatics): Colonel and Mrs R. P. Kegley-Bassington' told their own story; and the same thing applied to 'Imitations: Watkyn Kegley-Bassington'; 'Card Tricks: Percival Kegley-Bassington' and 'Rhythmic Dance: Miss Poppy Kegley-Bassington'. Master George Kegley-Bassington, who was down for a recitation, I absolved from blame. I strongly suspected that he, like me, had been thrust into his painful position by *force majeure* and would have been equally willing to make a cash settlement.

In the intervals of feeling a brotherly sympathy for Master George and wishing I could run across him and stand him a commiserating gingerbeer, I devoted my time to studying the faces of my neighbours, hoping to detect in them some traces of ruth and pity and what is known as kind indulgence. But not a glimmer. Like all rustic standees, these were stern, implacable men, utterly incapable of taking the broad, charitable view and realizing that a fellow who comes on a platform and starts reciting about Christopher Robin going hoppity-hoppity-hop (or, alternatively, saying his prayers) does not do so from sheer wantonness but because he is a helpless victim of circumstances beyond his control.

I was gazing with considerable apprehension at a particularly dangerous specimen on my left, a pleasure-seeker with hair oil on his head and those mobile lips to which the raspberry springs automatically, when a mild splatter of applause from the two-bob seats showed that we were off. The vicar was opening the proceedings with a short address.

Apart from the fact that I was aware that he played chess and shared with Catsmeat's current *fiancée* a dislike for hearing policemen make cracks about Jonah and the Whale, the Rev. Sidney Pirbright had hitherto been a sealed book to me, and this was, of course, the first time I had seen him in action. A tall, drooping man, looking as if he had been stuffed in a hurry by an incompetent taxidermist, it became apparent immediately that he was not one of those boisterous vicars who, when opening a village concert, bound on the stage with a whoop and a holler, give the parishioners a huge Hallo, slam across a couple of travelling-salesman-and-farmer's-daughter stories and bound off, beaming. He seemed low-spirited, as I suppose he had every right to be. With Corky permanently on the premises, doing the little Mother, and Gussie rolling up for practically every meal, and on top of that a gorilla like young Thos coming and parking himself in the spare bedroom, you could scarcely expect him to bubble over with *joie de vivre*. These things take their toll.

At any rate, he didn't. His theme was the Church Organ, in aid of which these grim doings had been set afoot, and it was in a vein of pessimism that he spoke of its prospects. The Church Organ, he told us frankly, was in a hell of a bad way. For years it had been going around with holes in its socks, doing the Brother-can-you-spare-a-dime stuff, and now it was about due to hand in its dinner pail. There had been a time when he had hoped that the pull-together spirit might have given it a shot in the arm, but the way it looked to him at the moment, things had gone too far and he was prepared to bet his shirt on the bally contrivance going down the drain and staying there.

He concluded by announcing sombrely that the first item on the programme would be a Violin Solo by Miss Eustacia Pulbrook, managing to convey the suggestion that, while he knew as well as we did that Eustacia was going to be about as corny as they come, he advised us to make the most of her, because after that we should have the Kegley-Bassington family at our throats.

Except for knowing that when you've heard one, you've heard them all, I'm not really an authority on violin solos, so cannot state definitely whether La Pulbrook's was or was not a credit to the accomplices who had taught her the use of the instrument. It was loud in spots and less loud in other spots, and it had that quality which I have noticed in all violin solos, of seeming to last much longer than it actually did. When it eventually blew over, one saw what the sainted Sidney had meant about the Kegley-Bassingtons. A minion came on the stage carrying a table. On this table he placed a framed photograph, and I knew that we were for it. Show Bertram Wooster a table and a framed photograph, and you don't have to tell him what the upshot is going to be. Muriel Kegley-Bassington stood revealed as a 'My Hero' from *The Chocolate Soldier* addict.

I thought the boys behind the back row behaved with extraordinary dignity and restraint, and their suavity gave me the first faint hope I had had that when my turn came to face the firing-squad I might be spared the excesses which I had been anticipating. I would rank 'My Hero' next after 'The Yeoman's Wedding Song' as a standee-rouser, and when a large blonde appeared and took up the photograph and gave it a soulful look and rubbed her hands in the rosin and inflated her lungs, I was expecting big things. But these splendid fellows apparently did not war on women. Not only did they refrain from making uncouth noises with the tongue between the lips, one or two actually clapped – an imprudent move, of course, because, taken in conjunction with the applause of the two-bobbers, who applaud everything, it led to 'Oh, who will o'er the downs with me' as an encore.

Inflamed by this promising start, Muriel would, I think, willingly have continued, probably with 'The Indian Love Call', but something in our manner must have shown her that she couldn't do that here, for she shrank back and withdrew. There was a brief stage wait, and then a small, bullet-headed boy in an Eton jacket came staggering on like Christopher Robin going hoppity-hoppity-hop, in a manner that suggested that blood relations in the background had overcome his reluctance to appear by putting a hand between his shoulder-blades and shoving. Master George Kegley-Bassington, and no other. My heart went out to the little fellow. I knew just how he was feeling.

One could picture so clearly all that must have led up to this rash act. The first fatal suggestion by his mother that it would please the vicar if George gave that recitation which he did so nicely. The agonized 'Hoy!' The attempted rebuttal. The family pressure. The sullen scowl. The calling in of Father to exercise his authority. The reluctant acquiescence. The dash for freedom at the eleventh hour, foiled, as we have seen, by that quick thrust between the shoulder-blades.

And here he was, out in the middle.

He gave us an unpleasant look, and said:

' "Ben Battle".'

I pursed the lips and shook the head. I knew this 'Ben Battle', for it had been in my own repertoire in my early days. One of those gruesome antiques with a pun in every other line, the last thing to which any right-minded boy would wish to lend himself, and quite unsuited to this artiste's style. If I had had the ear of Colonel and Mrs R. P. Kegley-Bassington, I would have said to them: 'Colonel, Mrs Kegley-Bassington, be advised by an old friend. Keep George away from comedy, and stick to good sound "Dangerous Dan McGrews". His forte is grimness.'

Having said 'Ben Battle', he paused and repeated the

unpleasant look. I could see what was passing through
his mind. He wished to know if anybody out front
wanted to make anything of this. The pause was a
belligerent pause. But it was evident that it had been
misinterpreted by his nearest and dearest, for two voices,
both loud and carrying, spoke simultaneously from the
wings. One had a parade-ground rasp, the other was that
of the songstress who had so recently My-Hero-ed.

'Ben Battle was a soldier bold . . .'

'All *right*!' said George, transferring the unpleasant
look in that direction. '*I* know.
Ben-Battle-was-a-soldier-bold-and-used-to-war's-alarms,
A-cannon-ball-took-off-his-legs-so-he-laid-down-his-arms,'
he added, crowding the thing into a single word. He then
proceeded.

Well, really, come, come, I felt, as he did so, this is
most encouraging. Can it be, I asked myself, that these
rugged exteriors around me hide hearts of gold? It
certainly seemed so, for despite the fact that it would
have been difficult, nay impossible, to imagine anything
lousier than Master George Kegley-Bassington's
performance, it was producing nothing in the nature of a
demonstration from the standees. They had not warred
on women, and they did not war on children. Might it
not quite easily happen, I mused, that they would not
war on Woosters? Tails up, Bertram, I said to myself, and
it was with almost a light heart that I watched George
forget the last three stanzas and shamble off, giving us
that unpleasant look again over his shoulder, and in the
exuberance with which I greeted the small man with the
face like an anxious marmoset – Adrian Higgins, I
gathered from my programme; by profession, I
subsequently learned, King's Deverill's courteous and
popular grave-digger – there was something that came
very close to being carefree.

Adrian Higgins solicited our kind attention for
Impressions of Woodland Songsters Which Are Familiar

To You All, and while these did not go with any
particular bang, the farmyard imitations which followed
were cordially received, and the drawing of a cork and
pouring out a bottle of beer which took him off made a
solid hit, leaving the customers in excellent mood. With
the conclusion of George's recitation, they were feeling
that the worst was behind them and a few clenched
teeth would see them through the remainder of the
Kegley-Bassington offensive. There was a general sense
of relaxation, and Gussie and Catsmeat could not have
had a better spot. When they came on, festooned in
green beards, they got a big hand.

It was the last time they did. The act died standing
up. Right from the start I saw that it was going to be a
turkey, and so it proved. It was listless. It lacked fire and
oomph. The very opening words struck a chill.

'Hallo, Pat,' said Catsmeat in a dull, toneless voice.

'Hallo, Mike,' said Gussie, with equal moodiness.
'How's your father?'

'He's not enjoying himself just now.'

'What's he doing?'

'Seven years,' said Catsmeat glumly, and went on in
the same depressed way to speak of his brother Jim,
who, having obtained employment as a swimming
teacher, was now often in low water.

Well, I couldn't see what Gussie could have on his
mind, unless he was brooding on the Church Organ, but
Catsmeat's despondency was, of course, susceptible of a
ready explanation. From where he stood he had an
excellent view of Gertrude Winkworth in row one of the
two-bob seats, and the sight of her, looking pale and
proud in something which I should say at a venture was
mousseline, must have been like a sword-thrust through
the bosom. Just as you allow a vicar a wide latitude in
the way of gloom when his private life has become
cluttered up with Corkies and Gussies and Thoses, so
should you, if a fairminded man, permit a tortured lover,

confronted with the girl he has lost, to sink into the depths a bit.

Well, that's all right. I'm not saying you shouldn't, and, as a matter of fact, I did. If you had come along and asked me, 'Has Claude Cattermole Pirbright your heartfelt sympathy, Wooster?' I would have replied, 'You betcher he has my heartfelt sympathy. I mourn in spirit.' All I do say is that this Byronic outlook doesn't help you bang across your points in a Pat and Mike knockabout cross-talk act.

The whole performance gave one a sort of grey, hopeless feeling, like listening to the rain at three o'clock on a Sunday afternoon in November. Even the standees, tough, rugged men who would not have recognized the finer feelings if you had served them up on a plate with watercress round them, obviously felt the pathos of it all. They listened in dejected silence, shuffling their feet, and I didn't blame them. There should be nothing so frightfully heartrending in one fellow asking another fellow who that lady was he saw him coming down the street with and the other fellow replying that there was no lady, that was his wife. An amusing little misunderstanding, you would say. But when Gussie and Catsmeat spoke the lines, they seemed to bring home to you all the underlying sadness of life.

At first, I couldn't think what the thing reminded me of. Then I got it. At the time when I was engaged to Florence Craye and she was trying to jack up my soul, one of the methods she employed to this end was to take me on Sunday nights to see Russian plays; the sort of things where the old home is being sold up and people stand around saying how sad it all is. If I had to make a criticism of Catsmeat and Gussie, I should say that they got too much of the Russian spirit into their work. It was a relief to one and all when the poignant slice of life drew to a close.

'My sister's in the ballet,' said Catsmeat despondently.

There was a pause here, because Gussie had fallen into a sort of trance and was standing staring silently before him as if the Church Organ had really got him down at last, and Catsmeat, realizing that only moral support, if that, was to be expected from this quarter, was obliged to carry on the conversation by himself, a thing which I always think spoils the effect on these occasions. The essence of a cross-talk act is that there should be wholesome give and take, and you never get the same snappy zip when one fellow is asking the questions and answering them himself.

'You say your sister's in the ballet?' said Catsmeat with a catch in his voice. 'Yes, begorrah, my sister's in the ballet. What does your sister do in the ballet?' he went on, taking a look at Gertrude Winkworth and quivering in agony. 'She comes rushin' in and she goes rushin' out. What does she have to rush like that for?' asked Catsmeat with a stifled sob. 'Faith and begob, because it's a Rushin' ballet.'

And, too broken in spirit to hit Gussie with his umbrella, he took him by the elbow and directed him to the exit. They moved slowly off with bowed heads, like a couple of pallbearers who have forgotten their coffin and had to go back for it, and to the rousing strains of 'Hallo, hallo, hallo, hallo, a-hunting we will go, pom pom', Esmond Haddock strode masterfully onto the stage.

Esmond looked terrific. Anxious to omit no word or act which would assist him in socking the clientele on the button, he had put on full hunting costume, pink coat and everything, and the effect was sensational. He seemed to bring into that sombre hall a note of joy and hope. After all, you felt, there was still happiness in the world. Life, you told yourself, was not all men in green beards saying 'Faith' and 'Begorrah'.

To the practised eye like mine it was apparent that in the interval since the conclusion of the scratch meal which had taken the place of dinner the young Squire had been having a couple, but, as I often say, why not? There is no occasion on which a man of retiring disposition with an inferiority complex and all the trimmings needs the old fluid more than when he is about to perform at a village concert, and with so much at stake it would have been madness on his part not to get moderately ginned.

It is to the series of quick ones which he had absorbed that I attribute the confident manner of his entry, but the attitude of the audience must speedily have convinced him that he could really have got by perfectly well on limejuice. Any doubt lingering in his mind as to his being the popular pet must have been dispelled instantly by the thunders of applause from all parts of the house. I noted twelve distinct standees who were whistling through their fingers, and those who were not whistling were stamping on the floor. The fellow with the hair oil on my left was doing both.

And now, of course, came the danger spot. A feeble piping at this point, like gas escaping from a pipe, or let us say a failure to remember more than an odd word or two of the subject matter, and a favourable first impression might well be undone. True, the tougher portion of the audience had been sedulously stood beers over a period of days and in return had entered into a gentleman's agreement to be indulgent, but nevertheless it was unquestionably up to Esmond Haddock to deliver the goods.

He did so abundantly and in heaping measure. That first night over the port, when we had been having our run-through, my thoughts at the outset had been centred on the lyric and I had been too busy polishing up Aunt Charlotte's material to give much attention to the quality of his voice. And later on, of course, I had been singing myself, which always demands complete concentration. When I was on the chair, waving my decanter, I had been aware in a vague sort of way of some kind of disturbance in progress on the table, but if Dame Daphne Winkworth on her entry had asked me my opinion of Esmond Haddock's timbre and brio, I should have had to reply that I really hadn't noticed them much.

He now stood forth as the possessor of a charming baritone – full of life and feeling and, above all, loud. And volume of sound is what you want at a village concert. Make the lights flicker and bring plaster down from the ceiling, and you are home. Esmond Haddock did not cater simply for those who had paid the price of admission, he took in strollers along the High Street and even those who had remained at their residences, curled up with a good book. Catsmeat, you may recall, in speaking of the yells which Dame Daphne and the Misses Deverill had uttered on learning of his betrothal to Gertrude Winkworth, had hazarded the opinion that they could have been heard at Basingstoke. I should say that Basingstoke got Esmond Haddock's hunting song nicely.

If so, it got a genuine treat and one of some duration, for he took three encores, a couple of bows, a fourth encore, some bows and then the chorus once over again by way of one for the road. And even then his well-wishers seemed reluctant to let him go.

This reluctance made itself manifest during the next item on the programme – Glee (Oh, come unto these yellow sands) by the Church Choir, conducted by the school-mistress – in murmurs at the back and an occasional 'Hallo', but it was not until Miss Poppy Kegley-Bassington was performing her rhythmic dance that it found full expression.

Unlike her sister Muriel, who had resembled a Criterion barmaid of the old school, Poppy

Kegley-Bassington was long and dark and supple, with a
sinuous figure suggestive of a snake with hips; one of
those girls who do rhythmic dances at the drop of a hat
and can be dissuaded from doing them only with a
meat-axe. The music that accompanied her act was
Oriental in nature, and I should be disposed to think
that the thing had started out in life as a straight Vision
of Salome but had been toned down and had the whistle
blown on it in spots in deference to the sensibilities of
the Women's Institute. It consisted of a series of
slitherings and writhings, punctuated with occasional
pauses when, having got herself tied in a clove-hitch, she
seemed to be waiting for someone who remembered the
combination to come along and disentangle her.

It was during one of these pauses that the plug-ugly
with the hair oil made an observation. Since Esmond's
departure he had been standing with a rather morose
expression on his face, like an elephant that has had its
bun taken from it, and you could see how deeply he was
regretting that the young Squire was no longer with us.
From time to time he would mutter in a peevish
undertone, and I seemed to catch Esmond's name. He
now spoke, and I found that my hearing had not been at
fault.

'We want Haddock,' he said. 'We want Haddock,
we want Haddock, we want Haddock, we want
HADDOCK!'

He uttered the words in a loud, clear, penetrating
voice, not unlike that of a costermonger informing the
public that he has blood oranges for sale, and the
sentiment expressed evidently chimed in with the views
of those standing near him. It was not long before
perhaps twenty or more discriminating concert-goers
were also chanting:

'We want Haddock, we want Haddock, we want
Haddock, we want Haddock, we want HADDOCK!'

And it just shows you how catching this sort of thing

is. It wasn't more than about five seconds later that I
heard another voice intoning.

'We want Haddock, we want Haddock, we want
Haddock, we want Haddock, we want HADDOCK!'
and discovered with a mild surprise that it was mine.
And as the remainder of the standees, some thirty in
number, also adopted the slogan, this made us
unanimous.

To sum up, then, the fellow with the hair oil, fifty
other fellows, also with hair oil, and I had begun to
speak simultaneously and what we said was:

'We want Haddock, we want Haddock, we want
Haddock, we want Haddock, we want HADDOCK!'

There was some shushing from the two-bobbers, but
we were firm, and though Miss Kegley-Bassington
pluckily continued to slither for a few moments longer,
the contest of wills could have but one ending. She
withdrew, getting a nice hand, for we were generous in
victory, and Esmond came on, all boots and pink coat.
And what with him going a-hunting at one end of the
hall and our group of thinkers going a-hunting at the
other, the thing might have occupied the rest of the
evening quite agreeably, had not some quick-thinking
person dropped the curtain for the intermission.

You might have supposed that my mood, as I strolled
from the building to enjoy a smoke, would have been
one of elation. And so, for some moments, it was. The
whole aim of my foreign policy had been to ensure the
making of a socko by Esmond, and he had made a socko.
He had slain them and stopped the show. For perhaps
the space of a quarter of a cigarette I rejoiced
unstintedly.

Then my uplifted mood suddenly left me. The
cigarette fell from my nerveless fingers, and I stood
rooted to the spot, the lower jaw resting negligently on
the shirt front. I had just realized that, what with one
thing and another – my disturbed night, my taxing day,

the various burdens weighing on my mind and so forth – every word of those Christopher Robin poems had been expunged from my memory.

And I was billed next but two after intermission.

23

How long I stood there, rooted to the s., I cannot say. A goodish while, no doubt, for this wholly unforeseen development had unmanned me completely. I was roused from my reverie by the sound of rustic voices singing 'Hallo, hallo, hallo, hallo, a-hunting we will go, my lads, a-hunting we will go' and discovered that the strains were proceeding from the premises of the Goose and Cowslip on the other side of the road. And it suddenly struck me – I can't think why it hadn't before – that here might possibly be the mental tonic of which I was in need. It might be that all that was wrong with me was that I was faint for lack of nourishment. Hitching up the lower jaw, I hurried across and plunged into the saloon bar.

The revellers who were singing the gem of the night's Hit Parade were doing so in the public bar. The only occupant of the more posh saloon bar was a godlike man in a bowler hat with grave, finely chiselled features and a head that stuck out at the back, indicating great brain power. To cut a long story short, Jeeves. He was having a meditative beer at the table by the wall.

'Good evening, sir,' he said, rising with his customary polish. 'I am happy to inform you that I was successful in obtaining the cosh from Master Thomas. I have it in my pocket.'

I raised a hand.

'This is no time for talking about coshes.'

'No, sir. I merely mentioned it in passing. Mr Haddock's was an extremely gratifying triumph, did you not think, sir?'

'Nor is it a time for talking about Esmond Haddock,
Jeeves,' I said, 'I'm sunk.'

'Indeed, sir?'

'Jeeves!'

'I beg your pardon, sir. I should have said "Really,
sir?"'

'"Really, sir?" is just as bad. What the crisis calls for
is a "Gosh!" or a "Gorblimey!" There have been
occasions, numerous occasions, when you have beheld
Bertram Wooster in the bouillon, but never so deeply
immersed in it as now. You know those damned poems I
was to recite? I've forgotten every word of them. I need
scarcely stress the gravity of the situation. Half an hour
from now I shall be up on that platform with the Union
Jack behind me and before me an expectant audience,
waiting to see what I've got. And I haven't got anything.
I shan't have a word to say. And while an audience at a
village concert justifiably resents having Christopher
Robin poems recited at it, its resentment becomes
heightened if the reciter merely stands there opening
and shutting his mouth in silence like a goldfish.'

'Very true, sir. You cannot jog your memory?'

'It was in the hope of jogging it that I came in here. Is
there brandy in this joint?'

'Yes, sir. I will procure you a double.'

'Make it two doubles.'

'Very good, sir.'

He moved obligingly to the little hatch thing in the
wall and conveyed his desire to the unseen provider on
the other side, and presently a hand came through with a
brimming glass and he brought it to the table.

'Let's see what this does,' I said. 'Skin off your nose,
Jeeves.'

'Mud in your eye, sir, if I may use the expression.'

I drained the glass and laid it down.

'The ironical thing,' I said, while waiting for the stuff
to work, 'is that though, except for remembering in a

broad, general way that he went hoppity-hoppity-hop, I am a spent force as regards Christopher Robin, I could do them "Ben Battle" without a hitch. Did you hear Master George Kegley-Bassington on the subject of "Ben Battle"?'

'Yes, sir. A barely adequate performance, I thought.'

'That is not the point, Jeeves. What I'm trying to tell you is that listening to him has had the effect of turning back time in its flight, if you know what I mean, so that from the reciting angle I am once more the old Bertram Wooster of bygone days and can remember every word of "Ben Battle" as clearly as in the epoch when it was constantly on my lips. I could do the whole thing without fluffing a syllable. But does that profit me?'

'No, sir.'

'No, sir, is correct. Thanks to George, saturation point has been reached with this particular audience as far as "Ben Battle" is concerned. If I started to give it them, too, I shouldn't get beyond the first stanza. There would be an ugly rush for the platform, and I should be roughly handled. So what do you suggest?'

'You have obtained no access of mental vigour from the refreshment which you have been consuming, sir?'

'Not a scrap. The stuff might have been water.'

'In that case, I think you would be well advised to refrain from attempting to entertain the audience, sir. It would be best to hand the whole conduct of the affair over to Mr Haddock.'

'Eh?'

'I am confident that Mr Haddock would gladly deputize for you. In the uplifted frame of mind in which he now is, he would welcome an opportunity to appear again before his public.'

'But he couldn't learn the stuff in a quarter of an hour.'

'No, sir, but he could read it from the book. I have a copy of the book on my person, for I had been intending to station myself at the side of the stage in order to prompt you, as I believe the technical expression is, should you have need of my services.'

'Dashed good of you, Jeeves. Very white. Very feudal.'

'Not at all, sir. Shall I step across and explain the position of affairs to Mr Haddock and hand him the book?'

I mused. The more I examined his suggestion, the better I liked it. When you are slated to go over Niagara Falls in a barrel, the idea of getting a kindly friend to take your place is always an attractive one; the only thing that restrains you, as a rule, from making the switch being the thought that it is a bit tough on the kindly f. But in the present case this objection did not apply. On this night of nights Esmond Haddock could get away with anything. There was, I seemed to remember dimly, a poem in the book about Christopher Robin having ten little toes. Even that, dished out by the idol of King's Deverill, would not provoke mob violence.

'Yes, buzz straight over and fix up the deal, Jeeves,' I said, hesitating no longer. 'As always, you have found the way.'

He adjusted the bowler hat which he had courteously doffed at my entry, and went off on his errand of mercy. And I, too agitated to remain sitting, wandered out into the street and began to pace up and down outside the hostelry. And I had paused for a moment to look at the stars, wondering, as I always did when I saw stars, why Jeeves had once described them to me as quiring to the young-eyed Cherubim, when a tapping on my arm and a bleating voice saying 'I say, Bertie' told me that some creature of the night was trying to arrest my attention. I turned and beheld something in a green beard and a check suit of loud pattern which, as it was not tall enough to be Catsmeat, the only other person likely to be going about in that striking get-up, I took correctly to be Gussie.

'I say, Bertie,' said Gussie, speaking with obvious emotion, 'do you think you could get me some brandy?'

'You mean orange juice?'

'No, I do not mean orange juice. I mean brandy. About a bucketful.'

Puzzled, but full of the St-Bernard-dog spirit, I returned to the saloon bar and came back with the snifter. He accepted it gratefully and downed about half of it at a gulp, gasping in a struck-by-lightning manner, as I have seen men gasp after taking one of Jeeves's special pick-me-ups.

'Thanks,' he said, when he had recovered. 'I needed that. And I didn't like to go in myself with this beard on.'

'Why don't you take it off?'

'I can't get it off. I stuck it on with spirit gum, and it hurts like sin when I pull at it. I shall have to get Jeeves to see what he can do about it later. Is this stuff brandy?'

'That's what they told me.'

'What appalling muck. Like vitriol. How on earth can you and your fellow topers drink it for pleasure?'

'What are you drinking it for? Because you promised your mother you would?'

'I am drinking it, Bertie, to nerve myself for a frightful ordeal.'

I gave his shoulder a kindly pat. It seemed to me that the man's mind was wandering.

'You're forgetting, Gussie. Your ordeal is over. You've done your act. And pretty lousy it was,' I said, unable to check the note of censure. 'What was the matter with you?'

He blinked like a chidden codfish.

'Wasn't I good?'

'No, you were not good. You were cheesy. Your work lacked fire and snap.'

'Well, so would your work lack fire and snap, if you had to play in a knockabout cross-talk act and knew that directly the thing was over, you were going to break into a police station and steal a dog.'

The stars, ceasing for a moment to quire to the young-eyed Cherubim, did a quick buck-and-wing.

'Say that again!'

'What's the point of saying it again? You heard. I've promised Corky I'll go to Dobbs's cottage and extract that dog of hers. She will be waiting in her car near at hand and will gather the animal in and whisk it off to the house of some friends of hers who live about twenty miles along the London road, well out of Dobbs's sphere of influence. So now you know why I wanted brandy.'

I wanted brandy, too. Either that or something equally restorative. Oh, I was saying to myself, for a beaker full of the warm south, full of the true, the blushful Hippocrene. I have spoken earlier of the tendency of the spirit of the Woosters to rise when crushed to earth, but there is a limit, and this limit had now been reached. At these frightful words, the spirit of the Woosters felt as if it had been sat on by an elephant. And not one of your streamlined, schoolgirl-figured elephants, either. A big, fat one.

'Gussie! You mustn't!'

'What do you mean, I mustn't? Of course I must. Corky wishes it.'

'But you don't realize the peril. Dobbs is laying for you. Esmond Haddock is laying for you. They're just waiting to spring.'

'How do you know that?'

'Esmond Haddock told me so himself. He dislikes you intensely and it is his dearest hope some day to catch you bending and put you behind the bars. And he's a J.P., so is in a strong position to bring about the happy ending. You'll look pretty silly when you find yourself doing thirty days in the jug.'

'For Corky's sake I'd do a year. As a matter of fact,' said Gussie in a burst of confidence, 'though you might not think it from the way I've been calling for brandy, there's no chance of my being caught. Dobbs is watching the concert.'

This, of course, improved the outlook. I don't say I breathed freely, but I breathed more freely than I had been breathing.

'You're sure of that?'

'I saw him myself.'

'You couldn't have been mistaken?'

'My dear Bertie, when Dobbs has come into a room in which you have been strewing frogs and stood face to face with you for an eternity, chewing his moustache and grinding his teeth at you, you know him when you see him again.'

'But all the same –'

'It's no good saying "All the same". Corky wants me to extract her dog, and I'm going to do it. "Gussie", she said to me, "you're such a *help*", and I intend to be worthy of those words.'

And, having spoken thus, he gave his beard a hitch and vanished into the silent night, leaving me to pay for the brandy.

I had just finished doing so when Jeeves returned.

'Everything has been satisfactorily arranged, sir,' he said. 'I have seen Mr Haddock, and, as I anticipated, he is more than willing to deputize for you.'

A great weight seemed to roll off my mind.

'Then God bless Mr Haddock!' I said. 'There is splendid stuff in these young English landowners, Jeeves, is there not?'

'Unquestionably, sir.'

'The backbone of the country, I sometimes call them. But I gather from the fact that you have been gone the dickens of a time that you had to do some heavy persuading.'

'No, sir. Mr Haddock consented immediately and with enthusiasm. My delay in returning was due to the

fact that I was detained in conversation by Police
Constable Dobbs. There were a number of questions of a
theological nature on which he was anxious to canvass
my views. He appears particularly interested in Jonah
and the Whale.'

'Is he enjoying the concert?'

'No, sir. He spoke in disparaging terms of the quality
of the entertainment provided.'

'He didn't like George Kegley-Bassington much?'

'No, sir. On the subject of Master Kegley-Bassington
he expressed himself strongly, and was almost equally
caustic when commenting upon Miss Kegley-
Bassington's rhythmic dance. It is in order to avoid
witnessing the efforts of the remaining members of the
family that he has returned to his cottage, where he
plans to pass what is left of the evening with a pipe and
the works of Colonel Robert G. Ingersoll.'

24

So that was that. You get the picture. Above, in the serene
sky, the stars quiring to the Cherubim. Off-stage, in the
public bar, the local toughies quiring to the potboy. And
down centre Jeeves, having exploded his bombshell,
regarding me with the eye of concern, as if he feared that
all was not well with the young master, in which
conjecture he was one hundred per cent right. The young
master was feeling as if his soul had just received the
Cornish Riviera express on the seat of its pants.

I gulped perhaps half a dozen times before I was able
to utter.

'Jeeves, you didn't really say that, did you?'

'Sir?'

'About Constable Dobbs going back to his cottage.'

'Yes, sir. He informed me that it was his intention to
do so. He said he desired solitude.'

'Solitude!' I said. 'Ha!'

And in a dull, toneless voice, like George Kegley-
Bassington reciting 'Ben Battle', I gave him the
lowdown.

'That is the situation in what is sometimes called a
nutshell, Jeeves,' I concluded. 'And, not that it matters,
for nothing matters now, I wonder if you have spotted
how extraordinarily closely the present set-up resembles
that of Alfred, Lord Tennyson's well-known poem, "The
Charge of the Light Brigade", which is another of the
things I used to recite in happier days. I mean to say,
someone has blundered and Gussie, like the Six
Hundred, is riding into the Valley of Death. His not to
reason why, his but to do or –'

'Pardon me, sir, for interrupting you – '

'Not at all, Jeeves. I had nearly finished.'

' – but would it not be advisable to take some form of action?'

I gave him the lack-lustre eye.

'Action, Jeeves? How can that help us now? And what form of it would you suggest? I should have said the thing had got beyond the scope of human power.'

'It might be possible to overtake Mr Fink-Nottle, sir, and apprise him of his peril.'

I shrugged the shoulders.

'We can try, if you like. I see little percentage in it, but I suppose one should leave no stone unturned. Can you find your way to *chez* Dobbs?'

'Yes, sir.'

'Then shift ho,' I said listlessly.

As we made our way out of the High Street into the dark regions beyond, we chatted in desultory vein.

'I noticed, Jeeves, that when I started telling you the bad news just now, one of your eyebrows flickered.'

'Yes, sir. I was much exercised.'

'Don't you ever get exercised enough to say "Coo!"?'

'No, sir.'

'Or "Crumbs!"?'

'No, sir.'

'Strange. I should have thought you might have done so at a moment like that. I would say this was the end, wouldn't you?'

'While there is life, there is hope, sir.'

'Neatly put, but I disagree with you. I see no reason for even two-pennorth of hope. We shan't overtake Gussie. He must have got there long ago. About now, Dobbs is sitting on his chest and slipping the handcuffs on him.'

'The officer may not have proceeded directly to his home, sir.'

'You think there is a possibility that he paused at a

pub for a gargle? It may be so, of course, but I am not
sanguine. It would mean that Fate was handing out
lucky breaks, and my experience of Fate – '

I would have spoken further and probably been pretty
deepish, for the subject of Fate and its consistent
tendency to give good men the elbow was one to which I
had devoted considerable thought, but at this moment I
was accosted by another creature of the night, a soprano
one this time, and I perceived a car drawn up at the side
of the road.

'Yoo-hoo, Bertie,' said a silvery voice. 'Hi-ya, Jeeves.'

'Good evening, miss,' said Jeeves in his suave way.
'Miss Pirbright, sir,' he added, giving me the office in an
undertone.

I had already recognized the silvery v.

'Hallo, Corky,' I said moodily. 'You are waiting for
Gussie?'

'Yes, he went by just now. What did you say?'

'Oh, nothing,' I replied, for I had merely remarked by
way of a passing comment that cannons to left of him,
cannons to right of him volleyed and thundered. 'I
suppose you know that you have lured him on to a doom
so hideous that the brain reels, contemplating it?'

'What do you mean?'

'He will find Dobbs at journey's end reading Robert G.
Ingersoll. How long the officer will continue reading
Robert G. Ingersoll after discovering that Gussie has
broken in and is de-dogging the premises, one cannot – '

'Don't be an ass. Dobbs is at the concert.'

'He *was* at the concert. But he left early and is now – '

Once more I was interrupted when about to speak
further. From down the road there had begun to make
itself heard in the silent night a distant barking. It grew
in volume, indicating that the barker was heading our
way, and Corky sprang from the car and established
herself as a committee of welcome in the middle of the
fairway.

'What a chump you are, Bertie,' she said with some heat, 'pulling a girl's leg and trying to scare her stiff. Everything has gone according to plan. Here comes Sam. I'd know his voice anywhere. At-a-boy, Sam! This way. Come to Mother.'

What ensued was rather like the big scene in *The Hound of the Baskervilles*. The baying and the patter of feet grew louder, and suddenly out of the darkness Sam Goldwyn clocked in, coming along at a high rate of speed and showing plainly in his manner how keenly he appreciated the termination of the sedentary life he had been leading these last days. He looked good for about another fifty miles at the same pace, but the sight of us gave him pause. He stopped, looked and listened. Then, as our familiar odour reached his nostrils, he threw his whole soul into a cry of ecstasy. He bounded at Jeeves as if contemplating licking his face, but was checked by the latter's quiet dignity. Jeeves views the animal kingdom with a benevolent eye and is the first to pat its head and offer it a slice of whatever is going, but he does not permit it to lick his face.

'Inside, Sam,' said Corky, when the rapture of reunion had had the first keen edge taken off it and we had all simmered down a bit. She boosted him into the car, and resumed her place at the wheel. 'Time to be leaving,' she said. 'The quick fade-out is what the director would suggest here, I think. I'll be seeing you at the Hall later, Bertie. Uncle Sidney has been asked to look in for coffee and sandwiches after the show, and I was included in the invitation, I don't think. Still, I shall assume I was.'

She clapped spurs to her two-seater and vanished into the darkness. Sam Goldwyn's vocal solo died away, and all was still once more.

No, not all, to be absolutely accurate, for at this moment there came to the ear-drum an odd sort of hammering noise in the distance which at first I couldn't classify. It sounded as if someone was doing a

tap-dance, but it seemed improbable that people would
be doing tap-dances out of doors at this hour. Then I got
it. Somebody – no, two people – was – or I should say
were – hareing towards us along the road, and I was
turning to cock an enquiring eyebrow at Jeeves, when he
drew me into the shadows.

'I fear the worst, sir,' he said in a hushed voice, and,
sure enough, along it came.

In addition to the stars quiring to the young-eyed
Cherubim, there was now in the serene sky a fair-sized
moon, and as always happens under these conditions the
visibility was improved. By its light one could see what
was in progress.

Gussie and Constable Dobbs were in progress, in the
order named. Not having been present at the outset of
the proceedings, I can only guess at what had occurred in
the early stages, but anyone entering a police station to
steal a dog and finding Constable Dobbs on the premises
would have lost little time in picking up the feet, and I
think we can assume that Gussie had got off to a good
start. At any rate, at the moment when the runners
came into view he had established a nice lead and
appeared to be increasing it.

It is curious how you can be intimate with a fellow
from early boyhood and yet remain unacquainted with
one side of him. Mixing constantly with Gussie through
the years, I had come to know him as a newt-fancier, a
lover and a fathead, but I had never suspected him of
possessing outstanding qualities as a sprinter on the flat,
and I was amazed at the high order of ability he was
exhibiting in this very specialized form of activity. He
was coming along like a jack-rabbit of the western
prairie, his head back and his green beard floating in the
breeze. I liked his ankle work.

Dobbs, on the other hand, was more laboured in his
movements and to an eye like mine, trained in the
watching of point-to-point races, had all the look of an

also-ran. One noted symptoms of roaring, and I am
convinced that had Gussie had the intelligence to stick
to his job and make a straight race of it, he would soon
have out-distanced the field and come home on a tight
rein. Police constables are not built for speed. Where you
catch them at their best is standing on street corners
saying 'Pass along there'.

But, as I was stressing a moment ago, Augustus
Fink-Nottle, in addition to being a flat racer of marked
ability, was also a fathead, and now, when he had
victory in his grasp, the fat-headed streak in him came
uppermost. There was a tree standing at the roadside
and, suddenly swerving off the course, he made for it and
hoisted himself into its branches. And what he supposed
that was going to get him, only his diseased mind knew.
Ernest Dobbs may not have been one of Hampshire's
brightest thinkers, but he was smart enough to stand
under a tree.

And this he proceeded to do. Determination to fight it
out on these lines if it took all summer was written on
every inch of his powerful frame. His back being towards
me, I couldn't see his face, but I have no doubt it was
registering an equal amount of resolution, and nothing
could have been firmer than his voice as he urged upon
the rooster above the advisability of coming down
without further waste of time. It was a fair cop, said
Ernest Dobbs, and I agreed with him. To shut out the
painful scene which must inevitably ensue, I closed my
eyes.

It was an odd, chunky sound, like some solid
substance striking another solid substance, that made
me open them. And when they were opened, I could
hardly believe them. Ernest Dobbs, who a moment
before had been standing with his feet apart and his
thumbs in his belt like a statue of Justice Putting It
Across the Evil-Doer, had now assumed what I have
heard described as a recumbent position. To make what

I am driving at clear to the meanest intelligence, he was lying in the road with his face to the stars, while Jeeves, like a warrior sheathing his sword, replaced in his pocket some object which instinct told me was small but serviceable and constructed of india-rubber.

I tottered across, and drew the breath in sharply as I viewed the remains. The best you could have said of Constable Ernest Dobbs was that he looked peaceful.

'Good Lord, Jeeves!' I said.

'I took the liberty of coshing the officer, sir,' he explained respectfully. 'I considered it advisable in the circumstances as the simplest method of averting unpleasantness. You will find it safe to descend now, sir,' he proceeded, addressing Gussie. 'If I might offer the suggestion, speed is of the essence. One cannot guarantee that the constable will remain indefinitely immobile.'

This opened up a new line of thought.

'You don't mean he'll recover?'

'Why, yes, sir, almost immediately.'

'I'd have said that all he wanted was a lily in the right hand, and he'd be set.'

'Oh, no, sir. The cosh produces merely a passing malaise. Permit me, sir,' he said, assisting Gussie to alight. 'I anticipate that Dobbs, on coming to his senses, will experience a somewhat severe headache, but –'

'Into each life some rain must fall?'

'Precisely, sir. I think it would be prudent of Mr Fink-Nottle to remove his beard. It presents too striking a means of identification.'

'But he can't. It's stuck on with spirit gum.'

'If Mr Fink-Nottle will permit me to escort him to his room, sir, I shall be able to adjust that without difficulty.'

'You will? Then get on with it, Gussie.'

'Eh?' said Gussie, being just the sort of chap who

would stand about saying 'Eh?' at a moment like this.
He had a dazed air, as if he, too, had stopped one.

'Push off.'

'Eh?'

I gave a weary gesture.

'Remove him, Jeeves,' I said.

'Very good, sir.'

'I would come along with you, but I shall be occupied
elsewhere. I need about six more of those brandies, and I
need them quick. You're sure about this living corpse?'

'Sir?'

'I mean, "living" really is the *mot juste*?'

'Oh, yes, sir. If you will notice, the officer is already
commencing to regain consciousness.'

I did notice it. Ernest Dobbs was plainly about to
report for duty. He moved, he stirred, he seemed to feel
the rush of life along his keel. And, this being so, I
deemed it best to withdraw. I had no desire to be found
standing at the sick-bed when a fellow of his muscular
development and uncertain temper came to and started
looking about for responsible parties. I returned to the
Goose and Cowslip at a good speed, and proceeded to
put big business in the way of the hand that came
through the hatch. Then, feeling somewhat restored, I
went back to the Hall and dug in in my room.

I had, as you will readily understand, much food for
thought. The revelation of this deeper, coshing side to
Jeeves's character had come as something of a shock to
me. One found oneself wondering how far the thing
would spread. He and I had had our differences in the
past, failing to see eye to eye on such matters as purple
socks and white dinner jackets, and it was inevitable,
both of us being men of high spirit, that similar
differences would arise in the future. It was a disquieting
thought that in the heat of an argument about, say,
soft-bosomed shirts for evening wear he might forget the
decencies of debate and elect to apply the closure by

hauling off and socking me on the frontal bone with
something solid. One could but trust that the feudal
spirit would serve to keep the impulse in check.

I was still trying to adjust the faculties to the idea
that I had been nursing in my bosom all these years
something that would be gratefully accepted as a muscle
guy by any gang on the lookout for new blood, when
Gussie appeared, minus the shrubbery. He had changed
the check suit for a dinner jacket, and with a start I
realized that I ought to be dressing, too. I had forgotten
that Corky had said that a big coffee-and-sandwiches
binge was scheduled to take place in the drawing-room
at the conclusion of the concert, which must by now be
nearing the 'God Save The King' stage.

There seemed to be something on Gussie's mind. His
manner was nervous. As I hurriedly socked, shirted and
evening shoe-ed myself, he wandered about the room,
fiddling with the *objets d'art* on the mantelpiece, and as
I slid into the form-fitting trousers there came to my
ears the familiar sound of a hollow groan – whether
hollower than those recently uttered by self and
Catsmeat I couldn't say, but definitely hollow. He had
been staring for some moments at a picture on the wall
of a girl in a poke bonnet cooing to a pigeon with a
fellow in a cocked hat and tight trousers watching her
from the background, such as you will always find in
great profusion in places like Deverill Hall, and he now
turned and spoke.

'Bertie, do you know what it is to have the scales fall
from your eyes?'

'Why, yes. Scales have frequently fallen from my
eyes.'

'They have fallen from mine,' said Gussie. 'And I'll
tell you the exact moment when it happened. It was
when I was up in that tree gazing down at Constable
Dobbs and hearing him describe the situation as a fair
cop. That was when the scales fell from my eyes.'

I ventured to interrupt.

'Half a second,' I said. 'Just to keep the record straight, what are you talking about?'

'I'm telling you. The scales fell from my eyes. Something happened to me. In a flash, with no warning, love died.'

'Whose love?'

'Mine, you ass. For Corky. I felt that a girl who could subject a man to such an ordeal was not the wife for me. Mind you, I still admire her enormously, and I think she would make an excellent helpmeet for somebody of the Ernest Hemingway type who likes living dangerously, but after what has occurred tonight, I am quite clear in my mind that what I require as a life partner is someone slightly less impulsive. If you could have seen Constable Dobbs's eyes glittering in the moonlight!' he said, and broke off with a strong shudder.

A silence ensued, for my ecstasy at this sensational news item was so profound that for an instant I was unable to utter. Then I said 'Whoopee!' and in doing so may possibly have raised my voice a little, for he leaped somewhat and said he wished I wouldn't suddenly yell 'Whoopee!' like that, because I had made him bite his tongue.

'I'm sorry,' I said, 'but I stick to it. I said "Whoopee!" and I meant "Whoopee!" "Whoopee!" with the possible exception of "Hallelujah!" is the only word that meets the case, and if I yelled it, it was merely because I was deeply stirred. I don't mind telling you now, Gussie, that I have viewed your passion for young Corky with concern, pursing the lips and asking myself dubiously if you were on the right lines. Corky is fine and, as you say, admirably fitted to be the bride of the sort of man who won't object to her landing him on the whim of the moment in a cell in one of our popular prisons, but the girl for you is obviously Madeline Bassett. Now you can go back to her and live happily ever after. It will be a

genuine pleasure to me to weigh in with the silver
egg-boiler or whatever you may suggest as a wedding
gift, and during the ceremony you can rely on me to be
in a ringside pew, singing "Now the labourer's task is
o'er" like nobody's business.'

I paused at this point, for I noticed that he was
writhing rather freely. I asked him why he writhed, and
he said, Well, wouldn't anybody writhe who had got
himself into the jam he had, and he wished I wouldn't
stand there talking rot about going back to Madeline.

'How can I go back to Madeline, dearly as I would like
to, after writing that letter telling her it was all off?'

I saw that the time had come to slip him the good news.

'Gussie,' I said, 'all is well. No need for concern.
Others have worked while you slept.'

And without further preamble I ran through the
Wimbledon continuity.

At the outset he listened dumbly, his eyes bulging,
his lips moving like those of a salmon in the spawning
season.

Then, as the gist penetrated, his face lit up, his
horn-rimmed spectacles flashed fire and he clasped my
hand, saying rather handsomely that while as a general
rule he yielded to none in considering me the world's
premier half-wit, he was bound to own that on this
occasion I had displayed courage, resource, enterprise
and an almost human intelligence.

'You've saved my life, Bertie!'

'Quite all right, old man.'

'But for you –'

'Don't mention it. Just the Wooster service.'

'I'll go and telephone her.'

'A sound move.'

He mused for a moment.

'No, I won't, by Jove. I'll pop right off and see her. I'll
get my car and drive to Wimbledon.'

'She'll be in bed.'

'Well, I'll sleep in London and go out there first thing in the morning.'

'You'll find her up and about shortly after eight. Don't forget your sprained wrist.'

'By Jove, no. I'm glad you reminded me. What sort of a child was it you told her I had saved?'

'Small, blue-eyed, golden-haired and lisping.'

'Small, blue-eyed, golden-haired and lisping. Right.'

He clasped my hand once more and bounded off, pausing at the door to tell me to tell Jeeves to send on his luggage, and I, having completed the toilet, sank into a chair to enjoy a quick cigarette before leaving for the drawing-room.

I suppose in this moment of *bien être*, with the heart singing within me and the good old blood coursing through my veins, as I believe the expression is, I ought to have been saying to myself, 'Go easy on the rejoicing, cocky. Don't forget that the tangled love-lives of Catsmeat, Esmond Haddock, Gertrude Winkworth, Constable Dobbs and Queenie the parlourmaid remain still unstraightened out', but you know how it is. There come times in a man's life when he rather tends to think only of self, and I must confess that the anguish of the above tortured souls was almost completely thrust into the background of my consciousness by the reflection that Fate after a rocky start had at last done the square thing by Bertram Wooster.

My mental attitude, in short, was about that of an African explorer who by prompt shinning up a tree has just contrived to elude a quick-tempered crocodile and gathers from a series of shrieks below that his faithful native bearer had not been so fortunate. I mean to say he mourns, no doubt, as he listens to the doings, but though his heart may bleed, he cannot help his primary emotion being one of sober relief that, however sticky life may have become for native bearers, he, personally, is sitting on top of the world.

I was crushing out the cigarette and preparing to leave, feeling just ripe for a cheery sandwich and an invigorating cup of coffee, when there was a flash of pink in the doorway, and Esmond Haddock came in.

25

In dishing up this narrative for family consumption, it has been my constant aim throughout to get the right word in the right place and to avoid fobbing the customers off with something weak and inexpressive when they have a right to expect the telling phrase. It means a bit of extra work, but one has one's code.

We will therefore expunge that 'came' at the conclusion of the previous spasm and substitute for it 'curvetted'. There was a flash of pink, and Esmond Haddock curvetted in. I don't know if you have ever seen a fellow curvet, but war-horses used to do it rather freely in the old days, and Esmond Haddock was doing it now. His booted feet spurned the carpet in a sort of rhythmic dance something on the lines of that of the recent Poppy Kegley-Bassington, and it scarcely needed the ringing hunting cries which he uttered to tell me that here stood a bird who was about as full of beans and buck as a bird could be.

I Hallo-Esmonded and invited him to take a seat, and he stared at me in an incredulous sort of way.

'You don't seriously think that on this night of nights I can *sit down*?' he said. 'I don't suppose I shall sit down again for months and months and months. It's only by the exercise of the greatest will-power that I'm keeping myself from floating up to the ceiling. Yoicks!' he proceeded, changing the subject. 'Hard for'ard! Tally ho! Loo-loo-loo-loo-loo-loo!'

It had become pretty plain by now that Jeeves and I, while budgeting for a certain uplift of the spirit as the result of the success on the concert platform, had

underestimated the heady results of a popular triumph.
Watching this Haddock as he curvetted and listening to
his animal cries, I felt that it was lucky for him that my
old buddy Sir Roderick Glossop did not happen to be
among those present. That zealous loony doctor would
long ere this have been on the telephone summoning
horny-handed assistants to rally round with the straight
waistcoat and dust off the padded cell.

'Well, be that as it may,' I said, after he had loo-loo-
looed for perhaps another minute and a quarter, 'I should
like, before going any further, to express my gratitude to
you for your gallant conduct in taking on those poems of
mine. Was everything all right?'

'Terrific.'

'No mob violence?'

'Not a scrap. They ate 'em.'

'That's good. One felt that you were so solidly
established with the many-headed that you would be in
no real danger. Still, you were taking a chance, and
thank Heaven that all has ended well. I don't wonder
you're bucked,' I said, interrupting him in a fresh
outbreak of loo-loo-looing. 'Anyone would be after
making the sort of hit you did. You certainly wowed
them.'

He paused in his curvetting to give me another
incredulous look.

'My good Gussie,' he said, 'you don't think I'm
floating about like this just because my song got over?'

'Aren't you?'

'Certainly not.'

'Then why do you float?'

'Because of Corky, of course. Good Lord!' he said,
smiting his brow and seeming a moment later to wish
he hadn't, for he had caught it a rather juicy wallop.
'Good Lord! I haven't told you, have I? And that'll give
you a rough idea of the sort of doodah I'm in, because it
was simply in order to tell you that I came here. You

aren't abreast, Gussie. You haven't heard the big news.
The most amazing front-page stuff has been happening,
and you know nothing about it. Let me tell you the
whole story.'

'Do,' I said, adding that I was agog.

He simmered down a bit, not sufficiently to enable
him to take a seat but enough to make him cheese the
curvetting for a while.

'I wonder, Gussie, if you remember a conversation we
had the first night you were here? To refresh your
memory, it was the last time we were allowed to get at
the port; the occasion when you touched up that lyric of
my Aunt Charlotte's in such a masterly way,
strengthening the weak spots and making it box-office. If
you recall?'

I said I recalled.

'In the course of that conversation I told you that
Corky had given me the brusheroo. If you recollect?'

I said I recollected.

'Well, tonight – You know, Gussie,' he said, breaking
off, 'it's the most extraordinary sensation, swaying a
vast audience . . .'

'Would you call it a vast audience?'

The question seemed to ruffle him.

'Well, the two bob, shilling and eightpenny seats were
all sold out and there must have been fully fifty
threepenny standees at the back,' he said, a bit stiffly.
'Still, call it a fairly vast audience, if you prefer. It makes
no difference to the argument. It's the most extraordinary sensation, swaying a fairly vast audience. It
does something to you. It fills you with a sense of power.
It makes you feel that you're a pretty hot number and
that you aren't going to stand any nonsense from
anyone. And under the head of nonsense you find
yourself classing girls giving you the brusheroo. I
mention this so that you will be able to understand
what follows.'

I smiled one of my subtle smiles.

'I know what follows. You got hold of Corky and took a strong line.'

'Why, yes,' he said, seeming a little flattened. 'As a matter of fact that was what I was leading up to. How did you guess?'

I smiled another subtle one.

'I foresaw what would happen if you slew that fairly vast audience. I knew you were one of those birds on whom popular acclamation has sensational effects. Yours has been a repressed life, and you have, no doubt, a marked inferiority complex. The cheers of the multitude frequently act like a powerful drug upon bimbos with inferiority complexes.'

I had rather expected this to impress him, and it did. His lower jaw fell a notch, and he gazed at me in a reverent sort of way.

'You're a deep thinker, Gussie.'

'I always have been. From a child.'

'One wouldn't suspect it, just to look at you.'

'It doesn't show on the surface. Yes,' I said, getting back to the *res*, 'matters have taken precisely the course which I anticipated. With the cheers of the multitude ringing in your ears, you came off that platform a changed man, full of yeast and breathing flame through the nostrils. You found Corky. You backed her into a corner. You pulled a dominant male on her and fixed everything up. Right?'

'Yes, that was just what happened. Amazing how you got it all taped out.'

'Oh, well, one studies the psychology of the individual, you know.'

'Only I didn't back her into a corner. She was in her car, just driving off somewhere, and I shoved my head in at the window.'

'And –?'

'Oh, we kidded back and forth,' he said a little

awkwardly, as if reluctant to reveal what had passed at that sacred scene. 'I told her she was the lodestar of my life and all that sort of thing, adding that I intended to have no more rot about her not marrying me, and after a bit of pressing she came clean and admitted that I was the tree on which the fruit of her life hung.'

Those who know Bertram Wooster best are aware that he is not an indiscriminate back-slapper. He picks and chooses. But there was no question in my mind that here before me stood a back which it would be churlish not to slap. So I slapped it.

'Nice work,' I said. 'Then everything's all right?'

'Yes,' he assented. 'Everything's fine . . . except for one small detail.'

'What is that in round numbers?'

'Well, it's a thing I don't know if you will quite understand. To make it clear I shall have to go back to that time when we were engaged before. She severed relations then because she considered that I was a bit too much under the domination of my aunts, and she didn't like it.'

Well, of course, I knew this, having had it from her personal lips, but I wore the mask and weighed in with a surprised 'Really?'

'Yes. And unfortunately she hasn't changed her mind. Nothing doing in the orange-blossom and wedding-cake line, she says, until I have defied my aunts.'

'Well, go ahead. Defy them.'

My words seemed to displease him. With a certain show of annoyance he picked up a statuette of a shepherdess on the mantelpiece and hurled it into the fireplace, reducing it to hash and removing it from the active list.

'It's all very well to say that. It's a thing that presents all sorts of technical difficulties. You can't just walk up to an aunt and say "I defy you". You need a cue of some sort. I'm dashed if I know how to set about it.'

I mused.

'I'll tell you what,' I said. 'It seems to me that here is a matter on which you would do well to seek advice from Jeeves.'

'Jeeves?'

'My man.'

'I thought your man's name was Meadowes.'

'A slip of the tongue,' I said hastily. 'I meant to say Wooster's man. He is a bird of extraordinary sagacity and never fails to deliver the goods.'

He frowned a bit.

'Doesn't one rather want to keep visiting valets out of this?'

'No, one does not want to keep visiting valets out of this,' I said firmly. 'Not when they're Jeeves. If you didn't live all the year round in this rural morgue, you'd know that Jeeves isn't so much a valet as a Mayfair consultant. The highest in the land bring their problems to him. I shouldn't wonder if they didn't give him jewelled snuff-boxes.'

'And you think he would have something to suggest?'

'He always has something to suggest.'

'In that case,' said Esmond Haddock, brightening, 'I'll go and find him.'

With a brief 'Loo-loo-loo' he pushed off, clicking his spurs, and I settled down to another cigarette and a pleasant reverie.

Really, I told myself, things were beginning to straighten out. Deverill Hall still housed, no doubt, its quota of tortured souls, but the figures showed a distinct downward trend. I was all right. Gussie was all right. It was only on the Catsmeat front that the outlook was still unsettled and the blue bird a bit slow in picking up its cues.

I pondered on Catsmeat's affairs for a while, then turned to the more agreeable theme of my own, and I was still doing so, feeling more braced every moment, when the door opened.

There was no flash of pink this time, because it wasn't Esmond home from the hunt. It was Jeeves.

'I have extricated Mr Fink-Nottle from his beard, sir,' he said, looking modestly pleased with himself, like a man who has fought the good fight, and I said Yes, Gussie had been paying me a neighbourly call and I had noticed the absence of the fungoid growth.

'He told me to tell you to pack his things and send them on. He's gone back to London.'

'Yes, sir. I saw Mr Fink-Nottle and received his instructions in person.'

'Did he tell you why he was going to London?'

'No, sir.'

I hesitated. I yearned to share the good news with him, but I was asking myself if it wouldn't involve bandying a woman's name. And, as I have explained earlier, Jeeves and I do not bandy women's names.

I put out a feeler.

'You've been seeing a good deal of Gussie recently, Jeeves?'

'Yes, sir.'

'Constantly together, swapping ideas, what?'

'Yes, sir.'

'I wonder if by any chance . . . in some moment of expansiveness, if that's the word . . . he ever happened to let fall anything that gave you the impression that his heart, instead of sticking like glue to Wimbledon, had skidded a bit in another direction?'

'Yes, sir. Mr Fink-Nottle was good enough to confide in me regarding the emotions which Miss Pirbright had aroused in his bosom. He spoke freely on the subject.'

'Good. Then I can speak freely, too. All that's off.'

'Indeed, sir?'

'Yes. He came down from that tree feeling that Corky was not the dream mate he had supposed her to be. The

scales fell from his eyes. He still admires her many fine
qualities and considers that she would make a good wife
for Sinclair Lewis, but –'

'Precisely, sir. I must confess that I had rather
anticipated some such contingency. Mr Fink-Nottle is of
the quiet, domestic type that enjoys a calm, regular life,
and Miss Pirbright is perhaps somewhat –'

'More than somewhat. Considerably more. He sees
that now. He realizes that association with young
Corky, though having much to be said for it, must
inevitably lead in the end to a five-year stretch in
Wormwood Scrubs or somewhere, and his object in
going to London to-night is to get a good flying start for
an early morning trip to Wimbledon Common
to-morrow. He is very anxious to see Miss Bassett as
soon as possible. No doubt they will breakfast together,
and having downed a couple of rashers and a pot of
coffee, saunter side by side through the sunlit grounds.'

'Most gratifying, sir.'

'Most. And I'll tell you something else that's
gratifying. Esmond Haddock and Corky are engaged.'

'Indeed, sir?'

'Provisionally, perhaps I ought to say.'

And I sketched out for him the set-up at the moment
of going to press.

'I advised him to consult you,' I said, 'and he went off
to find you. You see the posish, Jeeves? As he rightly
says, however much you may want to defy a bunch of
aunts, you can't get started unless they give you
something to defy them about. What we want is some
situation where they're saying "Go", like the chap in the
Bible, and instead of going he cometh. If you see what I
mean?'

'I interpret your meaning exactly, sir, and I will devote
my best thought to the problem. Meanwhile, I fear I
must be leaving you, sir. I promised to help my Uncle
Charlie serve the refreshments in the drawing-room.'

'Scarcely your job, Jeeves?'

'No, sir. But one is glad to stretch a point to oblige a relative.'

'Blood is thicker than water, you mean?'

'Precisely, sir.'

He withdrew, and about a minute later Esmond blew in again, looking baffled, like a Master of Hounds who has failed to locate the fox.

'I can't find the blighter,' he said.

'He has just this moment left. He's gone to the drawing-room to help push around the sandwiches.'

'And that's where we ought to be, my lad,' said Esmond. 'We're a bit late.'

He was right. Silversmith, whom we encountered in the hall, informed us that he had just shown out the last batch of alien guests, the Kegley-Bassington gang, and that apart from members of the family only the vicar, Miss Pirbright and what he called 'the young gentleman', a very loose way of describing my cousin Thomas, remained on the burning deck. Esmond exhibited pleasure at the news, saying that now we should have a bit of elbow room.

'Smooth work, missing those stiffs, Gussie. What England needs is fewer and better Kegley-Bassingtons. You agree with me, Silversmith?'

'I fear I have not formulated an opinion on the subject, sir.'

'Silversmith,' said Esmond, 'you're a pompous old ass,' and, incredible as it may seem, he poised a finger and with a cheery 'Yoicks!' drove it into the other's well-covered ribs.

And it was as the stricken butler reeled back and tottered off with an incredulous stare of horror in his gooseberry eyes, no doubt to restore himself with a quick one in the pantry, that Dame Daphne came out of the drawing-room.

'Esmond!' she said in the voice which in days gone by

had reduced so many Janes and Myrtles and Gladyses
to tearful pulp in the old study. 'Where have you
been?'

It was a situation which in the pre-Hallo-hallo epoch
would have had Esmond Haddock tying himself in
apologetic knots and perspiring at every pore: and no
better evidence of the changed conditions prevailing in
the soul of King's Deverill's Bing Crosby could have
been afforded than by the fact that his brow remained
unmoistened and he met her eye with a pleasant
smile.

'Oh, hallo, Aunt Daphne,' he said. 'Where are you off
to?'

'I am going to bed. I have a headache. Why are you so
late, Esmond?'

'Well, if you ask me,' said Esmond cheerily, 'I'd say it
was because I didn't arrive sooner.'

'Colonel and Mrs Kegley-Bassington were most
surprised. They could not understand why you were not
here.'

Esmond uttered a ringing laugh.

'Then they must be the most priceless fatheads,' he
said. 'You'd think a child would have realized that
the solution was that I was somewhere else. Come
along, Gussie. Loo-loo-loo-loo-loo,' he added in a
dispassionate sort of way, and led me into the drawing-
room.

Even though the drawing-room had been cleansed of
Kegley-Bassingtons, it still gave the impression of being
fairly well filled up. Four aunts, Corky, young Thos,
Gertrude Winkworth and the Rev. Sidney Pirbright
might not be absolute capacity, but it was not at all
what you would call a poor house. Add Esmond and self
and Jeeves and Queenie moving to and fro with the
refreshments, and you had quite a quorum.

I had taken a couple of sandwiches (sardine) off Jeeves
and was lolling back in my chair, feeling how jolly this

all was, when Silversmith appeared in the doorway, still pale after his recent ordeal.

He stood to attention and inflated his chest.

'Constable Dobbs,' he announced.

26

The reactions of a gaggle of coffee and sandwich
chewers in the drawing-room of an aristocratic home
who, just as they are getting down to it, observe the
local flatty muscling in through the door, vary according
to what Jeeves calls the psychology of the individual.
Thus, while Esmond Haddock welcomed the
newcomer with a genial 'Loo-loo-loo', the aunts raised
their eyebrows with a good deal of To-what-are-we-
indebted-for-the-honour-of-this-visitness and the vicar
drew himself up austerely, suggesting in his manner
that one crack out of the zealous officer about Jonah
and the Whale and he would know what to do about it.
Gertrude Winkworth, who had been listless, continued
listless, Silversmith preserved the detached air which
butlers wear on all occasions, and the parlourmaid
Queenie turned pale and uttered a stifled 'Oo-er!'
giving the impression of a woman on the point of
wailing for her demon lover. I, personally, put in a
bit of quick gulping. The mood of *bien être* left
me, and I was conscious of a coolness about the feet.
When the run of events has precipitated, as Jeeves
would say, a situation of such delicacy as existed at
Deverill Hall, it jars you to find the place filling up with
rozzers.

It was to Esmond Haddock that the constable directed
his opening remark.

'I've come on an unpleasant errand, sir,' he said, and
the chill in the Wooster feet became accentuated. 'But
before I go into that there,' he proceeded, now addressing
himself to the Rev. Sidney Pirbright, 'there's this here. I

wonder if I might have a word with you, sir, on a spiritual subject?'

I saw the sainted Sidney stiffen, and knew that he was saying to himself 'Here it comes'.

'It's with ref to my having seen the light, sir.'

Somebody gave a choking gasp, like a Pekingese that has taken on a chump chop too large for its frail strength, and looking around I saw that it was Queenie. She was staring at Constable Dobbs wide-eyed and parted-lipped.

This choking gasp might have attracted more attention had it not dead-heated with another, equally choking, which proceeded from the thorax of the Rev. Sidney. He, too, was staring wide-eyed. He looked like a vicar who has just seen the outsider on whom he has placed his surplice nose its way through the throng of runners and flash in the lead past the judge's box.

'Dobbs! What did you say? You have seen the light?'

I could have told the officer he was a chump to nod so soon after taking that juicy one on the napper from the serviceable rubber instrument, but he did so, and the next thing he said was 'Ouch!' But the English policeman is made of splendid stuff, and after behaving for a moment like a man who has just swallowed one of Jeeves's morning specials he resumed his normal air, which was that of a stuffed gorilla.

'R,' he said. 'And I'll tell you how it come about, sir. On the evening of the twenty-third inst . . . well, to-night, as a matter of fact . . . I was proceeding about my duties, chasing a marauder up a tree, when I was unexpectedly struck by a thunderbolt.'

That, as might have been expected, went big. The vicar said 'A thunderbolt', two of the aunts said 'A *thunderbolt*?' and Esmond Haddock said 'Yoicks'.

'Yes, sir,' proceeded the officer, 'a thunderbolt. Caught me on the back of the head, it did, and hasn't half raised a lump.'

The vicar said 'Most extraordinary', the other two aunts said 'Tch, tch' and Esmond said 'Tally ho'.

'Well, sir, I'm no fool,' continued Ernest Dobbs. 'I can take a hint. "Dobbs," I said to myself, "no use kidding yourself about what *this* is, Dobbs. It's a warning from above, Dobbs," I said to myself. "If it's got as far as thunderbolts, Dobbs," I said to myself, "it's time you made a drawstic revision of your spiritual outlook, Dobbs," I said to myself. So, if you follow my meaning, sir, I've seen the light, and what I wanted to ask you, sir, was Do I have to join the Infants' Bible Class or can I start singing in the choir right away?'

I mentioned earlier in this narrative that I had never actually seen a shepherd welcoming a strayed lamb back into the fold, but watching Dame Daphne Winkworth on the occasion to which I allude I had picked up a pointer or two about the technique, so was able to recognize that this was what was going to happen now. You could see from his glowing eyes and benevolent smile, not to mention the hand raised as if about to bestow a blessing, that this totally unexpected reversal of form on the part of the local backslider had taken the Rev. Sidney's mind right off the church organ. I think that in about another couple of ticks he would have come across with something pretty impressive in the way of simple, manly words, but, as it so happened, he hadn't time to get set. Even as his lips parted, there was a noise like a rising pheasant from the outskirts and some solid object left the ranks and hurled itself on Constable Dobbs's chest.

Closer inspection showed this to be Queenie. She was clinging to the representative of the Law like a poultice, and from the fact that she was saying 'Oh, Ernie!' and bedewing his uniform with happy tears I deduced, being pretty shrewd, that what she was trying to convey was that all was forgiven and forgotten and that she was expecting the prompt return of the ring, the letters and the china ornament with 'A Present from Blackpool' on it. And as it did not escape my notice that he, on his side, was covering her upturned face with burning kisses and saying 'Oh, Queenie!' I gathered that Tortured Souls Preferred had taken another upward trend and that one could chalk up on the slate two more sundered hearts reunited in the springtime.

These tender scenes affect different people in different ways. I myself, realizing Catsmeat's honourable obligations to this girl might now be considered cancelled, was definitely bucked by the spectacle. But the emotion aroused in Silversmith was plainly a shuddering horror that such goings-on should be going on in the drawing-room of Deverill Hall. Pulling a quick Stern Father, he waddled up to the happy pair and with a powerful jerk of the wrist detached his child and led her from the room.

Constable Dobbs, though still dazed, recovered himself sufficiently to apologize for his display of naked emotion, and the Rev. Sidney said he quite, quite understood.

'Come and see me to-morrow, Dobbs,' he said benevolently, 'and we will have a long talk.'

'Very good, sir.'

'And now,' said the Rev. Sidney, 'I think I will be wending my way homeward. Will you accompany me, Cora?'

Corky said she thought she would stick on for a bit, and Thos, keenly alive to the fact that there were still stacks of sandwiches on tap, also declined to shift, so he beamed his way out of the room by himself, and it was only after the door had closed that I realized that Constable Dobbs was still standing there and remembered that his opening words had been that he had come upon an unpleasant errand. Once more the temperature of the feet fell, and I eyed him askance.

He was not long in getting down to the agenda. These flatties are trained to snap into it.

'Sir,' he said, addressing Esmond.

Esmond interrupted to ask him if he would like a sardine sandwich, and he said 'No, sir, I thank you', and when Esmond said that he did not insist on sardine but would be equally gratified if the other would wade into the ham, tongue, cucumber or potted meat, explained that he would prefer to take no nourishment of any kind, because of this unpleasant errand he had come on. Apparently, when policemen come on unpleasant errands, they lay off the vitamins.

'I'm looking for Mr Wooster, sir,' he said.

In the ecstasy of this recent reunion with the woman he loved I imagine that Esmond had temporarily forgotten how much he disliked Gussie, but at these words it was plain that all the old distaste for one who had made passes at the adored object had come flooding back, for his eyes gleamed, his face darkened and he did a spot of brow-knitting. The sweet singer of King's Deverill had vanished, leaving in his place the stern, remorseless Justice of the Peace.

'Wooster, eh?' he said, and I saw him lick his lips. 'You wish to see him officially?'

'Yes, sir.'

'What has he been doing?'

'Effecting burglarious entries, sir.'

'Has he, by Jove!'

'Yes, sir. On the twenty . . . This evening, sir a burglarious entry was effected by the accused into my police station and certain property of the Crown abstracted – to wit, one dog, what was in custody for having effected two bites. I copped him in the very act, sir,' said Constable Dobbs, simplifying his narrative style. 'He was the marauder I was chasing up trees at the moment when I was inadvertently struck by that thunderbolt.'

Esmond continued to knit his brow. It was evident that he took a serious view of the matter. And when Justices of the Peace take serious views of matters, you want to get out from under.

'You actually found him abstracting this to wit one dog?' he said keenly, looking like Judge Jeffreys about to do his stuff.

'Yes, sir. I come into my police station and he was in the act of unloosing it and encouraging it to buzz off. It proceeded to buzz off, and I proceeded to say "Ho!" whereupon, becoming cognizant of my presence, he also proceeded to buzz off, with me after him lickerty-split. I proceeded to pursue him up a tree and was about to effect an arrest, when along come this here thunderbolt, stunning me and depriving me of my senses. When I come to, the accused had departed.'

'And what makes you think it was Wooster?'

'He was wearing a green beard, sir, and a check suit. This rendered him conspicuous.'

'I see. He had not changed after his performance.'

'No, sir.'

Esmond licked his lips again.

'Then the first thing to do,' he said, 'is to find Wooster. Has anybody seen him?'

'Yes, sir. Mr Wooster has gone to London in his car.'

It was Jeeves who spoke, and Esmond gave him a rather surprised look.

'Who are you?' he asked.

'My name is Jeeves, sir. I am Mr Wooster's personal attendant.'

Esmond eyed him with interest.

'Oh, you're Jeeves? I'd like a word with you, Jeeves, some time.'

'Very good, sir.'

'Not now. Later on. So Wooster has gone to London, has he?'

'Yes, sir.'

241

'Fleeing from justice, eh?'

'No, sir. Might I make a remark, sir?'

'Carry on, Jeeves.'

'Thank you, sir. I merely wished to say that the officer is mistaken in supposing that the miscreant responsible for the outrage was Mr Wooster. I was continuously in Mr Wooster's society from the time he left the concert hall. I accompanied him to his room, and we remained together until he took his departure for London. I was assisting him to remove his beard, sir.'

'You mean you give him an alibi?'

'A complete alibi, sir.'

'Oh?' said Esmond, looking baffled, like the villain in a melodrama. One could sense that the realization that he was not to be able to dish out a sharp sentence on Gussie had cut him to the quick.

'Ho!' said Constable Dobbs, not, probably, with an idea of contributing anything vital to the debate but just because policemen never lose a chance of saying 'Ho!' Then suddenly a strange light came into his face and he said 'Ho!' again, this time packing a lot of meaning into the word.

'Ho!' he said. 'Then if it wasn't the accused Wooster, it must have been the other chap. That fellow Meadowes, who was doing Mike. He was wearing a green beard, too.'

'Ah!' said Esmond.

'Ha!' said the aunts.

'Oh!' said Gertrude Winkworth, starting visibly.

'Hoy!' said Corky, also starting visibly.

I must say I felt like saying 'Hoy!' too. It astonished me that Jeeves had not spotted what must inevitably ensue if he gave Gussie that alibi. Just throwing Catsmeat to the wolves, I mean to say. It was not like him to overlook a snag like that.

I caught Corky's eye. It was the eye of a girl seeing a loved brother going down for the third time in the soup.

And then my gaze, swivelling round, picked up Gertrude Winkworth.

Gertrude Winkworth was plainly wrestling with some strong emotion. Her face was drawn, her bosom heaved. Her fragile handkerchief, torn by a sudden movement of the fingers, came apart in her hands.

Esmond was being very Justice-of-the-Peace-y.

'Bring Meadowes here,' he said curtly.

'Very good, sir,' said Jeeves, and pushed off.

When he had gone, the aunts started to question Constable Dobbs, demanding more details, and when it had been brought home to them that the dog in question was none other than the one which had barged into the drawing-room on the night of my arrival and chased Aunt Charlotte to and fro, they were solidly in favour of Esmond sentencing this Meadowes to the worst the tariff would allow, Aunt Charlotte being particularly vehement.

They were still urging Esmond to display no weakness, when Jeeves returned, ushering in Catsmeat. Esmond gave him the bleak eye.

'Meadowes?'

'Yes, sir. You wished to speak to me?'

'I not only wished to speak to you,' said Esmond nastily, 'I wished to give you thirty days without the option.'

I heard Constable Dobbs snort briefly, and recognized his snort as a snort of ecstasy. The impression I received was that a weaker man, not trained in the iron discipline of the Force, would have said 'Whoopee!' For, just as Esmond Haddock had got it in for Gussie for endeavouring to move in on Corky, so had Constable Dobbs got it in for Catsmeat for endeavouring to move in on the parlourmaid, Queenie. Both were strong men, who believed in treating rivals rough.

Catsmeat seemed puzzled.

'I beg your pardon, sir?'

'You heard,' said Esmond. He intensified the
bleakness of his eye. 'Let me ask you a few simple
questions. You sustained the role of Pat in the
Pat-and-Mike entertainment this evening?'

'Yes, sir.'

'You wore a green beard?'

'Yes, sir.'

'And a check suit?'

'Yes, sir.'

'Then you're for it,' said Esmond crisply, and the four
aunts said So they should think, indeed, Aunt Charlotte
going on to ask Esmond rather pathetically if thirty days
was really all that the book of rules permitted. She had
been reading a story about life in the United States, she
said, and there, it seemed, even comparatively trivial
offences rated ninety.

She was going on to say that the whole trend of
modern life in England was towards a planned
Americanization and that she, for one, approved of this,
feeling that we had much to learn from our cousins
across the sea, when there was a brusque repetition of
that rising pheasant effect which had preceded the
Hobbs-Queenie one-act sketch and the eye noted that
Gertrude Winkworth had risen from her seat and
precipitated herself into Catsmeat's arms. No doubt she
had picked up a hint or two from watching Queenie's
work for in its broad lines her performance was
modelled on that of the recent parlourmaid. The main
distinction was that whereas Silversmith's ewe lamb
had said 'Oh, Ernie!' she was saying 'Oh, Claude!'

Esmond Haddock stared.

'Hallo!' he said, adding another three hallos from force
of habit.

You might have thought that a fellow in Catsmeat's
position, faced with the prospect of going up the river for
a calendar month, would have been too perturbed to
have time for hugging girls, and it would scarcely have

surprised me if he had extricated himself from Gertrude
Winkworth's embrace with a 'Yes, yes, quite, but some
other time, what?' Not so, however. To clasp her to his
bosom was with him the work of a moment, and you
could see that he was regarding this as the important
part of the evening's proceedings, giving him little scope
for attending to Justices of the Peace.

'Oh, Gertrude!' he said. 'Be with you in a minute,' he
added to Esmond. 'Oh, Gertrude!' he proceeded, once
more addressing his remarks to the lovely burden. And,
precisely as Constable Dobbs had done in a similar
situation, he covered her upturned face with burning
kisses.

'Eeek!' said the aunts, speaking as one aunt.

I didn't blame them for being fogged and unable to
follow the run of the scenario. It is unusual for a niece to
behave towards a visiting valet as their niece Gertrude
was behaving as of even date, and if they squeaked like
mice, I maintain they had every right to do so. Theirs had
been a sheltered life, and this was all new stuff to them.

Esmond, too, seemed a bit not abreast.

'What's all this?' he said, a remark which would have
proceeded more fittingly from the lips of Constable
Dobbs. In fact, I saw the officer shoot a sharp look at
him, as if stung by this infringement of copyright.

Corky came forward and slipped her arm through his.
It was plain that she felt the time had come for a frank,
manly explanation.

'It's my brother Catsmeat, Esmond.'

'What is?'

'This is.'

'What, that?'

'Yes. He came here as a valet for love of Gertrude, and
a darned good third-reel situation, if you ask me.'

Esmond wrinkled his brow. He looked rather as he
had done when discussing that story of mine with me on
the night of my arrival.

'Let's go into this,' he said. 'Let's thresh it out. This character is not Meadowes?'

'No.'

'He's not a valet?'

'No.'

'But he *is* your brother Catsmeat?'

'Yes.'

Esmond's face cleared.

'Now I've got it,' he said. 'Now it's all straight. How are you, Catsmeat?'

'I'm fine,' said Catsmeat.

'That's good,' said Esmond heartily. 'That's splendid.'

He paused, and started. I suppose the baying that arose at this point from the pack of aunts, together with the fact that he had just tripped over his spurs, had given him the momentary illusion that he was in the hunting field, for a 'Yoicks' trembled on his lips and he raised an arm as if about to give his horse one on the spot where it would do most good.

The aunts were a bit on the incoherent side, but gradually what you might call a message emerged from their utterances. They were trying to impress on Esmond that the fact that the accused was Corky's brother Catsmeat merely deepened the blackness of his crime and that he was to carry on and administer the sentence as planned.

Their observations would have gone stronger with Esmond if he had been listening to them. But he wasn't. His attention was riveted on Catsmeat and Gertrude, who had seized the opportunity afforded by the lull in the proceedings to exchange a series of burning kisses.

'Are you and Gertrude going to get married?' he asked.

'Yes,' said Catsmeat.

'Yes,' said Gertrude.

'No,' said the aunts.

'Please,' said Esmond, raising a hand. 'What's the

procedure?' he asked, once more addressing himself to Catsmeat.

Catsmeat said he thought the best scheme would be for them to nip up to London right away and put the thing through on the morrow. He had the licence all ready and waiting, he explained, and he saw no difficulties ahead that a good registry office couldn't solve. Esmond said he agreed with him, and suggested that they should borrow his car, and Catsmeat said that was awfully good of him, and Esmond said Not at all. 'Please,' he added to the aunts, who were now shrieking like Banshees.

It was at this point that Constable Dobbs thrust himself forward.

'Hoy,' said Constable Dobbs.

Esmond proved fully equal to the situation.

'I see what you're driving at, Dobbs. You very naturally wish to make a pinch. But consider, Dobbs how slender is the evidence which you can bring forward to support your charge. You say you chased a man in a green beard and a check suit up a tree. But the visibility was very poor, and you admit yourself that you were being struck by thunderbolts all the time, which must have distracted your attention, so it is more than probable that you were mistaken. I put it to you, Dobbs, that when you thought you saw a man in a green beard and a check suit, it may quite easily have been a clean-shaven man in something quiet and blue?'

He paused for a reply, and one could divine that the officer was thinking it over.

The thing that poisons life for a country policeman, the thing that makes him pick at the coverlet and brings him out in rashes, is the ever-present fear that one of these days he may talk out of turn and get in wrong with a Justice of the Peace. He knows what happens when you get in wrong with Justices of the Peace. They lay for you. They bide their time. And sooner or later they catch you bending, and the next thing you know you've drawn a strong rebuke from the Bench. And if there is one experience the young copper wishes to avoid, it is being in the witness-box and having the Bench look coldly at him and say something beginning with 'Then are we to understand, officer . . . ?' and culminating in the legal equivalent of the raspberry or Bronx cheer. And it was evident to him that defiance of Esmond on the present occasion must inevitably lead to that.

'I put it to you, Dobbs,' said Esmond.

Constable Dobbs sighed. There is, I suppose, no spiritual agony so keen as that of the rozzer who has made a cop and seen it turn blue on him. But he bowed to the inev.

'Perhaps you're right, sir.'

'Of course I'm right,' said Esmond heartily. 'I knew you would see it when it was pointed out to you. We don't want any miscarriages of justice, what?'

'No, sir.'

'I should say not. If there's one thing that gives me the pip, it's a miscarriage of justice. Catsmeat, you are dismissed without a stain on your character.'

Catsmeat said that was fine, and Esmond said he thought he would be pleased.

'I suppose you and Gertrude aren't going to hang around, spending a lot of time packing?'

'No, we thought we'd leg it instanter.'

'Exactly what I would suggest.'

'If Gertrude wants clothes,' said Corky, 'she can get them at my apartment.'

'Splendid,' said Esmond. 'Then the quickest way to the garage is along there.'

He indicated the french windows, which, the night being balmy, had been left open. He slapped Catsmeat on the back, and shook Gertrude by the hand, and they trickled out.

Constable Dobbs, watching them recede, heaved another sigh, and Esmond slapped his back, too.

'I know just how you're feeling, Dobbsy,' he said. 'But when you think it over, I'm sure that you'll be glad you haven't been instrumental in throwing a spanner into the happiness of two young hearts in springtime. If I were you, I'd pop off to the kitchen and have a word with Queenie. There must be much that you want to discuss.'

Constable Dobbs's was not a face that lent itself readily to any great display of emotion. It looked as if it had been carved out of some hard kind of wood by a sculptor who had studied at a Correspondence School and had got to about Lesson Three. But at this suggestion it definitely brightened.

'You're right, sir,' he said, and with a brief 'Good night, all' vanished in the direction indicated, his air that of a policeman who is feeling that life, while greyish in spots, is not without its compensations.

'So that's that,' said Esmond.

'That's that,' said Corky. 'I think your aunts are trying to attract your attention, angel.'

All through the preceding scene, though pressure of other matter prevented me mentioning it, the aunts had been extremely vocal. Indeed, it would not be putting it too strongly to say that they had been kicking up the hell of a row. And this row must have penetrated to the upper regions of the house, for at this moment the door suddenly opened, revealing Dame Daphne Winkworth. She wore a pink dressing-gown, and had the appearance of a woman who has been taking aspirins and bathing her temples with eau-de-Cologne.

'Really!' she said. She spoke with a goodish bit of asperity, and one couldn't fairly blame her. When you go up to your bedroom with a headache, you don't want to be dragged down again half an hour later by disturbances from below. 'Will someone be so kind as to tell me what is the reason for this uproar?'

Four simultaneous aunts were so kind. The fact that they all spoke together might have rendered their remarks hard to follow, had not the subject matter been identical. Gertrude, they said, had just eloped with Miss Pirbright's brother, and Esmond had not only expressed his approval of the move but had actually offered the young couple his car.

'There!' they said, as the sound of an engine gathering speed and the cheery toot-toot of a klaxon made themselves heard in the silent night, pointing up their statement.

Dame Daphne blinked as if she had been struck on the mazard with a wet dishcloth. She turned on the young squire menacingly, and one could understand her peevishness. There are few things more sickening for a mother than to learn that her only child has eloped with a man whom she has always regarded as a blot on the species. Not surprising if it spoils her day.

'Esmond! Is this true?'

The voice in which she spoke would have had me clambering up the wall and seeking refuge on the chandelier, had she been addressing me, but Esmond Haddock did not wilt. The man seemed fearless. He was like the central figure in one of those circus posters which show an intrepid bozo in a military uniform facing with death-defying determination twelve murderous, man-eating monarchs of the jungle.

'Quite true,' he replied. 'And I really cannot have any discussion and argument about it. I acted as I deemed best, and the subject is closed. Silence, Aunt Daphne. Less of it, Aunt Emmeline. Quiet, Aunt Charlotte. Desist, Aunt Harriet. Aunty Myrtle, put a sock in it. Really, the way you're going on, one would scarcely suppose that I was the master of the house and the head of the family and that my word was law. I don't know if

you happen to know it, but in Turkey all this
insubordinate stuff, these attempts to dictate to the
master of the house and the head of the family, would
have led long before this to you being strangled with
bowstrings and bunged into the Bosporus. Aunt Daphne,
you have been warned. One more yip out of you, Aunt
Myrtle, and I stop your pocket-money. Now, then,' said
Esmond Haddock, having obtained silence, 'let me give
you the strength of this. The reason I abetted young
Gertrude in her matrimonial plans was that the man she
loves is a good egg. I have this on the authority of his
sister Corky, who speaks extremely well of him. And, by
the way, before I forget, his sister Corky and I are going
to be married ourselves. Correct?'

'In every detail,' said Corky.

She was gazing at him with shining eyes. One got the
feeling that if she had had a table with a photograph on
it, she would have been singing 'My Hero'.

'Come, come,' said Esmond kindly, as the yells of the
personnel died away, 'no need to be upset about it. It
won't affect you dear old souls. You will go on living
here, if you call it living, just as you have always done.
All that'll happen is that you will be short one Haddock.
I propose to accompany my wife to Hollywood. And
when she's through with her contract there, we shall set
up a shack in some rural spot and grow pigs and cows
and things. I think that covers everything, doesn't it?'

Corky said she thought it did.

'Right,' said Esmond. 'Then how about a short stroll
in the moonlight?'

He led her lovingly through the french windows,
kissing her en route and I edged to the door and made
my way upstairs to my room. I could have stayed on and
chatted with the aunts, if I had wanted to, but I didn't
feel in the mood.

27

My first act on reaching the sleeping quarters was to take pencil and paper and sit down and make out a balance sheet. As follows:

Sundered Hearts	Reunited Hearts
(1) Esmond	(1) Esmond
(2) Corky	(2) Corky
(3) Gussie	(3) Gussie
(4) Madeline	(4) Madeline
(5) Officer Dobbs	(5) Officer Dobbs
(6) Queenie	(6) Queenie
(7) Catsmeat	(7) Catsmeat
(8) Gertrude	(8) Gertrude

It came out exactly square. Not a single loose end left over. With a not unmanly sigh, for if there is one thing that is the dish of the decent-minded man, it is seeing misunderstanding between loving hearts cleared up, especially in the springtime, I laid down the writing materials and was preparing to turn in for the night, when Jeeves came shimmering in.

'Oh, hallo, Jeeves,' I said, greeting him cordially. 'I was rather wondering if you would show up. A big night, what?'

'Extremely, sir.'

I showed him the balance sheet.

'No flaws in that, I think?'

'None, sir.'

'Gratifying, what?'

'Most gratifying, sir.'

'And, as always, due to your unremitting efforts.'

'It is very kind of you to say so, sir.'

'Not at all, Jeeves. We chalk up one more of your triumphs on the slate. I will admit that for an instant during the proceedings, when you gave Gussie that alibi, I experienced a momentary doubt as to whether you were on the right lines, feeling that you were but landing Catsmeat in the bouillon. But calmer reflection told me what you were up to. You felt that if Catsmeat stood in peril of receiving an exemplary sentence, Gertrude Winkworth would forget all that had passed and would cluster round him, her gentle heart melted by his distress. Am I right?'

'Quite right, sir. The poet Scott –'

'Pigeon-hole the poet Scott for a moment, or I shall be losing the thread of my remarks.'

'Very good, sir.'

'But I know what you mean. Oh, Woman in our hours of ease, what?'

'Precisely, sir. Uncertain, coy and hard to please. When –'

' – pain and anguish wring the brow, a ministering angel thou and so on and so forth. You can't stump me on the poet Scott. That is one more of the things I used to recite in the old days. First "Charge of Light Brigade" or "Ben Battle": then, in response to gales of applause, the poet Scott as an encore. But to return to what I was saying . . . There, as I suspected would be the case, Jeeves, I can't remember what I was saying. I warned you what would happen if you steered the conversation to the poet Scott.'

'You were speaking of the reconciliation between Miss Winkworth and Mr Pirbright, sir.'

'Of course. Well, I was about to say that having studied the psychology of the individual you foresaw what would occur. And you knew that Catsmeat wouldn't be in any real peril. Esmond Haddock was not going to jug the brother of the woman he loved.'

'Exactly, sir.'

'You can't get engaged to a girl with one hand and send her brother up for thirty days with the other.'

'No, sir.'

'And your subtle mind also spotted that this would lead to Esmond Haddock defying his aunts. I thought the intrepid Haddock was splendidly firm, didn't you?'

'Unquestionably, sir.'

'It's nice to think that he and Corky are now headed for the centre aisle.' I paused, and looked at him sharply. 'You sighed, Jeeves.'

'Yes, sir.'

'Why did you sigh?'

'I was thinking of Master Thomas, sir. The announcement of Miss Pirbright's betrothal came as a severe blow to him.'

I refused to allow my spirits to be lowered by any such side issues.

'Waste no time commiserating with young Thos, Jeeves. His is a resilient nature, and the agony will pass. He may have lost Corky, but there's always Betty Grable and Dorothy Lamour and Jennifer Jones.'

'I understand those ladies are married, sir.'

'That won't affect Thos. He'll be getting their autographs, just the same. I see a bright future ahead of him. Or, rather,' I said, correcting myself, 'fairly bright. There is that interview with his mother to be got over first.'

'It has already occurred, sir.'

I goggled at the man.

'What do you mean?'

'My primary motive in intruding upon you at this late hour, sir, was to inform you that her ladyship is downstairs.'

I quivered from brilliantine to shoe sole.

'Aunt Agatha?'

'Yes, sir.'

'Downstairs?'

'Yes, sir. In the drawing-room. Her ladyship arrived some few moments ago. It appears that Master Thomas, unwilling to occasion her anxiety, wrote her a letter informing her that he was safe and well, and unfortunately the postmark "King's Deverill" on the envelope –'

'Oh, my gosh! She came racing down?'

'Yes, sir.'

'And –?'

'A somewhat painful scene took place between mother and son, in the course of which Master Thomas happened to –'

'Mention me?'

'Yes, sir.'

'He blew the gaff?'

'Yes, sir. And I was wondering whether in these circumstances you might not consider it advisable to take an immediate departure down the waterpipe. I understand there is an excellent milk train at two fifty-four. Her ladyship is expressing a desire to see you, sir.'

It would be deceiving my public to say that for an instant I did not quail. I quailed, as a matter of fact, like billy-o. And then, suddenly, it was as if strength had descended upon me.

'Jeeves,' I said, 'this is grave news, but it comes at a moment when I am well fitted to receive it. I have just witnessed Esmond Haddock pound the stuffing out of five aunts, and I feel that after an exhibition like that it would ill beseem a Wooster to curl up before a single aunt. I feel strong and resolute, Jeeves. I shall now go downstairs and pull an Esmond Haddock on Aunt Agatha. And if things look like becoming too sticky, I can always borrow that cosh of yours, what?'

I squared the shoulders and strode to the door, like Childe Roland about to fight the paynim.

The Code of the Woosters

I

I reached out a hand from under the blankets, and rang the bell for Jeeves.

'Good evening, Jeeves.'

'Good morning, sir.'

This surprised me.

'Is it morning?'

'Yes, sir.'

'Are you sure? It seems very dark outside.'

'There is a fog, sir. If you will recollect, we are now in Autumn – season of mists and mellow fruitfulness.'

'Season of what?'

'Mists, sir, and mellow fruitfulness.'

'Oh? Yes. Yes, I see. Well, be that as it may, get me one of those bracers of yours, will you?'

'I have one in readiness, sir, in the ice-box.'

He shimmered out, and I sat up in bed with that rather unpleasant feeling you get sometimes that you're going to die in about five minutes. On the previous night, I had given a little dinner at the Drones to Gussie Fink-Nottle as a friendly send-off before his approaching nuptials with Madeline, only daughter of Sir Watkyn Bassett, CBE, and these things take their toll. Indeed, just before Jeeves came in, I had been dreaming that some bounder was driving spikes through my head – not just ordinary spikes, as used by Jael the wife of Heber, but red-hot ones.

He returned with the tissue-restorer. I loosed it down the hatch, and after undergoing the passing discomfort, unavoidable when you drink Jeeves's patent morning revivers, of having the top of the skull fly up to the

ceiling and the eyes shoot out of their sockets and
rebound from the opposite wall like racquet balls, felt
better. It would have been overstating it to say that even
now Bertram was back again in mid-season form, but I
had at least slid into the convalescent class and was
equal to a spot of conversation.

'Ha!' I said, retrieving the eyeballs and replacing them
in position. 'Well, Jeeves, what goes on in the great
world? Is that the paper you have there?'

'No, sir. It is some literature from the Travel Bureau. I
thought that you might care to glance at it.'

'Oh?' I said. 'You did, did you?'

And there was a brief and – if that's the word I want –
pregnant silence.

I suppose that when two men of iron will live in close
association with one another, there are bound to be
occasional clashes, and one of these had recently popped
up in the Wooster home. Jeeves was trying to get me to
go on a Round-The-World cruise, and I would have none
of it. But in spite of my firm statements to this effect,
scarcely a day passed without him bringing me a sheaf or
nosegay of those illustrated folders which the Ho-for-
the-open-spaces birds send out in the hope of drumming
up custom. His whole attitude recalled irresistibly to the
mind that of some assiduous hound who will persist in
laying a dead rat on the drawing-room carpet, though
repeatedly apprised by word and gesture that the market
for same is sluggish or even non-existent.

'Jeeves,' I said, 'this nuisance must now cease.'

'Travel is highly educational, sir.'

'I can't do with any more education. I was full up
years ago. No, Jeeves, I know what's the matter with
you. That old Viking strain of yours has come out again.
You yearn for the tang of the salt breezes. You see
yourself walking the deck in a yachting cap. Possibly
someone has been telling you about the Dancing Girls of
Bali. I understand, and I sympathize. But not for me. I

refuse to be decanted into any blasted ocean-going liner and lugged off round the world.'

'Very good, sir.'

He spoke with a certain what-is-it in his voice, and I could see that, if not actually disgruntled, he was far from being gruntled, so I tactfully changed the subject.

'Well, Jeeves, it was quite a satisfactory binge last night.'

'Indeed, sir?'

'Oh, most. An excellent time was had by all. Gussie sent his regards.'

'I appreciate the kind thought, sir. I trust Mr Fink-Nottle was in good spirits?'

'Extraordinarily good, considering that the sands are running out and that he will shortly have Sir Watkyn Bassett for a father-in-law. Sooner him than me, Jeeves, sooner him than me.'

I spoke with strong feeling, and I'll tell you why. A few months before, while celebrating Boat Race night, I had fallen into the clutches of the Law for trying to separate a policeman from his helmet, and after sleeping fitfully on a plank bed had been hauled up at Bosher Street next morning and fined five of the best. The magistrate who had inflicted this monstrous sentence – to the accompaniment, I may add, of some very offensive remarks from the bench – was none other than old Pop Bassett, father of Gussie's bride-to-be.

As it turned out, I was one of his last customers, for a couple of weeks later he inherited a pot of money from a distant relative and retired to the country. That, at least, was the story that had been put about. My own view was that he had got the stuff by sticking like glue to the fines. Five quid here, five quid there – you can see how it would mount up over a period of years.

'You have not forgotten that man of wrath, Jeeves? A hard case, eh?'

'Possibly Sir Watkyn is less formidable in private life, sir.'

'I doubt it. Slice him where you like, a hellhound is always a hellhound. But enough of this Bassett. Any letters today?'

'No, sir.'

'Telephone communications?'

'One, sir. From Mrs Travers.'

'Aunt Dahlia? She's back in town, then?'

'Yes, sir. She expressed a desire that you would ring her up at your earliest convenience.'

'I will do even better,' I said cordially. 'I will call in person.'

And half an hour later I was toddling up the steps of her residence and being admitted by old Seppings, her butler. Little knowing, as I crossed that threshold, that in about two shakes of a duck's tail I was to become involved in an imbroglio that would test the Wooster soul as it had seldom been tested before. I allude to the sinister affair of Gussie Fink-Nottle, Madeline Bassett, old Pop Bassett, Stiffy Byng, the Rev. H. P. ('Stinker') Pinker, the eighteenth-century cow-creamer and the small, brown, leather-covered notebook.

No premonition of an impending doom, however, cast a cloud on my serenity as I buzzed in. I was looking forward with bright anticipation to the coming reunion with this Dahlia – she, as I may have mentioned before, being my good and deserving aunt, not to be confused with Aunt Agatha, who eats broken bottles and wears barbed wire next to the skin. Apart from the mere intellectual pleasure of chewing the fat with her, there was the glittering prospect that I might be able to cadge an invitation to lunch. And owing to the outstanding virtuosity of Anatole, her French cook, the browsing at her trough is always of a nature to lure the gourmet.

The door of the morning room was open as I went through the hall, and I caught a glimpse of Uncle Tom messing about with his collection of old silver. For a moment I toyed with the idea of pausing to pip-pip and enquire after his indigestion, a malady to which he is extremely subject, but wiser counsels prevailed. This uncle is a bird who, sighting a nephew, is apt to buttonhole him and become a bit informative on the subject of sconces and foliation, not to mention scrolls, ribbon wreaths in high relief and gadroon borders, and it seemed to me that silence was best. I whizzed by, accordingly, with sealed lips, and headed for the library, where I had been informed that Aunt Dahlia was at the moment roosting.

I found the old flesh-and-blood up to her Marcelwave in proof sheets. As all the world knows, she is the courteous and popular proprietress of a weekly sheet for the delicately nurtured entitled *Milady's Boudoir*. I once contributed an article to it on 'What The Well-Dressed Man is Wearing'.

My entry caused her to come to the surface, and she greeted me with one of those cheery view-halloos which, in the days when she went in for hunting, used to make her so noticeable a figure of the Quorn, the Pytchley and other organizations for doing the British fox a bit of no good.

'Hullo, ugly,' she said. 'What brings you here?'

'I understood, aged relative, that you wished to confer with me.'

'I didn't want you to come barging in, interrupting my work. A few words on the telephone would have met the case. But I suppose some instinct told you that this was my busy day.'

'If you were wondering if I could come to lunch, have no anxiety. I shall be delighted, as always. What will Anatole be giving us?'

'He won't be giving you anything, my gay young

tapeworm. I am entertaining Pomona Grindle, the novelist, to the midday meal.'

'I should be charmed to meet her.'

'Well, you're not going to. It is to be a strictly *tête-à-tête* affair. I'm trying to get a serial out of her for the *Boudoir*. No, all I wanted was to tell you to go to an antique shop in the Brompton Road – it's just past the Oratory – you can't miss it – and sneer at a cow-creamer.'

I did not get her drift. The impression I received was that of an aunt talking through the back of her neck.

'Do what to a what?'

'They've got an eighteenth-century cow-creamer there that Tom's going to buy this afternoon.'

The scales fell from my eyes.

'Oh, it's a silver whatnot, is it?'

'Yes. A sort of cream jug. Go there and ask them to show it to you, and when they do, register scorn.'

'The idea being what?'

'To sap their confidence, of course, chump. To sow doubts and misgivings in their mind and make them clip the price a bit. The cheaper he gets the thing, the better he will be pleased. And I want him to be in cheery mood, because if I succeed in signing the Grindle up for this serial, I shall be compelled to get into his ribs for a biggish sum of money. It's sinful what these best-selling women novelists want for their stuff. So pop off there without delay and shake your head at the thing.'

I am always anxious to oblige the right sort of aunt, but I was compelled to put in what Jeeves would have called a *nolle prosequi*. Those morning mixtures of his are practically magical in their effect, but even after partaking of them one does not oscillate the bean.

'I can't shake my head. Not today.'

She gazed at me with a censorious waggle of the right eyebrow.

'Oh, so that's how it is? Well, if your loathsome

excesses have left you incapable of headshaking, you can
at least curl your lip.'

'Oh, rather.'

'Then carry on. And draw your breath in sharply. Also
try clicking the tongue. Oh, yes, and tell them you think
it's modern Dutch.'

'Why?'

'I don't know. Apparently it's something a cow-
creamer ought not to be.'

She paused, and allowed her eye to roam thoughtfully
over my perhaps somewhat corpse-like face.

'So you were out on the tiles last night, were you, my
little chickadee? It's an extraordinary thing – every time
I see you, you appear to be recovering from some
debauch. Don't you ever stop drinking? How about
when you are asleep?'

I rebutted the slur.

'You wrong me, relative. Except at times of special
revelry, I am exceedingly moderate in my potations. A
brace of cocktails, a glass of wine at dinner and possibly
a liqueur with the coffee – that is Bertram Wooster. But
last night I gave a small bachelor binge for Gussie Fink-
Nottle.'

'You did, did you?' She laughed – a bit louder than I
could have wished in my frail state of health, but then
she is always a woman who tends to bring plaster falling
from the ceiling when amused. 'Spink-Bottle, eh? Bless
his heart! How was the old newt-fancier?'

'Pretty roguish.'

'Did he make a speech at this orgy of yours?'

'Yes. I was astounded. I was all prepared for a blushing
refusal. But no. We drank his health, and he rose to his
feet as cool as some cucumbers, as Anatole would say,
and held us spellbound.'

'Tight as an owl, I suppose?'

'On the contrary. Offensively sober.'

'Well, that's a nice change.'

We fell into a thoughtful silence. We were musing on the summer afternoon down at her place in Worcestershire when Gussie, circumstances having so ordered themselves as to render him full to the back teeth with the right stuff, had addressed the young scholars of Market Snodsbury Grammar School on the occasion of their annual prize giving.

A thing I never know, when I'm starting out to tell a story about a chap I've told a story about before, is how much explanation to bung in at the outset. It's a problem you've got to look at from every angle. I mean to say, in the present case, if I take it for granted that my public knows all about Gussie Fink-Nottle and just breeze ahead, those publicans who weren't hanging on my lips the first time are apt to be fogged. Whereas if before kicking off I give about eight volumes of the man's life and history, other bimbos who were so hanging will stifle yawns and murmur 'Old stuff. Get on with it.'

I suppose the only thing to do is to put the salient facts as briefly as possible in the possession of the first gang, waving an apologetic hand at the second gang the while, to indicate that they had better let their attention wander for a minute or two and that I will be with them shortly.

This Gussie, then, was a fish-faced pal of mine who, on reaching man's estate, had buried himself in the country and devoted himself entirely to the study of newts, keeping the little chaps in a glass tank and observing their habits with a sedulous eye. A confirmed recluse you would have called him, if you had happened to know the word, and you would have been right. By all the rulings of the form book, a less promising prospect for the whispering of tender words into shell-like ears and the subsequent purchase of platinum ring and licence for wedding it would have seemed impossible to discover in a month of Sundays.

But Love will find a way. Meeting Madeline Bassett one day and falling for her like a ton of bricks, he had emerged from his retirement and started to woo, and after numerous vicissitudes had clicked and was slated at no distant date to don the spongebag trousers and gardenia for buttonhole and walk up the aisle with the ghastly girl.

I call her a ghastly girl because she was a ghastly girl. The Woosters are chivalrous, but they can speak their minds. A droopy, soupy, sentimental exhibit, with melting eyes and a cooing voice and the most extraordinary views on such things as stars and rabbits. I remember her telling me once that rabbits were gnomes in attendance on the Fairy Queen and that the stars were God's daisy chain. Perfect rot, of course. They're nothing of the sort.

Aunt Dahlia emitted a low, rumbling chuckle, for that speech of Gussie's down at Market Snodsbury has always been one of her happiest memories.

'Good old Spink-Bottle! Where is he now?'

'Staying at the Bassett's father's place – Totleigh Towers, Totleigh-in-the-Wold, Glos. He went back there this morning. They're having the wedding at the local church.'

'Are you going to it?'

'Definitely no.'

'No, I suppose it would be too painful for you. You being in love with the girl.'

I stared.

'In love? With a female who thinks that every time a fairy blows its wee nose a baby is born?'

'Well, you were certainly engaged to her once.'

'For about five minutes, yes, and through no fault of my own. My dear old relative,' I said, nettled, 'you are perfectly well aware of the inside facts of that frightful affair.'

I winced. It was an incident in my career on which I

267

did not care to dwell. Briefly, what had occurred was this. His nerve sapped by long association with newts, Gussie had shrunk from pleading his cause with Madeline Bassett, and had asked me to plead it for him. And when I did so, the fat-headed girl thought I was pleading mine. With the result that when, after that exhibition of his at the prize giving, she handed Gussie the temporary mitten, she had attached herself to me, and I had had no option but to take the rap. I mean to say, if a girl has got it into her nut that a fellow loves her, and comes and tells him that she is returning her *fiancé* to store and is now prepared to sign up with him, what can a chap do?

Mercifully, things had been straightened out at the eleventh hour by a reconciliation between the two pills, but the thought of my peril was one at which I still shuddered. I wasn't going to feel really easy in my mind till the parson had said: 'Wilt thou, Augustus?' and Gussie had whispered a shy 'Yes.'

'Well, if it is of any interest to you,' said Aunt Dahlia, 'I am not proposing to attend that wedding myself. I disapprove of Sir Watkyn Bassett, and don't think he ought to be encouraged. There's one of the boys, if you want one!'

'You know the old crumb, then?' I said, rather surprised, though of course it bore out what I often say – viz. that it's a small world.

'Yes, I know him. He's a friend of Tom's. They both collect old silver and snarl at one another like wolves about it all the time. We had him staying at Brinkley last month. And would you care to hear how he repaid me for all the loving care I lavished on him while he was my guest? Sneaked round behind my back and tried to steal Anatole!'

'No!'

'That's what he did. Fortunately, Anatole proved staunch – after I had doubled his wages.'

'Double them again,' I said earnestly. 'Keep on doubling them. Pour out money like water rather than lose that superb master of the roasts and hashes.'

I was visibly affected. The thought of Anatole, that peerless disher-up, coming within an ace of ceasing to operate at Brinkley Court, where I could always enjoy his output by inviting myself for a visit, and going off to serve under old Bassett, the last person in the world likely to set out a knife and fork for Bertram, had stirred me profoundly.

'Yes,' said Aunt Dahlia, her eye smouldering as she brooded on the frightful thing, 'that's the sort of hornswoggling high-binder Sir Watkyn Bassett is. You had better warn Spink-Bottle to watch out on the wedding day. The slightest relaxation of vigilance, and the old thug will probably get away with his tie-pin in the vestry. And now,' she said, reaching out for what had the appearance of being a thoughtful essay on the care of the baby in sickness and in health, 'push off. I've got about six tons of proofs to correct. Oh, and give this to Jeeves, when you see him. It's the "Husbands' Corner" article. It's full of deep stuff about braid on the side of men's dress trousers, and I'd like him to vet it. For all I know, it may be Red propaganda. And I can rely on you not to bungle that job? Tell me in your own words what it is you're supposed to do.'

'Go to antique shop –'

' – in the Brompton Road –'

' – in, as you say, the Brompton Road. Ask to see cow-creamer –'

' – and sneer. Right. Buzz along. The door is behind you.'

It was with a light heart that I went out into the street and hailed a passing barouche. Many men, no doubt, might have been a bit sick at having their morning cut into in this fashion, but I was conscious only of pleasure at the thought that I had it in my power to perform this little act of kindness. Scratch Bertram Wooster, I often say, and you find a Boy Scout.

The antique shop in the Brompton Road proved, as foreshadowed, to be an antique shop in the Brompton Road and, like all antique shops except the swanky ones in the Bond Street neighbourhood, dingy outside and dark and smelly within. I don't know why it is, but the proprietors of these establishments always seem to be cooking some sort of stew in the back room.

'I say,' I began, entering; then paused as I perceived that the bloke in charge was attending to two other customers.

'Oh, sorry,' I was about to add, to convey the idea that I had horned in inadvertently, when the words froze on my lips.

Quite a slab of misty fruitfulness had drifted into the emporium, obscuring the view, but in spite of the poor light I was able to note that the smaller and elder of these two customers was no stranger to me.

It was old Pop Bassett in person. Himself. Not a picture.

There is a tough, bulldog strain in the Woosters which has often caused comment. It came out in me now. A weaker man, no doubt, would have tiptoed from the scene and headed for the horizon, but I stood firm. After all, I felt, the dead past was the dead past. By forking out that fiver, I had paid my debt to Society and had nothing to fear from this shrimp-faced son of a whatnot. So I remained where I was, giving him the surreptitious once-over.

My entry had caused him to turn and shoot a quick look at me, and at intervals since then he had been peering at me sideways. It was only a question of time, I felt, before the hidden chord in his memory would be touched and he would realize that the slight distinguished-looking figure leaning on its umbrella in the background was an old acquaintance. And now it was plain that he was hep. The bird in charge of the shop had pottered off into an inner room, and he came across to where I stood, giving me the up-and-down through his wind-shields.

'Hullo, hullo,' he said. 'I know you, young man. I never forget a face. You came up before me once.'

I bowed slightly.

'But not twice. Good! Learned your lesson, eh? Going straight now? Capital. Now, let me see, what was it? Don't tell me. It's coming back. Of course, yes. Bag-snatching.'

'No, no. It was –'

'Bag-snatching,' he repeated firmly. 'I remember it distinctly. Still, it's all past and done with now, eh? We have turned over a new leaf, have we not? Splendid. Roderick, come over here. This is most interesting.'

His buddy, who had been examining a salver, put it down and joined the party.

He was, as I had already been able to perceive, a breath-taking cove. About seven feet in height, and swathed in a plaid ulster which made him look about six feet across, he caught the eye and arrested it. It was as if Nature had intended to make a gorilla, and had changed its mind at the last moment.

But it wasn't merely the sheer expanse of the bird that impressed. Close to, what you noticed more was his face, which was square and powerful and slightly moustached towards the centre. His gaze was keen and piercing. I don't know if you have even seen those pictures in the papers of Dictators with tilted chins and blazing eyes, inflaming the populace with fiery words on the occasion of the opening of a new skittle alley, but that was what he reminded me of.

'Roderick,' said old Bassett, 'I want you to meet this fellow. Here is a case which illustrates exactly what I have so often maintained – that prison life does not degrade, that it does not warp the character and prevent a man rising on stepping-stones of his dead self to higher things.'

I recognized the gag – one of Jeeves's – and wondered where he could have heard it.

'Look at this chap. I gave him three months not long ago for snatching bags at railway stations, and it is quite evident that his term in jail has had the most excellent effect on him. He has reformed.'

'Oh, yes?' said the Dictator.

Granted that it wasn't quite 'Oh, yeah?' I still didn't like the way he spoke. He was looking at me with a nasty sort of supercilious expression. I remember thinking that he would have been the ideal man to sneer at a cow-creamer.

'What makes you think he has reformed?'

'Of course he has reformed. Look at him. Well groomed, well dressed, a decent member of Society. What his present walk in life is, I do not know, but it is perfectly obvious that he is no longer stealing bags. What are you doing now, young man?'

'Stealing umbrellas, apparently,' said the Dictator. 'I notice he's got yours.'

And I was on the point of denying the accusation hotly – I had, indeed, already opened my lips to do so – when there suddenly struck me like a blow on the upper maxillary from a sock stuffed with wet sand the realization that there was a lot in it.

I mean to say, I remembered now that I had come out without my umbrella, and yet here I was, beyond any question of doubt, umbrellaed to the gills. What had caused me to take up the one that had been leaning against a seventeenth-century chair, I cannot say, unless it was the primeval instinct which makes a man without an umbrella reach out for the nearest one in sight, like a flower groping toward the sun.

A manly apology seemed in order. I made it as the blunt instrument changed hands.

'I say, I'm most frightfully sorry.'

Old Bassett said he was, too – sorry and disappointed. He said it was this sort of thing that made a man sick at heart.

The Dictator had to shove his oar in. He asked if he should call a policeman, and old Bassett's eyes gleamed for a moment. Being a magistrate makes you love the idea of calling policemen. It's like a tiger tasting blood. But he shook his head.

'No, Roderick. I couldn't. Not today – the happiest day of my life.'

The Dictator pursed his lips, as if feeling that the better the day, the better the deed.

'But listen,' I bleated, 'it was a mistake.'

'Ha!' said the Dictator.

'I thought that umbrella was mine.'

'That,' said old Bassett, 'is the fundamental trouble with you, my man. You are totally unable to distinguish between *meum* and *tuum*. Well, I am not going to have you arrested this time, but I advise you to be very careful. Come, Roderick.'

They biffed out, the Dictator pausing at the door to give me another look and say 'Ha!' again.

A most unnerving experience all this had been for a man of sensibility, as you may imagine, and my immediate reaction was a disposition to give Aunt Dahlia's commission the miss-in-balk and return to the flat and get outside another of Jeeves's pick-me-ups. You know how harts pant for cooling streams when heated in the chase. Very much that sort of thing. I realized now what madness it had been to go into the streets of London with only one of them under my belt, and I was on the point of melting away and going back to the fountain head, when the proprietor of the shop emerged from the inner room, accompanied by a rich smell of stew and a sandy cat, and enquired what he could do for me. And so, the subject having come up, I said that I understood that he had an eighteenth-century cow-creamer for sale.

He shook his head. He was a rather mildewed bird of gloomy aspect, almost entirely concealed behind a cascade of white whiskers.

'You're too late. It's promised to a customer.'

'Name of Travers?'

'Ah.'

'Then that's all right. Learn, O thou of unshuffled features and agreeable disposition,' I said, for one likes to be civil, 'that the above Travers is my uncle. He sent me here to have a look at the thing. So dig it out, will you? I expect it's rotten.'

'It's a beautiful cow-creamer.'

'Ha!' I said, borrowing a bit of the Dictator's stuff. 'That's what you think. We shall see.'

I don't mind confessing that I'm not much of a lad for old silver, and though I have never pained him by actually telling him so, I have always felt that Uncle Tom's fondness for it is evidence of a goofiness which he would do well to watch and check before it spreads. So I wasn't expecting the heart to leap up to any great extent at the sight of this exhibit. But when the whiskered ancient pottered off into the shadows and came back with the thing. I scarcely knew whether to laugh or weep. The thought of an uncle paying hard cash for such an object got right in amongst me.

It was a silver cow. But when I say 'cow', don't go running away with the idea of some decent, self-respecting cudster such as you may observe loading grass into itself in the nearest meadow. This was a sinister, leering, Underworld sort of animal, the kind that would spit out of the side of its mouth for twopence. It was about four inches high and six long. Its back opened on a hinge. Its tail was arched, so that the tip touched the spine – thus, I suppose, affording a handle for the cream-lover to grasp. The sight of it seemed to take me into a different and dreadful world.

It was, consequently, an easy task for me to carry out the programme indicated by Aunt Dahlia. I curled the lip and clicked the tongue, all in one movement. I also drew in the breath sharply. The whole effect was that of a man absolutely out of sympathy with this cow-creamer, and I saw the mildewed cove start, as if he had been wounded in a tender spot.

'Oh, tut, tut, tut!' I said, 'Oh, dear, dear, dear! Oh, no, no, no, no! I don't think much of this,' I said, curling and clicking freely. 'All wrong.'

'All wrong?'

'All wrong. Modern Dutch.'

'Modern Dutch?' He may have frothed at the mouth, or he may not. I couldn't be sure. But the agony of spirit was obviously intense. 'What do you mean, Modern Dutch? It's eighteenth-century English. Look at the hallmark.'

'I can't see any hallmark.'

'Are you blind? Here, take it outside in the street. It's lighter there.'

'Right ho,' I said, and started for the door, sauntering at first in a languid sort of way, like a connoisseur a bit bored at having his time wasted.

I say 'at first', because I had only taken a couple of steps when I tripped over the cat, and you can't combine tripping over cats with languid sauntering. Shifting abruptly into high, I shot out of the door like someone wanted by the police making for the car after a smash-and-grab raid. The cow-creamer flew from my hands, and it was a lucky thing that I happened to barge into a fellow citizen outside, or I should have taken a toss in the gutter.

Well, not absolutely lucky, as a matter of fact, for it turned out to be Sir Watkyn Bassett. He stood there goggling at me with horror and indignation behind the pince-nez, and you could almost see him totting up the score on his fingers. First, bag-snatching, I mean to say; then umbrella-pinching; and now this. His whole demeanour was that of a man confronted with the last straw.

'Call a policeman, Roderick!' he cried, skipping like the high hills.

The Dictator sprang to the task.

'Police!' he bawled.

'Police!' yipped old Bassett, up in the tenor clef.

'Police!' roared the Dictator, taking the bass.

And a moment later something large loomed up in the fog and said: 'What's all this?'

Well, I dare say I could have explained everything, if I had stuck around and gone into it, but I didn't want to stick around and go into it. Side-stepping nimbly, I picked up the feet and was gone like the wind. A voice shouted 'Stop!' but of course I didn't. Stop, I mean to say! Of all the damn silly ideas. I legged it down byways and along side streets, and eventually fetched up somewhere in the neighbourhood of Sloane Square. There I got aboard a cab and started back to civilization.

My original intention was to drive to the Drones and get a bite of lunch there, but I hadn't gone far when I realized that I wasn't equal to it. I yield to no man in my appreciation of the Drones Club . . . its sparkling conversation, its camaraderie, its atmosphere redolent of all that is best and brightest in the metropolis . . . but there would, I knew, be a goodish bit of bread thrown hither and thither at its luncheon table, and I was in no vein to cope with flying bread. Changing my strategy in a flash, I told the man to take me to the nearest Turkish bath.

It is always my practice to linger over a Turkish b., and it was consequently getting late by the time I returned to the flat. I had managed to put in two or three hours' sleep in my cubicle, and that, taken in conjunction with the healing flow of persp. in the hot room and the plunge into the icy tank, had brought the roses back to my cheeks to no little extent. It was, indeed, practically with a merry tra-la-la on my lips that I latchkeyed my way in and made for the sitting room.

And the next moment my fizziness was turned off at the main by the sight of a pile of telegrams on the table.

2

I don't know if you were among the gang that followed the narrative of my earlier adventures with Gussie Fink-Nottle – you may have been one of those who didn't happen to get around to it – but if you were you will recall that the dirty work on that occasion started with a tidal wave of telegrams, and you will not be surprised to learn that I found myself eyeing this mound of envelopes askance. Ever since then, telegrams in any quantity have always seemed to me to spell trouble.

I had had the idea at first glance that there were about twenty of the beastly things, but a closer scrutiny revealed only three. They had all been despatched from Totleigh-in-the-Wold, and they all bore the same signature.

They ran as follows:

The first:

> Wooster,
> Berkeley Mansions,
> Berkeley Square,
> London.
> Come immediately. Serious rift Madeline and self.
> Reply.
> GUSSIE

The second:

> Surprised receive no answer my telegram saying
> Come immediately serious rift Madeline and self. Reply.
> GUSSIE

And the third:

> I say, Bertie, why don't you answer my telegrams?
> Sent you two today saying Come immediately
> serious rift Madeline and self. Unless you come
> earliest possible moment prepared lend every effort
> effect reconciliation, wedding will be broken off.
> Reply.
>   GUSSIE

I have said that that sojourn of mine in the T. bath had
done much to re-establish the *mens sana in corpore*
whatnot. Perusal of these frightful communications
brought about an instant relapse. My misgivings, I saw,
had been well founded. Something had whispered to me
on seeing those bally envelopes that here we were again,
and here we were.

The sound of the familiar footsteps had brought
Jeeves floating out from the back premises. A glance was
enough to tell him that all was not well with ye
employer.

'Are you ill, sir?' he enquired solicitously.

I sank into a c. and passed an agitated h. over the b.

'Not ill, Jeeves, but all of a twitter. Read these.'

He ran his eye over the dossier, then transferred it to
mine, and I could read in it the respectful anxiety he was
feeling for the well-being of the young seigneur.

'Most disturbing, sir.'

His voice was grave. I could see that he hadn't missed
the gist. The sinister import of those telegrams was as
clear to him as it was to me.

We do not, of course, discuss the matter, for to do so
would rather come under the head of speaking lightly of
a woman's name, but Jeeves is in full possession of the
facts relating to the Bassett–Wooster mix-up and
thoroughly cognizant of the peril which threatens me
from that quarter. There was no need to explain to him

why I now lighted a feverish cigarette and hitched the lower jaw up with a visible effort.

'What do you suppose has happened, Jeeves?'

'It is difficult to hazard a conjecture, sir.'

'The wedding may be scratched, he says. Why? That is what I ask myself.'

'Yes, sir.'

'And I have no doubt that that is what you ask yourself?'

'Yes, sir.'

'Deep waters, Jeeves.'

'Extremely deep, sir.'

'The only thing we can say with any certainty is that in some way – how, we shall presumably learn later – Gussie has made an ass of himself again.'

I mused on Augustus Fink-Nottle for a moment, recalling how he had always stood by himself in the chump class. The best judges had been saying it for years. Why, at our private school, where I had first met him, he had been known as 'Fat-head', and that was in competition with fellows like Bingo Little, Freddie Widgeon and myself.

'What shall I do, Jeeves?'

'I think it would be best to proceed to Totleigh Towers, sir.'

'But how can I? Old Bassett would sling me out the moment I arrived.'

'Possibly if you were to telegraph to Mr Fink-Nottle, sir, explaining your difficulty, he might have some solution to suggest.'

This seemed sound. I hastened out to the post office, and wired as follows:

> Fink-Nottle,
> Totleigh Towers,
> Totleigh-in-the-Wold.
> Yes, that's all very well. You say come here

immediately, but how dickens can I? You don't
understand relations between Pop Bassett and self.
These not such as to make him welcome visit
Bertram. Would inevitably hurl out on ear and set
dogs on. Useless suggest putting on false whiskers
and pretending be fellow come inspect drains, as old
blighter familiar with features and would instantly
detect imposture. What is to be done? What has
happened? Why serious rift? What serious rift? How
do you mean wedding broken off? Why dickens?
What have you been doing to the girl? Reply.
    BERTIE

The answer to this came during dinner:

> Wooster,
> Berkeley Mansions,
> Berkeley Square,
> London.
> See difficulty, but think can work it. In spite
> strained relations, still speaking terms Madeline. Am
> telling her have received urgent letter from you
> pleading be allowed come here. Expect invitation
> shortly.
>   GUSSIE

And on the morrow, after a tossing-on-pillow night, I
received a bag of three.
The first ran:

> Have worked it. Invitation dispatched. When you
> come, will you bring book entitled *My Friends The
> Newts* by Loretta Peabody published Popgood and
> Grooly get any bookshop.
>   GUSSIE

The second:

281

Bertie, you old ass, I hear you are coming here. Delighted, as something very important want you do for me.
STIFFY

The third:

Please come here if you wish, but, oh Bertie, is this wise? Will not it cause you needless pain seeing me? Surely merely twisting knife wound.
MADELINE

Jeeves was bringing me the morning cup of tea when I read these missives, and I handed them to him in silence. He read them in same. I was able to imbibe about a fluid ounce of the hot and strengthening before he spoke.

'I think that we should start at once, sir.'

'I suppose so.'

'I will pack immediately. Would you wish me to call Mrs Travers on the telephone?'

'Why?'

'She has rung up several times this morning.'

'Oh? Then perhaps you had better give her a buzz.'

'I think it will not be necessary, sir. I fancy that this would be the lady now.'

A long and sustained peal had sounded from the front door, as if an aunt had put her thumb on the button and kept it there. Jeeves left the presence, and a moment later it was plain that his intuition had not deceived him. A booming voice rolled through the flat, the voice which once, when announcing the advent of a fox in their vicinity, had been wont to cause members of the Quorn and Pytchley to clutch their hats and bound in their saddles.

'Isn't that young hound awake yet, Jeeves? . . . Oh, there you are.'

Aunt Dahlia charged across the threshold.

At all times and on all occasions, owing to years of fox-chivvying in every kind of weather, this relative has a fairly purple face, but one noted now an even deeper mauve than usual. The breath came jerkily, and the eyes gleamed with a goofy light. A man with far less penetration than Bertram Wooster would have been able to divine that there before him stood an aunt who had got the pip about something.

It was evident that information which she yearned to uncork was bubbling within her, but she postponed letting it go for a moment in order to reproach me for being in bed at such an hour. Sunk, as she termed it in her forthright way, in hoggish slumber.

'Not sunk in hoggish slumber,' I corrected. 'I've been awake some little time. As a matter of fact, I was just about to partake of the morning meal. You will join me, I hope? Bacon and eggs may be taken as read, but say the word and we can do you a couple of kippers.'

She snorted with a sudden violence which twenty-four hours earlier would have unmanned me completely. Even in my present tolerably robust condition, it affected me rather like one of those gas explosions which slay six.

'Eggs! Kippers! What I want is a brandy and soda. Tell Jeeves to mix me one. And if he forgets to put in the soda, it will be all right with me. Bertie, a frightful thing has happened.'

'Push along into the dining saloon, my fluttering old aspen,' I said. 'We shall not be interrupted there. Jeeves will want to come in here to pack.'

'Are you off somewhere?'

'Totleigh Towers. I have had a most disturbing –'

'Totleigh Towers? Well, I'm dashed! That's just where I came to tell you you had jolly well got to go immediately.'

'Eh?'

'Matter of life and death.'

'How do you mean?'

'You'll soon see, when I've explained.'

'Then come along to the dining room and explain at your earliest convenience.'

'Now then, my dear old mysterious hinter,' I said, when Jeeves had brought the foodstuffs and withdrawn, 'tell me all.'

For an instant, there was silence, broken only by the musical sound of an aunt drinking brandy and soda and self lowering a cup of coffee. Then she put down her beaker, and drew a deep breath.

'Bertie,' she said, 'I wish to begin by saying a few words about Sir Watkyn Bassett, CBE. May greenfly attack his roses. May his cook get tight on the night of the big dinner party. May all his hens get the staggers.'

'Does he keep hens?' I said, putting a point.

'May his cistern start leaking, and may white ants, if there are any in England, gnaw away the foundations of Totleigh Towers. And when he walks up the aisle with his daughter Madeline, to give her away to that ass Spink-Bottle, may he get a sneezing fit and find that he has come out without a pocket handkerchief.'

She paused, and it seemed to me that all this, while spirited stuff, was not germane to the issue.

'Quite,' I said. 'I agree with you *in toto*. But what has he done?'

'I will tell you. You remember that cow-creamer?'

I dug into a fried egg, quivering a little.

'Remember it? I shall never forget it. You will scarcely believe this, Aunt Dahlia, but when I got to the shop, who should be there by the most amazing coincidence but this same Bassett –'

'It wasn't a coincidence. He had gone there to have a look at the thing, to see if it was all Tom had said it was. For – can you imagine such lunacy, Bertie? – that chump of an uncle of yours had told the man about it. He might have known that the fiend would hatch some devilish plot for his undoing. And he did. Tom lunched with Sir Watkyn Bassett at the latter's club yesterday. On the bill of fare was a cold lobster, and this Machiavelli sicked him onto it.'

I looked at her incredulously.

'You aren't going to tell me,' I said, astounded, for I was familiar with the intensely delicate and finely poised mechanism of his tummy, 'that Uncle Tom ate lobster? After what happened last Christmas?'

'At this man's instigation, he appears to have eaten not only pounds of lobster, but forests of sliced cucumber as well. According to his story, which he was able to tell me this morning – he could only groan when he came home yesterday – he resisted at first. He was strong and resolute. But then circumstances were too much for him. Bassett's club, apparently, is one of those clubs where they have the cold dishes on a table in the middle of the room, so placed that wherever you sit you can't help seeing them.'

I nodded.

'They do at the Drones, too. Catsmeat Potter-Pirbright once hit the game pie from the far window six times with six consecutive rolls.'

'That was what caused poor old Tom's downfall. Bassett's lobster sales-talk he might have been strong enough to ignore, but the sight of the thing was too much for him. He yielded, tucked in like a starving Eskimo, and at six o'clock I got a call from the hall porter, asking me if I would send the car round to fetch away the remains, which had been discovered by the page boy writhing in a corner of the library. He arrived half an hour later, calling weakly for bicarbonate of soda. Bicarbonate of soda, my foot!' said Aunt Dahlia, with a bitter, mirthless laugh. 'He had to have two doctors and a stomach-pump.'

'And in the meantime – ?' I said, for I could see whither the tale was tending.

'And in the meantime, of course, the fiend Bassett had nipped down and bought the cow-creamer. The man had promised to hold it for Tom till three o'clock, but naturally when three o'clock came and he didn't turn up and there was another customer clamouring for the thing, he let it go. So there you are. Bassett has the cow-creamer, and took it down to Totleigh last night.'

It was a sad story, of course, and one that bore out what I had so often felt about Pop Bassett – to wit, that a magistrate who could nick a fellow for five pounds, when a mere reprimand would more than have met the case, was capable of anything, but I couldn't see what she thought there was to be done about it. The whole situation seemed to me essentially one of those where you just clench the hands and roll the eyes mutely up to heaven and then start a new life and try to forget. I said as much, while marmalading a slice of toast.

She gazed at me in silence for a moment.

'Oh? So that's how you feel, is it?'

'I do, yes.'

'You admit, I hope, that by every moral law that cow-creamer belongs to Tom?'

'Oh, emphatically.'

'But you would take this foul outrage lying down? You would allow this stick-up man to get away with the swag? Confronted with the spectacle of as raw a bit of underhanded skulduggery as has ever been perpetrated in a civilized country, you would just sit tight and say "Well, well!" and do nothing?'

I weighed this.

'Possibly not "Well, well!" I concede that the situation is one that calls for the strongest comment. But I wouldn't do anything.'

'Well, I'm going to do something. I'm going to pinch the damn thing.'

I stared at her, astounded. I uttered no verbal rebuke, but there was a distinct 'Tut, tut!' in my gaze. Even though the provocation was, I admitted, severe, I could not approve of these strong-arm methods. And I was about to awaken her dormant conscience by asking her gently what the Quorn would think of these goings-on – or, for the matter of that, the Pytchley – when she added:

'Or, rather, you are!'

I had just lighted a cigarette as she spoke these words, and so, according to what they say in the advertisements, ought to have been nonchalant. But it must have been the wrong sort of cigarette, for I shot out of my chair as if somebody had shoved a bradawl through the seat.

'Who, me?'

'That's right. See how it all fits in. You're going to stay at Totleigh. You will have a hundred excellent opportunities of getting your hooks on the thing –'

'But, dash it!'

' – and I must have it, because otherwise I shall never be able to dig a cheque out of Tom for that Pomona Grindle serial. He simply won't be in the mood. And I signed the old girl up yesterday at a fabulous price, half the sum agreed upon to be paid in advance a week from current date. So snap into it, my lad. I can't see what you're making all this heavy weather about. It doesn't seem to me much to do for a loved aunt.'

'It seems to me a dashed lot to do for a loved aunt, and I'm jolly well not going to dream –'

'Oh, yes you are, because you know what will happen, if you don't.' She paused significantly. 'You follow me, Watson?'

I was silent. She had no need to tell me what she meant. This was not the first time she had displayed the velvet hand beneath the iron glove – or, rather, the other way about – in this manner.

For this ruthless relative has one all-powerful weapon which she holds constantly over my head like the sword of – who was the chap? – Jeeves would know – and by means of which she can always bend me to her will – viz. the threat that if I don't kick in she will bar me from her board and wipe Anatole's cooking from my lips. I shall not lightly forget the time when she placed sanctions on me for a whole month – right in the middle of the pheasant season, when this superman is at his incomparable best.

I made one last attempt to reason with her.

'But why does Uncle Tom want this frightful cow-creamer? It's a ghastly object. He would be far better without it.'

'He doesn't think so. Well, there it is. Perform this simple, easy task for me, or guests at my dinner table will soon be saying: "Why is it that we never seem to see Bertie Wooster here any more?" Bless my soul, what an amazing lunch that was that Anatole gave us yesterday! "Superb" is the only word. I don't wonder you're fond of his cooking. As you sometimes say, it melts in the mouth.'

I eyed her sternly.

'Aunt Dahlia, this is blackmail!'

'Yes, isn't it?' she said, and beetled off.

I resumed my seat, and ate a moody slice of cold bacon.

Jeeves entered.

'The bags are packed, sir.'

'Very good, Jeeves,' I said. 'Then let us be starting.'

'Man and boy, Jeeves,' I said, breaking a thoughtful silence which had lasted for about eighty-seven miles, 'I have been in some tough spots in my time, but this one wins the mottled oyster.'

We were bowling along in the two-seater on our way to Totleigh Towers, self at the wheel, Jeeves at my side,

the personal effects in the dicky. We had got off round
about eleven-thirty, and the genial afternoon was now at
its juiciest. It was one of those crisp, sunny, bracing days
with a pleasant tang in the air, and had circumstances
been different from what they were, I should no doubt
have been feeling at the peak of my form, chatting gaily,
waving to passing rustics, possibly even singing some
light snatch.

Unfortunately, however, if there was one thing
circumstances weren't, it was different from what they
were, and there was no suspicion of a song on the lips.
The more I thought of what lay before me at these bally
Towers, the bowed-downer did the heart become.

'The mottled oyster,' I repeated.

'Sir?'

I frowned. The man was being discreet, and this was
no time for discretion.

'Don't pretend you don't know all about it, Jeeves,' I
said coldly. 'You were in the next room throughout my
interview with Aunt Dahlia, and her remarks must have
been audible in Piccadilly.'

He dropped the mask.

'Well, yes, sir, I must confess that I did gather the
substance of the conversation.'

'Very well, then. You agree with me that the situation
is a lulu?'

'Certainly a somewhat sharp crisis in your affairs
would appear to have been precipitated, sir.'

I drove on, brooding.

'If I had my life to live again, Jeeves, I would start it as
an orphan without any aunts. Don't they put aunts in
Turkey in sacks and drop them in the Bosphorus?'

'Odalisques, sir, I understand. Not aunts.'

'Well, why not aunts? Look at the trouble they cause
in the world. I tell you, Jeeves, and you may quote me as
saying this – behind every poor, innocent, harmless
blighter who is going down for the first time in the soup,

you will find, if you look carefully enough, the aunt who shoved him into it.'

'There is much in what you say, sir.'

'It is no use telling me that there are bad aunts and good aunts. At the core, they are all alike. Sooner or later, out pops the cloven hoof. Consider this Dahlia, Jeeves. As sound an egg as ever cursed a foxhound for chasing a rabbit, I have always considered her. And she goes and hands me an assignment like this. Wooster, the pincher of policemen's helmets, we know. We are familiar with Wooster, the supposed bag-snatcher. But it was left for this aunt to present to the world a Wooster who goes to the houses of retired magistrates and, while eating their bread and salt, swipes their cow-creamers. Faugh!' I said, for I was a good deal overwrought.

'Most disturbing, sir.'

'I wonder how old Bassett will receive me, Jeeves.'

'It will be interesting to observe his reactions, sir.'

'He can't very well throw me out, I suppose, Miss Bassett having invited me?'

'No, sir.'

'On the other hand, he can – and I think he will – look at me over the top of his pince-nez and make rummy sniffing noises. The prospect is not an agreeable one.'

'No, sir.'

'I mean to say, even if this cow-creamer thing had not come up, conditions would be sticky.'

'Yes, sir. Might I venture to enquire if it is your intention to endeavour to carry out Mrs Travers's wishes?'

You can't fling the hands up in a passionate gesture when you are driving a car at fifty miles an hour. Otherwise, I should have done so.

'That is the problem which is torturing me, Jeeves. I can't make up my mind. You remember that fellow you've mentioned to me once or twice, who let

something wait upon something? You know who I mean
– the cat chap.'

'Macbeth, sir, a character in a play of that name by the
late William Shakespeare. He was described as letting "I
dare not" wait upon "I would", like the poor cat i' th'
adage.'

'Well, that's how it is with me. I wobble, and I
vacillate – if that's the word?'

'Perfectly correct, sir.'

'I think of being barred from those menus of
Anatole's, and I say to myself that I will take a pop.
Then I reflect that my name at Totleigh Towers is
already mud and that old Bassett is firmly convinced
that I am a combination of Raffles and a pea-and-
thimble man and steal everything I come upon that isn't
nailed down –'

'Sir?'

'Didn't I tell you about that? I had another encounter
with him yesterday, the worst to date. He now looks
upon me as the dregs of the criminal world – if not
Public Enemy Number One, certainly Number Two or
Three.'

I informed him briefly of what had occurred, and
conceive my emotion when I saw that he appeared to be
finding something humorous in the recital. Jeeves does
not often smile, but now a distinct simper had begun to
wreathe his lips.

'A laughable misunderstanding, sir.'

'Laughable, Jeeves?'

He saw that his mirth had been ill-timed. He
reassembled the features, ironing out the smile.

'I beg your pardon, sir. I should have said
"disturbing".'

'Quite.'

'It must have been exceedingly trying, meeting Sir
Watkyn in such circumstances.'

'Yes, and it's going to be a dashed sight more trying if

he catches me pinching his cow-creamer. I keep seeing a vision of him doing it.'

'I quite understand, sir. And thus the native hue of resolution is sicklied o'er with the pale cast of thought, and enterprises of great pitch and moment in this regard their currents turn awry and lose the name of action.'

'Exactly. You take the words out of my mouth.'

I drove on, brooding more than ever.

'And here's another point that presents itself, Jeeves. Even if I want to steal cow-creamers, how am I going to find the time? It isn't a thing you can just take in your stride. You have to plan and plot and lay schemes. And I shall need every ounce of concentration for this business of Gussie's.'

'Exactly, sir. One appreciates the difficulty.'

'And, as if that wasn't enough to have on my mind, there is that telegram of Stiffy's. You remember the third telegram that came this morning. It was from Miss Stephanie Byng, Miss Bassett's cousin, who resides at Totleigh Towers. You've met her. She came to lunch at the flat a week or two ago. Smallish girl of about the tonnage of Jessie Matthews.'

'Oh, yes, sir. I remember Miss Byng. A charming young lady.'

'Quite. But what does she want me to do for her? That's the question. Probably something completely unfit for human consumption. So I've got that to worry about, too. What a life!'

'Yes, sir.'

'Still, stiff upper lip, I suppose, Jeeves, what?'

'Precisely, sir.'

During these exchanges, we had been breezing along at a fairish pace, and I had not failed to note that on a signpost which we had passed some little while back there had been inscribed the words 'Totleigh-in-the-Wold, 8 miles'. There now appeared before us through the trees a stately home of E.

I braked the car.

'Journey's End, Jeeves?'

'So I should be disposed to imagine, sir.'

And so it proved. Having turned in at the gateway and fetched up at the front door, we were informed by the butler that this was indeed the lair of Sir Watkyn Bassett.

'Childe Roland to the dark tower came, sir,' said Jeeves, as we alighted, though what he meant I hadn't an earthly. Responding with a brief 'Oh, ah,' I gave my attention to the butler, who was endeavouring to communicate something to me.

What he was saying, I now gathered, was that if desirous of mixing immediately with the inmates I had chosen a bad moment for hitting the place. Sir Watkyn, he explained, had popped out for a breather.

'I fancy he is somewhere in the grounds with Mr Roderick Spode.'

I started. After that affair at the antique shop, the name Roderick was, as you may imagine, rather deeply graven on my heart.

'Roderick Spode? Big chap with a small moustache and the sort of eye that can open an oyster at sixty paces?'

'Yes, sir. He arrived yesterday with Sir Watkyn from London. They went out shortly after lunch. Miss Madeline, I believe, is at home, but it may take some little time to locate her.'

'How about Mr Fink-Nottle?'

'I think he has gone for a walk, sir.'

'Oh? Well, right ho. Then I'll just potter about a bit.'

I was glad of the chance of being alone for a while, for I wished to brood. I strolled off along the terrace, doing so.

The news that Roderick Spode was on the premises had shaken me a good deal. I had supposed him to be some mere club acquaintance of old Bassett's, who confined his activities exclusively to the metropolis, and his presence at the Towers rendered the prospect of trying to carry out Aunt Dahlia's commission, always one calculated to unnerve the stoutest, twice as intimidating as it had been before, when I had supposed that I should be under the personal eye of Sir Watkyn alone.

Well, you can see that for yourself, I mean to say. I mean, imagine how some unfortunate Master Criminal would feel, on coming down to do a murder at the old Grange, if he found that not only was Sherlock Holmes putting in the weekend there, but Hercule Poirot, as well.

The more I faced up to the idea of pinching that cow-creamer, the less I liked it. It seemed to me that there ought to be a middle course, and that what I had to do was explore avenues in the hope of finding some formula. To this end, I paced the terrace with bent bean, pondering.

Old Bassett, I noted, had laid out his money to excellent advantage. I am a bit of a connoisseur of country houses, and I found this one well up to sample. Nice façade, spreading grounds, smoothly shaven lawns, and a general atmosphere of what is known as old-world peace. Cows were mooing in the distance, sheep and birds respectively bleating and tootling, and from somewhere near at hand there came the report of a gun, indicating that someone was having a whirl at the local rabbits. Totleigh Towers might be a place where Man was vile, but undoubtedly every prospect pleased.

And I was strolling up and down, trying to calculate how long it would have taken the old bounder, fining, say, twenty people a day five quid apiece, to collect enough to pay for all this, when my attention was arrested by the interior of a room on the ground floor, visible through an open French window.

It was a sort of minor drawing room, if you know

what I mean, and it gave the impression of being overfurnished. This was due to the fact that it was stuffed to bursting point with glass cases, these in their turn stuffed to bursting point with silver. It was evident that I was looking at the Bassett collection.

I paused. Something seemed to draw me through the French window. And the next moment, there I was, *vis-à-vis*, as the expression is, with my old pal the silver cow. It was standing in a smallish case over by the door, and I peered in at it, breathing heavily on the glass.

It was with considerable emotion that I perceived that the case was not locked.

I turned the handle. I dipped in, and fished it out.

Now, whether it was my intention merely to inspect and examine, or whether I was proposing to shoot the works, I do not know. The nearest I can remember is that I had no really settled plans. My frame of mind was more or less that of a cat in an adage.

However, I was not accorded leisure to review my emotions in what Jeeves would call the final analysis, for at this point a voice behind me said 'Hands up!' and, turning, I observed Roderick Spode in the window. He had a shotgun in his hand, and this he was pointing in a negligent sort of way at my third waistcoat button. I gathered from his manner that he was one of those fellows who like firing from the hip.

3

I had described Roderick Spode to the butler as a man with an eye that could open an oyster at sixty paces, and it was an eye of this nature that he was directing at me now. He looked like a Dictator on the point of starting a purge, and I saw that I had been mistaken in supposing him to be seven feet in height. Eight, at least. Also the slowly working jaw muscles.

I hoped he was not going to say 'Ha!' but he did. And as I had not yet mastered the vocal cords sufficiently to be able to reply, that concluded the dialogue sequence for the moment. Then, still keeping his eyes glued on me, he shouted:

'Sir Watkyn!'

There was a distant sound of Eh-yes-here-I-am-what-is-it-ing.

'Come here, please. I have something to show you.'

Old Bassett appeared in the window, adjusting his pince-nez.

I had seen this man before only in the decent habiliments suitable to the metropolis, and I confess that even in the predicament in which I found myself I was able to shudder at the spectacle he presented in the country. It is, of course, an axiom, as I have heard Jeeves call it, that the smaller the man, the louder the check suit, and old Bassett's apparel was in keeping with his lack of inches. Prismatic is the only word for those frightful tweeds and, oddly enough, the spectacle of them had the effect of steadying my nerves. They gave me the feeling that nothing mattered.

'Look!' said Spode. 'Would you have thought such a thing possible?'

Old Bassett was goggling at me with a sort of stunned amazement.

'Good God! It's the bag-snatcher!'

'Yes. Isn't it incredible?'

'It's unbelievable. Why, damn it, it's persecution. Fellow follows me everywhere, like Mary's lamb. Never a free moment. How did you catch him?'

'I happened to be coming along the drive, and I saw a furtive figure slink in at the window. I hurried up, and covered him with my gun. Just in time. He had already begun to loot the place.'

'Well, I'm most obliged to you, Roderick. But what I can't get over is the chap's pertinacity. You would have thought that when we foiled that attempt of his in the Brompton Road, he would have given up the thing as a bad job. But no. Down he comes here next day. Well, he will be sorry he did.'

'I suppose this is too serious a case for you to deal with summarily?'

'I can issue a warrant for his arrest. Bring him along to the library, and I'll do it now. The case will have to go to the Assizes or the Sessions.'

'What will he get, do you think?'

'Not easy to say. But certainly not less than –'

'Hoy!' I said.

I had intended to speak in a quiet, reasonable voice – going on, after I had secured their attention, to explain that I was on these premises as an invited guest, but for some reason the word came out like something Aunt Dahlia might have said to a fellow member of the Pytchley half a mile away across a ploughed field, and old Bassett shot back as if he had been jabbed in the eye with a burned stick.

Spode commented on my methods of voice production.

'Don't shout like that!'

'Nearly broke my ear-drum,' grumbled old Bassett.

'But listen!' I yelled. 'Will you listen!'

A certain amount of confused argument then ensued, self trying to put the case for the defence and the opposition rather harping a bit on the row I was making. And in the middle of it all, just as I was showing myself in particularly good voice, the door opened and somebody said 'Goodness gracious!'

I looked round. Those parted lips . . . those saucer-like eyes . . . that slender figure, drooping slightly at the hinges . . .

Madeline Bassett was in our midst.

'Goodness gracious!' she repeated.

I can well imagine that a casual observer, if I had confided to him my qualms at the idea of being married to this girl, would have raised his eyebrows and been at a loss to understand. 'Bertie,' he would probably have said, 'you don't know what's good for you,' adding, possibly, that he wished he had half my complaint. For Madeline Bassett was undeniably of attractive exterior – slim, *svelte*, if that's the word, and bountifully equipped with golden hair and all the fixings.

But where the casual observer would have been making his bloomer was in overlooking that squashy soupiness of hers, that subtle air she had of being on the point of talking baby-talk. It was that that froze the blood. She was definitely the sort of girl who puts her hands over a husband's eyes, as he is crawling in to breakfast with a morning head, and says: 'Guess who!'

I once stayed at the residence of a newly married pal of mine, and his bride had had carved in large letters over the fireplace in the drawing room, where it was impossible to miss it, the legend: 'Two Lovers Built This Nest,' and I can still recall the look of dumb anguish in the other half of the sketch's eyes every time he came in and saw it. Whether Madeline Bassett, on entering the

marital state, would go to such an awful extreme, I
could not say, but it seemed most probable.

She was looking at us with a sort of pretty, wide-eyed
wonder.

'Whatever is all the noise about?' she said. 'Why,
Bertie! When did you get here?'

'Oh, hallo. I've just arrived.'

'Did you have a nice journey down?'

'Oh, rather, thanks. I came in the two-seater.'

'You must be quite exhausted.'

'Oh, no, thanks, rather not.'

'Well, tea will be ready soon. I see you've met Daddy.'

'And Mr Spode.'

'And Mr Spode.'

'I don't know where Augustus is, but he's sure to be in
to tea.'

'I'll count the moments.'

Old Bassett has been listening to these courtesies
with a dazed expression on the map – gulping a bit from
time to time, like a fish that has been hauled out of a
pond on a bent pin and isn't at all sure it is equal to the
pressure of events. One followed the mental processes,
of course. To him, Bertram was a creature of the
underworld who stole bags and umbrellas and, what
made it worse, didn't even steal them well. No father
likes to see his ewe lamb on chummy terms with such a
one.

'You don't mean you know this man?' he said.

Madeline Bassett laughed the tinkling, silvery laugh
which was one of the things that had got her so disliked
by the better element.

'Why, Daddy, you're too absurd. Of course I know
him. Bertie Wooster is an old, old, a very dear old friend
of mine. I told you he was coming here today.'

Old Bassett seemed not abreast. Spode didn't seem
any too abreast, either.

'This isn't your friend Mr Wooster?'

'Of course.'

'But he snatches bags.'

'Umbrellas,' prompted Spode, as if he had been the King's Remembrancer or something.

'And umbrellas,' assented old Bassett. 'And makes daylight raids on antique shops.'

Madeline was not abreast – making three in all.

'Daddy!'

Old Bassett stuck to it stoutly.

'He does, I tell you. I've caught him at it.'

'*I've* caught him at it,' said Spode.

'We've both caught him at it,' said old Bassett. 'All over London. Wherever you go in London, there you will find this fellow stealing bags and umbrellas. And now in the heart of Gloucestershire.'

'Nonsense!' said Madeline.

I saw that it was time to put an end to all this rot. I was about fed up with that bag-snatching stuff. Naturally, one does not expect a magistrate to have all the details about the customers at his fingers' ends – pretty good, of course, remembering his *clientèle* at all – but one can't just keep passing a thing like that off tactfully.

'Of course it's nonsense,' I thundered. 'The whole thing is one of those laughable misunderstandings.'

I must say I was expecting that my explanation would have gone better than it did. What I had anticipated was that after a few words from myself, outlining the situation, there would have been roars of jolly mirth, followed by apologies and backslappings. But old Bassett, like so many of these police court magistrates, was a difficult man to convince. Magistrates' natures soon get warped. He kept interrupting and asking questions, and cocking an eye at me as he asked them. You know what I mean – questions beginning with 'Just one moment –' and 'You say –' and 'Then you are asking us to believe –' Offensive, very.

However, after a good deal of tedious spadework, I managed to get him straight on the umbrella, and he conceded that he might have judged me unjustly about that.

'But how about the bags?'

'There weren't any bags.'

'I certainly sentenced you for something at Bosher Street. I remember it vividly.'

'I pinched a policeman's helmet.'

'That's just as bad as snatching bags.'

Roderick Spode intervened unexpectedly. Throughout this – well, dash it, this absolute Trial of Mary Dugan – he had been standing by, thoughtfully sucking the muzzle of his gun and listening to my statements as if he thought it all pretty thin; but now a flicker of human feeling came into his granite face.

'No,' he said, 'I don't think you can go so far as that. When I was at Oxford, I once stole a policeman's helmet myself.'

I was astounded. Nothing in my relations with this man had given me the idea that he, too, had, so to speak, once lived in Arcady. It just showed, as I often say, that there is good in the worst of us.

Old Bassett was plainly taken aback. Then he perked up.

'Well, how about that affair at the antique shop? Hey? Didn't we catch him in the act of running off with my cow-creamer? What has he got to say to that?'

Spode seemed to see the force of this. He removed the gun, which he had replaced between his lips, and nodded.

'The bloke at the shop had given it to me to look at,' I said shortly. 'He advised me to take it outside, where the light was better.'

'You were rushing out.'

'Staggering out. I trod on the cat.'

'What cat?'

'It appeared to be an animal attached to the personnel of the emporium.'

'H'm! I saw no cat. Did you see a cat, Roderick?'

'No, no cat.'

'Ha! Well, we will pass over the cat – '

'But I didn't,' I said, with one of my lightning flashes.

'We will pass over the cat,' repeated old Bassett, ignoring the gag and leaving it lying there, 'and come to another point. What were you doing with that cow-creamer? You say you were looking at it. You are asking us to believe that you were merely subjecting it to a perfectly innocent scrutiny. Why? What was your motive? What possible interest could it have for a man like you?'

'Exactly,' said Spode. 'The very question I was going to ask myself.'

This bit of backing-up from a pal had the worst effect on old Bassett. It encouraged him to so great an extent that he now yielded completely to the illusion that he was back in his bally police court.

'You say the proprietor of the shop handed it to you. I put it to you that you snatched it up and were making off with it. And now Mr Spode catches you here, with the thing in your hands. How do you explain that? What's your answer to that? Hey?'

'Why, Daddy!' said Madeline.

I dare say you have been wondering at this pancake's silence during all the cut-and-thrust stuff which had been going on. It is readily explained. What had occurred was that shortly after saying 'Nonsense!' in the earlier portion of the proceedings, she had happened to inhale some form of insect life, and since then had been choking quietly in the background. And as the situation was far too tense for us to pay any attention to choking girls, she had been left to carry on under her own steam while the men threshed out the subject on the agenda paper.

She now came forward, her eyes still watering a bit.

'Why, Daddy,' she said, 'naturally your silver would be the first thing Bertie would want to look at. Of course, he is interested in it. Bertie is Mr Travers's nephew.'

'What!'

'Didn't you know that? Your uncle has a wonderful collection hasn't he, Bertie? I suppose he has often spoken to you of Daddy's.'

There was a pause. Old Bassett was breathing heavily. I didn't like the look of him at all. He glanced from me to the cow-creamer, and from the cow-creamer to me, then back from me to the cow-creamer again, and it would have taken a far less astute observer than Bertram to fail to read what was passing in his mind. If ever I saw a bimbo engaged in putting two and two together, that bimbo was Sir Watkyn Bassett.

'Oh!' he said.

Just that. Nothing more. But it was enough.

'I say,' I said, 'could I send a telegram?'

'You can telephone it from the library,' said Madeline. 'I'll take you there.'

She conducted me to the instrument and left me, saying that she would be waiting in the hall when I had finished. I leaped at it, established connection with the post office, and after a brief conversation with what appeared to be the village idiot, telegraphed as follows:

Mrs Travers,
47, Charles Street,
Berkeley Square,
London.

I paused for a moment, assembling the ideas, then proceeded thus:

Deeply regret quite impossible carry out assignment re you know what. Atmosphere one of keenest suspicion and any sort of action instantly fatal. You ought to have seen old Bassett's eye just now on learning of blood relationship of self and Uncle Tom. Like ambassador finding veiled woman snooping round safe containing secret treaty. Sorry and all that, but nothing doing. Love.

    BERTIE

I then went down to the hall to join Madeline Bassett.

She was standing by the barometer, which, if it had had an ounce of sense in its head, would have been pointing to 'Stormy' instead of 'Set Fair': and as I hove alongside she turned and gazed at me with a tender goggle which sent a thrill of dread creeping down the Wooster spine. The thought that there stood one who was on distant terms with Gussie and might 'ere long return the ring and presents afflicted me with a nameless horror.

I resolved that if a few quiet words from a man of the world could heal the breach, they should be spoken.

'Oh, Bertie,' she said, in a low voice like beer trickling out of a jug, 'you ought not to be here!'

My recent interview with old Bassett and Roderick Spode had rather set me thinking along those lines myself. But I hadn't time to explain that this was no idle social visit, and that if Gussie hadn't been sending out SOSs I wouldn't have dreamed of coming within a hundred miles of the frightful place. She went on, looking at me as if I were a rabbit which she was expecting shortly to turn into a gnome.

'Why did you come? Oh, I know what you are going to say. You felt that, cost what it might, you had to see me again, just once. You could not resist the urge to take away with you one last memory, which you could cherish down the lonely years. Oh, Bertie, you remind me of Rudel.'

The name was new to me.'

'Rudel?'

'The Seigneur Geoffrey Rudel, Prince of Blay-en-Saintonge.'

I shook my head.

'Never met him, I'm afraid. Pal of yours?'

'He lived in the Middle Ages. He was a great poet. And he fell in love with the wife of the Lord of Tripoli.'

I stirred uneasily. I hoped she was going to keep it clean.

'For years he loved her, and at last he could resist no longer. He took ship to Tripoli, and his servants carried him ashore.'

'Not feeling so good?' I said, groping. 'Rough crossing?'

'He was dying. Of love.'

'Oh, ah.'

'They bore him into the Lady Melisande's presence on a litter, and he had just strength enough to reach out and touch her hand. Then he died.'

She paused, and heaved a sigh that seemed to come straight up from the cami-knickers. A silence ensued.

'Terrific,' I said, feeling I had to say something, though personally I didn't think the story a patch on the one about the travelling salesman and the farmer's daughter. Different, of course, if one had known the chap.

She sighed again.

'You see now why I said you reminded me of Rudel. Like him, you came to take one last glimpse of the woman you loved. It was dear of you, Bertie, and I shall never forget it. It will always remain with me as a fragrant memory, like a flower pressed between the leaves of an old album. But was it wise? should you not have been strong? Would it not have been better to have ended it all cleanly, that day when we said goodbye at Brinkley Court, and not to have reopened the wound? We had met, and you have loved me, and I had had to

tell you that my heart was another's. That should have
been our farewell.'

'Absolutely,' I said. I mean to say, all that was
perfectly sound, as far as it went. If her heart really was
another's, fine. Nobody more pleased than Bertram. The
whole nub of the thing was – was it? 'But I had a
communication from Gussie, more or less indicating
that you and he were *p'fft*.'

She looked at me like someone who has just solved
the crossword puzzle with a shrewd 'Emu' in the top
right-hand corner.

'So that was why you came! You thought that there
might still be hope? Oh, Bertie, I'm sorry . . . sorry . . . so
sorry.' Her eyes were misty with the unshed, and about
the size of soup plates. 'No, Bertie, really there is no
hope, none. You must not build dream castles. It can
only cause you pain. I love Augustus. He is my man.'

'And you haven't parted brass rags?'

'Of course not.'

'Then what did he mean by saying "Serious rift
Madeline and self"?'

'Oh, that?' She laughed another tinkling, silvery one.
'That was nothing. It was all too perfectly silly and
ridiculous. Just the teeniest, weeniest little
misunderstanding. I thought I had found him flirting
with my cousin Stephanie, and I was silly and jealous.
But he explained everything this morning. He was only
taking a fly out of her eye.'

I suppose I might legitimately have been a bit shirty
on learning that I had been hauled all the way down here
for nothing, but I wasn't. I was amazingly braced. As I
have indicated, that telegram of Gussie's had shaken me
to my foundations, causing me to fear the worst. And
now the All Clear had been blown, and I had received
absolute inside information straight from the horse's
mouth that all was hotsy-totsy between this blister and
himself.

'So everything's all right, is it?'

'Everything. I have never loved Augustus more than I do now.'

'Haven't you, by Jove?'

'Each moment I am with him, his wonderful nature seems to open before me like some lovely flower.'

'Does it, egad?'

'Every day I find myself discovering some new facet of his extraordinary character. For instance . . . you have seen him quite lately, have you not?'

'Oh, rather. I gave him a dinner at the Drones only the night before last.'

'I wonder if you noticed any difference in him?'

I threw my mind back to the binge in question. As far as I could recollect, Gussie had been the same fish-faced freak I had always known.

'Difference? No, I don't think so. Of course, at that dinner I hadn't the chance to observe him very closely – subject his character to the final analysis, if you know what I mean. He sat next to me, and we talked of this and that, but you know how it is when you're a host – you have all sorts of things to divert your attention . . . keeping an eye on the waiters, trying to make the conversation general, heading Catsmeat Potter-Pirbright off from giving his imitation of Beatrice Lillie . . . a hundred little duties. But he seemed to me much the same. What sort of difference?'

'An improvement, if such a thing were possible. Have you not sometimes felt in the past, Bertie, that, if Augustus had a fault, it was a tendency to be a little timid?'

I saw what she meant.

'Oh, ah, yes, of course, definitely.' I remembered something Jeeves had once called Gussie. 'A sensitive plant, what?'

'Exactly. You know your Shelley, Bertie.'

'Oh, am I?'

'That is what I have always thought him – a sensitive plant, hardly fit for the rough and tumble of life. But recently - in this last week, in fact – he has shown, together with that wonderful dreamy sweetness of his, a force of character which I had not suspected that he possessed. He seems completely to have lost his diffidence.'

'By Jove, yes,' I said, remembering. 'That's right. Do you know, he actually made a speech at that dinner of mine, and a most admirable one. And, what is more –'

I paused. I had been on the point of saying that, what was more, he had made it from start to finish on orange juice, and not – as had been the case at the Market Snodsbury prize giving – with about three quarts of mixed alcoholic stimulants lapping about inside him: and I saw that the statement might be injudicious. That Market Snodsbury exhibition on the part of the adored object was, no doubt, something which she was trying to forget.

'Why, only this morning,' she said, 'he spoke to Roderick Spode quite sharply.'

'He did?'

'Yes. They were arguing about something, and Augustus told him to go and boil his head.'

'Well, well!' I said.

Naturally, I didn't believe it for a moment. Well, I mean to say! Roderick Spode, I mean – a chap who even in repose would have made an all-in wrestler pause and pick his words. The thing wasn't possible.

I saw what had happened, of course. She was trying to give the boyfriend a build-up and, like all girls, was overdoing it. I've noticed the same thing in young wives, when they're trying to kid you that Herbert or George or whatever the name may be has hidden depths which the vapid and irreflective observer might overlook. Women never know when to stop on these occasions.

I remember Mrs Bingo Little once telling me, shortly

after their marriage, that Bingo said poetic things to her about sunsets – his best friends being perfectly well aware, of course, that the old egg never noticed a sunset in his life and that, if he did by a fluke ever happen to do so, the only thing he would say about it would be that it reminded him of a slice of roast beef, cooked just right.

However, you can't call a girl a liar; so, as I say, I said: 'Well, well!'

'It was the one thing that was needed to make him perfect. Sometimes, Bertie, I ask myself if I am worthy of so rare a soul.'

'Oh, I wouldn't ask yourself rot like that,' I said heartily. 'Of course you are.'

'It's sweet of you to say so.'

'Not a bit. You two fit like pork and beans. Anyone could see that it was a what-d'you-call-it . . . ideal union. I've known Gussie since we were kids together, and I wish I had a bob for every time I've thought to myself that the girl for him was somebody just like you.'

'Really?'

'Absolutely. And when I met you, I said: "That's the bird! There she spouts!" When is the wedding to be?'

'On the twenty-third.'

'I'd make it earlier.'

'You think so?'

'Definitely. Get it over and done with, and then you'll have it off your mind. You can't be married too soon to a chap like Gussie. Great chap. Splendid chap. Never met a chap I respected more. They don't often make them like Gussie. One of the fruitiest.'

She reached out and grabbed my hand and pressed it. Unpleasant, of course, but one had to take the rough with the smooth.

'Ah, Bertie! Always the soul of generosity!'

'No, no, rather not. Just saying what I think.'

'It makes me so happy to feel that . . . all this . . . has not interfered with your affection for Augustus.'

'I should say not.'

'So many men in your position might have become embittered.'

'Silly asses.'

'But you are too fine for that. You can still say these wonderful things about him.'

'Oh, rather.'

'Dear Bertie!'

And on this cheery note we parted, she to go messing about on some domestic errand, I to head for the drawing room and get a spot of tea. She, it appeared, did not take tea, being on a diet.

And I had reached the drawing room, and was about to shove open the door, which was ajar, when from the other side there came a voice. And what it was saying was:

'So kindly do not talk rot, Spode!'

There was no possibility of mistake as to whose voice it was. From his earliest years, there has always been something distinctive and individual about Gussie's *timbre*, reminding the hearer partly of an escape of gas from a gas pipe and partly of a sheep calling to its young in the lambing season.

Nor was there any possibility of mistake about what he had said. The words were precisely as I have stated, and to say that I was surprised would be to put it too weakly. I saw now that it was perfectly possible that there might be something, after all, in that wild story of Madeline Bassett's. I mean to say, an Augustus Fink-Nottle who told Roderick Spode not to talk rot was an Augustus Fink-Nottle who might quite well have told him to go and boil his head.

I entered the room, marvelling.

Except for some sort of dim female abaft the teapot, who looked as if she might be a cousin by marriage or something of that order, only Sir Watkyn Bassett,

Roderick Spode and Gussie were present. Gussie was straddling the hearth rug with his legs apart, warming himself at the blaze which should, one would have said, been reserved for the trouser seat of the master of the house, and I saw immediately what Madeline Bassett had meant when she said that he had lost his diffidence. Even across the room one could see that, when it came to self-confidence, Mussolini could have taken his correspondence course.

He sighted me as I entered, and waved what seemed to me a dashed patronizing hand. Quite the ruddy Squire graciously receiving the deputation of tenantry.

'Ah, Bertie. So here you are.'

'Yes.'

'Come in, come in and have a crumpet.'

'Thanks.'

'Did you bring that book I asked you to?'

'Awfully sorry. I forgot.'

'Well, of all the muddle-headed asses that ever stepped, you certainly are the worst. Others abide our question, thou art free.'

And dismissing me with a weary gesture, he called for another potted-meat sandwich.

I have never been able to look back on my first meal at Totleigh Towers as among my happiest memories. The cup of tea on arrival at a country house is a thing which, as a rule, I particularly enjoy. I like the crackling logs, the shaded lights, the scent of buttered toast, the general atmosphere of leisured cosiness. There is something that seems to speak to the deeps in me in the beaming smile of my hostess and the furtive whisper of my host, as he plucks at my elbow and says 'Let's get out of here and go and have a whisky and soda in the gun room.' It is on such occasions as this, it has often been said, that you catch Bertram Wooster at his best.

But now all sense of *bien-être* was destroyed by Gussie's peculiar manner – that odd suggestion he

conveyed of having bought the place. It was a relief
when the gang had finally drifted away, leaving us alone.
There were mysteries here which I wanted to probe.

I thought it best, however, to begin by taking a
second opinion on the position of affairs between
himself and Madeline. She had told me that everything
was now hunky-dory once more, but it was one of those
points on which you cannot have too much assurance.

'I saw Madeline just now,' I said. 'She tells me that
you are sweethearts still. Correct?'

'Quite correct. There was a little temporary coolness
about my taking a fly out of Stephanie Byng's eye, and I
got a bit panicked and wired you to come down. I
thought you might possibly plead. However, no need for
that now. I took a strong line, and everything is all right.
Still, stay a day or two, of course, as you're here.'

'Thanks.'

'No doubt you will be glad to see your aunt. She
arrives tonight, I understand.'

I could make nothing of this. My Aunt Agatha, I
knew, was in a nursing home with jaundice. I had taken
her flowers only a couple of days before. And naturally it
couldn't be Aunt Dahlia, for she had mentioned nothing
to me about any plans for infesting Totleigh Towers.

'Some mistake,' I said.

'No mistake at all. Madeline showed me the telegram
that came from her this morning, asking if she could be
put up for a day or two. It was dispatched from London, I
noticed, so I suppose she has left Brinkley.'

I stared.

'You aren't talking about my Aunt Dahlia?'

'Of course I'm talking about your Aunt Dahlia.'

'You mean Aunt Dahlia is coming here tonight?'

'Exactly.'

This was nasty news, and I found myself chewing the
lower lip a bit in undisguised concern. This sudden
decision to follow me to Totleigh Towers could mean

only one thing, that Aunt Dahlia, thinking things over, had become mistrustful of my will to win, and had felt it best to come and stand over me and see that I did not shirk the appointed task. And as I was fully resolved to shirk it, I could envisage some dirty weather ahead. Her attitude towards a recalcitrant nephew would, I feared, closely resemble that which in the old tally-ho days she had been wont to adopt towards a hound which refused to go to cover.

'Tell me,' continued Gussie, 'what sort of voice is she in these days? I ask, because if she is going to make those hunting noises of hers at me during her visit, I shall be compelled to tick her off pretty sharply. I had enough of that sort of thing when I was staying at Brinkley.'

I would have liked to go on musing on the unpleasant situation which had arisen, but it seemed to me that I had been given the cue to begin my probe.

'What's happened to you, Gussie?' I asked.

'Eh?'

'Since when have you been like this?'

'I don't understand you.'

'Well, to take an instance, saying you're going to tick Aunt Dahlia off. At Brinkley, you cowered before her like a wet sock. And, to take another instance, telling Spode not to talk rot. By the way, what was he talking rot about?'

'I forget. He talks so much rot.'

'I wouldn't have the nerve to tell Spode not to talk rot,' I said frankly. My candour met with an immediate response.

'Well, to tell you the truth, Bertie,' said Gussie, coming clean, 'neither would I, a week ago.'

'What happened a week ago?'

'I had a spiritual rebirth. Thanks to Jeeves. There's a chap, Bertie!'

'Ah!'

'We are as little children, frightened of the dark, and Jeeves is the wise nurse who takes us by the hand and –'

'Switches the light on?'

'Precisely. Would you care to hear about it?'

I assured him that I was all agog. I settled myself in my chair and, putting match to gasper, awaited the inside story.

Gussie stood silent for a moment. I could see that he was marshalling his facts. He took off his spectacles and polished them.

'A week ago, Bertie,' he began, 'my affairs had reached a crisis. I was faced by an ordeal, the mere prospect of which blackened the horizon. I discovered that I would have to make a speech at the wedding breakfast.'

'Well, naturally.'

'I know, but for some reason I had not foreseen it, and the news came as a stunning blow. And shall I tell you why I was so overcome by stark horror at the idea of making a speech at the wedding breakfast? It was because Roderick Spode and Sir Watkyn Bassett would be in the audience. Do you know Sir Watkyn intimately?'

'Not very. He once fined me five quid at his police court.'

'Well, you can take it from me that he is a hard nut, and he strongly objects to having me as a son-in-law. For one thing, he would have liked Madeline to marry Spode – who, I may mention, has loved her since she was so high.'

'Oh, yes?' I said, courteously concealing my astonishment that anyone except a certified boob like himself could deliberately love this girl.

'Yes. But apart from the fact that she wanted to marry me, he didn't want to marry her. He looks upon himself as a Man of Destiny, you see, and feels that marriage would interfere with his mission. He takes a line through Napoleon.'

I felt that before proceeding further I must get the low-down on this Spode. I didn't follow all this Man of Destiny stuff.

'How do you mean, his mission? Is he someone special?'

'Don't you ever read the papers? Roderick Spode is the founder and head of the Saviours of Britain, a Fascist organization better known as the Black Shorts. His general idea, if he doesn't get knocked on the head with a bottle in one of the frequent brawls in which he and his followers indulge, is to make himself a Dictator.'

'Well, I'm blowed!'

I was astounded at my keenness of perception. The moment I had set eyes on Spode, if you remember, I had said to myself 'What ho! A Dictator!' and a Dictator he had proved to be. I couldn't have made a better shot, if I had been one of those detectives who see a chap walking along the street and deduce that he is a retired manufacturer of poppet valves named Robinson with rheumatism in one arm, living at Clapham.

'Well, I'm dashed! I thought he was something of that sort. That chin . . . Those eyes . . . And, for the matter of that, that moustache. By the way, when you say "shorts", you mean "shirts", of course.'

'No. By the time Spode formed his association, there were no shirts left. He and his adherents wear black shorts.'

'Footer bags, you mean?'

'Yes.'

'How perfectly foul.'

'Yes.'

'Bare knees?'

'Bare knees.'

'Golly!'

'Yes.'

A thought struck me, so revolting that I nearly dropped my gasper.

'Does old Bassett wear black shorts?'

'No. He isn't a member of the Saviours of Britain.'

'Then how does he come to be mixed up with Spode? I met them going around London like a couple of sailors on shore leave.'

'Sir Watkyn is engaged to be married to his aunt – a Mrs Wintergreen, widow of the late Colonel H. H. Wintergreen, of Pont Street.'

I mused for a moment, reviewing in my mind the scene in the antique-bin.

When you are standing in the dock, with a magistrate looking at you over his pince-nez and talking about you as 'the prisoner Wooster', you have ample opportunity for drinking him in, and what had struck me principally about Sir Watkyn Bassett that day at Bosher Street had been his peevishness. In that shop, on the other hand, he had given the impression of a man who has found the blue bird. He had hopped about like a carefree cat on hot bricks, exhibiting the merchandise to Spode with little chirps of 'I think your aunt would like this?' and 'How about this?' and so forth. And now a clue to that fizziness had been provided.

'Do you know, Gussie,' I said, 'I've an idea he must have clicked yesterday.'

'Quite possibly. However, never mind about that. That is not the point.'

'No, I know. But it's interesting.'

'No, it isn't.'

'Perhaps you're right.'

'Don't let us go wandering off into side issues,' said Gussie, calling the meeting to order. 'Where was I?'

'I don't know.'

'I do. I was telling you that Sir Watkyn disliked the idea of having me for a son-in-law. Spode also was opposed to the match. Nor did he make any attempt to

conceal the fact. He used to come popping out at me
from round corners and muttering threats.'

'You couldn't have liked that.'

'I didn't.'

'Why did he mutter threats?'

'Because though he would not marry Madeline, even if
she would have him, he looks on himself as a sort of
knight, watching over her. He keeps telling me that the
happiness of that little girl is very dear to him, and that
if ever I let her down, he will break my neck. That is the
gist of the threats he mutters, and that was one of the
reasons why I was a bit agitated when Madeline became
distant in her manner, on catching me with Stephanie
Byng.'

'Tell me, Gussie, what were you and Stiffy actually
doing?'

'I was taking a fly out of her eye.'

I nodded. If that was his story, no doubt he was wise
to stick to it.

'So much for Spode. We now come to Sir Watkyn
Bassett. At our very first meeting I could see that I was
not his dream man.'

'Me, too.'

'I became engaged to Madeline, as you know, at
Brinkley Court. The news of the betrothal was,
therefore, conveyed to him by letter, and I imagine that
the dear girl must have hauled up her slacks about me in
a way that led him to suppose that what he was getting
was a sort of cross between Robert Taylor and Einstein.
At any rate, when I was introduced to him as the man
who was to marry his daughter, he just stared for a
moment and said "What?" Incredulously, you know, as
if he were hoping that this was some jolly practical joke
and that the real chap would shortly jump out from
behind a chair and say "Boo!" When he at last got onto it
that there was no deception, he went off into a corner
and sat there for some time, holding his head in his

hands. After that I used to catch him looking at me over the top of his pince-nez. It unsettled me.'

I wasn't surprised. I have already alluded to the effect that over-the-top-of-the-pince-nez look of old Bassett's had had on me, and I could see that, if directed at Gussie, it might quite conceivably have stirred the old egg up a good deal.

'He also sniffed. And when he learned from Madeline that I was keeping newts in my bedroom, he said something very derogatory – under his breath, but I heard him.'

'You've got the troupe with you, then?'

'Of course. I am in the middle of a very delicate experiment. An American professor has discovered that the full moon influences the love life of several undersea creatures, including one species of fish, two starfish groups, eight kinds of worms and a ribbon-like seaweed called Dictyota. The moon will be full in two or three days, and I want to find out if it affects the love life of newts, too.'

'But what *is* the love life of newts, if you boil it right down? Didn't you tell me once that they just waggled their tails at one another in the mating season?'

'Quite correct.'

I shrugged my shoulders.

'Well, all right, if they like it. But it's not my idea of molten passion. So old Bassett didn't approve of the dumb chums?'

'No. He didn't approve of anything about me. It made things most difficult and disagreeable. Add Spode, and you will understand why I was beginning to get thoroughly rattled. And then, out of a blue sky, they sprang it on me that I would have to make a speech at the wedding breakfast – to an audience, as I said before, of which Roderick Spode and Sir Watkyn Bassett would form a part.'

He paused, and swallowed convulsively, like a Pekingese taking a pill.

'I am a shy man, Bertie. Diffidence is the price I pay for having a hyper-sensitive nature. And you know how I feel about making speeches under any conditions. The mere idea appals me. When you lugged me into that prize-giving affair at Market Snodsbury, the thought of standing on a platform, faced by a mob of pimply boys, filled me with a panic terror. It haunted my dreams. You can imagine, then, what it was like for me to have to contemplate that wedding breakfast. To the task of haranguing a flock of aunts and cousins I might have steeled myself. I don't say it would have been easy, but I might have managed it. But to get up with Spode on one side of me and Sir Watkyn Bassett on the other . . . I didn't see how I was going to face it. And then out of the night that covered me, black as the pit from pole to pole, there shone a tiny gleam of hope. I thought of Jeeves.'

His hand moved upwards, and I think this idea was to bare his head reverently. The project was, however, rendered null and void by the fact that he hadn't a hat on.

'I thought of Jeeves,' he repeated, 'and I took the train to London and placed my problem before him. I was fortunate to catch him in time.'

'How do you mean, in time?'

'Before he left England.'

'He isn't leaving England.'

'He told me that you and he were starting off almost immediately on one of those Round-The-World cruises.'

'Oh, no, that's all off. I didn't like the scheme.'

'Does Jeeves say it's all off?'

'No, but I do.'

'Oh?'

He looked at me rather oddly, and I thought he was

going to say something more on the subject. But he only gave a rummy sort of short laugh, and resumed his narrative.

'Well, as I say, I went to Jeeves, and put the facts before him. I begged him to try to find some way of getting me out of this frightful situation in which I was enmeshed – assuring him that I would not blame him if he failed to do so, because it seemed to me, after some days of reviewing the matter, that I was beyond human aid. And you will scarcely credit this, Bertie, I hadn't got more than halfway through the glass of orange juice with which he had supplied me, when he solved the whole thing. I wouldn't have believed it possible. I wonder what that brain of his weighs?'

'A good bit, I fancy. He eats a lot of fish. So it was a winner, was it, this idea?'

'It was terrific. He approached the matter from the psychological angle. In the final analysis, he said, disinclination to speak in public is due to fear of one's audience.'

'Well, I could have told you that.'

'Yes, but he indicated how this might be cured. We do not, he said, fear those whom we despise. The thing to do, therefore, is to cultivate a lofty contempt for those who will be listening to one.'

'How?'

'Quite simple. You fill your mind with scornful thoughts about them. You keep saying to yourself: "Think of that pimple on Smith's nose" . . . "Consider Jones's flapping ears" . . . "Remember the time Robinson got hauled up before the beak for travelling first-class with a third-class ticket" . . . "Don't forget you once saw the child Brown being sick at a children's party" . . . and so on. So that when you are called upon to address Smith, Jones, Robinson and Brown, they have lost their sting. You dominate them.'

I pondered on this.

'I see. Well, yes, it sounds good, Gussie. But would it work in practice?'

'My dear chap, it works like a charm. I've tested it. You recall my speech at that dinner of yours?'

I started.

'You weren't despising us?'

'Certainly I was. Thoroughly.'

'What, me?'

'You, and Freddie Widgeon, and Bingo Little, and Catsmeat Potter-Pirbright, and Barmy Fotheringay-Phipps, and all the rest of those present. "Worms!" I said to myself. "What a crew!" I said to myself. "There's old Bertie," I said to myself. "Golly!" I said to myself, "what I know about *him*!" With the result that I played on you as on a lot of stringed instruments, and achieved an outstanding triumph.'

I must say I was conscious of a certain chagrin. A bit thick, I mean, being scorned by a goof like Gussie – and that at a moment when he had been bursting with one's meat and orange juice.

But soon more generous emotions prevailed. After all, I told myself, the great thing – the fundamental thing to which all other considerations must yield – was to get this Fink-Nottle safely under the wire and off on his honeymoon. And but for this advice of Jeeves's, the muttered threats of Roderick Spode and the combined sniffing and looking over the top of the pince-nez of Sir Watkyn Bassett might well have been sufficient to destroy his morale entirely and cause him to cancel the wedding arrangements and go off hunting newts in Africa.

'Well, yes,' I said, 'I see what you mean. But dash it, Gussie, conceding the fact that you might scorn Barmy Fotheringay-Phipps and Catsmeat Potter-Pirbright and – stretching the possibilities a bit – me, you couldn't despise Spode.'

'Couldn't I?' He laughed a light laugh. 'I did it on my

head. And Sir Watkyn Bassett, too. I tell you, Bertie, I approach this wedding breakfast without a tremor. I am gay, confident, debonair. There will be none of that blushing and stammering and twiddling the fingers and plucking at the tablecloth which you see in most bridegrooms on these occasions. I shall look these men in the eye, and make them wilt. As for the aunts and cousins, I shall have them rolling in the aisles. The moment Jeeves spoke those words, I settled down to think of all the things about Roderick Spode and Sir Watkyn Bassett which expose them to the just contempt of their fellow men. I could tell you fifty things about Sir Watkyn alone which would make you wonder how such a moral and physical blot on the English scene could have been tolerated all these years. I wrote them down in a notebook.'

'You wrote them down in a notebook?'

'A small, leather-covered notebook. I bought it in the village.'

I confess that I was a bit agitated. Even though he presumably kept it under lock and key, the mere existence of such a book made one uneasy. One did not care to think what the upshot and outcome would be were it to fall into the wrong hands. A brochure like that would be dynamite.

'Where do you keep it?'

'In my breast pocket. Here it is. Oh, no, it isn't. That's funny,' said Gussie. 'I must have dropped it somewhere.'

4

I don't know if you have had the same experience, but a thing I have found in life is that from time to time, as you jog along, there occur moments which you are able to recognize immediately with the naked eye as high spots. Something tells you that they are going to remain etched, if etched is the word I want, for ever on the memory and will come back to you at intervals down the years, as you are dropping off to sleep, banishing that drowsy feeling and causing you to leap on the pillow like a gaffed salmon.

One of these well-remembered moments in my own case was the time at my first private school when I sneaked down to the headmaster's study at dead of night, my spies having informed me that he kept a tin of biscuits in the cupboard under the bookshelf; to discover, after I was well inside and a modest and unobtrusive withdrawal impossible, that the old bounder was seated at his desk and – by what I have always thought a rather odd coincidence – actually engaged in the composition of my end-of-term report, which subsequently turned out a stinker.

It was a situation in which it would be paltering with the truth to say that Bertram retained unimpaired his customary *sang-froid*. But I'm dashed if I can remember staring at the Rev. Aubrey Upjohn on that occasion with half the pallid horror which had shot into the map at these words of Gussie's.

'Dropped it?' I quavered.

'Yes, but it's all right.'

'All right?'

'I mean, I can remember every word of it.'

'Oh, I see. That's fine.'

'Yes.'

'Was there much of it?'

'Oh, lots.'

'Good stuff?'

'Of the best.'

'Well, that's splendid.'

I looked at him with growing wonder. You would have thought that by this time even this pre-eminent sub-normal would have spotted the frightful peril that lurked. But no. His tortoiseshell-rimmed spectacles shone with a jovial light. He was full of *élan* and *espièglerie*, without a care in the world. All right up to the neck, but from there on pure concrete – that was Augustus Fink-Nottle.

'Oh, yes,' he said, 'I've got it all carefully memorized, and I'm extremely pleased with it. During this past week I have been subjecting the characters of Roderick Spode and Sir Watkyn Bassett to a pitiless examination. I have probed these two gumboils to the very core of their being. It's amazing the amount of material you can assemble, once you begin really analysing people. Have you ever heard Sir Watkyn Bassett dealing with a bowl of soup? It's not unlike the Scottish express going through a tunnel. Have you ever seen Spode eat asparagus?'

'No.'

'Revolting. It alters one's whole conception of Man as Nature's last word.'

'Those were two of the things you wrote in the book?'

'I gave them about half a page. They were just trivial, surface faults. The bulk of my researches went much deeper.'

'I see. You spread yourself?'

'Very much so.'

'And it was all bright, snappy stuff?'

'Every word of it.'

'That's great. I mean to say, no chance of old Bassett being bored when he reads it.'

'Reads it?'

'Well, he's just as likely to find the book as anyone, isn't he?'

I remember Jeeves saying to me once, apropos of how you can never tell what the weather's going to do, that full many a glorious morning had he seen flatter the mountain tops with sovereign eye and then turn into a rather nasty afternoon. It was the same with Gussie now. He had been beaming like a searchlight until I mentioned this aspect of the matter, and the radiance suddenly disappeared as if it had been switched off at the main.

He stood gaping at me very much as I had gaped at the Rev. A. Upjohn on the occasion to which I have alluded above. His expression was almost identical with that which I had once surprised on the face of a fish, whose name I cannot recall, in the royal aquarium at Monaco.

'I never thought of that!'

'Start now.'

'Oh, my gosh!'

'Yes.'

'Oh, my golly!'

'Quite.'

'Oh, my sainted aunt!'

'Absolutely.'

He moved to the tea table like a man in a dream, and started to eat a cold crumpet. His eyes, as they sought mine, were bulging.

'Suppose old Bassett does find that book, what do you think will ensue?'

I could answer that one.

'He would immediately put the bee on the wedding.'

'You don't really think that?'

'I do.'

He choked over his crumpet.

'Of course he would,' I said. 'You say he has never been any too sold on you as a son-in-law. Reading that book isn't going to cause a sudden change for the better. One glimpse of it, and he will be countermanding the cake and telling Madeline that she shall marry you over his dead body. And she isn't the sort of girl to defy a parent.'

'Oh, my gosh!'

'Still, I wouldn't worry about that, old man,' I said, pointing out the bright side, 'because long before it happened, Spode would have broken your neck.'

He plucked feebly at another crumpet.

'This is frightful, Bertie.'

'Not too good, no.'

'I'm in the soup.'

'Up to the thorax.'

'What's to be done?'

'I don't know.'

'Can't you think of anything?'

'Nothing. We must just put our trust in a higher power.'

'Consult Jeeves, you mean?'

I shook the lemon.

'Even Jeeves cannot help us here. It is a straight issue of finding and recovering that notebook before it can get to old Bassett. Why on earth didn't you keep it locked up somewhere?'

'I couldn't. I was always writing fresh stuff in it. I never knew when the inspiration would come, and I had to have it handy.'

'You're sure it was in your breast pocket?'

'Quite sure.'

'It couldn't be in your bedroom, by any chance?'

'No. I always kept it on me – so as to have it safe.'

'Safe. I see.'

'And also, as I said before, because I had constant need

of it. I'm trying to think where I saw it last. Wait a
minute. It's beginning to come back. Yes, I remember.
By the pump.'

'What pump?'

'The one in the stable yard, where they fill the
buckets for the horses. Yes, that is where I saw it last,
before lunch yesterday. I took it out to jot down a note
about the way Sir Watkyn slopped his porridge about at
breakfast, and I had just completed my critique when I
met Stephanie Byng and took the fly out of her eye.
Bertie!' he cried, breaking off. A strange light had come
into his spectacles. He brought his fist down with a bang
on the table. Silly ass. Might have known he would
upset the milk. 'Bertie, I've just remembered something.
It is as if a curtain had been rolled up and all was
revealed. The whole scene is rising before my eyes. I
took the book out, and entered the porridge item. I then
put it back in my breast pocket. Where I keep my
handkerchief.'

'Well?'

'Where I keep my handkerchief,' he repeated. 'Don't
you understand? Use your intelligence, man. What is the
first thing you do, when you find a girl with a fly in her
eye?'

I uttered an exclamash.

'Reach for your handkerchief!'

'Exactly. And draw it out and extract the fly with the
corner of it. And if there is a small, brown leather-
covered notebook alongside the handkerchief –'

'It shoots out –'

'And falls to earth –'

'– you know not where.'

'But I do know where. That's just the point. I could
lead you to the exact spot.'

For an instant I felt braced. Then moodiness returned.

'Yesterday before lunch, you say? Then someone must
have found it by this time.'

'That's just what I'm coming to. I've remembered something else. Immediately after I had coped with the fly, I recollect hearing Stephanie saying "Hullo, what's that?" and seeing her stoop and pick something up. I didn't pay much attention to the episode at the time, for it was just at that moment that I caught sight of Madeline. She was standing in the entrance of the stable yard, with a distant look on her face. I may mention that in order to extract the fly I had been compelled to place a hand under Stephanie's chin, in order to steady the head.'

'Quite.'

'Essential on these occasions.'

'Definitely.'

'Unless the head is kept rigid, you cannot operate. I tried to point this out to Madeline, but she wouldn't listen. She swept away, and I swept after her. It was only this morning that I was able to place the facts before her and make her accept my explanation. Meanwhile, I had completely forgotten the Stephanie-stooping-picking-up incident. I think it is obvious that the book is now in the possession of this Byng.'

'It must be.'

'Then everything's all right. We just seek her out and ask her to hand it back, and she does so. I expect she will have got a good laugh out of it.'

'Where is she?'

'I seem to remember her saying something about walking down to the village. I think she goes and hobnobs with the curate. If you're not doing anything, you might stroll and meet her.'

'I will.'

'Well, keep an eye open for that Scottie of hers. It probably accompanied her.'

'Oh, yes. Thanks.'

I remembered that he had spoken to me of this animal at my dinner. Indeed, at the moment when the *sole meunière* was being served, he had shown me the sore place on his leg, causing me to skip that course.

'It biteth like a serpent.'

'Right ho. I'll be looking out. And I might as well start at once.'

It did not take me long to get to the end of the drive. At the gates, I paused. It seemed to me that my best plan would be to linger here until Stiffy returned. I lighted a cigarette, and gave myself up to meditation.

Although slightly easier in the mind than I had been, I was still much shaken. Until that book was back in safe storage, there could be no real peace for the Wooster soul. Too much depended on its recovery. As I had said to Gussie, if old Bassett started doing the heavy father and forbidding banns, there wasn't a chance of Madeline sticking out her chin and riposting with a modern 'Is zat so?' A glance at her was enough to tell one that she belonged to that small group of girls who still think a parent should have something to say about things: and I was willing to give a hundred to eight that, in the circumstances which I had outlined, she would sigh and drop a silent tear, but that when all the smoke had cleared away Gussie would be at liberty.

I was still musing in sombre and apprehensive vein, when my meditations were interrupted. A human drama was developing in the road in front of me.

The shades of evening were beginning to fall pretty freely by now, but the visibility was still good enough to enble me to observe that up the road there was approaching a large, stout, moon-faced policeman on a bicycle. And he was, one could see, at peace with all the world. His daily round of tasks may or may not have been completed, but he was obviously off duty for the moment, and his whole attitude was that of a policeman with nothing on his mind but his helmet.

Well, when I tell you that he was riding without his

hands, you will gather to what lengths the careless gaiety of this serene slop had spread.

And where the drama came in was that it was patent that his attention had not yet been drawn to the fact that he was being chivvied – in the strong, silent, earnest manner characteristic of this breed of animal – by a fine Aberdeen terrier. There he was, riding comfortably along, sniffing the fragrant evening breeze; and there was the Scottie, all whiskers and eyebrows, haring after him hell-for-leather. As Jeeves said later, when I described the scene to him, the whole situation resembled some great moment in a Greek tragedy, where somebody is stepping high, wide and handsome, quite unconscious that all the while Nemesis is at his heels, and he may be right.

The constable, I say, was riding without his hands: and but for this the disaster, when it occurred, might not have been so complete. I was a bit of a cyclist myself in my youth – I think I have mentioned that I once won a choir boys' handicap at some village sports – and I can testify that when you are riding without your hands, privacy and a complete freedom from interruption are of the essence. The merest suggestion of an unexpected Scottie connecting with the ankle bone at such a time, and you swoop into a sudden swerve. And, as everybody knows, if the hands are not firmly on the handlebars, a sudden swerve spells a smeller.

And so it happened now. A smeller – and among the finest I have ever been privileged to witness – was what this officer of the law came. One moment he was with us, all merry and bright; the next he was in the ditch, a sort of *macédoine* of arms and legs and wheels, with the terrier standing on the edge, looking down at him with that rather offensive expression of virtuous smugness which I have often noticed on the faces of Aberdeen terriers in their clashes with humanity.

And as he threshed about in the ditch, endeavouring

to unscramble himself, a girl came round the corner, an attractive young prune upholstered in heather-mixture tweeds, and I recognized the familiar features of S. Byng.

After what Gussie had said, I ought to have been expecting Stiffy, of course. Seeing an Aberdeen terrier, I should have gathered that it belonged to her. I might have said to myself: If Scotties come, can Stiffy be far behind?

Stiffy was plainly vexed with the policeman. You could see it in her manner. She hooked the crook of her stick over the Scottie's collar and drew him back; then addressed herself to the man, who had now begun to emerge from the ditch like Venus rising from the foam.

'What on earth,' she demanded, 'did you do that for?'

It was no business of mine, of course, but I couldn't help feeling that she might have made a more tactful approach to what threatened to be a difficult and delicate conference. And I could see that the policeman felt the same. There was a good deal of mud on his face, but not enough to hide the wounded expression.

'You might have scared him out of his wits, hurling yourself about like that. Poor old Bartholomew, did the ugly man nearly squash him flat?'

Again I missed the tactful note. In describing this public servant as ugly, she was undoubtedly technically correct. Only if the competition had consisted of Sir Watkyn Bassett, Oofy Prosser of the Drones, and a few more fellows like that, could he have hoped to win to success in a beauty contest. But one doesn't want to rub these things in. Suavity is what you need on these occasions. You can't beat suavity.

The policeman had now lifted himself and bicycle out of the abyss, and was putting the latter through a series of tests, to ascertain the extent of the damage. Satisfied that it was slight, he turned and eyed Stiffy rather as old Bassett had eyed me on the occasion when I had occupied the Bosher Street dock.

'I was proceeding along the public highway,' he began, in a slow, measured tone, as if he were giving evidence in court, 'and the dorg leaped at me in a verlent manner. I was zurled from my bersicle – '

Stiffy seized upon the point like a practised debater.

'Well, you shouldn't ride a bicycle. Bartholomew hates bicycles.'

'I ride a bersicle, miss, because if I didn't I should have to cover my beat on foot.'

'Do you good. Get some of the fat off you.'

'That,' said the policeman, no mean debater himself, producing a notebook from the recesses of his costume and blowing a water-beetle off it, 'is not the point at tissue. The point at tissue is that this makes twice that the animal has committed an aggravated assault on my person, and I shall have to summons you once more, miss, for being in possession of a savage dorg not under proper control.'

The thrust was a keen one, but Stiffy came back strongly.

'Don't be an ass, Oates. You can't expect a dog to pass up a policeman on a bicycle. It isn't human nature. And I'll bet you started it, anyway. You must have teased him, or something, and I may as well tell you that I intend to fight this case to the House of Lords. I shall call this gentleman as a material witness.' She turned to me, and for the first time became aware that I was no gentleman, but an old friend. 'Oh, hallo, Bertie.'

'Hallo, Stiffy.'

'When did you get here?'

'Oh, recently.'

'Did you see what happened?'

'Oh, rather. Ringside seat throughout.'

'Well, stand by to be subpoenaed.'

'Right ho.'

The policeman had been taking a sort of inventory

and writing it down in the book. He was now in a
position to call the score.

'Piecer skin scraped off right knee. Bruise or contusion
on left elbow. Scratch on nose. Uniform covered with
mud and'll have to go and be cleaned. Also shock –
severe. You will receive the summons in due course,
miss.'

He mounted his bicycle and rode off, causing the dog
Bartholomew to make a passionate bound that nearly
unshipped him from the restraining stick. Stiffy stood
for a moment looking after him a bit yearningly, like a
girl who wished that she had half a brick handy. Then
she turned away, and I came straight down to brass
tacks.

'Stiffy,' I said, 'passing lightly over all the guff about
being charmed to see you again and how well you're
looking and all that, have you got a small, brown,
leather-covered notebook that Gussie Fink-Nottle
dropped in the stable yard yesterday?'

She did not reply, seeming to be musing – no doubt
on the recent Oates. I repeated the question, and she
came out of the trance.

'Notebook?'

'Small, brown, leather-covered one.'

'Full of a lot of breezy personal remarks?'

'That's the one.'

'Yes, I've got it.'

I flung the hands heavenwards and uttered a joyful
yowl. The dog Bartholomew gave me an unpleasant look
and said something under his breath in Gaelic, but I
ignored him. A kennel of Aberdeen terriers could have
rolled their eyes and bared the wisdom tooth without
impairing this ecstatic moment.

'Gosh, what a relief!'

'Does it belong to Gussie Fink-Nottle?'

'Yes.'

'You mean to say that it was Gussie who wrote those

really excellent character studies of Roderick Spode and Uncle Watkyn? I wouldn't have thought he had it in him.'

'Nobody would. It's a most interesting story. It appears –'

'Though why anyone should waste time on Spode and Uncle Watkyn when there was Oates simply crying out to be written about, I can't imagine. I don't think I have ever met a man, Bertie, who gets in the hair so consistently as this Eustace Oates. He makes me tired. He goes swanking about on that bicycle of his, simply asking for it, and then complains when he gets it. And why should he discriminate against poor Bartholomew in this sickening way? Every red-blooded dog in the village has had a go at his trousers, and he knows it.'

'Where's that book, Stiffy?' I said, returning to the *res*.

'Never mind about books. Let's stick to Eustace Oates. Do you think he means to summons me?'

I said that, reading between the lines, that was rather the impression I had gathered, and she made what I believe is known as a *moue*. . . Is it *moue*? . . . Shoving out the lips, I mean, and drawing them quickly back again.

'I'm afraid so, too. There is only one word for Eustace Oates, and that is "malignant". He just goes about seeking whom he may devour. Oh, well, more work for Uncle Watkyn.'

'How do you mean?'

'I shall come up before him.'

'Then he does still operate, even though retired?' I said, remembering with some uneasiness the conversation between this ex-beak and Roderick Spode in the collection room.

'He only retired from Bosher Street. You can't choke a man off magistrating, once it's in his blood. He's a Justice of the Peace now. He holds a sort of Star Chamber court in the library. That's where I always come up. I'll be flitting about, doing the flowers, or sitting in my room with a good book, and the butler comes and says I'm wanted in the library. And there's Uncle Watkyn at the desk, looking like Judge Jeffreys, with Oates waiting to give evidence.'

I could picture the scene. Unpleasant, of course. The sort of thing that casts a gloom over a girl's home life.

'And it always ends the same way, with him putting on the black cap and soaking me. He never listens to a word I say. I don't believe the man understands the ABC of justice.'

'That's how he struck me, when I attended his tribunal.'

'And the worst of it is, he knows just what my allowance is, so can figure out exactly how much the purse will stand. Twice this year he's skinned me to the bone, each time at the instigation of this man Oates – once for exceeding the speed limit in a built-up area, and once because Bartholomew gave him the teeniest little nip on the ankle.'

I tut-tutted sympathetically, but I was wishing that I could edge the conversation back to that notebook. One so frequently finds in girls a disinclination to stick to the important subject.

'The way Oates went on about it, you would have thought Bartholomew had taken his pound of flesh. And I suppose it's all going to happen again now. I'm fed up with this police persecution. One might as well be in Russia. Don't you loathe policemen, Bertie?'

I was not prepared to go quite so far as this in my attitude towards an, on the whole, excellent body of men.

'Well, not *en masse*, if you understand the expression. I suppose they vary, like other sections of the community, some being full of quiet charm, others not so full. I've met some very decent policemen. With the one on duty outside the Drones I am distinctly chummy.

In re this Oates of yours, I haven't seen enough of him,
of course, to form an opinion.'

'Well, you can take it from me that he's one of the
worst. And a bitter retribution awaits him. Do you
remember the time you gave me lunch at your flat? You
were telling me about how you tried to pinch that
policeman's helmet in Leicester Square.'

'That was when I first met your uncle. It was that that
brought us together.'

'Well, I didn't think much of it at the time, but the
other day it suddenly came back to me, and I said to
myself: "Out of the mouths of babes and sucklings!" For
months I had been trying to think of a way of getting
back at this man Oates, and you had showed it to me.'

I started. It seemed to me that her words could bear
but one interpretation.

'You aren't going to pinch his helmet?'

'Of course not.'

'I think you're wise.'

'It's man's work. I can see that. So I've told Harold to
do it. He has often said he would do anything in the
world for me, bless him.'

Stiffy's map, as a rule, tends to be rather grave and
dreamy, giving the impression that she is thinking deep,
beautiful thoughts. Quite misleading, of course. I don't
suppose she would recognize a deep, beautiful thought,
if you handed it to her on a skewer with tartare sauce.
Like Jeeves, she doesn't often smile, but now her lips
had parted – ecstatically, I think – I should have to check
up with Jeeves – and her eyes were sparkling.

'What a man!' she said. 'We're engaged, you know.'

'Oh, are you?'

'Yes, but don't tell a soul. It's frightfully secret. Uncle
Watkyn mustn't know about it till he has been well
sweetened.'

'And who is this Harold?'

'The curate down in the village.' She turned to the dog

Bartholomew. 'Is lovely kind curate going to pinch bad, ugly policeman's helmet for his muzzer, zen, and make her very, very happy?' she said.

Or words to that general trend. I can't do the dialect of course.

I stared at the young pill, appalled at her moral code, if you could call it that. You know, the more I see of women, the more I think that there ought to be a law. Something has got to be done about this sex, or the whole fabric of Society will collapse, and then what silly asses we shall all look.

'Curate?' I said. 'But, Stiffy, you can't ask a curate to go about pinching policemen's helmets.'

'Why not?'

'Well, it's most unusual. You'll get the poor bird unfrocked.'

'Unfrocked?'

'It's something they do to parsons when they catch them bending. And this will inevitably be the outcome of the frightful task you have apportioned to the sainted Harold.'

'I don't see that it's a frightful task.'

'You aren't telling me that it's the sort of thing that comes naturally to curates?'

'Yes, I am. It ought to be right up Harold's street. When he was at Magdalen, before he saw the light, he was the dickens of a chap. Always doing things like that.'

Her mention of Magdalen interested me. It had been my own college.

'Magdalen man, is he? What year? Perhaps I know him.'

'Of course you do. He often speaks of you, and was delighted when I told him you were coming here. Harold Pinker.'

I was astounded.

'Harold Pinker? Old Stinker Pinker? Great Scott! One

of my dearest pals. I've often wondered where he had got to. And all the while he had sneaked off and become a curate. It just shows you how true it is that one-half of the world doesn't know how the other three-quarters lives. Stinker Pinker, by Jove! You really mean that old Stinker cures souls?'

'Certainly. And jolly well, too. The nibs think very highly of him. Any moment now, he may get a vicarage, and then watch his smoke. He'll be a Bishop some day.'

The excitement of discovering a long-lost buddy waned. I found myself returning to the practical issues. I became grave.

And I'll tell you why I became grave. It was all very well for Stiffy to say that this thing would be right up old Stinker's street. She didn't know him as I did. I had watched Harold Pinker through the formative years of his life, and I knew him for what he was – a large, lumbering, Newfoundland puppy of a chap – full of zeal, yes: always doing his best, true; but never quite able to make the grade; a man, in short, who if there was a chance of bungling an enterprise and landing himself in the soup, would snatch at it. At the idea of him being turned on to perform the extraordinarily delicate task of swiping Constable Oates's helmet, the blood froze. He hadn't a chance of getting away with it.

I thought of Stinker, the youth. Built rather on the lines of Roderick Spode, he had played Rugby football not only for his University but also for England, and at the art of hurling an opponent into a mud puddle and jumping on his neck with cleated boots had had few, if any, superiors. If I had wanted someone to help me out with a mad bull, he would have been my first choice. If by some mischance I had found myself trapped in the underground den of the Secret Nine, there was nobody I would rather have seen coming down the chimney than the Rev. Harold Pinker.

But mere thews and sinews do not qualify a man to pinch policemen's helmets. You need finesse.

'He will, will he?' I said. 'A fat lot of bishing he's going to do, if he's caught sneaking helmets from members of his flock.'

'He won't be caught.'

'Of course he'll be caught. At the old Alma Mater he was always caught. He seemed to have no notion whatsoever of going about a thing in a subtle, tactful way. Chuck it, Stiffy. Abandon the whole project.'

'No.'

'Stiffy!'

'No. The show must go on.'

I gave it up. I could see plainly that it would be mere waste of time to try to argue her out of her girlish daydreams. She had the same type of mind, I perceived, as Roberta Wickham, who once persuaded me to go by night to the bedroom of a fellow guest at a country house and puncture his hot-water bottle with a darning needle on the end of a stick.

'Well, if it must be, it must be, I suppose,' I said resignedly. 'But at least impress upon him that it is essential, when pinching policemen's helmets, to give a forward shove before applying the upwards lift. Otherwise, the subject's chin catches in the strap. It was to overlooking this vital point that my own downfall in Leicester Square was due. The strap caught, the cop was enabled to turn and clutch, and before I knew what had happened I was in the dock, saying "Yes, your Honour" and "No, your Honour" to your Uncle Watkyn.'

I fell into a thoughtful silence, as I brooded on the dark future lying in wait for an old friend. I am not a weak man, but I was beginning to wonder if I had been right in squelching so curtly Jeeves's efforts to get me off on a Round-The-World cruise. Whatever you may say against these excursions – the cramped conditions of shipboard, the possibility of getting mixed up with a

crowd of bores, the nuisance of having to go and look at
the Taj Mahal – at least there is this to be said in their
favour, that you escape the mental agony of watching
innocent curates dishing their careers and forfeiting all
chance of rising to great heights in the Church by
getting caught bonneting their parishioners.

I heaved a sigh, and resumed the conversation.

'So you and Stinker are engaged, are you? Why didn't
you tell me when you lunched at the flat?'

'It hadn't happened then. Oh, Bertie, I'm so happy I
could bite a grape. At least, I shall be, if we can get
Uncle Watkyn thinking along "Bless you, my children"
lines.'

'Oh, yes, you were saying, weren't you? About him
being sweetened. How do you mean, sweetened?'

'That's what I want to have a talk with you about.
You remember what I said in my telegram, about there
being something I wanted you to do for me?'

I started. A well-defined uneasiness crept over me. I
had forgotten all about that telegram of hers.

'It's something quite simple.'

I doubted it. I mean to say, if her idea of a suitable job
for curates was the pinching of policemen's helmets,
what sort of an assignment, I could not but ask myself,
was she likely to hand to me? It seemed that the
moment had come for a bit of in-the-bud-nipping.

'Oh, yes?' I said. 'Well, let me tell you here and now
that I'm jolly well not going to do it.'

'Yellow, eh?'

'Bright yellow. Like my Aunt Agatha.'

'What's the matter with her?'

'She's got jaundice.'

'Enough to give her jaundice, having a nephew like
you. Why, you don't even know what it is.'

'I would prefer not to know.'

'Well, I'm going to tell you.'

'I do not wish to listen.'

'You would rather I unleashed Bartholomew? I notice he has been looking at you in that odd way of his. I don't believe he likes you. He does take sudden dislikes to people.'

The Woosters are brave, but not rash. I allowed her to lead me to the stone wall that bordered the terrace, and we sat down. The evening, I remember, was one of perfect tranquillity, featuring a sort of serene peace. Which just shows you.

'I won't keep you long,' she said. 'It's all quite simple and straightforward. I shall have to begin, though, by telling you why we have had to be so dark and secret about the engagement. That's Gussie's fault.'

'What has he done?'

'Just been Gussie, that's all. Just gone about with no chin, goggling through his spectacles and keeping newts in his bedroom. You can understand Uncle Watkyn's feelings. His daughter tells him she is going to get married. "Oh, yes?" he says. "Well, let's have a dekko at the chap." And along rolls Gussie. A nasty jar for a father.'

'Quite.'

'Well, you can't tell me that a time when he is reeling under the blow of having Gussie for a son-in-law is the moment for breaking it to him that I want to marry the curate.'

I saw her point. I recollected Freddie Threepwood telling me that there had been trouble at Blandings about a cousin of his wanting to marry a curate. In that case, I gathered, the strain had been eased by the discovery that the fellow was the heir of a Liverpool shipping millionaire; but, as a broad, general rule, parents do not like their daughters marrying curates, and I take it that the same thing applies to uncles with their nieces.

'You've got to face it. Curates are not so hot. So before anything can be done in the way of removing the veil of secrecy, we have got to sell Harold to Uncle Watkyn. If we play our cards properly, I am hoping that he will give him a vicarage which he has in his gift. Then we shall begin to get somewhere.'

I didn't like her use of the word 'we', but I saw what she was driving at, and I was sorry to have to insert a spanner in her hopes and dreams.

'You wish me to put in a word for Stinker? You would like me to draw your uncle aside and tell him what a splendid fellow Stinker is? There is nothing I would enjoy more, my dear Stiffy, but unfortunately we are not on those terms.'

'No, no, nothing like that.'

'Well, I don't see what more I can do.'

'You will,' she said, and again I was conscious of that subtle feeling of uneasiness. I told myself that I must be firm. But I could not but remember Roberta Wickham and the hot-water bottle. A man thinks he is being chilled steel – or adamant, if you prefer the expression – and suddenly the mists clear away and he finds that he has allowed a girl to talk him into something frightful. Samson had the same experience with Delilah.

'Oh?' I said, guardedly.

She paused in order to tickle the dog Bartholomew under the left ear. Then she resumed.

'Just praising Harold to Uncle Watkyn isn't any use. You need something much cleverer than that. You want to engineer some terrifically brainy scheme that will put him over with a bang. I thought I had got it a few days ago. Do you ever read *Milady's Boudoir*?'

'I once contributed an article to it on "What The Well-Dressed Man Is Wearing", but I am not a regular reader. Why?'

'There was a story in it last week about a Duke who wouldn't let his daughter marry the young secretary, so the secretary got a friend of his to take the Duke out on the lake and upset the boat, and then he dived in and saved the Duke, and the Duke said "Right ho".'

I resolved that no time should be lost in quashing this idea.

'Any notion you may have entertained that I am going to take Sir W. Bassett out in a boat and upset him can be dismissed instanter. To start with, he wouldn't come out on a lake with me.'

'No. And we haven't a lake. And Harold said that if I was thinking of the pond in the village, I could forget it, as it was much too cold to dive into ponds at this time of year. Harold is funny in some ways.'

'I applaud his sturdy common sense.'

'Then I got an idea from another story. It was about a young lover who gets a friend of his to dress up as a tramp and attack the girl's father, and then he dashes in and rescues him.'

I patted her hand gently.

'The flaw in all these ideas of yours,' I pointed out, 'is that the hero always seems to have a half-witted friend who is eager to place himself in the foulest positions on his behalf. In Stinker's case, this is not so. I am fond of Stinker – you could even go so far as to say that I love him like a brother – but there are sharply defined limits to what I am prepared to do to further his interests.'

'Well, it doesn't matter, because he put the presidential veto on that one, too. Something about what the vicar would say if it all came out. But he loves my new one.'

'Oh, you've got a new one?'

'Yes, and it's terrific. The beauty of it is that Harold's part in it is above reproach. A thousand vicars couldn't get the goods on him. The only snag was that he has to have someone working with him, and until I heard you were coming down here I couldn't think who we were to get. But now you have arrived, all is well.'

'It is, is it? I informed you before, young Byng, and I

now inform you again that nothing will induce me to mix myself up with your loathsome schemes.'

'Oh, but, Bertie, you must! We're relying on you. And all you have to do is practically nothing. Just steal Uncle Watkyn's cow-creamer.'

I don't know what you would have done, if a girl in heather-mixture tweeds had sprung this on you, scarcely eight hours after a mauve-faced aunt had sprung the same. It is possible that you would have reeled. Most chaps would, I imagine. Personally, I was more amused than aghast. Indeed, if memory serves me aright, I laughed. If so, it was just as well, for it was about the last chance I had.

'Oh, yes?' I said. 'Tell me more,' I said, feeling that it would be entertaining to allow the little blighter to run on. 'Steal his cow-creamer, eh?'

'Yes. It's a thing brought back from London yesterday for his collection. A sort of silver cow with a kind of blotto look on its face. He thinks the world of it. He had it on the table in front of him at dinner last night, and was gassing away about it. And it was then that I got the idea. I thought that if Harold could pinch it, and then bring it back, Uncle Watkyn would be so grateful that he would start spouting vicarages like a geyser. And then I spotted the catch.'

'Oh, there was a catch?'

'Of course. Don't you see? How would Harold be supposed to have got the thing? If a silver cow is in somebody's collection, and it disappears, and next day a curate rolls round with it, that curate has got to do some good, quick explaining. Obviously, it must be made to look like an outside job.'

'I see. You want me to put on a black mask and break in through the window and snitch this *objet d'art* and hand it over to Stinker? I see. I see.'

I spoke with satirical bitterness, and I should have thought that anyone could have seen that satirical

bitterness was what I was speaking with, but she merely
looked at me with admiration and approval.

'You are clever, Bertie. That's exactly it. Of course,
you needn't wear a mask.'

'You don't think it would help me throw myself into
the part?' I said with s. b., as before.

'Well, it might. That's up to you. But the great thing is
to get through the window. Wear gloves, of course,
because of the fingerprints.'

'Of course.'

'Then Harold will be waiting outside, and he will take
the thing from you.'

'And after that I go off and do my stretch at
Dartmoor?'

'Oh, no. You escape in the struggle, of course.'

'What struggle?'

'And Harold rushes into the house, all over blood –'

'Whose blood?'

'Well, I said yours, and Harold thought his. There
have got to be signs of a struggle to make it more
interesting, and my idea was that he should hit you on
the nose. But he said the thing would carry greater
weight if he was all covered with gore. So how we've left
it is that you both hit each other on the nose. And then
Harold rouses the house and comes in and shows Uncle
Watkyn the cow-creamer and explains what happened,
and everything's fine. Because, I mean, Uncle Watkyn
couldn't just say "Oh, thanks" and leave it at that, could
he? He would be compelled, if he had a spark of decency
in him, to cough up that vicarage. Don't you think it's a
wonderful scheme, Bertie?'

I rose. My face was cold and hard.

'Most. But I'm sorry –'

'You don't mean you won't do it, now that you see
that it will cause you practically no inconvenience at
all? It would only take about ten minutes of your time.'

'I do mean I won't do it.'

'Well, I think you're a pig.'

'A pig, maybe, but a shrewd, level-headed pig. I wouldn't touch the project with a bargepole. I tell you I know Stinker. Exactly how he would muck the thing up and get us all landed in the jug, I cannot say, but he would find a way. And now I'll take that book, if you don't mind.'

'What book? Oh, that one of Gussie's.'

'Yes.'

'What do you want it for?'

'I want it,' I said gravely, 'because Gussie is not fit to be in charge of it. He might lose it again, in which event it might fall into the hands of your uncle, in which event he would certainly kick the stuffing out of the Gussie–Madeline wedding arrangements, in which event I would be up against it as few men have ever been up against it before.'

'You?'

'None other.'

'How do you come into it?'

'I will tell you.'

And in a few terse words I outlined for her the events which had taken place at Brinkley Court, the situation which had arisen from those events and the hideous peril which threatened me if Gussie's entry were to be scratched.

'You will understand,' I said, 'that I am implying nothing derogatory to your cousin Madeline, when I say that the idea of being united to her in the bonds of holy wedlock is one that freezes the gizzard. The fact is in no way to her discredit. I should feel just the same about marrying many of the world's noblest women. There are certain females whom one respects, admires, reveres, but only from a distance. If they show any signs of attempting to come closer, one is prepared to fight them off with a blackjack. It is to this group that your cousin Madeline belongs. A charming girl, and the ideal mate

for Augustus Fink-Nottle, but ants in the pants to
Bertram.'

She drank this in.

'I see. Yes, I suppose Madeline is a bit of a Gawd-help-us.'

'The expresion "Gawd-help-us" is one which I would
not have gone so far as to use myself, for I think a
chivalrous man ought to stop somewhere. But since you
have brought it up, I admit that it covers the facts.'

'I never realized that that was how things were. No
wonder you want that book.'

'Exactly.'

'Well, all this has opened up a new line of thought.'

That grave, dreamy look had come into her face. She
massaged the dog Bartholomew's spine with a pensive
foot.

'Come on,' I said, chafing at the delay. 'Slip it across.'

'Just a moment. I'm trying to straighten it all out in
my mind. You know, Bertie, I really ought to take that
book to Uncle Watkyn.'

'What!'

'That's what my conscience tells me to do. After all, I
owe a lot to him. For years he has been a second father
to me. And he ought to know how Gussie feels about
him, oughtn't he? I mean to say, a bit tough on the old
buster, cherishing what he thinks is a harmless newt-
fancier in his bosom, when all the time it's a snake that
goes about criticizing the way he drinks soup. However,
as you're being so sweet and are going to help Harold
and me by stealing that cow-creamer, I suppose I shall
have to stretch a point.'

We Woosters are pretty quick. I don't suppose it was
more than a couple of minutes before I figured out what
she meant. I read her purpose, and shuddered.

She was naming the Price of the Papers. In other
words, after being blackmailed by an aunt at breakfast, I
was now being blackmailed by a female crony before

dinner. Pretty good going, even for this lax post-war world.

'Stiffy!' I cried.

'It's no good saying "Stiffy!" Either you sit in and do your bit, or Uncle Watkyn gets some racy light reading over his morning egg and coffee. Think it over, Bertie.'

She hoisted the dog Bartholomew to his feet, and trickled off towards the house. The last I saw of her was a meaning look, directed at me over her shoulder, and it went through me like a knife.

I had slumped back onto the wall, and I sat there, stunned. Just how long, I don't know, but it was a goodish time. Winged creatures of the night barged into me, but I gave them little attention. It was not till a voice suddenly spoke a couple of feet or so above my bowed head that I came out of the coma.

'Good evening, Wooster,' said the voice.

I looked up. The cliff-like mass looming over me was Roderick Spode.

I suppose even Dictators have their chummy moments, when they put their feet up and relax with the boys, but it was plain from the outset that if Roderick Spode had a sunnier side, he had not come with any idea of exhibiting it now. His manner was curt. One sensed the absence of the bonhomous note.

'I should like a word with you, Wooster.'

'Oh, yes?'

'I have been talking to Sir Watkyn Bassett, and he has told me the whole story of the cow-creamer.'

'Oh, yes?'

'And we know why you are here.'

'Oh, yes?'

'Stop saying "Oh, yes?" you miserable worm, and listen to me.'

Many chaps might have resented his tone. I did myself, as a matter of fact. But you know how it is.

There are some fellows you are right on your toes to tick off when they call you a miserable worm, others not quite so much.

'Oh, yes,' he said, saying it himself, dash it, 'it is perfectly plain to us why you are here. You have been sent by your uncle to steal this cow-creamer for him. You needn't trouble to deny it. I found you with the thing in your hands this afternoon. And now, we learn, your aunt is arriving. The muster of the vultures, ha!'

He paused a moment, then repeated 'The muster of the vultures,' as if he thought pretty highly of it as a gag. I couldn't see that it was so very hot myself.

'Well, what I came to tell you, Wooster, was that you are being watched – watched closely. And if you are caught stealing that cow-creamer, I can assure you that you will go to prison. You need entertain no hope that Sir Watkyn will shrink from creating a scandal. He will do his duty as a citizen and a Justice of the Peace.'

Here he laid a hand upon my shoulder, and I can't remember when I have experienced anything more unpleasant. Apart from what Jeeves would have called the symbolism of the action, he had a grip like the bite of a horse.

'Did you say "Oh, yes?"' he asked.

'Oh, no,' I assured him.

'Good. Now, what you are saying to yourself, no doubt, is that you will not be caught. You imagine that you and this precious aunt of yours will be clever enough between you to steal the cow-creamer without being detected. It will do you no good, Wooster. If the thing disappears, however cunningly you and your female accomplice may have covered your traces, I shall know where it has gone, and I shall immediately beat you to a jelly. To a jelly,' he repeated, rolling the words round his tongue as if they were vintage port. 'Have you got that clear?'

'Oh, quite.'

'You are sure you understand?'

'Oh, definitely.'

'Splendid.'

A dim figure was approaching across the terrace, and he changed his tone to one of a rather sickening geniality.

'What a lovely evening, is it not? Extraordinarily mild for the time of year. Well, I mustn't keep you any longer. You will be wanting to go and dress for dinner. Just a black tie. We are quite informal here. Yes?'

The word was addressed to the dim figure. A familiar cough revealed its identity.

'I wished to speak to Mr Wooster, sir. I have a message for him from Mrs Travers. Mrs Travers presents her compliments, sir, and desires me to say that she is in the Blue Room and would be glad if you could make it convenient to call upon her there as soon as possible. She has a matter of importance which she wishes to discuss.'

I heard Spode snort in the darkness.

'So Mrs Travers has arrived?'

'Yes, sir.'

'And has a matter of importance to discuss with Mr Wooster?'

'Yes, sir.'

'Ha!' said Spode, and biffed off with a short, sharp laugh.

I rose from my seat.

'Jeeves,' I said, 'stand by to counsel and advise. The plot has thickened.'

5

I slid into the shirt, and donned the knee-length under-wear.

'Well, Jeeves,' I said, 'how about it?'

During the walk to the house I had placed him in possession of the latest developments, and had left him to turn them over in his mind with a view to finding a formula, while I went along the passage and took a hasty bath. I now gazed at him hopefully, like a seal awaiting a bit of fish.

'Thought of anything, Jeeves?'

'Not yet, sir, I regret to say.'

'What, no results whatever?'

'None, sir, I fear.'

I groaned a hollow one, and shoved on the trousers. I had become so accustomed to having this gifted man weigh in with the ripest ideas at the drop of the hat that the possibility of his failing to deliver on this occasion had not occurred to me. The blow was a severe one, and it was with a quivering hand that I now socked the feet. A strange frozen sensation had come over me, rendering the physical and mental processes below par. It was as though both limbs and bean had been placed in a refrigerator and overlooked for several days.

'It may be, Jeeves,' I said, a thought occurring, 'that you haven't got the whole scenario clear in your mind. I was able to give you only the merest outline before going off to scour the torso. I think it would help if we did what they do in the thrillers. Do you ever read thrillers?'

'Not very frequently, sir.'

'Well, there's always a bit where the detective, in order to clarify his thoughts, writes down a list of suspects, motives, times when, alibis, clues and what not. Let us try this plan. Take pencil and paper, Jeeves, and we will assemble the facts. Entitle the thing "Wooster, B. – position of." Ready?'

'Yes, sir.'

'Right. Now, then. Item One – Aunt Dahlia says that if I don't pinch that cow-creamer and hand it over to her, she will bar me from her table, and no more of Anatole's cooking.'

'Yes, sir.'

'We now come to Item Two – viz., if I do pinch the cow-creamer and hand it over to her, Spode will beat me to a jelly.'

'Yes, sir.'

'Furthermore – Item Three – if I pinch it and hand it over to her and don't pinch it and hand it over to Harold Pinker, not only shall I undergo the jellying process alluded to above, but Stiffy will take that notebook of Gussie's and hand it over to Sir Watkyn Bassett. And you know and I know what the result of that would be. Well, there you are. That's the set-up. You've got it?'

'Yes, sir. It is certainly a somewhat unfortunate state of affairs.'

I gave him one of my looks.

'Jeeves,' I said, 'don't try me too high. Not at a moment like this. Somewhat unfortunate, forsooth! Who was it you were telling me about the other day, on whose head all the sorrows of the world had come?'

'The Mona Lisa, sir.'

'Well, if I met the Mona Lisa at this moment, I would shake her by the hand and assure her that I knew just how she felt. You see before you, Jeeves, a toad beneath the harrow.'

'Yes, sir. The trousers perhaps a quarter of an inch higher, sir. One aims at the carelessly graceful break over the instep. It is a matter of the nicest adjustment.'

'Like that?'

'Admirable, sir.'

I sighed.

'There are moments, Jeeves, when one asks oneself "Do trousers matter?"'

'The mood will pass, sir.'

'I don't see why it should. If you can't think of a way out of this mess, it seems to me that it is the end. Of course,' I proceeded on a somewhat brighter note, 'you haven't really had time to get your teeth into the problem yet. While I am at dinner, examine it once more from every angle. It is just possible that an inspiration might pop up. Inspirations do, don't they? All in a flash, as it were?'

'Yes, sir. The mathematician Archimedes is related to have discovered the principle of displacement quite suddenly one morning, while in his bath.'

'Well, there you are. And I don't suppose he was such a devil of a chap. Compared with you, I mean.'

'A gifted man, I believe, sir. It has been a matter of general regret that he was subsequently killed by a common soldier.'

'Too bad. Still, all flesh is as grass, what?'

'Very true, sir.'

I lighted a thoughtful cigarette and, dismissing Archimedes for the nonce, allowed my mind to dwell once more on the ghastly jam into which I had been thrust by young Stiffy's ill-advised behaviour.

'You know, Jeeves,' I said, 'when you really start to look into it, it's perfectly amazing how the opposite sex seems to go out of its way to snooter me. You recall Miss Wickham and the hot-water bottle?'

'Yes, sir.'

'And Gwladys what-was-her-name, who put her boyfriend with the broken leg to bed in my flat?'

'Yes, sir.'

'And Pauline Stoker, who invaded my rural cottage at dead of night in a bathing suit?'

'Yes, sir.'

'What a sex! What a sex, Jeeves! But none of that sex, however deadlier than the male, can be ranked in the same class with this Stiffy. Who was the chap lo whose name led all the rest – the bird with the angel?'

'Abou ben Adhem, sir.'

'That's Stiffy. She's the top. Yes, Jeeves?'

'I was merely about to enquire, sir, if Miss Byng, when she uttered her threat of handing over Mr Fink-Nottle's notebook to Sir Watkyn, by any chance spoke with a twinkle in her eye?'

'A roguish one, you mean, indicating that she was merely pulling my leg? Not a suspicion of it. No, Jeeves, I have seen untwinkling eyes before, many of them, but never a pair so totally free from twinkle as hers. She wasn't kidding. She meant business. She was fully aware that she was doing something which even by female standards was raw, but she didn't care. The whole fact of the matter is that all this modern emancipation of women has resulted in them getting it up their noses and not giving a damn what they do. It was not like this in Queen Victoria's day. The Prince Consort would have had a word to say about a girl like Stiffy, what?'

'I can conceive that His Royal Highness might quite possibly not have approved of Miss Byng.'

'He would have had her over his knee, laying into her with a slipper, before she knew where she was. And I wouldn't put it past him to have treated Aunt Dahlia in a similar fashion. Talking of which, I suppose I ought to be going and seeing the aged relative.'

'She appeared very desirous of conferring with you, sir.'

'Far from mutual, Jeeves, that desire. I will confess frankly that I am not looking forward to the *séance*.'

'No, sir?'

'No. You see, I sent her a telegram just before tea, saying that I wasn't going to pinch that cow-creamer, and she must have left London long before it arrived. In other words, she has come expecting to find a nephew straining at the leash to do her bidding, and the news will have to be broken to her that the deal is off. She will not like this, Jeeves, and I don't mind telling you that the more I contemplate the coming chat, the colder the feet become.'

'If I might suggest, sir – it is, of course, merely a palliative – but it has often been found in times of despondency that the assumption of formal evening dress has a stimulating effect on the morale.'

'You think I ought to put on a white tie? Spode told me black.'

'I consider that the emergency justifies the departure, sir.'

'Perhaps you're right.'

And, of course, he was. In these delicate matters of psychology he never errs. I got into the full soup and fish, and was immediately conscious of a marked improvement. The feet became warmer, a sparkle returned to the lack-lustre eyes, and the soul seemed to expand as if someone had got to work on it with a bicycle pump. And I was surveying the effect in the mirror, kneading the tie with gentle fingers and running over in my mind a few things which I proposed to say to Aunt Dahlia if she started getting tough, when the door opened and Gussie came in.

At the sight of this bespectacled bird, a pang of compassion shot through me, for a glance was enough to tell me that he was not abreast of stop-press events. There was visible in his demeanour not one of the earmarks of a man to whom Stiffy had been confiding her plans. His bearing was buoyant, and I exchanged a swift, meaning glance with Jeeves. Mine said 'He little knows!' and so did his.

'What ho!' said Gussie. 'What ho! Hallo, Jeeves.'

'Good evening, sir.'

'Well, Bertie, what's the news? Have you seen her?'

The pang of compash became more acute. I heaved a silent sigh. It was to be my mournful task to administer to this old friend a very substantial sock on the jaw, and I shrank from it.

Still, these things have to be faced. The surgeon's knife, I mean to say.

'Yes,' I said. 'Yes, I've seen her. Jeeves, have we any brandy?'

'No, sir.'

'Could you get a spot?'

'Certainly, sir.'

'Better bring the bottle.'

'Very good, sir.'

He melted away, and Gussie stared at me in honest amazement.

'What's all this? You can't start swigging brandy just before dinner.'

'I do not propose to. It is for you, my suffering old martyr at the stake, that I require the stuff.'

'I don't drink brandy.'

'I'll bet you drink this brandy – yes, and call for more. Sit down, Gussie, and let us chat awhile.'

And depositing him in the armchair, I engaged him in desultory conversation about the weather and the crops. I didn't want to spring the thing on him till the restorative was handy. I prattled on, endeavouring to infuse into my deportment a sort of bedside manner which would prepare him for the worst, and it was not long before I noted that he was looking at me oddly.

'Bertie, I believe you're pie-eyed.'

'Not at all.'

'Then what are you babbling like this for?'

'Just filling in till Jeeves gets back with the fluid. Ah, thank you, Jeeves.'

I took the brimming beaker from his hand, and gently placed Gussie's fingers round the stem.

'You had better go and inform Aunt Dahlia that I shall not be able to keep our tryst, Jeeves. This is going to take some time.'

'Very good, sir.'

I turned to Gussie, who was now looking like a bewildered halibut.

'Gussie,' I said, 'drink that down, and listen. I'm afraid I have bad news for you. About that notebook.'

'About the notebook?'

'Yes.'

'You don't mean she hasn't got it?'

'That is precisely the nub or crux. She has, and she is going to give it to Pop Bassett.'

I had expected him to take it fairly substantially, and he did. His eyes, like stars, started from their spheres and he leaped from the chair, spilling the contents of the glass and causing the room to niff like the saloon bar of a pub on a Saturday night.

'What!'

'That is the posish, I fear.'

'But, my gosh!'

'Yes.'

'You don't really mean that?'

'I do.'

'But why?'

'She has her reasons.'

'But she can't realize what will happen.'

'Yes, she does.'

'It will mean ruin!'

'Definitely.'

'Oh, my gosh!'

It has often been said that disaster brings out the best

in the Woosters. A strange calm descended on me. I patted his shoulder.

'Courage, Gussie! Think of Archimedes.'

'Why?'

'He was killed by a common soldier.'

'What of it?'

'Well, it can't have been pleasant for him, but I have no doubt he passed out smiling.'

My intrepid attitude had a good effect. He became more composed. I don't say that even now we were exactly like a couple of French aristocrats waiting for the tumbril, but there was a certain resemblance.

'When did she tell you this?'

'On the terrace not long ago.'

'And she really meant it?'

'Yes.'

'There wasn't –'

'A twinkle in her eyes? No. No twinkle.'

'Well, isn't there any way of stopping her?'

I had been expecting him to bring this up, but I was sorry he had done so. I foresaw a period of fruitless argument.

'Yes,' I said. 'There is. She says she will forgo her dreadful purpose if I steal old Bassett's cow-creamer.'

'You mean that silver cow thing he was showing us at dinner last night?'

'That's the one.'

'But why?'

I explained the position of affairs. He listened intelligently, his face brightening.

'Now I see! Now I understand! I couldn't imagine what her idea was. Her behaviour seemed so absolutely motiveless. Well, that's fine. That solves everything.'

I hated to put a crimp in his happy exuberance, but it had to be done.

'Not quite, because I'm jolly well not going to do it.'

'What! Why not?'

'Because, if I do, Roderick Spode says he will beat me to a jelly.'

'What's Roderick Spode got to do with it?'

'He appears to have espoused that cow-creamer's cause. No doubt from esteem for old Bassett.'

'H'm! Well, you aren't afraid of Roderick Spode.'

'Yes, I am.'

'Nonsense! I know you better than that.'

'No, you don't.'

He took a turn up and down the room.

'But, Bertie, there's nothing to be afraid of in a man like Spode, a mere mass of beef and brawn. He's bound to be slow on his feet. He would never catch you.'

'I don't intend to try him out as a sprinter.'

'Besides, it isn't as if you had to stay on here. You can be off the moment you've put the thing through. Send a note down to this curate after dinner, telling him to be on the spot at midnight, and then go to it. Here is the schedule, as I see it. Steal cow-creamer – say, twelve-fifteen to twelve-thirty, or call it twelve-forty, to allow for accidents. Twelve-forty-five, be at stables, starting up your car. Twelve-fifty, out on the open road, having accomplished a nice, smooth job. I can't think what you're worrying about. The whole thing seems childishly simple to me.'

'Nevertheless –'

'You won't do it?'

'No.'

He moved to the mantelpiece, and began fiddling with a statuette of a shepherdess of sorts.

'Is this Bertie Wooster speaking?' he asked.

'It is.'

'Bertie Wooster whom I admired so at school – the boy we used to call "Daredevil Bertie"?'

'That's right.'

'In that case, I suppose there is nothing more to be said.'

'No.'

'Our only course is to recover the book from the Byng.'

'How do you propose to do that?'

He pondered, frowning. Then the little grey cells seemed to stir.

'I know. Listen. That book means a lot to her, doesn't it?'

'It does.'

'This being so, she would carry it on her person, as I did.'

'I suppose so.'

'In her stocking, probably. Very well, then.'

'How do you mean, very well, then?'

'Don't you see what I'm driving at?'

'No.'

'Well, listen. You could easily engage her in a sort of friendly romp, if you know what I mean, in the course of which it would be simple to . . . well, something in the nature of a jocular embrace . . .'

I checked him sharply. There are limits, and we Woosters recognize them.

'Gussie, are you suggesting that I prod Stiffy's legs?'

'Yes.'

'Well, I'm not going to.'

'Why not?'

'We need not delve into my reasons,' I said, stiffly. 'Suffice it that the shot is not on the board.'

He gave me a look, a kind of wide-eyed, reproachful look, such as a dying newt might have given him, if he had forgotten to change its water regularly. He drew in his breath sharply.

'You certainly have altered completely from the boy I knew at school,' he said. 'You seem to have gone all to pieces. No pluck. No dash. No enterprise. Alcohol, I suppose.'

360

He sighed and broke the shepherdess, and we moved to the door. As I opened it, he gave me another look.

'You aren't coming down to dinner like that, are you? What are you wearing a white tie for?'

'Jeeves recommended it, to keep up the spirits.'

'Well, you're going to feel a perfect ass. Old Bassett dines in a velvet smoking-jacket with soup stains across the front. Better change.'

There was a good deal in what he said. One does not like to look conspicuous. At the risk of lowering the morale, I turned to doff the tails. And as I did so there came to us from the drawing room below the sound of a fresh young voice chanting, to the accompaniment of a piano, what exhibited all the symptoms of being an old English folk song. The ear detected a good deal of 'Hey nonny nonny', and all that sort of thing.

This uproar had the effect of causing Gussie's eyes to smoulder behind the spectacles. It was as if he were feeling that this was just that little bit extra which is more than man can endure.

'Stephanie Byng!' he said bitterly. 'Singing at a time like this!'

He snorted, and left the room. And I was just finishing tying the black tie, when Jeeves entered.

'Mrs Travers,' he announced formally.

An 'Oh, golly!' broke from my lips. I had known, of course, hearing that formal announcement, that she was coming, but so does a poor blighter taking a stroll and looking up and seeing a chap in an aeroplane dropping a bomb on his head know that that's coming, but it doesn't make it any better when it arrives.

I could see that she was a good deal stirred up – all of a doodah would perhaps express it better – and I hastened to bung her civilly into the armchair and make my apologies.

'Frightfully sorry I couldn't come and see you, old

ancestor,' I said. 'I was closeted with Gussie Fink-Nottle
upon a matter deeply affecting our mutual interests.
Since we last met, there have been new developments,
and my affairs have become somewhat entangled, I
regret to say. You might put it that Hell's foundations
are quivering. That is not overstating it, Jeeves?'

'No, sir.'

She dismissed my protestations with a wave of the
hand.

'So you're having your troubles, too, are you? Well, I
don't know what new developments there have been at
your end, but there has been a new development at
mine, and it's a stinker. That's why I've come down
here in such a hurry. The most rapid action has
got to be taken, or the home will be in the melting-
pot.'

I began to wonder if even the Mona Lisa could have
found the going so sticky as I was finding it. One thing
after another, I mean to say.

'What is it?' I asked. 'What's happened?'

She choked for a moment, then contrived to utter a
single word.

'Anatole!'

'Anatole?' I took her hand and pressed it soothingly.
'Tell me, old fever patient,' I said, 'what, if anything, are
you talking about? How do you mean, Anatole?'

'If we don't look slippy, I shall lose him.'

A cold hand seemed to clutch at my heart.

'Lose him?'

'Yes.'

'Even after doubling his wages?'

'Even after doubling his wages. Listen, Bertie. Just
before I left home this afternoon, a letter arrived for Tom
from Sir Watkyn Bassett. When I say "just before I left
home", that was what made me leave home. Because do
you know what was in it?'

'What?'

'It contained an offer to swap the cow-creamer for Anatole, and Tom is seriously considering it!'

I stared at her.

'What? Incredulous!'

'Incredible, sir.'

'Thank you, Jeeves. Incredible! I don't believe it. Uncle Tom would never contemplate such a thing for an instant.'

'Wouldn't he? That's all you know. Do you remember Pomeroy, the butler we had before Seppings?'

'I should say so. A noble fellow.'

'A treasure.'

'A gem. I never could think why you let him go.'

'Tom traded him to the Bessington-Copes for an oviform chocolate pot on three scroll feet.'

I struggled with a growing despair.

'But surely the delirious old ass – or, rather Uncle Tom – wouldn't fritter Anatole away like that?'

'He certainly would.'

She rose, and moved restlessly to the mantelpiece. I could see that she was looking for something to break as a relief to her surging emotions – what Jeeves would have called a palliative – and courteously drew her attention to a terra cotta figure of the Infant Samuel at Prayer. She thanked me briefly, and hurled it against the opposite wall.

'I tell you, Bertie, there are no lengths to which a really loony collector will not go to secure a coveted specimen. Tom's actual words, as he handed me the letter to read, were that it would give him genuine pleasure to skin old Bassett alive and personally drop him into a vat of boiling oil, but that he saw no alternative but to meet his demands. The only thing that stopped him wiring him there and then that it was a deal was my telling him that you had gone to Totleigh Towers expressly to pinch the cow-creamer, and that he would have it in his hands almost immediately. How are you coming along in that direction, Bertie? Formed your schemes? All your plans cut and dried? We can't afford to waste time. Every moment is precious.'

I felt a trifle boneless. The news, I saw, would now have to be broken, and I hoped that that was all there would be. This aunt is a formidable old creature, when stirred, and I could not but recall what had happened to the Infant Samuel.

'I was going to talk to you about that,' I said. 'Jeeves, have you that document we prepared?'

'Here it is, sir.'

'Thank you, Jeeves. And I think it might be a good thing if you were to go and bring a spot more brandy.'

'Very good, sir.'

He withdrew, and I slipped her the paper, bidding her read it attentively. She gave it the eye.

'What's all this?'

'You will soon see. Note how it is headed. "Wooster, B. – position of." Those words tell the story. They explain,' I said, backing a step and getting ready to duck, 'why it is that I must resolutely decline to pinch that cow-creamer.'

'What!'

'I sent you a telegram to that effect this afternoon, but, of course, it missed you.'

She was looking at me pleadingly, like a fond mother at an idiot child who has just pulled something exceptionally goofy.

'But, Bertie, dear, haven't you been listening? About Anatole? Don't you realize the position?'

'Oh, quite.'

'Then have you gone cuckoo? When I say "gone", of course – '

I held up a checking hand.

'Let me explain, aged r. You will recall that I mentioned to you that there had been some recent developments. One of these is that Sir Watkyn Bassett knows all about this cow-creamer-pinching scheme and is watching my every movement. Another is that he has confided his suspicions to a pal of his named Spode. Perhaps on your arrival here you met Spode?'

'That big fellow?'

'Big is right, though perhaps "supercolossal" would be more the *mot juste*. Well, Sir Watkyn, as I say, has confided his suspicions to Spode, and I have it from the latter personally that if that cow-creamer disappears, he will beat me to a jelly. That is why nothing constructive can be accomplished.'

A silence of some duration followed these remarks. I could see that she was chewing on the thing and reluctantly coming to the conclusion that it was no idle whim of Bertram's that was causing him to fail her in her hour of need. She appreciated the cleft stick in which he found himself and, unless I am vastly mistaken, shuddered at it.

This relative is a woman who, in the days of my boyhood and adolescence, was accustomed frequently to clump me over the side of the head when she considered that my behaviour warranted this gesture, and I have often felt in these days that she was on the point of doing it again. But beneath this earhole-sloshing exterior there beats a tender heart, and her love for Bertram is, I know, deep-rooted. She would be the last person to wish to see him get his eyes bunged up and have that well-shaped nose punched out of position.

'I see,' she said, at length. 'Yes. That makes things difficult, of course.'

'Extraordinarily difficult. If you care to describe the situation as an *impasse*, it will be all right with me.'

'Said he would beat you to a jelly, did he?'

'That was the expression he used. He repeated it, so that there should be no mistake.'

'Well, I wouldn't for the world have you manhandled by that big stiff. You wouldn't have a chance against a gorilla like that. He would tear the stuffing out of you before you could say "Pip-pip". He would rend you limb from limb and scatter the fragments to the four winds.'

I winced a little.

'No need to make a song about it, old flesh and blood.'

'You're sure he meant what he said?'

'Quite.'

'His bark may be worse than his bite.'

I smiled sadly.

'I see where you're heading, Aunt Dahlia,' I said. 'In another minute you will be asking if there wasn't a twinkle in his eye as he spoke. There wasn't. The policy which Roderick Spode outlined to me at our recent interview is the policy which he will pursue and fulfil.'

'Then we seem to be stymied. Unless Jeeves can think of something.' She addressed the man, who had just entered with the brandy – not before it was time. I couldn't think why he had taken so long over it. 'We are talking of Mr Spode, Jeeves.'

'Yes, madam?'

'Jeeves and I have already discussed the Spode menace,' I said moodily, 'and he confesses himself baffled. For once, that substantial brain has failed to click. He has brooded, but no formula.'

Aunt Dahlia had been swigging the brandy gratefully, and there now came into her face a thoughtful look.

'You know what has just occurred to me?' she said.

'Say on, old thicker than water,' I replied, still with that dark moodiness. 'I'll bet it's rotten.'

'It's not rotten at all. It may solve everything. I've been wondering if this man Spode hasn't some shady secret. Do you know anything about him, Jeeves?'

'No, madam.'

'How do you mean, a secret?'

'What I was turning over in my mind was the thought that, if he had some chink in his armour, one might hold him up by means of it, thus drawing his fangs. I remember, when I was a girl, seeing your Uncle George kiss my governess, and it was amazing how it eased the strain later on, when there was any question of her keeping me in after school to write out the principal imports and exports of the United Kingdom. You see what I mean? Suppose we knew that Spode had shot a fox, or something? You don't think much of it?' she said, seeing that I was pursing my lips dubiously.

'I can see it as an idea. But there seems to me to be one fatal snag – viz. that we don't know.'

'Yes, that's true.' She rose. 'Oh, well, it was just a random thought, I merely threw it out. And now I think I will be returning to my room and spraying my temples with *eau-de-Cologne*. My head feels as if it were about to burst like shrapnel.'

The door closed. I sank into the chair which she had vacated, and mopped the b.

'Well, that's over,' I said thankfully. 'She took the blow better than I had hoped, Jeeves. The Quorn trains its daughters well. But, stiff though her upper lip was, you could see that she felt it deeply, and that brandy came in handy. By the way, you were the dickens of a while bringing it. A St Bernard dog would have been there and back in half the time.'

'Yes, sir. I am sorry. I was detained in conversation by Mr Fink-Nottle.'

I sat pondering.

'You know, Jeeves,' I said, 'that wasn't at all a bad idea of Aunt Dahlia's about getting the goods on Spode. Fundamentally, it was sound. If Spode had buried the body and we knew where, it would unquestionably render him a negligible force. But you say you know nothing about him.'

'No, sir.'

'And I doubt if there is anything to know, anyway. There are some chaps, one look at whom is enough to tell you that they are pukka sahibs who play the game and do not do the things that aren't done, and prominent among these, I fear, is Roderick Spode. I shouldn't imagine that the most rigorous investigation would uncover anything about him worse than that moustache of his, and to the world's scrutiny of that he obviously has no objection, or he wouldn't wear the damned thing.'

'Very true, sir. Still, it might be worth while to institute enquiries.'

'Yes, but where?'

'I was thinking of the Junior Ganymede, sir. It is a club for gentlemen's personal gentlemen in Curzon Street, to which I have belonged for some years. The personal attendant of a gentleman of Mr Spode's prominence would be sure to be a member, and he would, of course, have confided to the secretary a good deal of material concerning him, for insertion in the club book.'

'Eh?'

'Under Rule Eleven, every new member is required to supply the club with full information regarding his employer. This not only provides entertaining reading, but serves as a warning to members who may be contemplating taking service with gentlemen who fall short of the ideal.'

A thought struck me, and I started. Indeed, I started rather violently.

'What happened when you joined?'

'Sir?'

'Did you tell them all about me?'

'Oh, yes, sir.'

'What, everything? The time when old Stoker was after me and I had to black up with boot polish in order to assume a rudimentary disguise?'

'Yes, sir.'

'And the occasion on which I came home after Pongo

Twistleton's birthday party and mistook the standard lamp for a burglar?'

'Yes, sir. The members like to have these things to read on wet afternoons.'

'They do, do they? And suppose some wet afternoon Aunt Agatha reads them? Did that occur to you?'

'The contingency of Mrs Spenser Gregson obtaining access to the club book is a remote one.'

'I dare say. But recent events under this very roof will have shown you how women do obtain access to books.'

I relapsed into silence, pondering on this startling glimpse he had accorded of what went on in institutions like the Junior Ganymede, of the existence of which I had previously been unaware. I had known, of course, that at nights, after serving the frugal meal, Jeeves would put on the old bowler hat and slip round the corner, but I had always supposed his destination to have been the saloon bar of some neighbouring pub. Of clubs in Curzon Street I had had no inkling.

Still less had I had an inkling that some of the fruitiest of Bertram Wooster's possibly ill-judged actions were being inscribed in a book. The whole thing to my mind smacked rather unpleasantly of Abou ben Adhem and Recording Angels, and I found myself frowning somewhat.

Still, there didn't seem much to be done about it, so I returned to what Constable Oates would have called the point at tissue.

'Then what's your idea? To apply to the Secretary for information about Spode?'

'Yes, sir.'

'You think he'll give it to you?'

'Oh, yes, sir.'

'You mean he scatters these data – these extraordinarily dangerous data – these data that might spell ruin if they fell into the wrong hands – broadcast to whoever asks for them?'

'Only to members, sir.'

'How soon could you get in touch with him?'

'I could ring him up on the telephone immediately, sir.'

'Then do so, Jeeves, and if possible chalk the call up to Sir Watkyn Bassett. And don't lose your nerve when you hear the girl say "Three minutes". Carry on regardless. Cost what it may, ye Sec. must be made to understand – and understand thoroughly – that now is the time for all good men to come to the aid of the party.'

'I think I can convince him that an emergency exists, sir.'

'If you can't, refer him to me.'

'Very good, sir.'

He started off on his errand of mercy.

'Oh, by the way, Jeeves,' I said, as he was passing through the door, 'did you say you had been talking to Gussie?'

'Yes, sir.'

'Had he anything new to report?'

'Yes, sir. It appears that his relations with Miss Bassett have been severed. The engagement is broken off.'

He floated out, and I leaped three feet. A dashed difficult thing to do, when you're sitting in an armchair, but I managed it.

'Jeeves!' I yelled.

But he had gone, leaving not a wrack behind.

From downstairs there came the sudden booming of the dinner gong.

6

It has always given me a bit of a pang to look back at
that dinner and think that agony of mind prevented me
sailing into it in the right carefree mood, for it was one
which in happier circumstances I would have got my
nose down to with a will. Whatever Sir Watkyn Bassett's
moral shortcomings, he did his guests extraordinarily
well at the festive board, and even in my preoccupied
condition it was plain to me in the first five minutes
that his cook was a woman who had the divine fire in
her. From a Grade A soup we proceeded to a toothsome
fish, and from the toothsome fish to a salmi of game
which even Anatole might have been proud to sponsor.
Add asparagus, a jam omelette and some spirited
sardines on toast, and you will see what I mean.

All wasted on me, of course. As the fellow said, better
a dinner of herbs when you're all buddies together than a
regular blow-out when you're not, and the sight of
Gussie and Madeline Bassett sitting side by side at the
other end of the table turned the food to ashes in my m.
I viewed them with concern.

You know what engaged couples are like in mixed
company, as a rule. They put their heads together and
converse in whispers. They slap and giggle. They pat and
prod. I have even known the female member of the duo
to feed her companion with a fork. There was none of
this sort of thing about Madeline Bassett and Gussie. He
looked pale and corpse-like, she cold and proud and
aloof. They put in the time for the most part making
bread pills and, as far as I was able to ascertain, didn't
exchange a word from start to finish. Oh, yes, once –

when he asked her to pass the salt, and she passed the pepper, and he said 'I meant the salt,' and she said 'Oh, really?' and passed the mustard.

There could be no question whatever that Jeeves was right. Brass rags had been parted by the young couple, and what was weighing upon me, apart from the tragic aspect, was the mystery of it all. I could think of no solution, and I looked forward to the conclusion of the meal, when the women should have legged it and I would be able to get together with Gussie over the port and learn the inside dope.

To my surprise, however, the last female had no sooner passed through the door than Gussie, who had been holding it open, shot through after her like a diving duck and did not return, leaving me alone with my host and Roderick Spode. And as they sat snuggled up together at the far end of the table, talking to one another in low voices, and staring at me from time to time as if I had been a ticket-of-leave man who had got in by crashing the gate and might be expected, unless carefully watched, to pocket a spoon or two, it was not long before I, too, left. Murmuring something about fetching my cigarette case, I sidled out and went up to my room. It seemed to me that either Gussie or Jeeves would be bound to look in there sooner or later.

A cheerful fire was burning in the grate, and to while away the time I pulled the armchair up and got out the mystery story I had brought with me from London. As my researches in it had already shown me, it was a particularly good one, full of crisp clues and meaty murders, and I was soon absorbed. Scarcely, however, had I really had time to get going on it, when there was a rattle at the door handle, and who should amble in but Roderick Spode.

I looked at him with not a little astonishment. I mean to say, the last chap I was expecting to invade my bedchamber. And it wasn't as if he had come to apologize for his offensive attitude on the terrace, when in addition to muttering menaces he had called me a miserable worm, or for those stares at the dinner table. One glance at his face told me that. The first thing a chap who has come to apologize does is to weigh in with an ingratiating simper, and of this there was no sign.

As a matter of fact, he seemed to me to be looking slightly more sinister than ever, and I found his aspect so forbidding that I dug up an ingratiating simper myself. I didn't suppose it would do much towards conciliating the blighter, but every little helps.

'Oh, hallo, Spode,' I said affably. 'Come on in. Is there something I can do for you?'

Without replying, he walked to the cupboard, threw it open with a brusque twiddle and glared into it. This done, he turned and eyed me, still in that unchummy manner.

'I thought Fink-Nottle might be here.'

'He isn't.'

'So I see.'

'Did you expect to find him in the cupboard?'

'Yes.'

'Oh?'

There was a pause.

'Any message I can give him if he turns up?'

'Yes. You can tell him that I am going to break his neck.'

'Break his neck?'

'Yes. Are you deaf? Break his neck.'

I nodded pacifically.

'I see. Break his neck. Right. And if he asks why?'

'He knows why. Because he is a butterfly who toys with women's hearts and throws them away like soiled gloves.'

'Right ho.' I hadn't had a notion that that was what butterflies did. Most interesting. 'Well, I'll let him know if I run across him.'

'Thank you.'

He withdrew, slamming the door, and I sat musing on the odd way in which history repeats itself. I mean to say, the situation was almost identical with the one which had arisen some few months earlier at Brinkley, when young Tuppy Glossop had come in to my room with a similar end in view. True, Tuppy, if I remembered rightly, had wanted to pull Gussie inside out and make him swallow himself, while Spode had spoken of breaking his neck, but the principle was the same.

I saw what had happened, of course. It was a development which I had rather been anticipating. I had not forgotten what Gussie had told me earlier in the day about Spode informing him of his intention of leaving no stone unturned to dislocate his cervical vertebrae should he ever do Madeline Bassett wrong. He had doubtless learned the facts from her over the coffee, and was now setting out to put his policy into operation.

As to what these facts were, I still had not the remotest. But it was evident from Spode's manner that they reflected little credit on Gussie. He must, I realized, have been making an ass of himself in a big way.

A fearful situation, beyond a doubt, and if there had been anything I could have done about it, I would have done same without hesitation. But it seemed to me that I was helpless, and that Nature must take its course. With a slight sigh, I resumed my goose-flesher, and was making fair progress with it, when a hollow voice said: 'I say, Bertie!' and I sat up quivering in every limb. It was as if a family spectre had edged up and breathed down the back of my neck.

Turning, I observed Augustus Fink-Nottle appearing from under the bed.

Owing to the fact that the shock had caused my tongue to get tangled up with my tonsils, inducing an

unpleasant choking sensation, I found myself
momentarily incapable of speech. All I was able to do
was goggle at Gussie, and it was immediately evident to
me, as I did so, that he had been following the recent
conversation closely. His whole demeanour was that of a
man vividly conscious of being just about half a jump
ahead of Roderick Spode. The hair was ruffled, the eyes
wild, the nose twitching. A rabbit pursued by a weasel
would have looked just the same – allowing, of course,
for the fact that it would not have been wearing
tortoiseshell-rimmed spectacles.

'That was a close call, Bertie,' he said, in a low,
quivering voice. He crossed the room, giving a little at
the knees. His face was a rather pretty greenish colour. 'I
think I'll lock the door, if you don't mind. He might
come back. Why he didn't look under the bed, I can't
imagine. I always thought these Dictators were so
thorough.'

I managed to get the tongue unhitched.

'Never mind about beds and Dictators. What's all this
about you and Madeline Bassett?'

He winced.

'Do you mind not talking about that?'

'Yes, I do mind not talking about it. It's the only thing
I want to talk about. What on earth has she broken off
the engagement for? What did you do to her?'

He winced again. I could see that I was probing an
exposed nerve.

'It wasn't so much what I did to her – it was what I
did to Stephanie Byng.'

'To Stiffy?'

'Yes.'

'What did you do to Stiffy?'

He betrayed some embarrassment.

'I – er . . . Well, as a matter of fact, I . . . Mind you, I
can see now that it was a mistake, but it seemed a good
idea at the time . . . You see, the fact is . . .'

'Get on with it.'

He pulled himself together with a visible effort.

'Well, I wonder if you remember, Bertie, what we were saying up here before dinner . . . about the possibility of her carrying that notebook on her person . . . I put forward the theory, if you recall, that it might be in her stocking . . . and I suggested if you recollect, that one might ascertain . . .'

I reeled. I had got the gist. 'You didn't –'

'Yes.'

'When?'

Again that look of pain passed over his face.

'Just before dinner. You remember we heard her singing folk songs in the drawing room. I went down there, and there she was at the piano, all alone . . . At least, I thought she was all alone . . . And it suddenly struck me that this would be an excellent opportunity to . . . What I didn't know, you see, was that Madeline, though invisible for the moment, was also present. She had gone behind the screen in the corner to get a further supply of folk songs from the chest in which they are kept . . . and . . . well, the long and short of it is that, just as I was . . . well, to cut a long story short, just as I was . . . How shall I put it? . . . Just as I was, so to speak, getting on with it, out she came . . . and . . . Well, you see what I mean . . . I mean, coming so soon after that taking-the-fly-out-of-the-girl's-eye-in-the-stable-yard business, it was not easy to pass it off. As a matter of fact, I didn't pass it off. That's the whole story. How are you on knotting sheets, Bertie?'

I could not follow what is known as the transition of thought.

'Knotting sheets?'

'I was thinking it over under the bed, while you and Spode were chatting, and I came to the conclusion that the only thing to be done is for us to take the sheets off

your bed and tie knots in them, and then you can lower
me down from the window. They do it in books, and I
have an idea I've seen it in the movies. Once outside, I
can take your car and drive up to London. After that, my
plans are uncertain. I may go to California.'

'California?'

'It's seven thousand miles away. Spode would hardly
come to California.'

I stared at him aghast.

'You aren't going to do a bolt?'

'Of course I'm going to do a bolt. Immediately. You
heard what Spode said?'

'You aren't afraid of Spode?'

'Yes, I am.'

'But you were saying yourself that he's a mere mass of
beef and brawn, obviously slow on his feet.'

'I know. I remember. But that was when I thought he
was after you. One's views change.'

'But, Gussie, pull yourself together. You can't just run
away.'

'What else can I do?'

'Why, stick around and try to effect a reconciliation.
You haven't had a shot at pleading with the girl yet.'

'Yes, I have. I did it at dinner. During the fish course.
No good. She just gave me a cold look, and made bread
pills.'

I racked the bean. I was sure there must be an avenue
somewhere, waiting to be explored, and in about half a
minute I spotted it.

'What you've got to do,' I said, 'is to get the notebook.
If you secured that book and showed it to Madeline, its
contents would convince her that your motives in acting
as you did towards Stiffy were not what she supposed,
but pure to the last drop. She would realize that your
behaviour was the outcome of . . . it's on the tip of my
tongue . . . of a counsel of desperation. She would
understand and forgive.'

For a moment, a faint flicker of hope seemed to illumine his twisted features.

'It's a thought,' he agreed. 'I believe you've got something there, Bertie. That's not a bad idea.'

'It can't fail. *Tout comprendre, c'est tout pardonner* about sums it up.'

The flicker faded.

'But how can I get the book? Where is it?'

'It wasn't on her person?'

'I don't think so. Though my investigations were, in the circumstances, necessarily cursory.'

'Then it's probably in her room.'

'Well, there you are. I can't go searching a girl's room.'

'Why not? You see that book I was reading when you popped up. By an odd coincidence – I call it a coincidence, but probably these things are sent to us for a purpose – I had just come to a bit where a gang had been doing that very thing. Do it now, Gussie. She's probably fixed in the drawing room for the next hour or so.'

'As a matter of fact, she's gone to the village. The curate is giving an address on the Holy Land with coloured slides to the Village Mothers at the Working Men's Institute, and she is playing the piano accompaniment. But even so . . . No, Bertie, I can't do it. It may be the right thing to do . . . in fact, I can see that it is the right thing to do . . . but I haven't the nerve. Suppose Spode came in and caught me.'

'Spode would hardly wander into a young girl's room.'

'I don't know so much. You can't form plans on any light-hearted assumption like that. I see him as a chap who wanders everywhere. No. My heart is broken, my future a blank, and there is nothing to be done but accept the fact and start knotting sheets. Let's get at it.'

'You don't knot any of my sheets.'

'But, dash it, my life is at stake.'

'I don't care. I decline to be a party to this craven scooting.'

'Is this Bertie Wooster speaking?'

'You said that before.'

'And I say it again. For the last time, Bertie, will you lend me a couple of sheets and help knot them?'

'No.'

'Then I shall just have to go off and hide somewhere till dawn, when the milk train leaves. Goodbye, Bertie. You have disappointed me.'

'You have disappointed *me*. I thought you had guts.'

'I have, and I don't want Roderick Spode fooling about with them.'

He gave me another of those dying-newt looks, and opened the door cautiously. A glance up and down the passage having apparently satisfied him that it was, for the moment, Spodeless, he slipped out and was gone. And I returned to my book. It was the only thing I could think of that would keep me from sitting torturing myself with agonizing broodings.

Presently I was aware that Jeeves was with me. I hadn't heard him come in, but you often don't with Jeeves. He just streams silently from spot A to spot B, like some gas.

7

I wouldn't say that Jeeves was actually smirking, but there was a definite look of quiet satisfaction on his face, and I suddenly remembered what this sickening scene with Gussie had caused me to forget – viz. that the last time I had seen him he had been on his way to the telephone to ring up the Secretary of the Junior Ganymede Club. I sprang to my feet eagerly. Unless I had misread that look, he had something to report.

'Did you connect with the Sec., Jeeves?'

'Yes, sir. I have just finished speaking to him.'

'And did he dish the dirt?'

'He was most informative, sir.'

'Has Spode a secret?'

'Yes, sir.'

I smote the trouser leg emotionally.

'I should have known better than to doubt Aunt Dahlia. Aunts always know. It's a sort of intuition. Tell me all.'

'I fear I cannot do that, sir. The rules of the club regarding the dissemination of material recorded in the book are very rigid.'

'You mean your lips are sealed?'

'Yes, sir.'

'Then what was the use of telephoning?'

'It is only the details of the matter which I am precluded from mentioning, sir. I am at perfect liberty to tell you that it would greatly lessen Mr Spode's potentiality for evil, if you were to inform him that you know all about Eulalie, sir.'

'Eulalie?'

'Eulalie, sir.'

'That would really put the stopper on him?'

'Yes, sir.'

I pondered. It didn't sound much to go on.

'You're sure you can't go a bit deeper into the subject?'

'Quite sure, sir. Were I to do so, it is probable that my resignation would be called for.'

'Well, I wouldn't want that to happen, of course.' I hated to think of a squad of butlers forming a hollow square while the Committee snipped his buttons off. 'Still, you really are sure that if I look Spode in the eye and spring this gag, he will be baffled? Let's get this quite clear. Suppose you're Spode, and I walk up to you and say "Spode, I know all about Eulalie," that would make you wilt?'

'Yes, sir. The subject of Eulalie, sir, is one which the gentleman, occupying the position he does in the public eye, would, I am convinced, be most reluctant to have ventilated.'

I practised it for a bit. I walked up to the chest of drawers with my hands in my pockets, and said, 'Spode, I know all about Eulalie.' I tried again, waggling my finger this time. I then had a go with folded arms, and I must say it still didn't sound too convincing.

However, I told myself that Jeeves always knew.

'Well, if you say so, Jeeves. Then the first thing I had better do is find Gussie and give him this life-saving information.'

'Sir?'

'Oh, of course, you don't know anything about that, do you? I must tell you, Jeeves, that, since we last met, the plot has thickened again. Were you aware that Spode has long loved Miss Bassett?'

'No, sir.'

'Well, such is the case. The happiness of Miss Bassett is very dear to Spode, and now that her engagement has gone phut for reasons highly discreditable to the male contracting party, he wants to break Gussie's neck.'

'Indeed, sir?'

'I assure you. He was in here just now, speaking of it, and Gussie, who happened to be under the bed at the time, heard him. With the result that he now talks of getting out of the window and going to California. Which, of course, would be fatal. It is imperative that he stays on and tries to effect a reconciliation.'

'Yes, sir.'

'He can't effect a reconciliation, if he is in California.'

'No, sir.'

'So I must go and try to find him. Though, mark you, I doubt if he will be easily found at this point in his career. He is probably on the roof, wondering how he can pull it up after him.'

My misgivings were proved abundantly justified. I searched the house assiduously, but there were no signs of him. Somewhere, no doubt, Totleigh Towers hid Augustus Fink-Nottle, but it kept its secret well. Eventually, I gave it up, and returned to my room, and stap my vitals if the first thing I beheld on entering wasn't the man in person. He was standing by the bed, knotting sheets.

The fact that he had his back to the door and that the carpet was soft kept him from being aware of my entry till I spoke. My 'Hey!' – a pretty sharp one, for I was aghast at seeing my bed thus messed about – brought him spinning round, ashen to the lips.

'Woof!' he exclaimed. 'I thought you were Spode!'

Indignation succeeded panic. He gave me a hard stare. The eyes behind the spectacles were cold. He looked like an annoyed turbot.

'What do you mean, you blasted Wooster,' he demanded, 'by sneaking up on a fellow and saying "Hey!" like that? You might have given me heart failure.'

'And what do you mean, you blighted Fink-Nottle,' I demanded in my turn, 'by mucking up my bed linen after I specifically forbade it? You have sheets of your own. Go and knot those.'

'How can I? Spode is sitting on my bed.'

'He is?'

'Certainly he is. Waiting for me. I went there after I left you, and there he was. If he hadn't happened to clear his throat, I'd have walked right in.'

I saw that it was high time to set this disturbed spirit at rest.

'You needn't be afraid of Spode, Gussie.'

'What do you mean, I needn't be afraid of Spode? Talk sense.'

'I mean just that. Spode, *qua* menace, if *qua* is the word I want, is a thing of the past. Owing to the extraordinary perfection of Jeeves's secret system, I have learned something about him which he wouldn't care to have generally known.'

'What?'

'Ah, there you have me. When I said I had learned it, I should have said that Jeeves had learned it, and unfortunately Jeeves's lips are sealed. However, I am in a position to slip it across the man in no uncertain fashion. If he attempts any rough stuff, I will give him the works.' I broke off, listening. Footsteps were coming along the passage. 'Ah!' I said. 'Someone approaches. This may quite possibly be the blighter himself.'

An animal cry escaped Gussie.

'Lock that door!'

I waved a fairly airy hand.

'It will not be necessary,' I said. 'Let him come. I positively welcome this visit. Watch me deal with him, Gussie. It will amuse you.'

I had guessed correctly. It was Spode, all right. No doubt he had grown weary of sitting on Gussie's bed, and had felt that another chat with Bertram might serve to vary the monotony. He came in, as before, without knocking, and as he perceived Gussie, uttered a wordless exclamation of triumph and satisfaction. He then stood for a moment, breathing heavily through the nostrils.

He seemed to have grown a bit since our last meeting, being now about eight foot six, and had my advices *in re* getting the bulge on him proceeded from a less authoritative source, his aspect might have intimidated me quite a good deal. But so sedulously had I been trained through the years to rely on Jeeves's lightest word that I regarded him without a tremor.

Gussie, I was sorry to observe, did not share my sunny confidence. Possibly I had not given him a full enough explanation of the facts in the case, or it may have been that, confronted with Spode in the flesh, his nerve had failed him. At any rate, he now retreated to the wall and seemed, as far as I could gather, to be trying to get through it. Foiled in this endeavour, he stood looking as if he had been stuffed by some good taxidermist, while I turned to the intruder and gave him a long, level stare, in which surprise and hauteur were nicely blended.

'Well, Spode,' I said, 'what is it now?'

I had put a considerable amount of top spin on the final word, to indicate displeasure, but it was wasted on the man. Giving the question a miss like the deaf adder of Scripture, he began to advance slowly, his gaze concentrated on Gussie. The jaw muscles, I noted, were working as they had done on the occasion when he had come upon me toying with Sir Watkyn Bassett's collection of old silver: and something in his manner suggested that he might at any moment start beating his chest with a hollow drumming sound, as gorillas do in moments of emotion.

'Ha!' he said.

Well, of course, I was not going to stand any rot like that. This habit of his of going about the place saying

'Ha!' was one that had got to be checked, and checked promptly.

'Spode!' I said sharply, and I have an idea that I rapped the table.

He seemed for the first time to become aware of my presence. He paused for an instant, and gave me an unpleasant look.

'Well, what do *you* want?'

I raised an eyebrow or two.

'What do I want? I like that. That's good. Since you ask, Spode, I want to know what the devil you mean by keeping coming into my private apartment, taking up space which I require for other purposes and interrupting me when I am chatting with my personal friends. Really, one gets about as much privacy in this house as a strip-tease dancer. I assume that you have a room of your own. Get back to it, you fat slob, and stay there.'

I could not resist shooting a swift glance at Gussie, to see how he was taking all this, and was pleased to note on his face the burgeoning of a look of worshipping admiration, such as a distressed damsel of the Middle Ages might have directed at a knight on observing him getting down to brass tacks with the dragon. I could see that I had once more become to him the old Daredevil Wooster of our boyhood days, and I had no doubt that he was burning with shame and remorse as he recalled those sneers and jeers of his.

Spode, also, seemed a good deal impressed, though not so favourably. He was staring incredulously, like one bitten by a rabbit. He seemed to be asking himself if this could really be the shrinking violet with whom he had conferred on the terrace.

He asked me if I had called him a slob, and I said I had.

'A fat slob?'

'A fat slob. It is about time,' I proceeded, 'that some public-spirited person came along and told you where you got off. The trouble with you, Spode, is that just because you have succeeded in inducing a handful of half-wits to disfigure the London scene by going about in black shorts, you think you're someone. You hear them shouting, "Heil, Spode!" and you imagine it is the Voice of the People. That is where you make your bloomer. What the Voice of the People is saying is: "Look at that frightful ass Spode swanking about in footer bags! Did you ever in your puff see such a perfect perisher?"'

He did what is known as struggling for utterance.

'Oh?' he said. 'Ha! Well, I will attend to you later.'

'And I,' I retorted, quick as a flash, 'will attend to you now.' I lit a cigarette. 'Spode,' I said, unmasking my batteries, 'I know your secret!'

'Eh?'

'I know all about –'

'All about what?'

It was to ask myself precisely that question that I had paused. For, believe me or believe me not, in this tense moment, when I so sorely needed it, the name which Jeeves had mentioned to me as the magic formula for coping with this blister had completely passed from my mind. I couldn't even remember what letter it began with.

It's an extraordinary thing about names. You've probably noticed it yourself. You think you've got them, I mean to say, and they simply slither away. I've often wished I had a quid for every time some bird with a perfectly familiar map has come up to me and Hallo-Woostered, and had me gasping for air because I couldn't put a label to him. This always makes one feel at a loss, but on no previous occasion had I felt so much at a loss as I did now.

'All about what?' said Spode.

'Well, as a matter of fact,' I had to confess, 'I've forgotten.'

A sort of gasping gulp from up-stage directed my

attention to Gussie again, and I could see that the
significance of my words had not been lost on him. Once
more he tried to back: and as he realized that he had
already gone as far as he could go, a glare of despair came
into his eyes. And then, abruptly, as Spode began to
advance upon him, it changed to one of determination
and stern resolve.

I like to think of Augustus Fink-Nottle at the
moment. He showed up well. Hitherto, I am bound to
say, I had never regarded him highly as a man of action.
Essentially the dreamer type, I should have said. But
now he couldn't have smacked into it with a
prompter gusto if he had been a rough-and-tumble
fighter on the San Francisco waterfront from early
childhood.

Above him, as he stood glued to the wall, there hung
a fairish-sized oil-painting of a chap in knee-breeches
and a three-cornered hat gazing at a female who
appeared to be chirruping to a bird of sorts – a dove,
unless I am mistaken, or a pigeon. I had noticed it once
or twice since I had been in the room, and had, indeed,
thought of giving it to Aunt Dahlia to break instead of
the Infant Samuel at Prayer. Fortunately, I had not done
so, or Gussie would not now have been in a position to
tear it from its moorings and bring it down with a nice
wristy action on Spode's head.

I say 'fortunately', because if ever there was a fellow
who needed hitting with oil paintings, that fellow was
Roderick Spode. From the moment of our first meeting,
his every word and action had proved abundantly that
this was the stuff to give him. But there is always a
catch in these good things, and it took me only an
instant to see that this effort of Gussie's, though well
meant, had achieved little of constructive importance.
What he should have done, of course, was to hold the
picture sideways, so as to get the best out of the stout
frame. Instead of which, he had used the flat of the

weapon, and Spode came through the canvas like a
circus rider going through a paper hoop. In other words,
what had promised to be a decisive blow had turned out
to be merely what Jeeves would call a gesture.

It did, however, divert Spode from his purpose for a
few seconds. He stood there blinking, with the thing
round his neck like a ruff, and the pause was sufficient
to enable me to get into action.

Give us a lead, make it quite clear to us that the party
has warmed up and that from now on anything goes, and
we Woosters do not hang back. There was a sheet lying
on the bed where Gussie had dropped it when disturbed
at his knotting, and to snatch this up and envelop Spode
in it was with me the work of a moment. It is a long
time since I studied the subject, and before committing
myself definitely I should have to consult Jeeves, but I
have an idea that ancient Roman gladiators used to do
much the same sort of thing in the arena, and were
rather well thought of in consequence.

I suppose a man who has been hit over the head with
a picture of a girl chirruping to a pigeon and almost
immediately afterwards enmeshed in a sheet can never
really retain the cool, intelligent outlook. Any friend of
Spode's, with his interests at heart, would have advised
him at this juncture to keep quite still and not stir till
he had come out of the cocoon. Only thus, in a terrain so
liberally studded with chairs and things, could a purler
have been avoided.

He did not do this. Hearing the rushing sound caused
by Gussie exiting, he made a leap in its general direction
and took the inevitable toss. At the moment when
Gussie, moving well, passed through the door, he was on
the ground, more inextricably entangled than ever.

My own friends, advising me, would undoubtedly
have recommended an immediate departure at this
point, and looking back, I can see that where I went
wrong was in pausing to hit the bulge which, from the

remarks that were coming through at that spot, I took to
be Spode's head, with a china vase that stood on the
mantelpiece not far from where the Infant Samuel had
been. It was a strategical error. I got home all right and
the vase broke into a dozen pieces, which was all to the
good – for the more of the property of a man like Sir
Watkyn Bassett that was destroyed, the better – but the
action of dealing this buffet caused me to overbalance.
The next moment, a hand coming out from under the
sheet had grabbed my coat.

It was a serious disaster, of course, and one which
might well have caused a lesser man to feel that it was
no use going on struggling. But the whole point about
the Woosters, as I have had occasion to remark before, is
that they are not lesser men. They keep their heads.
They think quickly, and they act quickly. Napoleon was
the same. I have mentioned that at the moment when I
was preparing to inform Spode that I knew his secret, I
had lighted a cigarette. This cigarette, in its holder, was
still between my lips. Hastily removing it, I pressed the
glowing end on the ham-like hand which was impeding
my getaway.

The results were thoroughly gratifying. You would
have thought that the trend of recent events would have
put Roderick Spode in a frame of mind to expect
anything and be ready for it, but this simple manœuvre
found him unprepared. With a sharp cry of anguish, he
released the coat, and I delayed no longer. Bertram
Wooster is a man who knows when and when not to be
among those present. When Bertram Wooster sees a lion
in his path, he ducks down a side street. I was off at an
impressive speed, and would no doubt have crossed the
threshold with a burst which would have clipped a
second or two off Gussie's time, had I not experienced a
head-on collision with a solid body which happened to
be entering at the moment. I remember thinking, as we
twined our arms about each other, that at Totleigh

Towers, if it wasn't one thing, it was bound to be something else.

I fancy that it was the scent of *eau-de-Cologne* that still clung to her temples that enabled me to identify this solid body as that of Aunt Dahlia, though even without it the rich, hunting-field expletive which burst from her lips would have put me on the right track. We came down in a tangled heap, and must have rolled inwards to some extent, for the next thing I knew, we were colliding with the sheeted figure of Roderick Spode, who when last seen had been at the other end of the room. No doubt the explanation is that we had rolled nor'-nor'-east and he had been rolling sou'-sou'-west, with the result that we had come together somewhere in the middle.

Spode, I noticed, as Reason began to return to her throne, was holding Aunt Dahlia by the left leg, and she didn't seem to be liking it much. A good deal of breath had been knocked out of her by the impact of a nephew on her midriff, but enough remained to enable her to expostulate, and this she was doing with all the old fire.

'What is this joint?' she was demanding heatedly. 'A loony bin? Has everybody gone crazy? First I meet Spink-Bottle racing along the corridor like a mustang. Then you try to walk through me as if I were thistledown. And now the gentleman in the burnous has started tickling my ankle – a thing that hasn't happened to me since the York and Ainsty Hunt Ball of the year nineteen-twenty-one.'

These protests must have filtered through to Spode, and presumably stirred his better nature, for he let go, and she got up, dusting her dress.

'Now, then,' she said, somewhat calmer. 'An explanation, if you please, and a categorical one. What's the idea? What's it all about? Who the devil's that inside the winding-sheet?'

I made the introductions.

'You've met Spode, haven't you? Mr Roderick Spode, Mrs Travers.'

Spode had now removed the sheet, but the picture was still in position, and Aunt Dahlia eyed it wonderingly.

'What on earth have you got that thing round your neck for?' she asked. Then, in more tolerant vein: 'Wear it if you like, of course, but it doesn't suit you.'

Spode did not reply. He was breathing heavily. I didn't blame him, mind you – in his place, I'd have done the same – but the sound was not agreeable, and I wished he wouldn't. He was also gazing at me intently, and I wished he wouldn't do that, either. His face was flushed, his eyes were bulging, and one had the odd illusion that his hair was standing on end – like quills upon the fretful porpentine, as Jeeves once put it when describing to me the reactions of Barmy Fotheringay-Phipps on seeing a dead snip, on which he had invested largely, come in sixth in the procession at the Newmarket Spring Meeting.

I remember once, during a temporary rift with Jeeves, engaging a man from the registry office to serve me in his stead, and he hadn't been with me a week when he got blotto one night and set fire to the house and tried to slice me up with a carving knife. Said he wanted to see the colour of my insides, of all bizarre ideas. And until this moment I had always looked on that episode as the most trying in my experience. I now saw that it must be ranked second.

This bird of whom I speak was a simple, untutored soul and Spode a man of good education and upbringing, but it was plain that there was one point at which their souls touched. I don't suppose they would have seen eye to eye on any other subject you could have brought up, but in the matter of wanting to see the colour of my insides their minds ran on parallel lines. The only difference seemed to be that whereas my employee had planned to use a carving knife for his excavations, Spode appeared to be satisfied that the job could be done all right with the bare hands.

'I must ask you to leave us, madam,' he said.

'But I've only just come,' said Aunt Dahlia.

'I am going to thrash this man within an inch of his life.'

It was quite the wrong tone to take with the aged relative. She has a very clannish spirit and, as I have said, is fond of Bertram. Her brow darkened.

'You don't touch a nephew of mine.'

'I am going to break every bone in his body.'

'You aren't going to do anything of the sort. The idea! . . . Here, you!'

She raised her voice sharply as she spoke the concluding words, and what had caused her to do so was the fact that Spode at this moment made a sudden move in my direction.

Considering the manner in which his eyes were gleaming and his moustache bristling, not to mention the gritting teeth and the sinister twiddling of the fingers, it was a move which might have been expected to send me flitting away like an adagio dancer. And had it occurred somewhat earlier, it would undoubtedly have done so. But I did not flit. I stood where I was, calm and collected. Whether I folded my arms or not, I cannot recall, but I remember that there was a faint, amused smile upon my lips.

For that brief monosyllable 'you' had accomplished what a quarter of an hour's research had been unable to do – viz. the unsealing of the fount of memory. Jeeve's words came back to me with a rush. One moment, the mind a blank: the next, the fount of memory spouting like nobody's business. It often happens this way.

'One minute, Spode,' I said quietly. 'Just one minute.

Before you start getting above yourself, it may interest you to learn that I know all about Eulalie.'

It was stupendous. I felt like one of those chaps who press buttons and explode mines. If it hadn't been that my implicit faith in Jeeves had led me to expect solid results, I should have been astounded at the effect of this pronouncement on the man. You could see that it had got right in amongst him and churned him up like an egg whisk. He recoiled as if he had run into something hot, and a look of horror and alarm spread slowly over his face.

The whole situation recalled irresistibly to my mind something that had happened to me once up at Oxford, when the heart was young. It was during Eights Week, and I was sauntering on the river-bank with a girl named something that has slipped my mind, when there was a sound of barking and a large, hefty dog came galloping up, full of beans and buck and obviously intent on mayhem. And I was just commending my soul to God, and feeling that this was where the old flannel trousers got about thirty bob's worth of value bitten out of them, when the girl, waiting till she saw the whites of its eyes, with extraordinary presence of mind suddenly opened a coloured Japanese umbrella in the animal's face. Upon which, it did three back somersaults and retired into private life.

Except that he didn't do any back somersaults, Roderick Spode's reactions were almost identical with those of this nonplussed hound. For a moment, he just stood gaping. Then he said 'Oh?' Then his lips twisted into what I took to be his idea of a conciliatory smile. After that, he swallowed six – or it may have been seven – times, as if he had taken aboard a fish bone. Finally, he spoke. And when he did so, it was the nearest thing to a cooing dove that I have ever heard – and an exceptionally mild-mannered dove, at that.

'Oh, do you?' he said.

'I do,' I replied.

If he had asked me what I knew about her, he would have had me stymied, but he didn't.

'Er – how did you find out?'

'I have my methods.'

'Oh?' he said.

'Ah,' I replied, and there was silence again for a moment.

I wouldn't have believed it possible for so tough an egg to sidle obsequiously, but that was how he now sidled up to me. There was a pleading look in his eyes.

'I hope you will keep this to yourself, Wooster? You will keep it to yourself, won't you, Wooster?'

'I will –'

'Thank you, Wooster.'

'– provided,' I continued, 'that we have no more of these extraordinary exhibitions on your part of – what's the word?'

He sidled a bit closer.

'Of course, of course. I'm afraid I have been acting rather hastily.' He reached out a hand and smoothed my sleeve. 'Did I rumple your coat, Wooster? I'm sorry. I forgot myself. It shall not happen again.'

'It had better not. Good Lord! Grabbing fellows' coats and saying you're going to break chaps' bones. I never heard of such a thing.'

'I know, I know. I was wrong.'

'You bet you were wrong. I shall be very sharp on that sort of thing in the future, Spode.'

'Yes, yes, I understand.'

'I have not been at all satisfied with your behaviour since I came to this house. The way you were looking at me at dinner. You may think people don't notice these things, but they do.'

'Of course, of course.'

'And calling me a miserable worm.'

'I'm sorry I called you a miserable worm, Wooster. I spoke without thinking.'

'Always think, Spode. Well, that is all. You may withdraw.'

'Good night, Wooster.'

'Good night, Spode.'

He hurried out with bowed head, and I turned to Aunt Dahlia, who was making noises like a motor-bicycle in the background. She gazed at me with the air of one who has been seeing visions. And I suppose the whole affair must have been extraordinarily impressive to the casual bystander.

'Well, I'll be –'

Here she paused – fortunately, perhaps, for she is a woman who, when strongly moved, sometimes has a tendency to forget that she is no longer in the hunting-field, and the verb, had she given it utterance, might have proved a bit too fruity for mixed company.

'Bertie! What was all that about?'

I waved a nonchalant hand.

'Oh, I just put it across the fellow. Merely asserting myself. One has to take a firm line with chaps like Spode.'

'Who is this Eulalie?'

'Ah, there you've got me. For information on that point you will have to apply to Jeeves. And it won't be any good, because the club rules are rigid and members are permitted to go only just so far. Jeeves,' I went on, giving credit where credit was due, as is my custom, 'came to me some little while back and told me that I had only to inform Spode that I knew all about Eulalie to cause him to curl up like a burnt feather. And a burnt feather, as you have seen, was precisely what he did curl up like. As to who the above may be, I haven't the foggiest. All that I can say is that she is a chunk of Spode's past – and, one fears, a highly discreditable one.'

I sighed, for I was not unmoved.

'One can fill in the picture for oneself, I think, Aunt Dahlia? The trusting girl who learned too late that men betray . . . the little bundle . . . the last mournful walk to the river-bank . . . the splash . . . the bubbling cry . . . I fancy so, don't you? No wonder the man pales beneath the tan a bit at the idea of the world knowing of that.'

Aunt Dahlia drew a deep breath. A sort of Soul's Awakening look had come into her face.

'Good old blackmail! You can't beat it. I've always said so and I always shall. It works like magic in an emergency. Bertie,' she cried, 'do you realize what this means?'

'Means, old relative?'

'Now that you have got the goods on Spode, the only obstacle to your sneaking that cow-creamer has been removed. You can stroll down and collect it tonight.'

I shook my head regretfully. I had been afraid she was going to take that view of the matter. It compelled me to dash the cup of joy from her lips, always an unpleasant thing to have to do to an aunt who dandled one on her knee as a child.

'No,' I said. 'There you're wrong. There, if you will excuse me saying so, you are talking like a fathead. Spode may have ceased to be a danger to traffic, but that doesn't alter the fact that Stiffy still has the notebook. Before taking any steps in the direction of the cow-creamer, I have got to get it.'

'But why? Oh, but I suppose you haven't heard. Madeline Bassett has broken off her engagement with Spink-Bottle. She told me so in the strictest confidence just now. Well, then. The snag before was that young Stephanie might cause the engagement to be broken by showing old Bassett the book. But if it's broken already –'

I shook the bean again.

'My dear old faulty reasoner,' I said, 'you miss the gist by a mile. As long as Stiffy retains that book, it cannot

be shown to Madeline Bassett. And only by showing it
to Madeline Bassett can Gussie prove to her that his
motive in pinching Stiffy's legs was not what she
supposed. And only by proving to her that his motive
was not what she supposed can he square himself and
effect a reconciliation. And only if he squares himself
and effects a reconciliation can I avoid the distasteful
necessity of having to marry this bally Bassett myself.
No, I repeat. Before doing anything else, I have got to
have that book.'

My pitiless analysis of the situation had its effect. It
was plain from her manner that she had got the strength.
For a space, she sat chewing the lower lip in silence,
frowning like an aunt who has drained the bitter cup.

'Well, how are you going to get it?'

'I propose to search her room.'

'What's the good of that?'

'My dear old relative, Gussie's investigations have
already revealed that the thing is not on her person.
Reasoning closely, we reach the conclusion that it must
be in her room.'

'Yes, but, you poor ass, whereabouts in her room? It
may be anywhere, And wherever it is, you can be jolly
sure it's carefully hidden. I suppose you hadn't thought
of that.'

As a matter of fact, I hadn't, and I imagine that my
sharp 'Oh ah!' must have revealed this, for she snorted
like a bison at the water trough.

'No doubt you thought it would be lying out on the
dressing table. All right, search her room, if you like.
There's no actual harm in it, I suppose. It will give you
something to do and keep you out of the public houses.
I, meanwhile, will be going off and starting to think of
something sensible. It's time one of us did.'

Pausing at the mantelpiece to remove a china horse
which stood there and hurl it to the floor and jump on it,
she passed along. And I, somewhat discomposed, for I

had thought I had got everything neatly planned out and it was a bit of a jar to find that I hadn't, sat down and began to bend the brain.

The longer I bent it the more I was forced to admit that the flesh and blood had been right. Looking round this room of my own, I could see at a glance a dozen places where, if I had had a small object to hide like a leather-covered notebook full of criticisms of old Bassett's method of drinking soup, I could have done so with ease. Presumably, the same conditions prevailed in Stiffy's lair. In going thither, therefore, I should be embarking on a quest well calculated to baffle the brightest bloodhound, let alone a chap who from childhood up had always been rotten at hunt-the-slipper.

To give the brain a rest before having another go at the problem, I took up my goose-flesher again. And, by Jove, I hadn't read more than half a page when I uttered a cry. I had come upon a significant passage.

'Jeeves,' I said, addressing him as he entered a moment later, 'I have come upon a significant passage.'

'Sir?'

I saw that I had been too abrupt, and that footnotes would be required.

'In this thriller I'm reading,' I explained. 'But wait. Before showing it to you, I would like to pay you a stately tribute on the accuracy of your information *re* Spode. A hearty vote of thanks, Jeeves. You said the name Eulalie would make him wilt, and it did. Spode, *qua* menace . . . is it *qua*?'

'Yes, sir. Quite correct.'

'I thought so. Well, Spode, *qua* menace, is a spent egg. He has dropped out and ceased to function.'

'That is very gratifying, sir.'

'Most. But we are still faced by this Becher's Brook, that young Stiffy continues in possession of the notebook. That notebook, Jeeves, must be located and re-snitched before we are free to move in any other direction. Aunt Dahlia has just left in despondent mood, because, while she concedes that the damned thing is almost certainly concealed in the little pimple's sleeping quarters, she sees no hope of fingers being able to be laid upon it. She says it may be anywhere and is undoubtedly carefully hidden.'

'That is the difficulty, sir.'

'Quite. But that is where this significant passage comes in. It points the way and sets the feet upon the right path. I'll read it to you. The detective is speaking to his pal, and the "they" refers to some bounders at present unidentified, who have been ransacking a girl's room, hoping to find the missing jewels. Listen attentively, Jeeves. "They seem to have looked everywhere, my dear Postlethwaite, except in the one place where they might have expected to find something. Amateurs, Postlethwaite, rank amateurs. They never thought of the top of the cupboard, the thing any experienced crook thinks of at once, because" – note carefully what follows – "because he knows it is every woman's favourite hiding-place." '

I eyed him keenly.

'You see the profound significance of that, Jeeves?'

'If I interpret your meaning aright, sir, you are suggesting the Mr Fink-Nottle's notebook may be concealed at the top of the cupboard in Miss Byng's apartment?'

'Not "may", Jeeves, "must". I don't see how it can be concealed anywhere else but. That detective is no fool. If he says a thing is so, it is so. I have the utmost confidence in the fellow, and am prepared to follow his lead without question.'

'But surely, sir, you are not proposing – '

'Yes, I am. I'm going to do it immediately. Stiffy has gone to the Working Men's Institute, and won't be back for ages. It's absurd to suppose that a gaggle of Village Mothers are going to be sated with coloured slides of the

Holy Land, plus piano accompaniment, in anything under two hours. So now is the time to operate while the coast is clear. Gird up your loins, Jeeves, and accompany me.'

'Well, really, sir – '

'And don't say "Well, really, sir". I have had occasion to rebuke you before for this habit of yours of saying "Well, really, sir" in a soupy sort of voice, when I indicate some strategic line of action. What I want from you is less of the "Well, really, sir" and more of the buckling-to spirit. Think feudally, Jeeves. Do you know Stiffy's room?'

'Yes, sir.'

'Then Ho for it!'

I cannot say, despite the courageous dash which I had exhibited in the above slab of dialogue, that it was in any too bobbish a frame of mind that I made my way to our destination. In fact, the nearer I got, the less bobbish I felt. It had been just the same the time I allowed myself to be argued by Roberta Wickham into going and puncturing that hot-water bottle. I hate these surreptitious prowlings. Bertram Wooster is a man who likes to go through the world with his chin up and both feet on the ground, not to sneak about on tiptoe with his spine tying itself into reefer knots.

It was precisely because I had anticipated some such reactions that I had been so anxious that Jeeves should accompany me and lend moral support, and I found myself wishing that he would buck up and lend a bit more than he was doing. Willing service and selfless co-operation were what I had hoped for, and he was not giving me them. His manner from the very start betrayed an aloof disapproval. He seemed to be dissociating himself entirely from the proceedings, and I resented it.

Owing to this aloofness on his part and this resentment on mine, we made the journey in silence, and it was in silence that we entered the room and switched on the light.

The first impression I received on giving the apartment the once-over was that for a young shrimp of her shaky moral outlook Stiffy had been done pretty well in the matter of sleeping accommodation. Totleigh Towers was one of those country houses which had been built at a time when people planning a little nest had the idea that a bedroom was not a bedroom unless you could give an informal dance for about fifty couples in it, and this sanctum could have accommodated a dozen Stiffys. In the rays of the small electric light up in the ceiling, the bally thing seemed to stretch for miles in every direction, and the thought that if that detective had not called his shots correctly, Gussie's notebook might be concealed anywhere in these great spaces, was a chilling one.

I was standing there, hoping for the best, when my meditations were broken in upon by an odd, gargling sort of noise, something like static and something like distant thunder, and to cut a long story short this proved to proceed from the larynx of the dog Bartholomew.

He was standing on the bed, stropping his front paws on the coverlet, and so easy was it to read the message in his eyes that we acted like two minds with but a single thought. At the exact moment when I soared like an eagle onto the chest of drawers, Jeeves was skimming like a swallow onto the top of the cupboard. The animal hopped from the bed and, advancing into the middle of the room, took a seat, breathing through the nose with a curious whistling sound, and looking at us from under his eyebrows like a Scottish elder rebuking sin from the pulpit.

And there for a while the matter rested.

8

Jeeves was the first to break a rather strained silence.

'The book does not appear to be here, sir.'

'Eh?'

'I have searched the top of the cupboard, sir, but I have not found the book.'

It may be that my reply erred a trifle on the side of acerbity. My narrow escape from those slavering jaws had left me a bit edgy.

'Blast the book, Jeeves! What about this dog?'

'Yes, sir.'

'What do you mean – "Yes, sir"?'

'I was endeavouring to convey that I appreciate the point which you have raised, sir. The animal's unexpected appearance unquestionably presents a problem. While he continues to maintain his existing attitude, it will not be easy for us to prosecute the search for Mr Fink-Nottle's notebook. Our freedom of action will necessarily be circumscribed.'

'Then what's to be done?'

'It is difficult to say, sir.'

'You have no ideas?'

'No, sir.'

I could have said something pretty bitter and stinging at this – I don't know what, but something – but I refrained. I realized that it was rather tough on the man, outstanding though his gifts were, to expect him to ring the bell every time, without fail. No doubt that brilliant inspiration of his which had led to my signal victory over the forces of darkness as represented by R. Spode had taken it out of him a good deal, rendering the brain for the nonce a bit flaccid. One could but wait and hope that the machinery would soon get going again, enabling him to seek new high levels of achievement.

And, I felt as I continued to turn the position of affairs over in my mind, the sooner, the better, for it was plain that nothing was going to budge this canine excrescence except an offensive on a major scale, dashingly conceived and skilfully carried out. I don't think I have ever seen a dog who conveyed more vividly the impression of being rooted to the spot and prepared to stay there till the cows – or, in this case, his proprietress – came home. And what I was going to say to Stiffy if she returned and found me roosting on her chest of drawers was something I had not yet thought out in any exactness of detail.

Watching the animal sitting there like a bump on a log, I soon found myself chafing a good deal. I remember Freddie Widgeon, who was once chased onto the top of a wardrobe by an Alsatian during a country house visit, telling me that what he had disliked most about the thing was the indignity of it all – the blow to the proud spirit, if you know what I mean – the feeling, in fine, that he, the Heir of the Ages, as you might say, was camping out on a wardrobe at the whim of a bally dog.

It was the same with me. One doesn't want to make a song and dance about one's ancient lineage, of course, but after all the Woosters did come over with the Conqueror and were extremely pally with him: and a fat lot of good it is coming over with Conquerors, if you're simply going to wind up by being given the elbow by Aberdeen terriers.

These reflections had the effect of making me rather peevish, and I looked down somewhat sourly at the animal.

'I call it monstrous, Jeeves,' I said, voicing my train of thought, 'that this dog should be lounging about in a bedroom. Most unhygienic.'

'Yes, sir.'

'Scotties are smelly, even the best of them. You will
recall how my Aunt Agatha's McIntosh niffed to heaven
while enjoying my hospitality. I frequently mentioned it
to you.'

'Yes, sir.'

'And this one is even riper. He should obviously have
been bedded out in the stables. Upon my Sam, what
with Scotties in Stiffy's room and newts in Gussie's,
Totleigh Towers is not far short of being a lazar
house.'

'No, sir.'

'And consider the matter from another angle,' I said,
warming to my theme. 'I refer to the danger of keeping a
dog of this nature and disposition in a bedroom, where it
can spring out ravening on anyone who enters. You and I
happen to be able to take care of ourselves in an
emergency such as has arisen, but suppose we had been
some highly strung house-maid.'

'Yes, sir.'

'I can see her coming into the room to turn down the
bed. I picture her as a rather fragile girl with big eyes and
a timid expression. She crosses the threshold. She
approaches the bed. And out leaps this man-eating dog.
One does not like to dwell upon the sequel.'

'No, sir.'

I frowned.

'I wish,' I said, 'that instead of sitting there saying
"Yes, sir" and "No, sir", Jeeves, you would do
something.'

'But what can I do, sir?'

'You can get action, Jeeves. That is what is required
here – sharp, decisive action. I wonder if you recall a
visit we once paid to the residence of my Aunt Agatha at
Woollam Chersey in the county of Herts. To refresh
your memory, it was the occasion on which, in company
with the Right Honourable A. B. Filmer, the Cabinet

Minister, I was chivvied onto the roof of a shack on the island in the lake by an angry swan.'

'I recall the incident vividly, sir.'

'So do I. And the picture most deeply imprinted on my mental retina – is that the correct expression?'

'Yes, sir.'

' – is of you facing that swan in the most intrepid "You-can't-do-that-there-here" manner and bunging a raincoat over its head, thereby completely dishing its aims and plans and compelling it to revise its whole strategy from the bottom up. It was a beautiful bit of work. I don't know when I have seen a finer.'

'Thank you, sir. I am glad if I gave satisfaction.'

'You certainly, did, Jeeves, in heaping measure. And what crossed my mind was that a similar operation would make this dog feel pretty silly.'

'No doubt, sir. But I have no raincoat.'

'Then I would advise seeing what you can do with a sheet. And in case you are wondering if a sheet would work as well, I may tell you that just before you came to my room I had had admirable results with one in the case of Mr Spode. He just couldn't seem to get out of the thing.'

'Indeed, sir?'

'I assure you, Jeeves. You could wish no better weapon than a sheet. There are some on the bed.'

'Yes, sir. On the bed.'

There was a pause. I was loath to wrong the man, but if this wasn't a *nolle prosequi*, I didn't know one when I saw one. The distant and unenthusiastic look on his face told me that I was right, and I endeavoured to sting his pride, rather as Gussie in our *pourparlers* in the matter of Spode had endeavoured to sting mine.

'Are you afraid of a tiny little dog, Jeeves?'

He corrected me respectfully, giving it as his opinion that the undersigned was not a tiny little dog, but well above the average in muscular development. In particular, he drew my attention to the animal's teeth.

I reassured him.

'I think you would find that if you were to make a sudden spring, his teeth would not enter into the matter. You could leap onto the bed, snatch up a sheet, roll him up in it before he knew what was happening, and there we would be.'

'Yes, sir.'

'Well, are you going to make a sudden spring?'

'No, sir.'

A rather stiff silence ensued, during which the dog Bartholomew continued to gaze at me unwinkingly, and once more I found myself noticing – and resenting – the superior, sanctimonious expression on his face. Nothing can ever render the experience of being treed on top of a chest of drawers by an Aberdeen terrier pleasant, but it seemed to me that the least you can expect on such an occasion is that the animal will meet you halfway and not drop salt into the wound by looking at you as if he were asking if you were saved.

It was in the hope of wiping this look off his face that I now made a gesture. There was a stump of candle standing in the parent candlestick beside me, and I threw this at the little blighter. He ate it with every appearance of relish, took time out briefly in order to be sick, and resumed his silent stare. And at this moment the door opened and in came Stiffy – hours before I had expected her.

The first thing that impressed itself upon one on seeing her was that she was not in her customary buoyant spirits. Stiffy, as a rule, is a girl who moves jauntily from spot to spot – youthful elasticity is, I believe, the expression – but she entered now with a slow and dragging step like a Volga boatman. She cast a dull eye at us, and after a brief 'Hullo, Bertie. Hullo, Jeeves,' seemed to dismiss us from her thoughts. She made for the dressing-table and having removed her hat, sat looking at herself in the mirror with sombre eyes. It was plain that for some reason the soul had got a flat tyre, and seeing that unless I opened the conversation there was going to be one of those awkward pauses, I did so.

'What ho, Stiffy.'

'Hullo.'

'Nice evening. Your dog's just been sick on the carpet.'

All this, of course, was merely by way of leading into the main theme, which I now proceeded to broach.

'Well, Stiffy, I suppose you're surprised to see us here?'

'No, I'm not. Have you been looking for that book?'

'Why, yes. That's right. We have. Though, as a matter of fact, we hadn't got really started. We were somewhat impeded by the bow-wow.' (Keeping it light, you notice. Always the best way on these occasions.) 'He took our entrance in the wrong spirit.'

'Oh?'

'Yes. Would it be asking too much of you to attach a stout lead to his collar, thus making the world safe for democracy?'

'Yes, it would.'

'Surely you wish to save the lives of two fellow creatures?'

'No, I don't. Not if they're men. I loathe all men. I hope Bartholomew bites you to the bone.'

I saw that little was to be gained by approaching the matter from this angle. I switched to another *point d'appui*.

'I wasn't expecting you,' I said. 'I thought you had gone to the Working Men's Institute, to tickle the ivories in accompaniment to old Stinker's coloured lecture on the Holy Land.'

'I did.'

'Back early, aren't you?'

407

'Yes. The lecture was off. Harold broke the slides.'

'Oh?' I said, feeling that he was just the sort of chap who would break slides. 'How did that happen?'

She passed a listless hand over the brow of the dog Bartholomew, who had stepped up to fraternize.

'He dropped them.'

'What made him do that?'

'He had a shock, when I broke off our engagement.'

'What!'

'Yes.' A gleam came into her eyes, as if she were reliving unpleasant scenes, and her voice took on the sort of metallic sharpness which I have so often noticed in that of my Aunt Agatha during our get-togethers. Her listlessness disappeared, and for the first time she spoke with a girlish vehemence. 'I got to Harold's cottage, and I went in, and after we'd talked of this and that for a while, I said "When are you going to pinch Eustace Oates's helmet, darling?" And would you believe it, he looked at me in a horrible, sheepish, hang-dog way and said that he had been wrestling with his conscience in the hope of getting its OK, but that it simply wouldn't hear of him pinching Eustace Oates's helmet, so it was all off. "Oh?" I said, drawing myself up. "All off, is it? Well, so is our engagement," and he dropped a double handful of coloured slides of the Holy Land, and I came away.'

'You don't mean that?'

'Yes, I do. And I consider that I have had a very lucky escape. If he is the sort of man who is going to refuse me every little thing I ask, I'm glad I found it out in time. I'm delighted about the whole thing.'

Here, with a sniff like the tearing of a piece of calico, she buried the bean in her hands, and broke into what are called uncontrollable sobs.

Well, dashed painful, of course, and you wouldn't be far wrong in saying that I ached in sympathy with her distress. I don't suppose there is a man in the WI postal

district of London more readily moved by a woman's
grief than myself. For two pins, if I'd been a bit nearer, I
would have patted her head. But though there is this
kindly streak in the Woosters, there is also a practical
one, and it didn't take me long to spot the bright side to
all this.

'Well, that's too bad,' I said. 'The heart bleeds. Eh,
Jeeves?'

'Distinctly, sir.'

'Yes, by Jove, it bleeds profusely, and I suppose all that
one can say is that one hopes that Time, the great
healer, will eventually stitch up the wound. However, as
in these circs you will, of course, no longer have any use
for that notebook of Gussie's, how about handing it
over?'

'What?'

'I said that if your projected union with Stinker is off,
you will, of course, no longer wish to keep that
notebook of Gussie's among your effects –'

'Oh, don't bother me about notebooks now.'

'No, no, quite. Not for the world. All I'm saying is
that if – at your leisure – choose the time to suit yourself
– you wouldn't mind slipping it across –'

'Oh, all right. I can't give it you now, though. It isn't
here.'

'Not here?'

'No. I put it . . . Hallo, what's that?'

What had caused her to suspend her remarks just at
the point when they were becoming fraught with
interest was a sudden tapping sound. A sort of tap-tap-
tap. It came from the direction of the window.

This room of Stiffy's, I should have mentioned, in
addition to being equipped with four-poster beds,
valuable pictures, richly upholstered chairs and all sorts
of things far too good for a young squirt who went about
biting the hand that had fed her at luncheon at its flat by
causing it the utmost alarm and despondency, had a

balcony outside its window. It was from this balcony
that the tapping sound proceeded, leading one to infer
that someone stood without.

That the dog Bartholomew had reached this
conclusion was shown immediately by the lissom agility
with which he leaped at the window and started trying
to bite his way through. Up till this moment he had
shown himself a dog of strong reserves, content merely
to sit and stare, but now he was full of strange oaths.
And I confess that as I watched his champing and
listened to his observations I congratulated myself on
the promptitude with which I had breezed onto that
chest of drawers. A bone-crusher, if ever one drew
breath, this Bartholomew Byng. Reluctant as one always
is to criticize the acts of an all-wise Providence, I was
dashed if I could see why a dog of his size should have
been fitted out with the jaws and teeth of a crocodile.
Still, too late of course to do anything about it now.

Stiffy, after that moment of surprised inaction which
was to be expected in a girl who hears tapping sounds at
her window, had risen and gone to investigate. I couldn't
see a thing from where I was sitting, but she was
evidently more fortunately placed. As she drew back the
curtain, I saw her clap a hand to her throat, like
someone in a play, and a sharp cry escaped her, audible
even above the ghastly row which was proceeding from
the lips of the frothing terrier.

'Harold!' she yipped, and putting two and two
together I gathered that the bird on the balcony must be
old Stinker Pinker, my favourite curate.

It was with a sort of joyful yelp, like that of a woman
getting together with her demon lover, that the little
geezer had spoken his name, but it was evident that
reflection now told her that after what had occurred
between this man of God and herself this was not quite
the tone. Her next words were uttered with a cold,
hostile intonation. I was able to hear them, because she

had stooped and picked up the bounder Bartholomew, clamping a hand over his mouth to still his cries – a thing I wouldn't have done for a goodish bit of money.

'What do you want?'

Owing to the lull in Bartholomew, the stuff was coming through well now. Stinker's voice was a bit muffled by the intervening sheet of glass, but I got it nicely.

'Stiffy!'

'Well?'

'Can I come in?'

'No, you can't.'

'But I've brought you something.'

A sudden yowl of ecstasy broke from the young pimple.

'Harold! You angel lamb! You haven't got it, after all?'

'Yes.'

'Oh, Harold, my dream of joy!'

She opened the window with eager fingers, and a cold draught came in and played about my ankles. It was not followed, as I had supposed it would be, by old Stinker. He continued to hang about on the outskirts, and a moment later his motive in doing so was made clear.

'I say, Stiffy, old girl, is that hound of yours under control?'

'Yes, rather. Wait a minute.'

She carried the animal to the cupboard and bunged him in, closing the door behind him. And from the fact that no further bulletins were received from him, I imagine he curled up and went to sleep. These Scotties are philosophers, well able to adapt themselves to changing conditions. They can take it as well as dish it out.

'All clear, angel,' she said, and returned to the window, arriving there just in time to be folded in the embrace of the Incoming Stinker.

It was not easy for some moments to sort out the

male from the female ingredients in the ensuing tangle, but eventually he disengaged himself and I was able to see him steadily and see him whole. And when I did so, I noticed that there was rather more of him than there had been when I had seen him last. Country butter and the easy life these curates lead had added a pound or two to an always impressive figure. To find the lean, finely trained Stinker of my nonage, I felt that one would have to catch him in Lent.

But the change in him, I soon perceived, was purely superficial. The manner in which he now tripped over a rug and cannoned into an occasional table, upsetting it with all the old thoroughness, showed me that at heart he still remained the same galumphing man with two left feet, who had always been constitutionally incapable of walking through the great Gobi desert without knocking something over.

Stinker's was a face which in the old College days had glowed with health and heartiness. The health was still there – he looked like a clerical beetroot – but of heartiness at this moment one noted rather a shortage. His features were drawn, as if Conscience were gnawing at his vitals. And no doubt it was, for in one hand he was carrying the helmet which I had last observed perched on the dome of Constable Eustace Oates. With a quick, impulsive movement, like that of a man trying to rid himself of a dead fish, he thrust it at Stiffy, who received it with a soft tender squeal of ecstasy.

'I brought it,' he said dully.

'Oh, Harold!'

'I brought your gloves, too. You left them behind. At least, I've brought one of them. I couldn't find the other.'

'Thank you, darling. But never mind about gloves, my wonder man. Tell me everything that happened.'

He was about to do so, when he paused, and I saw that he was staring at me with a rather feverish look in his eyes. Then he turned and stared at Jeeves. One could read what was passing in his mind. He was debating within himself whether we were real, or whether the nervous strain to which he had been subjected was causing him to see things.

'Stiffy,' he said, lowering his voice, 'don't look now, but is there something on top of that chest of drawers?'

'Eh? Oh, yes, that's Bertie Wooster.'

'Oh, it is?' said Stinker, brightening visibly. 'I wasn't quite sure. Is that somebody on the cupboard, too?'

'That's Bertie's man Jeeves.'

'How do you do?' said Stinker.

'How do you do, sir?' said Jeeves.

We climbed down, and I came forward with outstretched hand, anxious to get the reunion going.

'What ho, Stinker.'

'Hullo, Bertie.'

'Long time since we met.'

'It is a bit, isn't it?'

'I hear you're a curate now.'

'Yes, that's right.'

'How are the souls?'

'Oh, fine, thanks.'

There was a pause, and I suppose I would have gone on to ask him if he had seen anything of old So-and-so lately or knew what had become of old What's-his-name, as one does when the conversation shows a tendency to drag on these occasions of ancient College chums meeting again after long separation, but before I could do so, Stiffy, who had been crooning over the helmet like a mother over the cot of her sleeping child, stuck it on her head with a merry chuckle, and the spectacle appeared to bring back to Stinker like a slosh in the waistcoat the realization of what he had done. You've probably heard the expression 'The wretched man seemed fully conscious of his position.' That was Harold Pinker at this juncture. He shied like a startled horse, knocked over another table, tottered to a chair, knocked that over, picked it up and sat down, burying his face in his hands.

'If the Infants' Bible Class should hear of this!' he said, shuddering strongly.

I saw what he meant. A man in his position has to watch his step. What people expect from a curate is a zealous performance of his parochial duties. They like to think of him as a chap who preaches about Hivites, Jebusites and what not, speaks the word in season to the backslider, conveys soup and blankets to the deserving bed-ridden and all that sort of thing. When they find him de-helmeting policemen, they look at one another with the raised eyebrow of censure, and ask themselves if he is quite the right man for the job. That was what was bothering Stinker and preventing him being the old effervescent curate whose jolly laugh had made the last School Treat go with such a bang.

Stiffy endeavoured to hearten him.

'I'm sorry, darling. If it upsets you, I'll put it away.' She crossed to the chest of drawers, and did so. 'But why it should,' she said, returning, 'I can't imagine. I should have thought it would have made you so proud and happy. And now tell me everything that happened.'

'Yes,' I said. 'One would like the first-hand story.'

'Did you creep up behind him like a leopard?' asked Stiffy.

'Of course he did,' I said, admonishing the silly young shrimp. 'You don't suppose he pranced up in full view of the fellow? No doubt you trailed him with unremitting snakiness, eh, Stinker, and did the deed when he was relaxing on a stile or somewhere over a quiet pipe?'

Stinker sat staring straight before him, that drawn look still on his face.

'He wasn't on the stile. He was leaning against it. After you left me, Stiffy, I went for a walk to think things over, and I had just crossed Plunkett's meadow and was going to climb the stile into the next one, when

414

I saw something dark in front of me, and there he was.'

I nodded. I could visualize the scene.

'I hope,' I said, 'that you remembered to give the forward shove before the upwards lift?'

'It wasn't necessary. The helmet was not on his head. He had taken it off and put it on the ground. And, I just crept up and grabbed it.'

I started, pursing the lips a bit.

'Not quite playing the game, Stinker.'

'Yes, it was,' said Stiffy, with a good deal of warmth. 'I call it very clever of him.'

I could not recede from my position. At the Drones, we hold strong views on these things.

'There is a right way and a wrong way of pinching policemen's helmets,' I said firmly.

'You're talking absolute nonsense,' said Stiffy. 'I think you were wonderful, darling.'

I shrugged my shoulders.

'How do you feel about it, Jeeves?'

'I scarcely think that it would be fitting for me to offer an opinion, sir.'

'No,' said Stiffy. 'And it jolly well isn't fitting for you to offer an opinion, young pie-faced Bertie Wooster. Who do you think you are,' she demanded, with renewed warmth, 'coming strolling into a girl's bedroom, sticking on dog about the right way and wrong way of pinching helmets? It isn't as if you were such a wonder at it yourself, considering that you got collared and hauled up next morning at Bosher Street, where you had to grovel to Uncle Watkyn in the hope of getting off with a fine.'

I took this up promptly.

'I did not grovel to the old disease. My manner throughout was calm and dignified, like that of a Red Indian at the stake. And when you speak of me hoping to get off with a fine –'

Here Stiffy interrupted, to beg me to put a sock in it.

'Well, all I was about to say was that the sentence

stunned me. I felt so strongly that it was a case for a
mere reprimand. However, this is beside the point –
which is that Stinker in the recent encounter did not
play to the rules of the game. I consider his behaviour
morally tantamount to shooting a sitting bird. I cannot
alter my opinion.'

'And I can't alter my opinion that you have no
business in my bedroom. What are you doing here?'

'Yes, I was wondering that,' said Stinker, touching on
the point for the first time. And I could see, of course,
how he might quite well be surprised at finding this mob
scene in what he had supposed the exclusive sleeping
apartment of the loved one.

I eyed her sternly.

'You know what I am doing here. I told you. I came –'

'Oh, yes. Bertie came to borrow a book, darling. But' –
here her eyes lingered on mine in a cold and sinister
manner – 'I'm afraid I can't let him have it just yet. I
have not finished with it myself. By the way,' she
continued, still holding me with that compelling stare,
'Bertie says he will be delighted to help us with that
cow-creamer scheme.'

'Will you, old man?' said Stinker eagerly.

'Of course he will,' said Stiffy. 'He was saying only
just now what a pleasure it would be.'

'You won't mind me hitting you on the nose?'

'Of course he won't.'

'You see, we must have blood. Blood is of the
essence.'

'Of course, of course, of course,' said Stiffy. Her
manner was impatient. She seemed in a hurry to
terminate the scene. 'He quite understands that.'

'When would you feel like doing it, Bertie?'

'He feels like doing it tonight,' said Stiffy. 'No sense
in putting things off. Be waiting outside at midnight,
darling. Everybody will have gone to bed by then.
Midnight will suit you, Bertie? Yes, Bertie says it will

suit him splendidly. So that's all settled. And now you really must be going, precious. If somebody came in and found you here, they might think it odd. Good night, darling.'

'Good night, darling.'

'Good night, darling.'

'Good night, darling.'

'Wait!' I said, cutting in on these revolting exchanges, for I wished to make a last appeal to Stinker's finer feelings.

'He can't wait. He's got to go. Remember, angel. On the spot, ready to the last button, at twelve pip emma. Good night, darling.'

'Good night, darling.'

'Good night, darling.'

'Good night, darling.'

They passed onto the balcony, the nauseous endearments receding in the distance, and I turned to Jeeves, my face stern and hard.

'Faugh, Jeeves!'

'Sir?'

'I said "Faugh!" I am a pretty broadminded man, but this has shocked me – I may say to the core. It is not so much the behaviour of Stiffy that I find so revolting. She is a female, and the tendency of females to be unable to distinguish between right and wrong is notorious. But that Harold Pinker, a clerk in Holy Orders, a chap who buttons his collar at the back, should countenance this thing appals me. He knows she has got that book. He knows that she is holding me up with it. But does he insist on her returning it? No! He lends himself to the raw work with open enthusiasm. A nice look-out for the Totleigh-in-the-Wold flock, trying to keep on the straight and narrow path with a shepherd like that! A pretty example he sets to this Infants' Bible Class of which he speaks! A few years of sitting at the feet of Harold Pinker and imbibing his extraordinary views on morality and ethics, and every bally child on the list will be serving a long stretch at Wormwood Scrubs for blackmail.'

I paused, much moved. A bit out of breath, too.

'I think you do the gentleman an injustice, sir.'

'Eh?'

'I am sure that he is under the impression that your acquiescence in the scheme is due entirely to goodness of heart and a desire to assist an old friend.'

'You think she hasn't told him about the notebook?'

'I am convinced of it, sir. I could gather that from the lady's manner.'

'I didn't notice anything about her manner.'

'When you were about to mention the notebook, it betrayed embarrassment, sir. She feared lest Mr Pinker might enquire into the matter and, learning the facts, compel her to make restitution.'

'By Jove, Jeeves, I believe you're right.'

I reviewed the recent scene. Yes, he was perfectly correct. Stiffy, though one of those girls who enjoy in equal quantities the gall of an army mule and the calm *insouciance* of a fish on a slab of ice, had unquestionably gone up in the air a bit when I had seemed about to explain to Stinker my motives for being in the room. I recalled the feverish way in which she had hustled him out, like a small bouncer at a pub ejecting a large customer.

'Egad, Jeeves!' I said, impressed.

There was a muffled crashing sound from the direction of the balcony. A few moments later, Stiffy returned.

'Harold fell off the ladder,' she explained, laughing heartily. 'Well, Bertie, you've got the programme all clear? Tonight's the night!'

I drew out a gasper and lit it.

'Wait!' I said. 'Not so fast. Just one moment, young Stiffy.'

*

The ring of quiet authority in my tone seemed to take her aback. She blinked twice, and looked at me questioningly, while I, drawing in a cargo of smoke, expelled it nonchalantly through the nostrils.

'Just one moment,' I repeated.

In the narrative of my earlier adventures with Augustus Fink-Nottle at Brinkley Court, with which you may or may not be familiar, I mentioned that I had once read a historical novel about a Buck or Beau or some such cove who, when it became necessary for him to put people where they belonged, was in the habit of laughing down from lazy eyelids and flicking a speck of dust from the irreproachable Mechlin lace at his wrists. And I think I stated that I had had excellent results from modelling myself on this bird.

I did so now.

'Stiffy,' I said, laughing down from lazy eyelids and flicking a speck of cigarette ash from my irreproachable cuff, 'I will trouble you to disgorge that book.'

The questioning look became intensified. I could see that all this was perplexing her. She had supposed that she had Bertram nicely ground beneath the iron heel, and here he was, popping up like a two-year-old, full of the fighting spirit.

'What do you mean?'

I laughed down a bit more.

'I should have supposed,' I said, flicking, 'that my meaning was quite clear. I want that notebook of Gussie's, and I want it immediately, without any more back chat.'

Her lips tightened.

'You will get it tomorrow – if Harold turns in a satisfactory report.'

'I shall get it now.'

'Ha jolly ha!'

'"Ha jolly ha!" to you, young Stiffy, with knobs on,' I

retorted with quiet dignity. 'I repeat, I shall get it now. If I don't, I shall go to old Stinker and tell him all about it.'

'All about what?'

'All about everything. At present, he is under the impression that my acquiescence in your scheme is due entirely to goodness of heart and a desire to assist an old friend. You haven't told him about the notebook. I am convinced of it. I could gather that from your manner. When I was about to mention the notebook, it betrayed embarrassment. You feared lest Stinker might enquire into the matter and, learning the facts, compel you to make restitution.'

Her eyes flickered. I saw that Jeeves had been correct in his diagnosis.

'You're talking absolute rot,' she said, but it was with a quaver on the v.

'All right. Well, toodle-oo. I'm off to find Stinker.'

I turned on my heel and, as I expected, she stopped me with a pleading yowl.

'No, Bertie, don't! You mustn't!'

I came back.

'So! You admit it? Stinker knows nothing of your . . .' The powerful phrase which Aunt Dahlia had employed when speaking of Sir Watkyn Bassett occurred to me – 'of your underhanded skulduggery.'

'I don't see why you call it underhanded skulduggery.'

'I call it underhanded skulduggery because that is what I consider it. And that is what Stinker, dripping as he is with high principles, will consider it when the facts are placed before him.' I turned on the h. again. 'Well, toodle-oo once more.'

'Bertie, wait!'

'Well?'

'Bertie, darling –'

I checked her with a cold wave of the cigarette-holder.

'Less of the "Bertie, darling". "Bertie, darling",
forsooth! Nice time to start the "Bertie, darling"-ing.'

'But, Bertie darling, I want to explain. Of course I
didn't dare tell Harold about the book. He would have
had a fit. He would have said it was a rotten trick, and of
course I knew it was. But there was nothing else to do.
There didn't seem any other way of getting you to help
us.'

'There wasn't.'

'But you are going to help us, aren't you?'

'I am not.'

'Well, I do think you might.'

'I dare say you do, but I won't.'

Somewhere about the first or second line of this
chunk of dialogue, I had observed her eyes begin to
moisten and her lips to tremble, and a pearly one had
started to steal down the cheek. The bursting of the
dam, of which that pearly one had been the first
preliminary trickle, now set in with great severity. With
a brief word to the effect that she wished she were dead
and that I would look pretty silly when I gazed down at
her coffin, knowing that my inhumanity had put her
there, she flung herself on the bed and started going
oomp.

It was the old uncontrollable sob-stuff which she had
pulled earlier in the proceedings, and once more I found
myself a bit unmanned. I stood there irresolute, plucking
nervously at the cravat. I have already alluded to the
effect of a woman's grief on the Woosters.

'Oomp,' she went.

'Oomp . . . Oomp . . .'

'But, Stiffy, old girl, be reasonable. Use the bean. You
can't seriously expect me to pinch that cow-creamer.'

'It oomps everything to us.'

'Very possibly. But listen. You haven't envisaged the
latent snags. Your blasted uncle is watching my every
move, just waiting for me to start something. And even

if he wasn't, the fact that I would be co-operating with
Stinker renders the thing impossible. I have already
given you my views on Stinker as a partner in crime.
Somehow, in some manner, he would muck everything
up. Why, look at what happened just now. He couldn't
even climb down a ladder without falling off.'

'Oomp.'

'And, anyway, just examine this scheme of yours in
pitiless analysis. You tell me the wheeze is for Stinker to
stroll in all over blood and say he hit the marauder on
the nose. Let us suppose he does so. What ensues? "Ha!"
says your uncle, who doubtless knows a clue as well as
the next man. "Hit him on the nose, did you? Keep your
eyes skinned, everybody, for a bird with a swollen nose."
And the first thing he sees is me with a beezer twice
the proper size. Don't tell me he wouldn't draw
conclusions.'

I rested my case. It seemed to me that I had made out
a pretty good one, and I anticipated the resigned. 'Right
ho. Yes, I see what you mean. I suppose you're right.'
But she merely oomped the more, and I turned to Jeeves,
who hitherto had not spoken.

'You follow my reasoning, Jeeves?'

'Entirely, sir.'

'You agree with me, that the scheme, as planned,
would merely end in disaster?'

'Yes, sir. It undoubtedly presents certain grave
difficulties. I wonder if I might be permitted to suggest
an alternative one.'

I stared at the man.

'You mean you have found a formula.'

'I think so, sir.'

His words had de-oomped Stiffy. I don't think
anything else in the world would have done it. She sat
up, looking at him with a wild surmise.

'Jeeves! Have you really?'

'Yes, miss.'

'Well, you certainly are the most wonderfully woolly baa-lamb that ever stepped.'

'Thank you, miss.'

'Well, let us have it, Jeeves,' I said, lighting another cigarette and lowering self into a chair. 'One hopes, of course, that you are right, but I should have thought personally that there were no avenues.'

'I think we can find one, sir, if we approach the matter from the psychological angle.'

'Oh, psychological?'

'Yes, sir.'

'The psychology of the individual?'

'Precisely, sir.'

'I see. Jeeves,' I explained to Stiffy, who, of course, knew the man only slightly, scarcely more, indeed, than as a silent figure that had done some smooth potato-handing when she had lunched at my flat, 'is and always has been a whale on the psychology of the individual. He eats it alive. What individual, Jeeves?'

'Sir Watkyn Bassett, sir.'

I frowned doubtfully.

'You propose to try to soften that old public enemy? I don't think it can be done, except with a knuckleduster.'

'No, sir. It would not be easy to soften Sir Watkyn, who, as you imply, is a man of strong character, not easily moulded. The idea I have in mind is to endeavour to take advantage of his attitude towards yourself. Sir Watkyn does not like you, sir.'

'I don't like him.'

'No, sir. But the important thing is that he has conceived a strong distaste for you, and would consequently sustain a severe shock, were you to inform him that you and Miss Byng were betrothed and were anxious to be united in matrimony.'

'What! You want me to tell him that Stiffy and I are that way?'

'Precisely, sir.'

I shook the head.

'I see no percentage in it, Jeeves. All right for a laugh, no doubt – watching the old bounder's reactions I mean – but of little practical value.'

Stiffy, too, seemed disappointed. It was plain that she had been hoping for better things.

'It sounds goofy to me,' she said. 'Where would that get us Jeeves?'

'If I might explain miss. Sir Watkyn's reactions would, as Mr Wooster suggests, be of a strongly defined character.'

'He would hit the ceiling.'

'Exactly, miss. A very colourful piece of imagery. And if you were then to assure him that there was no truth in Mr Wooster's statement, adding that you were, in actual fact, betrothed to Mr Pinker, I think the overwhelming relief which he would feel at the news would lead him to look with a kindly eye on your union with that gentleman.'

Personally, I had never heard anything so potty in my life, and my manner indicated as much. Stiffy, on the other hand, was all over it. She did the first few steps of a Spring dance.

'Why, Jeeves, that's marvellous!'

'I think it would prove effective, miss.'

'Of course, it would. It couldn't fail. Just imagine, Bertie, darling, how he would feel if you told him I wanted to marry you. Why, if after that I said "Oh, no, it's all right, Uncle Watkyn. The chap I really want to marry is the boy who cleans the boots," he would fold me in his arms and promise to come and dance at the wedding. And when he finds that the real fellow is a splendid, wonderful, terrific man like Harold, the thing will be a walk-over. Jeeves, you really are a specific dream-rabbit.'

'Thank you, miss. I am glad to have given satisfaction.'

I rose. It was my intention to say goodbye to all this. I don't mind people talking rot in my presence, but it must not be utter rot. I turned to Stiffy, who was now in the later stages of her Spring dance, and addressed her with curt severity.

'I will now take the book, Stiffy.'

She was over by the cupboard, strewing roses. She paused for a moment.

'Oh, the book. You want it?'

'I do. Immediately.'

'I'll give it you after you've seen Uncle Watkyn.'

'Oh?'

'Yes. It isn't that I don't trust you, Bertie, darling, but I should feel much happier if I knew that you knew I had still got it, and I'm sure you want me to feel happy. You toddle off and beard him, and then we'll talk.'

I frowned.

'I will toddle off,' I said coldly, 'but beard him, no. I don't seem to see myself bearding him!'

She stared.

'But Bertie, this sounds as if you weren't going to sit in.'

'It was how I meant it to sound.'

'You wouldn't fail me, would you?'

'I would. I would fail you like billy-o.'

'Don't you like the scheme?'

'I do not. Jeeves spoke a moment ago of his gladness at having given satisfaction. He has given me no satisfaction whatsoever. I consider that the idea he has advanced marks the absolute zero in human goofiness, and I am surprised that he should have entertained it. The book, Stiffy, if you please – and slippily.'

She was silent for a space.

'I was rather asking myself,' she said, 'if you might not take this attitude.'

'And now you know the answer,' I riposted. 'I have. The book, if you please.'

'I'm not going to give you the book.'

'Very well. Then I go to Stinker and tell him all.'

'All right. Do. And before you can get within a mile of him, I shall be up in the library, telling Uncle Watkyn all.'

She waggled her chin, like a girl who considers that she has put over a swift one: and, examining what she had said, I was compelled to realize that this was precisely what she had put over. I had overlooked this contingency completely. Her words gave me pause. The best I could do in the way of a comeback was to utter a somewhat baffled 'H'm!' There is no use attempting to disguise the fact – Bertram was nonplussed.

'So there you are. Now, how about it?'

It is never pleasant for a chap who has been doing the dominant male to have to change his stance and sink to ignoble pleadings, but I could see no other course. My voice, which had been firm and resonant, took on a melting tremolo.

'But, Stiffy, dash it! You wouldn't do that?'

'Yes, I would, if you don't go and sweeten Uncle Watkyn.'

'But how can I go and sweeten him? Stiffy, you can't subject me to this fearful ordeal.'

'Yes, I can. And what's so fearful about it? He can't eat you.'

I conceded this.

'True. But that's about the best you can say.'

'It won't be any worse than a visit to the dentist.'

'It'll be worse than six visits to six dentists.'

'Well, think how glad you will be when it's over.'

I drew little consolation from this. I looked at her closely, hoping to detect some signs of softening. Not one. She had been as tough as a restaurant steak, and she continued as tough as a restaurant steak. Kipling was right. D. than them. No getting round it.

I made one last appeal.

'You won't recede from your position?'

'Not a step.'

'In spite of the fact – excuse me mentioning it – that I gave you a dashed good lunch at my flat, no expense spared?'

'No.'

I shrugged my shoulders, as some Roman gladiator – one of those chaps who threw knotted sheets over people, for instance – might have done on hearing the call-boy shouting his number in the wings.

'Very well, then,' I said.

She beamed at me maternally.

'That's the spirit. That's my brave little man.'

At a less preoccupied moment, I might have resented her calling me her brave little man, but in this grim hour it scarcely seemed to matter.

'Where is this frightful uncle of yours?'

'He's bound to be in the library now.'

'Very good. Then I will go to him.'

I don't know if you were ever told as a kid that story about the fellow whose dog chewed up the priceless manuscript of the book he was writing. The blow-out, if you remember, was that he gave the animal a pained look and said: 'Oh, Diamond, Diamond, you – or it may have been thou – little know – or possibly knowest – what you – or thou – has – or hast – done.' I heard it in the nursery, and it has always lingered in my mind. And why I bring it up now is that this was how I looked at Jeeves as I passed from the room. I didn't actually speak the gag, but I fancy he knew what I was thinking.

I could have wished that Stiffy had not said 'Yoicks! Tally-ho!' as I crossed the threshold. It seemed to me in the circumstances flippant and in dubious taste.

9

It has been well said of Bertram Wooster by those who know him best that there is a certain resilience in his nature that enables him as a general rule to rise on stepping-stones of his dead self in the most unfavourable circumstances. It isn't often that I fail to keep the chin up and the eye sparkling. But as I made my way to the library in pursuance of my dreadful task, I freely admit that Life had pretty well got me down. It was with leaden feet, as the expression is, that I tooled along.

Stiffy had compared the binge under advisement to a visit to the dentist, but as I reached journey's end I was feeling more as I had felt in the old days of school when going to keep a tryst with the head master in his study. You will recall me telling you of the time I sneaked down by night to the Rev. Aubrey Upjohn's lair in quest of biscuits and found myself unexpectedly cheek by jowl with the old bird, I in striped non-shrinkable pyjamas, he in tweeds and a dirty look. On that occasion, before parting, we had made a date for half-past four next day at the same spot, and my emotions were almost exactly similar to those which I had experienced on that far-off afternoon, as I tapped on the door and heard a scarcely human voice invite me to enter.

The only difference was that while the Rev. Aubrey had been alone, Sir Watkyn Bassett appeared to be entertaining company. As my knuckles hovered over the panel, I seemed to hear the rumble of voices, and when I went in I found that my ears had not deceived me. Pop Bassett was seated at the desk, and by his side stood Constable Eustace Oates. It was a spectacle that rather put the lid on the shrinking feeling from which I was suffering. I don't know if you have ever been jerked before a tribunal of justice, but if you have you will bear me out when I say that the memory of such an experience lingers, with the result that when later you are suddenly confronted by a sitting magistrate and a standing policeman, the association of ideas gives you a bit of a shock and tends to unman.

A swift keen glance from old B. did nothing to still the fluttering pulse.

'Yes, Mr Wooster?'

'Oh – ah – could I speak to you for a moment?'

'Speak to me?' I could see that a strong distaste for having his sanctum cluttered up with Woosters was contending in Sir Watkyn Bassett's bosom with a sense of the obligations of a host. After what seemed a nip-and-tuck struggle, the latter got its nose ahead. 'Why, yes . . . That is . . . If you really . . . Oh, certainly . . . Pray take a seat.'

I did so, and felt a good deal better. In the dock, you have to stand. Old Bassett, after a quick look in my direction to see that I wasn't stealing the carpet, turned to the constable again.

'Well, I think that is all, Oates.'

'Very good, Sir Watkyn.'

'You understand what I wish you to do?'

'Yes, sir.'

'And with regard to that other matter, I will look into it very closely, bearing in mind what you have told me of your suspicions. A most rigorous investigation shall be made.'

The zealous officer clumped out. Old Bassett fiddled for a moment with the papers on his desk. Then he cocked an eye at me.

'That was Constable Oates, Mr Wooster.'

'Yes.'

'You know him?'

'I've seen him.'

'When?'

'This afternoon.'

'Not since then?'

'No.'

'Are you quite sure?'

'Oh, quite.'

He fiddled with the papers again, then touched on another topic.

'We were all disappointed that you were not with us in the drawing-room after dinner, Mr Wooster.'

This, of course, was a bit embarrassing. The man of sensibility does not like to reveal to this host that he has been dodging him like a leper.

'You were much missed.'

'Oh, was I? I'm sorry. I had a bit of a headache, and went and ensconced myself in my room.'

'I see. And you remained there?'

'Yes.'

'You did not by any chance go for a walk in the fresh air, to relieve your headache?'

'Oh, no. Ensconced all the time.'

'I see. Odd. My daughter Madeline tells me that she went twice to your room after the conclusion of dinner, but found it unoccupied.'

'Oh, really? Wasn't I there?'

'You were not.'

'I suppose I must have been somewhere else.'

'The same thought had occurred to me.'

'I remember now. I did saunter out on two occasions.'

'I see.'

He took up a pen and leaned forward, tapping it against his left forefinger.

'Somebody stole Constable Oates's helmet tonight,' he said, changing the subject.

'Oh, yes.'

'Yes. Unfortunately he was not able to see the miscreant.'

'No?'

'No. At the moment when the outrage took place, his back was turned.'

'Dashed difficult, of course, to see miscreants, if your back's turned.'

'Yes.'

'Yes.'

There was a pause. And as, in spite of the fact that we seemed to be agreeing on every point, I continued to sense a strain in the atmosphere, I tried to lighten things with a gag which I remembered from the old *in statu pupillari* days.

'Sort of makes you say to yourself *Quis custodiet ipsos custodes*, what?'

'I beg your pardon?'

'Latin joke,' I exclaimed. '*Quis* – who – *custodiet* – shall guard – *ipsos custodes* – the guardians themselves? Rather funny, I mean to say,' I proceeded, making it clear to the meanest intelligence, 'a chap who's supposed to stop chaps pinching things from chaps having a chap come along and pinch something from him.'

'Ah, I see your point. Yes, I can conceive that a certain type of mind might detect a humorous side to the affair. But I can assure you, Mr Wooster, that that is not the side which presents itself to me as a Justice of the Peace. I take the very gravest view of the matter, and this, when once he is apprehended and placed in custody, I shall do my utmost to persuade the culprit to share.'

I didn't like the sound of this at all. A sudden alarm for old Stinker's well-being swept over me.

'I say, what do you think he would get?'

'I appreciate your zeal for knowledge, Mr Wooster, but at the moment I am not prepared to confide in you. In the words of the late Lord Asquith, I can only say "Wait and see". I think it is possible that your curiosity may be gratified before long.'

I didn't want to rake up old sores, always being a bit of a lad for letting the dead past bury its dead, but I thought it might be as well to give him a pointer.

'You fined me five quid,' I reminded him.

'So you informed me this afternoon,' he said, pince-nezing me coldly. 'But if I understood correctly what you were saying, the outrage for which you were brought before me at Bosher Street was perpetrated on the night of the annual boat race between the Universities of Oxford and Cambridge, when a certain licence is traditionally granted by the authorities. In the present case, there are no such extenuating circumstances. I should certainly not punish the wanton stealing of Government property from the person of Constable Oates with a mere fine.'

'You don't mean it would be chokey?'

'I said that I was not prepared to confide in you, but having gone so far I will. The answer to your question, Mr Wooster, is in the affirmative.'

There was a silence. He sat tapping his finger with the pen. I, if memory serves me correctly, straightening my tie. I was deeply concerned. The thought of poor old Stinker being bunged into the Bastille was enough to disturb anyone with a kindly interest in his career and prospects. Nothing retards a curate's advancement in his chosen profession more surely than a spell in the jug.

He lowered the pen.

'Well, Mr Wooster, I think that you were about to tell me what brings you here?'

I started a bit. I hadn't actually forgotten my mission, of course, but all this sinister stuff had caused me to shove it away at the back of my mind, and the suddenness with which it now came popping out gave me a bit of a jar.

I saw that there would have to be a few preliminary

pourparlers before I got down to the nub. When relations
between a bloke and another bloke are of a strained
nature, the second bloke can't charge straight into the
topic of wanting to marry the first bloke's niece. Not,
that is to say, if he has a nice sense of what is fitting, as
the Woosters have.

'Oh, ah, yes. Thanks for reminding me.'

'Not at all.'

'I just thought I'd drop in and have a chat.'

'I see.'

What the thing wanted, of course, was edging into,
and I found I had got the approach. I teed up with a
certain access of confidence.

'Have you ever thought about love, Sir Watkyn?'

'I beg your pardon?'

'About love. Have you ever brooded on it to any
extent?'

'You have not come here to discuss love?'

'Yes, I have. That's exactly it. I wonder if you have
noticed a rather rummy thing about it – viz. that it is
everywhere. You can't get away from it. Love, I mean.
Wherever you go, there it is, buzzing along in every
class of life. Quite remarkable. Take newts, for
instance.'

'Are you quite well, Mr Wooster?'

'Oh, fine, thanks. Take newts, I was saying. You
wouldn't think it, but Gussie Fink-Nottle tells me they
get it right up their noses in the mating season. They
stand in line by the hour, waggling their tails at the local
belles. Starfish, too. Also undersea worms.'

'Mr Wooster –'

'And, according to Gussie, even ribbonlike seaweed.
That surprises you, eh? It did me. But he assures me that
it is so. Just where a bit of ribbonlike seaweed thinks it
is going to get by pressing its suit is more than I can tell
you, but at the time of the full moon it hears the voice
of Love all right and is up and doing with the best of

433

them. I suppose it builds on the hope that it will look good to other bits of ribbonlike seaweed, which, of course, would also be affected by the full moon. Well, be that as it may, what I'm working round to is that the moon is pretty full now, and if that's how it affects seaweed you can't very well blame a chap like me for feeling the impulse, can you?'

'I am afraid –'

'Well, can you?' I repeated, pressing him strongly. And I threw in an 'eh, what?' to clinch the thing.

But there was no answering spark of intelligence in his eye. He had been looking like a man who had missed the finer shades, and he still looked like a man who had missed the finer shades.

'I am afraid, Mr Wooster, that you will think me dense, but I have not the remotest notion what you are talking about.'

Now that the moment for letting him have it in the eyeball had arrived, I was pleased to find that the all-of-a-twitter feeling which had gripped me at the outset had ceased to function. I don't say that I had become exactly debonair and capable of flicking specks of dust from the irreproachable Mechlin lace at my wrists, but I felt perfectly calm.

What had soothed the system was the realization that in another half-jiffy I was about to slip a stick of dynamite under this old buster which would teach him that we are not put into the world for pleasure alone. When a magistrate has taken five quid off you for what, properly looked at, was a mere boyish peccadillo which would have been amply punished by a waggle of the forefinger and a brief 'Tut, tut!' it is always agreeable to make him jump like a pea on a hot shovel.

'I'm talking about me and Stiffy.'

'Stiffy?'

'Stephanie.'

'Stephanie? My niece?'

434

'That's right. Your niece. Sir Watkyn,' I said, remembering a good one, 'I have the honour to ask you for your niece's hand.'

'You – what?'

'I have the honour to ask you for your niece's hand.'

'I don't understand.'

'It's quite simple. I want to marry young Stiffy. She wants to marry me. Surely you've got it now? Take a line through that ribbonlike seaweed.'

There was no question as to its being value for money. On the cue 'niece's hand', he had come out of his chair like a rocketing pheasant. He now sank, back, fanning himself with the pen. He seemed to have aged quite a lot.

'She wants to marry you?'

'That's the idea.'

'But I was not aware that you knew my niece.'

'Oh, rather. We two, if you care to put it that way, have plucked the gowans fine. Oh, yes, I know Stiffy, all right. Well, I mean to say, if I didn't, I shouldn't want to marry her, should I?'

He seemed to see the justice of this. He became silent, except for a soft, groaning noise. I remembered another good one.

'You will not be losing a niece. You will be gaining a nephew.'

'But I don't want a nephew, damn it!'

Well, there was that, of course.

He rose, and muttering something which sounded like 'Oh, dear! Oh, dear!' went to the fireplace and pressed the bell with a weak finger. Returning to his seat, he remained holding his head in his hands until the butler blew in.

'Butterfield,' he said in a low, hoarse voice, 'find Miss Stephanie and tell her that I wish to speak to her.'

A stage wait then occurred, but not such a long one as you might have expected. It was only about a minute

before Stiffy appeared. I imagine she had been lurking in
the offing, expectant of his summons. She tripped in, all
merry and bright.

'You want to see me, Uncle Watkyn? Oh, hallo,
Bertie.'

'Hallo.'

'I didn't know you were here. Have you and Uncle
Watkyn been having a nice talk?'

Old Bassett, who had gone into a coma again, came
out of it and uttered a sound like the death-rattle of a
dying duck.

' "Nice",' he said, 'is not the adjective I would have
selected.' He moistened his ashen lips. 'Mr Wooster has
just informed me that he wishes to marry you.'

I must say that young Stiffy gave an extemely
convincing performance. She stared at him. She stared at
me. She clasped her hands. I rather think she blushed.

'Why Bertie!'

Old Bassett broke the pen. I had been wondering
when he would.

'Oh, Bertie! You have made me very proud.'

'Proud?' I detected an incredulous note in old Bassett's
voice. 'Did you say "proud"?'

'Well, it's the greatest compliment a man can pay a
woman, you know. All the nibs are agreed on that. I'm
tremendously flattered and grateful . . . and, well, all that
sort of thing. But, Bertie dear, I'm terribly sorry. I'm
afraid it's impossible.'

I hadn't supposed that there was anything in the
world capable of jerking a man from the depths so
effectively as one of those morning mixtures of Jeeves's,
but these words acted on old Bassett with an even
greater promptitude and zip. He had been sitting in his
chair in a boneless, huddled sort of way, a broken man.
He now started up, with gleaming eyes and twitching
lips. You could see that hope had dawned.

'Impossible? Don't you want to marry him?'

'No.'

'He said you did.'

'He must have been thinking of a couple of other fellows. No, Bertie, darling, it cannot be. You see, I love somebody else.'

Old Bassett started.

'Eh? Who?'

'The most wonderful man in the world.'

'He has a name, I presume?'

'Harold Pinker.'

'Harold Pinker? . . . Pinker . . . The only Pinker I know is – '

'The curate. That's right. He's the chap.'

'You love the curate?'

'Ah!' said Stiffy, rolling her eyes up and looking like Aunt Dahlia when she had spoken of the merits of blackmail. 'We've been secretly engaged for weeks.'

It was plain from old Bassett's manner that he was not prepared to classify this under the heading of tidings of great joy. His brows were knitted, like those of some diner in a restaurant who, sailing into his dozen oysters, finds that the first one to pass his lips is a wrong 'un. I saw that Stiffy had shown a shrewd knowledge of human nature, if you could call his that, when she had told me that this man would have to be heavily sweetened before the news could be broken. You could see that he shared the almost universal opinion of parents and uncles that curates were nothing to start strewing roses out of a hat about.

'You know that vicarage that you have in your gift, Uncle Watkyn? What Harold and I were thinking was that you might give him that, and then we could get married at once. You see, apart from the increased dough, it would start him off on the road to higher things. Up till now, Harold has been working under wraps. As a curate, he has had no scope. But slip him a vicarage, and watch him let himself out. There is literally no eminence to which that boy will not rise, once he spits on his hands and starts in.'

She wriggled from base to apex with girlish enthusiasm, but there was no girlish enthusiasm in old Bassett's demeanour. Well, there wouldn't be, of course, but what I mean is there wasn't.

'Ridiculous!'

'Why?'

'I could not dream –'

'Why not?'

'In the first place, you are far too young –'

'What nonsense. Three of the girls I was at school with were married last year. I'm senile compared with some of the infants you see toddling up the aisle nowadays.'

Old Bassett thumped the desk – coming down, I was glad to see, on an upturned paper fastener. The bodily anguish induced by this lent vehemence to his tone.

'The whole thing is quite absurd and utterly out of the question. I refuse to consider the idea for an instant.'

'But what have you got against Harold?'

'I have nothing, as you put it, against him. He seems zealous in his duties and popular in the parish –'

'He's a baa-lamb.'

'No doubt.'

'He played football for England.'

'Very possibly.'

'And he's marvellous at tennis.'

'I dare say he is. But that is not a reason why he should marry my niece. What means has he, if any, beyond his stipend?'

'About five hundred a year.'

'Tchah!'

'Well, I don't call that bad. Five hundred's pretty good sugar, if you ask me. Besides, money doesn't matter.'

'It matters a great deal.'

'You really feel that, do you?'

'Certainly. You must be practical.'

'Right ho, I will. If you'd rather I married for money, I'll marry for money. Bertie, it's on. Start getting measured for the wedding trousers.'

Her words created what is known as a genuine sensation. Old Bassett's 'What!' and my 'Here, I say, dash it!' popped out neck and neck and collided in mid air, my heart-cry having, perhaps, an even greater horse-power than his. I was frankly appalled. Experience has taught me that you never know with girls, and it might quite possibly happen, I felt, that she would go through with this frightful project as a gesture. Nobody could teach me anything about gestures. Brinkley Court in the preceding summer had crawled with them.

'Bertie is rolling in the stuff and, as you suggest, one might do worse than take a whack at the Wooster millions. Of course, Bertie dear, I am only marrying you to make you happy. I can never love you as I love Harold. But as Uncle Watkyn has taken this violent prejudice against him –'

Old Bassett hit the paper fastener again, but this time didn't seem to notice it.

'My dear child, don't talk such nonsense. You are quite mistaken. You must have completely misunderstood me. I have no prejudice against this young man Pinker. I like and respect him. If you really think your happiness lies in becoming his wife, I would be the last man to stand in your way. By all means, marry him. The alternative –'

He said no more, but gave me a long, shuddering look. Then, as if the sight of me were more than his frail strength could endure, he removed his gaze, only to bring it back again and give me a short quick one. He then closed his eyes and leaned back in his chair, breathing stertorously. And as there didn't seem anything to keep me, I sidled out. The last I saw of him, he was submitting without any great animation to a niece's embrace.

I suppose that when you have an uncle like Sir Watkyn Bassett on the receiving end, a niece's embrace is a thing you tend to make pretty snappy. It wasn't more than about a minute before Stiffy came out and immediately went into her dance.

'What a man! What a man! What a man! What a man! What a man!' she said, waving her arms and giving other indications of *bien-être*. 'Jeeves,' she explained, as if she supposed that I might imagine her to be alluding to the recent Bassett. 'Did he say it would work? He did. And was he right? He was. Bertie, could one kiss Jeeves?'

'Certainly not.'

'Shall I kiss you?'

'No, thank you. All I require from you, young Byng, is that notebook.'

'Well, I must kiss someone, and I'm dashed if I'm going to kiss Eustace Oates.'

She broke off. A graver look came into her dial.

'Eustace Oates!' she repeated meditatively. 'That reminds me. In the rush of recent events, I had forgotten him. I exchanged a few words with Eustace Oates just now, Bertie, while I was waiting on the stairs for the balloon to go up, and he was sinister to a degree.'

'Where's that notebook?'

'Never mind about the notebook. The subject under discussion is Eustace Oates and his sinisterness. He's on my trail about that helmet.'

'What!'

'Absolutely. I'm Suspect Number One. He told me that he reads a lot of detective stories, and he says that the first thing a detective makes a bee-line for is motive. After that, opportunity. And finally clues. Well, as he pointed out, with that high-handed behaviour of his about Bartholomew rankling in my bosom, I had a motive all right, and seeing that I was out and about at the time of the crime I had the opportunity, too. And as for clues, what do you think he had with him, when I saw him? One of my gloves! He had picked it up on the scene of the outrage – while measuring footprints or looking for cigar ash, I suppose. You remember when Harold brought me back my gloves, there was only one of them. The other he apparently dropped while scooping in the helmet.'

A sort of dull, bruised feeling weighed me down as I mused on this latest manifestation of Harold Pinker's goofiness, as if a strong hand had whanged me over the cupola with a blackjack. There was such a sort of hideous ingenuity in the way he thought up new methods of inviting ruin.

'He would!'

'What do you mean, he would?'

'Well, he did, didn't he?'

'That's not the same as saying he would – in a beastly sneering, supercilious tone, as if you were so frightfully hot yourself. I can't understand you, Bertie – the way you're always criticizing poor Harold. I thought you were so fond of him.'

'I love him like a b. But that doesn't alter my opinion that of all the pumpkin-headed foozlers who ever preached about Hivites and Jebusites, he is the foremost.'

'He isn't half as pumpkin-headed as you.'

'He is, at a conservative estimate, about twenty-seven times as pumpkin-headed as me. He begins where I leave off. It may be a strong thing to say, but he's more pumpkin-headed than Gussie.'

With a visible effort, she swallowed the rising choler.

'Well, never mind about that. The point is that Eustace Oates is on my trail, and I've got to look slippy and find a better safe-deposit vault for that helmet than my chest of drawers. Before I know where I am, the

Ogpu will be searching my room. Where would be a good place, do you think?'

I dismissed the thing wearily.

'Oh dash it, use your own judgement. To return to the main issue, where is that notebook?'

'Oh, Bertie, you're a perfect bore about that notebook. Can't you talk of anything else?'

'No, I can't. Where is it?'

'You're going to laugh when I tell you.'

I gave her an austere look.

'It is possible that I may some day laugh again – when I have got well away from this house of terror, but there is a fat chance of my doing so at this early date. Where is that book?'

'Well, if you really must know, I hid it in the cow-creamer.'

Everyone, I imagine, has read stories in which things turned black and swam before people. As I heard these words, Stiffy turned black and swam before me. It was as if I had been looking at a flickering negress.

'You – what?'

'I hid it in the cow-creamer.'

'What on earth did you do that for?'

'Oh, I thought I would.'

'But how am I to get it?'

A slight smile curved the young pimple's mobile lips.

'Oh, dash it, use your own judgement,' she said. 'Well, see you soon, Bertie.'

She biffed off, and I leaned limply against the banisters, trying to rally from this frightful wallop. But the world still flickered, and a few moments later I became aware that I was being addressed by a flickering butler.

'Excuse me, sir. Miss Madeline desired me to say that she would be glad if you could spare her a moment.'

I gazed at the man dully, like someone in a prison cell when the jailer has stepped in at dawn to notify him that the firing squad is ready. I knew what this meant, of course. I had recognized this butler's voice for what it was – the voice of doom. There could be only one thing that Madeline Bassett would be glad if I could spare her a moment about.

'Oh, did she?'

'Yes, sir.'

'Where is Miss Bassett?'

'In the drawing-room, sir.'

'Right ho.'

I braced myself with the old Wooster grit. Up came the chin, back went the shoulders.

'Lead on,' I said to the butler, and the butler led on.

10

The sound of soft and wistful music percolating through
the drawing-room door as I approached did nothing to
brighten the general outlook: and when I went in and
saw Madeline Bassett seated at the piano, drooping on
her stem a goodish deal, the sight nearly caused me to
turn and leg it. However, I fought down the impulse and
started things off with a tentative 'What ho.'

The observation elicited no immediate response. She
had risen, and for perhaps half a minute stood staring at
me in a sad sort of way, like the Mona Lisa on one of the
mornings when the sorrows of the world had been
coming over the plate a bit too fast for her. Finally, just
as I was thinking I had better try to fill in with
something about the weather, she spoke.

'Bertie – '

It was, however, only a flash in the pan. She blew a
fuse, and silence supervened again.

'Bertie – '

No good. Another wash-out.

I was beginning to feel the strain a bit. We had had
one of these deaf-mutes-getting-together sessions before,
at Brinkley Court, in the summer, but on that occasion I
had been able to ease things along by working in a spot
of stage business during the awkward gaps in the
conversation. Our previous chat as you may or possibly
may not recall, had taken place in the Brinkley dining-
room in the presence of a cold collation, and it had
helped a lot being in a position to bound forward at
intervals with a curried egg or a cheese straw. In the
absence of these food stuffs, we were thrown back a good

deal on straight staring, and this always tends to
embarrass.

Her lips parted. I saw that something was coming to
the surface. A couple of gulps, and she was off to a good
start. 'Bertie, I wanted to see you . . . I asked you to come
because I wanted to say . . . I wanted to tell you . . .
Bertie, my engagement to Augustus is at an end.'

'Yes.'

'You knew?'

'Oh, rather. He told me.'

'Then you know why I asked you to come here. I
wanted to say –'

'Yes.'

'That I am willing –'

'Yes.'

'To make you happy.'

She appeared to be held up for a moment by a slight
return of the old tonsil trouble, but after another brace of
gulps she got it out.

'I will be your wife, Bertie.'

I suppose that after this most chaps would have
thought it scarcely worthwhile to struggle against the
inev., but I had a dash at it. With such vital issues at
stake, one would have felt a chump if one had left any
stone unturned.

'Awfully decent of you,' I said civilly. 'Deeply sensible
of the honour, and what not. But have you thought?
Have you reflected? Don't you feel you're being a bit
rough on poor old Gussie?'

'What! After what happened this evening?'

'Ah, I wanted to talk to you about that. I always
think, don't you, that it is as well on these occasions,
before doing anything drastic, to have a few words with
a seasoned man of the world and get the real low-down.
You wouldn't like later on to have to start wringing your
hands and saying "Oh, if I had only known!" In my
opinion, the whole thing should be re-examined with a

view to threshing out. If you care to know what I think,
you're wronging Gussie.'

'Wronging him? When I saw him with my own eyes –'

'Ah, but you haven't got the right angle. Let me
explain.'

'There can be no explanation. We will not talk about
it any more, Bertie. I have blotted Augustus from my
life. Until tonight I saw him only through the golden
mist of love, and thought him the perfect man. This
evening he revealed himself as what he really is – a
satyr.'

'But that's just what I'm driving at. That's just where
you're making your bloomer. You see –'

'We will not talk about it any more.'

'But –'

'Please!'

I tuned out. You can't make any headway with that
tout comprendre, c'est tout pardonner stuff if the girl
won't listen.

She turned the bean away, no doubt to hide a silent
tear, and there ensued a brief interval during which she
swabbed the eyes with a pocket handerkchief and I,
averting my gaze, dipped the beak into a jar of *pot-pourri*
which stood on the piano.

Presently, she took the air again.

'It is useless, Bertie. I know, of course, why you are
speaking like this. It is that sweet, generous nature of
yours. There are no lengths to which you will not go to
help a friend, even though it may mean the wrecking of
your own happiness. But there is nothing you can say
that will change me. I have finished with Augustus.
From tonight he will be to me merely a memory – a
memory that will grow fainter and fainter through the
years as you and I draw ever closer together. You will
help me to forget. With you beside me, I shall be able in
time to exorcize Augustus's spell . . . And now I suppose
I had better go and tell Daddy.'

I started. I could still see Pop Bassett's face when he
had thought that he was going to draw me for a nephew.
It would be a bit thick, I felt, while he was still
quivering to the roots of the soul at the recollection of
that hair's-breadth escape, to tell him that I was about to
become his son-in-law. I was not fond of Pop Bassett,
but one has one's humane instincts.

'Oh, my aunt!' I said. 'Don't do that!'

'But I must. He will have to know that I am to be your
wife. He is expecting me to marry Augustus three weeks
from tomorrow.'

I chewed this over. I saw what she meant, of course.
You've got to keep a father posted about these things.
You can't just let it all slide and have the poor old egg
rolling up to the church in a topper and a buttonhole, to
find that the wedding is off and nobody bothered to
mention it to him.

'Well, don't tell him tonight,' I urged. 'Let him
simmer a bit. He's just had a pretty testing shock.'

'A shock?'

'Yes. He's not quite himself.'

A concerned look came into her eyes, causing them
to bulge a trifle.

'So I was right. I thought he was not himself, when I
met him coming out of the library just now. He was
wiping his forehead and making odd little gasping
noises. And when I asked him if anything was the
matter, he said that we all had our cross to bear in
this world, but that he supposed he ought not to
complain, because things were not so bad as they might
have been. I couldn't think what he meant. He then said
he was going to have a warm bath and take three
aspirins and go to bed. What was it? What had
happened?'

I saw that to reveal the full story would be to
complicate an already fairly well complicated situation.
I touched, accordingly, on only one aspect of it.

'Stiffy had just told him she wanted to marry the curate.'

'Stephanie? The curate? Mr Pinker?'

'That's right. Old Stinker Pinker. And it churned him up a good deal. He appears to be a bit allergic to curates.'

She was breathing emotionally, like the dog Bartholomew just after he had finished eating the candle.

'But . . . But . . .'

'Yes?'

'But does Stephanie love Mr Pinker?'

'Oh, rather. No question about that.'

'But then –'

I saw what was in her mind, and nipped in promptly.

'Then there can't be anything between her and Gussie, you were going to say? Exactly. This proves it, doesn't it? That's the very point I've been trying to work the conversation round to from the start.'

'But he –'

'Yes, I know he did. But his motives in doing so were as pure as the driven snow. Purer, if anything. I'll tell you all about it, and I am prepared to give you a hundred to eight that when I have finished you will admit that he was more to be pitied then censured.'

Give Bertram Wooster a good, clear story to unfold, and he can narrate it well. Starting at the beginning with Gussie's aghastness at the prospect of having to make a speech at the wedding breakfast, I took her step by step through the subsequent developments, and I may say that I was as limpid as dammit. By the time I had reached the final chapter, I had her a bit squiggle-eyed but definitely wavering on the edge of conviction.

'And you say Stephanie has hidden this notebook in Daddy's cow-creamer?'

'Plumb spang in the cow-creamer.'

'But I never heard such an extraordinary story in my life.'

448

'Bizarre, yes, but quite capable of being swallowed, don't you think? What you have got to take into consideration is the psychology of the individual. You may say that you wouldn't have a psychology like Stiffy's if you were paid for it, but it's hers all right.'

'Are you sure you are not making all this up, Bertie?'

'Why on earth?'

'I know your altruistic nature so well.'

'Oh, I see what you mean. No, rather not. This is the straight official stuff. Don't you believe it?'

'I shall, if I find the notebook where you say Stephanie put it. I think I had better go and look.'

'I would.'

'I will.'

'Fine.'

She hurried out, and I sat down at the piano and began to play 'Happy Days Are Here Again' with one finger. It was the only method of self-expression that seemed to present itself. I would have preferred to get outside a curried egg or two, for the strain had left me weak, but, as I have said, there were no curried eggs present.

I was profoundly braced. I felt like some Marathon runner who, after sweating himself to the bone for hours, at length breasts the tape. The only thing that kept my bracedness from being absolutely unmixed was the lurking thought that in this ill-omened house there was always the chance of something unforeseen suddenly popping up to mar the happy ending. I somehow couldn't see Totleigh Towers throwing in the towel quite so readily as it appeared to be doing. It must, I felt, have something up its sleeve.

Nor was I wrong. When Madeline Bassett returned a few minutes later, there was no notebook in her hand. She reported total inability to discover so much as a trace of a notebook in the spot indicated. And, I gathered

from her remarks, she had ceased entirely to be a
believer in that notebook's existence.

I don't know if you have ever had a bucket of cold
water right in the mazzard. I received one once in my
boyhood through the agency of a groom with whom I
had had some difference of opinion. That same feeling of
being knocked endways came over me now.

I was at a loss and nonplussed. As Constable Oates
had said, the first move the knowledgeable bloke makes
when rummy goings-on are in progress is to try to spot
the motive, and what Stiffy's motive could be for saying
the notebook was in the cow-creamer, when it wasn't, I
was unable to fathom. With a firm hand this girl had
pulled my leg, but why – that was the point that baffled
– why had she pulled my leg?

I did my best.

'Are you sure you really looked?'

'Perfectly sure.'

'I mean, carefully.'

'Very carefully.'

'Stiffy certainly swore it was there.'

'Indeed?'

'How do you mean, indeed?'

'If you want to know what I mean, I do not believe
there ever was a notebook.'

'You don't credit my story?'

'No, I do not.'

Well, after that, of course, there didn't seem much to
say. I may have said 'Oh?' or something along those
lines – I'm not sure – but if I did, that let me out. I
edged to the door, and pushed off in a sort of daze,
pondering.

You know how it is when you ponder. You become
absorbed, concentrated. Outside phenomena do not
register on the what-is-it. I suppose I was fully halfway
along the passage leading to my bedroom before the
beastly row that was going on there penetrated to

my consciousness, causing me to stop, look and
listen.

This row to which I refer was a kind of banging row, as if
somebody were banging on something. And I had
scarcely said to myself 'What ho, a banger!' when I saw
who this banger was. It was Roderick Spode, and what
he was banging on was the door of Gussie's bedroom. As
I came up, he was in the act of delivering another buffet
on the woodwork.

The spectacle had an immediate tranquillizing effect
on my jangled nervous system. I felt a new man. And I'll
tell you why.

Everyone, I suppose, has experienced the sensation of
comfort and relief which comes when you are being
given the run-around by forces beyond your control and
suddenly discover someone on whom you can work off
the pent-up feelings. The merchant prince, when things
are going wrong, takes it out of the junior clerk. The
junior clerk goes and ticks off the office boy. The office
boy kicks the cat. The cat steps down the street to find a
smaller cat, which in its turn, the interview concluded,
starts scouring the countryside for a mouse.

It was so with me now. Snootered to bursting point
by Pop Bassetts and Madeline Bassetts and Stiffy Byngs
and what not, and hounded like the dickens by a
remorseless Fate, I found solace in the thought that I
could still slip it across Roderick Spode.

'Spode!' I cried sharply.

He paused with lifted fist and turned an inflamed face
in my direction. Then, as he saw who had spoken, the
red light died out of his eyes. He wilted obsequiously.

'Well, Spode, what is all this?'

'Oh, hullo, Wooster. Nice evening.'

I proceeded to work off the pent-up f's.

'Never mind what sort of an evening it is,' I said.
'Upon my word, Spode, this is too much. This is just

451

that little bit above the odds which compels a man to take drastic steps.'

'But, Wooster –'

'What do you mean by disturbing the house with this abominable uproar? Have you forgotten already what I told you about checking this disposition of yours to run amok like a raging hippopotamus? I should have thought that after what I said you would have spent the remainder of the evening curled up with a good book. But no. I find you renewing your efforts to assault and batter my friends. I must warn you, Spode, that my patience is not inexhaustible.'

'But, Wooster, you don't understand.'

'What don't I understand?'

'You don't know the provocation I have received from this pop-eyed Fink-Nottle.' A wistful look came into his face. 'I must break his neck.'

'You are not going to break his neck.'

'Well, shake him like a rat.'

'Nor shake him like a rat.'

'But he says I'm a pompous ass.'

'When did Gussie say that to you?'

'He didn't exactly say it. He wrote it. Look. Here it is.'

Before my bulging eyes he produced from his pocket a small, brown, leather-covered notebook.

Harking back to Archimedes just once more, Jeeves's description of him discovering the principle of displacement, though brief, had made a deep impression on me, bringing before my eyes a very vivid picture of what must have happened on that occasion. I had been able to see the man testing the bath water with his toe ... stepping in ... immersing the frame. I had accompanied him in spirit through all the subsequent formalities – the soaping of the loofah, the shampooing of the head, the burst of song ...

And then, abruptly, as he climbs towards the high note, there is a silence. His voice has died away.

Through the streaming suds you can see that his eyes are glowing with a strange light. The loofah falls from his grasp, disregarded. He utters a triumphant cry. 'Got it! What ho! The principle of displacement!' And out he leaps, feeling like a million dollars.

In precisely the same manner did the miraculous appearance of this notebook affect me. There was that identical moment of stunned silence, followed by the triumphant cry. And I have no doubt that, as I stretched out a compelling hand, my eyes were glowing with a strange light.

'Give me that book, Spode!'

'Yes, I would like you to look at it, Wooster. Then you will see what I mean. I came upon this,' he said, 'in rather a remarkable way. The thought crossed my mind that Sir Watkyn might feel happier if I were to take charge of that cow-creamer of his. There have been a lot of burglaries in the neighbourhood,' he added hastily, 'a lot of burglaries, and those French windows are never really safe. So I – er – went to the collection-room, and took it out of its case. I was surprised to hear something bumping about inside it. I opened it, and found this book. Look,' he said, pointing a banana-like finger over my shoulder. 'There is what he says about the way I eat asparagus.'

I think Roderick Spode's idea was that we were going to pore over the pages together. When he saw me slip the volume into my pocket, I sensed the feeling of bereavement.

'Are you going to keep the book, Wooster?'

'I am.'

'But I wanted to show it to Sir Watkyn. There's a lot about him in it, too.'

'We will not cause Sir Watkyn needless pain, Spode.'

'Perhaps you're right. Then I'll be getting on with breaking this door down?'

'Certainly not,' I said sternly. 'All you do is pop off.'

'Pop off?'

'Pop off. Leave me, Spode. I would be alone.'

I watched him disappear round the bend, then rapped vigorously on the door.

'Gussie.'

No reply.

'Gussie, come out.'

'I'm dashed if I do.'

'Come out, you ass. Wooster speaking.'

But even this did not produce immediate results. He explained later that he was under the impression that it was Spode giving a cunning imitation of my voice. But eventually I convinced him that this was indeed the boyhood friend and no other, and there came the sound of furniture being dragged away, and presently the door opened and his head emerged cautiously, like that of a snail taking a look round after a thunderstorm.

Into the emotional scene which followed I need not go in detail. You will have witnessed much the same sort of thing in the pictures, when the United States Marines arrive in the nick of time to relieve the beleaguered garrison. I may sum it up by saying that he fawned upon me. He seemed to be under the impression that I had worsted Roderick Spode in personal combat and it wasn't worthwhile to correct it. Pressing the notebook into his hand, I sent him off to show it to Madeline Bassett, and proceeded to my room.

Jeeves was there, messing about at some professional task.

It had been my intention, on seeing this man again, to put him through it in no uncertain fashion for having subjected me to the tense nervous strain of my recent interview with Pop Bassett. But now I greeted him with the cordial smile rather than the acid glare. After all, I told myself, his scheme had dragged home the gravy, and in any case this was no moment for recriminations. Wellington didn't go about ticking people off after the battle of Waterloo. He slapped their backs and stood them drinks.

'Aha, Jeeves! You're there, are you?'

'Yes, sir.'

'Well, Jeeves, you may start packing the effects.'

'Sir?'

'For the homeward trip. We leave tomorrow.'

'You are not proposing, then, sir, to extend your stay at Totleigh Towers?'

I laughed one of my gay, jolly ones.

'Don't ask foolish questions, Jeeves. Is Totleigh Towers a place where people extend their stays, if they haven't got to? And there is now no longer any necessity for me to linger on the premises. My work is done. We leave first thing tomorrow morning. Start packing, therefore, so that we shall be in a position to get off the mark without an instant's delay. It won't take you long?'

'No, sir. There are merely the two suitcases.'

He hauled them from beneath the bed, and opening the larger of the brace began to sling coats and things into it, while I, seating myself in the armchair, proceeded to put him abreast of recent events.

'Well, Jeeves, that plan of yours worked all right.'

'I am most gratified to hear it, sir.'

'I don't say that the scene won't haunt me in my dreams for some little time to come. I make no comment on your having let me in for such a thing. I merely state that it proved a winner. An uncle's blessing came popping out like a cork out of a champagne bottle, and Stiffy and Stinker are headed for the altar rails with no more fences ahead.'

'Extremely satisfactory, sir. Then Sir Watkyn's reactions were as we had anticipated?'

'If anything, more so. I don't know if you have ever seen a stout bark buffeted by the waves?'

'No, sir. My visits to the seaside have always been made in clement weather.'

'Well, that was what he resembled on being informed by me that I wanted to become his nephew by marriage. He looked and behaved like the Wreck of the *Hesperus*. You remember? It sailed the wintry sea, and the skipper had taken his little daughter to bear him company.'

'Yes, sir. Blue were her eyes as the fairy-flax, her cheeks like the dawn of day, and her bosom was white as the hawthorn buds that open in the month of May.'

'Quite. Well, as I was saying, he reeled beneath the blow and let water in at every seam. And when Stiffy appeared, and told him that it was all a mistake and that the *promesso sposo* was in reality old Stinker Pinker, his relief knew no bounds. He instantly gave his sanction to their union. Could hardly get the words out quick enough. But why am I wasting time telling you all this, Jeeves? A mere side issue. Here's the real front-page stuff. Here's the news that will shock the *chancelleries*. I've got that notebook.'

'Indeed, sir?'

'Yes, absolutely got it. I found Spode with it and took it away from him, and Gussie is even now showing it to Miss Bassett and clearing his name of the stigma that rested upon it. I shouldn't be surprised if at this very moment they were locked in a close embrace.'

'A consummation devoutly to be wished, sir.'

'You said it, Jeeves.'

'Then you have nothing to cause you further concern, sir.'

'Nothing. The relief is stupendous. I feel as if a great weight had been rolled from my shoulders. I could dance and sing. I think there can be no question that exhibiting that notebook will do the trick.'

'None, I should imagine, sir.'

'I say, Bertie,' said Gussie, trickling in at this juncture with the air of one who has been passed through a wringer, 'a most frightful thing has happened. The wedding's off.'

11

I stared at the man, clutching the brow and rocking on my base.

'Off?'

'Yes.'

'Your wedding?'

'Yes.'

'It's off?'

'Yes.'

'What – *off*?'

'Yes.'

I don't know what the Mona Lisa would have done in my place. Probably just what I did.

'Jeeves,' I said. 'Brandy!'

'Very good, sir.'

He rolled away on his errand of mercy, and I turned to Gussie, who was tacking about the room in a dazed manner, as if filling in the time before starting to pluck straws from his hair.

'I can't bear it!' I heard him mutter. 'Life without Madeline won't be worth living.'

It was an astounding attitude, of course, but you can't argue about fellows' tastes. One man's peach is another man's poison, and *vice versa*. Even my Aunt Agatha, I remembered, had roused the red-hot spark of pash in the late Spenser Gregson.

His wandering had taken him to the bed, and I saw that he was looking at the knotted sheet which lay there.

'I suppose,' he said, in an absent, soliloquizing voice, 'a chap could hang himself with that.'

I resolved to put a stopper on this trend of thought promptly. I had got more or less used by now to my bedroom being treated as a sort of meeting-place of the nations, but I was dashed if I was going to have it turned into the spot marked with an X. It was a point on which I felt strongly.

'You aren't going to hang yourself here.'

'I shall have to hang myself somewhere.'

'Well, you don't hang yourself in my bedroom.'

He raised his eyebrows.

'Have you any objection to my sitting in your armchair?'

'Go ahead.'

'Thanks.'

He seated himself, and stared before him with glazed eyes.

'Now, then, Gussie,' I said, 'I will take your statement. What is all this rot about the wedding being off?'

'It is off.'

'But didn't you show her the notebook?'

'Yes. I showed her the notebook.'

'Did she read its contents?'

'Yes.'

'Well, didn't she *tout comprendre*?'

'Yes.'

'And *tout pardonner*?'

'Yes.'

'Then you must have got your facts twisted. The wedding can't be off.'

'It is, I tell you. Do you think I don't know when a wedding's off and when it isn't? Sir Watkyn has forbidden it.'

This was an angle I had not foreseen.

'Why? Did you have a row or something?'

'Yes. About newts. He didn't like me putting them in the bath.'

'You put newts in the bath?'

'Yes.'

Like a keen cross-examining counsel, I swooped on the point.

'Why?'

His hand fluttered, as if about to reach for a straw.

'I broke the tank. The tank in my bedroom. The glass tank I keep my newts in. I broke the glass tank in my bedroom, and the bath was the only place to lodge the newts. The basin wasn't large enough. Newts need elbow-room. So I put them in the bath. Because I had broken the tank. The glass tank in my bedroom. The glass tank I keep my – '

I saw that if allowed to continue in this strain he might go on practically indefinitely, so I called him to order with a sharp rap of a china vase on the mantelpiece.

'I get the idea,' I said, brushing the fragments into the fireplace. 'Proceed. How does Pop Bassett come into the picture?'

'He went to take a bath. It never occurred to me that anyone would be taking a bath as late as this. And I was in the drawing-room, when he burst in shouting: "Madeline, that blasted Fink-Nottle has been filling my bathtub with tadpoles!" And I lost my head a little, I'm afraid. I yelled: "Oh, my gosh, you silly old ass, be careful what you're doing with those newts. Don't touch them. I'm in the middle of a most important experiment."'

'I see. And then – '

'I went on to tell him how I wished to ascertain whether the full moon affected the love life of newts. And a strange look came into his face, and he quivered a bit, and then he told me that he had pulled out the plug and all my newts had gone down the waste pipe.'

I think he would have preferred at this point to fling

himself on the bed and turn his face to the wall, but I
headed him off. I was resolved to stick to the *res*.

'Upon which you did what?'

'I ticked him off properly. I called him every name I
could think of. In fact, I called him names that I hadn't a
notion I knew. They just seemed to come bubbling up
from my subconsciousness. I was hampered a bit at first
by the fact that Madeline was there, but it wasn't long
before he told her to go to bed, and then I was really able
to express myself. And when I finally paused for breath,
he forbade the banns and pushed off. And I rang the bell
and asked Butterfield to bring me a glass of orange juice.'

I started.

'Orange juice?'

'I wanted picking up.'

'But orange juice? At such a time?'

'It was what I felt I needed.'

I shrugged my shoulders.

'Oh, well,' I said.

Just another proof, of course, of what I often say –
that it takes all sorts to make a world.

'As a matter of fact, I could do with a good long drink
now.'

'The tooth-bottle is at your elbow.'

'Thanks . . . Ah! That's the stuff!'

'Have a go at the jug.'

'No, thanks. I know when to stop. Well, that's the
position, Bertie. He won't let Madeline marry me, and
I'm wondering if there is any possible way of bringing
him round. I'm afraid there isn't. You see, it wasn't only
that I called him names –'

'Such as?'

'Well, louse, I remember, was one of them. And
skunk, I think. Yes, I'm pretty sure I called him a wall-
eyed skunk. But he might forgive that. The real trouble
is that I mocked at that cow-creamer of his.'

'Cow-creamer!'

I spoke sharply. He had started a train of thought. An idea had begun to burgeon. For some little time I had been calling on all the resources of the Wooster intellect to help me to solve this problem, and I don't often do that without something breaking loose. At this mention of the cow-creamer, the brain seemed suddenly to give itself a shake and start off across country with its nose to the ground.

'Yes. Knowing how much he loved and admired it, and searching for barbed words that would wound him, I told him it was modern Dutch. I had gathered from his remarks at the dinner table last night that that was the last thing it ought to be. "You and your eighteen-century cow-creamers!" I said. "Pah! Modern Dutch!" or words to that effect. The thrust got home. He turned purple, and broke off the wedding.'

'Listen, Gussie,' I said. 'I think I've got it.'

His face lit up. I could see that optimism had stirred and was shaking a leg. This Fink-Nottle has always been of an optimistic nature. Those who recall his address to the boys of Market Snodsbury Grammar School will remember that it was largely an appeal to the little blighters not to look on the dark side.

'Yes, I believe I see the way. What you have got to do, Gussie, is pinch that cow-creamer.'

His lips parted, and I thought an 'Eh, what?' was coming through, but it didn't. Just silence and a couple of bubbles.

'That is the first, essential step. Having secured the cow-creamer, you tell him it is in your possession and say: "Now, how about it?" I feel convinced that in order to recover that foul cow he would meet any terms you care to name. You know what collectors are like. Practically potty, every one of them. Why, my Uncle Tom wants the thing so badly that he is actually prepared to yield up his supreme cook, Anatole, in exchange for it.'

'Not the fellow who was functioning at Brinkley when I was there?'

'That's right.'

'The chap who dished up those *nonettes de poulet Agnes Sorel*?'

'That very artist.'

'You really mean that your uncle would consider Anatole well lost if he could secure this cow-creamer?'

'I have it from Aunt Dahlia's own lips.'

He drew a deep breath.

'Then you're right. This scheme of yours would certainly solve everything. Assuming, of course, that Sir Watkyn values the thing equally highly.'

'He does. Doesn't he, Jeeves?' I said, putting it up to him, as he trickled in with the brandy. 'Sir Watkyn Bassett has forbidden Gussie's wedding,' I explained, 'and I've been telling him that all he has to do in order to make him change his mind is to get hold of that cow-creamer and refuse to give it back until he coughs up a father's blessing. You concur?'

'Undoubtedly, sir. If Mr Fink-Nottle possesses himself of the *objet d'art* in question, he will be in a position to dictate. A very shrewd plan, sir.'

'Thank you, Jeeves. Yes, not bad, considering that I had to think on my feet and form my strategy at a moment's notice. If I were you, Gussie, I would put things in train immediately.'

'Excuse me, sir.'

'You spoke, Jeeves?'

'Yes, sir. I was about to say that before Mr Fink-Nottle can put the arrangements in operation there is an obstacle to be surmounted.'

'What's that?'

'In order to protect his interests, Sir Watkyn has posted Constable Oates on guard in the collection-room.'

'What!'

'Yes, sir.'

The sunshine died out of Gussie's face, and he uttered a stricken sound like a gramophone record running down.

'However, I think that with a little finesse it will be perfectly possible to eliminate this factor. I wonder if you recollect, sir, the occasion at Chufnell Hall, when Sir Roderick Glossop had become locked up in the potting-shed, and your efforts to release him appeared likely to be foiled by the fact that Police Constable Dobson had been stationed outside the door?'

'Vividly, Jeeves.'

'I ventured to suggest that it might be possible to induce him to leave his post by conveying word to him that the parlourmaid Mary, to whom he was betrothed, wished to confer with him in the raspberry bushes. The plan was put into effect and proved successful.'

'True, Jeeves. But,' I said dubiously, 'I don't see how anything like that could be worked here. Constable Dobson, you will recall, was young, ardent, romantic – just the sort of chap who would automatically go leaping into raspberry bushes if you told him there were girls there. Eustace Oates has none of the Dobson fire. He is well stricken in years and gives the impression of being a settled married man who would rather have a cup of tea.'

'Yes, sir, Constable Oates is, as you say, of a more sober temperament. But it is merely the principle of the thing which I would advocate applying to the present emergency. It would be necessary to provide a lure suited to the psychology of the individual. What I would suggest is that Mr Fink-Nottle should inform the officer that he has seen his helmet in your possession.'

'Egad, Jeeves!'

'Yes, sir.'

'I see the idea. Yes, very hot. Yes, that would do it.'

Gussie's glassy eye indicating that all this was failing to register, I explained.

'Earlier in the evening, Gussie, a hidden hand snitched this *gendarme's* lid, cutting him to the quick. What Jeeves is saying is that a word from you to the effect that you have seen it in my room will bring him bounding up here like a tigress after its lost cub, thus leaving you a clear field in which to operate. That is your idea in essence, is it not, Jeeves?'

'Precisely, sir.'

Gussie brightened visibly.

'I see. It's a ruse.'

'That's right. One of the ruses, and not the worst of them. Nice work, Jeeves.'

'Thank you, sir.'

'That will do the trick, Gussie. Tell him I've got his helmet, wait while he bounds out, nip to the glass case and trouser the cow. A simple programme. A child could carry it out. My only regret, Jeeves, is that this appears to remove any chance Aunt Dahlia might have had of getting the thing. A pity there has been such a wide popular demand for it.'

'Yes, sir. But possibly Mrs Travers, feeling that Mr Fink-Nottle's need is greater than hers, will accept the disappointment philosophically.'

'Possibly. On the other hand, possibly not. Still, there it is. On these occasions when individual interests clash, somebody has got to draw the short straw.'

'Very true, sir.'

'You can't be expected to dish out happy endings all round – one per person, I mean.'

'No, sir.'

'The great thing is to get Gussie fixed. So buzz off, Gussie, and Heaven speed your efforts.'

I lit a cigarette.

'A very sound idea, that, Jeeves. How did you happen to think of it?'

'It was the officer himself who put it into my head, sir, when I was chatting with him not long ago. I gathered from what he said that he actually does suspect you of being the individual who purloined his helmet.'

'Me? Why on earth? Dash it, I scarcely know the man. I thought he suspected Stiffy.'

'Originally, yes, sir. And it is still his view that Miss Byng was the motivating force behind the theft. But he now believes that the young lady must have had a male accomplice, who did the rough work. Sir Watkyn, I understand, supports, him in this theory.'

I suddenly remembered the opening passages of my interview with Pop Bassett in the library, and at last got on to what he had been driving at. Those remarks of his which had seemed to me then mere idle gossip had had, I now perceived, a sinister undercurrent of meaning. I had supposed that we were just two of the boys chewing over the latest bit of hot news, and all the time the thing had been a probe or quiz.

'But what makes them think that I was the male accomplice?'

'I gather that the officer was struck by the cordiality which he saw to exist between Miss Byng and yourself, when he encountered you in the road this afternoon, and his suspicions became strengthened when he found the young lady's glove on the scene of the outrage.'

'I don't get you, Jeeves.'

'He supposes you to be enamoured of Miss Byng, sir, and thinks that you were wearing her glove next your heart.'

'If it had been next my heart, how could I have dropped it?'

'His view is that you took it out to press to your lips, sir.'

'Come, come, Jeeves. Would I start pressing gloves to my lips at the moment when I was about to pinch a policeman's helmet?'

465

'Apparently Mr Pinker did, sir.'

I was on the point of explaining to him that what old Stinker would do in any given situation and what the ordinary, normal person with a couple of ounces more brain than a cuckoo clock would do were two vastly different things, when I was interrupted by the re-entrance of Gussie. I could see by the buoyancy of his demeanour that matters had been progressing well.

'Jeeves was right, Bertie,' he said. 'He read Eustace Oates like a book.'

'The information stirred him up?'

'I don't think I have ever seen a more thoroughly roused policeman. His first impulse was to drop everything and come dashing up here right away.'

'Why didn't he?'

'He couldn't quite bring himself to, in view of the fact that Sir Watkyn had told him to stay there.'

I followed the psychology. It was the same as that of the boy who stood on the burning deck, whence all but he had fled.

'Then the procedure, I take it, will be that he will send word to Pop Bassett, notifying him of the facts and asking permission to go ahead?'

'Yes. I expect you will have him with you in a few minutes.'

'Then you ought not to be here. You should be lurking in the hall.'

'I'm going there at once. I only came to report.'

'Be ready to slip in the moment he is gone.'

'I will. Trust me. There won't be a hitch. It was a wonderful idea of yours, Jeeves.'

'Thank you, sir.'

'You can imagine how relieved I'm feeling, knowing that in about five minutes everything will be all right. The only thing I'm a bit sorry for now,' said Gussie thoughtfully, 'is that I gave the old boy that notebook.'

He threw out this appalling statement so casually

466

that it was a second or two before I got its import. When I did, a powerful shock permeated my system. It was as if I had been reclining in the electric chair and the authorities had turned on the juice.

'You gave him the notebook!'

'Yes. Just as he was leaving. I thought there might be some names in it which I had forgotten to call him.'

I supported myself with a trembling hand on the mantelpiece.

'Jeeves!'

'Sir?'

'More brandy!'

'Yes, sir.'

'And stop doling it out in those small glasses, as if it were radium. Bring the cask.'

Gussie was regarding me with a touch of surprise.

'Something the matter, Bertie?'

'Something the matter?' I let out a mirthless 'Ha! Well, this has torn it.'

'How do you mean? Why?'

'Can't you see what you've done, you poor chump? It's no use pinching that cow-creamer now. If old Bassett has read the contents of that notebook, nothing will bring him round.'

'Why not?'

'Well, you saw how they affected Spode. I don't suppose Pop Bassett is any fonder of reading home truths about himself than Spode is.'

'But he's had the home truths already. I told you how I ticked him off.'

'Yes, but you could have got away with that. Overlook it, please . . . spoken in hot blood . . . strangely forgot myself . . . all that sort of stuff. Coldly reasoned opinions, carefully inscribed day by day in a notebook, are a very different thing.'

I saw that it had penetrated at last. The greenish tinge was back in his face. His mouth opened and shut like

467

that of a goldfish which sees another goldfish nip in and get away with the ant's egg which it had been earmarking for itself.

'Oh, gosh!'

'Yes.'

'What can I do?'

'I don't know.'

'Think. Bertie, think!'

I did so, tensely, and was rewarded with an idea.

'Tell me,' I said, 'what exactly occurred at the conclusion of the vulgar brawl? You handed him the book. Did he dip into it on the spot?'

'No. He shoved it away in his pocket.'

'And did you gather that he still intended to take a bath?'

'Yes.'

'Then answer me this. What pocket? I mean the pocket of what garment? What was he wearing?'

'A dressing gown.'

'Over – think carefully, Fink-Nottle, for everything hangs on this – over shirt and trousers and things?'

'Yes, he had his trousers on. I remember noticing.'

'Then there is still hope. After leaving you, he would have gone to his room to shed the upholstery. He was pretty steamed up, you say?'

'Yes, very much.'

'Good. My knowledge of human nature, Gussie, tells me that a steamed-up man does not loiter about feeling in his pocket for notebooks and steeping himself in their contents. He flings off the garments, and legs it to the *salle de bain*. The book must still be in the pocket of his dressing gown – which, no doubt, he flung on the bed or over a chair – and all you have to do is nip into his room and get it.'

I had anticipated that this clear thinking would produce the joyous cry and the heartfelt burst of thanks. Instead of which, he merely shuffled his feet dubiously.

'Nip into his room?'

'Yes.'

'But dash it!'

'Now, what?'

'You're sure there isn't some other way?'

'Of course there isn't.'

'I see . . . You wouldn't care to do it for me, Bertie?'

'No, I would not.'

'Many fellows would, to help an old school friend.'

'Many fellows are mugs.'

'Have you forgotten those days at the dear old school?'

'Yes.'

'You don't remember the time I shared my last bar of milk chocolate with you?'

'No.'

'Well, I did, and you told me then that if ever you had an opportunity of doing anything for me . . . However, if these obligations – sacred, some people might consider them – have no weight with you, I suppose there is nothing more to be said.'

He pottered about for a while, doing the old cat-in-an-adage stuff: then, taking from his breast pocket a cabinet photograph of Madeline Bassett, he gazed at it intently. It seemed to be the bracer he required. He eyes lit up. His face lost its fishlike look. He strode out, to return immediately, slamming the door behind him. 'I say, Bertie, Spode's out there!'

'What of it?'

'He made a grab at me.'

'Made a grab at you?'

I frowned. I am a patient man, but I can be pushed too far. It seemed incredible, after what I had said to him, that Roderick Spode's hat was still in the ring. I went to the door, and threw it open. It was even as Gussie had said. The man was lurking.

He sagged a bit, as he saw me. I addressed him with cold severity.

'Anything I can do for you, Spode?'

'No. No, nothing, thanks.'

'Push along, Gussie,' I said, and stood watching him with a protective eye as he sidled round the human gorilla and disappeared along the passage. Then I turned to Spode.

'Spode,' I said in a level voice, 'did I or did I not tell you to leave Gussie alone?'

He looked at me pleadingly.

'Couldn't you possibly see your way to letting me do something to him, Wooster? If it was only to kick his spine up through his hat?'

'Certainly not.'

'Well, just as you say, of course.' He scratched his cheek discontentedly. 'Did you read that notebook, Wooster?'

'No.'

'He says my moustache is like the faint discoloured smear left by a squashed blackbeetle on the side of a kitchen sink.'

'He always was a poetic sort of chap.'

'And that the way I eat asparagus alters one's whole conception of Man as Nature's last word.'

'Yes, he told me that, I remember. He's about right, too. I was noticing at dinner. What you want to do, Spode, in future is lower the vegetable gently into the abyss. Take it easy. Don't snap at it. Try to remember that you are a human being and not a shark.'

'Ha, ha! "A human being and not a shark." Cleverly put, Wooster. Most amusing.'

He was still chuckling, though not frightfully heartily I thought, when Jeeves came along with a decanter on a tray.

'The brandy, sir.'

'And about time, Jeeves.'

'Yes, sir. I must once more apologize for my delay. I was detained by Constable Oates.'

'Oh? Chatting with him again?'

'Not so much chatting, sir, as staunching the flow of blood.'

'Blood?'

'Yes, sir. The officer had met with an accident.'

My momentary pique vanished, and in its place there came a stern joy. Life at Totleigh Towers had hardened me, blunting the gentler emotions, and I derived nothing but gratification from the news that Constable Oates had been meeting with accidents. Only one thing, indeed, could have pleased me more – if I had been informed that Sir Watkyn Bassett had trodden on the soap and come a purler in the bath tub.

'How did that happen?'

'He was assaulted while endeavouring to recover Sir Watkyn's cow-creamer from a midnight marauder, sir.'

Spode uttered a cry.

'The cow-creamer has not been stolen?'

'Yes, sir.'

It was evident that Roderick Spode was deeply affected by the news. His attitude towards the cow-creamer had, if you remember, been fatherly from the first. Not lingering to hear more, he galloped off, and I accompanied Jeeves into the room, agog for details.

'What happened, Jeeves?'

'Well, sir, it was a little difficult to extract a coherent narrative from the officer, but I gather that he found himself restless and fidgety – '

'No doubt owing to his inability to get in touch with Pop Bassett, who, as we know, is in his bath, and receive permission to leave his post and come up here after his helmet.'

'No doubt, sir. And being restless, he experienced a strong desire to smoke a pipe. Reluctant, however, to run the risk of being found to have smoked while on duty – as might have been the case had he done so in an

enclosed room, where the fumes would have lingered –
he stepped out into the garden.'

'A quick thinker, this Oates.'

'He left the French window open behind him. And
some little time later his attention was arrested by a
sudden sound from within.'

'What sort of sound?'

'The sound of stealthy footsteps, sir.'

'Someone stepping stealthily, as it were?'

'Precisely, sir. Followed by the breaking of glass. He
immediately hastened back to the room – which was, of
course, in darkness.'

'Why?'

'Because he had turned the light out, sir.'

I nodded. I followed the idea.

'Sir Watkyn's instruction to him had been to keep his
vigil in the dark, in order to convey to a marauder the
impression that the room was unoccupied.'

I nodded again. It was a dirty trick, but one which
would spring naturally to the mind of an ex-magistrate.

'He hurried to the case in which the cow-creamer had
been deposited, and struck a match. This almost
immediately went out, but not before he had been able
to ascertain that the *objet d'art* had disappeared. And he
was still in the process of endeavouring to adjust himself
to the discovery, when he heard a movement and,
turning, perceived a dim figure stealing out through the
French window. He pursued it into the garden, and was
overtaking it and might shortly have succeeded in
effecting an arrest, when there sprang from the darkness
a dim figure –'

'The same dim figure?'

'No, sir. Another one.'

'A big night for dim figures.'

'Yes, sir.'

'Better call them Pat and Mike, or we shall be getting
mixed.'

'A and B perhaps, sir?'

'If you prefer it, Jeeves. He was overtaking dim figure A, you say, when dim figure B sprang from the darkness – '

' – and struck him upon the nose.'

I uttered an exclamash. The thing was a mystery no longer.

'Old Stinker!'

'Yes, sir. No doubt Miss Byng inadvertently forgot to apprise him that there had been a change in the evening's arrangements.'

'And he was lurking there, waiting for me.'

'So one would be disposed to imagine, sir.'

I inhaled deeply, my thoughts playing about the constable's injured beezer. There, I was feeling, but for whatever it is, went Bertram Wooster, as the fellow said.

'This assault diverted the officer's attention, and the object of his pursuit was enabled to escape.'

'What became of Stinker?'

'On becoming aware of the officer's identity, he apologized, sir. He then withdrew.'

'I don't blame him. A pretty good idea, at that. Well, I don't know what to make of this, Jeeves. This dim figure. I am referring to dim figure A. Who could it have been? Had Oates any views on the subject?'

'Very definite views, sir. He is convinced that it was you.'

I stared.

'Me? Why the dickens has everything that happens in this ghastly house got to be me?'

'And it is his intention, as soon as he is able to secure Sir Watkyn's co-operation, to proceed here and search your room.'

'He was going to do that, anyway, for the helmet.'

'Yes, sir.'

'This is going to be rather funny, Jeeves. It will be entertaining to watch these two blighters ferret about,

473

feeling sillier and sillier asses as each moment goes by and they find nothing.'

'Most diverting, sir.'

'And when the search is over and they are standing there baffled, stammering out weak apologies, I shall get a bit of my own back. I shall fold my arms and draw myself up to my full height –'

There came from without the hoof beats of a galloping relative, and Aunt Dahlia whizzed in.

'Here, shove this away somewhere, young Bertie,' she panted, seeming touched in the wind.

And so saying, she thrust the cow-creamer into my hands.

12

In my recent picture of Sir Watkyn Bassett reeling beneath the blow of hearing that I wanted to marry into his family, I compared his garglings, if you remember, to the death rattle of a dying duck. I might now have been this duck's twin brother, equally stricken. For some moments I stood there, quacking feebly: then with a powerful effort of the will I pulled myself together and cheesed the bird imitation. I looked at Jeeves. He looked at me. I did not speak, save with the language of the eyes, but his trained senses enabled him to read my thoughts unerringly.

'Thank you, Jeeves.'

I took the tumbler from him, and lowered perhaps half an ounce of the raw spirit. Then, the dizzy spell overcome, I transferred my gaze to the aged relative, who was taking an easy in the armchair.

It is pretty generally admitted, both in the Drones Club and elsewhere, that Bertram Wooster in his dealings with the opposite sex invariably shows himself a man of the nicest chivalry – what you sometimes hear described as a *parfait gentil* knight. It is true that at the age of six, when the blood ran hot, I once gave my nurse a juicy one over the top knot with a porringer, but the lapse was merely a temporary one. Since then, though few men have been more sorely tried by the sex, I have never raised a hand against a woman. And I can give no better indication of my emotions at this moment than by saying that, *preux chevalier* though I am, I came within the veriest toucher of hauling off and letting a revered aunt have it on the side of the head with a *papier*

475

mâché elephant – the only object on the mantelpiece which the fierce rush of life at Totleigh Towers had left still unbroken.

She, while this struggle was proceeding in my bosom, was at her chirpiest. Her breath recovered, she had begun to prattle with a carefree gaiety which cut me like a knife. It was obvious from her demeanour that, stringing along with the late Diamond, she little knew what she had done.

'As nice a run,' she was saying, 'as I have had since the last time I was out with the Berks and Bucks. Not a check from start to finish. Good clean British sport at its best. It was a close thing though, Bertie. I could feel that cop's hot breath on the back of my neck. If a posse of curates hadn't popped up out of a trap and lent a willing hand at precisely the right moment, he would have got me. Well, God bless the clergy, say I. A fine body of men. But what on earth were policemen doing on the premises? Nobody ever mentioned policemen to me.'

'That was Constable Oates, the vigilant guardian of the peace of Totleigh-in-the-Wold,' I replied, keeping a tight hold on myself lest I should howl like a banshee and shoot up to the ceiling. 'Sir Watkyn had stationed him in the room to watch over his belongings. He was lying in the wait. I was the visitor he expected.'

'I'm glad you weren't the visitor he got. The situation would have been completely beyond you, my poor lamb. You would have lost your head and stood there like a stuffed wombat, to fall an easy prey. I don't mind telling you that when that man suddenly came in through the window, I myself was for a moment paralysed. Still, all's well that ends well.'

I shook a sombre head.

'You err, my misguided old object. This is not an end, but a beginning. Pop Bassett is about to spread a drag-net.'

'Let him.'

'And when he and the constable come and search this room?'

'They wouldn't do that.'

'They would and will. In the first place, they think the Oates helmet is here. In the second place, it is the officer's view, relayed to me by Jeeves, who had it from him first hand as he was staunching the flow of blood, that it was I whom he pursued.'

Her chirpiness waned. I had expected it would. She had been beaming. She beamed no longer. Eyeing her steadily, I saw that the native hue of resolution had become sicklied o'er with the pale cast of thought.

'H'm! This is awkward.'

'Most.'

'If they find the cow-creamer here, it may be a little difficult to explain.'

She rose, and broke the elephant thoughtfully.

'The great thing,' she said, 'is not to lose our heads. We must say to ourselves: "What would Napoleon have done?" He was the boy in a crisis. He knew his onions. We must do something very clever, very shrewd, which will completely baffle these bounders. Well, come on, I'm waiting for suggestions.'

'Mine is that you pop off without delay, taking that beastly cow with you.'

'And run into the search party on the stairs! Not if I know it. Have you any ideas, Jeeves?'

'Not at the moment, madam.'

'You can't produce a guilty secret of Sir Watkyn's out of the hat, as you did with Spode?'

'No, madam.'

'No, I suppose that's too much to ask. Then we've got to hide the thing somewhere. But where? It's the old problem, of course – the one that makes life so tough for murderers – what to do with the body. I suppose the old Purloined Letter stunt wouldn't work?'

'Mrs Travers is alluding to the well-known story by
the late Edgar Allan Poe, sir,' said Jeeves, seeing that I
was not abreast. 'It deals with the theft of an important
document, and the character who had secured it foiled
the police by placing it in full view in a letter-rack, his
theory being that what is obvious is often overlooked.
No doubt Mrs Travers wishes to suggest that we deposit
the object on the mantelpiece.'

I laughed a hollow one.

'Take a look at the mantelpiece! It is as bare as a
windswept prairie. Anything placed there would stick
out like a sore thumb.'

'Yes, that's true,' Aunt Dahlia was forced to admit.

'Put the bally thing in the suitcase, Jeeves.'

'That's no good. They're bound to look there.'

'Merely as a palliative,' I explained. 'I can't stand the
sight of it any longer. In with it, Jeeves.'

'Very good, sir.'

A silence ensued, and it was just after Aunt Dahlia
had broken it to say how about barricading the door and
standing a siege that there came from the passage the
sound of approaching footsteps.

'Here they are,' I said.

'They seem in a hurry,' said Aunt Dahlia.

She was correct. These were running footsteps. Jeeves
went to the door and looked out.

'It is Mr Fink-Nottle, sir.'

And the next moment Gussie entered, going strongly.

A single glance at him was enough to reveal to the
discerning eye that he had not been running just for the
sake of the exercise. His spectacles were glittering in a
hunted sort of way, and there was more than a touch of
the fretful porpentine about his hair.

'Do you mind if I hide here till the milk train goes,
Bertie?' he said. 'Under the bed will do. I shan't be in
your way.'

'What's the matter?'

'Or, still better, the knotted sheet. That's the stuff.'

A snort like a minute-gun showed that Aunt Dahlia was in no welcoming mood.

'Get out of here, you foul Spink-Bottle,' she said curtly. 'We're in conference. Bertie, if an aunt's wishes have any weight with you, you will stamp on this man with both feet and throw him out on his ear.'

I raised a hand.

'Wait! I want to get the strength of this. Stop messing about with those sheets, Gussie, and explain. Is Spode after you again? Because if so – '

'Not Spode. Sir Watkyn.'

Aunt Dahlia snorted again, like one giving an encore in response to a popular demand.

'Bertie – '

I raised another hand.

'Half a second, old ancestor. How do you mean Sir Watkyn? Why Sir Watkyn? What on earth is he chivvying you for?'

'He's read the notebook.'

'What!'

'Yes.'

'Bertie, I am only a weak woman – '

I raised a third hand. This was no time for listening to aunts.

'Go on, Gussie,' I said dully.

He took off his spectacles and wiped them with a trembling handkerchief. You could see that he was a man who had passed through the furnace.

'When I left you, I went to his room. The door was ajar, and I crept in. And when I had got in, I found that he hadn't gone to have a bath, after all. He was sitting on the bed in his underwear, reading the notebook. He looked up, and our eyes met. You've no notion what a frightful shock it gave me.'

'Yes, I have. I once had a very similar experience with the Rev. Aubrey Upjohn.'

'There was a long, dreadful pause. Then he uttered a sort of gurgling sound and rose, his face contorted. He made a leap in my direction. I pushed off. He followed. It was neck and neck down the stairs, but as we passed through the hall he stopped to get a hunting crop, and this enabled me to secure a good lead, which I –'

'Bertie,' said Aunt Dahlia, 'I am only a weak woman, but if you won't tread on this insect and throw the remains outside, I shall have to see what I can do. The most tremendous issues hanging in the balance . . . Our plan of action still to be decided on . . . Every second of priceless importance . . . and he comes in here, telling us the story of his life. Spink-Bottle, you ghastly goggle-eyed piece of gorgonzola, will you hop it or will you not?'

There is a compelling force about the old flesh and blood, when stirred, which generally gets her listened to. People have told me that in her hunting days she could make her wishes respected across two ploughed fields and a couple of spinneys. The word 'not' had left her lips like a high-powered shell, and Gussie, taking it between the eyes, rose some six inches into the air. When he returned to terra firma, his manner was apologetic and conciliatory.

'Yes, Mrs Travers. I'm just going, Mrs Travers. The moment we get the sheet working, Mrs Travers. If you and Jeeves will just hold this end, Bertie . . .'

'You want them to let you down from the window with a sheet?'

'Yes, Mrs Travers. Then I can borrow Bertie's car and drive to London.'

'It's a long drop.'

'Oh, not so very, Mrs Travers.'

'You may break your neck.'

'Oh, I don't think so, Mrs Travers.'

'But you may,' argued Aunt Dahlia. 'Come on, Bertie,' she said, speaking with real enthusiasm, 'hurry up. Let the man down with the sheet, can't you? What are you waiting for?'

I turned to Jeeves. 'Ready, Jeeves?'

'Yes, sir.' He coughed gently. 'And perhaps if Mr Fink-Nottle is driving your car to London, he might take your suitcase with him and leave it at the flat.'

I gasped. So did Aunt Dahlia. I stared at him. Aunt Dahlia the same. Our eyes met, and I saw in hers the same reverent awe which I have no doubt she viewed in mine.

I was overcome. A moment before, I had been dully conscious that nothing could save me from the soup. Already I had seemed to hear the beating of its wings. And now this!

Aunt Dahlia, speaking of Napoleon, had claimed that he was pretty hot in an emergency, but I was prepared to bet that not even Napoleon could have topped this superb effort. Once more, as so often in the past, the man had rung the bell and was entitled to the cigar or coconut.

'Yes, Jeeves,' I said, speaking with some difficulty, 'that is true. He might, mightn't he?'

'Yes, sir.'

'You won't mind taking my suitcase, Gussie? If you're borrowing the car, I shall have to go by train. I'm leaving in the morning myself. And it's a nuisance hauling about a lot of luggage.'

'Of course.'

'We'll just loose you down on the sheet and drop the suitcase after you. All set, Jeeves?'

'Yes, sir.'

'Then upsy-daisy!'

I don't think I have ever assisted at a ceremony which gave such universal pleasure to all concerned. The sheet didn't split, which pleased Gussie. Nobody came to interrupt us, which pleased me. And when I dropped the suitcase, it hit Gussie on the head, which delighted

Aunt Dahlia. As for Jeeves, one could see that the faithful fellow was tickled pink at having been able to cluster round and save the young master in his hour of peril. His motto is 'Service'.

The stormy emotions through which I had been passing had not unnaturally left me weak, and I was glad when Aunt Dahlia, after a powerful speech in which she expressed her gratitude to our preserver in well-phrased terms, said that she would hop along and see what was going on in the enemy's camp. Her departure enabled me to sink into the armchair in which, had she remained, she would unquestionably have parked herself indefinitely. I flung myself on the cushioned seat and emitted a woof that came straight from the heart.

'So that's that, Jeeves!'

'Yes, sir.'

'Once again your swift thinking has averted disaster as it loomed.'

'It is very kind of you to say so, sir.'

'Not kind, Jeeves. I am merely saying what any thinking man would say. I didn't chip in while Aunt Dahlia was speaking, for I saw that she wished to have the floor, but you may take it that I was silently subscribing to every sentiment she uttered. You stand alone, Jeeves. What size hat do you take?'

'A number eight, sir.'

'I should have thought larger. Eleven or twelve.'

I helped myself to a spot of brandy, and sat rolling it round my tongue luxuriantly. It was delightful to relax after the strain and stress I had been through.

'Well, Jeeves, the going has been pretty tough, what?'

'Extremely, sir.'

'One begins to get some idea of how the skipper of the *Hesperus*'s little daughter must have felt. Still, I suppose these tests and trials are good for the character.'

'No doubt, sir.'

'Strengthening.'

'Yes, sir.'

'However, I can't say I'm sorry it's all over. Enough is always enough. And it is all over, one feels. Even this sinister house can surely have no further shocks to offer.'

'I imagine not, sir.'

'No, this is the finish. Totleigh Towers has shot its bolt, and at long last we are sitting pretty. Gratifying, Jeeves.'

'Most gratifying, sir.'

'You bet it is. Carry on with the packing. I want to get it done and go to bed.'

He opened the small suitcase, and I lit a cigarette and proceeded to stress the moral lesson to be learned from all this rannygazoo.

'Yes, Jeeves, "gratifying" is the word. A short while ago, the air was congested with V-shaped depressions, but now one looks north, south, east and west and descries not a single cloud on the horizon – except the fact that Gussie's wedding is still off, and that can't be helped. Well, this should certainly teach us, should it not, never to repine, never to despair, never to allow the upper lip to unstiffen, but always to remember that, no matter how dark the skies may be, the sun is shining somewhere and will eventually come smiling through.'

I paused. I perceived that I was not securing his attention. He was looking down with an intent, thoughtful expression on his face.

'Something the matter, Jeeves?'

'Sir?'

'You appear preoccupied.'

'Yes, sir. I have just discovered that there is a policeman's helmet in this suitcase.'

13

I had been right about the strengthening effect on the character of the vicissitudes to which I had been subjected since clocking in at the country residence of Sir Watkyn Bassett. Little by little, bit by bit, they had been moulding me, turning me from a sensitive clubman and *boulevardier* to a man of chilled steel. A novice to conditions in this pest house, abruptly handed the news item which I had just been handed, would, I imagine, have rolled up the eyeballs and swooned where he sat. But I, toughened and fortified by the routine of one damn thing after another which constituted life at Totleigh Towers, was enabled to keep my head and face the issue.

I don't say I didn't leave my chair like a jack-rabbit that has sat on a cactus, but having risen I wasted no time in fruitless twitterings. I went to the door and locked it. Then, tight-lipped and pale, I came back to Jeeves, who had now taken the helmet from the suitcase and was oscillating it meditatively by its strap.

His first words showed me that he had got the wrong angle on the situation.

'It would be wiser, sir,' he said with a faint reproach, 'to have selected some more adequate hiding place.'

I shook my head. I may even have smiled – wanly, of course. My swift intelligence had enabled me to probe to the bottom of this thing.

'Not me, Jeeves. Stiffy.'

'Sir?'

'The hand that placed that helmet there was not

mine, but that of S. Byng. She had it in her room. She feared lest a search might be instituted, and when I last saw her was trying to think of a safer spot. This is her idea of one.'

I sighed.

'How do you imagine a girl gets a mind like Stiffy's, Jeeves?'

'Certainly the young lady is somewhat eccentric in her actions, sir.'

'Eccentric? She could step straight into Colney Hatch, and no questions asked. They would lay down the red carpet for her. The more the thoughts dwell on that young shrimp, the more the soul sickens in horror. One peers into the future, and shudders at what one sees there. One has to face it, Jeeves – Stiffy, who is pure padded cell from the foundations up, is about to marry the Rev. H. P. Pinker, himself about as pronounced a goop as ever broke bread, and there is no reason to suppose – one has to face this, too – that their union will not be blessed. There will, that is to say, 'ere long be little feet pattering about the home. And what one asks oneself is – Just how safe will human life be in the vicinity of those feet, assuming – as one is forced to assume – that they will inherit the combined loopiness of two such parents? It is with a sort of tender pity, Jeeves, that I think of the nurses, the governesses, the private-school masters and the public-school masters who will lightly take on the responsibility of looking after a blend of Stephanie Byng and Harold Pinker, little knowing that they are coming up against something hotter than mustard. However,' I went on, abandoning these speculations, 'all this, though of absorbing interest, is not really germane to the issue. Contemplating that helmet and bearing in mind the fact that the Oates-Bassett comedy duo will be arriving at any moment to start their search, what would you recommend?'

'It is a little difficult to say, sir. A really effective hiding place for so bulky an object does not readily present itself.'

'No. The damn thing seems to fill the room, doesn't it?'

'It unquestionably takes the eye, sir.'

'Yes. The authorities wrought well when they shaped this helmet for Constable Oates. They aimed to finish him off impressively, not to give him something which would balance on top of his head like a peanut, and they succeeded. You couldn't hide a lid like this in an impenetrable jungle. Ah, well,' I said, 'we will just have to see what tact and suavity will do. I wonder when these birds are going to arrive. I suppose we may expect them very shortly. Ah! That would be the hand of doom now, if I mistake not, Jeeves.'

But in assuming that the knocker who had just knocked on the door was Sir Watkyn Bassett, I had erred. It was Stiffy's voice that spoke.

'Bertie, let me in.'

There was nobody I was more anxious to see, but I did not immediately fling wide the gates. Prudence dictated a preliminary inquiry.

'Have you got that bally dog of yours with you?'

'No. He's being aired by the butler.'

'In that case, you may enter.'

When she did so, it was to find Bertram confronting her with folded arms and a hard look. She appeared, however, not to note my forbidding exterior.

'Bertie, darling –'

She broke off, checked by a fairly animal snarl from the Wooster lips.

'Not so much of the "Bertie, darling". I have just one thing to say to you, young Stiffy, and it is this: Was it you who put that helmet in my suitcase?'

'Of course it was. That's what I was coming to talk to you about. You remember I was trying to think of a good

486

place. I racked the brain quite a bit, and then suddenly I got it.'

'And now I've got it.'

The acidity of my tone seemed to surprise her. She regarded me with girlish wonder – the wide-eyed kind.

'But you don't mind do you, Bertie, darling?'

'Ha!'

'But why? I thought you would be so glad to help me out.'

'Oh, yes?' I said, and I meant it to sting.

'I couldn't risk having Uncle Watkyn find it in my room.'

'You preferred to have him find it in mine?'

'But how can he? He can't come searching your room.'

'He can't, eh?'

'Of course not. You're his guest.'

'And you suppose that that will cause him to hold his hand?' I smiled one of those bitter, sardonic smiles. 'I think you are attributing to the old poison germ a niceness of feeling and a respect for the laws of hospitality which nothing in his record suggests that he possesses. You can take it from me that he definitely is going to search the room, and I imagine that the only reason he hasn't arrived already is that he is still scouring the house for Gussie.'

'Gussie?'

'He is at the moment chasing Gussie with a hunting crop. But a man cannot go on doing that indefinitely. Sooner or later he will give it up, and then we shall have him here, complete with magnifying glass and bloodhounds.'

The gravity of the situash had at last impressed itself upon her. She uttered a squeak of dismay, and her eyes became a bit soup-platey.

'Oh, Bertie! Then I'm afraid I've put you in rather a spot.'

'That covers the facts like a dust-sheet.'

'I'm sorry now I ever asked Harold to pinch the thing. It was a mistake. I admit it. Still, after all, even if Uncle Watkyn does come here and find it, it doesn't matter much, does it?'

'Did you hear that, Jeeves?'

'Yes, sir.'

'Thank you, Jeeves. What makes you suppose that I shall meekly assume the guilt and not blazon the truth forth to the world?'

I wouldn't have supposed that her eyes could have widened any more, but they did perceptibly. Another dismayed squeak escaped her. Indeed, such was its volume that it might perhaps be better to call it a squeal.

'But Bertie!'

'Well?'

'Bertie, listen!'

'I'm listening.'

'Surely you will take the rap? You can't let Harold get it in the neck. You were telling me this afternoon that he would be unfrocked. I won't have him unfrocked. Where is he going to get if they unfrock him? That sort of thing gives a curate a frightful black eye. Why can't you say you did it? All it would mean is that you would be kicked out of the house, and I don't suppose you're so anxious to stay on, are you?'

'Possibly you are not aware that your bally uncle is proposing to send the perpetrator of this outrage to chokey.'

'Oh, no. At the worst, just a fine.'

'Nothing of the kind. He specifically told me chokey.'

'He didn't mean it. I expect there was –'

'No, there was not a twinkle in his eye.'

'Then that settles it. I can't have my precious, angel Harold doing a stretch.'

'How about your precious, angel Bertram?'

'But Harold's sensitive.'

'So am I sensitive.'

'Not half so sensitive as Harold. Bertie, surely you aren't going to be difficult about this? You're much too good a sport. Didn't you tell me once that the Code of the Woosters was "Never let a pal down"?'

She had found the talking point. People who appeal to the Code of the Woosters rarely fail to touch a chord in Bertram. My iron front began to crumble.

'That's all very fine – '

'Bertie, darling!'

'Yes, I know, but, dash it all – '

'Bertie!'

'Oh, well!'

'You will take the rap?'

'I suppose so.'

She yodelled ecstatically, and I think that if I had not side-stepped she would have flung her arms about my neck. Certainly she came leaping forward with some such purpose apparently in view. Foiled by my agility, she began to tear off a few steps of that Spring dance to which she was so addicted.

'Thank you, Bertie, darling. I knew you would be sweet about it. I can't tell you how grateful I am, and how much I admire you. You remind me of Carter Paterson . . . no, that's not it . . . Nick Carter . . . no, not Nick Carter . . . Who does Mr Wooster remind me of, Jeeves?'

'Sidney Carton, miss.'

'That's right. Sidney Carton. But he was small-time stuff compared with you, Bertie. And, anyway, I expect we are getting the wind up quite unnecessarily. Why are we taking it for granted that Uncle Watkyn will find the helmet, if he comes and searches the room? There are a hundred places where you can hide it.'

And before I could say 'Name three!' she had pirouetted to the door and pirouetted out. I could hear her dying away in the distance with a song on the lips.

My own, as I turned to Jeeves, were twisted in a bitter smile.

'Women, Jeeves!'

'Yes, sir.'

'Well, Jeeves,' I said, my hand stealing towards the decanter, 'this is the end!'

'No, sir.'

I started with a violence that nearly unshipped my front uppers.

'Not the end?'

'No, sir.'

'You don't mean you have an idea?'

'Yes, sir.'

'But you told me just now you hadn't.'

'Yes, sir. But since then I have been giving the matter some thought, and am now in a position to say "Eureka!"'

'Say what?'

'Eureka, sir. Like Archimedes.'

'Did he say Eureka? I thought it was Shakespeare.'

'No, sir. Archimedes. What I would recommend is that you drop the helmet out of the window. It is most improbable that it will occur to Sir Watkyn to search the exterior of the premises, and we shall be able to recover it at our leisure.' He paused, and stood listening. 'Should this suggestion meet with your approval, sir, I feel that a certain haste would be advisable. I fancy I can hear the sound of approaching footsteps.'

He was right. The air was vibrant with their clumping. Assuming that a herd of bison was not making its way along the second-floor passage of Totleigh Towers, the enemy were upon us. With the nippiness of a lamb in the fold on observing the approach of Assyrians, I snatched up the helmet, bounded to the window and loosed the thing into the night. And scarcely had I done so, when the door opened, and through it came – in the order named –

Aunt Dahlia, wearing an amused and indulgent look, as if she were joining in some game to please the children: Pop Bassett, in a purple dressing gown, and Police Constable Oates, who was dabbing at his nose with a pocket-handkerchief.

'So sorry to disturb you, Bertie,' said the aged relative courteously.

'Not at all,' I replied with equal suavity. 'Is there something I can do for the multitude?'

'Sir Watkyn has got some extraordinary idea into his head about wanting to search your room.'

'Search my room?'

'I intend to search it from top to bottom,' said old Bassett, looking very Bosher Street-y.

I glanced at Aunt Dahlia, raising the eyebrows.

'I don't understand. What's all this about?'

She laughed indulgently.

'You will scarcely believe it, Bertie, but he thinks that cow-creamer is here.'

'Is it missing?'

'It's been stolen.'

'You don't say!'

'Yes.'

'Well, well, well!'

'He's very upset about it.'

'I don't wonder.'

'Most distressed.'

'Poor old bloke!'

I placed a kindly hand on Pop Bassett's shoulder. Probably the wrong thing to do, I can see, looking back, for it did not soothe.

'I can do without your condolences, Mr Wooster, and I should be glad if you would not refer to me as a bloke. I have every reason to believe that not only is my cow-creamer in your possession, but Constable Oates's helmet, as well.'

A cheery guffaw seemed in order. I uttered it.

'Ha, ha!'

Aunt Dahlia came across with another.

'Ha, ha!'

'How dashed absurd!'

'Perfectly ridiculous.'

'What on earth would I be doing with cow-creamers?'

'Or policemen's helmets?'

'Quite.'

'Did you ever hear such a weird idea?'

'Never. My dear old host,' I said, 'let us keep perfectly calm and cool and get all this straightened out. In the kindliest spirit, I must point out that you are on the verge – if not slightly past the verge – of making an ass of yourself. This sort of thing won't do, you know. You can't dash about accusing people of nameless crimes without a shadow of evidence.'

'I have all the evidence I require, Mr Wooster.'

'That's what you think. And that, I maintain, is where you are making the floater of lifetime. When was this modern Dutch gadget of yours abstracted?'

He quivered beneath the thrust, pinkening at the tip of the nose.

'It is not modern Dutch!'

'Well, we can thresh that out later. The point is: when did it leave the premises?'

'It has not left the premises.'

'That, again, is what you think. Well, when was it stolen?'

'About twenty minutes ago.'

'Then there you are. Twenty minutes ago I was up here in my room.'

This rattled him. I had thought it would.

'You were in your room?'

'In my room.'

'Alone?'

'On the contrary. Jeeves was here.'

'Who is Jeeves?'

'Don't you know, Jeeves? This is Jeeves. Jeeves . . . Sir Watkyn Bassett.'

'And who may you be, my man?'

'That's exactly what he is – my man. May I say my right-hand man?'

'Thank you, sir.'

'Not at all, Jeeves. Well-earned tribute.'

Pop Bassett's face was disfigured, if you could disfigure a face like his, by an ugly sneer.

'I regret, Mr Wooster, that I am not prepared to accept as conclusive evidence of your innocence the unsupported word of your manservant.'

'Unsupported, eh? Jeeves, go and page Mr Spode. Tell him I want him to come and put a bit of stuffing into my alibi.'

'Very good, sir.'

He shimmered away, and Pop Bassett seemed to swallow something hard and jagged.

'Was Roderick Spode with you?'

'Certainly he was. Perhaps you will believe him?'

'Yes, I would believe Roderick Spode.'

'Very well, then. He'll be here in a moment.'

He appeared to muse.

'I see. Well, apparently I was wrong, then, in supposing that you are concealing my cow-creamer. It must have been purloined by somebody else.'

'Outside job, if you ask me,' said Aunt Dahlia.

'Possibly the work of an international gang,' I hazarded.

'Very likely.'

'I expect it was all over the place that Sir Watkyn had bought the thing. You remember Uncle Tom had been counting on getting it, and no doubt he told all sorts of people where it had gone. It wouldn't take long for the news to filter through to the international gangs. They keep their ear to the ground.'

'Damn clever, those gangs,' assented the aged relative.

Pop Bassett had seemed to me to wince a trifle at the mention of Uncle Tom's name. Guilty conscience doing its stuff, no doubt – gnawing, as these guilty consciences do.

'Well, we need not discuss the matter further,' he said. 'As regards the cow-creamer, I admit that you have established your case. We will now turn to Constable Oate's helmet. That, Mr Wooster, I happen to know positively, is in your possession.'

'Oh, yes?'

'Yes. The constable received specific information on the point from an eyewitness. I will proceed, therefore, to search your room without delay.'

'You really feel you want to?'

'I do.'

I shrugged the shoulders.

'Very well,' I said, 'very well. If that is the spirit in which you interpret the duties of a host, carry on. We invite inspection. I can only say that you appear to have extraordinarily rummy views on making your guests comfortable over the weekend. Don't count on my coming here again.'

I had expressed the opinion to Jeeves that it would be entertaining to stand by and watch this blighter and his colleague ferret about, and so it proved. I don't know when I have extracted more solid amusement from anything. But all these good things have to come to an end at last. About ten minutes later, it was plain that the bloodhounds were planning to call it off and pack up.

To say that Pop Bassett was wry, as he desisted from his efforts and turned to me, would be to understate it.

'I appear to owe you an apology, Mr Wooster,' he said.

'Sir W. Bassett,' I rejoined, 'you never spoke a truer word.'

And folding my arms and drawing myself up to my full height, I let him have it.

The exact words of my harangue have, I am sorry to

say, escaped my memory. It is a pity that there was nobody taking them down in shorthand, for I am not exaggerating when I say that I surpassed myself. Once or twice, when a bit lit at routs and revels, I have spoken with an eloquence which, rightly or wrongly, has won the plaudits of the Drones Club, but I don't think that I have ever quite reached the level to which I now soared. You could see the stuffing trickling out of old Bassett in great heaping handfuls.

But as I rounded into my peroration, I suddenly noticed that I was failing to grip. He had ceased to listen, and was staring past me at something out of my range of vision. And so worth looking at did this spectacle, judging from his expression, appear to be that I turned in order to take a dekko.

It was the butler who had so riveted Sir Watkyn Bassett's attention. He was standing in the doorway, holding in his right hand a silver salver. And on that salver was a policeman's helmet.

14

I remember old Stinker Pinker, who towards the end of his career at Oxford used to go in for social service in London's tougher districts, describing to me once in some detail the sensations he had experienced one afternoon, while spreading the light in Bethnal Green, on being unexpectedly kicked in the stomach by a costermonger. It gave him, he told me, a strange, dreamy feeling, together with an odd illusion of having walked into a thick fog. And the reason I mention it is that my own emotions at this moment were extraordinarily similar.

When I had last seen this butler, if you recollect, on the occasion when he had come to tell me that Madeline Bassett would be glad if I could spare her a moment, I mentioned that he had flickered. It was not so much at a flickering butler that I was gazing now as at a sort of heaving mist with a vague suggestion of something butlerine vibrating inside it. Then the scales fell from my eyes, and I was enabled to note the reactions of the rest of the company.

They were all taking it extremely big. Pop Bassett, like the chap in the poem which I had to write out fifty times at school for introducing a white mouse into the English Literature hour, was plainly feeling like some watcher of the skies when a new planet swims into his ken, while Aunt Dahlia and Constable Oates resembled respectively stout Cortez staring at the Pacific and all his men looking at each other with a wild surmise, silent upon a peak in Darien.

It was a goodish while before anybody stirred. Then,

with a choking cry like that of a mother spotting her
long-lost child in the offing, Constable Oates swooped
forward and grabbed the lid, clasping it to his bosom
with visible ecstasy.

The movement seemed to break the spell. Old Bassett
came to life as if someone had pressed a button.

'Where – where did you get that, Butterfield?'

'I found it in a flowerbed, Sir Watkyn.'

'In a flowerbed?'

'Odd,' I said. 'Very strange.'

'Yes, sir. I was airing Miss Byng's dog, and happening
to be passing the side of the house I observed Mr
Wooster drop something from his window. It fell into
the flowerbed beneath, and upon inspection proved to be
this helmet.'

Old Bassett drew a deep breath.

'Thank you, Butterfield.'

The butler breezed off, and old B., revolving on his
axis, faced me with gleaming pince-nez.

'So!' he said.

There is never very much you can do in the way of a
telling come-back when a fellow says 'So!' to you. I
preserved a judicious silence.

'Some mistake,' said Aunt Dahlia, taking the floor
with an intrepidity which became her well. 'Probably
came from one of the other windows. Easy to get
confused on a dark night.'

'Tchah!'

'Or it may be that the man was lying. Yes, that seems
a plausible explanation. I think I see it all. This
Butterfield of yours is the guilty man. He stole the
helmet, and knowing that the hunt was up and detection
imminent, decided to play a bold game and try to shove
it off on Bertie. Eh, Bertie?'

'I shouldn't wonder, Aunt Dahlia. I shouldn't wonder
at all.'

'Yes, that is what must have happened. It becomes

497

clearer every moment. You can't trust these saintly looking butlers an inch.'

'Not an inch.'

'I remember thinking the fellow had a furtive eye.'

'Me, too.'

'You noticed it yourself, did you?'

'Right away.'

'He reminds me of Murgatroyd. Do you remember Murgatroyd at Brinkley, Bertie?'

'The fellow before Pomeroy? Stoutish cove?'

'That's right. With a face like a more than usually respectable archbishop. Took us all in, that face. We trusted him implicitly. And what was the result? Fellow pinched a fish slice, put it up the spout and squandered the proceeds at the dog races. This Butterfield is another Murgatroyd.'

'Some relation, perhaps.'

'I shouldn't be surprised. Well, now that's all satisfactorily settled and Bertie dismissed without a stain on his character, how about all going to bed? It's getting late, and if I don't have my eight hours, I'm a rag.'

She had injected into the proceedings such a pleasant atmosphere of all-pals-together and hearty let's-say-no-more-about-it that it came quite as a shock to find that old Bassett was failing to see eye to eye. He proceeded immediately to strike the jarring note.

'With your theory that somebody is lying, Mrs Travers, I am in complete agreement. But when you assert that it is my butler, I must join issue with you. Mr Wooster has been exceedingly clever – most ingenious –'

'Oh, thanks.'

' – but I am afraid that I find myself unable to dismiss him, as you suggest, without a stain on his character. In fact, to be frank with you, I do not propose to dismiss him at all.'

He gave me the pince-nez in a cold and menacing

manner. I can't remember when I've seen a man I liked the look of less.

'You may possibly recall, Mr Wooster, that in the course of our conversation in the library I informed you that I took the very gravest view of this affair. Your suggestion that I might be content with inflicting a fine of five pounds, as was the case when you appeared before me at Bosher Street convicted of a similar outrage, I declared myself unable to accept. I assured you that the perpetrator of this wanton assault on the person of Constable Oates would, when apprehended, serve a prison sentence. I see no reason to revise that decision.'

This statement had a mixed press. Eustace Oates obviously approved. He looked up from the helmet with a quick encouraging smile and but for the iron restraint of discipline would, I think, have said 'Hear, hear!' Aunt Dahlia and I, on the other hand, didn't like it.

'Here, come, I say now, Sir Watkyn, really, dash it,' she expostulated, always on her toes when the interests of the clan were threatened. 'You can't do that sort of thing.'

'Madam, I both can and will.' He twiddled a hand in the direction of Eustace Oates. 'Constable!'

He didn't add 'Arrest this man!' or 'Do your duty!' but the officer got the gist. He clumped forward zealously. I was rather expecting him to lay a hand on my shoulder or to produce the gyves and apply them to my wrists, but he didn't. He merely lined up beside me as if we were going to do a duet and stood there looking puff-faced.

Aunt Dahlia continued to plead and reason.

'But you can't invite a man to your house and the moment he steps inside the door calmly bung him into the coop. If that is Gloucestershire hospitality, then heaven help Gloucestershire.'

'Mr Wooster is not here on my invitation, but on my daughter's.'

'That makes no difference. You can't wriggle out of it like that. He is your guest. He has eaten your salt. And let me tell you, while we are on the subject, that there was a lot too much of it in the soup tonight.'

'Oh, would you say that?' I said. 'Just about right, it seemed to me.'

'No. Too salty.'

Pop Bassett intervened.

'I must apologize for the shortcomings of my cook. I may be making a change before long. Meanwhile, to return to the subject with which we were dealing, Mr Wooster is under arrest, and tomorrow I shall take the necessary steps to – '

'And what's going to happen to him tonight?'

'We maintain a small but serviceable police station in the village, presided over by Constable Oates. Oates will doubtless be able to find him accommodation.'

'You aren't proposing to lug the poor chap off to a police station at this time of night? You could at least let him doss in a decent bed.'   'Yes, I see no objection to that. One does not wish to be unduly harsh. You may remain in this room until tomorrow, Mr Wooster.'

'Oh, thanks.'

'I shall lock the door – '

'Oh, quite.'

'And take charge of the key – '

'Oh, rather.'

'And Constable Oates will patrol beneath the window for the remainder of the night.'

'Sir?'

'This will check Mr Wooster's known propensity for dropping things from windows. You had better take up your station at once, Oates.'

'Very good, sir.'

There was a note of quiet anguish in the officer's voice, and it was plain that the smug satisfaction with which he had been watching the progress of events had waned. His views on getting his eight hours were apparently the same as Aunt Dahlia's. Saluting sadly, he left the room in a depressed sort of way. He had his helmet again, but you could see that he was beginning to ask himself if helmets were everything.

'And now, Mrs Travers, I should like, if I may, to have a word with you in private.'

They oiled off, and I was alone.

I don't mind confessing that my emotions, as the key turned in the lock, were a bit poignant. On the one hand, it was nice to feel that I had got my bedroom to myself for a few minutes, but against that you had to put the fact that I was in what is known as durance vile and not likely to get out of it.

Of course, this was not new stuff to me, for I had heard the bars clang outside my cell door that time at Bosher Street. But on that occasion I had been able to buoy myself up with the reflection that the worst the aftermath was likely to provide was a rebuke from the bench or, as subsequently proved to be the case, a punch in the pocket-book. I was not faced, as I was faced now, by the prospect of waking on the morrow to begin serving a sentence of thirty days' duration in a prison where it was most improbable that I would be able to get my morning cup of tea.

Nor did the consciousness that I was innocent seem to help much. I drew no consolation from the fact that Stiffy Byng thought me like Sidney Carton. I had never met the chap, but I gathered that he was somebody who had taken it on the chin to oblige a girl, and to my mind this was enough to stamp him as a priceless ass. Sidney Carton and Bertram Wooster, I felt – nothing to choose between them. Sidney, one of the mugs – Bertram, the same.

I went to the window and looked out. Recalling the moody distaste which Constable Oates had exhibited at the suggestion that he should stand guard during the night hours, I had a faint hope that, once the eye of authority was removed, he might have ducked the assignment and gone off to get his beauty sleep. But no. There he was, padding up and down on the lawn, the picture of vigilance. And I had just gone to the washhand-stand to get a cake of soap to bung at him, feeling that this might soothe the bruised spirit a little, when I heard the door handle rattle.

I stepped across and put my lips to the woodwork.

'Hallo.'

'It is I, sir. Jeeves.'

'Oh, hallo, Jeeves.'

'The door appears to be locked, sir.'

'And you can take it from me, Jeeves, that appearances do not deceive. Pop Bassett locked it, and has trousered the key.'

'Sir?'

'I've been pinched.'

'Indeed, sir?'

'What was that?'

'I said "Indeed, sir?"'

'Oh, did you? Yes. Yes, indeed. And I'll tell you why.'

I gave him a *précis* of what had happened. It was not easy to hear, with a door between us, but I think the narrative elicited a spot of respectful tut-tutting.

'Unfortunate, sir.'

'Most. Well, Jeeves, what is your news?'

'I endeavoured to locate Mr Spode, sir, but he had gone for a walk in the grounds. No doubt he will be returning shortly.'

'Well, we shan't require him now. The rapid march of events has taken us far past the point where Spode could have been of service. Anything else been happening at your end?'

'I have had a word with Miss Byng, sir.'

'I should like a word with her myself. What had she to say?'

'The young lady was in considerable distress of mind, sir, her union with the Reverend Mr Pinker having been forbidden by Sir Watkyn.'

'Good Lord, Jeeves! Why?'

'Sir Watkyn appears to have taken umbrage at the part played by Mr Pinker in allowing the purloiner of the cow-creamer to effect his escape.'

'Why do you say "his"?'

'From motives of prudence, sir. Walls have ears.'

'I see what you mean. That's rather neat, Jeeves.'

'Thank you, sir.'

I mused a while on this latest development. There were certainly aching hearts in Gloucestershire all right this p.m. I was conscious of a pang of pity. Despite the fact that it was entirely owing to Stiffy that I found myself in my present predic., I wished the young loony well and mourned for her in her hour of disaster.

'So he has bunged a spanner into Stiffy's romance as well as Gussie's, has he? That old bird has certainly been throwing his weight about tonight, Jeeves.'

'Yes, sir.'

'And not a thing to be done about it, as far as I can see. Can you see anything to be done about it?'

'No, sir.'

'And switching to another aspect of the affair, you haven't any immediate plans for getting me out of this, I suppose?'

'Not adequately formulated, sir. I am turning over an idea in my mind.'

'Turn well, Jeeves. Spare no effort.'

'But it is at present merely nebulous.'

'It involves finesse, I presume?'

'Yes, sir.'

I shook my head. Waste of time really, of course, because he couldn't see me. Still, I shook it.

'It's no good trying to be subtle and snaky now, Jeeves.

What is required is rapid action. And a thought has occurred to me. We were speaking not long since of the time when Sir Roderick Glossop was immured in the potting-shed, with Constable Dobson guarding every exit. Do you remember what old Pop Stoker's idea was for coping with the situation?'

'If I recollect rightly, sir, Mr Stoker advocated a physical assault upon the officer. "Bat him over the head with a shovel!" was, as I recall, his expression.'

'Correct, Jeeves. Those were his exact words. And though we scouted the idea at the time, it seemed to me now that he displayed a considerable amount of rugged good sense. These practical, self-made men have a way of going straight to the point and avoiding side issues. Constable Oates is on sentry go beneath my window. I still have the knotted sheets and they can readily be attached to the leg of the bed or something. So if you would just borrow a shovel somewhere and step down –'

'I fear, sir –'

'Come on, Jeeves. This is no time for *nolle prosequis*. I know you like finesse, but you must see that it won't help us now. The moment has arrived when only shovels can serve. You could go and engage him in conversation, keeping the instrument concealed behind your back, and waiting for the psychological –'

'Excuse me, sir. I think I hear somebody coming.'

'Well, ponder over what I have said. Who is coming?'

'It is Sir Watkyn and Mrs Travers, sir. I fancy they are about to call upon you.'

'I thought I shouldn't get this room to myself for long. Still, let them come. We Woosters keep open house.'

When the door was unlocked a few moments later, however, only the relative entered. She made for the old familiar armchair, and dumped herself heavily in it. Her demeanour was sombre, encouraging no hope that she had come to announce that Pop Bassett, wiser counsels having prevailed, had decided to set me free. And yet I'm

dashed if that wasn't precisely what she had come to
announce.

'Well, Bertie,' she said, having brooded in silence for a
space, 'you can get on with your packing.'

'Eh?'

'He's called it off.'

'Called it off?'

'Yes. He isn't going to press the charge.'

'You mean I'm not headed for chokey?'

'No.'

'I'm as free as the air, as the expression is?'

'Yes.'

I was so busy rejoicing in spirit that it was some
moments before I had leisure to observe that the buck-
and-wing dance which I was performing was not being
abetted by the old flesh and blood. She was still carrying
on with her sombre sitting, and I looked at her with a
touch of reproach.

'You don't seem very pleased.'

'Oh, I'm delighted.'

'I fail to detect the symptoms,' I said, rather coldly. 'I
should have thought that a nephew's reprieve at the foot
of the scaffold, as you might say, would have produced a
bit of leaping and springing about.'

A deep sigh escaped her.

'Well, the trouble is, Bertie, there is a catch in it. The
old buzzard has made a condition.'

'What is that?'

'He wants Anatole.'

I stared at her.

'Wants Anatole?'

'Yes. That is the price of your freedom. He says he
will agree not to press the charge if I let him have
Anatole. The darned old blackmailer!'

A spasm of anguish twisted her features. It was not so
very long since she had been speaking in high terms of
blackmail and giving it her hearty approval, but if you

want to derive real satisfaction from blackmail, you have to be at the right end of it. Catching it coming, as it were, instead of going, this woman was suffering.

I wasn't feeling any too good myself. From time to time in the course of this narrative I have had occasion to indicate my sentiments regarding Anatole, that peerless artist, and you will remember that the relative's account of how Sir Watkyn Bassett had basely tried to snitch him from her employment during his visit to Brinkley Court had shocked me to my foundations.

It is difficult, of course, to convey to those who have not tasted this wizard's products the extraordinary importance which his roasts and boileds assume in the scheme of things to those who have. I can only say that once having bitten into one of his dishes you are left with the feeling that life will be deprived of all its poetry and meaning unless you are in a position to go on digging in. The thought that Aunt Dahlia was prepared to sacrifice this wonder man merely to save a nephew from the cooler was one that struck home and stirred.

I don't know when I have been so profoundly moved. It was with a melting eye that I gazed at her. She reminded me of Sidney Carton.

'You were actually contemplating giving up Anatole for my sake?' I gasped.

'Of course.'

'Of course jolly well not! I wouldn't hear of such a thing.'

'But you can't go to prison.'

'I certainly can, if my going means that that supreme maestro will continue working at the old stand. Don't dream of meeting old Bassett's demands.'

'Bertie! Do you mean this?'

'I should say so. What's a mere thirty days in the second division? A bagatelle. I can do it on my head. Let Bassett do his worst. And,' I added in a softer voice, 'when my time is up and I come out into the world once

more a free man, let Anatole do his best. A month of
bread and water or skilly or whatever they feed you on
in these establishments will give me a rare appetite. On
the night when I emerge, I shall expect a dinner that will
live in legend and song.'

'You shall have it.'

'We might be sketching out the details now.'

'No time like the present. Start with caviare? Or
cantaloup?'

'And *cantaloup*. Followed by a strengthening soup.'

'Thick or clear?'

'Clear.'

'You aren't forgetting Anatole's *Velouté aux fleurs de
courgette*?'

'Not for a moment. But how about his *Consommé
aux Pommes d'Amour*?'

'Perhaps you're right.'

'I think I am. I feel I am.'

'I'd better leave the ordering to you.'

'It might be wisest.'

I took pencil and paper, and some ten minutes later I
was in a position to announce the result.

'This, then,' I said, 'subject to such additions as I may
think out in my cell, is the menu as I see it.'

And I read as follows:

Le Diner

Caviar Frais
Cantaloup
Consommé aux Pommes d'Amour
Sylphides à la crème d'Écrevisses
Mignonette de poulet petit Duc
Points d'ásperges à la Mistinguette
Suprême de fois gras au champagne
Neige aux Perles des Alpes
Timbale de ris de veau Toulousaine

Salade d'endive et de céleri
Le Plum Pudding
L'Etoile au Berger
Bénédictins Blancs
Bombe Néro
Friandises
Diablotins
Fruits

'That about covers it, Aunt Dahlia?'

'Yes, you don't seem to have missed out much.'

'Then let's have the man in and defy him. Bassett!' I cried.

'Bassett!' shouted Aunt Dahlia.

'Bassett!' I bawled, making the welkin ring.

It was still ringing when he popped in, looking annoyed.

'What the devil are you shouting at me like that for?'

'Oh, there you are, Bassett.' I wasted no time in getting down to the agenda. 'Bassett, we defy you.'

The man was plainly taken aback. He threw a questioning look at Aunt Dahlia. He seemed to be feeling that Bertram was speaking in riddles.

'He is alluding,' explained the relative, 'to that idiotic offer of yours to call the thing off if I let you have Anatole. Silliest idea I ever heard. We've been having a good laugh about it. Haven't we, Bertie?'

'Roaring our heads off,' I assented.

He seemed stunned.

'Do you mean that you refuse?'

'Of course we refuse. I might have known my nephew better than to suppose for an instant that he would consider bringing sorrow and bereavement to an aunt's home in order to save himself unpleasantness. The Woosters are not like that, are they, Bertie?'

'I should say not.'

'They don't put self first.'

'You bet they don't.'

'I ought never to have insulted him by mentioning the offer to him. I apologize, Bertie.'

'Quite all right, old flesh and blood.'

She wrung my hand.

'Good night, Bertie, and goodbye – or, rather *au revoir*. We shall meet again.'

'Absolutely. When the fields are white with daisies, if not sooner.'

'By the way, didn't you forget *Nomais de la Méditerranée au Fenouil*?'

'So I did. And *Selle d'Agneau aux laitues á la Grecque*. Shove them on the charge sheet, will you?'

Her departure, which was accompanied by a melting glance of admiration and esteem over her shoulder as she navigated across the threshold, was followed by a brief and, on my part, haughty silence. After a while, Pop Bassett spoke in a strained and nasty voice.

'Well, Mr Wooster, it seems that after all you will have to pay the penalty of your folly.'

'Quite.'

'I may say that I have changed my mind about allowing you to spend the night under my roof. You will go to the police station.'

'Vindictive, Bassett.'

'Not at all. I see no reason why Constable Oates should be deprived of his well-earned sleep merely to suit your convenience. I will send for him.' He opened the door. 'Here, you!'

It was a most improper way of addressing Jeeves, but the faithful fellow did not appear to resent it.

'Sir?'

'On the lawn outside the house you will find Constable Oates. Bring him here.'

'Very good, sir. I think Mr Spode wishes to speak to you, sir.'

'Eh?'

'Mr Spode, sir. He is coming along the passage now.'

Old Bassett came back into the room, seeming displeased.

'I wish Roderick would not interrupt me at a time like this,' he said querulously. 'I cannot imagine what reason he can have for wanting to see me.'

I laughed lightly. The irony of the thing amused me.

'He is coming – a bit late – to tell you that he was with me when the cow-creamer was pinched, thus clearing me of the guilt.'

'I see. Yes, as you say, he is somewhat late. I shall have to explain to him . . . Ah, Roderick.'

The massive frame of R. Spode had appeared in the doorway.

'Come in, Roderick, come in. But you need not have troubled, my dear fellow. Mr Wooster has made it quite evident that he had nothing to do with the theft of my cow-creamer. It was that that you wished to see me about, was it not?'

'Well – er – no,' said Roderick Spode.

There was an odd, strained look on the man's face. His eyes were glassy and, as far as a thing of that size was capable of being fingered, he was fingering his moustache. He seemed to be bracing himself for some unpleasant task.

'Well – er – no,' he said. 'The fact is, I hear there's been some trouble about that helmet I stole from Constable Oates.'

There was a stunned silence. Old Bassett goggled. I goggled. Roderick Spode continued to finger his moustache.

'It was a silly thing to do,' he said. 'I see that now. I – er – yielded to a uncontrollable impulse. One does sometimes, doesn't one? You remember I told you I once stole a policeman's helmet at Oxford. I was hoping I could keep quiet about it, but Wooster's man tells me that you have got the idea that Wooster did it, so of

course I had to come and tell you. That's all. I think I'll
go to bed,' said Roderick Spode. 'Good night.'

He edged off, and the stunned silence started
functioning again.

I suppose there have been men who looked bigger
asses than Sir Watkyn Bassett at this moment, but I
have never seen one myself. The tip of his nose had gone
bright scarlet, and his pince-nez were hanging limply to
the parent nose at an angle of forty-five. Consistently
though he had snootered me from the very inception of
our relations, I felt almost sorry for the poor old blighter.

'H'rrmph!' he said at length.

He struggled with the vocal cords for a space. They
seemed to have gone twisted on him.

'It appears that I owe you an apology, Mr Wooster.'

'Say no more about it, Bassett.'

'I am sorry that all this has occurred.'

'Don't mention it. My innocence is established. That
is all that matters. I presume that I am now at liberty to
depart?'

'Oh, certainly, certainly. Good night, Mr Wooster.'

'Good night, Bassett. I need scarcely say, I think, that I
hope this will be a lesson to you.'

I dismissed him with a distant nod, and stood there
wrapped in thought. I could make nothing of what had
occurred. Following the old and tried Oates method of
searching for the motive, I had to confess myself baffled.
I could only suppose that this was the Sidney Carton
spirit bobbing up again.

And then a sudden blinding light seemed to flash
upon me.

'Jeeves!'

'Sir?'

'Were you behind this thing?'

'Sir?'

'Don't keep saying "Sir?" You know what I'm talking
about. Was it you who egged Spode on to take the rap?'

I wouldn't say he smiled – he practically never does – but a muscle abaft the mouth did seem to quiver slightly for an instant.

'I did venture to suggest to Mr Spode that it would be a graceful act on his part to assume the blame, sir. My line of argument was that he would be saving you a great deal of unpleasantness, while running no risk himself. I pointed out to him that Sir Watkyn, being engaged to marry his aunt, would hardly be likely to inflict upon him the sentence which he had contemplated inflicting upon you. One does not send gentlemen to prison if one is betrothed to their aunts.'

'Profoundly true, Jeeves. But I still don't get it. Do you mean he just right-hoed? Without a murmur?'

'Not precisely without a murmur, sir. At first, I must confess, he betrayed a certain reluctance. I think I may have influenced his decision by informing him that I knew all about –'

I uttered a cry.

'Eulalie?'

'Yes, sir.'

A passionate desire to get to the bottom of this Eulalie thing swept over me.

'Jeeves, tell me. What did Spode actually do to the girl? Murder her?'

'I fear I am not at liberty to say, sir.'

'Come on, Jeeves.'

'I fear not, sir.'

I gave it up.

'Oh, well!'

I started shedding the garments. I climbed into the pyjamas. I slid into bed. The sheets being inextricably knotted, it would be necessary, I saw, to nestle between the blankets, but I was prepared to rough it for one night.

The rapid surge of events had left me pensive. I sat with my arms round my knees, meditating on Fortune's swift changes.

'An odd thing, life, Jeeves.'

'Very odd, sir.'

'You never know where you are with it, do you? To take a simple instance, I little thought half an hour ago that I would be sitting here in carefree pyjamas, watching you pack for the getaway. A very different future seemed to confront me.'

'Yes, sir.'

'One would have said that a curse had come upon me.'

'One would, indeed, sir.'

'But now my troubles, as you might say, have vanished like the dew on the what-is-it. Thanks to you.'

'I am delighted to have been able to be of service, sir.'

'You have delivered the goods as seldom before. And yet, Jeeves, there is always a snag.'

'Sir?'

'I wish you wouldn't keep saying "Sir?" What I mean is, Jeeves, loving hearts have been sundered in this vicinity and are still sundered. I may be all right – I am – but Gussie isn't all right. Nor is Stiffy all right. That is the fly in the ointment.'

'Yes, sir.'

'Though, pursuant on that, I never could see why flies shouldn't be in ointment. What harm do they do?'

'I wonder, sir –'

'Yes, Jeeves?'

'I was merely about to inquire if it is your intention to bring an action against Sir Watkyn for wrongful arrest and defamation of character before witnesses.'

'I hadn't thought of that. You think an action would lie?'

'There can be no question about it, sir. Both Mrs Travers and I could offer overwhelming testimony. You are undoubtedly in a position to mulct Sir Watkyn in heavy damages.'

'Yes, I suppose you're right. No doubt that was why

he went up in the air to such an extent when Spode did his act.'

'Yes, sir. His trained legal mind would have envisaged the peril.'

'I don't think I ever saw a man go so red in the nose. Did you?'

'No, sir.'

'Still, it seems a shame to harry him further. I don't know that I want actually to grind the old bird into the dust.'

'I was merely thinking, sir, that were you to threaten such an action, Sir Watkyn, in order to avoid unpleasantness, might see his way to ratifying the betrothals of Miss Bassett and Mr Fink-Nottle and Miss Byng and the Reverend Mr Pinker.'

'Golly, Jeeves! Put the bite on him, what?'

'Precisely, sir.'

'The thing shall be put in train immediately.'

I sprang from the bed and nipped to the door.

'Bassett!' I yelled.

There was no immediate response. The man had presumably gone to earth. But after I had persevered for some minutes, shouting 'Bassett!' at regular intervals with increasing volume, I heard the distant sound of pattering feet, and along he came, in a very different spirit from that which he had exhibited on the previous occasion. This time it was more like some eager waiter answering the bell.

'Yes, Mr Wooster?'

I led the way back into the room, and hopped into bed again.

'There is something you wish to say to me, Mr Wooster?'

'There are about a dozen things I wish to say to you, Bassett, but the one we will touch on at the moment is this. Are you aware that your headstrong conduct in sticking police officers on to pinch me and locking me in my room has laid you open to an action for – what was it, Jeeves?'

'Wrongful arrest and defamation of character before witnesses, sir.'

'That's the baby. I could soak you for millions. What are you going to do about it?'

He writhed like an electric fan.

'I'll tell you what you are going to do about it,' I proceeded. 'You are going to issue your OK on the union of your daughter Madeline and Augustus Fink-Nottle and also on that of your niece Stephanie and the Rev. H. P. Pinker. And you will do it now.'

A short struggle seemed to take place in him. It might have lasted longer, if he hadn't caught my eye.

'Very well, Mr Wooster.'

'And touching that cow-creamer. It is highly probable that the international gang that got away with it will sell it to my Uncle Tom. Their system of underground information will have told them that he is in the market. Not a yip out of you, Bassett, if at some future date you see that cow-creamer in his collection.'

'Very well, Mr Wooster.'

'And one other thing. You owe me a fiver.'

'I beg your pardon?'

'In repayment of the one you took off me at Bosher Street. I shall want that before I leave.'

'I will write you a cheque in the morning.'

'I shall expect it on the breakfast tray. Good night, Bassett.'

'Good night, Mr Wooster. Is that brandy I see over there? I think I should like a glass, if I may.'

'Jeeves, a snootful for Sir Watkyn Bassett.'

'Very good, sir.'

He drained the beaker gratefully, and tottered out. Probably quite a nice chap, if you knew him.

Jeeves broke the silence.

'I have finished the packing, sir.'

'Good. Then I think I'll curl up. Open the windows, will you?'

'Very good, sir.'

'What sort of a night is it?'

'Unsettled, sir. It has begun to rain with some violence.'

The sound of a sneeze came to my ears.

'Hallo, who's that Jeeves? Somebody out there?'

'Constable Oates, sir.'

'You don't mean he hasn't gone off duty?'

'No, sir. I imagine that in his preoccupation with other matters it escaped Sir Watkyn's mind to send word to him that there was no longer any necessity to keep his vigil.'

I sighed contentedly. It needed but this to complete my day. The thought of Constable Oates prowling in the rain like the troops of Midian, when he could have been snug in bed toasting his pink toes on the hot-water bottle, gave me a curiously mellowing sense of happiness.

'This is the end of a perfect day, Jeeves. What's that thing of yours about larks?'

'Sir?'

'And, I rather think, snails.'

'Oh, yes, sir. "The year's at the Spring, the day's at the morn, morning's at seven, the hill side's dew-pearled –"'

'But the larks, Jeeves? The snails? I'm pretty sure larks and snails entered into it.'

'I am coming to the larks and snails, sir. "The lark's on the wing, the snail's on the thorn –"'

'Now you're talking. And the tab line?'

'"God's in His heaven, all's right with the world."'

'That's it in a nutshell. I couldn't have put it better myself. And yet, Jeeves, there is just one thing. I do wish you would give me the inside facts about Eulalie.'

'I fear, sir –'

'I would keep it dark. You know me – the silent
tomb.'

'The rules of the Junior Ganymede are extremely
strict, sir.'

'I know. But you might stretch a point.'

'I am sorry, sir –'

I made the great decision.

'Jeeves,' I said, 'give me the low-down, and I'll come
on that World Cruise of yours.'

He wavered.

'Well, in the strictest confidence, sir –'

'Of course.'

'Mr Spode designs ladies' underclothing, sir. He has a
considerable talent in that direction, and has indulged it
secretly for some years. He is the founder and proprietor
of the emporium in Bond Street known as Eulalie
Sœurs.'

'You don't mean that?'

'Yes, sir.'

'Good Lord, Jeeves! No wonder he didn't want a thing
like that to come out.'

'No, sir. It would unquestionably jeopardize his
authority over his followers.'

'You can't be a successful Dictator and design
women's underclothing.'

'No, sir.'

'One or the other. Not both.'

'Precisely, sir.'

I mused.

'Well, it was worth it, Jeeves. I couldn't have slept,
wondering about it. Perhaps that cruise won't be so very
foul, after all?'

'Most gentlemen find them enjoyable, sir.'

'Do they?'

'Yes, sir. Seeing new faces.'

'That's true. I hadn't thought of that. The faces will be

new, won't they? Thousands and thousands of people,
but no Stiffy.'

'Exactly, sir.'

'You had better get the tickets tomorrow.'

'I have already procured them, sir. Good night, sir.'

The door closed. I switched off the light. For some
moments I lay there listening to the measured tramp of
Constable Oates's feet and thinking of Gussie and
Madeline Bassett and of Stiffy and old Stinker Pinker,
and of the hotsy-totsiness which now prevailed in their
love lives. I also thought of Uncle Tom being handed the
cow-creamer and of Aunt Dahlia seizing the
psychological moment and nicking him for a fat cheque
for *Milady's Boudoir*. Jeeves was right, I felt. The snail
was on the wing and the lark on the thorn – or, rather,
the other way round – and God was in His heaven and
all right with the world.

And presently the eyes closed, the muscles relaxed,
the breathing became soft and regular, and sleep which
does something which has slipped my mind to the
something sleeve of care poured over me in a healing
wave.

Right Ho, Jeeves

TO RAYMOND NEEDHAM, K. C.,
WITH AFFECTION AND ADMIRATION

I

'Jeeves,' I said, 'may I speak frankly?'

'Certainly, sir.'

'What I have to say may wound you.'

'Not at all, sir.'

'Well, then –'

No – wait. Hold the line a minute. I've gone off the rails.

I don't know if you have had the same experience, but the snag I always come up against when I'm telling a story is this dashed difficult problem of where to begin it. It's a thing you don't want to go wrong over, because one false step and you're sunk. I mean, if you fool about too long at the start, trying to establish atmosphere, as they call it, and all that sort of rot, you fail to grip and the customers walk out on you.

Get off the mark, on the other hand, like a scalded cat, and your public is at a loss. It simply raises its eyebrows, and can't make out what you're talking about.

And in opening my report of the complex case of Gussie Fink-Nottle, Madeline Bassett, my Cousin Angela, my Aunt Dahlia, my Uncle Thomas, young Tuppy Glossop, and the cook, Anatole, with the above spot of dialogue, I see that I have made the second of these two floaters.

I shall have to hark back a bit. And taking it for all in all, and weighing this against that, I suppose the affair may be said to have had its inception, if inception is the word I want, with that visit of mine to Cannes. If I hadn't gone to Cannes, I shouldn't have met the Bassett or bought that white mess jacket, and Angela wouldn't have met her shark, and Aunt Dahlia wouldn't have played baccarat.

Yes, most decidedly, Cannes was the *point d'appui*.

Right ho, then. Let me marshal my facts.

I went to Cannes – leaving Jeeves behind, he having intimated that he did not wish to miss Ascot – round about the beginning of June. With me travelled my Aunt Dahlia and her daughter Angela. Tuppy Glossop, Angela's betrothed, was to have been of the party, but at the last moment couldn't get away. Uncle Tom, Aunt Dahlia's husband, remained at home, because he can't stick the South of France at any price.

So there you have the layout – Aunt Dahlia, Cousin Angela, and self off to Cannes round about the beginning of June.

All pretty clear so far, what?

We stayed at Cannes about two months, and except for the fact that Aunt Dahlia lost her shirt at baccarat and Angela nearly got inhaled by a shark while aquaplaning, a pleasant time was had by all.

On July the twenty-fifth, looking bronzed and fit, I accompanied aunt and child back to London. At seven p.m. on July the twenty-sixth we alighted at Victoria. And at seven-twenty or thereabouts we parted with mutual expressions of esteem – they to shove off in Aunt Dahlia's car to Brinkley Court, her place in Worcestershire, where they were expecting to entertain Tuppy in a day or two; I to go to the flat, drop my luggage, clean up a bit, and put on the soup and fish preparatory to pushing round to the Drones for a bite of dinner.

And it was while I was at the flat, towelling the torso after a much-needed rinse, that Jeeves, as we chatted of this and that – picking up the threads, as it were – suddenly brought the name of Gussie Fink-Nottle into the conversation.

As I recall it, the dialogue ran something as follows:

SELF: Well, Jeeves, here we are, what?
JEEVES: Yes, sir.
SELF: I mean to say, home again.
JEEVES: Precisely, sir.
SELF: Seems ages since I went away.
JEEVES: Yes, sir.
SELF: Have a good time at Ascot?
JEEVES: Most agreeable, sir.
SELF: Win anything?
JEEVES: Quite a satisfactory sum, thank you, sir.
SELF: Good. Well, Jeeves, what news on the Rialto? Anybody been phoning or calling or anything during my abs?
JEEVES: Mr Fink-Nottle, sir, has been a frequent caller.

I stared. Indeed, it would not be too much to say that I gaped.

'Mr Fink-Nottle?'
'Yes, sir.'
'You don't mean Mr Fink-Nottle?'
'Yes, sir.'
'But Mr Fink-Nottle's not in London?'
'Yes, sir.'
'Well, I'm blowed.'

And I'll tell you why I was blowed. I found it scarcely possible to give credence to his statement. This Fink-Nottle, you see, was one of those freaks you come across from time to time during life's journey who can't stand London. He lived year in and year out, covered with moss, in a remote village down in Lincolnshire, never coming up even for the Eton and Harrow match. And when I asked him once if he didn't find the time hang a bit heavy on his hands, he said, no, because he had a pond in his garden and studied the habits of newts.

I couldn't imagine what could have brought the chap up to the great city. I would have been prepared to bet that as long as the supply of newts didn't give out, nothing could have shifted him from that village of his.

'Are you sure?'

'Yes, sir.'

'You got the name correctly? Fink-Nottle?'

'Yes, sir.'

'Well, it's the most extraordinary thing. It must be five years since he was in London. He makes no secret of the fact that the place gives him the pip. Until now, he has always stayed glued to the country, completely surrounded by newts.'

'Sir?'

'Newts, Jeeves. Mr Fink-Nottle has a strong newt complex. You must have heard of newts. Those little sort of lizard things that charge about in ponds.'

'Oh, yes, sir. The aquatic members of the family Salamandridae which constitute the genus Molge.'

'That's right. Well, Gussie has always been a slave to them. He used to keep them at school.'

'I believe young gentlemen frequently do, sir.'

'He kept them in his study in a kind of glass-tank arrangement, and pretty niffy the whole thing was, I recall. I suppose one ought to have been able to see what the end would be even then, but you know what boys are. Careless, heedless, busy about our own affairs, we scarcely gave this kink in Gussie's character a thought. We may have exchanged an occasional remark about it taking all sorts to make a world, but nothing more. You can guess the sequel. The trouble spread.'

'Indeed, sir?'

'Absolutely, Jeeves. The craving grew upon him. The newts got him. Arrived at man's estate, he retired to the depths of the country and gave his life up to these dumb chums. I suppose he used to tell himself that he could

526

take them or leave them alone, and then found – too late – that he couldn't.'

'It is often the way, sir.'

'Too true, Jeeves. At any rate, for the last five years he has been living at this place of his down in Lincolnshire, as confirmed a species-shunning hermit as ever put fresh water in the tank every second day and refused to see a soul. That's why I was so amazed when you told me he had suddenly risen to the surface like this. I still can't believe it. I am inclined to think that there must be some mistake, and that this bird who has been calling here is some different variety of Fink-Nottle. The chap I know wears horn-rimmed spectacles and has a face like a fish. How does that check up with your data?'

'The gentleman who came to the flat wore horn-rimmed spectacles, sir.'

'And looked like something on a slab?'

'Possibly there was a certain suggestion of the piscine, sir.'

'Then it must be Gussie, I suppose. But what on earth can have brought him up to London?'

'I am in a position to explain that, sir. Mr Fink-Nottle confided to me his motive in visiting the metropolis. He came because the young lady is here.'

'Young lady?'

'Yes, sir.'

'You don't mean he's in love?'

'Yes, sir.'

'Well, I'm dashed. I'm really dashed. I positively am dashed, Jeeves.'

And I was too. I mean to say, a joke's a joke, but there are limits.

Then I found my mind turning to another aspect of this rummy affair. Conceding the fact that Gussie Fink-Nottle, against all the ruling of the form book, might have fallen in love, why should he have been haunting my flat like this? No doubt the occasion was one of those when a fellow needs a friend, but I couldn't see what had made him pick on me.

It wasn't as if he and I were in any way bosom. We had seen a lot of each other at one time, of course, but in the last two years I hadn't had so much as a post card from him.

I put all this to Jeeves:

'Odd, his coming to me. Still, if he did, he did. No argument about that. It must have been a nasty jar for the poor perisher when he found I wasn't here.'

'No, sir. Mr Fink-Nottle did not call to see you, sir.'

'Pull yourself together, Jeeves. You've just told me that this is what he has been doing, and assiduously, at that.'

'It was I with whom he was desirous of establishing communication, sir.'

'You? But I didn't know you had ever met him.'

'I had not had that pleasure until he called here, sir. But it appears that Mr Sipperley, a fellow student of whose Mr Fink-Nottle had been at the university, recommended him to place his affairs in my hands.'

The mystery had conked. I saw all. As I dare say you know, Jeeves's reputation as a counsellor has long been established among the cognoscenti, and the first move of any of my little circle on discovering themselves in any form of soup is always to roll round and put the thing up to him. And when he's got A out of a bad spot, A puts B on to him. And then, when he has fixed up B, B sends C along. And so on, if you get my drift, and so forth.

That's how these big consulting practices like Jeeves's grow. Old Sippy, I knew, had been deeply impressed by the man's efforts on his behalf at the time when he was trying to get engaged to Elizabeth Moon, so it was not to be wondered at that he should have advised Gussie to apply. Pure routine, you might say.

'Oh, you're acting for him, are you?'

'Yes, sir.'

'Now I follow. Now I understand. And what is Gussie's trouble?'

'Oddly enough, sir, precisely the same as that of Mr Sipperley when I was enabled to be of assistance to him. No doubt you recall Mr Sipperley's predicament, sir. Deeply attached to Miss Moon, he suffered from a rooted diffidence which made it impossible for him to speak.'

I nodded.

'I remember. Yes, I recall the Sipperley case. He couldn't bring himself to the scratch. A marked coldness of the feet, was there not? I recollect you saying he was letting – what was it? – letting something do something. Cats entered into it, if I am not mistaken.'

'Letting "I dare not" wait upon "I would", sir.'

'That's right. But how about the cats?'

'Like the poor cat i' the adage, sir.'

'Exactly. It beats me how you think up these things. And Gussie, you say, is in the same posish?'

'Yes, sir. Each time he endeavours to formulate a proposal of marriage, his courage fails him.'

'And yet, if he wants this female to be his wife, he's got to say so, what? I mean, only civil to mention it.'

'Precisely, sir.'

I mused.

'Well, I suppose this was inevitable, Jeeves. I wouldn't have thought that this Fink-Nottle would ever have fallen a victim to the divine p, but, if he has, no wonder he finds the going sticky.'

'Yes, sir.'

'Look at the life he's led.'

'Yes, sir.'

'I don't suppose he has spoken to a girl for years. What a lesson this is to us, Jeeves, not to shut ourselves up in country houses and stare into glass tanks. You can't be the dominant male if you do that sort of thing. In this life, you can choose between two courses. You can either shut yourself up in a country house and stare into tanks, or you can be a dasher with the sex. You can't do both.'

'No, sir.'

I mused once more. Gussie and I, as I say, had rather lost touch, but all the same I was exercised about the poor fish, as I am about all my pals, close or distant, who find themselves treading upon Life's banana skins. It seemed to me that he was up against it.

I threw my mind back to the last time I had seen him. About two years ago, it had been. I had looked in at his place while on a motor trip, and he had put me right off my feed by bringing a couple of green things with legs to the luncheon table, crooning over them like a young mother and eventually losing one of them in the salad. That picture, rising before my eyes, didn't give me much confidence in the unfortunate goof's ability to woo and win, I must say. Especially if the girl he had earmarked was one of these tough modern thugs, all lipstick and cool, hard, sardonic eyes, as she probably was.

'Tell me, Jeeves,' I said, wishing to know the worst, 'what sort of a girl is this girl of Gussie's?'

'I have not met the young lady, sir. Mr Fink-Nottle speaks highly of her attractions.'

'Seemed to like her, did he?'

'Yes, sir.'

'Did he mention her name? Perhaps I know her.'

'She is a Miss Bassett, sir. Miss Madeline Bassett.'

'What?'

'Yes, sir.'

I was deeply intrigued.

'Egad, Jeeves! Fancy that. It's a small world, isn't it, what?'

'The young lady is an acquaintance of yours, sir?'

'I know her well. Your news has relieved my mind, Jeeves. It makes the whole thing begin to seem far more like a practical working proposition.'

'Indeed, sir?'

'Absolutely. I confess that until you supplied this information I was feeling profoundly dubious about poor old Gussie's chances of inducing any spinster of any parish to join him in the saunter down the aisle. You will agree with me that he is not everybody's money.'

'There may be something in what you say, sir.'

'Cleopatra wouldn't have liked him.'

'Possibly not, sir.'

'And I doubt if he would go any too well with Tallulah Bankhead.'

'No, sir.'

'But when you tell me that the object of his affections is Miss Bassett, why, then, Jeeves, hope begins to dawn a bit. He's just the sort of chap a girl like Madeline Bassett might scoop in with relish.'

This Bassett, I must explain, had been a fellow visitor of ours at Cannes; and as she and Angela had struck up one of those effervescent friendships which girls do strike up, I had seen quite a bit of her. Indeed, in my moodier moments it sometimes seemed to me that I could not move a step without stubbing my toe on the woman.

And what made it all so painful and distressing was that the more we met, the less did I seem able to find to say to her.

You know how it is with some girls. They seem to take the stuffing right out of you. I mean to say, there is something about their personality that paralyses the vocal cords and reduces the contents of the brain to cauliflower. It was like that with this Bassett and me; so much so that I have known occasions when for minutes at a stretch Bertram Wooster might have been observed fumbling with the tie, shuffling the feet, and behaving in all other respects in her presence like the complete dumb brick. When, therefore, she took her departure some two weeks before we did, you may readily imagine that, in Bertram's opinion, it was not a day too soon.

It was not her beauty, mark you, that thus numbed me. She was a pretty enough girl in a droopy, blonde, saucer-eyed way, but not the sort of breath-taker that takes the breath.

No, what caused this disintegration in a usually fairly fluent prattler with the sex was her whole mental attitude. I don't want to wrong anybody, so I won't go so far as to say that she actually wrote poetry, but her conversation, to my mind, was of a nature calculated to excite the liveliest suspicions. Well, I mean to say, when a girl suddenly asks you out of a blue sky if you don't somtimes feel that the stars are God's daisy-chain, you begin to think a bit.

As regards the fusing of her soul and mine, therefore, there was nothing doing. But with Gussie, the posish was entirely different. The thing that had stymied me – viz. that this girl was obviously all loaded down with ideals and sentiment and what not – was quite in order as far as he was concerned.

Gussie had always been one of those dreamy, soulful birds – you can't shut yourself up in the country and live only for newts, if you're not – and I could see no reason why, if he could somehow be induced to get the low, burning words off his chest, he and the Bassett shouldn't hit it off like ham and eggs.

'She's just the type for him,' I said.

'I am most gratified to hear it, sir.'

'And he's just the type for her. In fine, a good thing and one to be pushed along with the utmost energy. Strain every nerve, Jeeves.'

'Very good, sir,' replied the honest fellow. 'I will attend to the matter at once.'

Now up to this point, as you will doubtless agree, what you might call a perfect harmony had prevailed. Friendly gossip between employer and employed, and everything as sweet as a nut. But at this juncture, I regret to say, there was an unpleasant switch. The atmosphere suddenly changed, the storm clouds began to gather, and before we knew where we were, the jarring note had come bounding on the scene. I have known this to happen before in the Wooster home.

The first intimation I had that things were about to hot up was a pained and disapproving cough from the neighbourhood of the carpet. For, during the above exchanges, I should explain, while I, having dried the frame, had been dressing in a leisurely manner, donning here a sock, there a shoe, and gradually climbing into the vest, the shirt, the tie, and the knee-length, Jeeves had been down on the lower level, unpacking my effects.

He now rose, holding a white object. And at the sight of it, I realized that another of our domestic crises had arrived, another of those unfortunate clashes of will between two strong men, and that Bertram, unless he remembered his fighting ancestors and stood up for his rights, was about to be put upon.

I don't know if you were at Cannes this summer. If you were, you will recall that anybody with any pretensions to being the life and soul of the party was accustomed to attend binges at the Casino in the ordinary evening-wear trouserings topped to the north by a white mess jacket with brass buttons. And ever since I had stepped aboard the Blue Train at Cannes station, I had been wondering on and off how mine would go with Jeeves.

In the matter of evening costumes, you see, Jeeves is hidebound and reactionary. I had had trouble with him before about soft-bosomed shirts. And while these mess jackets had, as I say, been all the rage – *tout ce qu'il y a de chic* – on the Côte d'Azur, I had never concealed it from myself, even when treading the measure at the Palm Beach Casino in the one I had hastened to buy, that there might be something of an upheaval about it on my return.

I prepared to be firm.

'Yes, Jeeves?' I said. And though my voice was suave,
a close observer in a position to watch my eyes would
have noticed a steely glint. Nobody has a greater respect
for Jeeves's intellect than I have, but this disposition of
his to dictate to the hand that fed him had got, I felt, to
be checked. This mess jacket was very near to my heart,
and I jolly well intended to fight for it with all the vim
of grand old Sieur de Wooster at the Battle of Agincourt.

'Yes, Jeeves?' I said. 'Something on your mind,
Jeeves?'

'I fear that you inadvertently left Cannes in the
possession of a coat belonging to some other gentleman,
sir.'

I switched on the steely a bit more.

'No, Jeeves,' I said, in a level tone, 'the object under
advisement is mine. I bought it out there.'

'You wore it, sir?'

'Every night.'

'But surely you are not proposing to wear it in
England, sir?'

I saw that we had arrived at the nub.

'Yes, Jeeves.'

'But sir –'

'You were saying, Jeeves?'

'It is quite unsuitable, sir.'

'I do not agree with you, Jeeves. I anticipate a great
popular success for this jacket. It is my intention to
spring it on the public tomorrow at Pongo Twistleton's
birthday party, where I confidently expect it to be one
long scream from start to finish. No argument, Jeeves.
No discussion. Whatever fantastic objection you may
have taken to it, I wear this jacket.'

'Very good, sir.'

He went on with his unpacking. I said no more on the
subject. I had won the victory, and we Woosters do not
triumph over a beaten foe. Presently, having completed
my toilet, I bade the man a cheery farewell and in

generous mood suggested that, as I was dining out, why didn't he take the evening off and go to some improving picture or something. Sort of olive branch, if you see what I mean.

He didn't seem to think much of it.

'Thank you, sir, I will remain in.'

I surveyed him narrowly.

'Is this dudgeon, Jeeves?'

'No, sir, I am obliged to remain on the premises. Mr Fink-Nottle informed me that he would be calling to see me this evening.'

'Oh, Gussie's coming, is he? Well, give him my love.'

'Very good, sir.'

'And a whisky and soda, and so forth.'

'Very good, sir.'

'Right ho, Jeeves.'

I then set off for the Drones.

At the Drones I ran into Pongo Twistleton, and he talked so much about this forthcoming merry-making of his, of which good reports had already reached me through my correspondents, that it was nearing eleven when I got home again.

And scarcely had I opened the door when I heard voices in the sitting-room, and scarcely had I entered the sitting-room when I found that these proceeded from Jeeves and what appeared at first sight to be the Devil.

A closer scrutiny informed me that it was Gussie Fink-Nottle, dressed as Mephistopheles.

2

'What-ho Gussie, I said.

You couldn't have told it from my manner, but I was feeling more than a bit nonplussed. The spectacle before me was enough to nonplus anyone. I mean to say, this Fink-Nottle, as I remembered him, was the sort of shy, shrinking goop who might have been expected to shake like an aspen if invited to so much as a social Saturday afternoon at the vicarage. And yet here he was, if one could credit one's senses, about to take part in a fancy-dress ball, a form of entertainment notoriously a testing experience for the toughest.

And he was attending that fancy-dress ball, mark you – not, like every other well-bred Englishman, as a Pierrot, but as Mephistopheles – this involving, as I need scarcely stress, not only scarlet tights but a pretty frightful false beard.

Rummy, you'll admit. However, one masks one's feelings, I betrayed no vulgar astonishment, but, as I say, what-hoed with civil nonchalance.

He grinned through the fungus – rather sheepishly, I thought.

'Oh, hullo, Bertie.'

'Long time since I saw you. Have a spot?'

'No, thanks. I must be off in a minute. I just came round to ask Jeeves how he thought I looked. How do you think I look, Bertie?'

Well, the answer to that, of course, was 'perfectly foul'. But we Woosters are men of tact and have a nice sense of the obligations of a host. We do not tell old friends beneath our roof-tree that they are an offence to the eyesight. I evaded the question.

'I hear you're in London,' I said carelessly.

'Oh, yes.'

'Must be years since you came up.'

'Oh, yes.'

'And now you're off for an evening's pleasure.'

He shuddered a bit. He had, I noticed, a hunted air.

'Pleasure!'

'Aren't you looking forward to this rout or revel?'

'Oh, I suppose it'll be all right,' he said, in a toneless voice. 'Anyway, I ought to be off, I suppose. The thing starts round about eleven. I told my cab to wait . . . Will you see if it's there, Jeeves.'

'Very good, sir.'

There was something of a pause after the door had closed. A certain constraint. I mixed myself a beaker, while Gussie, a glutton for punishment, stared at himself in the mirror. Finally I decided that it would be best to let him know that I was abreast of his affairs. It might be that it would ease his mind to confide in a sympathetic man of experience. I have generally found, with those under the influence, that what they want more than anything is the listening ear.

'Well, Gussie, old leper,' I said, 'I've been hearing all about you.'

'Eh?'

'This little trouble of yours. Jeeves has told me everything.'

He didn't seem any too braced. It's always difficult to be sure, of course, when a chap has dug himself in behind a Mephistopheles beard, but I fancy he blushed a trifle.

'I wish Jeeves wouldn't go gassing all over the place. It was supposed to be confidential.'

I could not permit this tone.

537

'Dishing up the dirt to the young master can scarcely be described as gassing all over the place,' I said, with a touch of rebuke. 'Anyway, there it is. I know all. And I should like to begin,' I said, sinking my personal opinion that the female in question was a sloppy pest in my desire to buck and encourage, 'by saying that Madeline Bassett is a charming girl. A winner, and just the sort for you.'

'You don't know her?'

'Certainly I know her. What beats me is how you ever got in touch. Where did you meet?'

'She was staying at a place near mine in Lincolnshire the week before last.'

'Yes, but even so. I didn't know you called on the neighbours.'

'I don't. I met her out for a walk with her dog. The dog had got a thorn in its foot, and when she tried to take it out, it snapped at her. So, of course, I had to rally round.'

'You extracted the thorn?'

'Yes.'

'And fell in love at first sight?'

'Yes.'

'Well, dash it, with a thing like that to give you a send-off, why didn't you cash in immediately?'

'I hadn't the nerve.'

'What happened?'

'We talked for a bit.'

'What about?'

'Oh, birds.'

'Birds? What birds?'

'The birds that happened to be hanging round. And the scenery, and all that sort of thing. And she said she was going to London, and asked me to look her up if I was ever there.'

'And after that you didn't so much as press her hand?'

'Of course not.'

538

Well, I mean, it looked as though there was no more to be said. If a chap is such a rabbit that he can't get action when he's handed the thing on a plate, his case would appear to be pretty hopeless. Nevertheless, I reminded myself that this non-starter and I had been at school together. One must make an effort for an old school friend.

'Ah, well,' I said, 'we must see what can be done. Things may brighten. At any rate, you will be glad to learn that I am behind you in this enterprise. You have Bertram Wooster in your corner, Gussie.'

'Thanks, old man. And Jeeves, of course, which is the thing that really matters.'

I don't mind admitting that I winced. He meant no harm, I suppose, but I'm bound to say that this tactless speech nettled me not a little. People are always nettling me like that. Giving me to understand, I mean to say, that in their opinion Bertram Wooster is a mere cipher and that the only member of the household with brains and resources is Jeeves.

It jars on me.

And tonight it jarred on me more than usual, because I was feeling pretty dashed fed-up with Jeeves. Over that matter of the mess jacket, I mean. True, I had forced him to climb down, quelling him, as described, with the quiet strength of my personality, but I was still a trifle shirty at his having brought the thing up at all. It seemed to me that what Jeeves wanted was the iron hand.

'And what is he doing about it?' I inquired stiffly.

'He's been giving the position of affairs a lot of thought.'

'He has, has he?'

'It's on his advice that I'm going to this dance.'

'Why?'

'She is going to be there. In fact, it was she who sent me the ticket of invitation. And Jeeves considered –'

'And why not as a Pierrot?' I said, taking up the point which had struck me before. 'Why this break with a grand old tradition?'

'He particularly wanted me to go as Mephistopheles.'

I started.

'He did, did he? He specifically recommended that definite costume?'

'Yes.'

'Ha!'

'Eh?'

'Nothing. Just "Ha!" '

And I'll tell you why I said 'Ha!' Here was Jeeves making heavy weather about me wearing a perfectly ordinary white mess jacket, a garment not only *tout ce qu'il y a de chic*, but absolutely *de rigueur*, and in the same breath, as you might say, inciting Gussie Fink-Nottle to be a blot on the London scene in scarlet tights. Ironical, what? One looks askance at this sort of in-and-out running.

'What has he got against Pierrots?'

'I don't think he objects to Pierrots as Pierrots. But in my case he thought a Pierrot wouldn't be adequate.'

'I don't follow that.'

'He said that the costume of Pierrot, while pleasing to the eye, lacked the authority of the Mephistopheles costume.'

'I still don't get it.'

'Well, it's a matter of psychology, he said.'

There was a time when a remark like that would have had me snookered. But long association with Jeeves had developed the Wooster vocabulary considerably. Jeeves has always been a whale for the psychology of the individual, and I now follow him like a bloodhound when he snaps it out of the bag.

'Oh, psychology?'

'Yes. Jeeves is a great believer in the moral effect of clothes. He thinks I might be emboldened in a striking

540

costume like this. He said a Pirate Chief would be just
as good. In fact, a Pirate Chief was his first suggestion,
but I objected to the boots.'

I saw his point. There is enough sadness in life
without having fellows like Gussie Fink-Nottle going
about in sea boots.

'Are you emboldened?'

'Well, to be absolutely accurate, Bertie, old man, no.'

A gust of compassion shook me. After all, though we
had lost touch a bit of recent years, this man and I had
once thrown inked darts at each other.

'Gussie,' I said, 'take an old friend's advice, and don't
go within a mile of this binge.'

'But it's my last chance of seeing her. She's off
tomorrow to stay with some people in the country.
Besides, you don't know.'

'Don't know what?'

'That this idea of Jeeves's won't work. I feel a most
frightful chump now, yes, but who can say whether that
will not pass off when I get into a mob of other people in
fancy dress. I had the same experience as a child, one
year during the Christmas festivities. They dressed me
up as a rabbit, and the shame was indescribable. Yet
when I got to the party and found myself surrounded by
scores of other children, many in costumes even
ghastlier than my own, I perked up amazingly, joined
freely in the revels, and was able to eat so hearty a
supper that I was sick twice in the cab coming home.
What I mean is, you can't tell in cold blood.'

I weighed this. It was specious, of course.

'And you can't get away from it that, fundamentally,
Jeeves's idea is sound. In a striking costume like
Mephistopheles, I might quite easily pull off something
pretty impressive. Colour does make a difference. Look
at newts. During the courting season the male newt is
brilliantly coloured. It helps him a lot.'

'But you aren't a male newt.'

541

'I wish I were. Do you know how a male newt proposes, Bertie? He just stands in front of the female newt vibrating his tail and bending his body in a semicircle. I could do that on my head. No, you wouldn't find me grousing if I were a male newt.'

'But if you were a male newt, Madeline Bassett wouldn't look at you. Not with the eye of love, I mean.'

'She would, if she were a female newt.'

'But she isn't a female newt.'

'No, but suppose she was.'

'Well, if she was, you wouldn't be in love with her.'

'Yes, I would, if I were a male newt.'

A slight throbbing about the temples told me that this discussion had reached saturation point.

'Well, anyway,' I said, 'coming down to hard facts and cutting out all this visionary stuff about vibrating tails and what-not, the salient point that emerges is that you are booked to appear at a fancy-dress ball. And I tell you out of my riper knowledge of fancy-dress balls, Gussie, that you won't enjoy yourself.'

'It isn't a question of enjoying yourself.'

'I wouldn't go.'

'I must go. I keep telling you she's off to the country tomorrow.'

I gave it up.

'So be it,' I said. 'Have it your own way . . . Yes, Jeeves?'

'Mr Fink-Nottle's cab, sir.'

'Ah? The cab, eh? . . . Your cab, Gussie.'

'Oh, the cab? Oh, right. Of course, yes, rather . . . Thanks, Jeeves . . . Well, so long, Bertie.'

And giving me the sort of weak smile Roman gladiators used to give the Emperor before entering the arena, Gussie trickled off. And I turned to Jeeves. The moment had arrived for putting him in his place, and I was all for it.

It was a little difficult to know how to begin, of

course. I mean to say, while firmly resolved to tick him
off, I didn't want to gash his feelings too deeply. Even
when displaying the iron hand, we Woosters like to keep
the thing fairly matey.

However, on consideration, I saw that there was
nothing to be gained by trying to lead up to it gently. It
is never any use beating about the b.

'Jeeves,' I said, 'may I speak frankly?'

'Certainly, sir.'

'What I have to say may wound you.'

'Not at all, sir.'

'Well, then, I have been having a chat with Mr
Fink-Nottle, and he has been telling me about this
Mephistopheles scheme of yours.'

'Yes, sir?'

'Now let me get it straight. If I follow your reasoning
correctly, you think that, stimulated by being
upholstered throughout in scarlet tights, Mr
Fink-Nottle, on encountering the adored object, will
vibrate his tail and generally let himself go with a
whoop.'

'I am of opinion that he will lose much of his normal
diffidence, sir.'

'I don't agree with you, Jeeves.'

'No, sir?'

'No. In fact, not to put too fine a point upon it, I
consider that of all the dashed silly, drivelling ideas I
ever heard in my puff this is the most blithering and
futile. It won't work. Not a chance. All you have done is
to subject Mr Fink-Nottle to the nameless horrors of a
fancy-dress ball for nothing. And this is not the first
time this sort of thing has happened. To be quite candid,
Jeeves, I have frequently noticed before now a tendency
of disposition on your part to become – what's the
word?'

'I could not say, sir.'

'Eloquent? No, it's not eloquent. Elusive? No, it's not

543

elusive. It's on the tip of my tongue. Begins with an "e" and means being a jolly sight too clever.'

'Elaborate, sir?'

'That is the exact word I was after. Too elaborate, Jeeves – that is what you are frequently prone to become. Your methods are not simple, not straightforward. You cloud the issue with a lot of fancy stuff that is not of the essence. All that Gussie needs is the elder-brotherly advice of a seasoned man of the world. So what I suggest is that from now onwards you leave this case to me.'

'Very good, sir.'

'You lay off and devote yourself to your duties about the home.'

'Very good, sir.'

'I shall no doubt think of something quite simple and straightforward yet perfectly effective ere long. I will make a point of seeing Gussie tomorrow.'

'Very good, sir.'

'Right ho, Jeeves.'

But on the morrow all those telegrams started coming in, and I confess that for twenty-four hours I didn't give the poor chap a thought, having problems of my own to contend with.

3

The first of the telegrams arrived shortly after noon, and
Jeeves brought it in with the before-luncheon snifter. It
was from my Aunt Dahlia, operating from Market
Snodsbury, a small town of sorts a mile or two along the
main road as you leave her country seat.

It ran as follows:

Come at once. Travers.

And when I say it puzzled me like the dickens, I am
understating it, if anything. As mysterious a
communication, I considered, as was ever flashed over
the wires. I studied it in a profound reverie for the best
part of two dry Martinis and a dividend. I read it
backwards. I read it forwards. As a matter of fact, I have
a sort of recollection of even smelling it. But it still
baffled me.

Consider the facts, I mean. It was only a few hours
since this aunt and I had parted, after being in constant
association for nearly two months. And yet here she was
– with my farewell kiss still lingering on her cheek, so to
speak – pleading for another reunion. Bertram Wooster is
not accustomed to this gluttonous appetite for his
society. Ask anyone who knows me, and they will tell
you that after two months of my company, what the
normal person feels is that that will about do for the
present. Indeed, I have known people who couldn't stick
it out for more than a few days.

Before sitting down to the well-cooked, therefore, I
sent this reply:

Perplexed. Explain. Bertie.

To this I received an answer during the
after-luncheon sleep:

What on earth is there to be perplexed about, ass?
Come at once. Travers.

Three cigarettes and a couple of turns about the
room, and I had my response ready:

How do you mean come at once? Regards. Bertie.

I append the comeback:

I mean come at once, you maddening half-wit. What
did you think I meant? Come at once or expect an
aunt's curse first post tomorrow. Love. Travers.

I then dispatched the following message, wishing to
get everything quite clear:

When you say 'Come' do you mean 'Come to
Brinkley Court'? And when you say 'At once' do you
mean 'At once'? Fogged. At a loss. All the best.
Bertie.

I sent this one off on my way to the Drones, where I
spent a restful afternoon throwing cards into a top-hat
with some of the better element. Returning in the
evening hush, I found the answer waiting for me:

Yes, yes, yes, yes, yes, yes, yes. It doesn't matter
whether you understand or not. You just come at
once, as I tell you, and for heaven's sake stop this
backchat. Do you think I am made of money that I
can afford to send you telegrams every ten minutes.

Stop being a fat-head and come immediately. Love.
Travers.

It was at this point that I felt the need of getting a
second opinion. I pressed the bell.

'Jeeves,' I said, 'a V-shaped rumminess has manifested
itself from the direction of Worcestershire. Read these,' I
said, handing him the papers in the case.

He scanned them.

'What do you make of it, Jeeves?'

'I think Mrs Travers wishes you to come at once,
sir.'

'You gather that too, do you?'

'Yes, sir.'

'I put the same construction on the thing. But why,
Jeeves? Dash it all, she's just had nearly two months of
me.'

'Yes, sir.'

'And many people consider the medium dose for an
adult two days.'

'Yes, sir. I appreciate the point you raise.
Nevertheless, Mrs Travers appears very insistent. I think
it would be well to acquiesce in her wishes.'

'Pop down, you mean?'

'Yes, sir.'

'Well, I certainly can't go at once. I've an important
conference on at the Drones tonight. Pongo Twistleton's
birthday party, you remember.'

'Yes, sir.'

There was a slight pause. We were both recalling the
little unpleasantness that had arisen. I felt obliged to
allude to it.

'You're all wrong about that mess jacket, Jeeves.'

'These things are a matter of opinion, sir.'

'When I wore it at the Casino in Cannes, beautiful
women nudged one another and whispered: "Who is
he?"'

547

'The code at Continental casinos is notoriously lax, sir.'

'And when I described it to Pongo last night, he was fascinated.'

'Indeed, sir?'

'So were all the rest of those present. One and all admitted that I had got hold of a good thing. Not a dissentient voice.'

'Indeed, sir?'

'I am convinced that you will eventually learn to love this mess jacket, Jeeves.'

'I fear not, sir.'

I gave it up. It is never any use trying to reason with Jeeves on these occasions. 'Pig-headed' is the word that springs to the lips. One sighs and passes on.

'Well, anyway, returning to the agenda, I can't go down to Brinkley Court or anywhere else yet awhile. That's final. I'll tell you what, Jeeves. Give me form and pencil, and I'll wire her that I'll be with her some time next week or the week after. Dash it all, she ought to be able to hold out without me for a few days. It only requires will power.'

'Yes, sir.'

'Right ho, then. I'll wire "Expect me tomorrow fortnight" or words to some such effect. That ought to meet the case. Then if you will toddle round the corner and send it off, that will be that.'

'Very good, sir.'

And so the long day wore on till it was time for me to dress for Pongo's party.

Pongo had assured me, while chatting of the affair on the previous night, that this birthday binge of his was to be on a scale calculated to stagger humanity, and I must say I have participated in less fruity functions. It was well after four when I got home, and by that time I was about ready to turn in. I can just remember groping for the bed and crawling into it, and it seemed to me that the lemon had scarcely touched the pillow before I was aroused by the sound of the door opening.

I was barely ticking over, but I contrived to raise an eyelid.

'Is that my tea, Jeeves?'

'No, sir. It is Mrs Travers.'

And a moment later there was a sound like a mighty rushing wind, and the relative had crossed the threshold at fifty m.p.h. under her own steam.

4

It has been well said of Bertram Wooster that, while no one views his flesh and blood with a keener and more remorselessly critical eye, he is nevertheless a man who delights in giving credit where credit is due. And if you have followed these memoirs of mine with the proper care, you will be aware that I have frequently had occasion to emphasize the fact that Aunt Dahlia is all right.

She is the one, if you remember, who married old Tom Travers *en secondes noces*, as I believe the expression is, the year Bluebottle won the Cambridgeshire, and once induced me to write an article on What the Well-Dressed Man is Wearing for that paper she runs – *Milady's Boudoir*. She is a large, genial soul, with whom it is a pleasure to hob-nob. In her spiritual make-up there is none of that subtle gosh-awfulness which renders such an exhibit as, say, my Aunt Agatha the curse of the Home Counties and a menace to one and all. I have the highest esteem for Aunt Dahlia, and have never wavered in my cordial appreciation of her humanity, sporting qualities, and general good-eggishness.

This being so, you may conceive of my astonishment at finding her at my bedside at such an hour. I mean to say, I've stayed at her place many a time and oft, and she knows my habits. She is well aware that until I have had my cup of tea in the morning, I do not receive. This crashing in at a moment when she knew that solitude and repose were of the essence was scarcely, I could not but feel, the good old form.

Besides, what business had she being in London at all? That was what I asked myself. When a conscientious housewife has returned to her home after an absence of seven weeks, one does not expect her to start racing off again the day after her arrival. One feels that she ought to be sticking round, ministering to her husband, conferring with the cook, feeding the cat, combing and brushing the Pomeranian – in a word, staying put. I was more than a little bleary-eyed, but I endeavoured, as far as the fact that my eyelids were more or less glued together would permit, to give her an austere and censorious look.

She didn't seem to get it.

'Wake up, Bertie, you old ass!' she cried, in a voice that hit me between the eyebrows and went out at the back of my head.

If Aunt Dahlia has a fault, it is that she is apt to address a *vis-à-vis* as if he were somebody half a mile away whom she had observed riding over hounds. A throwback, no doubt, to the time when she counted the day lost that was not spent in chivvying some unfortunate fox over the countryside.

I gave her another of the austere and censorious, and this time it registered. All the effect it had, however, was to cause her to descend to personalities.

'Don't blink at me in that obscene way,' she said. 'I wonder, Bertie,' she proceeded, gazing at me as I should imagine Gussie would have gazed at some newt that was not up to sample, 'if you have the faintest conception how perfectly loathsome you look? A cross between an orgy scene in the movies and some low form of pond life. I suppose you were out on the tiles last night?'

'I attended a social function, yes,' I said coldly. 'Pongo Twistleton's birthday party. I couldn't let Pongo down. *Noblesse oblige.*'

'Well, get up and dress.'

I felt I could not have heard her aright.

'Get up and dress?'

'Yes.'

I turned on the pillow with a little moan, and at this juncture Jeeves entered with the vital oolong. I clutched at it like a drowning man at a straw hat. A deep sip or two, and I felt – I won't say restored, because a birthday party like Pongo Twistleton's isn't a thing you get restored after with a mere mouthful of tea, but sufficiently for the old Bertram to be able to bend the mind on this awful thing which had come upon me.

And the more I bent same, the less could I grasp the trend of the scenario.

'What is this, Aunt Dahlia?' I inquired.

'It looks to me like tea,' was her response. 'But you know best. You're drinking it.'

If I hadn't been afraid of spilling the healing brew, I have little doubt that I should have given an impatient gesture. I know I felt like it.

'Not the contents of this cup. All this. Your barging in and telling me to get up and dress, and all that rot.'

'I've barged in, as you call it, because my telegrams seemed to produce no effect. And I told you to get up and dress because I want you to get up and dress. I've come to take you back with me. I like your crust, wiring that you would come next year or whenever it was. You're coming now. I've got a job for you.'

'But I don't want a job.'

'What you want, my lad, and what you're going to get are two very different things. There is man's work for you to do at Brinkley Court. Be ready to the last button in twenty minutes.'

'But I can't possibly be ready to any buttons in twenty minutes. I'm feeling awful.'

She seemed to consider.

'Yes,' she said, 'I suppose it's only humane to give you a day or two to recover. All right, then, I shall expect you on the thirtieth at the latest.'

'But, dash it, what is all this? How do you mean, a job? Why a job? What sort of job?'

'I'll tell you if you'll only stop talking for a minute. It's quite an easy, pleasant job. You will enjoy it. Have you ever heard of Market Snodsbury Grammar School?'

'Never.'

'It's a grammar school at Market Snodsbury.'

I told her a little frigidly that I had divined as much.

'Well, how was I to know that a man with a mind like yours would grasp it so quickly?' she protested. 'All right, then. Market Snodsbury Grammar School is, as you have guessed, the grammar school at Market Snodsbury. I'm one of the governors.'

'You mean one of the governesses.'

'I don't mean one of the governesses. Listen, ass. There was a board of governors at Eton, wasn't there? Very well. So there is at Market Snodsbury Grammar School, and I'm a member of it. And they left the arrangements for the summer prize-giving to me. This prize-giving takes place on the last – or thirty-first – day of this month. Have you got that clear?'

I took another oz. of the life-saving and inclined my head. Even after a Pongo Twistleton birthday party, I was capable of grasping simple facts like these.

'I follow you, yes. I see the point you are trying to make, certainly. Market . . . Snodsbury . . . Grammar School . . . Board of Governors . . . Prize-giving . . . Quite. But what's it got to do with me?'

'You're going to give away the prizes.'

I goggled. Her words did not appear to make sense. They seemed the mere aimless vapouring of an aunt who has been sitting out in the sun without a hat.

'Me?'

'You.'

I goggled again.

'You don't mean me?'

'I mean you in person.'

553

I goggled a third time.

'You're pulling my leg.'

'I am not pulling your leg. Nothing would induce me to touch your beastly leg. The vicar was to have officiated, but when I got home I found a letter from him saying that he had strained a fetlock and must scratch his nomination. You can imagine the state I was in. I telephoned all over the place. Nobody would take it on. And then suddenly I thought of you.'

I decided to check all this rot at the outset. Nobody is more eager to oblige deserving aunts than Bertram Wooster, but there are limits, and sharply defined limits, at that.

'So you think I'm going to strew prizes at this bally Dotheboys Hall of yours?'

'I do.'

'And make a speech?'

'Exactly.'

I laughed derisively.

'For goodness' sake, don't start gargling now. This is serious.'

'I was laughing.'

'Oh, were you? Well, I'm glad to see you taking it in this merry spirit.'

'Derisively,' I explained. 'I won't do it. That's final. I simply will not do it.'

'You will do it, young Bertie, or never darken my doors again. And you know what that means. No more of Anatole's dinners for you.'

A strong shudder shook me. She was alluding to her *chef*, that superb artist. A monarch of his profession, unsurpassed – nay, unequalled – at dishing up the raw material so that it melted in the mouth of the ultimate consumer, Anatole had always been a magnet that drew me to Brinkley Court with my tongue hanging out. Many of my happiest moments had been those which I had spent champing this great man's roasts and ragouts, and the prospect of being barred from digging into them in the future was a numbing one.

'No, I say, dash it!'

'I thought that would rattle you. Greedy young pig.'

'Greedy young pigs have nothing to do with it,' I said with a touch of hauteur. 'One is not a greedy young pig because one appreciates the cooking of a genius.'

'Well, I will say I like it myself,' conceded the relative. 'But not another bite of it do you get, if you refuse to do this simple, easy, pleasant job. No, not so much as another sniff. So put that in your twelve-inch cigarette-holder and smoke it.'

I began to feel like some wild thing caught in a snare.

'But why do you want me? I mean, what am I? Ask yourself that.'

'I often have.'

'I mean to say, I'm not the type. You have to have some terrific nib to give away prizes. I seem to remember, when I was at school, it was generally a prime minister or somebody.'

'Ah, but that was at Eton. At Market Snodsbury we aren't nearly so choosy. Anybody in spats impresses us.'

'Why don't you get Uncle Tom?'

'Uncle Tom!'

'Well, why not? He's got spats.'

'Bertie,' she said, 'I will tell you why not Uncle Tom. You remember me losing all that money at baccarat at Cannes? Well, very shortly I shall have to sidle up to Tom and break the news to him. If, right after that, I ask him to put on lavender gloves and a topper and distribute the prizes at Market Snodsbury Grammar School, there will be a divorce in the family. He would pin a note to the pincushion and be off like a rabbit. No, my lad, you're for it, so you may as well make the best of it.'

'But, Aunt Dahlia, listen to reason. I assure you, you've got hold of the wrong man. I'm hopeless at a game like that. Ask Jeeves about that time I got lugged in to address a girls' school. I made the most colossal ass of myself.'

'And I confidently anticipate that you will make an equally colossal ass of yourself on the thirty-first of this month. That's why I want you. The way I look at it is that, as the thing is bound to be a frost, anyway, one may as well get a hearty laugh out of it. I shall enjoy seeing you distribute those prizes, Bertie. Well, I won't keep you, as, no doubt, you want to do your Swedish exercises. I shall expect you in a day or two.'

And with these heartless words she beetled off, leaving me a prey to the gloomiest emotions. What with the natural reaction after Pongo's party and this stunning blow, it is not too much to say that the soul was seared.

And I was still writhing in the depths, when the door opened and Jeeves appeared.

'Mr Fink-Nottle to see you, sir,' he announced.

5

I gave him one of my looks.

'Jeeves,' I said, 'I had scarcely expected this of you. You are aware that I was up to an advanced hour last night. You know that I have barely had my tea. You cannot be ignorant of the effect of that hearty voice of Aunt Dahlia's on a man with a headache. And yet you come bringing me Fink-Nottles. Is this a time for Fink or any other kind of Nottle?'

'But did you not give me to understand, sir, that you wished to see Mr Fink-Nottle to advise him on his affairs?'

This, I admit, opened up a new line of thought. In the stress of my emotions, I had clean forgotten about having taken Gussie's interests in hand. It altered things. One can't give the raspberry to a client. I mean, you didn't find Sherlock Holmes refusing to see clients just because he had been out late the night before at Doctor Watson's birthday party. I could have wished that the man had selected some more suitable hour for approaching me, but as he appeared to be a sort of human lark, leaving his watery nest at daybreak, I supposed I had better give him an audience.

'True,' I said. 'All right. Bung him in.'

'Very good, sir.'

'But before doing so, bring me one of those pick-me-ups of yours.'

'Very good, sir.'

And presently he returned with the vital essence.

I have had occasion, I fancy, to speak before now of these pick-me-ups of Jeeves's and their effect on a

557

fellow who is hanging to life by a thread on the morning after. What they consist of, I couldn't tell you. He says some kind of sauce, the yolk of a raw egg and a dash of red pepper, but nothing will convince me that the thing doesn't go much deeper than that. Be that as it may, however, the results of swallowing one are amazing.

For perhaps the split part of a second nothing happens. It is as though all Nature waited breathless. Then, suddenly, it is as if the Last Trump had sounded and Judgement Day set in with unusual severity.

Bonfires burst out in all parts of the frame. The abdomen becomes heavily charged with molten lava. A great wind seems to blow through the world, and the subject is aware of something resembling a steam hammer striking the back of the head. During this phase, the ears ring loudly, the eyeballs rotate and there is a tingling about the brow.

And then, just as you are feeling that you ought to ring up your lawyer and see that your affairs are in order before it is too late, the whole situation seems to clarify. The wind drops. The ears cease to ring. Birds twitter. Brass bands start playing. The sun comes up over the horizon with a jerk.

And a moment later all you are conscious of is a great peace.

As I drained the glass now, new life seemed to burgeon within me. I remember Jeeves, who, however much he may go off the rails at times in the matter of dress clothes and in his advice to those in love, has always had a neat turn of phrase, once speaking of someone rising on stepping-stones of his dead self to higher things. It was that way with me now. I felt that the Bertram Wooster who lay propped up against the pillows had become a better, stronger, finer Bertram.

'Thank you, Jeeves,' I said.

'Not at all, sir.'

'That touched the exact spot. I am now able to cope with life's problems.'

'I am gratified to hear it, sir.'

'What madness not to have had one of those before tackling Aunt Dahlia. However, too late to worry about that now. Tell me of Gussie. How did he make out at the fancy-dress ball?'

'He did not arrive at the fancy-dress ball, sir.'

I looked at him a bit austerely.

'Jeeves,' I said, 'I admit that after that pick-me-up of yours I feel better, but don't try me too high. Don't stand by my sick bed talking absolute rot. We shot Gussie into a cab and he started forth, headed for wherever this fancy-dress ball was. He must have arrived.'

'No, sir. As I gather from Mr Fink-Nottle, he entered the cab convinced in his mind that the entertainment to which he had been invited was to be held at No. 17 Suffolk Square, whereas the actual rendezvous was No. 71 Norfolk Terrace. These aberrations of memory are not uncommon with those who, like Mr Fink-Nottle, belong essentially to what one might call the dreamer type.'

'One might also call it the fatheaded type.'

'Yes, sir.'

'Well?'

'On reaching No. 17 Suffolk Square, Mr Fink-Nottle endeavoured to produce money to pay the fare.'

'What stopped him?'

'The fact that he had no money, sir. He discovered that he had left it, together with his ticket of invitation, on the mantelpiece of his bedchamber in the house of his uncle, where he was residing. Bidding the cabman to wait, accordingly, he rang the door-bell, and when the butler appeared, requested him to pay the cab, adding that it was all right, as he was one of the guests invited to the dance. The butler then disclaimed all knowledge of a dance on the premises.'

'And declined to unbelt?'

'Yes, sir.'

'Upon which – '

'Mr Fink-Nottle directed the cabman to drive him back to his uncle's residence.'

'Well, why wasn't that the happy ending? All he had to do was go in, collect cash and ticket, and there he would have been, on velvet.'

'I should have mentioned, sir, that Mr Fink-Nottle had also left his latchkey on the mantelpiece of his bedchamber.'

'He could have rung the bell.'

'He did ring the bell, sir, for some fifteen minutes. At the expiration of that period he recalled that he had given permission to the caretaker – the house was officially closed and all the staff on holiday – to visit his sailor son at Portsmouth.'

'Golly, Jeeves.'

'Yes, sir.'

'These dreamer-types do live, don't they.'

'Yes, sir.'

'What happened then?'

'Mr Fink-Nottle appears to have realized at this point that his position as regards the cabman had become equivocal. The figures on the clock had already reached a substantial sum, and he was not in a position to meet his obligations.'

'He could have explained.'

'You cannot explain to cabmen, sir. On endeavouring to do so, he found the fellow sceptical of his bona fides.'

'I should have legged it.'

'That is the policy which appears to have commended itself to Mr Fink-Nottle. He darted rapidly away, and the cabman, endeavouring to detain him, snatched at his overcoat. Mr Fink-Nottle contrived to extricate himself from the coat, and it would seem that his appearance in the masquerade costume beneath it came as something

of a shock to the cabman. Mr Fink-Nottle informs me
that he heard a species of whistling gasp, and, looking
round, observed the man crouching against the railings
with his hands over his face. Mr Fink-Nottle thinks he
was praying. No doubt an uneducated, superstitious
fellow, sir. Possibly a drinker.'

'Well, if he hadn't been one before, I'll bet he started
being one shortly afterwards. I expect he could scarcely
wait for the pubs to open.'

'Very possibly, in the circumstances he might have
found a restorative agreeable, sir.'

'And so, in the circumstances, might Gussie too, I
should think. What on earth did he do after that?
London late at night – or even in the daytime, for that
matter – is no place for a man in scarlet tights.'

'No, sir.'

'He invites comment.'

'Yes, sir.'

'I can see the poor old bird ducking down side-streets,
skulking in alley-ways, diving into dust-bins.'

'I gathered from Mr Fink-Nottle's remarks, sir, that
something very much on those lines was what occurred.
Eventually, after a trying night, he found his way to Mr
Sipperley's residence, where he was able to secure
lodging and a change of costume in the morning.'

I nestled against the pillows, the brow a bit drawn. It
is all very well to try to do old school friends a spot of
good, but I could not but feel that in espousing the cause
of a lunkhead capable of mucking things up as Gussie
had done, I had taken on a contract almost too big for
human consumption. It seemed to me that what Gussie
needed was not so much the advice of a seasoned man of
the world as a padded cell in Colney Hatch and a couple
of good keepers to see that he did not set the place on
fire.

Indeed, for an instant I had half a mind to withdraw
from the case and hand it back to Jeeves. But the pride of

the Woosters restrained me. When we Woosters put our hands to the plough, we do not readily sheathe the sword. Besides, after that business of the mess jacket, anything resembling weakness would have been fatal.

'I suppose you realize, Jeeves,' I said, for though one dislikes to rub it in, these things have to be pointed out, 'that all this was your fault?'

'Sir?'

'It's no good saying "Sir?" You know it was. If you had not insisted on his going to that dance – a mad project, as I spotted from the first – this would not have happened.'

'Yes, sir, but I confess I did not anticipate –'

'Always anticipate everything, Jeeves,' I said, a little sternly. 'It is the only way. Even if you had allowed him to wear a Pierrot costume, things would not have panned out as they did. A Pierrot costume has pockets. However,' I went on more kindly, 'we need not go into that now. If all this has shown you what comes of going about the place in scarlet tights, that is something gained. Gussie waits without, you say?'

'Yes, sir.'

'Then shoot him in, and I will see what I can do for him.'

6

Gussie, on arrival, proved to be still showing traces of his grim experience. The face was pale, the eyes gooseberrylike, the ears drooping, and the whole aspect that of a man who has passed through the furnace and been caught in the machinery. I hitched myself up a bit higher on the pillows and gazed at him narrowly. It was a moment, I could see, when first aid was required, and I prepared to get down to cases.

'Well, Gussie.'

'Hullo, Bertie.'

'What ho.'

'What ho.'

These civilities concluded, I felt that the moment had come to touch delicately on the past.

'I hear you've been through it a bit.'

'Yes.'

'Thanks to Jeeves.'

'It wasn't Jeeves's fault.'

'Entirely Jeeves's fault.'

'I don't see that. I forgot my money and latchkey –'

'And now you'd better forget Jeeves. For you will be interested to hear, Gussie,' I said, deeming it best to put him in touch with the position of affairs right away, 'that he is no longer handling your little problem.'

This seemed to slip it across him properly. The jaw fell, the ears drooped more limply. He had been looking like a dead fish. He now looked like a deader fish, one of last year's, cast up on some lonely beach and left there at the mercy of the wind and tides.

'What!'

'Yes.'

'You don't mean that Jeeves isn't going to – '

'No.'

'But, dash it – '

I was kind, but firm.

'You will be much better off without him. Surely your terrible experiences of that awful night have told you that Jeeves needs a rest. The keenest of thinkers strikes a bad patch occasionally. That is what has happened to Jeeves. I have seen it coming on for some time. He has lost his form. He wants his plugs decarbonized. No doubt this is a shock to you. I suppose you came here this morning to seek his advice?'

'Of course I did.'

'On what point?'

'Madeline Bassett has gone to stay with these people in the country, and I want to know what he thinks I ought to do.'

'Well, as I say, Jeeves is off the case.'

'But, Bertie, dash it – '

'Jeeves,' I said with a certain asperity, 'is no longer on the case. I am now in sole charge.'

'But what on earth can you do?'

I curbed my resentment. We Woosters are fair-minded. We can make allowances for men who have been parading London all night in scarlet tights.

'That,' I said quietly, 'we shall see. Sit down and let us confer. I am bound to say the thing seems quite simple to me. You say this girl has gone to visit friends in the country. It would appear obvious that you must go there too, and flock round her like a poultice. Elementary.'

'But I can't plant myself on a lot of perfect strangers.'

'Don't you know these people?'

'Of course I don't. I don't know anybody.'

I pursed the lips. This did seem to complicate matters somewhat.

'All that I know is that their name is Travers, and it's a place called Brinkley Court down in Worcestershire.'

I unpursed the lips.

'Gussie,' I said, smiling paternally, 'it was a lucky day for you when Bertram Wooster interested himself in your affairs. As I foresaw from the start, I can fix everything. This afternoon you shall go to Brinkley Court, an honoured guest.'

He quivered like a *mousse*. I suppose it must always be rather a thrilling experience for the novice to watch me taking hold.

'But, Bertie, you don't mean you know these Traverses?'

'They are my Aunt Dahlia.'

'My gosh!'

'You see now,' I pointed out, 'how lucky you were to get me behind you. You go to Jeeves, and what does he do? He dresses you up in scarlet tights and one of the foulest false beards of my experience, and sends you off to fancy-dress balls. Result, agony of spirit and no progress. I then take over and put you on the right lines. Could Jeeves have got you into Brinkley Court? Not a chance. Aunt Dahlia isn't his aunt. I merely mention these things.'

'By Jove, Bertie, I don't know how to thank you.'

'My dear chap!'

'But, I say.'

'Now what?'

'What do I do when I get there?'

'If you knew Brinkley Court, you would not ask that question. In those romantic surroundings you can't miss. Great lovers through the ages have fixed up the preliminary formalities at Brinkley. The place is simply ill with atmosphere. You will stroll with the girl in the shady walks. You will sit with her on the shady lawns. You will row on the lake with her. And gradually you will find yourself working up to a point where –'

'By Jove, I believe you're right.'

'Of course, I'm right. I've got engaged three times at Brinkley. No business resulted, but the fact remains. And I went there without the foggiest idea of indulging in the tender pash. I hadn't the slightest intention of proposing to anybody. Yet no sooner had I entered those romantic grounds than I found myself reaching out for the nearest girl in sight and slapping my soul down in front of her. It's something in the air.'

'I see exactly what you mean. That's just what I want to be able to do – work up to it. And in London – curse the place – everything's in such a rush that you don't get a chance.'

'Quite. You see a girl alone for about five minutes a day, and if you want to ask her to be your wife, you've got to charge into it as if you were trying to grab the gold ring on a merry-go-round.'

'That's right. London rattles one. I shall be a different man altogether in the country. What a bit of luck this Travers woman turning out to be your aunt.'

'I don't know what you mean, turning out to be my aunt. She has been my aunt all along.'

'I mean, how extraordinary that it should be your aunt that Madeline's going to stay with.'

'Not at all. She and my Cousin Angela are close friends. At Cannes she was with us all the time.'

'Oh, you met Madeline at Cannes, did you? By Jove, Bertie,' said the poor lizard devoutly, 'I wish I could have seen her at Cannes. How wonderful she must have looked in beach pyjamas! Oh, Bertie – '

'Quite,' I said, a little distantly. Even when restored by one of Jeeves's depth bombs, one doesn't want this sort of thing after a hard night. I touched the bell and, when Jeeves appeared, requested him to bring me telegraph form and pencil. I then wrote a well-worded communication to Aunt Dahlia, informing her that I was sending my friend, Augustus Fink-Nottle, down to

Brinkley today to enjoy her hospitality, and handed it to Gussie.

'Push that in at the first post office you pass,' I said. 'She will find it waiting for her on her return.'

Gussie popped along, flapping the telegram and looking like a close-up of Joan Crawford, and I turned to Jeeves and gave him a précis of my operations.

'Simple, you observe, Jeeves. Nothing elaborate.'

'No, sir.'

'Nothing far-fetched. Nothing strained or bizarre. Just Nature's remedy.'

'Yes, sir.'

'This is the attack as it should have been delivered. What do you call it when two people of opposite sexes are bunged together in close association in a secluded spot, meeting each other every day and seeing a lot of each other?'

'Is "propinquity" the word you wish, sir?'

'It is. I stake everything on propinquity, Jeeves. Propinquity, in my opinion, is what will do the trick. At the moment, as you are aware, Gussie is a mere jelly when in the presence. But ask yourself how he will feel in a week or so, after he and she have been helping themselves to sausages out of the same dish day after day at the breakfast sideboard. Cutting the same ham, ladling out communal kidneys and bacon – why –'

I broke off abruptly. I had one of my ideas.

'Golly, Jeeves!'

'Sir?'

'Here's an instance of how you have to think of everything. You heard me mention sausages, kidneys and bacon and ham.'

'Yes, sir.'

'Well, there must be nothing of that. Fatal. The wrong note entirely. Give me that telegraph form and pencil. I must warn Gussie without delay. What he's got to do is to create in this girl's mind the impression that he is

567

pining away for love of her. This cannot be done by
wolfing sausages.'

'No, sir.'

'Very well, then.'

And, taking form and p., I drafted the following:

> *Fink-Nottle*
> *Brinkley Court*
> *Market Snodsbury*
> *Worcestershire*
> *Lay off the sausages. Avoid the ham. Bertie*

'Send that off, Jeeves, instanter.'

'Very good, sir.'

I sank back on the pillows.

'Well, Jeeves,' I said, 'you see how I am taking hold.
You notice the grip I am getting on this case. No doubt
you realize now that it would pay you to study my
methods.'

'No doubt, sir.'

'And even now you aren't on to the full depths of the
extraordinary sagacity I've shown. Do you know what
brought Aunt Dahlia up here this morning? She came to
tell me I'd got to distribute the prizes at some beastly
seminary she's a governor of down at Market
Snodsbury.'

'Indeed, sir? I fear you will scarcely find that a
congenial task.'

'Ah, but I'm not going to do it. I'm going to shove it
off on to Gussie.'

'Sir?'

'I propose, Jeeves, to wire to Aunt Dahlia saying that
I can't get down, and suggesting that she unleashes
him on these young Borstal inmates of hers in my
stead.'

'But if Mr Fink-Nottle should decline, sir?'

'Decline? Can you see him declining? Just conjure up

the picture in your mind, Jeeves. Scene, the
drawing-room at Brinkley; Gussie wedged into a corner,
with Aunt Dahlia standing over him making hunting
noises. I put it to you, Jeeves, can you see him
declining?'

'Not readily, sir, I agree. Mrs Travers' is a forceful
personality.'

'He won't have a hope of declining. His only way out
would be to slide off. And he can't slide off, because he
wants to be with Miss Bassett. No, Gussie will have to
toe the line, and I shall be saved from a job at which I
confess the soul shuddered. Getting up on a platform
and delivering a short, manly speech to a lot of foul
school-kids! Golly, Jeeves. I've been through that sort of
thing once, what? You remember that time at the girls'
school?'

'Very vividly, sir.'

'What an ass I made of myself!'

'Certainly I have seen you to better advantage, sir.'

'I think you might bring me just one more of those
dynamite specials of yours, Jeeves. This narrow squeak
has made me come over all faint.'

I suppose it must have taken Aunt Dahlia three hours or
so to get back to Brinkley, because it wasn't till well
after lunch that her telegram arrived. It read like a
telegram that had been dispatched in a white-hot surge
of emotion some two minutes after she had read mine.
As follows:

*Am taking legal advice to ascertain whether
strangling an idiot nephew counts as murder. If it
doesn't look out for yourself. Consider your conduct
frozen limit. What do you mean by planting your
loathsome friends on me like this? Do you think
Brinkley Court is a leper colony or what is it? Who is
this Spink-Bottle? Love. Travers.*

I had expected some such initial reaction. I replied in temperate vein:

Not Bottle. Nottle. Regards. Bertie.

Almost immediately after she had dispatched the above heart cry, Gussie must have arrived, for it wasn't twenty minutes later when I received the following:

Cipher telegram signed by you has reached me here. Runs 'Lay off the sausages. Avoid the ham'. Wire key immediately. Fink-Nottle.

I replied:

Also Kidneys. Cheerio. Bertie.

I had staked all on Gussie making a favourable impression on his hostess, basing my confidence on the fact that he was one of those timid, obsequious, teacup-passing, thin-bread-and-butter-offering, yes-men whom women of my Aunt Dahlia's type nearly always like at first sight. That I had not overrated my acumen was proved by her next in order, which, I was pleased to note, assayed a markedly larger percentage of the milk of human kindness.

As follows:

Well, this friend of yours has got here, and I must say that for a friend of yours he seems less sub-human than I had expected. A bit of a pop-eyed bleater, but on the whole clean and civil, and certainly most informative about newts. Am considering arranging series of lectures for him in neighbourhood. All the same I like your nerve using my house as a summer-

hotel resort and shall have much to say to you on subject when you come down. Expect you thirtieth. Bring spats. Love. Travers.

To this I riposted:

On consulting engagement book find it impossible come Brinkley Court. Deeply regret. Toodle-oo. Bertie.

Hers in reply struck a sinister note:

Oh, so it's like that, is it? You and your engagement book, indeed. Deeply regret my foot. Let me tell you, my lad, that you will regret it a jolly sight more deeply if you don't come down. If you imagine for one moment that you are going to get out of distributing those prizes you are very much mistaken. Deeply regret Brinkley Court hundred miles from London as unable hit you with a brick. Love. Travers.

I then put my fortune to the test, to win or lose it all. It was not a moment for petty economies. I let myself go regardless of expense:

No, but dash it, listen. Honestly, you don't want me. Get Fink-Nottle distribute prizes. A born distributor, who will do you credit. Confidently anticipate Augustus Fink-Nottle as Master of Revels on thirty-first inst. would make genuine sensation. Do not miss this great chance, which may never occur again. Tinkerty-tonk. Bertie.

There was an hour of breathless suspense, and then the joyful tidings arrived:

Well, all right. Something in what you say, I suppose.
Consider you treacherous worm and contemptible,
spineless cowardy custard, but have booked
Spink-Bottle. Stay where you are, then, and I hope
you get run over by an omnibus. Love. Travers.

The relief, as you may well imagine, was stupendous.
A great weight seemed to have rolled off my mind. It
was as if somebody had been pouring Jeeves's
pick-me-ups into me through a funnel. I sang as I dressed
for dinner that night. At the Drones I was so gay and
cheery that there were several complaints. And when I
got home and turned into the old bed, I fell asleep like a
little child within five minutes of inserting the person
between the sheets. It seemed to me that the whole
distressing affair might now be considered definitely
closed.

Conceive my astonishment, therefore, when waking
on the morrow and sitting up to dig into the morning
tea-cup, I beheld on the tray another telegram.

My heart sank. Could Aunt Dahlia have slept on it
and changed her mind? Could Gussie, unable to face the
ordeal confronting him, have legged it during the night
down a water-pipe? With these speculations racing
through the bean, I tore open the envelope. And as I
noted contents I uttered a startled yip.

'Sir?' said Jeeves, pausing at the door.

I read the thing again. Yes, I had got the gist all right.
No, I had not been deceived in the substance.

'Jeeves,' I said, 'do you know what?'

'No, sir.'

'You know my Cousin Angela?'

'Yes, sir.'

'You know young Tuppy Glossop?'

'Yes, sir.'

'They've broken off their engagement.'

'I am sorry to hear that, sir.'

'I have here a communication from Aunt Dahlia, specifically stating this. I wonder what the row was about.'

'I could not say, sir.'

'Of course you couldn't. Don't be an ass, Jeeves.'

'No, sir.'

I brooded. I was deeply moved.

'Well, this means that we shall have to go down to Brinkley today. Aunt Dahlia is obviously all of a twitter, and my place is by her side. You had better pack this morning, and catch that 12.45 train with the luggage. I have a lunch engagement, so will follow in the car.'

'Very good, sir.'

I brooded some more.

'I must say this has come as a great shock to me, Jeeves.'

'No doubt, sir.'

'A very great shock. Angela and Tuppy . . . Tut, tut! Why, they seemed like the paper on the wall. Life is full of sadness, Jeeves.'

'Yes, sir.'

'Still, there it is.'

'Undoubtedly, sir.'

'Right ho, then. Switch on the bath.'

'Very good, sir.'

I meditated pretty freely as I drove down to Brinkley in the old two-seater that afternoon. The news of this rift or rupture of Angela's and Tuppy's had disturbed me greatly.

The projected match, you see, was one on which I had always looked with kindly approval. Too often, when a chap of your acquaintance is planning to marry a girl you know, you find yourself knitting the brow a bit and chewing the lower lip dubiously, feeling that he or she, or both, should be warned while there is yet time.

But I have never felt anything of this nature about Tuppy and Angela. Tuppy, when not making an ass of himself, is a soundish sort of egg. So is Angela a soundish sort of egg. And, as far as being in love was concerned, it had always seemed to me that you wouldn't have been far out in describing them as two hearts that beat as one.

True, they had had their little tiffs, notably on the occasion when Tuppy – with what he said was fearless honesty and I considered thorough goofiness – had told Angela that her new hat made her look like a Pekingese. But in every romance you have to budget for the occasional dust-up, and after that incident I had supposed that he had learned his lesson and that from then on life would be one grand, sweet song.

And now this wholly unforeseen severing of diplomatic relations had popped up through a trap.

I gave the thing the cream of the Wooster brain all the way down, but it continued to beat me what could have caused the outbreak of hostilities, and I bunged my foot sedulously on the accelerator in order to get to Aunt Dahlia with the greatest possible speed and learn the inside history straight from the horse's mouth. And what with all six cylinders hitting nicely, I made good time and found myself closeted with the relative shortly before the hour of the evening cocktail.

She seemed glad to see me. In fact, she actually said she was glad to see me – a statement no other aunt on the list would have committed herself to, the customary reaction of these near and dear ones to the spectacle of Bertram arriving for a visit being a sort of sick horror.

'Decent of you to rally round, Bertie,' she said.

'My place was by your side, Aunt Dahlia,' I responded.

I could see at a g. that the unfortunate affair had got in amongst her in no uncertain manner. Her usually cheerful map was clouded, and the genial smile conspic. by its a. I pressed her hand sympathetically, to indicate that my heart bled for her.

'Bad show this, my dear old flesh and blood,' I said. 'I'm afraid you've been having a sticky time. You must be worried.'

She snorted emotionally. She looked like an aunt who has just bitten into a bad oyster.

'Worried is right. I haven't had a peaceful moment since I got back from Cannes. Ever since I put my foot across this blasted threshold,' said Aunt Dahlia, returning for the nonce to the hearty *argot* of the hunting field, 'everything's been at sixes and sevens. First there was that mix-up about the prize-giving.'

She paused at this point and gave me a look. 'I had been meaning to speak freely to you about your behaviour in that matter, Bertie,' she said. 'I had some good things all stored up. But, as you've rallied round like this, I suppose I shall have to let you off. And, anyway, it is probably all for the best that you evaded your obligations in that sickeningly craven way. I have an idea that this Spink-Bottle of yours is going to be good. If only he can keep off newts.'

'Has he been talking about newts?'

'He has. Fixing me with a glittering eye, like the Ancient Mariner. But if that was the worst I had to bear, I wouldn't mind. What I'm worrying about is what Tom is going to say when he starts talking.'

'Uncle Tom?'

'I wish there was something else you could call him except "Uncle Tom",' said Aunt Dahlia a little testily. 'Every time you do it, I expect to see him turn black and start playing the banjo. Yes, Uncle Tom, if you must have it. I shall have to tell him soon about losing all that money at baccarat, and, when I do, he will go up like a rocket.'

'Still, no doubt Time, the great healer –'

'Time, the great healer, be blowed. I've got to get a cheque for five hundred pounds out of him for *Milady's Boudoir* by August the third at the latest.'

I was concerned. Apart from a nephew's natural interest in an aunt's refined weekly paper, I had always had a soft spot in my heart for *Milady's Boudoir* ever since I contributed that article to it on What the Well-Dressed Man is Wearing. Sentimental, possibly, but we old journalists do have these feelings.

'Is the *Boudoir* on the rocks?'

'It will be if Tom doesn't cough up. It needs help till it has turned the corner.'

'But wasn't it turning the corner two years ago?'

'It was. And it's still at it. Till you've run a weekly paper for women, you don't know what corners are.'

'And you think the chances of getting into Uncle – into my uncle by marriage's ribs are slight?'

'I'll tell you, Bertie. Up till now, when these subsidies were required, I have always been able to come to Tom in the gay, confident spirit of an only child touching an indulgent father for chocolate cream. But he's just had a demand from the income-tax people for an additional fifty-eight pounds, one and threepence, and all he's been talking about since I got back has been ruin and the sinister trend of socialistic legislation and what will become of us all.'

I could readily believe it. This Tom has a peculiarity I've noticed in other very oofy men. Nick him for the paltriest sum, and he lets out a squawk you can hear at Land's End. He has the stuff in gobs, but he hates giving it up.

'If it wasn't for Anatole's cooking, I doubt if he would bother to carry on. Thank God for Anatole, I say.'

I bowed my head reverently.

'Good old Anatole,' I said.

'Amen,' said Aunt Dahlia.

Then the look of holy ecstasy, which is always the result of letting the mind dwell, however briefly, on Anatole's cooking, died out of her face.

'But don't let me wander from the subject,' she resumed. 'I was telling you of the way hell's foundations have been quivering since I got home. First the prize-giving, then Tom, and now, on top of everything else, this infernal quarrel between Angela and young Glossop.'

I nodded gravely.

'I was frightfully sorry to hear of that. Terrible shock. What was the row about?'

'Sharks.'

'Eh?'

'Sharks. Or, rather, one individual shark. The brute that went for the poor child when she was aquaplaning at Cannes. You remember Angela's shark?'

Certainly I remembered Angela's shark. A man of sensibility does not forget about a cousin nearly being chewed by monsters of the deep. The episode was still green in my memory.

In a nutshell, what had occurred was this: You know

how you aquaplane. A motor-boat nips on ahead, trailing a rope. You stand on a board, holding the rope, and the boat tows you along. And every now and then you lose your grip on the rope and plunge into the sea and have to swim to your board again.

A silly process it has always seemed to me, though many find it diverting.

Well, on the occasion referred to, Angela had just regained her board after taking a toss, when a great beastly shark came along and cannoned into it, flinging her into the salty once more. It took her quite a bit of time to get on again and make the motor-boat chap realize what was up and haul her to safety, and during that interval you can readily picture her embarrassment.

According to Angela, the finny denizen kept snapping at her ankles virtually without cessation, so that by the time help arrived, she was feeling more like a salted almond at a public dinner than anything human. Very shaken the poor child had been, I recall, and had talked of nothing else for weeks.

'I remember the whole incident vividly,' I said. 'But how did that start the trouble?'

'She was telling him the story last night.'

'Well?'

'Her eyes shining and her little hands clasped in girlish excitement.'

'No doubt.'

'And instead of giving her the understanding and sympathy to which she was entitled, what do you think this blasted Glossop did? He sat listening like a lump of dough, as if she had been talking about the weather, and when she had finished, he took his cigarette holder out of his mouth and said, "I expect it was only a floating log!"'

'He didn't!'

'He did. And when Angela described how the thing had jumped and snapped at her, he took his cigarette holder out of his mouth again, and said, "Ah! Probably a flatfish. Quite harmless. No doubt it was just trying to play." Well, I mean! What would you have done if you had been Angela? She has pride, sensibility, all the natural feelings of a good woman. She told him he was an ass and a fool and an idiot, and didn't know what he was talking about.'

I must say I saw the girl's viewpoint. It's only about once in a lifetime that anything sensational ever happens to one, and when it does, you don't want people taking all the colour out of it. I remember at school having to read that stuff where that chap, Othello, tells the girl what a hell of a time he'd been having among the cannibals and what not. Well, imagine his feelings if, after he had described some particularly sticky passage with a cannibal chief and was waiting for the awe-struck 'Oh-h! Not really?' she had said that the whole thing had no doubt been greatly exaggerated and that the man had probably really been a prominent local vegetarian.

Yes, I saw Angela's point of view.

'But don't tell me that when he saw how shirty she was about it, the chump didn't back down?'

'He didn't. He argued. And one thing led to another until, by easy stages, they had arrived at the point where she was saying that she didn't know if he was aware of it, but if he didn't knock off starchy foods and do exercises every morning, he would be getting as fat as a pig, and he was talking about this modern habit of girls putting make-up on their faces, of which he had always disapproved. This continued for a while, and then there was a loud pop and the air was full of mangled fragments of their engagement. I'm distracted about it. Thank goodness you've come, Bertie.'

'Nothing could have kept me away,' I replied, touched. 'I felt you needed me.'

'Yes.'

'Quite.'

'Or, rather,' she said, 'not you, of course, but Jeeves. The minute all this happened, I thought of him. The situation obviously cries out for Jeeves. If ever in the whole history of human affairs there was a moment when that lofty brain was required about the home, this is it.'

I think, if I had been standing up, I would have staggered. In fact, I'm pretty sure I would. But it isn't so dashed easy to stagger when you're sitting in an arm-chair. Only my face, therefore, showed how deeply I had been stung by these words.

Until she spoke them, I had been all sweetness and light – the sympathetic nephew prepared to strain every nerve to do his bit. I now froze, and the face became hard and set.

'Jeeves!' I said, between clenched teeth.

'Oom beroofen,' said Aunt Dahlia.

I saw that she had got the wrong angle.

'I was not sneezing. I was saying "Jeeves!"'

'And well you may. What a man! I'm going to put the whole thing up to him. There's nobody like Jeeves.'

My frigidity became more marked.

'I venture to take issue with you, Aunt Dahlia.'

'You take what?'

'Issue.'

'You do, do you?'

'I emphatically do. Jeeves is hopeless.'

'What?'

'Quite hopeless. He has lost his grip completely. Only a couple of days ago I was compelled to take him off a case because his handling of it was so footling. And, anyway, I resent this assumption, if assumption is the word I want, that Jeeves is the only fellow with brain. I object to the way everybody puts things up to him without consulting me and letting me have a stab at them first.'

She seemed about to speak, but I checked her with a gesture.

'It is true that in the past I have sometimes seen fit to seek Jeeves's advice. It is possible that in the future I may seek it again. But I claim the right to have a pop at these problems, as they arise, in person, without having everybody behave as if Jeeves was the only onion in the hash. I sometimes feel that Jeeves, though admittedly not unsuccessful in the past, has been lucky rather than gifted.'

'Have you and Jeeves had a row?'

'Nothing of the kind.'

'You seem to have it in for him.'

'Not at all.'

And yet I must admit that there was a modicum of truth in what she said. I had been feeling pretty austere about the man all day, and I'll tell you why.

You remember that he caught that 12.45 train with the luggage, while I remained on in order to keep a luncheon engagement. Well, just before I started out to the tryst, I was pottering about the flat, and suddenly – I don't know what put the suspicion into my head, possibly the fellow's manner had been furtive – something seemed to whisper to me to go and have a look in the wardrobe.

And it was as I had suspected. There was the mess jacket still on its hanger. The hound hadn't packed it.

Well, as anybody at the Drones will tell you, Bertram Wooster is a pretty hard chap to outgeneral. I shoved the thing in a brown-paper parcel and put it in the back of the car, and it was on a chair in the hall now. But that didn't alter the fact that Jeeves had attempted to do the dirty on me, and I suppose a certain what-d'you-call-it had crept into my manner during the above remarks.

'There has been no breach,' I said. 'You might describe it as a passing coolness, but no more. We did not happen to see eye to eye with regard to my white mess jacket with the brass buttons and I was compelled to assert my personality. But –'

'Well, it doesn't matter, anyway. The thing that matters is that you are talking piffle, you poor fish. Jeeves lost his grip? Absurd. Why, I saw him for a moment when he arrived, and his eyes were absolutely glittering with intelligence. I said to myself "Trust Jeeves", and I intend to.'

'You would be far better advised to let me see what I can accomplish, Aunt Dahlia.'

'For heaven's sake, don't you start butting in. You'll only make matters worse.'

'On the contrary, it may interest you to know that while driving here I concentrated deeply on this trouble of Angela's and was successful in formulating a plan, based on the psychology of the individual, which I am proposing to put into effect at an early moment.'

'Oh, my God!'

'My knowledge of human nature tells me it will work.'

'Bertie,' said Aunt Dahlia, and her manner struck me as febrile, 'lay off, lay off! For pity's sake, lay off. I know these plans of yours. I suppose you want to shove Angela into the lake and push young Glossop in after her to save her life, or something like that.'

'Nothing of the kind.'

'It's the sort of thing you would do.'

'My scheme is far more subtle. Let me outline it for you.'

'No, thanks.'

'I say to myself –'

'But not to me.'

'Do listen for a second.'

'I won't.'

'Right ho, then. I am dumb.'

'And have been from a child.'

I perceived that little good could result from continuing the discussion. I waved a hand and shrugged a shoulder.

'Very well, Aunt Dahlia,' I said, with dignity, 'if you don't want to be in on the ground floor, that is your affair. But you are missing an intellectual treat. And, anyway, no matter how much you may behave like the deaf adder of Scripture which, as you are doubtless aware, the more one piped, the less it danced, or words to that effect, I shall carry on as planned. I am extremely fond of Angela, and I shall spare no effort to bring the sunshine back into her heart.'

'Bertie, you abysmal chump, I appeal to you once more. Will you please lay off? You'll only make things ten times as bad as they are already.'

I remember reading in one of those historical novels once about a chap – a buck he would have been, no doubt, or a macaroni or some such bird as that – who, when people said the wrong thing, merely laughed down from lazy eyelids and flicked a speck of dust from the irreproachable Mechlin lace at his wrists. This was practically what I did now. At least, I straightened my tie and smiled one of those inscrutable smiles of mine. I then withdrew and went out for a saunter in the garden.

And the first chap I ran into was young Tuppy. His brow was furrowed, and he was moodily bunging stones at a flowerpot.

8

I think I have told you before about young Tuppy
Glossop. He was the fellow, if you remember, who,
callously ignoring the fact that we had been friends since
boyhood, betted me one night at the Drones that I
couldn't swing myself across the swimming bath by the
rings – a childish feat for one of my lissomness – and
then, having seen me well on the way, looped back the
last ring, thus rendering it necessary for me to drop into
the deep end in formal evening costume.

To say that I had not resented this foul deed, which
seemed to me deserving of the title of the crime of the
century, would be paltering with the truth. I had
resented it profoundly, chafing not a little at the time
and continuing to chafe for some weeks.

But you know how it is with these things. The wound
heals. The agony abates.

I am not saying, mind you, that had the opportunity
presented itself of dropping a wet sponge on Tuppy from
some high spot or of putting an eel in his bed or finding
some other form of self-expression of a like nature, I
would not have embraced it eagerly; but that let me out.
I mean to say, grievously injured though I had been, it
gave me no pleasure to feel that the fellow's bally life
was being ruined by the loss of a girl whom, despite all
that had passed, I was convinced he still loved like the
dickens.

On the contrary, I was heart and soul in favour of
healing the breach and rendering everything hotsy-totsy
once more between these two young sundered blighters.
You will have gleaned that from my remarks to Aunt

Dahlia, and if you had been present at this moment and had seen the kindly commiserating look I gave Tuppy, you would have gleaned it still more.

It was one of those searching, melting looks, and was accompanied by the hearty clasp of the right hand and the gentle laying of the left on the collar-bone.

'Well, Tuppy, old chap,' I said. 'How are you, old man?'

My commiseration deepened as I spoke the words, for there had been no lighting up of the eye, no answering pressure of the palm, no sign whatever, in short, of any disposition on his part to do spring dances at the sight of an old friend. The man seemed sand-bagged. Melancholy, as I remember Jeeves saying once about Pongo Twistleton when he was trying to knock off smoking, had marked him for her own. Not that I was surprised, of course. In the circs, no doubt, a certain moodiness was only natural.

I released the hand, ceased to knead the shoulder, and, producing the old case, offered him a cigarette.

He took it dully.

'Are you here, Bertie?' he asked.

'Yes, I'm here.'

'Just passing through, or come to stay?'

I thought for a moment. I might have told him that I had arrived at Brinkley Court with the express intention of bringing Angela and himself together once more, of knitting up the severed threads, and so on and so forth; and for perhaps half the time required for the lighting of a gasper I had almost decided to do so. Then, I reflected, better, on the whole, perhaps not. To broadcast the fact that I proposed to take him and Angela and play on them as on a couple of stringed instruments might have been injudicious. Chaps don't always like being played on as on a stringed instrument.

'It all depends,' I said. 'I may remain. I may push on. My plans are uncertain.'

He nodded listlessly, rather in the manner of a man

who did not give a damn what I did, and stood gazing
out over the sunlit garden. In build and appearance,
Tuppy somewhat resembles a bulldog, and his aspect
now was that of one of these fine animals who has just
been refused a slice of cake. It was not difficult for a man
of my discernment to read what was in his mind, and it
occasioned me no surprise, therefore, when his next
words had to do with the subject marked with a cross on
the agenda paper.

'You've heard of this business of mine, I suppose? Me
and Angela?'

'I have, indeed, Tuppy, old man.'

'We've bust up.'

'I know. Some little friction, I gather, *in re* Angela's
shark.'

'Yes. I said it must have been a flatfish.'

'So my informant told me.'

'Who did you hear it from?'

'Aunt Dahlia.'

'I suppose she cursed me properly?'

'Oh, no. Beyond referring to you in one passage as
"this blasted Glossop", she was, I thought, singularly
temperate in her language for a woman who at one time
hunted regularly with the Quorn. All the same, I could
see, if you don't mind me saying so, old man, that
she felt you might have behaved with a little more
tact.'

'Tact!'

'And I must admit I rather agreed with her. Was it
nice, Tuppy, was it quite kind to take the bloom off
Angela's shark like that? You must remember that
Angela's shark is very dear to her. Could you not see
what a sock on the jaw it would be for the poor child to
hear it described by the man to whom she had given her
heart as a flatfish?'

I saw that he was struggling with some powerful
emotion.

'And what about my side of the thing?' he demanded, in a voice choked with feeling.

'Your side?'

'You don't suppose,' said Tuppy, with rising vehemence, 'that I would have exposed this dashed synthetic shark for the flatfish it undoubtedly was if there had not been causes that led up to it. What induced me to speak as I did was the fact that Angela, the little squirt, had just been most offensive, and I seized the opportunity to get a bit of my own back.'

'Offensive?'

'Exceedingly offensive. Purely on the strength of my having let fall some casual remark – simply by way of saying something and keeping the conversation going – to the effect that I wondered what Anatole was going to give us for dinner, she said that I was too material and ought not always to be thinking of food. Material, my elbow! As a matter of fact, I'm particularly spiritual.'

'Quite.'

'I don't see any harm in wondering what Anatole was going to give us for dinner. Do you?'

'Of course not. A mere ordinary tribute of respect to a great artist.'

'Exactly.'

'All the same –'

'Well?'

'I was only going to say that it seems a pity that the frail craft of love should come a stinker like this when a few manly words of contrition –'

He stared at me.

'You aren't suggesting that I should climb down?'

'It would be the fine, big thing, old egg.'

'I wouldn't dream of climbing down.'

'But, Tuppy –'

'No. I wouldn't do it.'

'But you love her, don't you?'

This touched the spot. He quivered noticeably, and his mouth twisted. Quite the tortured soul.

'I'm not saying I don't love the little blighter,' he said, obviously moved. 'I love her passionately. But that doesn't alter the fact that I consider that what she needs most in this world is a swift kick in the pants.'

A Wooster could scarcely pass this.

'Tuppy, old man!'

'It's no good saying "Tuppy, old man".'

'Well, I do say "Tuppy, old man". Your tone shocks me. One raises the eyebrows. Where is the fine, old, chivalrous spirit of the Glossops?'

'That's all right about the fine, old, chivalrous spirit of the Glossops. Where is the sweet, gentle, womanly spirit of the Angelas? Telling a fellow he was getting a double chin!'

'Did she do that?'

'She did.'

'Oh, well, girls will be girls. Forget it, Tuppy. Go to her and make it up.'

He shook his head.

'No. It is too late. Remarks have been passed about my tummy which it is impossible to overlook.'

'But, Tummy – Tuppy, I mean – be fair. You once told her her new hat made her look like a Pekingese.'

'It did make her look like a Pekingese. That was not vulgar abuse. It was sound, constructive criticism, with no motive behind it but the kindly desire to keep her from making an exhibition of herself in public. Wantonly to accuse a man of puffing when he goes up a flight of stairs is something very different.'

I began to see that the situation would require all my address and ingenuity. If the wedding bells were ever to ring out in the little church of Market Snodsbury, Bertram had plainly got to put in some shrewdish work. I had gathered, during my conversation with Aunt Dahlia, that there had been a certain amount of frank

speech between the two contracting parties, but I had
not realized till now that matters had gone so far.

The pathos of the thing gave me the pip. Tuppy had
admitted in so many words that love still animated the
Glossop bosom, and I was convinced that, even after all
that occurred, Angela had not ceased to love him. At the
moment, no doubt, she might be wishing that she could
hit him with a bottle, but deep down in her I was
prepared to bet that there still lingered all the old
affection and tenderness. Only injured pride was keeping
these two apart, and I felt that if Tuppy would make the
first move, all would be well.

I had another whack at it.

'She's broken-hearted about this rift, Tuppy.'

'How do you know? Have you seen her?'

'No, but I'll bet she is.'

'She doesn't look it.'

'Wearing the mask, no doubt. Jeeves does that when I
assert my authority.'

'She wrinkles her nose at me as if I were a drain that
had got out of order.'

'Merely the mask. I feel convinced she loves you
still, and that a kindly word from you is all that is
required.'

I could see that this had moved him. He plainly
wavered. He did a sort of twiddly on the turf with his
foot. And, when he spoke, one spotted the tremolo in
the voice:

'You really think that?'

'Absolutely.'

'H'm.'

'If you were to go to her –'

He shook his head.

'I can't do that. It would be fatal. Bing, instantly,
would go my prestige. I know girls. Grovel, and the best
of them get uppish.' He mused. 'The only way to work
the thing would be by tipping her off in some indirect

way that I am prepared to open negotiations. Should I sigh a bit when we meet, do you think?'

'She would think you were puffing.'

'That's true.'

I lit another cigarette and gave my mind to the matter. And first crack out of the box, as is so often the way with the Woosters, I got an idea. I remembered the counsel I had given Gussie in the matter of the sausages and ham.

'I've got it, Tuppy. There is one infallible method of indicating to a girl that you love her, and it works just as well when you've had a row and want to make it up. Don't eat any dinner tonight. You can see how impressive that would be. She knows how devoted you are to food.'

He started violently.

'I am not devoted to food!'

'No, no.'

'I am not devoted to food at all.'

'Quite. All I meant –'

'This rot about me being devoted to food,' said Tuppy warmly, 'has got to stop. I am young and healthy and have a good appetite, but that's not the same as being devoted to food. I admire Anatole as a master of his craft, and am always willing to consider anything he may put before me, but when you say I am devoted to food –'

'Quite, quite. All I meant was that if she sees you push away your dinner untasted, she will realize that your heart is aching, and will probably be the first to suggest blowing the all clear.'

Tuppy was frowning thoughtfully.

'Push my dinner away, eh?'

'Yes.'

'Push away a dinner cooked by Anatole?'

'Yes.'

'Push it away untasted?'

'Yes.'

'Let us get this straight. Tonight, at dinner, when the butler offers me a *ris de veau à la financière* or whatever it may be, hot from Anatole's hands, you wish me to push it away untasted?'

'Yes.'

He chewed his lip. One could sense the struggle going on within. And then suddenly a sort of glow came into his face. The old martyrs probably used to look like that.

'All right.'

'You'll do it?'

'I will.'

'Fine.'

'Of course, it will be agony.'

I pointed out the silver lining.

'Only for the moment. You could slip down tonight, after everyone is in bed, and raid the larder.'

He brightened.

'That's right. I could, couldn't I?'

'I expect there would be something cold there.'

'There is something cold there,' said Tuppy, with growing cheerfulness. 'A steak-and-kidney pie. We had it for lunch today. One of Anatole's ripest. The thing I admire about that man,' said Tuppy reverently, 'the thing that I admire so enormously about Anatole is that, though a Frenchman, he does not, like so many of these *chefs*, confine himself exclusively to French dishes, but is always willing and ready to weigh in with some good old simple English fare such as this steak-and-kidney pie to which I have alluded. A masterly pie, Bertie, and it wasn't more than half finished. It will do me nicely.'

'And at dinner you will push, as arranged?'

'Absolutely as arranged.'

'Fine.'

'It's an excellent idea. One of Jeeves's best. You can tell him from me, when you see him, that I'm much obliged.'

The cigarette fell from my fingers. It was as though somebody had slapped Bertram Wooster across the face with a wet dish-rag.

'You aren't suggesting that you think this scheme I have been sketching out is Jeeves's?'

'Of course it is. It's no good trying to kid me, Bertie. You wouldn't have thought of a wheeze like that in a million years.'

There was a pause. I drew myself up to my full height; then, seeing that he wasn't looking at me, lowered myself again.

'Come, Glossop,' I said coldly, 'we had better be going. It is time we were dressing for dinner.'

9

Tuppy's fatheaded words were still rankling in my bosom as I went up to my room. They continued rankling as I shed the form-fitting, and had not ceased to rankle when, clad in the old dressing-gown, I made my way along the corridor to the *salle de bain*.

It is not too much to say that I was piqued to the tonsils.

I mean to say, one does not court praise. The adulation of the multitude means very little to one. But, all the same, when one has taken the trouble to whack out a highly juicy scheme to benefit an in-the-soup friend in his hour of travail, it's pretty foul to find him giving the credit to one's personal attendant, particularly if that personal attendant is a man who goes about the place not packing mess jackets.

But after I had been splashing about in the porcelain for a bit, composure began to return. I have always found that in moments of heart-bowed-downness there is nothing that calms the bruised spirit like a good go at the soap and water. I don't say I actually sang in the tub, but there were times when it was a mere spin of the coin whether I would do so or not.

The spiritual anguish induced by that tactless speech had become noticeably lessened.

The discovery of a toy duck in the soap dish, presumably the property of some former juvenile visitor, contributed not a little to this new and happier frame of mind. What with one thing and another, I hadn't played with toy ducks in my bath for years, and I found the novel experience most invigorating. For the benefit of those interested, I may mention that if you shove the thing under the surface with the sponge and then let go, it shoots out of the water in a manner calculated to divert the most careworn. Ten minutes of this and I was enabled to return to the bedchamber much more the old merry Bertram.

Jeeves was there, laying out the dinner disguise. He greeted the young master with his customary suavity.

'Good evening, sir.'

I responded in the same affable key.

'Good evening, Jeeves.'

'I trust you had a pleasant drive, sir.'

'Very pleasant, thank you, Jeeves. Hand me a sock or two, will you?'

He did so, and I commenced to don.

'Well, Jeeves,' I said, reaching for the under-linen, 'here we are again at Brinkley Court in the county of Worcestershire.'

'Yes, sir.'

'A nice mess things seem to have gone and got themselves into in this rustic joint.'

'Yes, sir.'

'The rift between Tuppy Glossop and my cousin Angela would appear to be serious.'

'Yes, sir. Opinion in the servants' hall is inclined to take a grave view of the situation.'

'And the thought that springs to your mind, no doubt, is that I shall have my work cut out to fix things up?'

'Yes, sir.'

'You are wrong, Jeeves. I have the thing well in hand.'

'You surprise me, sir.'

'I thought I should. Yes, Jeeves, I pondered on the matter most of the way down here, and with the happiest results. I have just been in conference with Mr Glossop, and everything is taped out.'

'Indeed, sir? Might I inquire –'

594

'You know my methods, Jeeves. Apply them. Have you,' I asked, slipping into the shirt and starting to adjust the cravat, 'been gnawing on the thing at all?'

'Oh, yes, sir. I have always been much attached to Miss Angela, and I felt that it would afford me great pleasure were I to be able to be of service to her.'

'A laudable sentiment. But I suppose you drew blank?'

'No, sir. I was rewarded with an idea.'

'What was it?'

'It occurred to me that a reconciliation might be effected between Mr Glossop and Miss Angela by appealing to that instinct which prompts gentlemen in time of peril to hasten to the rescue of –'

I had to let go of the cravat in order to raise a hand. I was shocked.

'Don't tell me you were contemplating descending to that old he-saved-her-from-drowning gag? I am surprised, Jeeves. Surprised and pained. When I was discussing the matter with Aunt Dahlia on my arrival, she said in a sniffy sort of way that she supposed I was going to shove my Cousin Angela into the lake and push Tuppy in to haul her out, and I let her see pretty clearly that I considered the suggestion an insult to my intelligence. And now, if your words have the meaning I read into them, you are mooting precisely the same drivelling scheme. Really, Jeeves!'

'No, sir. Not that. But the thought did cross my mind, as I walked in the grounds and passed the building where the fire-bell hangs, that a sudden alarm of fire in the night might result in Mr Glossop endeavouring to assist Miss Angela to safety.'

I shivered.

'Rotten, Jeeves.'

'Well, sir –'

'No good. Not a bit like it.'

'I fancy, sir –'

595

'No, Jeeves. No more. Enough has been said. Let us drop the subj.'

I finished tying the tie in silence. My emotions were too deep for speech. I knew, of course, that this man had for the time being lost his grip, but I had never suspected that he had gone absolutely to pieces like this. Remembering some of the swift ones he had pulled in the past, I shrank with horror from the spectacle of his present ineptitude. Or is it ineptness? I mean this frightful disposition of his to stick straws in his hair and talk like a perfect ass. It was the old, old story, I supposed. A man's brain whizzes along for years exceeding the speed limit, and then something suddenly goes wrong with the steering-gear and it skids and comes a smeller in the ditch.

'A bit elaborate,' I said, trying to put the thing in as kindly a light as possible. 'Your old failing. You can see that it's a bit elaborate?'

'Possibly the plan I suggested might be considered open to that criticism, sir, but *faute de mieux* –'

'I don't get you, Jeeves.'

'A French expression, sir, signifying "for want of anything better".'

A moment before, I had been feeling for this wreck of a once fine thinker nothing but a gentle pity. These words jarred the Wooster pride, inducing asperity.

'I understand perfectly well what *faute de mieux* means, Jeeves. I did not recently spend two months among our Gallic neighbours for nothing. Besides, I remember that one from school. What caused my bewilderment was that you should be employing the expression, well knowing that there is no bally *faute de mieux* about it at all. Where do you get that *faute-de-mieux* stuff? Didn't I tell you I had everything taped out?'

'Yes, sir, but –'

'What do you mean – but?'

'Well, sir – '

'Push on, Jeeves. I am ready, even anxious, to hear your views.'

'Well, sir, if I may take the liberty of reminding you of it, your plans in the past have not always been uniformly successful.'

There was a silence – rather a throbbing one – during which I put on my waistcoat in a marked manner. Not till I had got the buckle at the back satisfactorily adjusted did I speak.

'It is true, Jeeves,' I said formally, 'that once or twice in the past I may have missed the bus. This, however, I attribute purely to bad luck.'

'Indeed, sir?'

'On the present occasion I shall not fail, and I'll tell you why I shall not fail. Because my scheme is rooted in human nature.'

'Indeed, sir?'

'It is simple. Not elaborate. And, furthermore, based on the psychology of the individual.'

'Indeed, sir?'

'Jeeves,' I said, 'don't keep saying "Indeed, sir?" No doubt nothing is further from your mind than to convey such a suggestion, but you have a way of stressing the "in" and then coming down with a thud on the "deed" which makes it virtually tantamount to "Oh, yeah?" Correct this, Jeeves.'

'Very good, sir.'

'I tell you I have everything nicely lined up. Would you care to hear what steps I have taken?'

'Very much, sir.'

'Then listen. Tonight at dinner I have recommended Tuppy to lay off the food.'

'Sir?'

'Tut, Jeeves, surely you can follow the idea, even though it is one that would never have occurred to yourself. Have you forgotten that telegram I sent to

Gussie Fink-Nottle, steering him away from the sausages and ham? This is the same thing. Pushing the food away untasted is a universally recognized sign of love. It cannot fail to bring home the gravy. You must see that?'

'Well, sir –'

I frowned.

'I don't want to seem always to be criticizing your methods of voice production, Jeeves,' I said, 'but I must inform you that that "Well, sir" of yours is in many respects fully as unpleasant as your "Indeed, sir?" Like the latter, it seems to be tinged with a definite scepticism. It suggests a lack of faith in my vision. The impression I retain after hearing you shoot it at me a couple of times is that you consider me to be talking through the back of my neck, and that only a feudal sense of what is fitting restrains you from substituting for it the words "Says you!"'

'Oh, no, sir.'

'Well, that's what it sounds like. Why don't you think this scheme will work?'

'I fear Miss Angela will merely attribute Mr Glossop's abstinence to indigestion, sir.'

I hadn't thought of that, and I must confess it shook me for a moment. Then I recovered myself. I saw what was at the bottom of all this. Mortified by the consciousness of his own ineptness – or ineptitude – the fellow was simply trying to hamper and obstruct. I decided to knock the stuffing out of him without further preamble.

'Oh?' I said. 'You do, do you? Well, be that as it may, it doesn't alter the fact that you've put out the wrong coat. Be so good, Jeeves,' I said, indicating with a gesture the gent's ordinary dinner jacket, or *smoking*, as we call it on the Côte d'Azur, which was suspended from the hanger on the knob of the wardrobe, 'as to shove that bally black thing in the cupboard and bring out my white mess jacket with the brass buttons.'

He looked at me in a meaning manner. And when I say a meaning manner, I mean there was a respectful but at the same time uppish glint in his eye and a sort of muscular spasm flickered across his face which wasn't quite a quiet smile and yet wasn't quite not a quiet smile. Also the soft cough.

'I regret to say, sir, that I inadvertently omitted to pack the garment to which you refer.'

The vision of that parcel in the hall seemed to rise before my eyes, and I exchanged a merry wink with it. I may even have hummed a bar or two. I'm not quite sure.

'I know you did, Jeeves,' I said, laughing down from lazy eyelids and flicking a speck of dust from the irreproachable Mechlin lace at my wrists. 'But I didn't. You will find it on a chair in the hall in a brown-paper parcel.'

The information that his low manoeuvres had been rendered null and void and that the thing was on the strength after all, must have been the nastiest of jars, but there was no play of expression on his finely chiselled to indicate it. There very seldom is on Jeeves's f-c. In moments of discomfort, as I had told Tuppy, he wears a mask, preserving throughout the quiet stolidity of a stuffed moose.

'You might just slide down and fetch it, will you?'

'Very good, sir.'

'Right ho, Jeeves.'

And presently I was sauntering towards the drawing-room with the good old j. nestling snugly abaft the shoulder blades.

Aunt Dahlia was in the drawing-room. She glanced up at my entrance.

'Hullo, eyesore,' she said. 'What do you think you're made up as?'

I did not get the purport.

'The jacket, you mean?' I queried, groping.

'I do. You look like one of the chorus of male guests at

Abernethy Towers in Act 2 of a touring musical
comedy.'

'You do not admire this jacket?'

'I do not.'

'You did at Cannes.'

'Well, this isn't Cannes.'

'But, dash it –'

'Oh, never mind. Let it go. If you want to give my
butler a laugh, what does it matter? What does anything
matter now?'

There was a death-where-is-thy-sting-fulness about
her manner which I found distasteful. It isn't often that I
score off Jeeves in the devastating fashion just described,
and when I do I like to see happy, smiling faces about
me.

'Tails up, Aunt Dahlia,' I urged buoyantly.

'Tails up be dashed,' was her sombre response. 'I've
just been talking to Tom.'

'Telling him?'

'No, listening to him. I haven't had the nerve to tell
him yet.'

'Is he still upset about that income-tax money?'

'Upset is right. He says that Civilization is in the
melting-pot and that all thinking men can read the
writing on the wall.'

'What wall?'

'Old Testament, ass. Belshazzar's feast.'

'Oh, that, yes. I've often wondered how that gag was
worked. With mirrors, I expect.'

'I wish I could use mirrors to break it to Tom about
this baccarat business.'

I had a word of comfort to offer here. I had been
turning the thing over in my mind since our last
meeting, and I thought I saw where she had got twisted.
Where she made her error, it seemed to me, was in
feeling she had got to tell Uncle Tom. To my way
of thinking, the matter was one on which it would

600

be better to continue to exercise a quiet reserve.

'I don't see why you need mention that you lost that money at baccarat.'

'What do you suggest, then? Letting *Milady's Boudoir* join Civilization in the melting-pot. Because that is what it will infallibly do unless I get a cheque by next week. The printers have been showing a nasty spirit for months.'

'You don't follow. Listen. It's an understood thing, I take it, that Uncle Tom foots the *Boudoir* bills. If the bally sheet has been turning the corner for two years, he must have got used to forking out by this time. Well, simply ask him for the money to pay the printers.'

'I did. Just before I went to Cannes.'

'Wouldn't he give it to you?'

'Certainly he gave it to me. He brassed up like an officer and a gentleman. That was the money I lost at baccarat.'

'Oh? I didn't know that.'

'There isn't much you do know.'

A nephew's love made me overlook the slur.

'Tut!' I said.

'What did you say?'

'I said "Tut!"'

'Say it once again, and I'll biff you where you stand. I've enough to endure without being tutted at.'

'Quite.'

'Any tutting that's required, I'll attend to myself. And the same applies to clicking the tongue, if you were thinking of doing that.'

'Far from it.'

'Good.'

I stood awhile in thought. I was concerned to the core. My heart, if you remember, had already bled once for Aunt Dahlia this evening. It now bled again. I knew how deeply attached she was to this paper of hers. Seeing it go down the drain would be for her like

watching a loved child sink for the third time in some
pond or mere.

And there was no question that, unless carefully
prepared for the touch, Uncle Tom would see a hundred
*Milady's Boudoir*s go phut rather than take the rap.

Then I saw how the thing could be handled. This
aunt, I perceived, must fall into line with my other
clients. Tuppy Glossop was knocking off dinner to melt
Angela. Gussie Fink-Nottle was knocking off dinner to
impress the Bassett. Aunt Dahlia must knock off dinner
to soften Uncle Tom. For the beauty of this scheme of
mine was that there was no limit to the number of
entrants. Come one, come all, the more the merrier, and
satisfaction guaranteed in every case.

'I've got it,' I said. 'There is only one course to pursue.
Eat less meat.'

She looked at me in a pleading sort of way. I wouldn't
swear that her eyes were wet with unshed tears, but I
rather think they were. Certainly she clasped her hands
in piteous appeal.

'Must you drivel, Bertie? Won't you stop it just this
once? Just for tonight, to please Aunt Dahlia.'

'I'm not drivelling.'

'I dare say that to a man of your high standards it
doesn't come under the head of drivel, but –'

I saw what had happened. I hadn't made myself quite
clear.

'It's all right,' I said. 'Have no misgivings. This is the
real Tabasco. When I said "Eat less meat", what I meant
was that you must refuse your oats at dinner tonight.
Just sit there, looking blistered, and wave away each
course as it comes with a weary gesture of resignation.
You see what will happen. Uncle Tom will notice your
loss of appetite, and I am prepared to bet that at the
conclusion of the meal he will come to you and say
"Dahlia, darling" – I take it he calls you "Dahlia" –
"Dahlia darling," he will say, "I noticed at dinner

tonight that you were a bit off your feed. Is anything the matter, Dahlia, darling?" "Why, yes, Tom, darling," you will reply. "It is kind of you to ask, darling. The fact is, darling, I am terribly worried." "My darling," he will say –'

Aunt Dahlia interrupted at this point to observe that these Traverses seemed to be a pretty soppy couple of blighters, to judge by their dialogue. She also wished to know when I was going to get to the point.

I gave her a look.

'"My darling," he will say tenderly, "is there anything I can do?" To which your reply will be that there jolly well is – viz. reach for his cheque-book and start writing.'

I was watching her closely as I spoke, and was pleased to note respect suddenly dawn in her eyes.

'But, Bertie, this is positively bright.'

'I told you Jeeves wasn't the only fellow with brain.'

'I believe it would work.'

'It's bound to work. I've recommended it to Tuppy.'

'Young Glossop?'

'In order to soften Angela.'

'Splendid!'

'And to Gussie Fink-Nottle, who wants to make a hit with the Bassett.'

'Well, well, well! What a busy little brain it is.'

'Always working, Aunt Dahlia, always working.'

'You're not the chump I took you for, Bertie.'

'When did you ever take me for a chump?'

'Oh, some time last summer. I forget what gave me the idea. Yes, Bertie, this scheme is bright. I suppose, as a matter of fact, Jeeves suggested it?'

'Jeeves did not suggest it. I resent these implications. Jeeves had nothing to do with it whatsoever.'

'Well, all right, no need to get excited about it. Yes, I think it will work. Tom's devoted to me.'

'Who wouldn't be?'

'I'll do it.'

And then the rest of the party trickled in, and we toddled down to dinner.

Conditions being as they were at Brinkley Court – I mean to say, the place being loaded down above the Plimsoll mark with aching hearts and standing room only as regarded tortured souls – I hadn't expected the evening meal to be particularly effervescent. Nor was it. Silent. Sombre. The whole thing more than a bit like Christmas dinner on Devil's Island.

I was glad when it was over.

What with having, on top of her other troubles, to rein herself back from the trough, Aunt Dahlia was a total loss as far as anything in the shape of brilliant badinage was concerned. The fact that he was fifty quid in the red and expecting Civilization to take a toss at any moment had caused Uncle Tom, who always looked a bit like a pterodactyl with a secret sorrow, to take on a deeper melancholy. The Bassett was a silent bread crumbler. Angela might have been hewn from the living rock. Tuppy had the air of a condemned murderer refusing to make the usual hearty breakfast before tooling off to the execution shed.

And as for Gussie Fink-Nottle, many an experienced undertaker would have been deceived by his appearance and started embalming him on sight.

This was the first glimpse I had had of Gussie since we parted at my flat, and I must say his demeanour disappointed me. I had been expecting something a great deal more sparkling.

At my flat, on the occasion alluded to, he had, if you recall, practically given me a signed guarantee that all he needed to touch him off was a rural setting. Yet in his aspect now I could detect no indication whatsoever that he was about to round into mid-season form. He still looked like a cat in an adage, and it did not take me long to realize that my very first act on escaping from this morgue must be to draw him aside and give him a pep talk.

If ever a chap wanted the clarion note, it looked as if it was this Fink-Nottle.

In the general exodus of mourners, however, I lost sight of him, and, owing to the fact that Aunt Dahlia roped me in for a game of backgammon, it was not immediately that I was able to institute a search. But after we had been playing for a while, the butler came in and asked her if she would speak to Anatole, so I managed to get away. And some ten minutes later, having failed to find scent in the house I started to throw out the drag-net through the grounds, and flushed him in the rose garden.

He was smelling a rose at the moment in a limp sort of way, but removed the beak as I approached.

'Well, Gussie,' I said.

I had beamed genially upon him as I spoke, such being my customary policy on meeting an old pal; but instead of beaming back genially, he gave me a most unpleasant look. His attitude perplexed me. It was as if he were not glad to see Bertram. For a moment he stood letting this unpleasant look play upon me, as it were, and then he spoke.

'You and your "Well, Gussie"!'

He said this between clenched teeth, always an unmatey thing to do, and I found myself more fogged than ever.

'How do you mean – me and my "Well, Gussie"?'

'I like your nerve, coming bounding about the place, saying "Well, Gussie". That's about all the "Well, Gussie" I shall require from you, Wooster. And it's no good looking like that. You know what I mean. That damned prize-giving! It was a dastardly act to crawl out as you did and shove it off on to me. I will not mince my words. It was the act of a hound and a stinker.'

Now, though, as I have shown, I had devoted most of

the time on the journey down to meditating upon the case of Angela and Tuppy, I had not neglected to give a thought or two to what I was going to say when I encountered Gussie. I had foreseen that there might be some little temporary unpleasantness when we met, and when a difficult interview is in the offing Bertram Wooster likes to have his story ready.

So now I was able to reply with a manly, disarming frankness. The sudden introduction of the topic had given me a bit of a jolt, it is true, for in the stress of recent happenings I had rather let that prize-giving business slide to the back of my mind; but I had speedily recovered and, as I say, was able to reply with a manly d.f.

'But, my dear chap,' I said, 'I took it for granted that you would understand that that was all part of my schemes.'

He said something about my schemes which I did not catch.

'Absolutely. "Crawling out" is entirely the wrong way to put it. You don't suppose I didn't want to distribute those prizes, do you? Left to myself, there is nothing I would find a greater treat. But I saw that the square, generous thing to do was to step aside and let you take it on, so I did so. I felt that your need was greater than mine. You don't mean to say you aren't looking forward to it?'

He uttered a coarse expression which I wouldn't have thought he would have known. It just shows that you can bury yourself in the country and still somehow acquire a vocabulary. No doubt one picks up things from the neigbours – the vicar, the local doctor, the man who brings the milk, and so on.

'But, dash it,' I said, 'can't you see what this is going to do for you? It will send your stock up with a jump. There you will be, up on that platform, a romantic, impressive figure, the star of the whole proceedings, the what-d'you-call-it of all eyes. Madeline Bassett will be all over you. She will see you in a totally new light.'

'She will, will she?'

'Certainly she will. Augustus Fink-Nottle, the newts' friend, she knows. She is acquainted with Augustus Fink-Nottle, the dogs' chiropodist. But Augustus Fink-Nottle, the orator – that'll knock her sideways, or I know nothing of the female heart. Girls go potty over a public man. If ever anyone did anyone else a kindness, it was I when I gave this extraordinarily attractive assignment to you.'

He seemed impressed by my eloquence. Couldn't have helped himself, of course. The fire faded from behind his horn-rimmed spectacles, and in its place appeared the old fishlike goggle.

''Myes,' he said meditatively. 'Have you ever made a speech, Bertie?'

'Dozens of times. It's pie. Nothing to it. Why, I once addressed a girls' school.'

'You weren't nervous?'

'Not a bit.'

'How did you go?'

'They hung on my lips. I held them in the hollow of my hand.'

'They didn't throw eggs, or anything?'

'Not a thing.'

He expelled a deep breath, and for a space stood staring in silence at a passing slug.

'Well,' he said, at length, 'it may be all right. Possibly I am letting the thing prey on my mind too much. I may be wrong in supposing it the fate that is worse than death. But I'll tell you this much: The prospect of that prize-giving on the thirty-first of this month has been turning my existence into a nightmare. I haven't been able to sleep or think or eat . . . By the way, that reminds me. You never explained that cipher telegram of yours about the sausages and ham.'

'It wasn't a cipher telegram. I wanted you to go light on the food, so that she would realize you were in love.'

He laughed hollowly.

'I see. Well, I've been doing that, all right.'

'Yes, I was noticing at dinner. Splendid.'

'I don't see what's splendid about it. It's not going to get me anywhere. I shall never be able to ask her to marry me. I couldn't find the nerve to do that if I lived on wafer biscuits for the rest of my life.'

'But, dash it, Gussie. In these romantic surroundings. I should have thought the whispering trees alone –'

'I don't care what you would have thought. I can't do it.'

'Oh, come!'

'I can't. She seems so aloof, so remote.'

'She doesn't.'

'Yes, she does. Especially when you see her sideways. Have you seen her sideways, Bertie? That cold, pure profile. It just takes all the heart out of one.'

'It doesn't.'

'I tell you it does. I catch sight of it, and the words freeze on my lips.'

He spoke with a sort of dull despair, and so manifest was his lack of ginger and the spirit that wins to success that for an instant, I confess, I felt a bit stymied. It seemed hopeless to go on trying to steam up such a human jellyfish. Then I saw the way. With that extraordinary quickness of mine, I realized exactl what must be done if this Fink-Nottle was to be enabled to push his nose past the judges' box.

'She must be softened up,' I said.

'Be what?'

'Softened up. Sweetened. Worked on. Preliminary spadework must be put in. Here, Gussie, is the procedure I propose to adopt: I shall now return to the house and lug this Bassett out for a stroll. I shall talk to her of hearts that yearn, intimating that there is one

actually on the premises. I shall pitch in strong, sparing
no effort. You, meanwhile, will lurk on the outskirts,
and in about a quarter of an hour you will come along
and carry on from there. By that time, her emotions
having been stirred, you ought to be able to do the rest
on your head. It will be like leaping on to a moving bus.'

I remember when I was a kid at school having to
learn a poem of sorts about a fellow named
Pig-something – a sculptor he would have been, no
doubt – who made a statue of a girl, and what should
happen one morning but that the bally thing suddenly
came to life. A pretty nasty shock for the chap, of
course, but the point I'm working round to is that there
were a couple of lines that went, if I remember correctly:

> She starts. She moves. She seems to feel
> The stir of life along her keel.

And what I'm driving at is that you couldn't get a better
description of what happened to Gussie as I spoke these
heartening words. His brow cleared, his eyes brightened,
he lost that fishy look, and he gazed at the slug, which
was still on the long, long trail, with something
approaching bonhomie. A marked improvement.

'I see what you mean. You will sort of pave the way,
as it were.'

'That's right. Spadework.'

'It's a terrific idea, Bertie. It will make all the
difference.'

'Quite. But don't forget that after that it will be up to
you. You will have to haul up your slacks and give her
the old oil, or my efforts will have been in vain.'

Something of his former Gawd-help-us-ness seemed
to return to him. He gasped a bit.

'That's true. What the dickens shall I say?'

I restrained my impatience with an effort. The man
had been at school with me.

'Dash it, there are hundreds of things you can say. Talk about the sunset.'

'The sunset?'

'Certainly. Half the married men you meet began by talking about the sunset.'

'But what can I say about the sunset?'

'Well, Jeeves got off a good one the other day. I met him airing the dog in the park one evening, and he said, "Now fades the glimmering landscape on the sight, sir, and all the air a solemn stillness holds." You might use that.'

'What sort of landscape?'

'Glimmering. *G* for "gastritis", *l* for "lizard" –'

'Oh, glimmering? Yes, that's not bad. Glimmering landscape . . . solemn stillness . . . Yes, I call that pretty good.'

'You could then say that you have often thought that the stars are God's daisy chain.'

'But I haven't.'

'I dare say not. But she has. Hand her that one, and I don't see how she can help feeling that you're a twin soul.'

'God's daisy chain?'

'God's daisy chain. And then you go on about how twilight always makes you sad. I know you're going to say it doesn't, but on this occasion it has jolly well got to.'

'Why?'

'That's just what she will ask, and you will then have got her going. Because you will reply that it is because yours is such a lonely life. It wouldn't be a bad idea to give her a brief description of a typical home evening at your Lincolnshire residence, showing how you pace the meadows with a heavy tread.'

'I generally sit indoors and listen to the wireless.'

'No, you don't. You pace the meadows with a heavy tread, wishing that you had someone to love you. And then you speak of the day when she came into your life.'

'Like a fairy princess.'

'Absolutely,' I said with approval. I hadn't expected such a hot one from such a quarter. 'Like a fairy princess. Nice work, Gussie.'

'And then?'

'Well, after that it's easy. You say you have something you want to say to her, and then you snap into it. I don't see how it can fail. If I were you, I should do it in this rose garden. It is well established that there is no sounder move than to steer the adored object into rose gardens in the gloaming. And you had better have a couple of quick ones first.'

'Quick ones?'

'Snifters.'

'Drinks, do you mean? But I don't drink.'

'What?'

'I've never touched a drop in my life.'

This made me a bit dubious, I must confess. On these occasions it is pretty generally conceded that a moderate skinful is of the essence.

However, if the facts were as he had stated, I supposed there was nothing to be done about it.

'Well, you'll have to make out as best you can on ginger pop.'

'I always drink orange juice.'

'Orange juice, then. Tell me, Gussie, to settle a bet, do you really like that muck?'

'Very much.'

'Then there is no more to be said. Now, let's just have a run through, to see that you've got the lay-out straight. Start off with the glimmering landscape.'

'Stars God's daisy chain.'

'Twilight makes you feel sad.'

'Because mine lonely life.'

'Describe life.'

'Talk about the day I met her.'

'Add fairy-princess gag. Say there's something you want to say to her. Heave a couple of sighs. Grab her hand. And give her the works. Right.'

And confident that he had grasped the scenario and that everything might now be expected to proceed through the proper channels, I picked up the feet and hastened back to the house.

It was not until I had reached the drawing-room and was enabled to take a square look at the Bassett that I found the debonair gaiety with which I had embarked on this affair beginning to wane a trifle. Beholding her at close range like this, I suddenly became cognizant of what I was in for. The thought of strolling with this rummy specimen undeniably gave me a most unpleasant sinking feeling. I could not but remember how often, when in her company at Cannes, I had gazed dumbly at her, wishing that some kindly motorist in a racing car would ease the situation by coming along and ramming her amidships. As I have already made abundantly clear, this girl was not one of my most congenial buddies.

However, a Wooster's word is his bond. Woosters may quail, but they do not edge out. Only the keenest ear could have detected the tremor in the voice as I asked her if she would care to come out for half an hour.

'Lovely evening,' I said.

'Yes, lovely, isn't it?'

'Lovely. Reminds me of Cannes.'

'How lovely the evenings were there.'

'Lovely,' I said.

'Lovely,' said the Bassett.

'Lovely,' I agreed.

That completed the weather and news bulletin for the French Riviera. Another minute, and we were out in the great open spaces, she cooing a bit about the scenery, and self replying, 'Oh, rather, quite,' and wondering how best to approach the matter in hand.

10

How different it all would have been, I could not but
reflect, if this girl had been the sort of girl one chirrups
cheerily to over the telephone and takes for spins in the
old two-seater. In that case, I would simply have said,
'Listen,' and she would have said, 'What?' and I would
have said, 'You know Gussie Fink-Nottle,' and she
would have said, 'Yes,' and I would have said, 'He loves
you,' and she would have said either, 'What, that mutt?
Well, thank heaven for one good laugh today!' or else, in
more passionate vein, 'Hot dog! Tell me more.'

I mean to say, in either event the whole thing over
and done with in under a minute.

But with the Bassett something less snappy and a
good deal more glutinous was obviously indicated. What
with all this daylight-saving stuff, we had hit the great
open spaces at a moment when the twilight had not yet
begun to cheese it in favour of the shades of night. There
was a fag-end of sunset still functioning. Stars were
beginning to peep out, bats were fooling round, the
garden was full of the aroma of those niffy white flowers
which only start to put in their heavy work at the end of
the day – in short, the glimmering landscape was fading
on the sight and all the air held a solemn stillness, and it
was plain that this was having the worst effect on her.
Her eyes were enlarged, and her whole map a good deal
too suggestive of the soul's awakening for comfort.

Her aspect was that of a girl who was expecting
something fairly fruity from Bertram.

In these circs, conversation inevitably flagged a bit. I
am never at my best when the situation seems to call for

a certain soupiness, and I've heard other members of the Drones say the same thing about themselves. I remember Pongo Twistleton telling me that he was out in a gondola with a girl by moonlight once, and the only time he spoke was to tell her that old story about the chap who was so good at swimming that they made him a traffic cop in Venice.

Fell rather flat, he assured me, and it wasn't much later when the girl said she thought it was getting a little chilly and how about pushing back to the hotel.

So now, as I say, the talk rather hung fire. It had been all very well for me to promise Gussie that I would cut loose to this girl about aching hearts, but you want a cue for that sort of thing. And when, toddling along, we reached the edge of the lake and she finally spoke, conceive my chagrin when I discovered that what she was talking about was stars.

Not a bit of good to me.

'Oh, look,' she said. She was a confirmed Oh-looker. I had noticed this at Cannes, where she had drawn my attention in this manner on various occasions to such diverse objects as a French actress, a Provençal filling station, the sunset over the Estorels, Michael Arlen, a man selling coloured spectacles, the deep velvet blue of the Mediterranean, and the late Mayor of New York in a striped one-piece bathing suit. 'Oh, look at that sweet little star up there all by itself.'

I saw the one she meant, a little chap operating in a detached sort of way above a spinney.

'Yes,' I said.

'I wonder if it feels lonely.'

'Oh, I shouldn't think so.'

'A fairy must have been crying.'

'Eh?'

'Don't you remember? "Every time a fairy sheds a tear, a wee bit star is born in the Milky Way." Have you ever thought that, Mr Wooster?'

I never had. Most improbable, I considered, and it didn't seem to me to check up with her statement that the stars were God's daisy chain. I mean, you can't have it both ways.

However, I was in no mood to dissect and criticize. I saw that I had been wrong in supposing that the stars were not germane to the issue. Quite a decent cue they had provided, and I leaped on it promptly:

'Talking of shedding tears – '

But she was now on the subject of rabbits, several of which were messing about in the park to our right.

'Oh, look. The little bunnies!'

'Talking of shedding tears – '

'Don't you love this time of the evening, Mr Wooster, when the sun has gone to bed and all the bunnies come out to have their little suppers? When I was a child, I used to think that rabbits were gnomes, and that if I held my breath and stayed quite still, I should see the fairy queen.'

Indicating with a reserved gesture that this was just the sort of loony thing I should have expected her to think as a child, I returned to the point.

'Talking of shedding tears,' I said firmly, 'it may interest you to know that there is an aching heart in Brinkley Court.'

This held her. She cheesed the rabbit theme. Her face, which had been aglow with what I supposed was a pretty animation, clouded. She unshipped a sigh that sounded like the wind going out of a rubber duck.

'Ah, yes. Life is very sad, isn't it?'

'It is for some people. This aching heart, for instance.'

'Those wistful eyes of hers! Drenched irises. And they used to dance like elves of delight. And all through a foolish misunderstanding about a shark. What a tragedy misunderstandings are. That pretty romance broken and over just because Mr Glossop would insist that it was a flatfish.'

615

I saw that she had got the wires crossed.

'I'm not talking about Angela.'

'But her heart is aching.'

'I know it's aching. But so is somebody else's.'

She looked at me, perplexed.

'Somebody's else? Mr Glossop's, you mean?'

'No, I don't.'

'Mrs Travers's?'

The exquisite code of politeness of the Woosters prevented me clipping her one on the ear-hole, but I would have given a shilling to be able to do it. There seemed to me something deliberately fatheaded in the way she persisted in missing the gist.

'No, not Aunt Dahlia's, either.'

'I'm sure she is dreadfully upset.'

'Quite. But this heart I'm talking about isn't aching because of Tuppy's row with Angela. It's aching for a different reason altogether. I mean to say – dash it, you know why hearts ache!'

She seemed to shimmy a bit. Her voice, when she spoke, was whispery:

'You mean – for love?'

'Absolutely. Right on the bull's-eye. For love.'

'Oh, Mr Wooster!'

'I take it you believe in love at first sight?'

'I do, indeed.'

'Well, that's what happened to this aching heart. It fell in love at first sight, and ever since it's been eating itself out, as I believe the expression is.'

There was a silence. She had turned away and was watching a duck out on the lake. It was tucking into weeds, a thing I've never been able to understand anyone wanting to do. Though I suppose, if you face it squarely, they're no worse than spinach. She stood drinking it in for a bit, and then it suddenly stood on its head and disappeared, and this seemed to break the spell.

'Oh, Mr Wooster!' she said again, and from the tone

of her voice, I could see that I had got her
going.

'For you, I mean to say,' I proceeded, starting to put in
the fancy touches. I dare say you have noticed on these
occasions that the difficulty is to plant the main idea, to
get the general outline of the thing well fixed. The rest is
mere detail work. I don't say I became glib at this
juncture, but I certainly became a dashed sight glibber
than I had been.

'It's having the dickens of a time. Can't eat, can't
sleep – all for love of you. And what makes it all so
particularly rotten is that it – this aching heart – can't
bring itself up to the scratch and tell you the position of
affairs, because your profile has gone and given it cold
feet. Just as it is about to speak, it catches sight of you
sideways, and words fail it. Silly, of course, but there it
is.'

I heard her give a gulp, and I saw that her eyes had
become moistish. Drenched irises, if you care to put it
that way.

'Lend you a handkerchief?'

'No, thank you. I'm quite all right.'

It was more than I could say for myself. My efforts
had left me weak. I don't know if you suffer in the same
way, but with me the act of talking anything in the
nature of real mashed potatoes always induces a sort of
prickly sensation and a hideous feeling of shame,
together with a marked starting of the pores.

I remember at my Aunt Agatha's place in
Hertfordshire once being put on the spot and forced to
enact the role of King Edward III saying good-bye to that
girl of his, Fair Rosamund, at some sort of pageant in aid
of the Distressed Daughters of the Clergy. It involved
some rather warmish medieval dialogue, I recall, racy of
the days when they called a spade a spade, and by the
time the whistle blew, I'll bet no Daughter of the Clergy
was half as distressed as I was. Not a dry stitch.

My reaction now was very similar. It was a highly
liquid Bertram who, hearing his *vis-à-vis* give a couple of
hiccups and start to speak, bent an attentive ear.

'Please don't say any more, Mr Wooster.'

Well, I wasn't going to, of course.

'I understand.'

I was glad to hear this.

'Yes, I understand. I won't be so silly as to pretend not
to know what you mean. I suspected this at Cannes,
when you used to stand and stare at me without
speaking a word, but with whole volumes in your
eyes.'

If Angela's shark had bitten me in the leg, I couldn't
have leaped more convulsively. So tensely had I been
concentrating on Gussie's interests that it hadn't so
much as crossed my mind that another and an
unfortunate construction could be placed on those words
of mine. The persp., already bedewing my brow, became
a regular Niagara.

My whole fate hung upon a woman's word. I mean to
say, I couldn't back out. If a girl thinks a man is
proposing to her, and on that understanding books him
up, he can't explain to her that she has got hold of
entirely the wrong end of the stick and that he hadn't
the smallest intention of suggesting anything of the
kind. He must simply let it ride. And the thought of
being engaged to a girl who talked openly about fairies
being born because stars blew their noses, or whatever it
was, frankly appalled me.

She was carrying on with her remarks, and as I
listened I clenched my fists till I shouldn't wonder if the
knuckles didn't stand out white under the strain. It
seemed as if she would never get to the nub.

'Yes, all through those days at Cannes I could see
what you were trying to say. A girl always knows. And
then you followed me down here, and there was that
same dumb, yearning look in your eyes when we met

this evening. And then you were so insistent that I
should come out and walk with you in the twilight. And
now you stammer out those halting words. No, this does
not come as a surprise. But I am sorry – '

The word was like one of Jeeves's pick-me-ups. Just
as if a glassful of meat sauce, red pepper, and the yolk of
an egg – though, as I say, I am convinced that these are
not the sole ingredients – had been shot into me, I
expanded like some lovely flower blossoming in the
sunshine. It was all right, after all. My guardian angel
had not been asleep at the switch.

' – but I am afraid it is impossible.'

She paused.

'Impossible,' she repeated.

I had been so busy feeling saved from the scaffold that
I didn't get on to it for a moment that an early reply was
desired.

'Oh, right ho,' I said hastily.

'I'm sorry.'

'Quite all right.'

'Sorrier than I can say.'

'Don't give it another thought.'

'We can still be friends.'

'Oh, rather.'

'Then shall we just say no more about it; keep what
has happened as a tender little secret between
ourselves?'

'Absolutely.'

'We will. Like something lovely and fragrant laid
away in lavender.'

'In lavender – right.'

There was a longish pause. She was gazing at me in a
divinely pitying sort of way, much as if I had been a
snail she had happened accidentally to bring her short
French vamp down on, and I longed to tell her that it
was all right, and that Bertram, so far from being the
victim of despair, had never felt fizzier in his life. But, of

course, one can't do that sort of thing. I simply said
nothing, and stood there looking brave.

'I wish I could,' she murmured.

'Could?' I said, for my attensh had been wandering.

'Feel towards you as you would like me to feel.'

'Oh, ah.'

'But I can't. I'm sorry.'

'Absolutely O.K. Faults on both sides, no doubt.'

'Because I am fond of you, Mr – no, I think I must call
you Bertie. May I?'

'Oh, rather.'

'Because we are real friends.'

'Quite.'

'I do like you, Bertie. And if things were different – I
wonder –'

'Eh?'

'After all, we are real friends . . . We have this
common memory . . . You have a right to know . . . I
don't want you to think – Life is such a muddle, isn't it?'

To many men, no doubt, these broken utterances
would have appeared mere drooling and would have
been dismissed as such. But the Woosters are
quicker-witted than the ordinary and can read between
the lines. I suddenly divined what it was that she was
trying to get off the chest.

'You mean there's someone else?'

She nodded.

'You're in love with some other bloke?'

She nodded.

'Engaged, what?'

This time she shook the pumpkin.

'No, not engaged.'

Well, that was something, of course. Nevertheless,
from the way she spoke, it certainly looked as if poor old
Gussie might as well scratch his name off the entry list,
and I didn't at all like the prospect of having to break the
bad news to him. I had studied the man closely, and it

was my conviction that this would about be his finish.

Gussie, you see, wasn't like some of my pals – the name of Bingo Little is one that springs to the lips – who, if turned down by a girl, would simply say, 'Well, bung-ho!' and toddle off quite happily to find another. He was so manifestly a bird who, having failed to score in the first chukker, would turn the thing up and spend the rest of his life brooding over his newts and growing long grey whiskers, like one of those chaps you read about in novels, who live in the great white house you can just see over there through the trees and shut themselves off from the world and have pained faces.

'I'm afraid he doesn't care for me in that way. At least, he has said nothing. You understand that I am only telling you this because – '

'Oh, rather.'

'It's odd that you should have asked me if I believed in love at first sight.' She half-closed her eyes. ' "Who ever loved that loved not at first sight?" ' she said in a rummy voice that brought back to me – I don't know why – the picture of my Aunt Agatha, as Boadicea, reciting at that pageant I was speaking of. 'It's a silly little story. I was staying with some friends in the country, and I had gone for a walk with my dog, and the poor wee mite got a nasty thorn in his little foot and I didn't know what to do. And then suddenly this man came along – '

Harking back once again to that pageant, in sketching out for you my emotions on that occasion, I showed you only the darker side of the picture. There was, I should now mention, a splendid aftermath when, having climbed out of my suit of chain mail and sneaked off to the local pub, I entered the saloon bar and requested mine host to start pouring. A moment later, a tankard of their special home-brewed was in my hand, and the ecstasy of that first gollup is still green in my memory. The recollection of the agony through which I had passed was just what was needed to make it perfect.

It was the same now. When I realized, listening to her words, that she must be referring to Gussie – I mean to say, there couldn't have been a whole platoon of men taking thorns out of her dog that day; the animal wasn't a pin-cushion – and became aware that Gussie, who an instant before had, to all appearances, gone so far back in the betting as not to be worth a quotation, was the big winner after all, a positive thrill permeated the frame and there escaped my lips a 'Wow!' so crisp and hearty that the Bassett leaped a liberal inch and a half from terra firma.

'I beg your pardon?' she said.

I waved a jaunty hand.

'Nothing,' I said. 'Nothing. Just remembered there's a letter I have to write tonight without fail. If you don't mind, I think I'll be going in. Here,' I said, 'comes Gussie Fink-Nottle. He will look after you.'

And, as I spoke, Gussie came sidling out from behind a tree.

I passed away and left them to it. As regards these two, everything was beyond a question absolutely in order. All Gussie had to do was keep his head down and not press. Already, I felt, as I legged it back to the house, the happy ending must have begun to function. I mean to say, when you leave a girl and a man, each of whom has admitted in set terms that she and he loves him and her, in close juxtaposition in the twilight, there doesn't seem much more to do but start pricing fish slices.

Something attempted, something done, seemed to me to have earned two-penn'orth of wassail in the smoking-room.

I proceeded thither.

The makings were neatly laid out on a side-table, and to pour into a glass an inch or so of the raw spirit and shoosh some soda-water on top of it was with me the work of a moment. This done, I retired to an arm-chair and put my feet up, sipping the mixture with carefree enjoyment, rather like Caesar having one in his tent the day he overcame the Nervii.

As I let the mind dwell on what must even now be taking place in that peaceful garden, I felt bucked and uplifted. Though never for an instant faltering in my opinion that Augustus Fink-Nottle was Nature's final word in cloth-headed guffins, I liked the man, wished him well, and could not have felt more deeply involved in the success of his wooing if I, and not he, had been the bloke under the ether.

The thought that by this time he might quite easily have completed the preliminary *pourparlers* and be deep in an informal discussion of honeymoon plans, was very pleasant to me.

Of course considering the sort of girl Madeline Bassett was – stars and rabbits and all that, I mean – you might say that a sober sadness would have been more fitting. But in these matters you have got to realize that tastes differ. The impulse of right-thinking men might be to run a mile when they saw the Bassett, but for some reason she appealed to the deeps in Gussie, so that was that.

I had reached this point in my meditations, when I was aroused by the sound of the door opening. Somebody came in and started moving like a leopard towards the side-table and, lowering the feet, I perceived that it was Tuppy Glossop.

The sight of him gave me a momentary twinge of remorse, reminding me, as it did, that in the excitement of getting Gussie fixed up I had rather forgotten about this other client. It is often that way when you're trying to run two cases at once.

However, Gussie now being off my mind, I was prepared to devote my whole attention to the Glossop problem.

I had been much pleased by the way he had carried out the task assigned him at the dinner-table. No easy one, I can assure you, for the browsing and sluicing had been of the highest quality, and there had been one dish in particular – I allude to the *nonnettes de poulet Agnès Sorel* – which might well have broken down the most iron resolution. But he had passed it up like a professional fasting man, and I was proud of him.

'Oh, hullo, Tuppy,' I said, 'I wanted to see you.'

He turned, snifter in hand, and it was easy to see that his privations had tried him sorely. He was looking like a wolf on the steppes of Russia which has seen its peasant shin up a high tree.

'Yes?' he said, rather unpleasantly. 'Well, here I am.'

'Well?'

'How do you mean – well?'

'Make your report.'

'What report?'

'Have you nothing to tell me about Angela?'

'Only that she's a blister.'

I was concerned.

'Hasn't she come clustering round you yet?'

'She has not.'

'Very odd.'

'Why odd?'

'She must have noted your lack of appetite.'

He barked raspingly, as if he were having trouble with the tonsils of the soul.

'Lack of appetite! I'm as hollow as the Grand Canyon.'

'Courage, Tuppy! Think of Gandhi.'

'What about Gandhi?'

'He hasn't had a square meal for years.'

'Nor have I. Or I could swear I hadn't. Gandhi, my left foot.'

I saw that it might be best to let the Gandhi *motif* slide. I went back to where we had started.

'She's probably looking for you now.'

'Who is? Angela?'

'Yes. She must have noticed your supreme sacrifice.'

'I don't suppose she noticed it at all, the little fathead. I'll bet it didn't register in any way whatsoever.'

'Come, Tuppy,' I urged, 'this is morbid. Don't take this gloomy view. She must at least have spotted that you refused those *nonnettes de poulet Agnès Sorel*. It was a sensational renunciation and stuck out like a sore thumb. And the *cèpes à la Rossini* –'

A hoarse cry broke from his twisted lips:

'Will you stop it, Bertie! Do you think I am made of marble? Isn't it bad enough to have sat watching one of Anatole's supremest dinners flit by, course after course, without having you making a song about it? Don't remind me of those *nonnettes*. I can't stand it.'

I endeavoured to hearten and console.

'Be brave, Tuppy. Fix your thoughts on that cold steak-and-kidney pie in the larder. As the Good Book says, it cometh in the morning.'

'Yes, in the morning. And it's now about half past nine at night. You would bring that pie up, wouldn't you? Just when I was trying to keep my mind off it.'

I saw what he meant. Hours must pass before he could dig into that pie. I dropped the subject, and we sat for a pretty good time in silence. Then he rose and began to pace the room in an overwrought sort of way, like a zoo lion who has heard the dinner-gong go and is hoping the keeper won't forget him in the general distribution. I averted my gaze tactfully, but I could hear him kicking chairs and things. It was plain that the man's soul was in travail and his blood pressure high.

Presently he returned to his seat, and I saw that he was looking at me intently. There was that about his demeanour that led me to think that he had something to communicate.

Nor was I wrong. He tapped me significantly on the knee and spoke:

'Bertie.'

'Hullo?'

'Shall I tell you something?'

'Certainly, old bird,' I said cordially. 'I was just beginning to feel that the scene could do with a bit more dialogue.'

'This business of Angela and me.'

'Yes?'

'I've been putting in a lot of solid thinking about it.'

'Oh, yes?'

'I have analysed the situation pitilessly, and one thing stands out as clear as dammit. There has been dirty work afoot.'

'I don't get you.'

'All right. Let me review the facts. Up to the time she went to Cannes Angela loved me. She was all over me. I was the blue-eyed boy in every sense of the term. You'll admit that?'

'Indisputably.'

'And directly she came back we had this bust-up.'

'Quite.'

'About nothing.'

'Oh, dash it, old man, nothing? You were a bit tactless, what, about her shark.'

'I was frank and candid about her shark. And that's just my point. Do you seriously believe that a trifling disagreement about sharks would make a girl hand a man his hat, if her heart were really his?'

'Certainly.'

It beat me why he couldn't see it. But then poor old Tuppy has never been very hot on the finer shades. He's one of those large, tough, football-playing blokes who lack the more delicate sensibilities, as I've heard Jeeves call them. Excellent at blocking a punt or walking across an opponent's face in cleated boots, but not so good when it comes to understanding the highly-strung female temperament. It simply wouldn't occur to him that a girl might be prepared to give up her life's happiness rather than waive her shark.

'Rot! It was just a pretext.'

'What was?'

'This shark business. She wanted to get rid of me, and grabbed at the first excuse.'

'No, no.'

'I tell you she did.'

'But what on earth would she want to get rid of you for?'

'Exactly. That's the very question I asked myself. And here's the answer: Because she has fallen in love with somebody else. It sticks out a mile. There's no other possible solution. She goes to Cannes all for me, she comes back all off me. Obviously, during those two months, she must have transferred her affections to some foul blister she met out there.'

'No, no.'

'Don't keep saying "No, no." She must have done. Well, I'll tell you one thing, and you can take this as official. If ever I find this slimy, slithery snake in the grass, he had better make all the necessary arrangements at his favourite nursing-home without delay, because I am going to be very rough with him. I propose, if and when found, to take him by his beastly neck, shake him till he froths, and pull him inside out and make him swallow himself.'

627

With which words he biffed off; and I, having given him a minute or two to get out of the way, rose and made for the drawing-room. The tendency of females to roost in drawing-rooms after dinner being well marked, I expected to find Angela there. It was my intention to have a word with Angela.

To Tuppy's theory that some insinuating bird had stolen the girl's heart from him at Cannes I had given, as I have indicated, little credence, considering it the mere unbalanced apple sauce of a bereaved man. It was, of course, the shark, and nothing but the shark, that had caused love's young dream to go temporarily off the boil, and I was convinced that a word or two with the cousin at this juncture would set everything right.

For, frankly, I thought it incredible that a girl of her natural sweetness and tender-heartedness should not have been moved to her foundations by what she had seen at dinner that night. Even Seppings, Aunt Dahlia's butler, a cold, unemotional man, had gasped and practically reeled when Tuppy waved aside those *nonnettes de poulet Agnès Sorel*, while the footman, standing by with the potatoes, had stared like one seeing a vision. I simply refused to consider the possibility of the significance of the thing having been lost on a nice girl like Angela. I fully expected to find her in the drawing-room with her heart bleeding freely, all ripe for an immediate reconciliation.

In the drawing-room, however, when I entered, only Aunt Dahlia met the eye. It seemed to me that she gave me rather a jaundiced look as I hove in sight, but this, having so recently beheld Tuppy in his agony, I attributed to the fact that she, like him, had been going light on the menu. You can't expect an empty aunt to beam like a full aunt.

'Oh, it's you, is it?' she said.

Well it was, of course.

'Where's Angela?' I asked.

'Gone to bed.'

'Already?'

'She said she had a headache.'

'H'm.'

I wasn't so sure that I liked the sound of that so much. A girl who has observed the sundered lover sensationally off his feed does not go to bed with headaches if love has been reborn in her heart. She sticks around and gives him the swift, remorseful glance from beneath the drooping eyelashes and generally endeavours to convey to him that, if he wants to get together across a round table and try to find a formula, she is all for it. Yes, I am bound to say I found that going-to-bed stuff a bit disquieting.

'Gone to bed, eh?' I murmured musingly.

'What did you want her for?'

'I thought she might like a stroll and a chat.'

'Are you going for a stroll?' said Aunt Dahlia, with a sudden show of interest. 'Where?'

'Oh, hither and thither.'

'Then I wonder if you would mind doing something for me.'

'Give it a name.'

'It won't take you long. You know that path that runs past the greenhouses into the kitchen garden. If you go along it you come to a pond.'

'That's right.'

'Well, will you get a good, stout piece of rope or cord and go down that path till you come to the pond –'

'To the pond. Right.'

'– and look about you till you find a nice, heavy stone. Or a fairly large brick would do.'

'I see,' I said, though I didn't, being still fogged. 'Stone or brick. Yes. And then?'

'Then,' said the relative, 'I want you, like a good boy, to fasten the rope to the brick and tie it round your damned neck and jump into the pond and drown

yourself. In a few days I will send and have you fished
up and buried because I shall need to dance on your
grave.'

I was more fogged than ever. And not only fogged –
wounded and resentful. I remember reading a book
where a girl 'suddenly fled from the room, afraid to stay
for fear dreadful things would come tumbling from her
lips; determined that she would not remain another day
in this house to be insulted and misunderstood'. I felt
much about the same.

Then I reminded myself that one has got to make
allowances for a woman with only about half a spoonful
of soup inside her, and I checked the red-hot crack that
rose to the lips.

'What,' I said gently, 'is this all about? You seem
pipped with Bertram.'

'Pipped!'

'Noticeably pipped. Why this ill-concealed animus?'

A sudden flame shot from her eyes, singeing my hair.

'Who was the ass, who was the chump, who was the
dithering idiot who talked me, against my better
judgement, into going without my dinner? I might have
guessed –'

I saw that I had divined correctly the basic cause of
her strange mood.

'It's all right, Aunt Dahlia. I know just how you're
feeling. A bit on the hollow side, what? But the agony
will pass. If I were you, I'd sneak down and raid the
larder, after the household have gone to bed. I am told
there's a pretty good steak-and-kidney pie there which
will repay inspection. Have faith, Aunt Dahlia,' I urged.
'Pretty soon Uncle Tom will be along, full of sympathy
and anxious inquiries.'

'Will he? Do you know where he is now?'

'I haven't seen him.'

'He is in the study with his face buried in his hands,
muttering about civilization and melting pots.'

'Eh? Why?'

'Because it has just been my painful duty to inform him that Anatole has given notice.'

I own that I reeled.

'What?'

'Given notice. As the result of that drivelling scheme of yours. What did you expect a sensitive, temperamental French cook to do, if you went about urging everybody to refuse all food? I hear that when the first two courses came back to the kitchen practically untouched, his feelings were so hurt that he cried like a child. And when the rest of the dinner followed, he came to the conclusion that the whole thing was a studied and calculated insult, and decided to hand in his portfolio.'

'Golly!'

'You may well say "Golly!" Anatole, God's gift to the gastric juices, gone like the dew off the petal of a rose, all through your idiocy. Perhaps you understand now why I want you to go and jump in that pond. I might have known that some hideous disaster would strike this house like a thunderbolt if once you wriggled your way into it and started trying to be clever.'

Harsh words, of course, as from aunt to nephew, but I bore her no resentment. No doubt, if you looked at it from a certain angle, Bertram might be considered to have made something of a floater.

'I am sorry.'

'What's the good of being sorry?'

'I acted for what I deemed the best.'

'Another time try acting for the worst. Then we may possibly escape with a mere flesh wound.'

'Uncle Tom's not feeling too bucked about it all, you say?'

'He's groaning like a lost soul. And any chance I ever had of getting that money out of him has gone.'

I stroked the chin thoughtfully. There was, I had to admit, reason in what she said. None knew better than I

how terrible a blow the passing of Anatole would be to
Uncle Tom.

I have stated earlier in this chronicle that this curious
object of the seashore with whom Aunt Dahlia has
linked her lot is a bloke who habitually looks like a
pterodactyl that has suffered, and the reason he does so
is that all those years he spent in making millions in the
Far East put his digestion on the blink, and the only
cook that has ever been discovered capable of pushing
food into him without starting something like Old
Home Week in Moscow under the third waistcoat
button is this uniquely gifted Anatole. Deprived of
Anatole's services, all he was likely to give the wife of
his b was a dirty look. Yes, unquestionably, things
seemed to have struck a somewhat rocky patch, and I
must admit that I found myself, at moment of going to
press, a little destitute of constructive ideas.

Confident, however, that these would come ere long,
I kept the stiff upper lip.

'Bad,' I conceded. 'Quite bad, beyond a doubt.
Certainly a nasty jar for one and all. But have no fear,
Aunt Dahlia, I will fix everything.'

I have alluded earlier to the difficulty of staggering
when you're sitting down, showing that it is a feat of
which I, personally, am not capable. Aunt Dahlia, to my
amazement, now did it apparently without an effort. She
was well wedged into a deep arm-chair, but,
nevertheless, she staggered like billy-o. A sort of spasm
of horror and apprehension contorted her face.

'If you dare to try any more of your lunatic schemes – '

I saw that it would be fruitless to try to reason with
her. Quite plainly, she was not in the vein. Contenting
myself, accordingly, with a gesture of loving sympathy, I
left the room. Whether she did or did not throw a
handsomely bound volume of the Works of Alfred, Lord
Tennyson, at me, I am not in a position to say. I had
seen it lying on the table beside her, and as I closed the

door I remember receiving the impression that some
blunt instrument had crashed against the woodwork, but
I was feeling too preoccupied to note and observe.

I blamed myself for not having taken into
consideration the possible effects of a sudden abstinence
on the part of virtually the whole strength of the
company on one of Anatole's impulsive Provençal
temperament. These Gauls, I should have remembered,
can't take it. Their tendency to fly off the handle at the
slightest provocation is well known. No doubt the man
had put his whole soul into those *nonnettes de poulet*,
and to see them come homing back to him must have
gashed him like a knife.

However, spilt milk blows nobody any good, and it is
useless to dwell upon it. The task now confronting
Bertram was to put matters right, and I was pacing the
lawn, pondering to this end, when I suddenly heard a
groan so lost-soulish that I thought it must have
proceeded from Uncle Tom, escaped from captivity and
come to groan in the garden.

Looking about me, however, I could discern no
uncles. Puzzled, I was about to resume my meditations,
when the sound came again. And peering into the
shadows I observed a dim form seated on one of the
rustic benches which so liberally dotted this pleasance
and another dim form standing beside same. A second
and more penetrating glance, and I had assembled the
facts.

These dim forms were, in the order named, Gussie
Fink-Nottle and Jeeves. And what Gussie was doing,
groaning all over the place like this, was more than I
could understand.

Because, I mean to say, there was no possibility of
error. He wasn't singing. As I approached, he gave an
encore, and it was beyond question a groan. Moreover, I
could now see him clearly, and his whole aspect was
definitely sand-bagged.

'Good evening, sir,' said Jeeves. 'Mr Fink-Nottle is not feeling well.'

Nor was I. Gussie had begun to make a low, bubbling noise, and I could no longer disguise it from myself that something must have gone seriously wrong with the works. I mean, I know marriage is a pretty solemn business and the realization that he is in for it frequently churns a chap up a bit, but I had never come across a case of a newly-engaged man taking it on the chin quite so completely as this.

Gussie looked up. His eye was dull. He clutched the thatch.

'Good-bye, Bertie,' he said, rising.

I seemed to spot an error.

'You mean "Hullo", don't you?'

'No, I don't. I mean good-bye. I'm off.'

'Off where?'

'To the kitchen garden. To drown myself.'

'Don't be an ass.'

'I'm not an ass . . . Am I an ass, Jeeves?'

'Possibly a little injudicious, sir.'

'Drowning myself, you mean?'

'Yes, sir.'

'You think, on the whole, not drown myself?'

'I should not advocate it, sir.'

'Very well, Jeeves. I accept your ruling. After all, it would be unpleasant for Mrs Travers to find a swollen body floating in her pond.'

'Yes, sir.'

'And she has been very kind to me.'

'Yes, sir.'

'And you have been very kind to me, Jeeves.'

'Thank you, sir.'

'So have you, Bertie. Very kind. Everybody has been very kind to me. Very, very kind. Very kind indeed. I have no complaints to make. All right, I'll go for a walk instead.'

I followed him with bulging eyes as he tottered off into the darkness.

'Jeeves,' I said, and I am free to admit that in my emotion I bleated like a lamb drawing itself to the attention of the parent sheep, 'what the dickens is all this?'

'Mr Fink-Nottle is not quite himself, sir. He has passed through a trying experience.'

I endeavoured to put together a brief synopsis of previous events.

'I left him out there with Miss Bassett.'

'Yes, sir.'

'I had softened her up.'

'Yes, sir.'

'He knew exactly what he had to do. I had coached him thoroughly in lines and business.'

'Yes, sir. So Mr Fink-Nottle informed me.'

'Well, then –'

'I regret to say, sir, that there was a slight hitch.'

'You mean, something went wrong?'

'Yes, sir.'

I could not fathom. The brain seemed to be tottering on its throne.

'But how could anything go wrong? She loves him, Jeeves.'

'Indeed, sir?'

'She definitely told me so. All he had to do was propose.'

'Yes, sir.'

'Well, didn't he?'

'No, sir.'

'Then what the dickens did he talk about?'

'Newts, sir.'

'Newts?'

'Yes, sir.'

'Newts?'

'Yes, sir.'

635

'But why did he want to talk about newts?'

'He did not want to talk about newts, sir. As I gather from Mr Fink-Nottle, nothing could have been more alien to his plans.'

I simply couldn't grasp the trend.

'But you can't force a man to talk about newts.'

'Mr Fink-Nottle was the victim of a sudden unfortunate spasm of nervousness, sir. Upon finding himself alone with the young lady, he admits to having lost his morale. In such circumstances, gentlemen frequently talk at random, saying the first thing that chances to enter their heads. This, in Mr Fink-Nottle's case, would seem to have been the newt, its treatment in sickness and in health.'

The scales fell from my eyes. I understood. I had had the same sort of thing happen to me in moments of crisis. I remember once detaining a dentist with the drill at one of my lower bicuspids and holding him up for nearly ten minutes with a story about a Scotchman, an Irishman, and a Jew. Purely automatic. The more he tried to jab, the more I said 'Hoots, mon', 'Begorrah', and 'Oy, oy'. When one loses one's nerve, one simply babbles.

I could put myself in Gussie's place. I could envisage the scene. There he and the Bassett were, alone together in the evening stillness. No doubt, as I had advised, he had shot the works about sunsets and fairy princesses, and so forth, and then had arrived at the point where he had to say that bit about having something to say to her. At this, I take it, she lowered her eyes and said, 'Oh, yes?'

He then, I should imagine, said it was something very important; to which her response would, one assumes, have been something on the lines of 'Really?' or 'Indeed?' or possibly just the sharp intake of the breath. And then their eyes met, just as mine met the dentist's, and something suddenly seemed to catch him in the pit

of the stomach and everything went black and he heard
his voice starting to drool about newts. Yes, I could
follow the psychology.

Nevertheless, I found myself blaming Gussie. On
discovering that he was stressing the newt note in this
manner, he ought, of course, to have tuned out, even if it
had meant sitting there saying nothing. No matter how
much of a twitter he was in, he should have had sense
enough to see that he was throwing a spanner into the
works. No girl, when she has been led to expect that a
man is about to pour forth his soul in a fervour of
passion, likes to find him suddenly shelving the whole
topic in favour of an address on aquatic Salamandridae.

'Bad, Jeeves.'

'Yes, sir.'

'And how long did this nuisance continue?'

'For some not inconsiderable time, I gather, sir.
According to Mr Fink-Nottle, he supplied Miss Bassett
with very full and complete information not only with
respect to the common newt, but also the crested and
palmated varieties. He described to her how newts,
during the breeding season, live in the water, subsisting
upon tadpoles, insect larvae, and crustaceans; how, later,
they make their way to the land and eat slugs and
worms; and how the newly born newt has three pairs of
long, plumelike, external gills. And he was just
observing that newts differ from salamanders in the
shape of the tail, which is compressed, and that a
marked sexual dimorphism prevails in most species,
when the young lady rose and said that she thought she
would go back to the house.'

'And then –'

'She went, sir.'

I stood musing. More and more, it was beginning to
be borne in upon me what a particularly difficult chap
Gussie was to help. He seemed to so marked an extent
to lack snap and finish. With infinite toil, you

manoeuvred him into a position where all he had to do was charge ahead, and he didn't charge ahead, but went off sideways, missing the objective completely.

'Difficult, Jeeves.'

'Yes, sir.'

In happier circs, of course, I would have canvassed his views on the matter. But after what had occurred in connexion with that mess jacket, my lips were sealed.

'Well, I must think it over.'

'Yes, sir.'

'Burnish the brain a bit and endeavour to find the way out.'

'Yes, sir.'

'Well, good night, Jeeves.'

'Good night, sir.'

He shimmered off, leaving a pensive Bertram Wooster standing motionless in the shadows. It seemed to me that it was hard to know what to do for the best.

12

I don't know if it has happened to you at all, but a thing
I've noticed with myself is that, when I'm confronted by
a problem which seems for the moment to stump and
baffle, a good sleep will often bring the solution in the
morning.

It was so on the present occasion.

The nibs who study these matters claim, I believe,
that this has got something to do with the subconscious
mind, and very possibly they may be right. I wouldn't
have said off-hand that I had a subconscious mind, but
I suppose I must without knowing it, and no doubt it
was there, sweating away diligently at the old stand, all
the while the corporeal Wooster was getting his eight
hours.

For directly I opened my eyes on the morrow, I saw
daylight. Well, I don't mean that exactly, because
naturally I did. What I mean is that I found I had the
thing all mapped out. The good old subconscious m. had
delivered the goods, and I perceived exactly what steps
must be taken in order to put Augustus Fink-Nottle
among the practising Romeos.

I should like you, if you can spare me a moment of
your valuable time, to throw your mind back to that
conversation he and I had had in the garden on the
previous evening. Not the glimmering landscape bit, I
don't mean that, but the concluding passages of it.
Having done so, you will recall that when he informed
me that he never touched alcoholic liquor, I shook the
head a bit, feeling that this must inevitably weaken him
as a force where proposing to girls was concerned.

And events had shown that my fears were well founded.

Put to the test, with nothing but orange juice inside him, he had proved a complete bust. In a situation calling for words of molten passion of a nature calculated to go through Madeline Bassett like a red-hot gimlet through half a pound of butter, he had said not a syllable that could bring a blush to the cheek of modesty, merely delivering a well-phrased but, in the circumstances, quite misplaced lecture on newts.

A romantic girl is not to be won by such tactics. Obviously, before attempting to proceed further, Augustus Fink-Nottle must be induced to throw off the shackling inhibitions of the past and fuel up. It must be a primed, confident Fink-Nottle who squared up to the Bassett for Round No. 2.

Only so could the *Morning Post* make its ten bob, or whatever it is, for printing the announcement of the forthcoming nuptials.

Having arrived at this conclusion I found the rest easy, and by the time Jeeves brought me my tea I had evolved a plan complete in every detail. This I was about to place before him – indeed, I had got as far as the preliminary 'I say, Jeeves' – when we were interrupted by the arrival of Tuppy.

He came listlessly into the room, and I was pained to observe that a night's rest had effected no improvement in the unhappy wreck's appearance. Indeed, I should have said, if anything, that he was looking rather more moth-eaten than when I had seen him last. If you can visualize a bulldog which has just been kicked in the ribs and had its dinner sneaked by the cat, you will have Hildebrand Glossop as he now stood before me.

'Stap my vitals, Tuppy, old corpse,' I said, concerned, 'you're looking pretty blue round the rims.'

Jeeves slid from the presence in that tactful, eel-like way of his, and I motioned the remains to take a seat.

'What's the matter?' I said.

He came to anchor on the bed, and for a while sat picking at the coverlet in silence.

'I've been through hell, Bertie.'

'Through where?'

'Hell.'

'Oh, hell? And what took you there?'

Once more he became silent, staring before him with sombre eyes. Following his gaze, I saw that he was looking at an enlarged photograph of my Uncle Tom in some sort of Masonic uniform which stood on the mantelpiece. I've tried to reason with Aunt Dahlia about this photograph for years, placing before her two alternative suggestions: (a) to burn the beastly thing; or (b) if she must preserve it, to shove me in another room when I come to stay. But she declines to accede. She says it's good for me. A useful discipline, she maintains, teaching me that there is a darker side to life and that we were not put into this world for pleasure only.

'Turn it to the wall, if it hurts you, Tuppy,' I said gently.

'Eh?'

'That photograph of Uncle Tom as the bandmaster.'

'I didn't come here to talk about photographs. I came for sympathy.'

'And you shall have it. What's the trouble? Worrying about Angela, I suppose? Well, have no fear. I have another well-laid plan for encompassing that young shrimp. I'll guarantee that she will be weeping on your neck before yonder sun has set.'

He barked sharply.

'A fat chance!'

'Tup, Tushy!'

'Eh?'

'I mean "Tush, Tuppy". I tell you I will do it. I was just going to describe this plan of mine to Jeeves when you came in. Care to hear it?'

'I don't want to hear any more of your beastly plans. Plans are no good. She's gone and fallen in love with this other bloke, and now hates my gizzard.'

'Rot.'

'It isn't rot.'

'I tell you, Tuppy, as one who can read the female heart, that this Angela loves you still.'

'Well, it didn't look much like it in the larder last night.'

'Oh, you went to the larder last night?'

'I did.'

'And Angela was there?'

'She was. And your aunt. Also your uncle.'

I saw that I should require foot-notes. All this was new stuff to me. I had stayed at Brinkley Court quite a lot in my time, but I had no idea the larder was such a social vortex. More like a snack bar on a race-course than anything else, it seemed to have become.

'Tell me the whole story in your own words,' I said, 'omitting no detail, however apparently slight, for one never knows how important the most trivial detail may be.'

He inspected the photograph for a moment with growing gloom.

'All right,' he said. 'This is what happened. You know my views about that steak-and-kidney pie.'

'Quite.'

'Well, round about one a.m. I thought the time was ripe. I stole from my room and went downstairs. The pie seemed to beckon to me.'

I nodded. I knew how pies do.

'I got to the larder. I fished it out. I set it on the table. I found knife and fork. I collected salt, mustard, and pepper. There were some cold potatoes. I added those. And I was about to pitch in when I heard a sound behind me, and there was your aunt at the door. In a blue-and-yellow dressing gown.'

'Embarrassing.'

'Most.'

'I suppose you didn't know where to look.'

'I looked at Angela.'

'She came in with my aunt?'

'No. With your uncle, a minute or two later. He was wearing mauve pyjamas and carried a pistol. Have you ever seen your uncle in pyjamas and a pistol?'

'Never.'

'You haven't missed much.'

'Tell me, Tuppy,' I asked, for I was anxious to ascertain this, 'about Angela. Was there any momentary softening in her gaze as she fixed it on you?'

'She didn't fix it on me. She fixed it on the pie.'

'Did she say anything?'

'Not right away. Your uncle was the first to speak. He said to your aunt, "God bless my soul, Dahlia, what are you doing here?" To which she replied, "Well, if it comes to that, my merry somnambulist, what are you?" Your uncle then said that he thought there must be burglars in the house, as he had heard noises.'

I nodded again. I could follow the trend. Ever since the scullery window was found open the year Shining Light was disqualified in the Cesarewitch for boring, Uncle Tom has had a marked complex about burglars. I can still recall my emotions when, paying my first visit after he had had bars put on all the windows and attempting to thrust the head out in order to get a sniff of country air, I nearly fractured my skull on a sort of iron grille, as worn by the tougher kinds of medieval prison.

' "What sort of noises?" said your aunt. "Funny noises," said your uncle. Whereupon Angela – with a nasty, steely tinkle in her voice, the little buzzard – observed, "I expect it was Mr Glossop eating." And then she did give me a look. It was the sort of wondering, revolted look a very spiritual woman would give a fat man gulping soup in a restaurant. The kind of look that makes a fellow feel he's forty-six round the waist and has great rolls of superfluous flesh pouring down over the back of his collar. And, still speaking in the same unpleasant tone, she added, "I ought to have told you, Father, that Mr Glossop always likes to have a good meal three or four times during the night. It helps to keep him going till breakfast. He has the most amazing appetite. See, he has practically finished a large steak-and-kidney pie already." '

As he spoke these words, a feverish animation swept over Tuppy. His eyes glittered with a strange light, and he thumped the bed violently with his fist, nearly catching me a juicy one on the leg.

'That was what hurt, Bertie. That was what stung. I hadn't so much as started on that pie. But that's a woman all over.'

'The eternal feminine.'

'She continued her remarks. "You've no idea," she said, "how Mr Glossop loves food. He just lives for it. He always eats six or seven meals a day, and then starts in again after bedtime. I think it's rather wonderful." Your aunt seemed interested, and said it reminded her of a boa constrictor. Angela said, didn't she mean a python? And then they argued as to which of the two it was. Your uncle, meanwhile, poking about with that damned pistol of his till human life wasn't safe in the vicinity. And the pie lying there on the table, and me unable to touch it. You begin to understand why I said I had been through hell.'

'Quite. Can't have been at all pleasant.'

'Presently your aunt and Angela settled their discussion, deciding that Angela was right and that it was a python that I reminded them of. And shortly after that we all pushed back to bed, Angela warning me in a motherly voice not to take the stairs too quickly. After seven or eight solid meals, she said a man of my build ought to be very careful, because of the danger of apoplectic fits. She said it was the same with dogs. When they became very fat and overfed, you had to see that they didn't hurry upstairs, as it made them puff and pant, and that was bad for their hearts. She asked your aunt if she remembered the late spaniel, Ambrose; and your aunt said, "Poor old Ambrose, you couldn't keep him away from the garbage pail"; and Angela said, "Exactly, so do please be careful, Mr Glossop." And you tell me she loves me still!'

I did my best to encourage.

'Girlish banter, what?'

'Girlish banter be dashed. She's right off me. Once her ideal, I am now less than the dust beneath her chariot wheels. She became infatuated with this chap, whoever he was, at Cannes, and now she can't stand the sight of me.'

I raised the eyebrows.

'My dear Tuppy, you are not showing your usual good sense in this Angela-chap-at-Cannes matter. If you will forgive me saying so, you have got an *idée fixe*.'

'A what?'

'An *idée fixe*. You know. One of those things fellows get. Like Uncle Tom's delusion that everybody who is known even slightly to the police is lurking in the garden, waiting for a chance to break into the house. You keep talking about this chap at Cannes, and there never was a chap at Cannes, and I'll tell you why I'm so sure about this. During those two months on the Riviera, it so happens that Angela and I were practically inseparable. If there had been somebody nosing round her, I should have spotted it in a second.'

He started. I could see that this had impressed him.

'Oh, she was with you all the time at Cannes, was she?'

'I don't suppose she said two words to anybody else, except, of course, idle conv. at the crowded dinner table or a chance remark in a throng at the Casino.'

'I see. You mean that anything in the shape of mixed bathing and moonlight strolls she conducted solely in your company?'

'That's right. It was quite a joke in the hotel.'

'You must have enjoyed that.'

'Oh, rather. I've always been devoted to Angela.'

'Oh, yes?'

'When we were kids, she used to call herself my little sweetheart.'

'She did?'

'Absolutely.'

'I see.'

He sat plunged in thought, while I, glad to have set his mind at rest, proceeded with my tea. And presently there came the banging of a gong from the hall below, and he started like a war horse at the sound of the bugle.

'Breakfast!' he said, and was off to a flying start, leaving me to brood and ponder. And the more I brooded and pondered, the more did it seem to me that everything now looked pretty smooth. Tuppy, I could see, despite that painful scene in the larder, still loved Angela with all the old fervour.

This meant that I could rely on that plan to which I had referred to bring home the bacon. And as I had found the way to straighten out the Gussie-Bassett difficulty, there seemed nothing more to worry about.

It was with an uplifted heart that I addressed Jeeves as he came in to remove the tea tray.

13

'Jeeves,' I said.

'Sir?'

'I've just been having a chat with young Tuppy, Jeeves. Did you happen to notice that he wasn't looking very roguish this morning?'

'Yes, sir. It seemed to me that Mr Glossop's face was sicklied o'er with the pale cast of thought.'

'Quite. He met my Cousin Angela in the larder last night, and a rather painful interview ensued.'

'I am sorry, sir.'

'Not half so sorry as he was. She found him closeted with a steak-and-kidney pie, and appears to have been a bit caustic about fat men who lived for food alone.'

'Most disturbing, sir.'

'Very. In fact, many people would say that things had gone so far between these two that nothing now could bridge the chasm. A girl who could make cracks about human pythons who ate nine or ten meals a day and ought to be careful not to hurry upstairs because of the danger of apoplectic fits is a girl, many people would say, in whose heart love is dead. Wouldn't many people say that, Jeeves?'

'Undeniably, sir.'

'They would be wrong.'

'You think so, sir?'

'I am convinced of it. I know these females. You can't go by what they say.'

'You feel that Miss Angela's strictures should not be taken too much *au pied de la lettre*, sir?'

'Eh?'

'In English, we should say "literally".'

'Literally. That's exactly what I mean. You know what girls are. A tiff occurs, and they shoot their heads off. But underneath it all the old love still remains. Am I correct?'

'Quite correct, sir. The poet Scott –'

'Right ho, Jeeves.'

'Very good, sir.'

'And in order to bring that old love whizzing to the surface once more, all that is required is the proper treatment.'

'By "proper treatment", sir, you mean –'

'Clever handling, Jeeves. A spot of the good old snaky work. I see what must be done to jerk my Cousin Angela back to normalcy. I'll tell you, shall I?'

'If you would be so kind, sir.'

I lit a cigarette, and eyed him keenly through the smoke. He waited respectfully for me to unleash the words of wisdom. I must say for Jeeves that – till, as he is so apt to do, he starts shoving his oar in and cavilling and obstructing – he makes a very good audience. I don't know if he is actually agog, but he looks agog, and that's the great thing.

'Suppose you were strolling through the illimitable jungle, Jeeves, and happened to meet a tiger cub.'

'The contingency is a remote one, sir.'

'Never mind. Let us suppose it.'

'Very good, sir.'

'Let us now suppose that you sloshed that tiger cub, and let us suppose further that word reached its mother that it was being put upon. What would you expect the attitude of that mother to be? In what frame of mind do you consider that that tigress would approach you?'

'I should anticipate a certain show of annoyance, sir.'

'And rightly. Due to what is known as the maternal instinct, what?'

'Yes, sir.'

648

'Very good, Jeeves. We will now suppose that there
has recently been some little coolness between this tiger
cub and this tigress. For some days, let us say, they have
not been on speaking terms. Do you think that that
would make any difference to the vim with which the
latter would leap to the former's aid?'

'No, sir.'

'Exactly. Here, then, in brief, is my plan, Jeeves. I am
going to draw my Cousin Angela aside to a secluded spot
and roast Tuppy properly.'

'Roast, sir?'

'Knock. Slam. Tick off. Abuse. Denounce. I shall be
very terse about Tuppy, giving it as my opinion that in
all essentials he is more like a wart-hog than an
ex-member of a fine old English public school. What will
ensue? Hearing him attacked, my Cousin Angela's
womanly heart will be as sick as mud. The maternal
tigress in her will awake. No matter what differences
they may have had, she will remember only that he is
the man she loves, and will leap to his defence. And
from that to falling into his arms and burying the dead
past will be but a step. How do you react to that?'

'The idea is an ingenious one, sir.'

'We Woosters are ingenious, Jeeves, exceedingly
ingenious.'

'Yes, sir.'

'As a matter of fact, I am not speaking without a
knowledge of the form book. I have tested this theory.'

'Indeed, sir?'

'Yes, in person. And it works. I was standing on the
Eden rock at Antibes last month, idly watching the
bathers disport themselves in the water, and a girl I
knew slightly pointed at a male diver and asked me if I
didn't think his legs were about the silliest-looking pair
of props ever issued to a human being. I replied that I
did, indeed, and for the space of perhaps two minutes
was extraordinarily witty and satirical about this bird's

underpinning. At the end of that period, I suddenly felt as if I had been caught up in the tail of a cyclone.

'Beginning with a *critique* of my own limbs, which she said, justly enough, were nothing to write home about, this girl went on to dissect my manners, morals, intellect, general physique, and method of eating asparagus with such acerbity that by the time she had finished the best you could say of Bertram was that, so far as was known, he had never actually committed murder or set fire to an orphan asylum. Subsequent investigation proved that she was engaged to the fellow with the legs and had had a slight disagreement with him the evening before on the subject of whether she should or should not have made an original call of two spades, having seven, but without the ace. That night I saw them dining together with every indication of relish, their differences made up and the lovelight once more in their eyes. That shows you, Jeeves.'

'Yes, sir.'

'I expect precisely similar results from my Cousin Angela when I start roasting Tuppy. By lunchtime, I should imagine, the engagement will be on again and the diamond-and-platinum ring glittering as of yore on her third finger. Or is it the fourth?'

'Scarcely by luncheon time, sir. Miss Angela's maid informs me that Miss Angela drove off in her car early this morning with the intention of spending the day with friends in the vicinity.'

'Well, within half an hour of whatever time she comes back, then. These are mere straws, Jeeves. Do not let us chop them.'

'No, sir.'

'The point is that, as far as Tuppy and Angela are concerned, we may say with confidence that everything will shortly be hotsy-totsy once more. And what an agreeable thought that is, Jeeves.'

'Very true, sir.'

'If there is one thing that gives me the pip, it is two loving hearts being estranged.'

'I can readily appreciate the fact, sir.'

I placed the stub of my gasper in the ash tray and lit another, to indicate that that completed Chap. I.

'Right ho, then. So much for the western front. We now turn to the eastern.'

'Sir?'

'I speak in parables, Jeeves. What I mean is, we now approach the matter of Gussie and Miss Bassett.'

'Yes, sir.'

'Here, Jeeves, more direct methods are required. In handling the case of Augustus Fink-Nottle, we must keep always in mind the fact that we are dealing with a poop.'

'A sensitive plant would, perhaps, be a kinder expression, sir.'

'No, Jeeves, a poop. And with poops one has to employ the strong, forceful, straightforward policy. Psychology doesn't get you anywhere. You, if I may remind you without wounding your feelings, fell into the error of mucking about with psychology in connexion with this Fink-Nottle, and the result was a washout. You attempted to push him over the line by rigging him out in a Mephistopheles costume and sending him off to a fancy-dress ball, your view being that scarlet tights would embolden him. Futile.'

'The matter was never actually put to the test, sir.'

'No. Because he didn't get to the ball. And that strengthens my argument. A man who can set out in a cab for a fancy-dress ball and not get there is manifestly a poop of no common order. I don't think I have ever known anybody else who was such a dashed silly ass that he couldn't even get to a fancy-dress ball. Have you, Jeeves?'

'No, sir.'

'But don't forget this, because it is the point I wish,

above all, to make: Even if Gussie had got to that ball;
even if those scarlet tights, taken in conjunction with
his horn-rimmed spectacles, hadn't given the girl a fit of
some kind; even if she had rallied from the shock and he
had been able to dance and generally hobnob with her;
even then your efforts would have been fruitless,
because Mephistopheles costume or no Mephistopheles
costume, Augustus Fink-Nottle would never have been
able to summon up the courage to ask her to be his. All
that would have resulted would have been that she
would have got that lecture on newts a few days earlier.
And why, Jeeves? Shall I tell you why?'

'Yes, sir.'

'Because he would have been attempting the hopeless
task of trying to do the thing on orange juice.'

'Sir?'

'Gussie is an orange-juice addict. He drinks nothing
else.'

'I was not aware of that, sir.'

'I have it from his own lips. Whether from some
hereditary taint, or because he promised his mother he
wouldn't, or simply because he doesn't like the taste of
the stuff, Gussie Fink-Nottle has never in the whole
course of his career pushed so much as the simplest gin
and tonic over the larynx. And he expects – this poop
expects, Jeeves – this wabbling, shrinking, diffident
rabbit in human shape expects under these conditions to
propose to the girl he loves. One hardly knows whether
to smile or weep, what?'

'You consider total abstinence a handicap to a
gentleman who wishes to make a proposal of marriage,
sir?'

The question amazed me.

'Why, dash it,' I said, astounded, 'you must know it is.
Use your intelligence, Jeeves. Reflect what proposing
means. It means that a decent, self-respecting chap has
got to listen to himself saying things which, if spoken on

the silver screen, would cause him to dash to the
box-office and demand his money back. Let him attempt
to do it on orange juice, and what ensues? Shame seals
his lips, or, if it doesn't do that, makes him lose his
morale and start to babble. Gussie, for example, as we
have seen, babbles of syncopated newts.'

'Palmated newts, sir.'

'Palmated or syncopated, it doesn't matter which. The
point is that he babbles and is going to babble again, if
he has another try at it. Unless – and this is where I
want you to follow me very closely, Jeeves – unless steps
are taken at once through the proper channels. Only
active measures, promptly applied, can provide this
poor, pusillanimous poop with the proper pep. And that
is why, Jeeves, I intend tomorrow to secure a bottle of
gin and lace his luncheon orange juice with it liberally.'

'Sir?'

I clicked the tongue.

'I have already had occasion, Jeeves,' I said rebukingly,
'to comment on the way you say "Well, sir" and
"Indeed, sir?" I take this opportunity of informing you
that I object equally strongly to your "Sir?" pure and
simple. The word seems to suggest that in your opinion I
have made a statement or mooted a scheme so bizarre
that your brain reels at it. In the present instance, there
is absolutely nothing to say "Sir?" about. The plan I
have put forward is entirely reasonable and icily logical,
and should excite no sirring whatsoever. Or don't you
think so?'

'Well, sir –'

'Jeeves?'

'I beg your pardon, sir. The expression escaped me
inadvertently. What I intended to say, since you press
me, was that the action which you propose does seem to
me somewhat injudicious.'

'Injudicious? I don't follow you, Jeeves.'

'A certain amount of risk would enter into it, in my

opinion, sir. It is not always a simple matter to gauge the effect of alcohol on a subject unaccustomed to such stimulant. I have known it to have distressing results in the case of parrots.'

'Parrots?'

'I was thinking of an incident of my earlier life, sir, before I entered your employment. I was in the service of the late Lord Brancaster at the time, a gentleman who owned a parrot to which he was greatly devoted, and one day the bird chanced to be lethargic, and his lordship, with the kindly intention of restoring it to its customary animation, offered it a portion of seed cake steeped in the '84 port. The bird accepted the morsel gratefully and consumed it with every indication of satisfaction. Almost immediately afterwards, however, its manner became markedly feverish. Having bitten his lordship in the thumb and sung part of a sea-chanty, it fell to the bottom of the cage and remained there for a considerable period of time with its legs in the air, unable to move. I merely mention this, sir, in order to – '

I put my finger on the flaw. I had spotted it all along.

'But Gussie isn't a parrot.'

'No, sir, but – '

'It is high time, in my opinion, that this question of what young Gussie really is was threshed out and cleared up. He seems to think he is a male newt, and you appear to suggest that he is a parrot. The truth of the matter being that he is just a plain, ordinary poop and needs a snootful as badly as ever man did. So no more discussion, Jeeves. My mind is made up. There is only one way of handing this difficult case, and that is the way I have outlined.'

'Very good, sir.'

'Right ho, Jeeves. So much for that, then. Now, here's something else: You noticed that I said I was going to put this project through tomorrow, and no doubt you wondered why I said tomorrow. Why did I, Jeeves?'

'Because you feel that if it were done when 'tis done, then 'twere well it were done quickly, sir?'

'Partly, Jeeves, but not altogether. My chief reason for fixing the date as specified is that tomorrow, though you have doubtless forgotten it, is the day of the distribution of prizes at Market Snodsbury Grammar School, at which, as you know, Gussie is to be the male star and master of the revels. So you see we shall, by lacing that juice, not only embolden him to propose to Miss Bassett, but also put him so into shape that he will hold that Market Snodsbury audience spellbound.'

'In fact, you will be killing two birds with one stone, sir.'

'Exactly. A very neat way of putting it. And now here is a minor point. On second thoughts, I think the best plan will be for you, not me, to lace the juice.'

'Sir?'

'Jeeves!'

'I beg your pardon, sir.'

'And I'll tell you why that will be the best plan. Because you are in a position to obtain ready access to the stuff. It is served to Gussie daily, I have noticed, in an individual jug. This jug will presumably be lying about the kitchen or somewhere before lunch tomorrow. It will be the simplest of tasks for you to slip a few fingers of gin in it.'

'No doubt, sir, but –'

'Don't say "but", Jeeves.'

'I fear, sir –'

' "I fear, sir" is just as bad.'

'What I am endeavouring to say, sir, is that I am sorry, but I am afraid I must enter an unequivocal *nolle prosequi*.'

'Do what?'

'The expression is a legal one, sir, signifying the resolve not to proceed with a matter. In other words, eager though I am to carry out your instructions, sir, as a general rule, on this occasion I must respectfully decline to cooperate.'

'You won't do it, you mean?'

'Precisely, sir.'

I was stunned. I began to understand how a general must feel when he has ordered a regiment to charge and has been told that it isn't in the mood.

'Jeeves,' I said, 'I had not expected this of you.'

'No, sir?'

'No, indeed. Naturally, I realize that lacing Gussie's orange juice is not one of those regular duties for which you receive the monthly stipend, and if you care to stand on the strict letter of the contract, I suppose there is nothing to be done about it. But you will permit me to observe that this is scarcely the feudal spirit.'

'I am sorry, sir.'

'It is quite all right, Jeeves, quite all right. I am not angry, only a little hurt.'

'Very good, sir.'

'Right ho, Jeeves.'

14

Investigation proved that the friends Angela had gone to spend the day with were some stately-home owners of the name of Stretchley-Budd, hanging out in a joint called Kingham Manor, about eight miles distant in the direction of Pershore. I didn't know these birds, but their fascination must have been considerable, for she tore herself away from them only just in time to get back and dress for dinner. It was, accordingly, not until coffee had been consumed that I was able to get matters moving. I found her in the drawing-room and at once proceeded to put things in train.

It was with very different feelings from those which had animated the bosom when approaching the Bassett twenty-four hours before in the same manner in this same drawing-room, that I headed for where she sat. As I had told Tuppy, I have always been devoted to Angela, and there is nothing I like better than a ramble in her company.

And I could see by the look of her now how sorely in need she was of my aid and comfort.

Frankly, I was shocked by the unfortunate young prune's appearance. At Cannes she had been a happy, smiling English girl of the best type, full of beans and buck. Her face now was pale and drawn, like that of a hockey centre-forward at a girls' school who, in addition to getting a fruity one on the shin, has just been penalized for 'sticks'. In any normal gathering, her demeanour would have excited instant remark, but the standard of gloom at Brinkley Court had become so high that it passed unnoticed. Indeed, I shouldn't wonder if

Uncle Tom, crouched in his corner waiting for the end, didn't think she was looking indecently cheerful.

I got down to the agenda in my debonair way.

'What ho, Angela, old girl.'

'Hullo, Bertie, darling.'

'Glad you're back at last. I missed you.'

'Did you, darling?'

'I did, indeed. Care to come for a saunter?'

'I'd love it.'

'Fine. I have much to say to you that is not for the public ear.'

I think at this moment poor old Tuppy must have got a sudden touch of cramp. He had been sitting hard by, staring at the ceiling, and he now gave a sharp leap like a gaffed salmon and upset a small table containing a vase, a bowl of potpourri, two china dogs, and a copy of Omar Khayyàm bound in limp leather.

Aunt Dahlia uttered a startled hunting cry. Uncle Tom, who probably imagined from the noise that this was civilization crashing at last, helped things along by breaking a coffee-cup.

Tuppy said he was sorry. Aunt Dahlia, with a deathbed groan, said it didn't matter. And Angela, having stared haughtily for a moment like a princess of the old regime confronted by some notable example of gaucherie on the part of some particularly foul member of the underworld, accompanied me across the threshold. And presently I had deposited her and self on one of the rustic benches in the garden, and was ready to snap into the business of the evening.

I considered it best, however, before doing so, to ease things along with a little informal chitchat. You don't want to rush a delicate job like the one I had in hand. And so for a while we spoke of neutral topics. She said that what had kept her so long at the Stretchley-Budds was that Hilda Stretchley-Budd had made her stop on and help with the arrangements for their servants' ball

tomorrow night, a task which she couldn't very well
decline, as all the Brinkley Court domestic staff were to
be present. I said that a jolly night's revelry might be just
what was needed to cheer Anatole up and take his mind
off things. To which she replied that Anatole wasn't
going. On being urged to do so by Aunt Dahlia, she said,
he had merely shaken his head sadly and gone on talking
of returning to Provence, where he was appreciated.

It was after the sombre silence induced by this
statement that Angela said the grass was wet and she
thought she would go in.

This, of course, was entirely foreign to my policy.

'No, don't do that. I haven't had a chance to talk to
you since you arrived.'

'I shall ruin my shoes.'

'Put your feet up on my lap.'

'All right. And you can tickle my ankles.'

'Quite.'

Matters were accordingly arranged on these lines, and
for some minutes we continued chatting in desultory
fashion. Then the conversation petered out. I made a few
observations *in re* the scenic effects, featuring the
twilight hush, the peeping stars, and the soft glimmer of
the waters of the lake, and she said yes. Something
rustled in the bushes in front of us, and I advanced the
theory that it was possibly a weasel, and she said it
might be. But it was plain that the girl was distrait, and I
considered it best to waste no more time.

'Well, old thing,' I said, 'I've heard all about your little
dust-up. So those wedding bells are not going to ring out,
what?'

'No.'

'Definitely over, is it?'

'Yes.'

'Well, if you want my opinion, I think that's a bit of
goose for you, Angela, old girl. I think you're extremely
well out of it. It's a mystery to me how you stood this

Glossop so long. Take him for all in all, he ranks very low down among the wines and spirits. A washout, I should describe him as. A frightful oik, and a mass of side to boot. I'd pity the girl who was linked for life to a bargee like Tuppy Glossop.'

And I emitted a hard laugh – one of the sneering kind.

'I always thought you were such friends,' said Angela.

I let go another hard one, with a bit more top spin on it than the first time:

'Friends. Absolutely not. One was civil, of course, when one met the fellow, but it would be absurd to say one was a friend of his. A club acquaintance, and a mere one at that. And then one was at school with the man.'

'At Eton?'

'Good heavens, no. We wouldn't have a fellow like that at Eton. At a kids' school before I went there. A grubby little brute he was, I recollect. Covered with ink and mire generally, and washing only on alternate Thursdays. In short, a notable outsider, shunned by all.'

I paused. I was more than a bit perturbed. Apart from the agony of having to talk in this fashion of one who, except when he was looping back rings and causing me to plunge into swimming baths in correct evening costume, had always been a very dear and esteemed crony, I didn't seem to be getting anywhere. Business was not resulting. Staring into the bushes without a yip, she appeared to be bearing these slurs and innuendoes of mine with an easy calm.

I had another pop at it:

'"Uncouth" about sums it up. I doubt if I've ever seen an uncoucher kid than this Glossop. Ask anyone who knew him in those days to describe him in a word, and the word they will use is "uncouth". And he's just the same today. It's the old story. The boy is the father of the man.'

She appeared not to have heard.

'The boy,' I repeated, not wishing her to miss that one, 'is the father of the man.'

'What are you talking about?'

'I'm talking about this Glossop.'

'I thought you said something about somebody's father.'

'I said the boy was the father of the man.'

'What boy?'

'The boy Glossop.'

'He hasn't got a father.'

'I never said he had. I said he was the father of the boy – or, rather, of the man.'

'What man?'

I saw that the conversation had reached a point where, unless care was taken, we should be muddled.

'The point I am trying to make,' I said, 'is that the boy Glossop is the father of the man Glossop. In other words, each loathsome fault and blemish that led the boy Glossop to be frowned upon by his fellows is present in the man Glossop, and causes him – I am speaking now of the man Glossop – to be a hissing and a byword at places like the Drones, where a certain standard of decency is demanded from the inmates. Ask anyone at the Drones, and they will tell you that it was a black day for the dear old club when this chap Glossop somehow wriggled into the list of members. Here you will find a man who dislikes his face; there one who could stand his face if it wasn't for his habits. But the universal consensus of opinion is that the fellow is a bounder and a tick, and that the moment he showed signs of wanting to get into the place he should have been met with a firm *nolle prosequi* and heartily blackballed.'

I had to pause again here, partly in order to take in a spot of breath, and partly to wrestle with the almost physical torture of saying these frightful things about poor old Tuppy.

'There are some chaps,' I resumed, forcing myself

661

once more to the nauseous task, 'who, in spite of looking as if they had slept in their clothes, can get by quite nicely because they are amiable and suave. There are others who, for all that they excite adverse comment by being fat and uncouth, find themselves on the credit side of the ledger owing to their wit and sparkling humour. But this Glossop, I regret to say, falls into neither class. In addition to looking like one of those things that come out of hollow trees, he is universally admitted to be a dumb brick of the first water. No soul. No conversation. In short, any girl who, having been rash enough to get engaged to him, has managed at the eleventh hour to slide out is justly entitled to consider herself dashed lucky.'

I paused once more, and cocked an eye at Angela to see how the treatment was taking. All the while I had been speaking, she had sat gazing silently into the bushes, but it seemed to me incredible that she should not now turn on me like a tigress, according to specifications. It beat me why she hadn't done it already. It seemed to me that a mere tithe of what I had said, if said to a tigress about a tiger of which she was fond, would have made her – the tigress, I mean – hit the ceiling.

And the next moment you could have knocked me down with a toothpick.

'Yes,' she said, nodding thoughtfully, 'you're quite right.'

'Eh?'

'That's exactly what I've been thinking myself.'

'What!'

'"Dumb brick." It just describes him. One of the six silliest asses in England, I should think he must be.'

I did not speak. I was endeavouring to adjust the faculties, which were in urgent need of a bit of first-aid treatment.

I mean to say, all this had come as a complete

surprise. In formulating the well-laid plan which I had just been putting into effect, the one contingency I had not budgeted for was that she might adhere to the sentiments which I expressed. I had braced myself for a gush of stormy emotion. I was expecting the tearful ticking off, the girlish recriminations and all the rest of the bag of tricks along those lines.

But this cordial agreement with my remarks I had not foreseen, and it gave me what you might call pause for thought.

She proceeded to develop her theme, speaking in ringing, enthusiastic tones, as if she loved the topic. Jeeves could tell you the word I want. I think it's 'ecstatic', unless that's that sort of rash you get on your face and have to use ointment for. But if that is the right word, then that's what her manner was as she ventilated the subject of poor old Tuppy. If you had been able to go simply by the sound of her voice, she might have been a court poet cutting loose about an Oriental monarch, or Gussie Fink-Nottle describing his last consignment of newts.

'It's so nice, Bertie, talking to somebody who really takes a sensible view about this man Glossop. Mother says he's a good chap, which is simply absurd. Anybody can see that he's absolutely impossible. He's conceited and opinionative and argues all the time, even when he knows perfectly well that he's talking through his hat, and he smokes too much and eats too much and drinks too much, and I don't like the colour of his hair. Not that he'll have any hair in a year or two, because he's pretty thin on the top already, and before he knows where he is he'll be as bald as an egg, and he's the last man who can afford to go bald. And I think it's simply disgusting, the way he gorges all the time. Do you know, I found him in the larder at one o'clock this morning, absolutely wallowing in a steak-and-kidney pie? There was hardly any of it left. And you remember what an enormous dinner he had. Quite disgusting, I call it. But I can't stop out here all night, talking about men who aren't worth wasting a word on and haven't even enough sense to tell sharks from flatfish. I'm going in.'

And gathering about her slim shoulders the shawl which she had put on as a protection against the evening dew, she buzzed off, leaving me alone in the silent night.

Well, as a matter of fact, not absolutely alone, because a few moments later there was a sort of upheaval in the bushes in front of me, and Tuppy emerged.

I5

I gave him the eye. The evening had begun to draw in a
bit by now and the visibility, in consequence, was not so
hot, but there still remained ample light to enable me to
see him clearly. And what I saw convinced me that I
should be a lot easier in my mind with a stout rustic
bench between us. I rose, accordingly, modelling my
style on that of a rocketing pheasant, and proceeded to
deposit myself on the other side of the object named.

My prompt agility was not without its effect. He
seemed somewhat taken aback. He came to a halt, and,
for about the space of time required to allow a bead of
persp. to trickle from the top of the brow to the tip of
the nose, stood gazing at me in silence.

'So!' he said, at length, and it came as a complete
surprise to me that fellows ever really do say 'So!' I had
always thought it was just a thing you read in books.
Like 'Quotha!' I mean to say, or 'Odds bodikins!' or even
'Eh ba goom!'

Still, there it was. Quaint or not quaint, bizarre or not
bizarre, he had said 'So!' and it was up to me to cope
with the situation on those lines.

It would have been a duller man than Bertram
Wooster who had failed to note that the dear old chap
was a bit steamed up. Whether his eyes were actually
shooting forth flame, I couldn't tell you, but there
appeared to me to be a distinct incandescence. For the
rest, his fists were clenched, his ears quivering, and the
muscles of his jaw rotating rhythmically, as if he were
making an early supper off something.

His hair was full of twigs, and there was a beetle

hanging to the side of his head which would have
interested Gussie Fink-Nottle. To this, however, I paid
scant attention. There is a time for studying beetles and
a time for not studying beetles.

'So!' he said again.

Now, those who know Bertram Wooster best will tell
you that he is always at his shrewdest and most
level-headed in moments of peril. Who was it who,
when gripped by the arm of the law on boat-race night
not so many years ago and hauled off to Vine Street
police station, assumed in a flash the identity of Eustace
H. Plimsoll, of The Laburnums, Alleyn Road, West
Dulwich, thus saving the grand old name of Wooster
from being dragged in the mire and avoiding wide
publicity of the wrong sort? Who was it . . .

But I need not labour the point. My record speaks for
itself. Three times pinched, but never once sentenced
under the correct label. Ask anyone at the Drones about
this.

So now, in a situation threatening to become every
moment more scaly, I did not lose my head. I preserved
the old sang-froid. Smiling a genial and affectionate
smile, and hoping that it wasn't too dark for it to
register, I spoke with a jolly cordiality:

'Why, hallo, Tuppy. You here?'

He said, yes, he was here.

'Been here long?'

'I have.'

'Fine. I wanted to see you.'

'Well, here I am. Come out from behind that bench.'

'No, thanks, old man. I like leaning on it. It seems to
rest the spine.'

'In about two seconds,' said Tuppy, 'I'm going to kick
your spine up through the top of your head.'

I raised the eybrows. Not much good, of course, in
that light, but it seemed to help the general
composition.

'Is this Hildebrand Glossop speaking?' I said.

He replied that it was, adding that if I wanted to make sure I might move a few feet over in his direction. He also called me an opprobrious name.

I raised the eyebrows again.

'Come, come, Tuppy, don't let us let this little chat become acrid. Is "acrid" the word I want?'

'I couldn't say,' he replied, beginning to sidle round the bench.

I saw that anything I might wish to say must be said quickly. Already he had sidled some six feet. And though, by dint of sidling, too, I had managed to keep the bench between us, who could predict how long this happy state of affairs would last?

I came to the point, therefore.

'I think I know what's on your mind, Tuppy,' I said. 'If you were in those bushes during my conversation with the recent Angela, I dare say you heard what I was saying about you.'

'I did.'

'I see. Well, we won't go into the ethics of the thing. Eavesdropping, some people might call it, and I can imagine stern critics drawing in the breath to some extent. Considering it – I don't want to hurt your feelings, Tuppy – but considering it un-English. A bit un-English, Tuppy, old man, you must admit.'

'I'm Scotch.'

'Really?' I said. 'I never knew that before. Rummy how you don't suspect a man of being Scotch unless he's Mac-something and says "Och, aye" and things like that. I wonder,' I went on, feeling that an academic discussion on some neutral topic might ease the tension, 'if you can tell me something that has puzzled me a good deal. What exactly is it that they put into haggis? I've often wondered about that.'

From the fact that his only response to the question was to leap over the bench and make a grab at me,

I gathered that his mind was not on haggis.

'However,' I said, leaping over the bench in my turn, 'that is a side issue. If, to come back to it, you were in those bushes and heard what I was saying about you –'

He began to move round the bench in a nor'-nor'-easterly direction. I followed his example, setting a course sou'-sou'-west.

'No doubt you were surprised at the way I was talking.'

'Not a bit.'

'What? Did nothing strike you as odd in the tone of my remarks?'

'It was just the sort of stuff I should have expected a treacherous, sneaking hound like you to say.'

'My dear chap,' I protested, 'this is not your usual form. A bit slow in the uptake, surely? I should have thought you would have spotted right away that it was all part of a well-laid plan.'

'I'll get you in a jiffy,' said Tuppy, recovering his balance after a swift clutch at my neck. And so probable did this seem that I delayed no longer, but hastened to place all the facts before him.

Speaking rapidly and keeping moving, I related my emotions on receipt of Aunt Dahlia's telegram, my instant rush to the scene of the disaster, my meditations in the car, and the eventual framing of this well-laid plan of mine. I spoke clearly and well, and it was with considerable concern, consequently, that I heard him observe – between clenched teeth, which made it worse – that he didn't believe a damned word of it.

'But, Tuppy,' I said, 'why not? To me the thing rings true to the last drop. What makes you sceptical? Confide in me, Tuppy.'

He halted and stood taking a breather. Tuppy, pungently though Angela might have argued to the contrary, isn't really fat. During the winter months you will find him constantly booting the football with merry shouts, and in the summer the tennis racket is seldom out of his hand.

But at the recently concluded evening meal, feeling, no doubt, that after that painful scene in the larder there was nothing to be gained by further abstinence, he had rather let himself go and, as it were, made up leeway; and after really immersing himself in one of Anatole's dinners, a man of his sturdy build tends to lose elasticity a bit. During the exposition of my plans for his happiness a certain animation had crept into this round-and-round-the-mulberry-bush jamboree of ours – so much so, indeed, that for the last few minutes we might have been a rather oversized greyhound and a somewhat slimmer electric hare doing their stuff on a circular track for the entertainment of the many-headed.

This, it appeared, had taken it out of him a bit, and I was not displeased. I was feeling the strain myself, and welcomed a lull.

'It absolutely beats me why you don't believe it,' I said. 'You know we've been pals for years. You must be aware that, except at the moment when you caused me to do a nose dive into the Drones' swimming bath, an incident which I long since decided to put out of my mind and let the dead past bury its dead about, if you follow what I mean – except on that one occasion, as I say, I have always regarded you with the utmost esteem. Why, then, if not for the motives I have outlined, should I knock you to Angela? Answer me that. Be very careful.'

'What do you mean, be very careful?'

Well, as a matter of fact, I didn't quite know myself. It was what the magistrate had said to me on the occasion when I stood in the dock as Eustace Plimsoll, of The Laburnums: and as it had impressed me a good deal at the time, I just bunged it in now by way of giving the conversation a tone.

'All right. Never mind about being careful, then. Just

answer me that question. Why, if I had not your
interests sincerely at heart, should I have ticked you off,
as stated?'

A sharp spasm shook him from base to apex. The
beetle, which, during the recent exchanges, had been
clinging to his head, hoping for the best, gave it up at
this and resigned office. It shot off and was swallowed in
the night.

'Ah!' I said. 'Your beetle,' I explained. 'No doubt you
were unaware of it, but all this while there has been a
beetle of sorts parked on the side of your head. You have
now dislodged it.'

He snorted.

'Beetles!'

'Not beetles. One beetle only.'

'I like your crust!' cried Tuppy, vibrating like one of
Gussie's newts during the courting season. 'Talking of
beetles, when all the time you know you're a
treacherous, sneaking hound.'

It was a debatable point, of course, why treacherous,
sneaking hounds should be considered ineligible to talk
about beetles, and I dare say a good cross-examining
counsel would have made quite a lot of it.

But I let it go.

'That's the second time you've called me that. And,' I
said firmly, 'I insist on an explanation. I have told you
that I acted throughout from the best and kindliest
motives in roasting you to Angela. It cut me to the quick
to have to speak like that, and only the recollection of
our lifelong friendship would have made me do it. And
now you say you don't believe me and call me names for
which I am not sure I couldn't have you up before a beak
and jury and mulct you in very substantial damages. I
should have to consult my solicitor, of course, but it
would surprise me very much if an action did not lie. Be
reasonable, Tuppy. Suggest another motive I could have
had. Just one.'

'I will. Do you think I don't know? You're in love with Angela yourself.'

'What?'

'And you knocked me in order to poison her mind against me and finally remove me from your path.'

I had never heard anything so absolutely loopy in my life. Why, dash it, I've known Angela since she was so high. You don't fall in love with close relations you've known since they were so high. Besides, isn't there something in the book of rules about a man may not marry his cousin? Or am I thinking of grandmothers?

'Tuppy, my dear old ass,' I cried, 'this is pure banana oil! You've come unscrewed.'

'Oh, yes?'

'Me in love with Angela? Ha-ha!'

'You can't get out of it with any ha-ha's. She called you "darling".'

'I know. And I disapproved. This habit of the younger g. of scattering "darlings" about like birdseed is one that I deprecate. Lax is how I should describe it.'

'You tickled her ankles.'

'In a purely cousinly spirit. It didn't mean a thing. Why, dash it, you must know that in the deeper and truer sense I wouldn't touch Angela with a barge pole.'

'Oh? And why not? Not good enough for you?'

'You misunderstand me,' I hastened to reply. 'When I say I wouldn't touch Angela with a barge pole, I intend merely to convey that my feelings towards her are those of distant, though cordial, esteem. In other words, you may rest assured that between this young prune and myself there never has been and never could be any sentiment warmer and stronger than that of ordinary friendship.'

'I believe it was you who tipped her off that I was in the larder last night, so that she could find me there with that pie, thus damaging my prestige.'

'My dear Tuppy! A Wooster?' I was shocked. 'You
think a Wooster would to that?'

He breathed heavily.

'Listen,' he said. 'It's no good your standing there
arguing. You can't get away from the facts. Somebody
stole her from me at Cannes. You told me yourself that
she was with you all the time at Cannes and hardly saw
anybody else. You gloated over the mixed bathing, and
those moonlight walks you had together –'

'Not gloated. Just mentioned them.'

'So now you understand why, as soon as I can get you
clear of this damned bench, I am going to tear you limb
from limb. Why they have these bally benches in
gardens,' said Tuppy discontentedly, 'is more than I can
see. They only get in the way.'

He ceased, and, grabbing out, missed me by a hair's
breadth.

It was a moment for swift thinking, and it is at such
moments, as I have already indicated, that Bertram
Wooster is at his best. I suddenly remembered the recent
misunderstanding with the Bassett, and with a flash of
clear vision saw that this was where it was going to
come in handy.

'You've got it all wrong, Tuppy,' I said, moving to the
left. 'True, I saw a lot of Angela, but my dealings with
her were on a basis from start to finish of the purest and
most wholesome camaraderie. I can prove it. During
that sojourn in Cannes my affections were engaged
elsewhere.'

'What?'

'Engaged elsewhere. My affections. During that
sojourn.'

I had struck the right note. He stopped sidling. His
clutching hand fell to his side.

'Is that true?'

'Quite official.'

'Who was she?'

'My dear Tuppy, does one bandy a woman's name?'

'One does if one doesn't want one's ruddy head pulled off.'

I saw that it was a special case.

'Madeline Bassett,' I said.

'Who?'

'Madeline Bassett.'

He seemed stunned.

'You stand there and tell me you were in love with that Bassett disaster?'

'I wouldn't call her "that Bassett disaster", Tuppy. Not respectful.'

'Dash being respectful. I want facts. You deliberately assert that you loved that weird Gawd-help-us?'

'I don't see why you should call her a weird Gawd-help-us, either. A very charming and beautiful girl. Odd in some of her views, perhaps – one does not quite see eye to eye with her in the matter of stars and rabbits – but not a weird Gawd-help-us.'

'Anyway, you stick to it that you were in love with her?'

'I do.'

'It sounds thin to me, Wooster, very thin.'

I saw that it would be necessary to apply the finishing touch.

'I must ask you to treat this as entirely confidential, Glossop, but I may as well inform you that it is not twenty-four hours since she turned me down.'

'Turned you down?'

'Like a bedspread. In this very garden.'

'Twenty-four hours?'

'Call it twenty-five. So you will readily see that I can't be the chap, if any, who stole Angela from you at Cannes.'

And I was on the brink of adding that I wouldn't touch Angela with a barge pole, when I remembered I had said it already and it hadn't gone frightfully well. I desisted, therefore.

673

My manly frankness seemed to be producing good results. The homicidal glare was dying out of Tuppy's eyes. He had the aspect of a hired assassin who had paused to think things over.

'I see,' he said, at length. 'All right, then. Sorry you were troubled.'

'Don't mention it, old man,' I responded courteously.

For the first time since the bushes had begun to pour forth Glossops, Bertram Wooster could be said to have breathed freely. I don't say I actually came out from behind the bench, but I did let go of it, and with something of the relief which those three chaps in the Old Testament must have experienced after sliding out of the burning fiery furnace, I even groped tentatively for my cigarette case.

The next moment a sudden snort made me take my fingers off it as if it had bitten me. I was distressed to note in the old friend a return of the recent frenzy.

'What the hell did you mean by telling her that I used to be covered with ink when I was a kid?'

'My dear Tuppy – '

'I was almost finickingly careful about my personal cleanliness as a boy. You could have eaten your dinner off me.'

'Quite. But – '

'And all that stuff about having no soul. I'm crawling with soul. And being looked on as an outsider at the Drones – '

'But, my dear old chap, I explained that. It was all part of my ruse or scheme.'

'It was, was it? Well, in future do me a favour and leave me out of your foul ruses.'

'Just as you say, old boy.'

'All right, then. That's understood.'

He relapsed into silence, standing with folded arms, staring before him rather like a strong, silent man in a novel when he's just been given the bird by the girl and is thinking of looking in at the Rocky Mountains and bumping off a few bears. His manifest pippedness excited my compash, and I ventured a kindly word.

'I don't suppose you know what *au pied de la lettre* means, Tuppy, but that's how I don't think you ought to take all that stuff Angela was saying just now too much.'

He seemed interested.

'What the devil,' he asked, 'are you talking about?'

I saw that I should have to make myself clearer.

'Don't take all that guff of hers too literally, old man. You know what girls are like.'

'I do,' he said, with another snort that came straight up from his insteps. 'And I wish I'd never met one.'

'I mean to say, it's obvious that she must have spotted you in those bushes and was simply talking to score off you. There you were, I mean, if you follow the psychology, and she saw you, and in that impulsive way girls have, she seized the opportunity of ribbing you a bit – just told you a few home truths, I mean to say.'

'Home truths?'

'That's right.'

He snorted once more, causing me to feel rather like royalty receiving a twenty-one gun salute from the fleet. I can't remember ever having met a better right-and-left-hand snorter.

'What do you mean, "home truths"? I'm not fat.'

'No, no.'

'And what's wrong with the colour of my hair?'

'Quite in order, Tuppy, old man. The hair, I mean.'

'And I'm not a bit thin on the top . . . What the dickens are you grinning about?'

'Not grinning. Just smiling slightly. I was conjuring up a sort of vision, if you know what I mean, of you as seen through Angela's eyes. Fat in the middle and thin on the top. Rather funny.'

'You think it funny, do you?'

'Not a bit.'

'You'd better not.'

'Quite.'

It seemed to me that the conversation was becoming difficult again. I wished it could be terminated. And so it was. For at this moment something came shimmering through the laurels in the quiet evenfall, and I perceived that it was Angela.

She was looking sweet and saintlike, and she had a plate of sandwiches in her hand. Ham, I was to discover later.

'If you see Mr Glossop anywhere, Bertie,' she said, her eyes resting dreamily on Tuppy's façade, 'I wish you would give him these. I'm so afraid he may be hungry, poor fellow. It's nearly ten o'clock, and he hasn't eaten a morsel since dinner. I'll just leave them on this bench.'

She pushed off, and it seemed to me that I might as well go with her. Nothing to keep me there, I mean. We moved towards the house, and presently from behind us there sounded in the night the splintering crash of a well-kicked plate of ham sandwiches, accompanied by the muffled oaths of a strong man in his wrath.

'How still and peaceful everything is,' said Angela.

16

Sunshine was gilding the grounds of Brinkley Court and
the ear detected a marked twittering of birds in the ivy
outside the window when I woke next morning to a new
day. But there was no corresponding sunshine in
Bertram Wooster's soul and no answering twitter in his
heart as he sat up in bed, sipping his cup of
strengthening tea. It could not be denied that to Bertram,
reviewing the happenings of the previous night, the
Tuppy – Angela situation seemed more or less to have
slipped a cog. With every desire to look for the silver
lining, I could not but feel that the rift between these
two haughty spirits had now reached such impressive
proportions that the task of bridging same.would be
beyond even my powers.

I am a shrewd observer, and there had been
something in Tuppy's manner as he booted that plate of
ham sandwiches that seemed to tell me that he would
not lightly forgive.

In these circs, I deemed it best to shelve their
problem for the nonce and turn the mind to the
matter of Gussie, which presented a brighter
picture.

With regard to Gussie, everything was in train.
Jeeves's morbid scruples about lacing the chap's orange
juice had put me to a good deal of trouble, but I had
surmounted every obstacle in the old Wooster way. I had
secured an abundance of the necessary spirit, and it was
now lying in its flask in the drawer of the dressing table.
I had also ascertained that the jug, duly filled, would be
standing on a shelf in the butler's pantry round about

the hour of one. To remove it from that shelf, sneak it up to my room, and return it, laced, in good time for the midday meal would be a task calling, no doubt, for address, but in no sense an exacting one.

It was with something of the emotions of one preparing a treat for a deserving child that I finished my tea and rolled over for that extra spot of sleep which just makes all the difference when there is man's work to be done and the brain must be kept clear for it.

And when I came downstairs an hour or so later, I knew how right I had been to formulate this scheme for Gussie's bucking up. I ran into him on the lawn, and I could see at a glance that if ever there was a man who needed a snappy stimulant, it was he. All nature, as I have indicated, was smiling, but not Augustus Fink-Nottle. He was walking round in circles, muttering something about not proposing to detain us long, but on this auspicious occasion feeling compelled to say a few words.

'Ah, Gussie,' I said, arresting him as he was about to start another lap. 'A lovely morning, is it not?'

Even if I had not been aware of it already, I could have divined from the abruptness with which he damned the lovely morning that he was not in merry mood. I addressed myself to the task of bringing the roses back to his cheeks.

'I've got good news for you, Gussie.'

He looked at me with a sudden sharp interest.

'Has Market Snodsbury Grammar School burned down?'

'Not that I know of.'

'Have mumps broken out? Is the place closed on account of measles?'

'No, no.'

'Then what do you mean you've got good news?'

I endeavoured to soothe.

'You mustn't take it so hard, Gussie. Why worry

about a laughably simple job like distributing prizes at a school?'

'Laughably simple, eh? Do you realize I've been sweating for days and haven't been able to think of a thing to say yet, except that I won't detain them long. You bet I won't detain them long. What the devil am I to say, Bertie? What do you say when you're distributing prizes?'

I considered. Once, at my private school, I had won a prize for Scripture knowledge, so I suppose I ought to have been full of inside stuff. But memory eluded me.

Then something emerged from the mists.

'You say the race is not always to the swift.'

'Why?'

'Well, it's a good gag. It generally gets a hand.'

'I mean, why isn't it? Why isn't the race to the swift?'

'Ah, there you have me. But the nibs say it isn't.'

'But what does it mean?'

'I take it it's supposed to console the chaps who haven't won prizes.'

'What's the good of that to me? I'm not worrying about them. It's the ones that have won prizes that I'm worrying about, the little blighters who will come up on the platform. Suppose they make faces at me.'

'They won't.'

'How do you know they won't? It's probably the first thing they'll think of. And even if they don't – Bertie, shall I tell you something?'

'What?'

'I've a good mind to take that tip of yours and have a drink.'

I smiled subtly. He little knew, about summed up what I was thinking.

'Oh, you'll be all right,' I said.

He became fevered again.

'How do you know I'll be all right? I'm sure to blow up in my lines.'

'Tush!'

'Or drop a prize.'

'Tut!'

'Or something. I can feel it in my bones. As sure as I'm standing here, something is going to happen this afternoon which will make everybody laugh themselves sick at me. I can hear them now. Like hyenas . . . Bertie!'

'Hullo?'

'Do you remember that kids' school we went to before Eton?'

'Quite. It was there I won my Scripture prize.'

'Never mind about your Scripture prize. I'm not talking about your Scripture prize. Do you recollect the Bosher incident?'

I did, indeed. It was one of the high spots of my youth.

'Major-General Sir Wilfred Bosher came to distribute the prizes at that school,' proceeded Gussie in a dull, toneless voice. 'He dropped a book. He stooped to pick it up. And, as he stooped, his trousers split up the back.'

'How we roared!'

Gussie's face twisted.

'We did, little swine that we were. Instead of remaining silent and exhibiting a decent sympathy for a gallant officer at a peculiarly embarrassing moment, we howled and yelled with mirth. I loudest of any. That is what will happen to me this afternoon, Bertie. It will be a judgement on me for laughing like that at Major-General Sir Wilfred Bosher.'

'No, no, Gussie, old man. Your trousers won't split.'

'How do you know they won't? Better men than I have split their trousers. General Bosher was a DSO, with a fine record of service on the north-western frontier of India, and his trousers split. I shall be a mockery and a scorn. I know it. And you, fully cognizant of what I am in for, come babbling about good news. What news could possibly be good to me at this moment except the information that bubonic plague had broken out among the scholars of Market Snodsbury Grammar School, and that they were all confined to their beds with spots?'

The moment had come for me to speak. I laid a hand gently on his shoulder. He brushed it off. I laid it on again. He brushed it off once more. I was endeavouring to lay it on for the third time, when he moved aside and desired, with a certain petulance, to be informed if I thought I was a ruddy osteopath.

I found his manner trying, but one has to make allowances. I was telling myself that I should be seeing a very different Gussie after lunch.

'When I said I had good news, old man, I meant about Madeline Bassett.'

The febrile gleam died out of his eyes, to be replaced by a look of infinite sadness.

'You can't have good news about her. I've dished myself there completely.'

'Not at all. I am convinced that if you take another whack at her, all will be well.'

And, keeping it snappy, I related what had passed between the Bassett and myself on the previous night.

'So all you have to do is play a return date, and you cannot fail to swing the voting. You are her dream man.'

He shook his head.

'No.'

'What?'

'No use.'

'What do you mean?'

'Not a bit of good trying.'

'But I tell you she said in so many words – '

'It doesn't make any difference. She may have loved me once. Last night will have killed all that.'

'Of course it won't.'

'It will. She despises me now.'

'Not a bit of it. She knows you simply got cold feet.'

'And I should get cold feet if I tried again. It's no good, Bertie. I'm hopeless, and there's an end of it. Fate made me the sort of chap who can't say "bo" to a goose.'

'It isn't a question of saying "bo" to a goose. The point doesn't arise at all. It is simply a matter of –'

'I know, I know. But it's no good. I can't do it. The whole thing is off. I am not going to risk a repetition of last night's fiasco. You talk in a light way of taking another whack at her, but you don't know what it means. You have not been through the experience of starting to ask the girl you love to marry you and then suddenly finding yourself talking about the plumelike external gills of the newly-born newt. It's not a thing you can do twice. No, I accept my destiny. It's all over. And now, Bertie, like a good chap, shove off. I want to compose my speech. I can't compose my speech with you mucking around. If you are going to continue to muck around, at least give me a couple of stories. The little hell hounds are sure to expect a story or two.'

'Do you know the one about –'

'No good. I don't want any of your off-colour stuff from the Drones' smoking-room. I need something clean. Something that will be a help to them in their after lives. Not that I care a damn about their after lives, except that I hope they'll all choke.'

'I heard a story the other day. I can't quite remember it, but it was about a chap who snored and disturbed the neighbours, and it ended, "It was his adenoids that adenoid them."'

He made a weary gesture.

'You expect me to work that in, do you, into a speech to be delivered to an audience of boys, every one of whom is probably riddled with adenoids? Damn it, they'd rush the platform. Leave me, Bertie. Push off. That's all I ask you to do. Push off . . . Ladies and gentlemen,' said Gussie, in a low, soliloquizing sort of way, 'I do not propose to detain this auspicious occasion long –'

It was a thoughtful Wooster who walked away and left him at it. More than ever I was congratulating myself on having had the sterling good sense to make all my arrangements so that I could press a button and set things moving at an instant's notice.

Until now, you see, I had rather entertained a sort of hope that when I had revealed to him the Bassett's mental attitude, Nature would have done the rest, bracing him up to such an extent that artificial stimulants would not be required. Because, naturally, a chap doesn't want to have to sprint about country houses lugging jugs of orange juice, unless it is absolutely essential.

But now I saw that I must carry on as planned. The total absence of pep, ginger, and the right spirit which the man had displayed during these conversational exchanges convinced me that the strongest measures would be necessary. Immediately upon leaving him, therefore, I proceeded to the pantry, waited till the butler had removed himself elsewhere, and nipped in and secured the vital jug. A few moments later, after a wary passage of the stairs, I was in my room. And the first thing I saw there was Jeeves, fooling about with trousers.

He gave the jug a look which – wrongly, as it was to turn out – I diagnosed as censorious. I drew myself up a bit. I intended to have no rot from the fellow.

'Yes, Jeeves?'

'Sir?'

'You have the air of one about to make a remark, Jeeves.'

'Oh, no, sir. I note that you are in possession of Mr Fink-Nottle's orange juice. I was merely about to observe that in my opinion it would be injudicious to add spirit to it.'

'That is a remark, Jeeves, and it is precisely – '

'Because I have already attended to the matter, sir.'

'What?'

'Yes, sir. I decided, after all, to acquiesce in your wishes.'

I stared at the man, astounded. I was deeply moved. Well, I mean, wouldn't any chap who had been going about thinking that the old feudal spirit was dead and then suddenly found it wasn't have been deeply moved?

'Jeeves,' I said, 'I am touched.'

'Thank you, sir.'

'Touched and gratified.'

'Thank you very much, sir.'

'But what caused this change of heart?'

'I chanced to encounter Mr Fink-Nottle in the garden, sir, while you were still in bed, and we had a brief conversation.'

'And you came away feeling that he needed a bracer?'

'Very much so, sir. His attitude struck me as defeatist.'

I nodded.

'I felt the same. "Defeatist" sums it up to a nicety. Did you tell him his attitude struck you as defeatist?'

'Yes, sir.'

'But it didn't do any good?'

'No, sir.'

'Very well, then, Jeeves. We must act. How much gin did you put in the jug?'

'A liberal tumblerful, sir.'

'Would that be a normal dose for an adult defeatist, do you think?'

'I fancy it should prove adequate, sir.'

'I wonder. We must not spoil the ship for a ha'porth of tar. I think I'll add just another fluid ounce or so.'

'I would not advocate it, sir. In the case of Lord Brancaster's parrot –'

'You are falling into your old error, Jeeves, of thinking that Gussie is a parrot. Fight against this. I shall add the oz.'

'Very good, sir.'

'And, by the way, Jeeves, Mr Fink-Nottle is in the
market for bright, clean stories to use in his speech. Do
you know any?'

'I know a story about two Irishmen, sir.'

'Pat and Mike?'

'Yes, sir.'

'Who were walking along Broadway?'

'Yes, sir.'

'Just what he wants. Any more?'

'No, sir.'

'Well, every little helps. You had better go and tell it
to him.'

'Very good, sir.'

He passed from the room, and I unscrewed the flask
and tilted into the jug a generous modicum of its
contents. And scarcely had I done so, when there came
to my ears the sound of footsteps without. I had only
just time to shove the jug behind the photograph of
Uncle Tom on the mantelpiece before the door opened
and in came Gussie, curveting like a circus horse.

'What-ho, Bertie,' he said. 'What-ho, what-ho,
what-ho, and again what-ho. What a beautiful world this
is, Bertie. One of the nicest I ever met.'

I stared at him, speechless. We Woosters are as quick
as lightning, and I saw at once that something had
happened.

I mean to say, I told you about him walking round it
circles. I recorded what passed between us on the lawn.
And if I portrayed the scene with anything like adequate
skill, the picture you will have retained of this Fink-
Nottle will have been that of a nervous wreck, sagging at
the knees, green about the gills, and picking feverishly at
the lapels of his coat in an ecstasy of craven fear. In a
word, defeatist. Gussie, during that interview, had, in
fine, exhibited all the earmarks of one licked to a
custard.

685

Vastly different was the Gussie who stood before me now. Self-confidence seemed to ooze from the fellow's every pore. His face was flushed, there was a jovial light in his eyes, the lips were parted in a swashbuckling smile. And when with a genial hand he sloshed me on the back before I could sidestep, it was as if I had been kicked by a mule.

'Well, Bertie,' he proceeded, as blithely as a linnet without a thing on his mind, 'you will be glad to hear that you were right. Your theory has been tested and proved correct. I feel like a fighting cock.'

My brain ceased to reel. I saw all.

'Have you been having a drink?'

'I have. As you advised. Unpleasant stuff. Like medicine. Burns your throat, too, and makes one as thirsty as the dickens. How anyone can mop it up, as you do, for pleasure beats me. Still, I would be the last to deny that it tunes up the system. I could bite a tiger.'

'What did you have?'

'Whisky. At least, that was the label on the decanter, and I have no reason to suppose that a woman like your aunt – staunch, true-blue, British – would deliberately deceive the public. If she labels her decanters Whisky, then I consider that we know where we are.'

'A whisky and soda, eh? You couldn't have done better.'

'Soda?' said Gussie thoughtfully. 'I knew there was something I had forgotten.'

'Didn't you put any soda in it?'

'It never occurred to me. I just nipped into the dining-room and drank out of the decanter.'

'How much?'

'Oh, about ten swallows. Twelve, maybe. Or fourteen. Say sixteen medium-sized gulps. Gosh, I'm thirsty.'

He moved over to the wash-hand stand and drank deeply out of the water bottle. I cast a covert glance at Uncle Tom's photograph behind his back. For the first time since it had come into my life, I was glad that it was so large. It hid its secret well. If Gussie had caught sight of that jug of orange juice, he would unquestionably have been on to it like a knife.

'Well, I'm glad you're feeling braced,' I said.

He moved buoyantly from the wash-hand stand, and endeavoured to slosh me on the back again. Foiled by my nimble footwork, he staggered to the bed and sat down upon it.

'Braced? Did I say I could bite a tiger?'

'You did.'

'Make it two tigers. I could chew holes in a steel door. What an ass you must have thought me out there in the garden. I see now you were laughing in your sleeve.'

'No, no.'

'Yes,' insisted Gussie. 'That very sleeve,' he said, pointing. 'And I don't blame you. I can't imagine why I made all that fuss about a potty job like distributing prizes at a rotten little country grammar school. Can you imagine, Bertie?'

'No.'

'Exactly. Nor can I imagine. There's simply nothing to it. I just shin up on the platform, drop a few gracious words, hand the little blighters their prizes, and hop down again, admired by all. Not a suggestion of split trousers from start to finish. I mean, why should anybody split his trousers? I can't imagine. Can you imagine?'

'No.'

'Nor can I imagine. I shall be a riot. I know just the sort of stuff that's needed – simple, manly, optimistic stuff straight from the shoulder. This shoulder,' said Gussie, tapping. 'Why I was so nervous this morning I can't imagine. For anything simpler than distributing a few footling books to a bunch of grimy-faced kids I can't imagine. Still, for some reason I can't imagine, I was feeling a little nervous, but now I feel fine, Bertie – fine,

fine, fine – and I say this to you as an old friend. Because
that's what you are, old man, when all the smoke has
cleared away – an old friend. I don't think I've ever met
an older friend. How long have you been an old friend of
mine, Bertie?'

'Oh, years and years.'

'Imagine? Though, of course, there must have been a
time when you were a new friend . . . Hullo, the
luncheon gong. Come on, old friend.'

And, rising from the bed like a performing flea, he
made for the door.

I followed rather pensively. What had occurred was,
of course, so much velvet, as you might say. I mean, I
had wanted a braced Fink-Nottle – indeed, all my plans
had had a braced Fink-Nottle as their end and aim – but I
found myself wondering a little whether the Fink-Nottle
now sliding down the banister wasn't, perhaps, a shade
too braced. His demeanour seemed to me that of a man
who might quite easily throw bread about at lunch.

Fortunately, however, the settled gloom of those
round him exercised a restraining effect upon him at the
table. It would have needed a far more plastered man to
have been rollicking at such a gathering. I had told the
Bassett that there were aching hearts in Brinkley Court,
and it now looked probable that there would shortly be
aching tummies. Anatole, I learned, had retired to his
bed with a fit of the vapours, and the meal now before us
had been cooked by the kitchen maid – as C3 a
performer as ever wielded a skillet.

This, coming on top of their other troubles, induced
in the company a pretty unanimous silence – a solemn
stillness, as you might say – which even Gussie did not
seem prepared to break. Except, therefore, for one short
snatch of song on his part, nothing untoward marked the
occasion, and presently we rose, with instructions from
Aunt Dahlia to put on festal raiment and be at Market
Snodsbury not later than 3.30. This leaving me ample

time to smoke a gasper or two in a shady bower beside the lake, I did so, repairing to my room round about the hour of three.

Jeeves was on the job, adding the final polish to the old topper, and I was about to apprise him of the latest developments in the matter of Gussie, when he forestalled me by observing that the latter had only just concluded an agreeable visit to the Wooster bed-chamber.

'I found Mr Fink-Nottle seated here when I arrived to lay out your clothes, sir.'

'Indeed, Jeeves? Gussie was in here, was he?'

'Yes, sir. He left only a few moments ago. He is driving to the school with Mr and Mrs Travers in the large car.'

'Did you give him your story of the two Irishmen?'

'Yes, sir. He laughed heartily.'

'Good. Had you any other contributions for him?'

'I ventured to suggest that he might mention to the young gentlemen that education is a drawing out, not a putting in. The late Lord Brancaster was much addicted to presenting prizes at schools, and he invariably employed this dictum.'

'And how did he react to that?'

'He laughed heartily, sir.'

'This surprised you, no doubt? This practically incessant merriment, I mean.'

'Yes, sir.'

'You thought it odd in one who, when you last saw him, was well up in Group A of the defeatists.'

'Yes, sir.'

'There is a ready explanation, Jeeves. Since you last saw him, Gussie has been on a bender. He's as tight as an owl.'

'Indeed, sir?'

'Absolutely. His nerve cracked under the strain, and he sneaked into the dining-room and started mopping the stuff up like a vacuum cleaner. Whisky would seem to be what he filled the radiator with. I gather that he used up most of the decanter. Golly, Jeeves, it's lucky he didn't get at that laced orange juice on top of that, what?'

'Extremely, sir.'

I eyed the jug. Uncle Tom's photograph had fallen into the fender, and it was standing there right out in the open, where Gussie couldn't have helped seeing it. Mercifully, it was empty now.

'It was a most prudent act on your part, if I may say so, sir, to dispose of the orange juice.'

I stared at the man.

'What? Didn't you?'

'No, sir.'

'Jeeves, let us get this clear. Was it not you who threw away that o.j.?'

'No, sir. I assumed, when I entered the room and found the pitcher empty, that you had done so.'

We looked at each other, awed. Two minds with but a single thought.

'I very much fear, sir –'

'So do I, Jeeves.'

'It would seem almost certain –'

'Quite certain. Weigh the facts. Sift the evidence. The jug was standing on the mantelpiece, for all eyes to behold. Gussie had been complaining of thirst. You found him in here, laughing heartily. I think that there can be little doubt, Jeeves, that the entire contents of that jug are at this moment reposing on top of the existing cargo in that already brilliantly lit man's interior. Disturbing, Jeeves.'

'Most disturbing, sir.'

'Let us face the position, forcing ourselves to be calm. You inserted in that jug – shall we say a tumblerful of the right stuff?'

'Fully a tumblerful, sir.'

'And I added of my plenty about the same amount.'

'Yes, sir.'

'And in two shakes of a duck's tail Gussie, with all that lapping about inside him, will be distributing the prizes at Market Snodsbury Grammar School before an audience of all that is fairest and most refined in the county.'

'Yes, sir.'

'It seems to me, Jeeves, that the ceremony may be one fraught with considerable interest.'

'Yes, sir.'

'What, in your opinion, will the harvest be?'

'One finds it difficult to hazard a conjecture, sir.'

'You mean imagination boggles?'

'Yes, sir.'

I inspected my imagination. He was right. It boggled.

17

'And yet, Jeeves,' I said, twiddling a thoughtful steering
wheel, 'there is always the bright side.'

Some twenty minutes had elapsed, and having picked
the honest fellow up outside the front door, I was driving
in the two-seater to the picturesque town of Market
Snodsbury. Since we had parted – he to go to his lair and
fetch his hat, I to remain in my room and complete the
formal costume – I had been doing some close thinking.

The results of this I now proceeded to hand on to
him.

'However dark the prospect may be, Jeeves, however
murkily the storm clouds may seem to gather, a keen
eye can usually discern the blue bird. It is bad, no doubt,
that Gussie should be going, some ten minutes from
now, to distribute prizes in a state of advanced
intoxication, but we must never forget that these things
cut both ways.'

'You imply, sir –'

'Precisely. I am thinking of him in his capacity of
wooer. All this ought to have put him in rare shape for
offering his hand in marriage. I shall be vastly surprised
if it won't turn him into a sort of caveman. Have you
ever seen James Cagney in the movies?'

'Yes, sir.'

'Something on those lines.'

I heard him cough, and sniped him with a sideways
glance. He was wearing that informative look of his.

'Then you have not heard, sir?'

'Eh?'

'You are not aware that a marriage has been arranged

and will shortly take place between Mr Fink-Nottle and
Miss Bassett?'

'What?'

'Yes, sir.'

'When did this happen?'

'Shortly after Mr Fink-Nottle had left your room, sir.'

'Ah! In the post-orange-juice era?'

'Yes, sir.'

'But are you sure of your facts? How do you know?'

'My informant was Mr Fink-Nottle himself, sir. He
appeared anxious to confide in me. His story was
somewhat incoherent, but I had no difficulty in
apprehending its substance. Prefacing his remarks with
the statement that this was a beautiful world, he
laughed heartily and said that he had become formally
engaged.'

'No details?'

'No, sir.'

'But one can picture the scene.'

'Yes, sir.'

'I mean, imagination doesn't boggle.'

'No, sir.'

And it didn't. I could see exactly what must have
happened. Insert a liberal dose of mixed spirits in a
normally abstemious man, and he becomes a force. He
does not stand round, twiddling his fingers and
stammering. He acts. I had no doubt that Gussie must
have reached for the Bassett and clasped her to him like
a stevedore handling a sack of coals. And one could
readily envisage the effect of that sort of thing on a girl
of romantic mind.

'Well, well, well, Jeeves.'

'Yes, sir.'

'This is splendid news.'

'Yes, sir.'

'You see now how right I was.'

'Yes, sir.'

'It must have been rather an eye-opener for you,
watching me handle this case.'

'Yes, sir.'

'The simple, direct method never fails.'

'No, sir.'

'Whereas the elaborate does.'

'Yes, sir.'

'Right ho, Jeeves.'

We had arrived at the main entrance of Market
Snodsbury Grammar School. I parked the car, and went
in, well content. True, the Tuppy–Angela problem still
remained unsolved and Aunt Dahlia's five hundred quid
seemed as far off as ever, but it was gratifying to feel that
good old Gussie's troubles were over, at any rate.

The Grammar School at Market Snodsbury had, I
understood, been built somewhere in the year 1416, and,
as with so many of these ancient foundations, there still
seemed to brood over its Great Hall, where the
afternoon's festivities were to take place, not a little of
the fug of the centuries. It was the hottest day of the
summer, and though somebody had opened a tentative
window or two, the atmosphere remained distinctive
and individual.

In this hall the youth of Market Snodsbury had been
eating its daily lunch for a matter of five hundred years,
and the flavour lingered. The air was sort of heavy and
languorous, if you know what I mean, with the scent of
Young England and boiled beef and carrots.

Aunt Dahlia, who was sitting with a bevy of the local
nibs in the second row, sighted me as I entered and
waved to me to join her, but I was too smart for that. I
wedged myself in among the standees at the back,
leaning up against a chap who, from the aroma, might
have been a corn chandler or something of that order.
The essency of strategy on these occasions is to be as
near the door as possible.

The hall was gaily decorated with flags and coloured

paper, and the eye was further refreshed by the spectacle of a mixed drove of boys, parents, and what not, the former running a good deal to shiny faces and Eton collars, the latter stressing the black-satin note rather when female, and looking as if their coats were too tight, if male. And presently there was some applause – sporadic, Jeeves has since told me it was – and I saw Gussie being steered by a bearded bloke in a gown to a seat in the middle of the platform.

And I confess that as I beheld him and felt that there but for the grace of God went Bertram Wooster, a shudder ran through the frame. It all reminded me so vividly of the time I had addressed that girls' school.

Of course, looking at it dispassionately, you may say that for horror and peril there is no comparison between an almost human audience like the one before me and a mob of small girls with pigtails down their backs, and this, I concede, is true. Nevertheless, the spectacle was enough to make me feel like a fellow watching a pal going over Niagara Falls in a barrel, and the thought of what I had escaped caused everything for a moment to go black and swim before my eyes.

When I was able to see clearly once more, I perceived that Gussie was now seated. He had his hands on his knees, with his elbows out at right angles, like a nigger minstrel of the old school about to ask Mr Bones why a chicken crosses the road, and he was staring before him with a smile so fixed and pebble-beached that I should have thought that anybody could have guessed that there sat one in whom the old familiar juice was splashing up against the back of the front teeth.

In fact, I saw Aunt Dahlia, who, having assisted at so many hunting dinners in her time, is second to none as a judge of the symptoms, give a start and gaze long and earnestly. And she was just saying something to Uncle Tom on her left when the bearded bloke stepped to the footlights and started making a speech. From the fact that he spoke as if he had a hot potato in his mouth without getting the raspberry from the lads in the ringside seats, I deduced that he must be the headmaster.

With his arrival in the spotlight, a sort of perspiring resignation seemed to settle on the audience. Personally, I snuggled up against the chandler and let my attention wander. The speech was on the subject of the doings of the school during the past term, and this part of a prize-giving is always apt rather to fail to grip the visiting stranger. I mean, you know how it is. You're told that J. B. Brewster has won an Exhibition for Classics at Cat's, Cambridge, and you feel that it's one of those stories where you can't see how funny it is unless you really know the fellow. And the same applies to G. Bullett being awarded the Lady Jane Wix Scholarship at the Birmingham College of Veterinary Science.

In fact, I and the corn chandler, who was looking a bit fagged, I thought, as if he had had a hard morning chandling the corn, were beginning to doze lightly when things suddenly brisked up, bringing Gussie into the picture for the first time.

'Today,' said the bearded bloke, 'we are all happy to welcome as the guest of the afternoon Mr Fitz-Wattle – '

At the beginning of the address, Gussie had subsided into a sort of daydream, with his mouth hanging open. About halfway through, faint signs of life had begun to show. And for the last few minutes he had been trying to cross one leg over the other and failing and having another shot and failing again. But only now did he exhibit any real animation. He sat up with a jerk.

'Fink-Nottle,' he said, opening his eyes.

'Fitz-Nottle.'

'Fink-Nottle.'

'I should say Fink-Nottle.'

'Of course you should, you silly ass,' said Gussie genially. 'All right, get on with it.'

And closing his eyes, he began trying to cross his legs again.

I could see that this little spot of friction had rattled the bearded bloke a bit. He stood for a moment fumbling at the fungus with a hesitating hand. But they make these headmasters of tough stuff. The weakness passed. He came back nicely and carried on.

'We are all happy, I say, to welcome as the guest of the afternoon Mr Fink-Nottle, who has kindly consented to award the prizes. This task, as you know, is one that should have devolved upon that well-beloved and vigorous member of our board of governors, the Rev. William Plomer, and we are all, I am sure, very sorry that illness at the last moment should have prevented him from being here today. But, if I may borrow a familiar metaphor from the – if I may employ a homely metaphor familiar to you all – what we lose on the swings we gain on the roundabouts.'

He paused, and beamed rather freely, to show that this was comedy. I could have told the man it was no use. Not a ripple. The corn chandler leaned against me and muttered 'Whoddidesay?' but that was all.

It's always a nasty jar to wait for the laugh and find that the gag hasn't got across. The bearded bloke was visibly discomposed. At that, however, I think he would have got by, had he not, at this juncture, unfortunately stirred Gussie up again.

'In other words, though deprived of Mr Plomer, we have with us this afternoon Mr Fink-Nottle. I am sure that Mr Fink-Nottle's name is one that needs no introduction to you. It is, I venture to assert, a name that is familiar to us all.'

'Not to you,' said Gussie.

And the next moment I saw what Jeeves had meant when he had described him as laughing heartily. 'Heartily' was absolutely the *mot juste*. It sounded like a gas explosion.

'You didn't seem to know it so dashed well, what, what?' said Gussie. And, reminded apparently by the word 'what' of the word 'Wattle', he repeated the latter some sixteen times with a rising inflexion.

'Wattle, Wattle, Wattle,' he concluded. 'Right-ho. Push on.'

But the bearded bloke had shot his bolt. He stood there, licked at last; and, watching him closely, I could see that he was now at the crossroads. I could spot what he was thinking as clearly as if he had confided it to my personal ear. He wanted to sit down and call it a day, I mean, but the thought that gave him pause was that, if he did, he must then either uncork Gussie or take the Fink-Nottle speech as read and get straight on to the actual prize-giving.

It was a dashed tricky thing, of course, to have to decide on the spur of the moment. I was reading in the paper the other day about those birds who are trying to split the atom, the nub being that they haven't the foggiest as to what will happen if they do. It may be all right. On the other hand, it may not be all right. And pretty silly a chap would feel, no doubt, if, having split the atom, he suddenly found the house going up in smoke and himself torn limb from limb.

So with the bearded bloke. Whether he was abreast of the inside facts in Gussie's case, I don't know, but it was obvious to him by this time that he had run into something pretty hot. Trial gallops had shown that Gussie had his own way of doing things. Those interruptions had been enough to prove to the perspicacious that here, seated on the platform at the big binge of the season, was one who, if pushed forward to make a speech, might let himself go in a rather epoch-making manner.

On the other hand, chain him up and put a green-baize cloth over him, and where were you? The proceeding would be over about half an hour too soon.

It was, as I say, a difficult problem to have to solve, and, left to himself, I don't know what conclusion he would have come to. Personally, I think he would have played it safe. As it happened, however, the thing was taken out of his hands, for at this moment, Gussie, having stretched his arms and yawned a bit, switched on that pebble-beached smile again and tacked down to the edge of the platform.

'Speech,' he said affably.

He then stood with his thumbs in the armholes of his waistcoat, waiting for the applause to die down.

It was some time before this happened, for he had got a very fine hand indeed. I suppose it wasn't often that the boys of Market Snodsbury Grammar School came across a man public-spirited enough to call their headmaster a silly ass, and they showed their appreciation in no uncertain manner. Gussie may have been one over the eight, but as far as the majority of those present were concerned he was sitting on top of the world.

'Boys,' said Gussie, 'I mean ladies and gentlemen and boys, I will not detain you long, but I propose on this occasion to feel compelled to say a few auspicious words. Ladies – boys and ladies and gentlemen – we have all listened with interest to the remarks of our friend here who forgot to shave this morning – I don't know his name, but then he didn't know mine – Fitz-Wattle, I mean, absolutely absurd – which squares things up a bit – and we are all sorry that the Reverend What-ever-he-was-called should be dying of adenoids, but after all, here today, gone tomorrow, and all flesh is as grass, and what not, but that wasn't what I wanted to say. What I wanted to say was this – and I say it confidently – without fear of contradiction – I say, in short, I am happy to be here on this auspicious occasion and I take much pleasure in kindly awarding the prizes, consisting of the handsome books you see laid out on that table. As Shakespeare says, there are sermons in books, stones in the running brooks, or, rather, the other way about, and there you have it in a nutshell.'

It went well, and I wasn't surprised. I couldn't quite follow some of it, but anybody could see that it was real ripe stuff, and I was amazed that even the course of treatment he had been taking could have rendered so normally tongue-tied a dumb brick as Gussie capable of it.

It just shows, what any member of Parliament will tell you, that if you want real oratory, the preliminary noggin is essential. Unless pie-eyed, you cannot hope to grip.

'Gentlemen,' said Gussie, 'I mean ladies and gentlemen and, of course, boys, what a beautiful world this is. A beautiful world, full of happiness on every side. Let me tell you a little story. Two Irishmen, Pat and Mike, were walking along Broadway, and one said to the other, "Begorrah, the race is not always to the swift," and the other replied, "Faith and begob, education is a drawing out, not a putting in."'

I must say it seemed to me the rottenest story I had ever heard, and I was surprised that Jeeves should have considered it worth shoving into a speech. However, when I taxed him with this later, he said that Gussie had altered the plot a good deal, and I dare say that accounts for it.

At any rate, that was the *conte* as Gussie told it, and when I say that it got a very fair laugh, you will understand what a popular favourite he had become with the multitude. There might be a bearded bloke or so on the platform and a small section in the second row who were wishing the speaker would conclude his remarks and resume his seat, but the audience as a whole was for him solidly.

There was applause, and a voice cried: 'Hear, hear!'

'Yes,' said Gussie, 'it is a beautiful world. The sky is

blue, the birds are singing, there is optimism
everywhere. And why not, boys and ladies and
gentlemen? I'm happy, you're happy, we're all happy,
even the meanest Irishman that walks along Broadway.
Though as I say, there were two of them – Pat and Mike,
one drawing out, the other putting in. I should like you
boys, taking the time from me, to give three cheers for
this beautiful world. All together now.'

Presently the dust settled down and the plaster
stopped falling from the ceiling, and he went on.

'People who say it isn't a beautiful world don't know
what they are talking about. Driving here in the car
today to award the kind prizes, I was reluctantly
compelled to tick off my host on this very point. Old
Tom Travers. You will see him sitting there in the
second row next to the large lady in beige.'

He pointed helpfully, and the hundred or so Market
Snodsburyians who craned their necks in the direction
indicated were able to observe Uncle Tom blushing
prettily.

'I ticked him off properly, the poor fish. He expressed
the opinion that the world was in a deplorable state. I
said, "Don't talk rot, old Tom Travers." "I am not
accustomed to talk rot," he said. "Then, for a beginner,"
I said, "you do it dashed well." And I think you will
admit, boys and ladies and gentlemen, that that was
telling him.'

The audience seemed to agree with him. The point
went big. The voice that had said 'Hear, hear' said 'Hear,
hear' again, and my corn chandler hammered the floor
vigorously with a large-size walking stick.

'Well, boys,' resumed Gussie, having shot his cuffs
and smirked horribly, 'this is the end of the summer
term, and many of you, no doubt, are leaving the school.
And I don't blame you, because there's a froust in here
you could cut with a knife. You are going out into the
great world. Soon many of you will be walking along

Broadway. And what I want to impress upon you is that, however much you may suffer from adenoids, you must all use every effort to prevent yourselves becoming pessimists and talking rot like old Tom Travers. There in the second row. The fellow with a face rather like a walnut.'

He paused to allow those wishing to do so to refresh themselves with another look at Uncle Tom, and I found myself musing in some little perplexity. Long association with the members of the Drones has put me pretty well in touch with the various ways in which an overdose of the blushful Hippocrene can take the individual, but I had never seen anyone react quite as Gussie was doing.

There was a sort of snap about his work which I had never witnessed before, even in Barmy Fotheringay-Phipps on New Year's Eve.

Jeeves, when I discussed the matter with him later, said it was something to do with inhibitions, if I caught the word correctly, and the suppression of, I think he said, the ego. What he meant, I gathered, was that, owing to the fact that Gussie had just completed a five years' stretch of blameless seclusion among the newts, all the goofiness which ought to have been spread out thin over those five years and had been bottled up during that period came to the surface on this occasion in a lump – or, if you prefer to put it that way, like a tidal wave.

There may be something in this. Jeeves generally knows.

Anyway, be that as it may, I was dashed glad I had had the shrewdness to keep out of that second row. It might be unworthy of the prestige of a Wooster to squash in among the proletariat in the standing-room-only section, but at least, I felt, I was out of the danger zone. So thoroughly had Gussie got it up his nose by now that it seemed to me that had he sighted me he might have become personal about even an old school friend.

'If there's one thing in the world I can't stand,' proceeded Gussie, 'it's a pessimist. Be optimists, boys. You all know the difference between an optimist and a pessimist. An optimist is a man who – well, take the case of two Irishmen walking along Broadway. One is an optimist and one is a pessimist, just as one's name is Pat and the other's Mike . . . Why, hullo, Bertie; I didn't know you were here.'

Too late, I endeavoured to go to earth behind the chandler, only to discover that there was no chandler there. Some appointment, suddenly remembered – possibly a promise to his wife that he would be home to tea – had caused him to ooze away while my attention was elsewhere, leaving me right out in the open.

Between me and Gussie, who was now pointing in an offensive manner, there was nothing but a sea of interested faces looking up at me.

'Now, there,' boomed Gussie, continuing to point, 'is an instance of what I mean. Boys and ladies and gentlemen, take a good look at that object standing up there at the back – morning coat, trousers as worn, quiet grey tie, and carnation in buttonhole – you can't miss him. Bertie Wooster, that is, and as foul a pessimist as ever bit a tiger. I tell you I despise that man. And why do I despise him? Because, boys and ladies and gentlemen, he is a pessimist. His attitude is defeatist. When I told him I was going to address you this afternoon, he tried to dissuade me. And do you know why he tried to dissuade me? Because he said my trousers would split up the back.'

The cheers that greeted this were the loudest yet. Anything about splitting trousers went straight to the simple hearts of the young scholars of Market Snodsbury Grammar School. Two in the row in front of me turned purple, and a small lad with freckles seated beside them asked me for my autograph.

'Let me tell you a story about Bertie Wooster.'

A Wooster can stand a good deal, but he cannot stand having his name bandied in a public place. Picking my feet up softly, I was in the very process of executing a quiet sneak for the door, when I perceived that the bearded bloke had at last decided to apply the closure.

Why he hadn't done so before is beyond me. Spellbound, I take it. And, of course, when a chap is going like a breeze with the public, as Gussie had been, it's not so dashed easy to chip in. However, the prospect of hearing another of Gussie's anecdotes seemed to have done the trick. Rising rather as I had risen from my bench at the beginning of that painful scene with Tuppy in the twilight, he made a leap for the table, snatched up a book and came bearing down on the speaker.

He touched Gussie on the arm, and Gussie, turning sharply and seeing a large bloke with a beard apparently about to bean him with a book, sprang back in an attitude of self-defence.

'Perhaps, as time is getting on, Mr Fink-Nottle, we had better –'

'Oh, ah,' said Gussie, getting the trend. He relaxed. 'The prizes, eh? Of course, yes. Right ho. Yes, might as well be shoving along with it. What's this one?'

'Spelling and dictation – P. K. Purvis,' announced the bearded bloke.

'Spelling and dictation – P. K. Purvis,' echoed Gussie, as if he were calling coals. 'Forward, P. K. Purvis.'

Now that the whistle had been blown on his speech, it seemed to me that there was no longer any need for the strategic retreat which I had been planning. I had no wish to tear myself away unless I had to. I mean, I had told Jeeves that this binge would be fraught with interest, and it was fraught with interest. There was a fascination about Gussie's methods which gripped and made one reluctant to pass the thing up provided personal innuendoes were steered clear of. I decided, accordingly, to remain, and presently there was a musical squeaking and P. K. Purvis climbed the platform.

The spelling-and-dictation champ was about three foot six in his squeaking shoes, with a pink face and sandy hair.

Gussie patted this hair. He seemed to have taken an immediate fancy to the lad.

'You P. K. Purvis?'

'Sir, yes, sir.'

'It's a beautiful world, P. K. Purvis.'

'Sir, yes, sir.'

'Ah, you've noticed it, have you? Good. You married, by any chance?'

'Sir, no, sir.'

'Get married, P. K. Purvis,' said Gussie earnestly. 'It's the only life . . . Well, here's your book. Looks rather bilge to me from a glance at the title page, but, such as it is, here you are.'

P. K. Purvis squeaked off amidst sporadic applause, but one could not fail to note that the sporadic was followed by a rather strained silence. It was evident that Gussie was striking something of a new note in Market Snodsbury scholastic circles. Looks were exchanged between parent and parent. The bearded bloke had the air of one who has drained the bitter cup. As for Aunt Dahlia, her demeanour now told only too clearly that her last doubts had been resolved and her verdict was in. I saw her whisper to the Bassett, who sat on her right, and the Bassett nodded sadly and looked like a fairy about to shed a tear and add another star to the Milky Way.

Gussie, after the departure of P. K. Purvis, had fallen into a sort of daydream and was standing with his mouth open and his hands in his pockets. Becoming abruptly aware that a fat kid in knickerbockers was at his elbow, he started violently.

'Hullo!' he said, visibly shaken. 'Who are you?'

'This,' said the bearded bloke, 'is R. V. Smethurst.'

'What's he doing here?' asked Gussie suspiciously.

'You are presenting him with the drawing prize, Mr Fink-Nottle.'

This apparently struck Gussie as a reasonable explanation. His face cleared.

'That's right too,' he said . . . 'Well, here it is, cocky. You off?' he said, as the kid prepared to withdraw.

'Sir, yes, sir.'

'Wait, R. V. Smethurst. Not so fast. Before you go, there is a question I wish to ask you.'

But the bearded bloke's aim now seemed to be to rush the ceremonies a bit. He hustled R. V. Smethurst off stage rather like a chucker-out in a pub regretfully ejecting an old and respected customer, and started paging G. G. Simmons. A moment later the latter was up and coming, and conceive my emotion when it was announced that the subject on which he had clicked was Scripture knowledge. One of us, I mean to say.

G. G. Simmons was an unpleasant, perky-looking stripling, mostly front teeth and spectacles, but I gave him a big hand. We Scripture-knowledge sharks stick together.

Gussie, I was sorry to see, didn't like him. There was in his manner, as he regarded G. G. Simmons, none of the chumminess which had marked it during his interview with P. K. Purvis or, in a somewhat lesser degree, with R. V. Smethurst. He was cold and distant.

'Well, G. G. Simmons,'

'Sir, yes, sir.'

'What do you mean – sir, yes, sir? Dashed silly thing to say. So you've won the Scripture-knowledge prize, have you?'

'Sir, yes, sir,'

'Yes,' said Gussie, 'you look just the sort of little tick

who would. And yet,' he said, pausing and eyeing the
child keenly, 'how are we to know that this has all been
open and above board? Let me test you, G. G. Simmons.
Who was What's-His-Name – the chap who begat
Thingummy? Can you answer me that, Simmons?'

'Sir, no, sir.'

Gussie turned to the bearded bloke.

'Fishy,' he said. 'Very fishy. This boy appears to be
totally lacking in Scripture knowledge.'

The bearded bloke passed a hand across his
forehead.

'I can assure you, Mr Finkle-Nottle, that every care
was taken to ensure a correct marking and that Simmons
outdistanced his competitors by a wide margin.'

'Well, if you say so,' said Gussie doubtfully. 'All right,
G. G. Simmons, take your prize.'

'Sir, thank you, sir.'

'But let me tell you that there's nothing to stick on
side about in winning a prize for Scripture knowledge.
Bertie Wooster – '

I don't know when I've had a nastier shock. I had
been going on the assumption that, now that they had
stopped him making his speech, Gussie's fangs had been
drawn, as you might say. To duck my head down and
resume my edging towards the door was with me the
work of a moment.

'Bertie Wooster won the Scripture-knowledge prize at
a kids' school we were at together, and you know what
he's like. But, of course, Bertie frankly cheated. He
succeeded in scrounging that Scripture-knowledge
trophy over the heads of better men by means of some of
the rawest and most brazen swindling methods ever
witnessed even at a school where such things were
common. If that man's pockets, as he entered the
examination-room, were not stuffed to bursting point
with lists of the kings of Judah – '

I heard no more. A moment later I was out in God's

air, fumbling with a fevered foot at the self-starter of the old car.

The engine raced. The clutch slid into position. I tooted and drove off.

My ganglions were still vibrating as I ran the car into the stables of Brinkley Court, and it was a much shaken Bertram who tottered up to his room to change into something loose. Having donned flannels, I lay down on the bed for a bit, and I suppose I must have dozed off, for the next thing I remember is finding Jeeves at my side.

I sat up.

'My tea, Jeeves?'

'No, sir. It is nearly dinner-time.'

The mists cleared away.

'I must have been asleep.'

'Yes, sir.'

'Nature taking its toll of the exhausted frame.'

'Yes, sir.'

'And enough to make it.'

'Yes, sir.'

'And now it's nearly dinner-time, you say? All right. I am in no mood for dinner, but I suppose you had better lay out the clothes.'

'It will not be necessary, sir. The company will not be dressing tonight. A cold collation has been set out in the dining-room.'

'Why's that?'

'It was Mrs Travers's wish that this should be done in order to minimize the work for the staff, who are attending a dance at Sir Percival Stretchley-Budd's residence tonight.'

'Of course, yes. I remember. My Cousin Angela told me. Tonight's the night, what? You going, Jeeves?'

'No, sir. I am not very fond of this form of entertainment in the rural districts, sir.'

'I know what you mean. These country binges are all

the same. A piano, one fiddle, and a floor like sandpaper.
Is Anatole going? Angela hinted not.'

'Miss Angela was correct, sir. Monsieur Anatole is in
bed.'

'Temperamental blighters, these Frenchmen.'

'Yes, sir.'

There was a pause.

'Well, Jeeves,' I said, 'it was certainly one of those
afternoons, what?'

'Yes, sir.'

'I cannot recall one more packed with incident. And I
left before the finish.'

'Yes, sir. I observed your departure.'

'You couldn't blame me for withdrawing.'

'No, sir. Mr Fink-Nottle had undoubtedly become
embarrassingly personal.'

'Was there much more of it after I went?'

'No, sir. The proceedings terminated very shortly. Mr
Fink-Nottle's remarks with reference to Master G. G.
Simmons brought about an early closure.'

'But he had finished his remarks about G. G.
Simmons.'

'Only temporarily, sir. He resumed them immediately
after your departure. If you recollect, sir, he had already
proclaimed himself suspicious of Master Simmons's
bona fides, and he now proceeded to deliver a violent
verbal attack upon the young gentleman, asserting that
it was impossible for him to have won the
Scripture-knowledge prize without systematic cheating
on an impressive scale. He went so far as to suggest that
Master Simmons was well known to the police.'

'Golly, Jeeves!'

'Yes, sir. The words did create a considerable
sensation. The reaction of those present to this
accusation I should describe as mixed. The young
students appeared pleased and applauded vigorously, but
Master Simmons's mother rose from her seat and

addressed Mr Fink-Nottle in terms of strong protest.'

'Did Gussie seem taken aback? Did he recede from his position?'

'No, sir. He said that he could see it all now, and hinted at a guilty liaison between Master Simmons's mother and the headmaster, accusing the latter of having cooked the marks, as his expression was, in order to gain favour with the former.'

'You don't mean that?'

'Yes, sir.'

'Egad, Jeeves! And then –'

'They sang the national anthem, sir.'

'Surely not?'

'Yes, sir.'

'At a moment like that?'

'Yes, sir.'

'Well, you were there and you know, of course, but I should have thought the last thing Gussie and this woman would have done in the circs would have been to start singing duets.'

'You misunderstand me, sir. It was the entire company who sang. The headmaster turned to the organist and said something to him in a low tone. Upon which the latter began to play the national anthem, and the proceedings terminated.'

'I see. About time, too.'

'Yes, sir. Mrs Simmons's attitude had become unquestionably menacing.'

I pondered. What I had heard was, of course, of a nature to excite pity and terror, not to mention alarm and despondency, and it would be paltering with the truth to say that I was pleased about it. On the other hand, it was all over now, and it seemed to me that the thing to do was not to mourn over the past but to fix the mind on the bright future. I mean to say, Gussie might have lowered the existing Worcestershire record for goofiness and definitely forfeited all chance of becoming

Market Snodsbury's favourite son, but you couldn't get away from the fact that he had proposed to Madeline Bassett, and you had to admit that she had accepted him.

I put this to Jeeves.

'A frightful exhibition,' I said, 'and one which will very possibly ring down history's pages. But we must not forget, Jeeves, that Gussie, though now doubtless looked upon in the neighbourhood as the world's worst freak, is all right otherwise.'

'No, sir.'

I did not quite get this.

'When you say "No, sir", do you mean "Yes, sir"?'

'No, sir. I mean "No, sir".'

'He is not all right otherwise?'

'No, sir.'

'But he's betrothed.'

'No longer, sir. Miss Bassett has severed the engagement.'

'You don't mean that?'

'Yes, sir.'

I wonder if you have noticed a rather peculiar thing about this chronicle. I allude to the fact that at one time or another practically everybody playing a part in it has had occasion to bury his or her face in his or her hands. I have participated in some pretty glutinous affairs in my time, but I think that never before or since have I been mixed up with such a solid body of brow clutchers.

Uncle Tom did it, if you remember. So did Gussie. So did Tuppy. So, probably, though I have no data, did Anatole, and I wouldn't put it past the Bassett. And Aunt Dahlia, I have no doubt, would have done it, too, but for the risk of disarranging the carefully fixed coiffure.

Well, what I am trying to say is that at this juncture I did it myself. Up went the hands and down went the head, and in another jiffy I was clutching as energetically as the best of them.

And it was while I was still massaging the coconut and wondering what the next move was that something barged up against the door like the delivery of a ton of coals.

'I think this may very possibly be Mr Fink-Nottle himself, sir,' said Jeeves.

His intuition, however, had led him astray. It was not Gussie but Tuppy. He came in and stood breathing asthmatically. It was plain that he was deeply stirred.

18

I eyed him narrowly. I didn't like his looks. Mark you, I don't say I ever had, much, because Nature, when planning this sterling fellow, shoved in a lot more lower jaw than was absolutely necessary and made the eyes a bit too keen and piercing for one who was neither an Empire builder nor a traffic policeman. But on the present occasion, in addition to offending the aesthetic sense, this Glossop seemed to me to be wearing a distinct air of menace, and I found myself wishing that Jeeves wasn't always so dashed tactful.

I mean, it's all very well to remove yourself like an eel sliding into mud when the employer has a visitor, but there are moments – and it looked to me as if this was going to be one of them – when the truer tact is to stick round and stand ready to lend a hand in the free-for-all.

For Jeeves was no longer with us. I hadn't seen him go, and I hadn't heard him go, but he had gone. As far as the eye could reach, one noted nobody but Tuppy. And in Tuppy's demeanour, as I say, there was a certain something that tended to disquiet. He looked to me very much like a man who had come to reopen that matter of my tickling Angela's ankles.

However, his opening remark told me that I had been alarming myself unduly. It was of a pacific nature, and came as a great relief.

'Bertie,' he said, 'I owe you an apology. I have come to make it.'

My relief on hearing these words, containing as they did no reference of any sort to tickled ankles, was, as I

say, great. But I don't think it was any greater than my
surprise. Months had passed since that painful episode at
the Drones, and until now he hadn't given a sign of
remorse and contrition. Indeed, word had reached me
through private sources that he frequently told the story
at dinners and other gatherings and, when doing so,
laughed his silly head off.

I found it hard to understand, accordingly, what could
have caused him to abase himself at this later date.
Presumably he had been given the elbow by his better
self, but why?

Still, there it was.

'My dear chap,' I said, gentlemanly to the gills, 'don't
mention it.'

'What's the sense of saying, "Don't mention it"? I
have mentioned it.'

'I mean, don't mention it any more. Don't give the
matter another thought. We all of us forget ourselves
sometimes and do things which, in our calmer
moments, we regret. No doubt you were a bit tight at
the time.'

'What the devil do you think you're talking about?'

I didn't like his tone. Brusque.

'Correct me if I am wrong,' I said, with a certain
stiffness, 'but I assumed that you were apologizing for
your foul conduct in looping back the last ring that night
in the Drones, causing me to plunge into the swimming
b. in the full soup and fish.'

'Ass! Not that, at all.'

'Then what?'

'This Bassett business.'

'What Bassett business?'

'Bertie,' said Tuppy, 'when you told me last night that
you were in love with Madeline Bassett, I gave you the
impression that I believed you, but I didn't. The thing
seemed too incredible. However, since then I have made
inquiries and the facts appear to square with your

statement. I have now come to apologize for doubting you.'

'Made inquiries?'

'I asked her if you had proposed to her, and she said, yes, you had.'

'Tuppy! You didn't?'

'I did.'

'Have you no delicacy, no proper feeling?'

'No.'

'Oh? Well, right-ho, of course, but I think you ought to have.'

'Delicacy be dashed. I wanted to be certain that it was not you who stole Angela from me. I now know it wasn't.'

So long as he knew that, I didn't so much mind him having no delicacy.

'Ah,' I said. 'Well, that's fine. Hold that thought.'

'I have found out who it was.'

'What?'

He stood brooding for a moment. His eyes were smouldering with a dull fire. His jaw stuck out like the back of Jeeves's head.

'Bertie,' he said, 'do you remember what I swore I would do to the chap who stole Angela from me?'

'As nearly as I recall, you planned to pull him inside out –'

' – and make him swallow himself. Correct. The programme still holds good.'

'But, Tuppy, I keep assuring you, as a competent eyewitness, that nobody snitched Angela from you during that Cannes trip.'

'No. But they did after she got back.'

'What?'

'Don't keep saying, "What?" You heard.'

'But she hasn't seen anybody since she got back.'

'Oh, no? How about that newt bloke?'

'Gussie?'

'Precisely. The serpent Fink-Nottle.'

This seemed to me absolute gibbering.

'But Gussie loves the Bassett.'

'You can't all love this blighted Bassett. What astonishes me is that anyone can do it. He loves Angela, I tell you. And she loves him.'

'But Angela handed you your hat before Gussie ever got here.'

'No, she didn't. Couple of hours after.'

'He couldn't have fallen in love with her in a couple of hours.'

'Why not? I fell in love with her in a couple of minutes. I worshipped her immediately we met, the pop-eyed little excrescence.'

'But, dash it –'

'Don't argue, Bertie. The facts are all docketed. She loves this newt-nuzzling blister.'

'Quite absurd, laddie – quite absurd.'

'Oh?' He ground a heel into the carpet – thing I've often read about, but had never seen done before.

'Then perhaps you will explain how it is that she happens to come to be engaged to him?'

You could have knocked me down with a f.

'Engaged to him?'

'She told me herself.'

'She was kidding you.'

'She was not kidding me. Shortly after the conclusion of this afternoon's binge at Market Snodsbury Grammar School he asked her to marry him, and she appears to have right-hoed without a murmur.'

'There must be some mistake.'

'There was. The snake Fink-Nottle made it, and by now I bet he realizes it. I've been chasing him since 5.30.'

'Chasing him?'

'All over the place. I want to pull his head off.'

'I see. Quite.'

'You haven't seen him, by any chance?'

'No.'

'Well, if you do, say good-bye to him quickly and put in your order for lilies . . . Oh, Jeeves.'

'Sir?'

I hadn't heard the door open, but the man was on the spot once more. My private belief, as I think I have mentioned before, is that Jeeves doesn't have to open doors. He's like one of those birds in India who bung their astral bodies about – the chaps, I mean, who having gone into thin air in Bombay, reassemble the parts and appear two minutes later in Calcutta. Only some such theory will account for the fact that he's not there one moment and is there the next. He just seems to float from Spot A to Spot B like some form of gas.

'Have you seen Mr Fink-Nottle, Jeeves?'

'No, sir.'

'I'm going to murder him.'

'Very good, sir.'

Tuppy withdrew, banging the door behind him, and I put Jeeves abreast.

'Jeeves,' I said, 'do you know what? Mr Fink-Nottle is engaged to my Cousin Angela.'

'Indeed, sir?'

'Well, how about it? Do you grasp the psychology? Does it make sense? Only a few hours ago he was engaged to Miss Bassett.'

'Gentlemen who have been discarded by one young lady are often apt to attach themselves without delay to another, sir. It is what is known as a gesture.'

I began to grasp.

'I see what you mean. Defiant stuff.'

'Yes, sir.'

'A sort of "Oh, right-ho, please yourself, but if you don't want me, there are plenty who do."'

'Precisely, sir. My cousin George –'

'Never mind about your Cousin George, Jeeves.'

'Very good, sir.'

'Keep him for the long winter evenings, what?'

'Just as you wish, sir.'

'And, anyway, I bet your Cousin George wasn't a shrinking, non-goose-bo-ing jellyfish like Gussie. That is what astounds me, Jeeves – that it should be Gussie who has been putting in all this heavy gesture-making stuff.'

'You must remember, sir, that Mr Fink-Nottle is in a somewhat inflamed cerebral condition.'

'That's true. A bit above par at the moment, as it were?'

'Exactly, sir.'

'Well, I'll tell you one thing – he'll be in a jolly sight more inflamed cerebral condition if Tuppy gets hold of him . . . What's the time?'

'Just on eight o'clock, sir.'

'Then Tuppy has been chasing him for two hours and a half. We must save the unfortunate blighter, Jeeves.'

'Yes, sir.'

'A human life is a human life, what?'

'Exceedingly true, sir.'

'The first thing, then, is to find him. After that we can discuss plans and schemes. Go forth, Jeeves, and scour the neighbourhood.'

'It will not be necessary, sir. If you will glance behind you, you will see Mr Fink-Nottle coming out from beneath your bed.'

And, by Jove, he was absolutely right.

There was Gussie, emerging as stated. He was covered with fluff and looked like a tortoise popping forth for a bit of a breather.

'Gussie!' I said.

'Jeeves,' said Gussie.

'Sir?' said Jeeves.

'Is that door locked, Jeeves?'

'No, sir, but I will attend to the matter immediately.'

Gussie sat down on the bed, and I thought for a

moment that he was going to be in the mode by burying his face in his hands. However, he merely brushed a dead spider from his brow.

'Have you locked the door, Jeeves?'

'Yes, sir.'

'Because you can never tell that that ghastly Glossop may not take it into his head to come –'

The word 'back' froze on his lips. He hadn't got any further than a *b*-ish sound, when the handle of the door began to twist and rattle. He sprang from the bed, and for an instant stood looking exactly like a picture my Aunt Agatha has in her dining-room – The Stag at Bay – Landseer. Then he made a dive for the cupboard and was inside it before one really got on to it that he had started leaping. I have seen fellows late for the 9.15 move less nippily.

I shot a glance at Jeeves. He allowed his right eyebrow to flicker slightly, which is as near as he ever gets to a display of the emotions.

'Hullo?' I yipped.

'Let me in, blast you!' responded Tuppy's voice from without. 'Who locked this door?'

I consulted Jeeves once more in the language of the eyebrow. He raised one of his. I raised one of mine. He raised his other. I raised my other. Then we both raised both. Finally, there seeming no other policy to pursue, I flung wide the gates and Tuppy came shooting in.

'Now what?' I said, as nonchalantly as I could manage.

'Why was the door locked?' demanded Tuppy.

I was in pretty good eyebrow-raising form by now, so I gave him a touch of it.

'Is one to have no privacy, Glossop?' I said coldly. 'I instructed Jeeves to lock the door because I was about to disrobe.'

'A likely story!' said Tuppy, and I'm not sure he didn't add 'Forsooth!' 'You needn't try to make me believe that you're afraid people are going to run excursion trains to see you in your underwear. You locked that door because you've got the snake Fink-Nottle in here. I suspected it the moment I'd left, and I decided to come back and investigate. I'm going to search this room from end to end. I believe he's in that cupboard . . . What's in this cupboard?'

'Just clothes,' I said, having another stab at the nonchalant, though extremely dubious as to whether it would come off. 'The usual wardrobe of the English gentleman paying a country-house visit.'

'You're lying!'

Well, I wouldn't have been if he had only waited a minute before speaking, because the words were hardly out of his mouth before Gussie was out of the cupboard. I have commented on the speed with which he had gone in. It was as nothing to the speed with which he emerged. There was a sort of whir and blur, and he was no longer with us.

I think Tuppy was surprised. In fact, I'm sure he was. Despite the confidence with which he had stated his view that the cupboard contained Fink-Nottle, it plainly disconcerted him to have the chap fizzing out at him like this. He gargled sharply, and jumped back about five feet. The next moment, however, he had recovered his poise and was galloping down the corridor in pursuit. It only needed Aunt Dahlia after them, shouting 'Yoicks!' or whatever is customary on these occasions, to complete the resemblance to a brisk run with the Quorn.

I sank into a handy chair. I am not a man whom it is easy to discourage, but it seemed to me that things had at last begun to get too complex for Bertram.

'Jeeves,' I said, 'all this is a bit thick.'

'Yes, sir.'

'The head rather swims.'

'Yes, sir.'

'I think you had better leave me, Jeeves. I shall need to devote the very closest thought to the situation which has arisen.'

'Very good, sir.'

The door closed. I lit a cigarette and began to ponder.

19

Most chaps in my position, I imagine, would have pondered all the rest of the evening without getting a bite, but we Woosters have an uncanny knack of going straight to the heart of things, and I don't suppose it was much more than ten minutes after I had started pondering before I saw what had to be done.

What was needed to straighten matters out, I perceived, was a heart-to-heart talk with Angela. She had caused all the trouble by her mutton-headed behaviour in saying 'Yes' instead of 'No' when Gussie, in the grip of mixed drinks and cerebral excitement, had suggested teaming up. She must obviously be properly ticked off and made to return him to store. A quarter of an hour later, I had tracked her down to the summer-house in which she was taking a cooler, and was seating myself by her side.

'Angela,' I said, and if my voice was stern, well, whose wouldn't have been, 'this is all perfect drivel.'

She seemed to come out of a reverie. She looked at me inquiringly.

'I'm sorry, Bertie, I didn't hear. What were you talking drivel about?'

'I was not talking drivel.'

'Oh, sorry, I thought you said you were.'

'Is it likely that I would come out here in order to talk drivel?'

'Very likely.'

I thought it best to haul off and approach the matter from another angle.

'I've just been seeing Tuppy.'

'Oh?'

'And Gussie Fink-Nottle.'

'Oh, yes?'

'It appears that you have gone and got engaged to the latter.'

'Quite right.'

'Well, that's what I meant when I said it was all perfect drivel. You can't possibly love a chap like Gussie.'

'Why not?'

'You simply can't.'

Well, I mean to say, of course she couldn't. Nobody could love a freak like Gussie except a similar freak like the Bassett. The shot wasn't on the board. A splendid chap, of course, in many ways – courteous, amiable, and just the fellow to tell you what to do till the doctor came, if you had a sick newt on your hands – but quite obviously not of Mendelssohn's March timbre. I have no doubt that you could have flung bricks by the hour in England's most densely-populated districts without endangering the safety of a single girl capable of becoming Mrs Augustus Fink-Nottle without an anaesthetic.

I put this to her, and she was forced to admit the justice of it.

'All right, then. Perhaps I don't.'

'Then what,' I said keenly, 'did you want to go and get engaged to him for, you unreasonable young fathead?'

'I thought it would be fun.'

'Fun!'

'And so it has been. I've had a lot of fun out of it. You should have seen Tuppy's face when I told him.'

A sudden bright light shone upon me.

'Ha! A gesture!'

'What?'

'You got engaged to Gussie just to score off Tuppy?'

'I did.'

'Well, then, that was what I was saying. It was a gesture.'

'Yes, I suppose you could call it that.'

'And I'll tell you something else I'll call it – viz. a dashed low trick. I'm surprised at you, young Angela.'

'I don't see why.'

I curled the lip about half an inch. 'Being a female, you wouldn't. You gentler sexers are like that. You pull off the rawest stuff without a pang. You pride yourselves on it. Look at Jael, the wife of Heber.'

'Where did you ever hear of Jael, the wife of Heber?'

'Possibly you are not aware that I once won a Scripture-knowledge prize at school?'

'Oh, yes. I remember Augustus mentioning it in his speech.'

'Quite,' I said, a little hurriedly. I had no wish to be reminded of Augustus's speech. 'Well, as I say, look at Jael, the wife of Heber. Dug spikes into the guest's coconut while he was asleep, and then went swanking about the place like a Girl Guide. No wonder they say "Oh, woman, woman!"'

'Who?'

'The chaps who do. Coo, what a sex! But you aren't proposing to keep this up, of course?'

'Keep what up?'

'This rot of being engaged to Gussie.'

'I certainly am,'

'Just to make Tuppy look silly.'

'Do you think he looks silly?'

'I do.'

'So he ought to.'

I began to get the idea that I wasn't making real headway. I remember when I won that Scripture-knowledge prize, having to go into the facts about Balaam's ass. I can't quite recall what they were, but I still retain a sort of general impression of something digging its feet in and putting its ears back and refusing to cooperate; and it seemed to me that this was what Angela was doing now. She and Balaam's ass were, so to speak, sisters under the skin. There's a word beginning with *r* – 're' something – 'recal' something – No, it's gone. But what I am driving at is that is what this Angela was showing herself.

'Silly young geezer,' I said.

She pinkened.

'I'm not a silly young geezer.'

'You are a silly young geezer. And, what's more, you know it.'

'I don't know anything of the kind.'

'Here you are, wrecking Tuppy's life, wrecking Gussie's life, all for the sake of a cheap score.'

'Well, it's no business of yours.'

I sat on this promptly:

'No business of mine when I see two lives I used to go to school with wrecked? Ha! Besides, you know you're potty about Tuppy.'

'I'm not!'

'Is that so? If I had a quid for every time I've seen you gaze at him with the lovelight in your eyes – '

She gazed at me, but without the lovelight.

'Oh, for goodness' sake, go away and boil your head, Bertie!'

I drew myself up.

'That,' I replied, with dignity, 'is just what I am going to go away and boil. At least, I mean, I shall now leave you. I have said my say.'

'Good.'

'But permit me to add – '

'I won't.'

'Very good,' I said coldly. 'In that case, tinkerty tonk.'

And I meant it to sting.

'Moody' and 'discouraged' were about the two

adjectives you would have selected to describe me as I left the summer-house. It would be idle to deny that I had expected better results from this little chat.

I was surprised at Angela. Odd how you never realize that every girl is at heart a vicious specimen until something goes wrong with her love affair. This cousin and I had been meeting freely since the days when I wore sailor suits and she hadn't any front teeth, yet only now was I beginning to get on to her hidden depths. A simple, jolly, kindly young pimple she had always struck me as – the sort you could more or less rely on not to hurt a fly. But here she was now laughing heartlessly – at least, I seemed to remember hearing her laugh heartlessly – like something cold and callous out of a sophisticated talkie, and fairly spitting on her hands in her determination to bring Tuppy's grey hairs in sorrow to the grave.

I've said it before, and I'll say it again – girls are rummy. Old Pop Kipling never said a truer word than when he made that crack about the f. of the s. being more d. than the m.

It seemed to me in the circs that there was but one thing to do – that is head for the dining-room and take a slash at that cold collation of which Jeeves had spoken. I felt in urgent need of sustenance, for the recent interview had pulled me down a bit. There is no gainsaying the fact that all this naked-emotion stuff reduces a chap's vitality and puts him in the vein for a good whack at the beef and ham.

To the dining-room, accordingly, I repaired, and had barely crossed the threshold when I perceived Aunt Dahlia at the sideboard, tucking into salmon mayonnaise.

The spectacle drew from me a quick 'Oh, ah,' for I was somewhat embarrassed. The last time this relative and I had enjoyed a *tête-à-tête*, it will be remembered, she had sketched out plans for drowning me in the kitchen-garden pond, and I was not quite sure what my present standing with her was.

I was relieved to find her in genial mood. Nothing could have exceeded the cordiality with which she waved her fork.

'Hallo, Bertie, you old ass,' was her very matey greeting. 'I thought I shouldn't find you far away from the food. Try some of this salmon. Excellent.'

'Anatole's?' I queried.

'No. He's still in bed. But the kitchen maid has struck an inspired streak. It suddenly seems to have come home to her that she isn't catering for a covey of buzzards in the Sahara Desert, and she has put out something quite fit for human consumption. There is good in the girl, after all, and I hope she enjoys herself at the dance.'

I ladled out a portion of salmon, and we fell into pleasant conversation, chatting of this servants' ball at the Stretchley-Budds and speculating idly, I recall, as to what Seppings, the butler, would look like, doing the rumba.

It was not till I had cleaned up the first platter and was embarking on a second that the subject of Gussie came up. Considering what had passed at Market Snodsbury that afternoon, it was one which I had been expecting her to touch on earlier. When she did touch on it, I could see that she had not yet been informed of Angela's engagement.

'I say, Bertie,' she said, meditatively chewing fruit salad. 'This Spink-Bottle.'

'Nottle.'

'Bottle,' insisted the aunt firmly. 'After that exhibition of his this afternoon, Bottle, and nothing but Bottle, is how I shall always think of him. However, what I was going to say was that, if you see him, I wish you would tell him that he has made an old woman

very, very happy. Except for the time when the curate
tripped over a loose shoelace and fell down the pulpit
steps, I don't think I have ever had a more wonderful
moment than when good old Bottle suddenly started
ticking Tom off from the platform. In fact, I thought his
whole performance in the most perfect taste.'

I could not but demur.

'Those references to myself – '

'Those were what I liked next best. I thought they
were fine. Is it true that you cheated when you won that
Scripture-knowledge prize?'

'Certainly not. My victory was the outcome of the
most strenuous and unremitting efforts.'

'And how about this pessimism we hear of? Are you a
pessimist, Bertie?'

I could have told her that what was occurring in this
house was rapidly making me one, but I said no, I
wasn't.

'That's right. Never be a pessimist. Everything is for
the best in this best of all possible worlds. It's a long
lane that has no turning. It's always darkest before the
dawn. Have patience and all will come right. The sun
will shine, although the day's a grey one . . . Try some of
this salad.'

I followed her advice, but even as I plied the spoon
my thoughts were elsewhere. I was perplexed. It may
have been the fact that I had recently been hobnobbing
with so many bowed-down hearts that made this
cheeriness of hers seem so bizarre, but bizarre was
certainly what I found it.

'I thought you might have been a trifle peeved,' I said.

'Peeved?'

'By Gussie's manoeuvres on the platform this
afternoon. I confess that I had rather expected the
tapping foot and the drawn brow.'

'Nonsense. What was there to be peeved about? I took
the whole thing as a great compliment, proud to feel

728

that any drink from my cellars could have produced
such a majestic jag. It restores one's faith in post-war
whisky. Besides, I couldn't be peeved at anything
tonight. I am like a little child clapping its hands and
dancing in the sunshine. For though it has been some
time getting a move on, Bertie, the sun has at last
broken through the clouds. Ring out those joy bells.
Anatole has withdrawn his notice.'

'What? Oh, very hearty congratulations.'

'Thanks. Yes. I worked on him like a beaver after I got
back this afternoon, and finally, vowing he would ne'er
consent, he consented. He stays on, praises be, and the
way I look at it now is that God's in His heaven and all's
right with –'

She broke off. The door had opened, and we were plus
a butler.

'Hullo, Seppings,' said Aunt Dahlia. 'I thought you
had gone.'

'Not yet, madam.'

'Well, I hope you will all have a good time.'

'Thank you, madam.'

'Was there something you wanted to see me about?'

'Yes, madam. It is with reference to Monsieur
Anatole. Is it by your wish, madam, that Mr Fink-Nottle
is making faces at Monsieur Anatole through the
skylight of his bedroom?'

20

There was one of those long silences. Pregnant, I believe, is what they're generally called. Aunt looked at butler. Butler looked at aunt. I looked at both of them. An eerie stillness seemed to envelop the room like a linseed poultice. I happened to be biting on a slice of apple in my fruit salad at the moment, and it sounded as if Carnera had jumped off the top of the Eiffel Tower on to a cucumber frame.

Aunt Dahlia steadied herself against the sideboard, and spoke in a low, husky voice:

'Faces?'

'Yes, madam.'

'Through the skylight?'

'Yes, madam.'

'You mean he's sitting on the roof?'

'Yes, madam. It has upset Monsieur Anatole very much.' I suppose it was that word 'upset' that touched Aunt Dahila off. Experience had taught her what happened when Anatole got upset. I had always known her as a woman who was quite active on her pins, but I had never suspected her of being capable of the magnificent burst of speed which she now showed. Pausing merely to get a rich hunting-field expletive off her chest, she was out of the room and making for the stairs before I could swallow a sliver of – I think – banana. And feeling, as I had felt when I got that telegram of hers about Angela and Tuppy, that my place was by her side, I put down my plate and hastened after her. Seppings following at a loping gallop.

I say that my place was by her side, but it was not so dashed easy to get there, for she was setting a cracking pace. At the top of the first flight she must have led by a matter of half a dozen lengths, and was still shaking off my challenge when she rounded into the second. At the next landing, however, the gruelling going appeared to tell on her, for she slackened off a trifle and showed symptoms of roaring, and by the time we were in the straight we were running practically neck and neck. Our entry into Anatole's room was as close a finish as you could have wished to see.

Result:

1. *Aunt Dahlia.*
2. *Bertram.*
3. *Seppings.*

Won by a short head. Half a staircase separated second and third.

The first thing that met the eye on entering was Anatole. This wizard of the cooking-stove is a tubby little man with a moustache of the outsize or soup-strainer type, and you can generally take a line through it as to the state of his emotions. When all is well, it turns up at the ends like a sergeant-major's. When the soul is bruised, it droops.

It was drooping now, striking a sinister note. And if any shadow of doubt had remained as to how he was feeling, the way he was carrying on would have dispelled it. He was standing by the bed in pink pyjamas, waving his fists at the skylight. Through the glass, Gussie was staring down. His eyes were bulging and his mouth was open, giving him so striking a resemblance to some rare fish in an aquarium that one's primary impulse was to offer him an ant's egg.

Watching this fist-waving cook and this goggling

guest, I must say that my sympathies were completely with the former. I considered him thoroughly justified in waving all the fists he wanted to.

Review the facts, I mean to say. There he had been, lying in bed, thinking idly of whatever French cooks do think about when in bed, and he had suddenly become aware of that frightful face at the window. A thing to jar the most phlegmatic. I know I should hate to be lying in bed and have Gussie popping up like that. A chap's bedroom – you can't get away from it – is his castle, and he has every right to look askance if gargoyles come glaring in at him.

While I stood musing thus, Aunt Dahlia, in her practical way, was coming straight to the point:

'What's all this?'

Anatole did a sort of Swedish exercise, starting at the base of the spine, carrying on through the shoulder-blades and finishing up among the back hair.

Then he told her.

In the chats I have had with this wonder man, I have always found his English fluent, but a bit on the mixed side. If you remember, he was with Mrs Bingo Little for a time before coming to Brinkley, and no doubt he picked up a good deal from Bingo. Before that, he had been a couple of years with an American family at Nice and had studied under their chauffeur, one of the Maloneys of Brooklyn. So, what with Bingo and what with Maloney, he is, as I say, fluent but a bit mixed.

He spoke, in part, as follows:

'Hot dog! You ask me what is it? Listen. Make some attention a little. Me, I have hit the hay, but I do not sleep so good, and presently I wake and up I look, and there is one who make faces against me through the dashed window. Is that a pretty affair? Is that convenient? If you think I like it, you jolly well mistake yourself. I am so mad as a wet hen. And why not? I am somebody, isn't it? This is a bedroom, what-what, not a

house for some apes? Then for what do blighters sit on
my window so cool as a few cucumbers, making some
faces?'

'Quite,' I said. Dashed reasonable, was my verdict.

He threw another look up at Gussie, and did Exercise
2 – the one where you clutch the moustache, give it a
tug and then start catching flies.

'Wait yet a little. I am not finish. I say I see this type
on my window, making a few faces. But what then?
Does he buzz off when I shout a cry, and leave me
peaceable? Not on your life. He remain planted there,
not giving any damns, and sit regarding me like a cat
watching a duck. He make faces against me and again he
make faces against me, and the more I command that he
should get to hell out of here, the more he do not get to
hell out of here. He cry something towards me, and I
demand what is his desire, but he do not explain. Oh,
no, that arrives never. He does but shrug his head. What
damn silliness! Is this amusing for me? You think I like
it? I am not content with such folly. I think the poor
mutt's loony. *Je me fiche de ce type infect. C'est idiot de
faire comme ça l'oiseau . . . Allez-vous-en,
louffier. . .* Tell the boob to go away. He is mad as some
March hatters.'

I must say I thought he was making out a jolly good
case, and evidently Aunt Dahlia felt the same. She laid a
quivering hand on his shoulder.

'I will, Monsieur Anatole, I will,' she said, and I
couldn't have believed that robust voice capable of
sinking to such an absolute coo. More like a turtle dove
calling to its mate than anything else. 'It's quite all
right.'

She had said the wrong thing. He did Exercise 3.

'All right? *Nom d'un nom d'un nom!* The hell you say
it's all right? Of what use to pull stuff like that? Wait
one half-moment. Not yet quite so quick, my old sport.
It is by no means all right. See yet again a little. It is

some very different dishes of fish. I can take a few
smooths with a rough, it is true, but I do not find it
agreeable when one play larks against me on my
windows. That cannot do. A nice thing, no. I am a
serious man. I do not wish a few larks on my windows. I
enjoy larks on my windows worse as any. It is very little
all right. If such rannygazoo is to arrive, I do not remain
any longer in this house no more. I buzz off and do not
stay planted.'

Sinister words, I had to admit, and I was not surprised
that Aunt Dahlia, hearing them, should have uttered a
cry like the wail of a master of hounds seeing a fox shot.
Anatole had begun to wave his fists again at Gussie, and
she now joined him. Seppings, who was puffing
respectfully in the background, didn't actually wave his
fists, but he gave Gussie a pretty austere look. It was
plain to the thoughtful observer that this Fink-Nottle, in
getting on to that skylight, had done a mistaken thing.
He couldn't have been more unpopular in the home of
G. G. Simmons.

'Go away, you crazy loon!' cried Aunt Dahlia, in that
ringing voice of hers which had once caused nervous
members of the Quorn to lose stirrups and take tosses
from the saddle.

Gussie's reply was to waggle his eyebrows. I could
read the message he was trying to convey.

'I think he means,' I said – reasonable old Bertram,
always trying to throw oil on the troubled w's – 'that if
he does he will fall down the side of the house and break
his neck.'

'Well, why not?' said Aunt Dahlia.

I could see her point, of course, but it seemed to me
that there might be a neater solution. This skylight
happened to be the only window in the house which
Uncle Tom had not festooned with his bally bars. I
suppose he felt that if a burglar had the nerve to climb
up as far as this, he deserved what was coming to him.

'If you opened the skylight, he could jump in.'

The idea got across.

'Seppings, how does this skylight open?'

'With a pole, madam.'

'Then get a pole. Get two poles. Ten.'

And presently Gussie was mixing with the company. Like one of those chaps you read about in the papers, the wretched man seemed deeply conscious of his position.

I must say Aunt Dahlia's bearing and demeanour did nothing to assist towards a restored composure. Of the amiability which she had exhibited when discussing this unhappy chump's activities with me over the fruit salad, no trace remained, and I was not surprised that speech more or less froze on the Fink-Nottle lips. It isn't often that Aunt Dahlia, normally as genial a bird as ever encouraged a gaggle of hounds to get their noses down to it, lets her angry passions rise, but when she does, strong men climb trees and pull them up after them.

'Well?' she said.

In answer to this, all that Gussie could produce was a sort of strangled hiccough.

'Well?'

Aunt Dahlia's face grew darker. Hunting, if indulged in regularly over a period of years, is a pastime that seldom fails to lend a fairly deepish tinge to the patient's complexion, and her best friends could not have denied that even at normal times the relative's map tended a little towards the crushed strawberry. But never had I seen it take on so pronounced a richness as now. She looked like a tomato struggling for self-expression.

'Well?'

Gussie tried hard. And for a moment it seemed as if something was going to come through. But in the end it turned out nothing more than a sort of death-rattle.

'Oh, take him away, Bertie, and put ice on his head,' said Aunt Dahlia, giving the thing up. And she turned to tackle what looked like the rather man's size job of soothing Anatole, who was now carrying on a muttered conversation with himself in a rapid sort of way.

Seeming to feel that the situation was one to which he could not do justice in Bingo-cum-Maloney Anglo-American, he had fallen back on his native tongue. Words like '*marmiton de Domange*', '*pignouf*', '*burluberlu*', and '*roustisseur*' were fluttering from him like bats out of a barn. Lost on me, of course, because, though I sweated a bit at the Gallic language during that Cannes visit, I'm still more or less in the Esker-vous-avez stage. I regretted this, for they sounded good.

I assisted Gussie down the stairs. A cooler thinker than Aunt Dahlia, I had already guessed the hidden springs and motives which had led him to the roof. Where she had seen only a cockeyed reveller indulging himself in a drunken prank or whimsy, I had spotted the hunted fawn.

'Was Tuppy after you?' I asked sympathetically.

What I believe is called a *frisson* shook him.

'He nearly got me on the top landing. I shinned out through a passage window and scrambled along a sort of ledge.'

'That baffled him, what?'

'Yes. But then I found I had stuck. The roof sloped down in all directions. I couldn't go back. I had to go on, crawling along this ledge. And then I found myself looking down the skylight. Who was that chap?'

'That was Anatole, Aunt Dahlia's chef.'

'French?'

'To the core.'

'That explains why I couldn't make him understand. What asses these Frenchmen are. They don't seem able to grasp the simplest thing. You'd have thought if a chap saw a chap on a skylight, the chap would realize the chap wanted to be let in. But no, he just stood there.'

'Waving a few fists.'

'Yes. Silly idiot. Still, here I am.'

'Here you are, yes – for the moment.'

'Eh?'

'I was thinking that Tuppy is probably lurking somewhere.'

He leaped like a lamb in springtime.

'What shall I do?'

I considered this.

'Sneak back to your room and barricade the door. That is the manly policy.'

'Suppose that's where he's lurking?'

'In that case, move elsewhere.'

But on arrival at the room, it transpired that Tuppy, if anywhere, was infesting some other portion of the house. Gussie shot in, and I heard the key turn. And feeling that there was no more that I could do in that quarter, I returned to the dining-room for further fruit salad and a quiet think. And I had barely filled my plate when the door opened and Aunt Dahlia came in. She sank into a chair, looking a bit shopworn.

'Give me a drink, Bertie.'

'What sort?'

'Any sort, so long as it's strong.'

Approach Bertram Wooster along these lines, and you catch him at his best. St Bernard dogs doing the square thing by Alpine travellers could not have bustled about more assiduously. I filled the order, and for some moments nothing was to be heard but the sloshing sound of an aunt restoring her tissues.

'Shove it down, Aunt Dahlia,' I said sympathetically. 'These things take it out of one, don't they? You've had a toughish time, no doubt, soothing Anatole,' I proceeded, helping myself to anchovy paste on toast. 'Everything pretty smooth now, I trust?'

She gazed at me in a long, lingering sort of way, her brow wrinkled as if in thought.

'Attila,' she said at length. 'That's the name. Attila the Hun.'

'Eh?'

'I was trying to think who you reminded me of. Somebody who went about strewing ruin and desolation and breaking up homes which, until he came along, had been happy and peaceful. Attila is the man. It's amazing,' she said, drinking me in once more. 'To look at you, one would think you were just an ordinary sort of amiable idiot – certifiable, perhaps, but quite harmless. Yet, in reality, you are a worse scourge than the Black Death. I tell you, Bertie, when I contemplate you I seem to come up against all the underlying sorrow and horror of life with such a thud that I feel as if I had walked into a lamp post.'

Pained and surprised, I would have spoken, but the stuff I had thought was anchovy paste had turned out to be something far more gooey and adhesive. It seemed to wrap itself round the tongue and impede utterance like a gag. And while I was still endeavouring to clear the vocal cords for action, she went on:

'Do you realize what you started when you sent that Spink-Bottle man down here? As regards his getting blotto and turning the prize-giving ceremonies at Market Snodsbury Grammar School into a sort of two-reel comic film, I will say nothing, for frankly I enjoyed it. But when he comes leering at Anatole through skylights, just after I had with infinite pains and tact induced him to withdraw his notice, and makes him so temperamental that he won't hear of staying on after tomorrow –'

The paste stuff gave way. I was able to speak.

'What?'

'Yes, Anatole goes tomorrow, and I suppose poor old Tom will have indigestion for the rest of his life. And that is not all. I have just seen Angela, and she tells me she is engaged to this Bottle.'

'Temporarily, yes,' I had to admit.

'Temporarily be blowed. She's definitely engaged to him and talks with a sort of hideous coolness of getting married in October. So there it is. If the prophet Job were to walk into the room at this moment, I could sit swapping hard-luck stories with him till bedtime. Not that Job was in my class.'

'He had boils.'

'Well, what are boils?'

'Dashed painful, I understand.'

'Nonsense. I'd take all the boils on the market in exchange for my troubles. Can't you realize the position? I've lost the best cook in England. My husband, poor soul, will probably die of dyspepsia. And my only daughter, for whom I had dreamed such a wonderful future, is engaged to be married to an inebriated newt fancier. And you talk about boils!'

I corrected her on a small point:

'I don't absolutely talk about boils. I merely mentioned that Job had them. Yes, I agree with you, Aunt Dahlia, that things are not looking too oojah-cum-spiff at the moment, but be of good cheer. A Wooster is seldom baffled for more than the nonce.'

'You rather expect to be coming along shortly with another of your schemes?'

'At any minute.'

She sighed resignedly.

'I thought as much. Well, it needed but this. I don't see how things could possibly be worse than they are, but no doubt you will succeed in making them so. Your genius and insight will find the way. Carry on, Bertie. Yes, carry on. I am past caring now. I shall even find a faint interest in seeing into what darker and profounder abysses of hell you can plunge this home. Go to it, lad ... What's that stuff you're eating?'

'I find it a little difficult to classify. Some sort of paste on toast. Rather like glue flavoured with beef extract.'

'Gimme,' said Aunt Dahlia listlessly.

'Be careful how you chew,' I advised. 'It sticketh closer than a brother ... Yes, Jeeves?'

The man had materialized on the carpet. Absolutely noiseless, as usual.

'A note for you, sir.'

'A note for me, Jeeves?'

'A note for you, sir.'

'From whom, Jeeves?'

'From Miss Bassett, sir.'

'From whom, Jeeves?'

'From Miss Bassett, sir.'

'From Miss Bassett, Jeeves?'

'From Miss Bassett, sir.'

At this point, Aunt Dahlia, who had taken one nibble at her whatever-it-was-on-toast and laid it down, begged us – a little fretfully, I thought – for heaven's sake to cut out the cross-talk vaudeville stuff, as she had enough to bear already without having to listen to us doing our imitation of the Two Macs. Always willing to oblige, I dismissed Jeeves with a nod, and he flickered for a moment and was gone. Many a spectre would have been less slippy.

'But what,' I mused, toying with the envelope, 'can this female be writing to me about?'

'Why not open the damn thing and see?'

'A very excellent idea,' I said, and did so.

'And if you are interested in my movements,' proceeded Aunt Dahlia, heading for the door, 'I propose to go to my room, do some Yogi deep breathing, and try to forget.'

'Quite,' I said absently, skimming p.1. And then, as I turned over, a sharp howl broke from my lips, causing Aunt Dahlia to shy like a startled mustang.

'Don't do it!' she exclaimed, quivering in every limb.

'Yes, but dash it –'

'What a pest you are, you miserable object,' she sighed. 'I remember years ago, when you were in your cradle, being left alone with you one day and you nearly swallowed your rubber comforter and started turning purple. And I, ass that I was, took it out and saved your life. Let me tell you, young Bertie, it will go very hard with you if you ever swallow a rubber comforter again when only I am by to aid.'

'But, dash it!' I cried. 'Do you know what's happened? Madeline Bassett says she's going to marry me!'

'I hope it keeps fine for you,' said the relative, and passed from the room looking like something out of an Edgar Allan Poe story.

21

I don't suppose I was looking so dashed unlike
something out of an Edgar Allan Poe story myself, for, as
you can readily imagine, the news item which I have
just recorded had got in amongst me properly. If the
Bassett, in the belief that the Wooster heart had long
been hers and was waiting ready to be scooped in on
demand, had decided to take up her option, I should, as a
man of honour and sensibility, have no choice but to
come across and kick in. The matter was obviously not
one that could be straightened out with a curt *nolle
prosequi*. All the evidence, therefore, seemed to point to
the fact that the doom had come upon me and, what was
more, had come to stay.

And yet, though it would be idle to pretend that my
grip on the situation was quite the grip I would have
liked it to be, I did not despair of arriving at a solution. A
lesser man, caught in this awful snare, would no doubt
have thrown in the towel at once and ceased to struggle;
but the whole point about the Woosters is that they are
not lesser men.

By way of a start, I read the note again. Not that I had
any hope that a second perusal would enable me to place
a different construction on its contents, but it helped to
fill in while the brain was limbering up. I then, to assist
thought, had another go at the fruit salad, and in
addition ate a slice of sponge cake. And it was as I passed
on to the cheese that the machinery started working. I
saw what had to be done.

To the question which had been exercising the mind

– viz., can Bertram cope? – I was now able to reply with a confident 'Absolutely'.

The great wheeze on these occasions of dirty work at the crossroads is not to lose your head but to keep cool and try to find the ringleaders. Once find the ringleaders, and you know where you are.

The ringleader here was plainly the Bassett. It was she who started the whole imbroglio by chucking Gussie, and it was clear that before anything could be done to solve and clarify, she must be induced to revise her views and take him on again. This would put Angela back into circulation, and that would cause Tuppy to simmer down a bit, and then we could begin to get somewhere.

I decided that as soon as I had had another morsel of cheese I would seek this Bassett out and be pretty eloquent.

And at this moment in she came. I might have foreseen that she would be turning up shortly. I mean to say, hearts may ache, but if they know that there is a cold collation set out in the dining-room, they are pretty sure to come popping in sooner or later.

Her eyes, as she entered the room, were fixed on the salmon mayonnaise, and she would no doubt have made a bee-line for it and started getting hers, had I not, in the emotion of seeing her, dropped a glass of the best with which I was endeavouring to bring about a calmer frame of mind. The noise caused her to turn, and for an instant embarrassment supervened. A slight flush mantled the cheek, and the eyes popped a bit.

'Oh!' she said.

I have always found that there is nothing that helps to ease you over one of these awkward moments like a spot of stage business. Find something to do with your hands, and it's half the battle. I grabbed a plate and hastened forward.

'A touch of salmon?'

'Thank you.'

'With a suspicion of salad?'

'If you please.'

'And to drink? Name the poison.'

'I think I would like a little orange juice.'

She gave a gulp. Not at the orange juice, I don't mean, because she hadn't got it yet, but at all the tender associations those two words provoked. It was as if someone had mentioned spaghetti to the relict of an Italian organ-grinder. Her face flushed a deeper shade, she registered anguish, and I saw that it was no longer within the sphere of practical politics to try to confine the conversation to neutral topics like cold boiled salmon.

So did she, I imagine, for when I, as a preliminary to getting down to brass tacks, said 'Er', she said 'Er', too, simultaneously, the brace of 'Ers' clashing in mid-air.

'I'm sorry.'

'I beg your pardon.'

'You were saying –'

'You were saying –'

'No, please go on.'

'Oh, right-ho.'

I straightened the tie, my habit when in this girl's society, and had at it:

'With reference to yours of even date –'

She flushed again, and took a rather strained forkful of salmon.

'You got my note?'

'Yes, I got your note.'

'I gave it to Jeeves to give it to you.'

'Yes, he gave it to me. That's how I got it.'

There was another silence. And as she was plainly shrinking from talking turkey, I was reluctantly compelled to do so. I mean, somebody had got to. Too dashed silly, a male and female in our position simply standing eating salmon and cheese at one another without a word.

'Yes, I got it all right.'

'I see. You got it.'

'Yes, I got it. I've just been reading it. And what I was rather wanting to ask you, if we happened to run into each other, was – well, what about it?'

'What about it?'

'That's what I say: What about it?'

'But it was quite clear.'

'Oh, quite. Perfectly clear. Very well expressed and all that. But – I mean – Well, I mean, deeply sensible of the honour, and so forth – but – Well, dash it!'

She had polished off her salmon, and now put the plate down.

'Fruit salad?'

'No, thank you.'

'Spot of pie?'

'No, thanks.'

'One of those glue things on toast?'

'No, thank you.'

She took a cheese straw. I found a cold egg which I had overlooked. Then I said 'I mean to say' just as she said 'I think I know', and there was another collision.

'I beg your pardon.'

'I'm sorry.'

'Do go on.'

'No, you go on.'

I waved my cold egg courteously, to indicate that she had the floor, and she started again:

'I think I know what you are trying to say. You are surprised.'

'Yes.'

'You are thinking of –'

'Exactly.'

'– Mr Fink-Nottle.'

'The very man.'

'You find what I have done hard to understand.'

'Absolutely.'

'I don't wonder.'

'I do.'

'And yet it is quite simple.'

She took another cheese straw. She seemed to like cheese straws.

'Quite simple, really. I want to make you happy.'

'Dashed decent of you.'

'I am going to devote the rest of my life to making you happy.'

'A very matey scheme.'

'I can at least do that. But – may I be quite frank with you, Bertie?'

'Oh, rather.'

'Then I must tell you this. I am fond of you. I will marry you. I will do my best to make you a good wife. But my affection for you can never be the flame-like passion I felt for Augustus.'

'Just the very point I was working round to. There, as you say, is the snag. Why not chuck the whole idea of hitching up with me? Wash it out altogether. I mean, if you love old Gussie –'

'No longer.'

'Oh, come.'

'No. What happened this afternoon has killed my love. A smear of ugliness has been drawn across a thing of beauty, and I can never feel towards him as I did.'

I saw what she meant, of course. Gussie had bunged his heart at her feet; she had picked it up, and, almost immediately after doing so, had discovered that he had been stewed to the eyebrows all the time. The shock must have been severe. No girl likes to feel that a chap has got to be thoroughly plastered before he can ask her to marry him. It wounds the pride.

Nevertheless, I persevered.

'But have you considered,' I said, 'that you may have

got a wrong line on Gussie's performance this afternoon? Admitted that all the evidence points to a more sinister theory, what price him simply having got a touch of the sun? Chaps do get touches of the sun, you know, especially when the weather's hot.'

She looked at me, and I saw that she was putting in a bit of the old drenched-irises stuff.

'It was like you to say that, Bertie. I respect you for it.'

'Oh, no.'

'Yes. You have a splendid, chivalrous soul.'

'Not a bit.'

'Yes, you have. You remind me of Cyrano.'

'Who?'

'Cyrano de Bergerac.'

'The chap with the nose?'

'Yes.'

I can't say I was any too pleased. I felt the old beak furtively. It was a bit on the prominent side, perhaps, but, dash it, not in the Cyrano class. It began to look as if the next thing this girl would do would be to compare me to Schnozzle Durante.

'He loved, but pleaded another's cause.'

'Oh, I see what you mean now.'

'I like you for that, Bertie. It was fine of you – fine and big. But it is no use. There are things which kill love. I can never forget Augustus, but my love for him is dead. I will be your wife.'

Well, one has to be civil.

'Right ho,' I said. 'Thanks awfully.'

Then the dialogue sort of poofed out once more, and we stood eating cheese straws and cold eggs respectively in silence. There seemed to exist some little uncertainty as to what the next move was.

Fortunately, before embarrassment could do much more supervening, Angela came in, and this broke up the meeting. The Bassett announced our engagement, and Angela kissed her and said she hoped she would be very, very happy, and the Bassett kissed her and said she hoped she would be very, very happy with Gussie, and Angela said she was sure she would, because Augustus was such a dear, and the Bassett kissed her again, and Angela kissed her again, and, in a word, the whole thing got so bally feminine that I was glad to edge away.

I would have been glad to do so, of course, in any case, for if ever there was a moment when it was up to Bertram to think, and think hard, this moment was that moment.

It was, it seemed to me, the end. Not even on the occasion, some years earlier, when I had inadvertently become betrothed to Tuppy's frightful Cousin Honoria, had I experienced a deeper sense of being waist high in the gumbo and about to sink without trace. I wandered out into the garden, smoking a tortured gasper, with the iron well embedded in the soul. And I had fallen into a sort of trance, trying to picture what it would be like having the Bassett on the premises for the rest of my life and at the same time, if you follow me, trying not to picture what it would be like, when I charged into something which might have been a tree, but was not – being, in point of fact, Jeeves.

'I beg your pardon, sir,' he said. 'I should have moved to one side.'

I did not reply. I stood looking at him in silence. For the sight of him had opened up a new line of thought.

This Jeeves, now, I reflected. I had formed the opinion that he had lost his grip and was no longer the force he had been, but was it not possible, I asked myself, that I might be mistaken? Start him off exploring avenues and might he not discover one through which I would be enabled to sneak off to safety, leaving no hard feelings behind? I found myself answering that it was quite on the cards that he might.

After all, his head still bulged out at the back as of old. One noted in the eyes the same intelligent glitter.

Mind you, after what had passed between us in the matter of that white mess jacket with the brass buttons, I was not prepared absolutely to hand over to the man. I would, of course, merely take him into consultation. But, recalling some of his earlier triumphs – the Sipperley Case, the Episode of My Aunt Agatha and the Dog McIntosh, and the smoothly handled Affair of Uncle George and The Barmaid's Niece were a few that sprang to my mind – I felt justified at least in offering him the opportunity of coming to the aid of the young master in his hour of peril.

But before proceeding further, there was one thing that had got to be understood between us, and understood clearly.

'Jeeves,' I said, 'a word with you.'

'Sir?'

'I am up against it a bit, Jeeves.'

'I am sorry to hear that, sir. Can I be of any assistance?'

'Quite possibly you can, if you have not lost your grip. Tell me frankly, Jeeves, are you in pretty good shape mentally?'

'Yes, sir.'

'Still eating plenty of fish?'

'Yes, sir.'

'Then it may be all right. But there is just one point before I begin. In the past, when you have contrived to extricate self or some pal from some little difficulty, you have frequently shown a disposition to take advantage of my gratitude to gain some private end. Those purple socks, for instance. Also the plus fours and the Old Etonian spats. Choosing your moment with subtle cunning, you came to me when I was weakened by relief and got me to get rid of them. And what I am saying now is that if you are successful on the present occasion there must be no rot of that description about that mess jacket of mine.'

749

'Very good, sir.'

'You will not come to me when all is over and ask me to jettison the jacket?'

'Certainly not, sir.'

'On that understanding then, I will carry on. Jeeves, I'm engaged.'

'I hope you will be very happy, sir.'

'Don't be an ass. I'm engaged to Miss Bassett.'

'Indeed, sir? I was not aware – '

'Nor was I. It came as a complete surprise. However, there it is. The official intimation was in that note you brought me.'

'Odd, sir.'

'What is?'

'Odd, sir, that the contents of that note should have been as you describe. It seemed to me that Miss Bassett, when she handed me the communication, was far from being in a happy frame of mind.'

'She is far from being in a happy frame of mind. You don't suppose she really wants to marry me, do you? Pshaw, Jeeves! Can't you see that this is simply another of those bally gestures which are rapidly rendering Brinkley Court a hell for man and beast? Dash all gestures, is my view.'

'Yes, sir.'

'Well, what's to be done?'

'You feel that Miss Bassett, despite what has occurred, still retains a fondness for Mr Fink-Nottle, sir?'

'She's pining for him.'

'In that case, sir, surely the best plan would be to bring about a reconciliation between them.'

'How? You see. You stand silent and twiddle the fingers. You are stumped.'

'No, sir. If I twiddled my fingers, it was merely to assist thought.'

'Then continue twiddling.'

'It will not be necessary, sir.'

'You don't mean you've got a bite already?'

'Yes, sir.'

'You astound me, Jeeves. Let's have it.'

'The device which I have in mind is one that I have already mentioned to you, sir.'

'When did you ever mention any device to me?'

'If you will throw your mind back to the evening of our arrival, sir. You were good enough to inquire of me if I had any plan to put forward with a view to bringing Miss Angela and Mr Glossop together, and I ventured to suggest – '

'Good Lord! Not the old fire-alarm thing?'

'Precisely, sir.'

'You're still sticking to that?'

'Yes, sir.'

It shows how much the ghastly blow I had received had shaken me when I say that, instead of dismissing the proposal with a curt 'Tchah!' or anything like that, I found myself speculating as to whether there might not be something in it, after all.

When he had first mooted this fire-alarm scheme of his, I had sat upon it, if you remember, with the maximum of promptitude and vigour. 'Rotten' was the adjective I had employed to describe it, and you may recall that I mused a bit sadly, considering the idea conclusive proof of the general breakdown of a once fine mind. But now it somehow began to look as if it might have possibilities. The fact of the matter was that I had about reached the stage where I was prepared to try anything once, however goofy.

'Just run through that wheeze again, Jeeves,' I said thoughtfully. 'I remember thinking it cuckoo, but it may be that I missed some of the finer shades.'

'Your criticism of it at the time, sir, was that it was too elaborate, but I do not think it is so in reality. As I see it, sir, the occupants of the house, hearing the fire bell ring, will suppose that a conflagration has broken out.'

I nodded. One could follow the train of thought.

'Yes, that seems reasonable.'

'Whereupon, Mr Glossop will hasten to save Miss Angela, while Mr Fink-Nottle performs the same office for Miss Bassett.'

'Is that based on psychology?'

'Yes, sir. Possibly you may recollect that it was an axiom of the late Sir Arthur Conan Doyle's fictional detective, Sherlock Holmes, that the instinct of everyone, upon an alarm of fire, is to save the object dearest to them.'

'It seems to me that there is a grave danger of seeing Tuppy come out carrying a steak-and-kidney pie, but resume, Jeeves, resume. You think that this would clean everything up?'

'The relations of the two young couples could scarcely continue distant after such an occurrence, sir.'

'Perhaps you're right. But, dash it, if we go ringing fire bells in the night watches, shan't we scare half the domestic staff into fits? There is one of the housemaids – Jane, I believe – who already skips like the high hills if I so much as come on her unexpectedly round a corner.'

'A neurotic girl, sir, I agree. I have noticed her. But by acting promptly we should avoid such a contingency. The entire staff, with the exception of Monsieur Anatole, will be at the ball at Kingham Manor tonight.'

'Of course. That just shows the condition this thing has reduced me to. Forget my own name next. Well, then, let's just try to envisage. Bong goes the bell. Gussie rushes and grabs the Bassett . . . Wait. Why shouldn't she simply walk downstairs?'

'You are overlooking the effect of sudden alarm on the feminine temperament, sir.'

'That's true.'

'Miss Bassett's impulse, I would imagine, sir, would be to leap from her window.'

'Well, that's worse. We don't want her spread out in a sort of *purée* on the lawn. It seems to me that the flaw in this scheme of yours, Jeeves, is that it's going to litter the garden with mangled corpses.'

'No, sir. You will recall that Mr Travers's fear of burglars has caused him to have stout bars fixed to all the windows.'

'Of course, yes. Well, it sounds all right,' I said, though still a bit doubtfully. 'Quite possibly it may come off. But I have a feeling that it will slip up somewhere. However, I am in no position to cavil at even a 100 to 1 shot. I will adopt this policy of yours, Jeeves, though, as I say, with misgivings. At what hour would you suggest bonging the bell?'

'Not before midnight, sir.'

'That is to say, some time after midnight.'

'Yes, sir.'

'Right-ho, then. At 12.30 on the dot, I will bong.'

'Very good, sir.'

22

I don't know why it is, but there's something about the rural districts after dark that always has a rummy effect on me. In London I can stay out till all hours and come home with the milk without a tremor, but put me in the garden of a country house after the strength of the company has gone to roost and the place is shut up, and a sort of goose-fleshy feeling steals over me. The night wind stirs the treetops, twigs crack, bushes rustle, and before I know where I am, the morale has gone phut and I'm expecting the family ghost to come sneaking up behind me, making groaning noises.

Dashed unpleasant, the whole thing, and if you think it improves matters to know that you are shortly about to ring the loudest fire bell in England and start an all-hands-to-the-pumps panic in that quiet, darkened house, you err.

I knew all about the Brinkley Court fire bell. The dickens of a row it makes. Uncle Tom, in addition to not liking burglars, is a bloke who has always objected to the idea of being cooked in his sleep, so when he bought the place he saw to it that the fire bell should be something that might give you heart failure, but which you couldn't possibly mistake for the drowsy chirping of a sparrow in the ivy.

When I was a kid and spent my holidays at Brinkley, we used to have fire drills after closing time, and many is the night I've had it jerk me out of the dreamless like the Last Trump.

I confess that the recollection of what this bell could do when it buckled down to it gave me pause as I stood

that night at 12.30 a.m. prompt beside the outhouse
where it was located. The sight of the rope against the
whitewashed wall and the thought of the bloodsome
uproar which was about to smash the peace of the night
into hash served to deepen that rummy feeling to which
I have alluded.

Moreover, now that I had had time to meditate upon
it, I was more than ever defeatist about this scheme of
Jeeves's.

Jeeves seemed to take it for granted that Gussie and
Tuppy, faced with a hideous fate, would have no thought
beyond saving the Bassett and Angela.

I could not bring myself to share his sunny
confidence.

I mean to say, I know how moments when they're
faced with a hideous fate affect chaps. I remember
Freddie Widgeon, one of the most chivalrous birds in the
Drones, telling me how there was an alarm of fire once
at a seaside hotel where he was staying and, so far from
rushing about saving women, he was down the escape
within ten seconds of the kick-off, his mind concerned
with but one thing – viz., the personal well-being of F.
Widgeon.

As far as any idea of doing the delicately nurtured a
bit of good went, he tells me, he was prepared to stand
underneath and catch them in blankets, but no more.

Why, then, should this not be so with Augustus
Fink-Nottle and Hildebrand Glossop?

Such were my thoughts as I stood toying with the
rope, and I believe I should have turned the whole thing
up, had it not been that at this juncture there floated
into my mind a picture of the Bassett hearing that bell
for the first time. Coming as a wholly new experience, it
would probably startle her into a decline.

And so agreeable was this reflexion that I waited no
longer, but seized the rope, braced the feet, and snapped
into it.

Well, as I say, I hadn't been expecting that bell to
hush things up to any great extent. Nor did it. The last
time I had heard it, I had been in my room on the other
side of the house, and even so it had hoiked me out of
bed as if something had exploded under me. Standing
close to it like this, I got the full force and meaning of
the thing, and I've never heard anything like it in my
puff.

I rather enjoy a bit of noise, as a general rule. I
remember Catsmeat Potter-Pirbright bringing a police
rattle into the Drones one night and loosing it off behind
my chair, and I just lay back and closed my eyes with a
pleasant smile, like someone in a box at the opera. And
the same applies to the time when my Aunt Agatha's
son, young Thos, put a match to the parcel of Guy
Fawkes Day fireworks to see what would happen.

But the Brinkley Court fire bell was too much for me.
I gave about half a dozen tugs, and then, feeling that
enough was enough, sauntered round to the front lawn
to ascertain what solid results had been achieved.

Brinkley Court had given of its best. A glance told me
that we were playing to capacity. The eye, roving to and
fro, noted here Uncle Tom in a purple dressing gown,
there Aunt Dahlia in the old blue and yellow. It also fell
upon Anatole, Tuppy, Gussie, Angela, the Bassett, and
Jeeves, in the order named. There they all were present
and correct.

But – and this was what caused me immediate
concern – I could detect no sign whatever that there had
been any rescue work going on.

What I had been hoping, of course, was to see Tuppy
bending solicitously over Angela in one corner, while
Gussie fanned the Bassett with a towel in the other.
Instead of which, the Bassett was one of the group which
included Aunt Dahlia and Uncle Tom and seemed to be
busy trying to make Anatole see the bright side, while
Angela and Gussie were, respectively, leaning against

the sundial with a peeved look and sitting on the grass
rubbing a barked shin. Tuppy was walking up and down
the path, all by himself.

A disturbing picture, you will admit. It was with a
rather imperious gesture that I summoned Jeeves to my
side.

'Well, Jeeves?'

'Sir?'

I eyed him sternly. 'Sir?' forsooth!

'It's no good saying "Sir?", Jeeves. Look round you.
See for yourself. Your scheme has proved a bust.'

'Certainly it would appear that matters have not
arranged themselves quite as we anticipated, sir.'

'We?'

'As I had anticipated, sir.'

'That's more like it. Didn't I tell you it would be a
flop?'

'I remember that you did seem dubious, sir.'

'Dubious is no word for it, Jeeves. I hadn't a scrap of
faith in the idea from the start. When you first mooted
it, I said it was rotten, and I was right. I'm not blaming
you, Jeeves. It is not your fault that you have sprained
your brain. But after this – forgive me if I hurt your
feelings, Jeeves – I shall know better than to allow you
to handle any but the simplest and most elementary
problems. It is best to be candid about this, don't you
think? Kindest to be frank and straightforward?'

'Certainly, sir.'

'I mean, the surgeon's knife, what?'

'Precisely, sir.'

'I consider –'

'If you will pardon me for interrupting you, sir, I fancy
Mrs Travers is endeavouring to attract your attention.'

And at this moment a ringing 'Hoy!' which could
have proceeded only from the relative in question,
assured me that his view was correct.

'Just step this way a moment, Attila, if you don't

mind,' boomed that well-known – and under certain
conditions, well-loved – voice, and I moved over.

I was not feeling unmixedly at my ease. For the first
time it was beginning to steal upon me that I had not
prepared a really good story in support of my
questionable behaviour in ringing fire bells at such an
hour, and I have known Aunt Dahlia to express herself
with a hearty freedom upon far smaller provocation.

She exhibited, however, no signs of violence. More a
sort of frozen calm, if you know what I mean. You could
see that she was a woman who had suffered. 'Well,
Bertie, dear,' she said, 'here we all are.'

'Quite,' I replied guardedly.

'Nobody missing, is there?'

'I don't think so.'

'Splendid. So much healthier for us out in the open
like this than frowsting in bed. I had just dropped off
when you did your bell-ringing act. For it was you, my
sweet child, who rang that bell, was it not?'

'I did ring the bell, yes.'

'Any particular reason, or just a whim?'

'I thought there was a fire.'

'What gave you that impression, dear?'

'I thought I saw flames.'

'Where, darling? Tell Aunt Dahlia.'

'In one of the windows.'

'I see. So we have all been dragged out of bed and
scared rigid because you have been seeing things.'

Here Uncle Tom made a noise like a cork coming out
of a bottle, and Anatole, whose moustache had hit a new
low, said something about 'some apes', and, if I am not
mistaken, a '*rogommier*' – whatever that is.

'I admit I was mistaken. I am sorry.'

'Don't apologize, ducky. Can't you see how pleased
we all are. What were you doing out here, anyway?'

'Just taking a stroll.'

'I see. And are you proposing to continue your stroll?'

'No, I think I'll go in now.'

'That's fine. Because I was thinking of going in, too,
and I don't believe I could sleep knowing you were out
here giving rein to that powerful imagination of yours.
The next thing that would happen would be that you
would think you saw a pink elephant sitting on the
drawing-room window-sill and start throwing bricks at
it . . . Well, come on, Tom, the entertainment seems to
be over . . . Yes, Mr Fink-Nottle?'

Gussie, as he joined our little group, seemed upset
about something.

'I say!'

'Say on, Augustus.'

'I say, what are we going to do?'

'Speaking for myself, I intend to return to bed.'

'But the door's shut.'

'What door?'

'The front door. Somebody must have shut it.'

'Then I shall open it.'

'But it won't open.'

'Then I shall try another door.'

'But all the other doors are shut.'

'What? Who shut them?'

'I don't know.'

I advanced a theory:

'The wind?'

Aunt Dahlia's eye met mine.

'Don't try me too high,' she begged. 'Not now,
precious.' And, indeed, even as I spoke, it did strike me
that the night was pretty still.

Uncle Tom said we must get in through a window.
Aunt Dahlia sighed a bit.

'How? Could Lloyd George do it, could Winston do it,
could Baldwin do it? No. Not since you had those bars of
yours put on.'

'Well, well, well. God bless my soul, ring the bell,
then.'

'The fire bell?'

'The door bell.'

'To what end, Thomas? There's nobody in the house.
The servants are all at Kingham.'

'But, confound it all, we can't stop out here all night.'

'Can't we? You just watch us. There is nothing –
literally nothing – which a country house party can't do
with Attila here operating on the premises. Seppings
presumably took the back-door key with him. We must
just amuse ourselves till he comes back.'

Tuppy made a suggestion:

'Why not take out one of the cars and drive over to
Kingham and get the key from Seppings?'

It went well. No question about that. For the first
time, a smile lit up Aunt Dahlia's drawn face. Uncle
Tom grunted approvingly. Anatole said something in
Provençal that sounded complimentary. And I thought I
detected even on Angela's map a slight softening.

'A very excellent idea,' said Aunt Dahlia. 'One of the
best. Nip round to the garage at once.'

After Tuppy had gone, some extremely flattering
things were said about his intelligence and resource, and
there was a disposition to draw rather invidious
comparisons between him and Bertram. Painful for me,
of course, but the ordeal didn't last long, for it couldn't
have been more than five minutes before he was with us
again.

Tuppy seemed perturbed.

'I say, it's all off.'

'Why?'

'The garage is locked.'

'Unlock it.'

'I haven't the key.'

'Shout, then, and wake Waterbury.'

'Who's Waterbury?'

'The chauffeur, ass. He sleeps over the garage.'

'But he's gone to the dance at Kingham.'

It was the final wallop. Until this moment, Aunt Dahlia had been able to preserve her frozen calm. The dam now burst. The years rolled away from her, and she was once more the Dahlia Wooster of the old yoicks-and-tantivy days – the emotional, free-speaking girl who had so often risen in her stirrups to yell derogatory personalities at people who were heading hounds.

'Curse all dancing chauffeurs! What on earth does a chauffeur want to dance for? I mistrusted that man from the start. Something told me he was a dancer. Well, this finishes it. We're out here till breakfast-time. If those blasted servants come back before eight o'clock, I shall be vastly surprised. You won't get Seppings away from a dance till you throw him out. I know him. The jazz'll go to his head, and he'll stand clapping and demanding encores till his hands blister. Damn all dancing butlers! What is Brinkley Court? A respectable English country house or a crimson dancing school? One might as well be living in the middle of the Russian Ballet. Well, all right. If we must stay out here, we must. We shall all be frozen stiff, except' – here she directed at me not one of her friendliest glances – 'except dear old Attila, who is, I observe, well and warmly clad. We will resign ourselves to the prospect of freezing to death like the Babes in the Wood, merely expressing a dying wish that our old pal Attila will see that we are covered with leaves. No doubt he will also toll that fire bell of his as a mark of respect – And what might you want, my good man?'

She broke off, and stood glaring at Jeeves. During the latter portion of her address, he had been standing by in a respectful manner, endeavouring to catch the speaker's eye.

'If I might make a suggestion, madam.'

I am not saying that in the course of our long association I have always found myself able to view Jeeves with approval. There are aspects of his character which have frequently caused coldnesses to arise between us. He is one of those fellows who, if you give them a thingummy, take a what-d'you-call-it. His work is often raw, and he has been known to allude to me as 'mentally negligible'. More than once, as I have shown, it has been my painful task to squelch in him a tendency to get uppish and treat the young master as a serf or peon.

These are grave defects.

But one thing I have never failed to hand the man. He is magnetic. There is about him something that seems to soothe and hypnotize. To the best of my knowledge, he has never encountered a charging rhinoceros, but should this contingency occur, I have no doubt that the animal, meeting his eye, would check itself in mid-stride, roll over and lie purring with its legs in the air.

At any rate he calmed down Aunt Dahlia, the nearest thing to a charging rhinoceros, in under five seconds. He just stood there looking respectful, and though I didn't time the thing – not having a stop-watch on me – I should say it wasn't more than three seconds and a quarter before her whole manner underwent an astounding change for the better. She melted before one's eyes.

'Jeeves! You haven't got an idea?'

'Yes, madam.'

'That great brain of yours has really clicked as ever in the hour of need?'

'Yes, madam.'

'Jeeves,' said Aunt Dahlia in a shaking voice, 'I am sorry I spoke so abruptly. I was not myself. I might have known that you would not come simply trying to make conversation. Tell us this idea of yours, Jeeves. Join our little group of thinkers and let us hear what you have to say. Make yourself at home, Jeeves, and give us the good word. Can you really get us out of this mess?'

'Yes, madam, if one of the gentlemen would be willing to ride a bicycle.'

'A bicycle?'

'There is a bicycle in the gardener's shed in the kitchen garden, madam. Possibly one of the gentlemen might feel disposed to ride over to Kingham Manor and procure the back-door key from Mr Seppings.'

'Splendid, Jeeves!'

'Thank you, madam.'

'Wonderful!'

'Thank you, madam.'

'Attila!' said Aunt Dahlia, turning and speaking in a quiet, authoritative manner.

I had been expecting it. From the very moment those ill-judged words had passed the fellow's lips, I had had a presentiment that a determined effort would be made to elect me as the goat, and I braced myself to resist and obstruct.

And as I was about to do so, while I was in the very act of summoning up all my eloquence to protest that I didn't know how to ride a bike and couldn't possibly learn in the brief time at my disposal, I'm dashed if the man didn't go and nip me in the bud.

'Yes, madam, Mr Wooster would perform the task admirably. He is an expert cyclist. He has often boasted to me of his triumphs on the wheel.'

I hadn't. I hadn't done anything of the sort. It's simply monstrous how one's words get twisted. All I had ever done was to mention to him – casually, just as an interesting item of information, one day in New York when we were watching the six-day bicycle race – that at the age of fourteen, while spending my holidays with a vicar of sorts who had been told off to teach me Latin, I had won the Choir Boys' Handicap at the local school treat.

A very different thing from boasting of one's triumphs on the wheel.

I mean, he was a man of the world and must have known that the form at school treats is never of the hottest. And, if I'm not mistaken, I had specifically told him that on the occasion referred to I had received half a lap start and that Willie Punting, the odds-on favourite to whom the race was expected to be a gift, had been forced to retire, owing to having pinched his elder brother's machine without asking the elder brother, and the elder brother coming along just as the pistol went and giving him one on the side of the head and taking it away from him, thus rendering him a scratched-at-the-post non-starter. Yet, from the way he talked, you would have thought I was one of those chaps in sweaters with medals all over them, whose photographs bob up from time to time in the illustrated press on the occasion of their having ridden from Hyde Park Corner to Glasgow in three seconds under the hour, or whatever it is.

And as if this were not bad enough, Tuppy had to shove his oar in.

'That's right,' said Tuppy. 'Bertie has always been a great cyclist. I remember at Oxford he used to take all his clothes off on bump-supper nights and ride around the quad, singing comic songs. Jolly fast he used to go too.'

'Then he can go jolly fast now,' said Aunt Dahlia with animation. 'He can't go too fast for me. He may also sing comic songs, if he likes . . . And if you wish to take your clothes off, Bertie, my lamb, by all means do so. But whether clothed or in the nude, whether singing comic songs or not singing comic songs, get a move on.'

I found speech:

'But I haven't ridden for years.'

'Then it's high time you began again.'

'I've probably forgotten how to ride.'

'You'll soon get the knack after you've taken a toss or two. Trial and error. The only way.'

'But it's miles to Kingham.'

'So the sooner you're off, the better.'

'But –'

'Bertie, dear.'

'But, dash it –'

'Bertie, darling.'

'Yes, but dash it –'

'Bertie, my sweet.'

And so it was arranged. Presently I was moving sombrely off through the darkness, Jeeves at my side, Aunt Dahlia calling after me something about trying to imagine myself the man who brought the good news from Aix to Ghent. The first I had heard of the chap.

'So, Jeeves,' I said, as we reached the shed, and my voice was cold and bitter, 'this is what your great scheme has accomplished! Tuppy, Angela, Gussie and the Bassett not on speaking terms, and self faced with an eight-mile ride –'

'Nine, I believe, sir.'

' – a nine-mile ride, and another nine-mile ride back.'

'I am sorry, sir.'

'No good being sorry now. Where is this foul bone-shaker?'

'I will bring it out, sir.'

He did so. I eyed it sourly.

'Where's the lamp?'

'I fear there is no lamp, sir.'

'No lamp?'

'No, sir.'

'But I may come a fearful stinker without a lamp. Suppose I barge into something.'

I broke off and eyed him frigidly.

'You smile, Jeeves. The thought amuses you?'

'I beg your pardon, sir. I was thinking of a tale my Uncle Cyril used to tell me as a child. An absurd little story, sir, though I confess that I have always found it droll. According to my Uncle Cyril, two men named

Nicholls and Jackson set out to ride to Brighton on a tandem bicycle, and were so unfortunate as to come into collision with a brewer's van. And when the rescue party arrived on the scene of the accident, it was discovered that they had been hurled together with such force that it was impossible to sort them out at all adequately. The keenest eye could not discern which portion of the fragments was Nicholls and which Jackson. So they collected as much as they could, and called it Nixon. I remember laughing very much at that story when I was a child, sir.'

I had to pause a moment to master my feelings.

'You did, eh?'

'Yes, sir.'

'You thought it funny?'

'Yes, sir.'

'And your Uncle Cyril thought it funny?'

'Yes, sir.'

'Golly, what a family! Next time you meet your Uncle Cyril, Jeeves, you can tell him from me that his sense of humour is morbid and unpleasant.'

'He is dead, sir.'

'Thank heaven for that . . . Well, give me the blasted machine.'

'Very good, sir.'

'Are the tyres inflated?'

'Yes, sir.'

'The nuts firm, the brakes in order, the sprockets running true with the differential gear?'

'Yes, sir.'

'Right ho, Jeeves.'

In Tuppy's statement that, when at the University of Oxford, I had been known to ride a bicycle in the nude about the quadrangle of our mutual college, there had been, I cannot deny, a certain amount of substance. Correct, however, though his facts were, so far as they went, he had not told all. What he had omitted to mention was that I had invariably been well oiled at the time, and when in that condition a chap is capable of feats at which in cooler moments his reason would rebel.

Stimulated by the juice, I believe, men have even been known to ride alligators.

As I started now to pedal out into the great world, I was icily sober, and the old skill, in consequence, had deserted me entirely. I found myself wobbling badly, and all the stories I had ever heard of nasty bicycle accidents came back to me with a rush, headed by Jeeves's Uncle Cyril's cheery little anecdote about Nicholls and Jackson.

Pounding wearily through the darkness, I found myself at a loss to fathom the mentality of men like Jeeves's Uncle Cyril. What on earth he could see funny in a disaster which had apparently involved the complete extinction of a human creature – or, at any rate, of half a human creature and half another human creature – was more than I could understand. To me, the thing was one of the most poignant tragedies that had ever been brought to my attention, and I have no doubt that I should have continued to brood over it for quite a time, had my thoughts not been diverted by the sudden necessity of zigzagging sharply in order to avoid a pig in the fairway.

For a moment it looked like being real Nicholls-and-Jackson stuff, but, fortunately, a quick zig on my part, coinciding with an adroit zag on the part of the pig, enabled me to win through, and I continued my ride safe, but with the heart fluttering like a captive bird.

The effect of this narrow squeak upon me was to shake the nerve to the utmost. The fact that pigs were abroad in the night seemed to bring home to me the perilous nature of my enterprise. It set me thinking of all the other things that could happen to a man out and about on a velocipede without a lamp after lighting-up time. In particular, I recalled the statement of a pal of mine that in certain sections of the rural districts goats were accustomed to stray across the road to the extent of their chains, thereby forming about as sound a booby trap as one could well wish.

He mentioned, I remember, the case of a friend of his whose machine got entangled with a goat chain and who was dragged seven miles – like skijoring in Switzerland – so that he was never the same man again. And there was one chap who ran into an elephant, left over from a travelling circus.

Indeed, taking it for all in all, it seemed to me that, with the possible exception of being bitten by sharks, there was virtually no front-page disaster that could not happen to a fellow, once he had allowed his dear ones to override his better judgement and shove him out into the great unknown on a push-bike, and I am not ashamed to confess that, taking it by and large, the amount of quailing I did from this point on was pretty considerable.

However, in respect to goats and elephants, I must say things panned out unexpectedly well.

Oddly enough, I encountered neither. But when you have said that you have said everything, for in every other way the conditions could scarcely have been fouler.

Apart from the ceaseless anxiety of having to keep an eye skinned for elephants, I found myself much depressed by barking dogs, and once I received a most unpleasant shock when, alighting to consult a signpost, I saw sitting on top of it an owl that looked exactly like my Aunt Agatha. So agitated, indeed, had my frame of mind become by this time that I thought at first it was Aunt Agatha, and only when reason and reflexion told me how alien to her habits it would be to climb signposts and sit on them, could I pull myself together and overcome the weakness.

In short, what with all this mental disturbance added

to the more purely physical anguish in the billowy
portions and the calves and ankles, the Bertram Wooster
who eventually toppled off at the door of Kingham
Manor was a very different Bertram from the gay and
insouciant *boulevardier* of Bond Street and Piccadilly.

Even to one unaware of the inside facts, it would have
been evident that Kingham Manor was throwing its
weight about a bit tonight. Lights shone in the windows,
music was in the air, and as I drew nearer my ear
detected the sibilant shuffling of the feet of butlers,
footmen, chauffeurs, parlourmaids, housemaids,
tweenies, and, I have no doubt, cooks, who were busily
treading the measure. I suppose you couldn't sum it up
much better than by saying that there was a sound of
revelry by night.

The orgy was taking place in one of the ground-floor
rooms which had French windows opening on to the
drive, and it was to these French windows that I now
made my way. An orchestra was playing something with
a good deal of zip to it, and under happier conditions I
dare say my feet would have started twitching in time to
the melody. But I had sterner work before me than to
stand hoofing it by myself on gravel drives.

I wanted that back-door key, and I wanted it
instanter.

Scanning the throng within, I found it difficult for a
while to spot Seppings. Presently, however, he hove in
view, doing fearfully lissom things in mid-floor. I
'Hi-Seppings!'-ed a couple of times, but his mind was too
much on his job to be diverted, and it was only when the
swirl of the dance had brought him within prodding
distance of my forefinger that a quick one to the lower
ribs enabled me to claim his attention.

The unexpected buffet caused him to trip over his
partner's feet, and it was with marked austerity that he
turned. As he recognized Bertram, however, coldness
melted, to be replaced by astonishment.

'Mr Wooster!'

I was in no mood for bandying words.

'Less of the "Mr Wooster" and more back-door keys,'
I said curtly. 'Give me the key of the back door,
Seppings.'

He did not seem to grasp the gist.

'The key of the back door, sir?'

'Precisely. The Brinkley Court back-door key.'

'But it is at the Court, sir.'

I clicked the tongue, annoyed.

'Don't be frivolous, my dear old butler,' I said. 'I
haven't ridden nine miles on a push-bike to listen to you
trying to be funny. You've got it in your trousers
pocket.'

'No, sir. I left it with Mr Jeeves.'

'You did – what?'

'Yes, sir. Before I came away. Mr Jeeves said that he
wished to walk in the garden before retiring for the
night. He was to place the key on the kitchen
window-sill.'

I stared at the man dumbly. His eye was clear, his
hand steady. He had none of the appearance of a butler
who has had a couple.

'You mean that all this while the key has been in
Jeeves's possession?'

'Yes, sir.'

I could speak no more. Emotion had overmastered my
voice. I was at a loss and not abreast; but of one thing, it
seemed to me, there could be no doubt. For some reason,
not to be fathomed now, but most certainly to be gone
well into as soon as I had pushed this infernal
sewing-machine of mine over those nine miles of lonely
country road and got within striking distance of him,
Jeeves had been doing the dirty. Knowing that at any
given moment he could have solved the whole situation,
he had kept Aunt Dahlia and others roosting out on the
front lawn *en déshabille* and, worse still, had stood

calmly by and watched his young employer set out on a wholly unnecessary eighteen-mile bicycle ride.

I could scarcely believe such a thing of him. Of his Uncle Cyril, yes. With that distorted sense of humour of his, Uncle Cyril might quite conceivably have been capable of such conduct. But that it should be Jeeves –

I leaped into the saddle and, stifling the cry of agony which rose to the lips as the bruised person touched the hard leather, set out on the homeward journey.

23

I remember Jeeves saying on one occasion – I forget how the subject had arisen – he may simply have thrown the observation out, as he does sometimes, for me to take or leave – that hell hath no fury like a woman scorned. And until tonight I had always felt that there was a lot in it. I had never scorned a woman myself, but Pongo Twistleton once scorned an aunt of his, flatly refusing to meet her son Gerald at Paddington and give him lunch and see him off to school at Waterloo, and he never heard the end of it. Letters were written, he tells me, which had to be seen to be believed. Also two very strong telegrams and a bitter picture postcard with a view of the Little Chilbury War Memorial on it.

Until tonight, therefore, as I say, I had never questioned the accuracy of the statement. Scorned women first and the rest nowhere, was how it had always seemed to me.

But tonight I revised my views. If you want to know what hell can really do in the way of furies, look for the chap who has been hornswoggled into taking a long and unnecessary bicycle ride in the dark without a lamp.

Mark that word 'unnecessary'. That was the part of it that really jabbed the iron into the soul. I mean, if it was a case of riding to the doctor's to save the child with croup, or going off to the local pub to fetch supplies in the event of the cellar having run dry, no one would leap to the handlebars more readily than I. Young Lochinvar, absolutely. But this business of being put through it merely to gratify one's personal attendant's diseased sense of the amusing was a bit too thick, and I chafed from start to finish.

So, what I mean to say, although the providence which watches over good men saw to it that I was enabled to complete the homeward journey unscathed except in the billowy portions, removing from my path all goats, elephants and even owls that looked like my Aunt Agatha, it was a frowning and jaundiced Bertram who finally came to anchor at the Bingley Court front door. And when I saw a dark figure emerging from the porch to meet me, I prepared to let myself go and uncork all that was fizzing in the mind.

'Jeeves!' I said.

'It is I, Bertie.'

The voice which spoke sounded like warm treacle, and even if I had not recognized it immediately as that of the Bassett, I should have known that it did not proceed from the man I was yearning to confront. For this figure before me was wearing a simple tweed dress and had employed my first name in its remarks. And Jeeves, whatever his moral defects, would never go about in skirts calling me Bertie.

The last person, of course, whom I would have wished to meet after a long evening in the saddle, but I vouchsafed a courteous 'What ho!'

There was a pause, during which I massaged the calves. Mine, of course, I mean.

'You got in, then?' I said, in allusion to the change of costume.

'Oh, yes. About a quarter of an hour after you left Jeeves went searching about and found the back-door key on the kitchen window-sill.'

'Ha!'

'What?'

'Nothing.'

'I thought you said something.'

'No, nothing.'

And I continued to do so. For at this juncture, as had so often happened when this girl and I were closeted, the conversation once more went blue on us. The night breeze whispered, but not the Bassett. A bird twittered, but not so much as a chirp escaped Bertram. It was perfectly amazing, the way her mere presence seemed to wipe speech from my lips – and mine, for that matter, from hers. It began to look as if our married life together would be rather like twenty years among the Trappist monks.

'Seen Jeeves anywhere?' I asked, eventually coming through.

'Yes, he is in the dining-room.'

'The dining-room?'

'Waiting on everybody. They are having eggs and bacon and champagne . . . What did you say?'

I had said nothing – merely snorted. There was something about the thought of these people carelessly revelling at a time when, for all they knew, I was probably being dragged about the countryside by goats or chewed by elephants, that struck home at me like a poisoned dart. It was the sort of thing you read about as having happened just before the French Revolution – the haughty nobles in their castles callously digging in and quaffing while the unfortunate blighters outside were suffering frightful privations.

The voice of the Bassett cut in on these mordant reflexions:

'Bertie.'

'Hullo!'

Silence.

'Hullo!' I said again.

No response. Whole thing rather like one of those telephone conversations where you sit at your end of the wire saying: 'Hullo! Hullo!' unaware that the party of the second part has gone off to tea.

Eventually, however, she came to the surface again:

'Bertie, I have something to say to you.'

'What?'

'I have something to say to you.'

'I know. I said "What?"'

'Oh, I thought you didn't hear what I said.'

'Yes, I heard what you said, all right, but not what you were going to say.'

'Oh, I see.'

'Right-ho.'

So that was straightened out. Nevertheless, instead of proceeding, she took time off once more. She stood twisting the fingers and scratching the gravel with her foot. When finally she spoke, it was to deliver an impressive boost:

'Bertie, do you read Tennyson?'

'Not if I can help.'

'You remind me so much of those Knights of the Round Table in the *Idylls of the King*.'

Of course I had heard of them – Lancelot, Galahad, and all that lot, but I didn't see where the resemblance came in. It seemed to me that she must be thinking of a couple of other fellows.

'How do you mean?'

'You have such a great heart, such a fine soul. You are so generous, so unselfish, so chivalrous. I have always felt that about you – that you are one of the few really chivalrous men I have ever met.'

Well, dashed difficult, of course, to know what to say when someone is giving you the old oil on a scale like that. I muttered an 'Oh, yes?' or something on those lines, and rubbed the billowy portions in some embarrassment. And there was another silence, broken only by a sharp howl as I rubbed a bit too hard.

'Bertie.'

'Hullo?'

I heard her give a sort of gulp.

'Bertie, will you be chivalrous now?'

'Rather. Only too pleased. How do you mean?'

775

'I am going to try you to the utmost. I am going to test you as few men have ever been tested. I am going – '

I didn't like the sound of this.

'Well,' I said doubtfully, 'always glad to oblige, you know, but I've just had the dickens of a bicycle ride, and I'm a bit stiff and sore, especially in the – as I say, a bit stiff and sore. If it's anything to be fetched from upstairs – '

'No, no, you don't understand.'

'I don't, quite, no.'

'Oh, it's so difficult . . . How can I say it? . . . Can't you guess?'

'No, I'm dashed if I can.'

'Bertie – let me go!'

'But I haven't got hold of you.'

'Release me!'

'Re – '

And then I suddenly got it. I suppose it was fatigue that had made me so slow to apprehend the nub.

'What?'

I staggered, and the left pedal came up and caught me on the shin. But such was the ecstasy in the soul that I didn't utter a cry.

'Release you?'

'Yes.'

I didn't want any confusion on the point.

'You mean you want to call it all off? You're going to hitch up with Gussie, after all?'

'Only if you are fine and big enough to consent.'

'Oh, I am.'

'I gave you my promise.'

'Dash promises.'

'Then you really – '

'Absolutely.'

'Oh, Bertie!'

She seemed to sway like a sapling. It is saplings that sway, I believe.

'A very parfait knight!' I heard her murmur, and there

not being much to say after that, I excused myself on the
ground that I had got about two pecks of dust down my
back and would like to go and get my maid to put me
into something loose.

'You go back to Gussie,' I said, 'and tell him that all is
well.'

She gave a sort of hiccup and, darting forward, kissed
me on the forehead. Unpleasant, of course, but, as
Anatole would say, I can take a few smooths with a
rough. The next moment she was legging it for the
dining-room, while I, having bunged the bicycle into a
bush, made for the stairs.

I need not dwell upon my buckedness. It can be
readily imagined. Talk about chaps with the noose
round their necks and the hangman about to let her go
and somebody galloping up on a foaming horse, waving
the reprieve – not in it. Absolutely not in it at all. I don't
know that I can give you a better idea of the state of my
feelings than by saying that as I started to cross the hall I
was conscious of so profound a benevolence towards all
created things that I found myself thinking kindly
thoughts even of Jeeves.

I was about to mount the stairs when a sudden 'What
ho!' from my rear caused me to turn. Tuppy was
standing in the hall. He had apparently been down to the
cellar for reinforcements, for there were a couple of
bottles under his arm.

'Hullo, Bertie,' he said. 'You back?' He laughed
amusedly. 'You look like the Wreck of the Hesperus.
Get run over by a steam-roller or something?'

At any other time I might have found his coarse
badinage hard to bear. But such was my uplifted mood
that I waved it aside and slipped him the good news.

'Tuppy, old man, the Bassett's going to marry Gussie
Fink-Nottle.'

'Tough luck on both of them, what?'

'But don't you understand? Don't you see what this

means? It means that Angela is once more out of pawn, and you have only to play your cards properly –'

He bellowed rollickingly. I saw now that he was in the pink. As a matter of fact, I had noticed something of the sort directly I met him, but had attributed it to alcoholic stimulant.

'Good Lord! You're right behind the times, Bertie. Only to be expected, of course, if you will go riding bicycles half the night. Angela and I made it up hours ago.'

'What?'

'Certainly. Nothing but a passing tiff. All you need in these matters is a little give and take, a bit of reasonableness on both sides. We got together and talked things over. She withdrew my double chin. I conceded her shark. Perfectly simple. All done in a couple of minutes.'

'But –'

'Sorry, Bertie. Can't stop chatting with you all night. There is a rather impressive beano in progress in the dining-room, and they are waiting for supplies.'

Endorsement was given to this statement by a sudden shout from the apartment named. I recognized – as who would not – Aunt Dahlia's voice:

'Glossop!'

'Hullo?'

'Hurry up with that stuff.'

'Coming, coming.'

'Well, come, then. Yoicks! Hark for-rard!'

'Tallyho, not to mention tantivy. Your aunt,' said Tuppy, 'is a bit above herself. I don't know all the facts of the case, but it appears that Anatole gave notice and has now consented to stay on, and also your uncle has given her a cheque for that paper of hers. I didn't get the details, but she is much braced. See you later. I must rush.'

To say that Bertram was now definitely nonplussed would be but to state the simple truth. I could make nothing of this. I had left Brinkley Court a stricken home, with hearts bleeding wherever you looked, and I had returned to find it a sort of earthly paradise. It baffled me.

I bathed bewilderedly. The toy duck was still in the soap-dish, but I was too preoccupied to give it a thought. Still at a loss, I returned to my room, and there was Jeeves. And it is proof of my fogged condish that my first words to him were words not of reproach and stern recrimination but of inquiry:

'I say, Jeeves!'

'Good evening, sir. I was informed that you had returned. I trust you had an enjoyable ride.'

At any other moment, a crack like that would have woken the fiend in Bertram Wooster. I barely noticed it. I was intent on getting to the bottom of this mystery.

'But I say, Jeeves, what?'

'Sir?'

'What does all this mean?'

'You refer, sir – '

'Of course I refer. You know what I'm talking about. What has been happening here since I left? The place is positively stiff with happy endings.'

'Yes, sir. I am glad to say that my efforts have been rewarded.'

'What do you mean, your efforts? You aren't going to try to make out that that rotten fire bell scheme of yours had anything to do with it?'

'Yes, sir.'

'Don't be an ass, Jeeves. It flopped.'

'Not altogether, sir. I fear, sir, that I was not entirely frank with regard to my suggestion of ringing the fire bell. I had not really anticipated that it would in itself produce the desired results. I had intended it merely as a preliminary to what I might describe as the real business of the evening.'

'You gibber, Jeeves.'

'No, sir. It was essential that the ladies and gentlemen

should be brought from the house, in order that, once out of doors, I could ensure that they remained there for the necessary period of time.'

'How do you mean?'

'My plan was based on psychology, sir.'

'How?'

'It is a recognized fact, sir, that there is nothing that so satisfactorily unites individuals who have been so unfortunate as to quarrel amongst themselves as a strong mutual dislike for some definite person. In my own family, if I may give a homely illustration, it was a generally accepted axiom that in times of domestic disagreement it was necessary only to invite my Aunt Annie for a visit to heal all breaches between the other members of the household. In the mutual animosity excited by Aunt Annie, those who had become estranged were reconciled almost immediately. Remembering this, it occurred to me that were you, sir, to be established as the person responsible for the ladies and gentlemen being forced to spend the night in the garden, everybody would take so strong a dislike to you that in this common sympathy they would sooner or later come together.'

I would have spoken, but he continued.

'And such proved to be the case. All, as you see, sir, is now well. After your departure on the bicycle, the various estranged parties agreed so heartily in their abuse of you that the ice, if I may use the expression, was broken, and it was not long before Mr Glossop was walking beneath the trees with Miss Angela, telling her anecdotes of your career at the university in exchange for hers regarding your childhood; while Mr Fink-Nottle, leaning against the sundial, held Miss Bassett enthralled with stories of your school-days. Mrs Travers, meanwhile, was telling Monsieur Anatole –'

I found speech.

'Oh?' I said. 'I see. And now, I suppose, as the result of

this dashed psychology of yours, Aunt Dahlia is so sore with me that it will be years before I can dare to show my face here again – years, Jeeves, during which, night after night, Anatole will be cooking those dinners of his –'

'No, sir. It was to prevent any such contingency that I suggested that you should bicycle to Kingham Manor. When I informed the ladies and gentlemen that I had found the key, and it was borne in upon them that you were having that long ride for nothing, their animosity vanished immediately, to be replaced by cordial amusement. There was much laughter.'

'There was, eh?'

'Yes, sir. I fear you may possibly have to submit to a certain amount of good-natured chaff, but nothing more. All, if I may say so, is forgiven, sir.'

'Oh?'

'Yes, sir.'

I mused awhile.

'You certainly seem to have fixed things.'

'Yes, sir.'

'Tuppy and Angela are once more betrothed. Also Gussie and the Bassett. Uncle Tom appears to have coughed up that money for *Milady's Boudoir*. And Anatole is staying on.'

'Yes, sir.'

'I suppose you might say that all's well that ends well.'

'Very apt, sir.'

I mused again.

'All the same, your methods are a bit rough, Jeeves.'

'One cannot make an omelette without breaking eggs, sir.'

I started.

'Omelette! Do you think you could get me one?'

'Certainly, sir.'

'Together with half a bot. of something?'

'Undoubtedly, sir.'

'Do so, Jeeves, and with all speed.'

I climbed into bed and sank back against the pillows.
I must say that my generous wrath had ebbed a bit. I was
aching the whole length of my body, particularly
towards the middle, but against this you had to set the
fact that I was no longer engaged to Madeline Bassett. In
a good cause one is prepared to suffer. Yes, looking at the
thing from every angle, I saw that Jeeves had done well,
and it was with an approving beam that I welcomed him
as he returned with the needful.

He did not check up with this beam. A bit grave, he
seemed to me to be looking, and I probed the matter
with a kindly query:

'Something on your mind, Jeeves?'

'Yes, sir. I should have mentioned it earlier, but in the
evening's disturbance it escaped my memory. I fear I
have been remiss, sir.'

'Yes, Jeeves?' I said, champing contentedly.

'In the matter of your mess jacket, sir.'

A nameless fear shot through me, causing me to
swallow a mouthful of omelette the wrong way.

'I am sorry to say, sir, that while I was ironing it this
afternoon I was careless enough to leave the hot
instrument upon it. I very much fear that it will be
impossible for you to wear it again, sir.'

One of those old pregnant silences filled the room.

'I am extremely sorry, sir.'

For a moment, I confess, that generous wrath of mine
came bounding back, hitching up its muscles and
snorting a bit through the nose, but, as we say on the
Riviera, *à quoi sert-il*? There was nothing to be gained
by g. w. now.

We Woosters can bite the bullet. I nodded moodily
and speared another slab of omelette.

'Right ho, Jeeves.'

'Very good, sir.'